**FROM THE BLOODY TRENCHES OF WORLD WAR I TO A WILDERNESS PARADISE, IT WAS MAN AGAINST MAN, HUSBAND AGAINST WIFE, FATHER AGAINST SON . . .**

Wealthy, powerful General Sean Courtney, war hero, veteran of the African goldfields, dedicated to preserving the grandeur of his beloved homeland . . .

Mark Anders, Sean's loyal young friend, sworn to reclaim his birthright and repay a brutal blood debt . . .

Storm Courtney, Sean's beautiful daughter with the violent temperament of a talented artist and the hungers of untried womanhood . . .

And their relentless enemy, a man driven by murderous, rapacious greed—Dirk Courtney, Sean's son.

Three men and a woman locked in a magnificent struggle to possess tempestuous love, to win a fortune, to gain the fabulous wealth that was the treasure, the grandeur, of Africa.

Dell Books by Wilbur Smith

EAGLE IN THE SKY
EYE OF THE TIGER
SHOUT AT THE DEVIL
WHEN THE LION FEEDS
DARK OF THE SUN
THE ROAR OF THUNDER
CRY WOLF

# A SPARROW FALLS

*Wilbur Smith*

A DELL BOOK

Published by
Dell Publishing Co., Inc.
1 Dag Hammarskjold Plaza
New York, New York 10017

Dell ® TM 681510, Dell Publishing Co., Inc.

ISBN: 0-440-17707-3

Reprinted by arrangement with Doubleday & Company, Inc.

Printed in United States of America

First Dell printing—December 1979

*For Danielle*

A sky the colour of old bruises hung low over the battle-fields of France, and rolled with ponderous dignity towards the German lines.

Brigadier-General Sean Courtney had spent four winters in France and now, with the eye of a cattleman and a farmer, he could judge this weather almost as accurately as that of his native Africa.

"It will snow tonight," he grunted, and Lieutenant Nick van der Heever, his orderly officer, glanced back at him over his shoulder.

"I shouldn't wonder, sir."

Van der Heever was heavily laden. In addition to his service rifle and webbing, he carried a canvas kitbag across his shoulder, for General Courtney was on his way to dine as a mess guest of the 2nd Battalion. At this moment the Colonel and officers at the 2nd Battalion were completely unaware of the impending honour, and Sean grinned in wicked anticipation at the panic that his unannounced arrival would create. The contents of the kitbag would be some small compensation for the shock, for it included half a dozen bottles of pinch bottle Haig and a fat goose.

Nevertheless, Sean was aware that his officers found his informal behaviour and his habit of arriving suddenly in the front lines, unannounced and unattended by his staff, more than a little disconcerting. Only a week before, he had overheard a field telephone conversation on a crossed line between a major and a captain.

"The old bastard thinks he's still fighting the Boer War. Can't you keep him in a cage back there at H.Q.?"

"How do you cage a bull elephant?"

"Well, at least warn us when he's on his way—"

Sean grinned again and trudged on after his orderly officer, the folds of his great-coat flapping about his putteed legs and, for warmth, a silk scarf wrapped around his head beneath the soup-plate shape of his helmet. The boards bounced under his feet and the gluey mud sucked and gurgled beneath them at the passing weight of the two men.

This part of the line was unfamiliar, the brigade had moved in less than a week previously, but the stench was well remembered. The musty smell of earth and mud, overladen with the odour of rotting flesh and sewage, the stale lingering whiff of burned cordite and high explosive.

Sean sniffed it and spat with distaste. Within an hour he knew he would be so accustomed as not to notice it, but now it seemed to coat the back of his throat like cold grease. Once again he looked up at the sky, and now he frowned. Either the wind had shifted into the east a point or two, or they had taken a wrong turning within the maze of trenches, for the low cloud was no longer rolling in the direction that fitted with the map that Sean carried in his head.

"Nick!"

"Sir?"

"Are you still right?"

And he saw at once the uncertainty in the young subaltern's eyes as he looked back.

"Well, sir—"

The trenches had been deserted for the last quarter of a mile, not a single soul had they passed in the labyrinth of high earthen walls.

"We'd better take a look, Nick."

"I'll do it, sir." Van der Heever glanced ahead along the trench, and found what he was looking for. At the next intersection a wooden ladder was fastened into the wall. It reached to the top of the sand-bagged parapet. He started towards it.

"Careful, Nick," Sean called after him.

"Sir," the young man acknowledged, and propped his rifle before swarming upwards.

Sean calculated they were still three or four hundred yards from the front line yet, and the light was going fast. There was a purple velvet look to the air beneath the clouds, not shooting light at all, and he knew that, despite his age, van der Heever was an old soldier. The glance he took over the top would be swift as a meerkat looking out of its hole.

Sean watched him crouch at the top of the ladder, lift his head for a single quick sweep and then duck down again.

"The hill is too much on our left," he called down.

The hill was a low, rounded mound that rose a mere hundred and fifty feet above the almost featureless plain. Once it had been thickly forested, but now only the shattered stumps stood waist-high and the slopes were dimpled with shell craters.

"How far is the farm house?" Sean asked, still peering upwards. The farm house was a roofless rectangle of battered walls that stood foursquare facing the centre of the Battalion's sector. It was used as a central reference point for artillery, infantry and aircorps alike.

"I'll have another look," and van der Heever lifted his head again.

The Mauser has a distinctive cracking report, a high and vicious sound that Sean had heard so often as to be able to judge with accuracy its range and direction.

This was a single shot, at about five hundred yards, almost dead ahead.

Van der Heever's head snapped backwards as though he had taken a heavy punch, and the steel of his helmet rang like a gong. The chin-strap snapped as the round helmet spun high in the air and then dropped to the floorboards in the bottom of the trench and rolled on its rim into a pool of grey mud.

Van der Heever's hands remained locked closed on the top rung of the ladder for a moment, then the nerveless fingers opened, and he tumbled backwards, falling heavily into the bottom of the trench with the skirts of his greatcoat ballooning around him.

Sean stood frozen and disbelieving, his mind not yet accepting the fact that Nick was hit, but, as a soldier and a hunter, judging that single shot with awe.

What kind of shooting was that? Five hundred yards in this murky light; one fleeting glimpse of a helmeted head above the parapet; three seconds to set the range and line up, then another instant of time to sight and fire as the head bobbled up again. The Hun that fired that shot was either a superb marksman with reflexes like a leopard—or the flukiest sniper on the western front.

The thought was fleeting and Sean started forward heavily and knelt beside his officer. He turned him with a hand upon the shoulder and felt the sickening slide in his guts and the cold grip on his chest.

The bullet had entered at the temple and exited behind the opposite ear.

Sean lifted the shattered head into his lap, removed his own helmet and began to unwind the silk scarf from around his head. He felt a desolation of loss.

Slowly he wrapped the boy's head in the scarf, and immediately the blood soaked through the thin material. It was a futile gesture—but it served to keep his hands occupied and detract from his sense of helplessness.

He sat on the muddy floorboards, holding the boy's body, his heavy shoulders bowed forward. The size of Sean's bared head was accentuated by the thick curls of dark wiry hair shot through with splashes and strands of grey that sparkled frostily in the fading light. The short thick beard was laced with grey as well, and the big beaked nose was twisted and battered-looking.

Only the black curved eyebrows were sleek and unmarked, and the eyes were clear and dark cobalt blue, the eyes of a much younger man, steady and alert.

Sean Courtney sat for a long time holding the boy, and then he sighed once, deeply, and laid the broken head aside. He stood up, hefted the kitbag on to his own shoulder, and set off along the communications trench once again.

\* \* \*

At five minutes before midnight, the Colonel commanding the 2nd Battalion stooped through the blackout curtains that screened the entrance to the mess, and beat the snow from his shoulders with a gloved hand as he straightened.

The mess had been a German dugout six months before, and was the envy of the brigade. Thirty feet below ground level, it was impregnable, even to the heaviest artillery barrage. The floor was of heavy timber boarding and even the walls were panelled against the damp and the cold. A pot-bellied stove stood against the far wall, glowing cheerfully.

Gathered about it in a half circle of looted armchairs sat the off-duty officers.

However, the Colonel had eyes only for the burly figure of his General, seated in the largest and most comfortable chair closest to the stove, and he shed his great-coat as he hurried across the dugout.

"General, my apologies. If I'd known you were coming—I was making my rounds."

Sean Courtney chuckled and rose ponderously from the chair to shake his hand. "It's what I would expect of you, Charles, but your officers have made me very welcome—and we have kept a little of the goose for you."

The Colonel glanced quickly about the circle and frowned as he saw the hectic cheeks and sparkling eyes of some of his younger subalterns. He must warn them of the folly of trying to drink level with the General. The old man was steady as a rock, of course, and those eyes were like bayonets under the dark brows, but the Colonel knew him well enough to guess that he had a full quart of Dimple

Haig in his belly, and that something was troubling him deeply. Then it came to him. Of course—

"I'm terribly sorry to hear about young van der Heever, sir. Sergeant-Major told me what happened."

Sean made a gesture of dismissal, but for a moment the shadows darkened about his eyes.

"If I'd only known you were coming up into the line this evening, I would have warned you, sir. We have had the devil of trouble with that sniper ever since we moved up. It's the same fellow, of course—absolutely deadly. I've never heard of anything like it. Dreadful nuisance when everything else is so quiet. Only casualties we've had all week."

"What are you doing about him?" Sean asked harshly. They all saw the flush of anger darken his face, and the Adjutant intervened swiftly.

"I've been on to Colonel Caithness at 3rd Battalion, and we did a deal, sir. He has agreed to send us Anders and MacDonald—"

"You got them!" The Colonel looked delighted. "Oh, I say, that's excellent. I didn't think Caithness would part with his prize pair."

"They came in this morning—and the two of them have been studying the ground all day. I gave them a free hand, but I understand they are setting up the shoot for tomorrow."

The young Captain who commanded "A" Company pulled out his watch and studied it a moment. "They are going out from my section, sir. As a matter of fact, I was going to go down and give them a send-off, they will be moving into position at half past twelve. If you'll excuse me, sir."

"Yes, of course, off with you, Dicky—wish them good luck from me." Everybody in the brigade had heard of Anders and MacDonald.

"I'd like to meet that pair." Sean Courtney spoke suddenly, and dutifully the Colonel agreed.

"Of course, I'll come out with you, sir."

"No, no, Charles—you've been out in the cold all night as it is. I'll just go along with Dicky here."

* * *

The snow came down thickly out of the utter darkness of the midnight sky. It damped down the night sounds in its thick muffling cloak, muting the regular bursts of a Vickers firing at a hole in the wire on the battalion's left.

Mark Anders sat wrapped in his borrowed blankets and he bowed his head to the book in his lap, adjusting his eyes to the yellow wavering light of the candle-stump.

The rise in temperature that accompanied the first fall of snow and the changed quality of sound entering the small dugout awakened the man who slept beside him. He coughed, and rolled over to open a chink in the canvas curtain beside his head.

"Damn," he said, and coughed again, the harsh hammering sound of a heavy smoker. "Damn it to hell. It's snowing." Then he rolled back to Mark. "You still reading?" he demanded roughly. "Always with your nose in a bloody book. You'll ruin your shooting eyes."

Mark lifted his head. "It's been snowing for an hour already."

"What you want all that learning for?" Fergus MacDonald was not so easily distracted. "It won't do you no good."

"I don't like the snow," said Mark. "We didn't reckon on the snow."

The snow complicated the task ahead of them. It would cover the ground out there with a sensitive mantle of white. Anybody moving out from the trench into no-man's-land would leave tracks that the dawn light would instantly betray to an observant enemy.

A match flared and Fergus lit two Woodbines and passed one to Mark. They sat shoulder to shoulder, huddled in their blankets.

"You can call off the shoot, Mark. Tell 'em to shove it. You're a volunteer lad."

They smoked in silence for a full minute before Mark replied.

"That Hun is a bad one."

"If it's snowing, he probably won't be out tomorrow. Snow will keep him in bed also."

Mark shook his head slowly. "If he's that good, he'll be out."

"Yes." Fergus nodded. "He's that good. That shot he made last evening—after lying up all day in the cold, then five hundred yards if it was an inch, and in that light—" Fergus cut himself off, and then went on quickly, "But you're good also, lad. You're the best, boy."

Mark said nothing, but carefully pinched out the glowing tip of the Woodbine.

"You're going?" Fergus asked.

"Yes."

"Get some sleep then, lad. It's going to be a long day."

Mark blew out the candle flame as he lay back and pulled the blankets over his head.

"You get a good sleep," Fergus said again. "I'll wake you in plenty of time," and he resisted the paternal urge to pat the thin bony shoulder under the blanket.

\* \* \*

The young Captain spoke quietly with one of the sentries on the forward firing step, and the man whispered a reply and pointed with his chin along the darkened trench.

"This way, sir." He went on down the boards, swaddled in clothing so that he had the shape of a bear, and Sean towered head and shoulders above him as he followed.

Around the next revert, through the soft curtains of falling snow, there was the subdued red glow of a brazier from the shallow dugout in the side of the trench. Dark figures squatted close about it, like witches at a sabbat.

"Sergeant MacDonald?" One of the figures rose and stepped forward.

"That's me." There was a cocky, self-assured tone to the reply.

"Is Anders with you?"

"Present and correct," said MacDonald, and one of the other figures rose from the circle about the brazier and came forward. He was taller, but moved with grace, like an athlete or a dancer.

"You are ready, Anders?" the Captain went on, speaking in the soft half-whisper of the trenches, and MacDonald replied for him.

"The lad is fighting fit, sir." He spoke with the proprietary tone of the manager of a prize-fighter. It was clear that the boy was his property, and that ownership gave him a distinction he would never have achieved on his own.

At that moment another flare burst high overhead, a brilliant white and silent explosion of light, softened by the snow.

Sean could judge a man like he could a horse. He could pick the rotten ones, or the big-hearted, from the herd. It was a trick of experience and some deeper inexplicable insight.

In the light of the flare his eyes flickered across the face of the older Sergeant. MacDonald had the bony under-nourished features of the slum-dweller, the eyes too close set, the lips narrow and twisted downwards at the corners. There was nothing to interest Sean there and he looked at the other man.

The eyes were a pale golden brown, set wide, with the serene gaze of a poet or a man who had lived in the open country of long distant horizons. The lids were held wide open, so that they did not overlap the iris, leaving a clear glimpse of the clean white about the cornea so that it floated free like a full moon. Sean had seen it only a few times before, the effect was almost hypnotic, of such direct and searching candour that it seemed to reach deep into Sean's own soul.

After the impact of those eyes, other impressions crowded in. The first was of the man's extreme youth. He was nearer seventeen than twenty, Sean judged—and then saw immediately how finely drawn the boy was. Despite the serenity of his gaze, he was stretched out tight and hard, racked up with strain close to the snapping point. Sean had seen it so often in the past four years. They had found this child's special talent and exploited it ruthlessly, all of them—Caithness at 3rd Battalion, the ferrety Mac-Donald, Charles, Dicky and, by association, himself. They had worked him mercilessly, sending him out time and again.

The boy held a steaming tin mug of coffee in one hand, and the wrist that protruded from the sleeve of his coat was skeletal, and speckled with angry red bites of body lice. The neck was too long and thin for the head it supported, and the cheeks were hollow, the eye-sockets sunken.

"This is General Courtney," said the Captain; and as the light of the flare died, Sean saw the eyes shine suddenly with a new light, and heard the boy's breath catch with awe.

"Hello, Anders, I've heard a lot about you."

"And I've heard about you, sir." The transparent tones of hero-worship irritated Sean. The boy would have heard all the stories, of course. The regiment boasted of him, and every new recruit heard the tales. There was nothing he could do to prevent them circulating.

"It's a great honour to meet you, sir." The boy tripped on the words, stuttering a little—another sign of the terrible strain he was under—yet the words were completely sincere.

The legendary Sean Courtney, the man who had made five million pounds on the goldfields of the Witwatersrand and lost every penny of it in a morning at a single coup of fortune. Sean Courtney, who had chased the Boer General Leroux across half of Southern Africa and caught him at last after a terrible hand-to-hand fight. The soldier who had held Bombata's ravaging Zula impis at the gorge and then driven them on to the waiting Maxims, who had planned with his erstwhile enemy Leroux and helped build the

Charter of Union which united the four independent states
of Southern Africa into a single mighty whole, who had
built another vast personal fortune in land and cattle and
timber, who had given up his position in Louis Botha's
Cabinet and at the head of the Natal Legislative Council to
bring the regiment out to France—it was natural the boy's
eyes should shine that way and his tongue trip, but still it
annoyed Sean. At fifty-nine I'm too old to play the hero
now, he thought wryly—and the flare went down, plunging
them back into the darkness.

"If there's another mug of that coffee," said Sean. "It's
bloody cold tonight."

Sean accepted the chipped enamel mug and hunkered
down close to the brazier, cupped the mug between his
hands, blowing on the steaming liquid and sipping noisily,
and after a moment the others followed his example hesitantly. It was strange to be squatting like old mates with a
General and the silence was profound.

"You're from Zululand?" Sean asked the boy suddenly;
his ear had picked up the accent, and without waiting for a
reply went on in the Zulu tongue, *"Velapi wena?* Where
are you from?"

The Zulu language came naturally and easily to Mark's
lips though he had not spoken it for two years. "From the
north beyond Eshowe, on the Umfolosi River."

"Yes. I know it well. I have hunted there." Sean changed
back to English. "Anders? I knew another Anders. He rode
transport from Delagoa Bay back in '89. John? Yes, that's
it. Old Johnny Anders. Any relation? Your father?"

"My grandfather. My father's dead. My grandfather has
land on the Umfolosi. That's where I live." The boy was
relaxing now. In the brazier glow, Sean thought he saw the
lines of strain around his mouth ironing out.

"I didn't think you'd know poor folk, like us—sir." Fergus MacDonald spoke with cutting edge in his voice, leaning forward towards the brazier with his head turned towards him so that Sean could see the bitter line of his
mouth.

Sean nodded slowly. MacDonald was one of them then. One of those who were intent on the new order—trade unions and Karl Marx, Bolsheviks who threw bombs and called themselves comrades. Irrelevantly he noticed for the first time that MacDonald had ginger hair, and big golden freckles on the backs of his hands. He turned back to Mark Anders.

"He taught you to shoot?"

"Yes, sir." The lad grinned for the first time, warmed by the memory. "He gave me my first rifle, a Martini Hendry that blew a cloud of gunsmoke like a bush fire but would throw dead true at a hundred and fifty yards."

"I've hunted elephant with it. A great rifle," Sean agreed, and suddenly across an age difference of forty years they were friends.

Perhaps, for Sean, the recent death of that other bright young man, Nick van der Heever, had left an aching gap in his life, for now he felt a flood of paternal protection for the youngster. Fergus MacDonald seemed to sense it also, for he cut in like a jealous woman.

"You'd best be getting ready now, lad." The smile was gone from Mark's lips, the eyes were too calm, and he nodded his thin neck stiffly.

Fergus MacDonald fussed over the lad, and once again Sean was reminded of a trainer preparing his fighter in the dressing-room. He stripped off the heavy, voluminous greatcoat and the battle-dress jacket. Over the long woollen full-length underwear went a woollen shirt and two knitted jerseys. A woollen scarf around the throat.

Then a mechanic's boiler-suit which covered the layers of clothing in a single neat skin that would not snag, or flutter in a breeze to draw an enemy eye. A woollen balaclava over the head, and a leather airman's helmet, and Sean saw the reason. The British steel helmet had a distinctive brim, and anyway was no protection from a Mauser bullet.

"Keep your nut down, Mark, me boy."

Knitted mittens with fingers cut out, and then thick loose gloves over them.

"Keep the old fingers working, lad. Don't let them stiffen up on you."

A small leather shoulder bag that slung comfortably under the left armpit.

"Ham sandwiches with plenty of mustard, chocolate and barley sugar—just the way you like it. Don't forget to eat, keep you warm."

Four full clips of .303 cartridges, three slipped into the thigh pickets of the boiler-suit—and one into the special pocket sewn into the forearm of the left sleeve.

"I waxed each round myself," Fergus announced mainly for the benefit of the listening General. "They'll slide in like—" and the simile was crude and obscene, meant to show Fergus' scorn of rank and class. But Sean let it pass easily, he was too interested in the preparations for the hunt.

"I won't show Cuthbert until the sun is right."

"Cuthbert?" Sean asked, and Fergus chuckled and indicated a third figure that lay quietly at the back of the dugout. It was the first time Sean had noticed him and Fergus chuckled again at his puzzled expression and reached out to the reclining figure.

Only then Sean realized it was a dummy, but in the light of the brazier the features were realistic and the helmeted head rode at a natural angle on the shoulders. The model ended abruptly at the hips and below it there was only a broom handle.

"I'd like to know how you are going to do it?" Sean addressed the question to young Mark Anders, but Fergus replied importantly,

"Yesterday the Hun was shooting from low on the northern slope of the hill. Mark and me worked out the angles of the two shots he made and we've got him pegged to within fifty yards."

"He may change position," Sean pointed out.

"He'll not leave the north slope. It's in shadow all day, even if the sun comes out. He will want to shoot from shade into light." Sean nodded at the logic of it.

"Yes," he agreed, "but he may shoot from a stand in the German line."

And Mark answered quietly, "I don't think so, sir. The lines are too far apart here"—the German line ran across the crest of the hill—"he'd want a shorter range. No, sir, he's shooting from close in. He makes a stand in no-man's-land, probably changes it every day—but each time he comes close as he can get to our lines while still staying in the shadow." The boy had not tripped on a single word now that his mind had locked on to the problem. His voice was low and intense.

"I picked out a good stand for the lad, just beyond the farm house. He can cover the whole of the northern slope at less than two hundred yards. He'll move out now and settle in while it's still dark. I'm sending him out early. I want him to make his move before the Hun. I don't want the lad walking on top of the bastard in the dark." Fergus MacDonald took over from Mark with an air of authority. "Then we both wait until the light is good and clean, then I start working with Cuthbert here," he patted the dummy and chuckled again. "It's damned difficult to give him a nice natural look, like some stupid rooky sticking his head up to take a first look at France. If you let the Hun get too long a look at him, then he'll tumble to the trick, but if you make it too quick, he won't get a chance for a shot. No, it's not easy."

"Yes, I should imagine," Sean murmured wryly, "that it's the most dangerous and difficult part of the whole thing." And he saw the deadly expression flit across Fergus MacDonald's face before he turned to Mark Anders.

"Another mug of coffee, lad—and then it's time to be getting on. I want you in place before the snow stops."

Sean reached into the breast of his great-coat and brought out the silver flask that Ruth had given him on the day the regiment sailed.

"Put some fangs in the coffee." He offered the flask to Mark.

The boy shook his head shyly. "No thank you, sir. Makes me see squiff."

"Don't mind if I do, sir." Fergus MacDonald reached swiftly across the brazier. The clear brown liquid glugged freely into his own mug.

\* \* \*

The Sergeant-Major had sent out a patrol before midnight to cut a lane through the wire in front of "A" Company.

Mark stood at the foot of the trench ladder and changed his rifle from the right hand; another flare burst overhead and in its light Sean saw how intent the boy was on his task. He pulled back the bolt of the rifle, and Sean noted that he was not using the standard No. 1 short Lee-Enfield, which was the work-horse of the British army, but that he favoured the American P.14 which also fired the .303 calibre but had the longer barrel and finer balance.

Mark stripped two clips of ammunition into the magazine and closed the bolt, levering a round of carefully selected and waxed ammunition into the breach.

In the last light of the flare he looked across at Sean, and nodded slightly. The flare died and in the darkness that followed Sean heard the quick light steps on the wooden ladder. He wanted to call "good luck" after the boy, but suppressed the whim and instead patted his pockets for his cheroot case.

"Shall we get on back, sir?" the Captain asked quietly.

"Off with you," growled Sean, his voice gruff with the premonition of coming tragedy. "I'll stay on a while." Though he could give no help, somehow it seemed like deserting the boy to leave now.

Mark moved quickly along the line that the patrol had laid to guide him through the wire. He stooped to keep contact with the line in his left hand, and he carried the P.14 in his right. He lifted his feet carefully, and stepped lightly, trying not to scuff the snow, trying to spread his weight evenly on each foot so as not to break the crust.

Yet every time a flare went up, he had to fall face forward and lie still and huddled, a dark blot in the electric glare of light against the sheet of white, screened only by the persistently falling veils of snow. When he scrambled up in the darkness and moved on, he knew he left a disturbed area of snow. Ordinarily it would not have mattered, for in the barren, shell-churned wilderness of no-man's-land, such light scrabble marks passed unnoticed. But Mark knew that in the first cold light of dawn an unusual pair of eyes would be scrutinizing every inch of the ground, hunting for just this kind of sign.

Suddenly, colder than the icy snow-laden air against his cheeks, was the deep chill of loneliness. The sense of vulnerability, of being pitted against a skilled and implacable enemy, an invisible, terrifying, efficient adversary who would deliver instant death at the slightest error.

The latest flare sank and died, and he scrambled to his feet and blundered to the dark, jagged wall of the ruined farm house. He crouched against it, and tried to control his breathing for this newly conceived terror threatened to smother him. It was the first time it had come upon him. Fear he had known—had lived with it as his constant companion these last two years, but never this terrible paralysing terror.

When he touched his fingers of his right hand to his ice-cold cheek, he felt the tremble in them, and in sympathy his teeth chattered in a short staccato rhythm.

"I can't shoot like this," he thought wildly, clenching his jaw until it ached and locking his hands together and hold-

ing them hard against his groin, "and I can't stay here."
The ruin was too obvious a stand to make. It would be the
first point the German sniper would study. He had to get
out of there, and quickly. Back to the trenches. Suddenly
his terror was panic, and he lifted himself to begin the
crazed flight back, leaving his rifle propped against the ruined wall.

*"Bist du da?"* a voice whispered softly near him in the
darkness. Mark froze instantly.

*"Ja!"* The reply was further along the wall and Mark
found the rifle with his left hand settling naturally on to the
stock and his right curling about the pistol grip, forefinger
hooking over the trigger.

*"Komm, wir gehen zurück."* Close beside Mark, sensed
rather than seen in the darkness, passed a heavily laden
figure. Mark swung the rifle to follow him, his thumb on
the safety-catch ready to slip it. The German stumbled
stumbled heavily in the treacherous snowy footing, and the
wiring tools he carried clanked together. The man cursed.

*"Scheisse!"*

*"Halt den Mond,"* snapped the other, and they moved
on back toward the German line above them on the crest
of the hill.

Mark had not expected a wiring detail to be out in this
weather. His first thought had been for the German sniper,
but now his mind leaped forward at this sudden good fortune.

The patrol would lead him through the German wire,
and their heavy blundering tracks would hide his own from
the sniper.

It was only when he had decided this that he realized
with surprise that his panic had passed, his hands were
rock steady and his breathing was deep and slow. He
grinned without humour at his own frailty and moved forward lightly after the German patrol.

They were a hundred paces beyond the farm house when
it stopped snowing. Mark felt the slide of dismay in his
chest. He had relied heavily on the snow holding, at least

until dawn, but he kept on after the patrol. They were moving faster and more confidently as they neared their own lines.

Two hundred yards below the crest Mark left them to go on alone, and began working his way sideways around the slope, groping his way painstakingly through the heavily staked wire, until at last he recognized and reached the stand that he and Fergus had picked out through binoculars the previous afternoon.

The main trunk of one of the oaks that had covered the hill had fallen directly down the slope, pulling up a great matted tangle of roots from the soft high-explosive-ploughed earth.

Mark crawled among the tangle of roots; selecting the side which would be in deepest shadow from the winter-angled sun, he wriggled in on his belly until he was half covered by them, but with head and shoulders able to turn to cover the full curve of the northern slope ahead of him.

Now his first concern was to check the P.14 carefully, paying particular attention to the vulnerable, high-mounted Bisley-type rear sight to make sure that it had not been knocked or misaligned during the journey across no-man's-land. He ate two of the ham sandwiches, drank a few rationed mouthfuls of sweet coffee and adjusted the woollen scarf over his mouth and nose, for warmth and to prevent the steaming of his breath. Then he laid his forehead carefully against the wooden butt of his rifle. He had developed the knack of instant sleep, and while he slept it snowed again.

When Mark woke in the sickly grey light of dawn, he was blanketed by the fine white flakes. Careful not to disturb them, he lifted his head slowly, and blinked his eyes rapidly to clear them. His fingers were stiff and cold; he worked them steadily in the gloves, forcing warm blood to flow.

He had been lucky again—twice in one night was too much. First the patrol to lead him through the wire and now this thin white coat of natural camouflage to blend his shape with the tangled roots of the oak. Too much luck, the pendulum must swing.

Slowly the darkness drew back, widening his circle of vision, and as it expanded so the whole of Mark's existence came to centre in those two wide golden brown eyes. They moved quickly in the pattern of search, touching in turn each irregularity and fold, each feature, each object, each contrasting colour or texture of snow and mud and earth, each stump of shattered timber or fallen branch, the irregular rim of every shell hole, looking for shadows where they should not have been, seeking the evidence of disturbance beneath the new thin coat of snow, seeking, searching—for life, literally for life.

* * *

The snow stopped again a little before nine, and by noon the sky had lightened and there were holes in the cloud-cover, a single water ray of sun fell and moved like a searchlight across the southern slope of the hill.

"Right, Cuthbert, let's draw some Hun fire."

Fergus had marked each of the German sniper's kills on the trench map the Sergeant-Major had loaned him. There were two black spots close to each other in the same section of trench. At those places the parapet was too low for the commanding bulk of the hill that commanded the front line. After five men had been killed at those two spots the parapet had warned the unwary.

### "KEEP YOUR HEAD DOWN. SNIPER AT WORK."

The two black spots were only fifty paces apart, and Fergus guessed that the sniper had achieved his successes here by waiting for a victim to pass down the trench. He would get a glimpse of a head in the first gap, and would be aiming into the second gap with his finger on the hair-trigger as the man passed it. He explained this to Sean Courtney as he made his preparations, for by this time Sean was so intrigued by the hunt that only a major German offensive would have lured him back to his headquarters. During the morning he had spoken to his aides-de-camp over the field telephone, and told them where they could find him in an emergency.

"But make sure it's an emergency," he had growled ferociously into the headset.

"I'll draw him from south to north," Fergus explained, "that will force the bloody Hun to turn away from Mark's stand, it will give the lad an extra second while he swings back towards the ridge."

Fergus MacDonald was good with the dummy, Sean had to concede it. He carried it two feet higher than natural man height, to compensate for the raised parapet, and he gave it a realistic roll of the shoulders, like a hurrying man as he passed it through the first gap.

Sean, the young Captain and the beefy red-faced Sergeant-Major were waiting with a half dozen other ranks beyond the second gap, watching Fergus come down the boards towards them steadily.

Instinctively they all drew breath and held it as he came up to the second gap, all of them tensed with suspense.

Up the slope of the hill, the Mauser cracked, like a bull-whip on the icy air, and the dummy kicked sharply in Fergus MacDonald's hands.

Fergus jerked it down out of sight, and fell to his knees to examine the neat round hole punched through the papier-mâché head.

"Oh shit!" he whispered bitterly. "Oh, shit all over it!"

"What is it, MacDonald?"

"The bloody Hun—oh, the sodding bastard—"

"MacDonald!"

"He's picked the same stand as my boy."

Sean did not understand for a moment. "He's in among the oak trunks, he's sitting right on top of Mark. They picked the same stand."

The vicious stinging discharge of the Mauser was so close, so high and sharp, that for a few seconds afterwards, Mark's eardrums buzzed with the mosquito hum of auditory memory.

For seconds he was stunned, frozen with the shock of it. The German sniper was somewhere within twenty feet of where he lay. By some freak of coincidence, he had chosen the same point on the slope as Mark. No, it was no freak of coincidence. With the hunter's eye for ground, both men had selected the ideal position for their common purpose— to deliver swift death from hiding. The pendulum of Mark's fortune had swung to the other end of its arc.

Mark had not moved in the seconds since the Mauser shot, but every sense was heightened by the adrenalin that sang through his veins and his heart beat with a force that seemed to reverberate against the cage of his ribs.

The German was on his left, higher up the slope, slightly behind his shoulder. The left was his unprotected side, away from the tangled oak roots.

He trained his eyes around, without moving his head, and in the periphery of his vision saw another of the fallen oak trunks close by. He did not move for another full minute, watching for the flicker of movement in the corner of his eye. There was nothing, and the silence was awesome and oppressive—until a Spandau fired a short blast, a mile or more away down the line.

Mark began to turn his head towards the left, as slowly as a chameleon stalking a fly. Gradually the distortion of periphery vision cleared, and he could sweep the whole of the slope above him.

The nearest oak trunk had been savaged with shrapnel, all the bark was torn away and raw chunks of timber ripped from it. It had fallen across a hollow in the earth, forming a bridge; and although the snow had piled up against it, there was a narrow gap between earth and oak.

The gap was perhaps three inches wide at the centre, and Mark could see reflected light from the snow beyond.

At that moment, a minute blur of movement snapped his eyes in his skull. It was a fleeting movement of a mere sixteenth of an inch, but it riveted Mark's attention. He stared for fully five seconds, before he realized what he was seeing.

Beyond the screening end of the oak trunk, the very tip of a Mauser barrel protruded. It had been bound with burlap to break the stark outline and to prevent reflection of light off metal—but the cruel little mouth of the muzzle was uncovered.

The German was lying behind the oak log, like Mark his right flank protected, facing halfway from Mark—and less than twenty feet separated them.

Mark watched the tip of the Mauser barrel for ten minutes more, and it did not move again. The German had stillness and patience. Once he had reloaded, he had frozen again into that rigour of watchfulness.

"He's so good that there is no way I can clear the shot," Mark thought. "If I move an inch, he'll hear me, and he'll be fast. Very fast."

To get a clear shot, Mark would have to move back twenty feet or more, and then he would be looking directly into the muzzle of the Mauser; a head-on shot, with the German alerted by his movements. Mark knew he could not afford to give away that much advantage, not against an adversary of this calibre.

The long still minutes crawled by without any break in tension. Mark had the illusion that every nerve and sinew of his body was quivering visibly, but in reality the only movement was in the glove of his right hand. The fingers moved steadily in a kneading motion, keeping supple and warm, and the eyes moved in Mark's skull, swivelling slowly back and forth across the battered trunk of the oak, blinking regularly to clear the tears that tension and the icy air induced.

"What the hell is happening up there?" Fergus MacDonald fretted nervously, peering into the lens of the periscope that allowed the observer to keep well down below the sand-bagged parapet.

"The boy is pinned down." General Sean Courtney did not remove his own eyes from the other periscope, but swung it slightly, sweeping back and forth across the slope. "Try the Hun with Cuthbert again."

"I don't think he'll fall for it again," Fergus began to protest immediately, looking up with those close-set eyes, rimmed with pink now by the cold and the strain of wait-ing.

"That's an order, Sergeant." Sean Courtney's broad fore-head wrinkled and the dark brows drew sharply together, his voice growled like an old lion and the dark-blue eyes snapped. The power and presence of the man in this mood awed even Fergus MacDonald.

"Very well, sir," he muttered sulkily, and went to where the dummy was propped against the firing step.

\* \* \*

The lash of the Mauser cracked again, and at the shock Mark Anders' eyelids blinked twice very quickly and then flared wide open. The golden brown eyes stared fixedly up the slope, intent as those of the hunting peregrine.

The instant after the shot, he heard the rattle of the Mauser bolt being drawn back and then thrust forward to reload, and again the tip of the hessian-wrapped muzzle stirred slightly—but then Mark's eyes flicked sideways.

There had been another movement, so fine that it might have gone unnoticed by eyes less keen. The movement had been a mere breath, and it had been in the narrow three-inch gap between the oak trunk and the snow-coated earth. Just that one brief stir and then stillness once more.

Mark stared into the gap for long seconds, and saw nothing. Merely shadow and undefined shape, trickily reflected light from the snow beyond. Then suddenly, he was seeing something else.

It was the texture of cloth, a thin sliver of it in the narrow gap, then his eyes picked up the stitched seam in the grey cloth, bulging slightly over the living flesh beneath.

There was some small portion of the German's body showing through the gap. He was lying close up on the far side of the log, and his head was pointed in the direction from which the muzzle of the Mauser projected.

Carefully Mark proportioned the man's body in his imagination. Using the rifle muzzle as his only reference point, he placed the man's head and shoulders, his trunk and his hips—

"Yes, his hips," Mark thought. "That is his hip or upper thigh—" and then there was a change in the light. The sun found a weak spot in the cloud cover overhead and the light brightened briefly.

In the better light, Mark made out a small portion of a German service belt, with the empty loop which should have held a bayonet. It confirmed his guess. Now he knew that the slight bulge in the field grey material was caused by the head of the femur where it fitted into the cup of the pelvic girdle.

"Through both hips," Mark thought coldly. "It's a pinning shot, and then there is the femoral artery—" Carefully he began to work the glove off his right hand.

He must roll on his side, and swing the long barrel of the P.14 through an arc of over ninety degrees, without making the least sound.

"Please, God," Mark asked silently, and began to make the move. Achingly slowly, the barrel of his rifle swung and, at the same time, he began to transfer his weight on to his other elbow.

It seemed to be a complete round of eternity before the

P.14 pointed into the narrow gap below the oak trunk, and Mark was doubled up, straining to keep the barrel bearing from this unnatural position. He could not slip the safety-catch from the rifle before firing; even that tiny metallic snick would alert the German.

He curled his finger on the trigger, and took up the pull, feeling the dead lock of the safety mechanism. He aimed carefully, his head twisted awkwardly, and he began to push the safety-catch across with his thumb, while holding pressure on the hair trigger. It had to be done smoothly, so as not to pull his aim off the sliver of grey uniform cloth.

The thunder of the shot seemed to bounce against the low grey sky, and the bullet crashed through the tiny gap. Mark saw the impact of it, the rubbery shock of metal into flesh.

He heard the German cry out, a wild sound without form or meaning, and Mark swept back the bolt of the P.14, and reloaded with instinctive dexterity. The next shot blended with the echo of the first, coming so close together that they seemed as one. The jacketed bullet crashed through the gap, and this time Mark saw blood spurt, a bright scarlet spray of it that splattered the snow, turning swiftly to pale pink as it was diluted by the melt of its own heat.

Then there was nothing in the gap, the German had been thrown back by the impact—or had rolled aside. Only the smear of pink stained snow.

Mark waited, a fresh cartridge in the breach of the P.14, turned now to face the oak trunk, tensed for the next shot. If it had not been a decisive wound, the German would be coming after him, and he was ready for the snap shot.

He felt coldly unemotional, but vitally aware, his every fibre and nerve pitched to its utmost, his vision sharp and bright and his hearing enhanced.

The silence drew out for a while longer—and then there was a sound. For a moment Mark did not recognize it, then it came again. The sound of a man sobbing.

It came stronger now, more hysterical, gut-racking.

*"Ach, mein Gott—mein lieber Gott—"* the man's voice, pitiful, broken. *"Das Blut—ach Gott—das Blut."*

Suddenly the sound was tearing at Mark's soul, cutting deeply into his being. His hand began to shake, and he felt the tremor of his lips once again. He tried to clench his jaw, but now his teeth were chattering wildly.

"Stop it, oh God, stop it," he whispered, and the rifle fell from his hands. He pressed his mittened hands to his ears, trying to shut out the terrible sounds of the dying German.

"Please, please," Mark pleaded aloud. "Stop it, please."

And the German seemed to hear him.

*"Hilf mir, lieber Gott—das Blut!"* His voice was broken by the wet helpless sounds of his despair.

Suddenly Mark was crawling forward, through the snow, blindly up the slope.

"I'm coming. It's all right," he muttered. "Only stop it." He felt his senses swaying.

*"Ach mein lieber Gott, ach, meine Mutti . . ."*

"Oh Jesus—stop it. Stop it."

Mark dragged himself around the end of the oak log.

The German was half propped against the log. With both hands he was trying vainly to stem the fountain of bright pulsing arterial blood that flowed through his fumbling fingers. The two bullets had shattered both his hips, and the snow was a sodden mushy porridge of blood.

He turned his face to Mark, and already it was drained of all colour, a shiny greyish white, slick with a fine sheen of perspiration. The German was young, as young as Mark, but swiftly approaching death had smoothed out his features so he seemed younger still. It was the face of a marble angel, smooth and white, and strangely beautiful, with blue eyes in pale blue sockets, a burst of pale golden curls escaping from under the helmet on to the smooth pale forehead.

He opened his mouth and said something that Mark did not understand, and the teeth were white and even, beyond the full pale lips.

Then, slowly, the German sagged back against the log

still staring at Mark. His hands fell away from his groin and the regular pulsing spurt of blood from the shattered flesh slowed and shrivelled away. The pale blue eyes lost their feverish lustre, and dulled, no longer focused.

Mark felt a thread pull in the fabric of his mind, like silk beginning to tear. It was almost a physical thing—he could hear it beginning to give way inside him.

His vision wavered, the dead German's features seemed to run like melting wax, and then slowly reformed again. Mark felt the tear widening, the silken veil of his reason ripping through; beyond it was a dark and echoing chasm.

The dead German's features went on reforming, until they hardened and Mark was looking into his own face as through a wavering distorted mirror. His own haunted face, the eyes golden brown and terrified, the mouth that was his mouth opened—and a cry came from it that was the despair and the agony of all the world.

The last shreds of Mark's reason whipped away on the tempest of horror, and he heard himself screaming—and felt his feet running under him, but there was only blackness in his head, and his body was light and without weight, like the body of a bird in flight.

\* \* \*

The German machine-gunner cocked the Maxim with a single savage wrench on the crank handle, and traversed sharply left, at the same time depressing the thick water-jacketed barrel of the weapon until it pointed directly down the slope below the sand-bagged emplacement towards the British lines.

The single wildly running figure was angling away towards the left, and the gunner pulled the wooden butt of the Maxim into his shoulder and fired a single short traversing burst, aiming a fraction low to counteract the natural tendency to shoot high at a downhill target.

Mark Ander hardly felt the mighty hammer strokes of the two bullets that smashed into his back.

Fergus MacDonald was crying. That surprised Sean, he had not expected it. The tears slid slowly from pink-rimmed eyes, and he struck them away with a single angry movement.

"Permission to take out a patrol, sir?" he asked, and the young Captain glanced uncertainly at Sean over the Sergeant's shoulder.

Sean nodded slightly, a mere inclination of the head.

"Do you think you can find volunteers?" the Captain asked uncertainly, and the red-faced Sergeant answered gruffly.

"There'll be volunteers, sir, the lads have a feeling for what that youngster did."

"Very well, then—as soon as it's dark."

They found Mark a little after eight o'clock. He hung in the rusting barbed wire at the bottom of the slope, like a broken doll. Fergus MacDonald had to use a pair of wire-cutters to cut him down, and it took them nearly another hour to get him back to the British lines, dragging the stretcher between them through the mud and slushy snow.

"He's dead," said General Courtney, looking down at the white drained face on the stretcher in the lantern light.

"No, he's not," Fergus MacDonald denied it fiercely. "They don't kill my boy that easy."

\*   \*   \*

The locomotive whistled shrilly as it clattered over the steelwork of the bridge. Silver steam flew high in a bright plume, and then smeared back on the wind.

Mark Anders leaned far out over the balcony of the single passenger carriage and the same wind ruffled the soft brown wing of his hair and a spattering of ash particles from the furnace stung his cheek, but he screwed up his eyes and looked down into the bed of the river as they roared across.

The water flowed down under the dipping reeds, and then met the pylons of the bridge and swirled sullenly, flowing green and strong and full down to the sea.

"Water's high for this time of year," Mark muttered aloud. "Grandpapa will be happy," and he felt his lips tugging up into the unaccustomed smile. He had smiled only infrequently during the past months.

The locomotive hurtled across the steel bridge, and threw itself at the far slope. Immediately, the beat of its engine changed and its speed bled away.

Mark stooped and hefted his old military pack, opened the gate of the balcony and clambered down on to the steel steps, hanging with one arm over the racing gravel embankment.

The train slowed rapidly as the incline steepened and he swung the pack off his shoulder and leaned far out to let it drop as gently as possible on to the gravel. It bounced once and went bounding away down the embankment, crashing into the shrubbery like a living animal in flight.

Then he swung down towards the racing earth himself and, judging his moment finely as the train crested the ridge, he let go to hit the embankment on flying feet, throwing his weight forward to ride the impact and feel the gravel sliding under him.

He stayed upright, and came to a halt as the rest of the train clattered past him, and the guard looked out sternly from the last van and called a reprimand.

"Hey, that's against the law."

"Send the sheriff," Mark shouted back, and gave him an ironic salute as the locomotive picked up speed on the reverse slope with explosive grunts of power, the rhythm of the tracks rising sharply. The guard clenched a fist and Mark turned away.

The jolt had hurt his back again and he slipped a hand into his shirt and ran it around under his armpit as he started back along the tracks. He fingered the twin depressions below the shoulder blade and marvelled again at how close one of them was to the bony projections of the spine. The scar tissue had a silky, almost sensuous feel, but it had taken long months to close. Mark shuddered involuntarily as he remembered the rattle of the trolley that carried the dressings, and the impassive almost masculine face of the matron as she stuffed the long cotton plugs into the open mouths of the bullet wounds; he remembered also the slow tearing agony as the bloody dressing was pulled out again with the glittering steel forceps, and his own breathing sobbing in his ears and the matron's voice, harsh and impersonal.

"Oh, don't be a baby!"

Every day—day after day, week after week—until the hot feverish delirium of the pneumonia that had attacked his bullet-damaged lung had seemed a blessed relief. How long had it been—from the V.A.D. Station in a French field with the muddy snow deeply rutted by the ambulances and the burial details digging graves beyond the tented hospital—to the general hospital near Brighton and the dark mists of pneumonia, the hospital ship home down the length of the Atlantic, baking in the airless tropics, the convalescent hospital with its pleasant lawns and gardens— how long? Fourteen months in all, months during which the war which men were already misnaming "Great" had ended. Pain and delirium had clouded the passage of time, yet it seemed a whole lifetime.

He had lived one life in the killing and the carnage, in the pain and the suffering, and now he was reborn. The pain in his back abated swiftly. It was almost mended now, he thought happily, and he pushed away the dark and terrible memories and scrabbled down the embankment to retrieve his pack.

Andersland was almost forty miles downstream, and the train had been behind schedule, it was noon already. Mark knew that he would not make it before the following evening—and strangely, now that he was almost home, the sense of urgency was gone.

He moved easily, falling into that long, familiar stride of the hunter, easing the pack on his back slightly as soon as the newly healed wounds stiffened, feeling the good sweat springing cool on his face and through the thin cotton of his shirt.

Absence of so many years had sharpened his appreciation of the world through which he moved, so that which before had warranted only passing attention became now a new and unfamiliar delight.

Along the banks the dense riverine bush was alive with myriad life. The bejewelled dragonflies that skimmed the surface on transparent wings or coupled in flight, male upon female, his long glittering abdomen arched to join with hers; the hippopotamus that burst through the surface in an explosive exhalation of breath, and stared at Mark upon the bank with pink watery eyes, flicking the tiny ears, and wallowing like a gargantuan black balloon in the green swirling current.

It was like moving through an ancient Eden, before the coming of man, and suddenly Mark knew that this solitude was what his body and mind needed to complete the healing process.

He camped that night on a grassy bluff above the river, above the mosquitoes and the unpleasant darkness of the thick bush.

A leopard woke him after midnight, sawing hoarsely down in the river bottom, and he lay and listened to it moving slowly upstream until he lost it among the crags of high ground. He did not sleep again immediately, but lay and examined, with the pleasure of anticipation, the day ahead of him.

For every day of the past four years, even the very bad days of darkness and ghosts, he had thought of the old man. Some days it had been only a fleeting thought, on other days he had dwelt upon him as a homesick schoolboy tortures himself with thoughts of home. The old man was home, of course, both the mother and father Mark had never known. Always there from his first vaguest memory to the present, unchanging in his strength and quiet understanding.

Mark felt a deep physical pang of longing, as he recalled clearly a picture of the old man sitting on the hard carved rocker on the wide boarded stoep, the crumpled old khaki shirt, crudely patched and in need of laundering, open at the neck to expose a fuzz of silver-white chest hair; the neck and jowls wrinkled like those of a turkey cock, but burned dark brown and pelted with five days' growth of silver stubble that sparkled like glass chips; the huge moustaches of glistening white, the ends curled with beeswax into fearsome spikes, the wide terai hat pulled low over the bright toffee-coloured humorous eyes. The hat was always in place, sweat-soaked and greasy around the band, but never removed, not even at meal-times—nor, Mark suspected, in the big brass bed at night.

Mark remembered him pausing from working with the whittling knife, rolling the quid from one cheek to the other, then letting fly at the old five-gallon Tate and Lyle golden syrup can that was his spittoon. Hitting solidly at ten feet, spilling not a single drop of the dark brown juice, and then continuing the story as though there had been no interruption. And what stories! Stories to start a small boy's eyes popping from their sockets and wake him in the night to peer fearfully under the bed.

Mark remembered the old man in small things, stooping to take up a handful of his rich soil and let it run through his fingers, then wiping them on the seat of his pants with the proud fierce expression on his withered old features. "Goodland—Andersland," he would say, and nod like a sage. Mark remembered him in the big things, standing tall and skinny beside Mark in thick thorn bush with the big old Martini Hendry rifle bellowing and smoking, the recoil shaking his frail old body as, like a black mountain, the buffalo bull came down upon them, blood mad and crazed with its wounds.

Four years since last he had seen him, since last he had heard news of him. At first he had written, long homesick letters, but the old man could not read nor write. Mark had hoped that he might take them to a friend, the postmistress perhaps, and that they might read them to him and write back to Mark.

It had been a vain hope. The old man's pride would never allow him to admit to a stranger that he could not read. Nevertheless, Mark had continued to write, once every month for all those long years; but only tomorrow could he have his first news of the old man in all that time.

Mark slept again for another few hours, then built up the fire again in the darkness before dawn and brewed coffee. He was moving again as soon as it was light enough to see his feet on the path.

From the escarpment he watched the sun come up out of the sea. There were mountains of cumulus thunder clouds standing tall over the distant sea, and the sun came up behind them so that they glowed with red and roses, wine and deep purples, each cloud etched in outline by brilliant red-gold and shot through with shafts of light.

At Mark's feet the land dropped away into the coastal lowlands, that rich littoral of densely forested valleys and smooth golden grassy hills that stretched to the endless white beaches of the Indian Ocean.

Below where Mark stood, the river tumbled over the edge of the escarpment, leaping in sheets of white and silver from wet black rock to deep dark pools which turned upon themselves in foam like huge wheels, as though they rested before the next wild plunge downwards.

Mark began to hurry for the first time, following the steep path downwards with the same urgency as the river, but it was mid morning before he came out on to the warm and drowsing sweep of land below the escarpment.

The river widened, and became shallower, changing its mood completely as it meandered between the exposed sandbanks. There were new birds here, different beasts in the forest and upon the hills, but now Mark had no time for them. Hardly glancing at the flocks of long, heavy-beaked storks and scimitar-billed ibis on the sandbanks, even when the hadedah ibis rose with their wild insanely ringing shrieks of laughter, he hurried on.

There was a place, unmarked except for a small tumbled cairn at the foot of a huge wild fig tree, that had a special significance to Mark, for it marked the western boundary of Andersland.

Mark stopped to rebuild the cairn among the grey scaly roots that crawled across the earth like ancient reptiles, and while he worked, a flock of fat green pigeons exploded on noisy wings from the branches above him where they had been feeding on the bitter yellow fruit.

When Mark went on beyond the fig tree, he walked with a new lightness and resilience to his step, a new set to his shoulders and a new brightness in his eyes—for he walked once again on Andersland. Eight thousand acres of rich chocolate loamy ground, four miles of river frontage, water that never failed, softly rounded hills covered with thick sweet grass, Andersland, the name the old man had given it thirty years before.

Half a mile further on, Mark was about to leave the river and take a short cut across the next ridge to the homestead, when there was a distant but earth-trembling thud, and immediately afterwards the faint sound of human voices on the still warm air.

Puzzled, Mark paused to listen, and again the thudding sound—but this time preceded by the crackling and snapping of branches and undergrowth. The unmistakable sound of timber being felled.

Abandoning his original intention, Mark kept on down the river, until he emerged suddenly from forest into open country that reminded him at first of those terrible devastated fields of France, torn and ravaged by shell and high explosive until the raw earth lay exposed and churned.

There were gangs of dark men in white linen dhotis and turbans felling the heavy timber and clearing out the undergrowth along the river. For a moment Mark did not understand who these strange men were, and then he remembered reading a newspaper report that Hindu labourers were being brought out in the thousands from India to work for the new sugar cane estates. These were the wiry, very dark-skinned men that worked now like a colony of ants along the river. There were hundreds of them—no, Mark realized that they were in the thousands—and there were oxen teams as well. Big spans of heavy, strong-looking beasts plodding slowly as they dragged the fallen timber into rows for burning.

Not truly understanding what he was seeing, Mark left the river and climbed the slope beside it. From the crest he had a new uninterrupted view across Andersland—and beyond, eastwards towards the sea.

The devastation stretched as far as he could see, and now there was something else to ponder. The land was going to the plough, all of it. The forest and grazing land had been torn out, and the trek oxen moved slowly over the open ground, one team following the next, the rich chocolate earth turning up under the ploughshares in thick shiny welts. The cries of the ploughmen and the muted popping of the long trek whips carried to where Mark stood, bewildered, upon the slope of the hill.

He sat down on a boulder and for almost an hour watched the men and the oxen at work, and he was afraid. Afraid for what this all meant. The old man would never let this happen to his land. He had a hatred of the plough and the axe; he loved too deeply the stately trees which now groaned and crackled as they toppled. The old man hoarded his grazing like a miser, as though it were as precious as its golden colour suggested. He would never allow it to be turned under—not if he were alive.

That was why Mark was afraid. If he were alive. For, God knows, he would never sell Andersland.

Mark did not truly want to know the answer. He had to force himself to rise and go down the hill.

The dark turbaned labourers did not understand his questions, but they directed him with expressive gestures to a fat babu in a cotton jacket who strutted importantly from work gang to work gang, snapping at a naked black back with a light cane or pausing to write a laborious note in the huge black book he carried.

He looked up, startled, and then immediately became obsequious in the presence of a white man.

"Good day, master—" He would have gone on, but the shiny acquisitive eyes darted over Mark and they saw how young he was, unshaven, his cheap army issue suit was stained with travel and rumpled from having been slept in. It was obvious he carried his entire worldly possessions in his back-pack.

"To tell the truth, we are not needing more men here." His manner changed instantly, becoming lordly. "I am being in charge here—"

"Good." Mark nodded. "Then you can tell me what these men are doing on Andersland."

The man irritated him, he had known so many like him in the army—bully those below and lick the backsides of those above.

"Beyond doubt we are making ground clear for sugar."

"This ground belongs to my family," said Mark, and instantly the man's manner changed again.

"Ah, good young master, you are from the company at Ladyburg?"

"No, no—we live here. In the house," Mark pointed at the ridge of the hill, beyond which lay the homestead, "this is our ground."

The babu chuckled like a fat dark baby, and shook his head.

"Nobody living here now. Alas! The company owns everything." And he made a wide gesture that took in the whole landscape from escarpment to the sea. "Soon everything is sugar, you will see, man. Sugar, sugar." And he laughed again.

From the ridge the old homestead looked the same, just a green-painted roof of corrugated iron showing above the dark green of the orchard, but as Mark came up the overgrown path past the hen coops, he saw that all the window panes had been removed, leaving blank dark squares, and there was no furniture on the wide stoep. The rocker was gone, and there was a sag to the roof timbers at one end of the veranda; a drainpipe had come loose and hung away from the wall.

The garden had the wild untended look of neglect, the plants beginning to encroach on the house itself. The old man had always kept it trimmed and neat with the leaves swept up daily from under the trees and the white-painted beehives set up in orderly rows in the shade. Somebody had robbed the hives with brutal carelessness, smashing them open with an axe.

The rooms were bare, stripped of anything of possible value, even the old black wood-burning stove in the kitchen, everything except the Tate and Lyle spittoon on the stoep which lay on its side; its spilled contents had left a dark stain on the woodwork.

Mark wandered slowly from room to empty room, feeling a terrible sense of loss and desolation as the wind-blown leaves rustled under his feet, and big black and yellow spiders watched him with myriad glittering eyes from the webs they had spun in the corners and across the jambs of the doorways.

Mark left the house and went down to the small family graveyard, feeling a quick lift of relief when he realized there were no new graves there. Grandmother Alice, her eldest daughter, and her cousin who had died before Mark was born. Still three graves—the old man was not there.

Mark drew a bucket from the well and drank a little of the cold sweet water, then he wandered into the orchard and picked a hatful of guavas and a ripe yellow pineapple. In the backyard strutted a young cockerel who had escaped the plunderers. Mark had to hunt him for half an hour before a stone brought him down off the roof in a squawking flutter of feathers.

Plucked and cleaned, he went into the canteen over the fire that Mark made in the backyard—and while he boiled, Mark had a sudden thought.

He went back into the old man's bedroom and in the far

corner, where the big brass bed had once stood, he knelt and felt for the loose board. With his clasp knife he pried the single nail that held it down and then lifted the plank.

He reached down into the opening below and brought out first a thick bundle of envelopes tied with a strip of rawhide. Mark riffled the edge of the pack and saw that not a single envelope had been opened. They were all addressed in his own spiky hand. They had been carefully stored in this hiding place. Yet not all Mark's letters were there. The sequence ended abruptly and Mark, checking the last letter, found it postmarked eleven months previously. Mark felt a choking sensation in the base of his throat, and the sharp sting of tears.

He placed the bundle of letters aside and reached again into the opening to bring out the Mazzawatee tea caddy, with the picture of the grandmother in steel-rimmed spectacles on the lid. It was the old man's treasure-chest.

He carried the can and the bundle of letters out into the backyard for the late afternoon light was going fast in the unlit rooms. He sat on the kitchen step, and opened the tea caddy.

There were forty gold sovereigns in a leather purse. Some of them had the bearded head of Kruger the old president of the South African Republic, the others of Edward and George. Mark slipped the purse into the inner pocket of his jacket and in the fading light examined the rest of the old man's treasure. Photographs of grandmother Alice as a young woman, yellowed and dog-eared with age, a wedding certificate, old newspaper clippings from the Boer War, cheap articles of women's jewellery, the same as those that Alice wore in the photographs, a medal in a presentation case, a Queen's South Africa medal with six bars including those for Tugela, Ladysmith and the Transvaal campaigns, Mark's own school reports from the Ladyburg School and then the diploma from the University College at Port Natal—these the old man valued especially, with the illiterate's awe of learning and the written word. He had sold some of his prize livestock to pay for Mark's education, he rated it that highly. Nothing in the tea caddy, apart from the sovereigns, was of any value, but it had all been precious beyond price to the old man. Carefully Mark repacked the tin and placed it in his back-pack.

In the last light of day Mark ate the stringy cockerel and the fruit, and when he rolled into his blanket on the wooden kitchen floor he was still thinking.

He knew now that the old man, wherever he had gone, had intended returning to Andersland. He would never have left that precious hoard behind unless that had been his intention.

\* \* \*

A boot in the ribs brought Mark awake, and he rolled over and sat up, gasping with the pain of it.

"On your feet! Get your arse moving—and keep it going."

It was not yet fully light, but Mark could make out the man's features. He was clean-shaven with a heavy smooth jaw, and his teeth seemed to have been ground down to a flat even line—very white against the dark suntan. His head was round, like a cannon ball, and gave the impression of vast weightiness, for he carried it low on a thick neck like a heavyweight boxer shaping up.

"Up!" he repeated, and drew the scuffed brown riding-boot again. Mark came up on his feet and squared to defend himself. He found the man was shorter than he was, but he was stocky and solid, with broad thick shoulders and the same weightiness in his frame. "This is private property, we don't want tramps hanging about."

"I'm not a tramp," Mark started, but the man cut him short with a snort of brusque laughter.

"You with the fancy clothes, and the Rolls parked at the door—you had me fooled for a moment there."

"My name is Mark Anders," he said. "This land belongs to my grandfather—John Anders—"

He thought he saw something move in the man's eyes, a change in the set of his mouth, doubt or worry perhaps. He licked his lips, a quick nervous gesture, but when he spoke his voice was still flat and quiet.

"I don't know nothing about that—all I know is this land belongs to the Ladyburg Estates now, and I am the foreman for the company, and neither me nor the company wants you hanging around here," he paused and settled on his feet, dropping his shoulders and pushing out his heavy jaw, "and one other thing I know is I like to break a head now and then, and I haven't broken one for God knows a long time."

They stared at each other, and Mark felt a sudden hot rush of anger. He wanted to take up the man's challenge, even though he realized how powerful and dangerous he was. He had the look of a killer, and the weight and the strength, but Mark felt himself coming into balance, his own shoulders dropping.

His tormentor saw it also and his relish was obvious. He smiled thinly, clenching his jaw around the smile so that the cords stood out in his throat, swaying slightly up on to the balls of his feet. Then suddenly Mark felt revolted and sickened by the presence of violence. There had been too much of it in his life already—and there was no reason to fight now. He turned away and picked up his boots.

The man watched him dress, disappointed perhaps, but ready for further confrontation. When he swung his pack up on his shoulder, Mark asked,

"What's your name?"

The man answered him lightly, still keyed up for violence. "My friends call me Hobday," he said.

"Hobday who?"

"Just Hobday."

"I won't forget it," said Mark. "You've been a real brick, Hobday." He went down the steps into the yard, and fifteen minutes later when Mark looked back from the ridge where the Ladyburg road crossed on its way northwards,

Hobday was still standing in the kitchen yard of Anders-land, watching him intently.

\* \* \*

Fred Black watched Mark come up the hill. He leaned against the rail of the dipping tank and chewed steadily on his quid of tobacco, stringy and sun-blackened and dry as a stick of chewing tobacco himself.

Although he was one of John Anders' cronies, and had known Mark since he was a crawler, it was clear he did not recognize him now. Mark stopped fifteen paces off and lifted his hat.

"Hello, Uncle Fred," Mark greeted him, and still it was a moment before the older man let out a whoop and leapt to embrace Mark. "God, boy, they told me you'd got your-self killed in France."

They sat together on the rail of the cattle pen, while the Zulu herd boys drove the cattle below them through the narrow race, until they reached the ledge from which they made the wild scrambling leap into the deep stinking chem-ical bath, to come up again, snorting fearfully, and swim, nose up, for the slope ramp beyond.

"He's been dead almost a year—no, longer, over a year now—lad, I'm sorry. I never thought to let you know. Like I said, we thought you were dead in France."

"That's all right, Uncle Fred." Mark was surprised that he felt no shock. He had known it, accepted it already, but there was still the grief that lay heavy on his soul. They were both silent for a longer time, the old man beside him respecting his grief.

"How did he—" Mark hesitated over the word, "how did he go?"

"Well, now." Fred Black lifted his hat and rubbed the bald pink pate lovingly. "It was all a bit sudden like. He went off to poach a little biltong with Piet Greyling and his son up at Chaka's Gate." Vivid memories crowded back for Mark. Chaka's Gate was the vast wilderness area to the north where the old man had taught him the craft of the hunter. Years before, back in 1869 it had been declared a hunting reserve but no warden had been appointed, and the men of northern Natal and Zululand looked upon it as their private hunting reserve.

"On the fifth day, the old man did not come back into camp. They searched for him another four days before they found him." He paused again and glanced at Mark. "You feeling all right, boy?"

"Yes, I'm all right." Mark wondered how many men he had seen die, how many he had killed himself—and yet the death of one more old man could move him so. "Go on, please, Uncle Fred."

"Piet said it looked like he had slipped while he was climbing a steep place, and he had fallen on his rifle and it had gone off. It hit him in the stomach." They watched the last ox plunge into the dip, and Fred Black climbed stiffly down from the pole fence. He held the small of his back for a moment. "Getting old," he grunted, and Mark fell in beside him as they started up towards the house.

"Piet and his boy buried him there. He wasn't fit to bring back, he'd been in the sun four days. They marked the place and made a sworn statement to the magistrate when they got back to Ladyburg."

Fred Black was interrupted by a cry and the sight of a female figure racing down the avenue of blue gum trees towards them—slim and young, with honey brown hair in a thick braid bouncing on her back, long brown legs and grubby bare feet beneath the skirts of the faded cheap cotton skirt.

"Mark!" she cried again. "Oh Mark!" But she was close before he recognized her. She had changed in four years.

"Mary." The sadness was still on Mark, but he could not talk further now. There would be time later. Even in the sadness, he could not miss the fact that Mary Black was a big girl now, no longer the mischievous imp who once had been below his lordly notice when he had been a senior at Ladyburg High School.

She still had the freckled laughing face and the prominent, slightly crooked front teeth, but she had grown into a big, wide-hipped, earthy farm girl, with a resounding jolly laugh. She was as tall as Mark's shoulder and her shape under the thin, threadbare cotton was rounded and full; she had hips and buttocks that swung as she walked beside him, a waist like the flared neck of a vase and fat heavy breasts that bounced loosely at each stride. As they walked, she asked questions, endless questions in a demanding manner, and she kept touching Mark, her hand on his elbow, then grabbing his hand to shake out the answers to her questions, looking up at him with mischievous eyes, laughing her big ringing laugh. Mark felt strangely restless.

Fred Black's wife recognized him from across the yard and let out a sound like a milch cow too long deprived of her calf. She had nine daughters, and she had always pined for a son.

"Hello, Aunt Hilda," Mark began, and then was folded into her vast pneumatic embrace.

"You're starved," she cried, "and those clothes, they stink. You stink too, Marky—your hair, you'll be sitting on it next."

The four unmarried girls, supervised by Mary, set the galvanized bath in the centre of the kitchen floor and filled it with buckets of steaming water from the stove. Mark sat on a stool on the back veranda with a sheet around his shoulders, while Aunt Hilda sheared him of his long curling locks with a huge pair of blunt scissors.

Then she drove her daughters protesting from the kitchen. Mark fought desperately for his modesty, but she brushed his defence aside.

"An old woman like me, you haven't got anything I haven't seen bigger and better." She stripped him determinedly, hurling the soiled and rumpled clothing through the open doorway to where Mary hovered expectantly.

"Wash them, child—and you get yourself away from that door."

Mark blushed furiously and dropped quickly into the water.

In the dusk, Fred Black and Mark sat together on the coping of the well in the yard, with a bottle of brandy between them. The liquor was the fierce "Cape Smoke" with a bite like a zebra stallion, and after the first sip Mark did not touch his glass again.

"Yes, I've thought about that often," Fred agreed, already slightly owl-eyed with the brandy. "Old Johnny loved that land of his."

"Did he ever speak of selling it to you?"

"No, never did. I always thought he'd be there forever. Often talked of being buried next to Alice. He wanted that."

"When did you last see Grandpapa, Uncle Fred?"

"Well, now," he rubbed his bald head thoughtfully, "it would be about two weeks before he left for Chaka's Gate with the Greylings. Yes, that's right. He'd been into Ladyburg to buy cartridges and provisions. Pitched up here one night in the old scotch-cart, and we had a good old chat."

"He didn't say anything then—about selling?"

"No, not a word."

The kitchen door flew open, spilling yellow lantern light into the yard, and Aunt Hilda bellowed at them.

"Food's up. Come along now, Fred, don't you keep that boy out there, teaching him your evil ways—and don't you bring that bottle into this house. You hear me!"

Fred grimaced, poured the last three inches of dark brown liquor into his tumbler and shook his head at the empty bottle.

"Farewell, old friend." He sent it sailing over the hedge, and drained the tumbler like medicine.

Mark was crowded into the bench against the kitchen wall with Mary on the one side of him and another of the big buxom daughters on the other. Aunt Hilda sat directly

opposite him, shovelling food on to his plate, and loudly
berating him if his rate of ingestion faltered.

"Fred needs somebody here to help him now. He's getting old, though the old fool doesn't know it."

Mark nodded, his mouth so full he was unable to reply,
and Mary reached across him for another hunk of home-
baked bread that was still warm from the oven. Her big
loose breast pressed against Mark and he almost choked.

"The girls don't get much chance to meet nice boys—
stuck out here on the farm."

Mary shifted in her seat, and her upper thigh came
firmly against Mark's.

"Leave the lad alone, Hilda, you scheming old woman,"
Fred slurred amiably from the head of the table.

"Mary, give Mark some more gravy on those potatoes."
The girl poured the gravy, steadying herself as she leaned
over towards Mark by placing her free hand on Mark's leg
above the knee.

"Eat up! Mary's done you a special milk tart for afters."

Mary's hand still rested on his leg, and now it moved
slowly but purposefully upwards. Instantly Mark's entire
attention focused on the hand and the food turned to hot
ashes in his mouth.

"Some more pumpkin, Marky?" Aunt Hilda asked with
concern, and Mark shook his head weakly. He could not
believe what was happening below the level of the table—
and directly in front of Mary's mother.

He felt a rising sense of panic.

As casually as he could in the circumstances, he dropped
one hand into his lap, and without looking at the girl,
gripped her wrist firmly.

"Have you had enough, Mark?"

"Yes, oh yes, indeed," Mark agreed fervently, and tried
to drag Mary's hand away, but she was a big powerful lass
and not easily distracted.

"Clear Mark's plate, Mary love, and give him some of
your lovely tart."

Mary seemed not to hear. Her head was bowed de-

murely over her plate, her cheeks were flushed bright glowing pink, and her lips trembled slightly. Beside her, Mark
writhed and squirmed in his seat.

"Mary, what's wrong with you, girl?" Her mother
frowned with irritation. "Do you hear me, child?"

"Yes, Mother, I hear you." At last she sighed and roused
herself. She stood up slowly and reached for Mark's plate
with both hands, while he sagged slightly on the bench,
weak with relief.

\*   \*   \*

Mark was exhausted from the long day's march and the
subsequent excitement, but though he fell asleep almost instantly, it was a sleep troubled by dreams.

Through a ghostly, brooding landscape of swirling mist
and weird unnatural light, he pursued a dark wraith—but
his legs were slowed, as though he moved through a bath of
treacle, and each pace was an enormous effort.

He knew the wraith that flitted through the mist ahead
of him was the old man, and he tried to cry out, but
though he strained with open mouth no sound came. Suddenly a small red hole appeared in the wraith's dark back
and from it flowed a bright pulsing stream of blood, and
the wraith turned to face him.

For a moment he looked into the old man's face, the
intelligent yellow eyes smiled at him over the huge spiked
moustache, and then the face melted like hot wax and the
pale features of a beautiful marble statue came up like a
face through water. The face of the young German—at last
Mark cried out and fell to cover his face. In the darkness
he sobbed softly, until another sensation came through to
his tortured imagination.

He felt a slow cunning caress. The sobbing shrivelled in
his throat, and gradually he abandoned himself to the
wicked delight of his senses. He knew what was coming, it
had happened so often in the lonely nights and he welcomed it now, drifting up slowly out of the depths of sleep.

At the edge of his awareness there was a voice now, whispering, crooning gently.

"There now, don't fuss, there now—it's all right now, it's going to be all right. Don't make that terrible noise."

He came awake gradually, for long moments not realizing that the warm firm flesh was reality. Above him were heavy white breasts, hanging big and heavy to sweep across his chest, white bare skin shining in the moonlight that spilled through the window above his narrow steel bed.

"Mary will make it better," the voice whispered with husky intensity.

"Mary?" he choked out the name, and tried to sit up, but she pushed him back gently with her full weight on his chest. "You're mad."

He began to struggle, but her mouth came down over his, wet and warm and all engulfing, and his struggles abated at the shock of this new sensation. He felt his senses whirl giddily.

Against the rising turmoil within him, was balanced the terrible things that he knew about women. Those strange and awful things that the regimental chaplain had explained to him, the knowledge that had sustained him against all the blandishments of the bold little *poules* of France and the ladies who had beckoned to him from the dark doorways of London's back streets.

The chaplain had told them how two equally evil terrible consequences came from unlawful union with a woman. Either there was a disease that was without cure, which ate away the flesh, left a rotting hole in a man's groin and finally drove him insane, or there was a child without a father—a bastard to darken a man's honour.

The threat was too much, and Mark tore his mouth free from the girl's sucking hungry lips and the thrusting, driving tongue.

"Oh God!" he whispered. "You'll have a baby."

"That's all right, silly," she whispered in a cheerful husky voice. "We can get married."

She shifted suddenly as he lay stunned by this intelligence, and she swung one knee over his supine body, pinning him under the heavy soft cushion of her flesh, smothering him with the fall of bright clinging hair.

"No." He tried to wriggle out from under her. "No, this is mad. I don't want to marry—"

"Yes, there—oh yes."

For another instant he was paralysed by the feeling of it, and then with a violent wrench he toppled her over. She fell sideways, her hands clutched wildly at his shoulders for an instant before she went over the side of the bed.

The washstand crashed over, and the thud of the girl's big body upon the floorboards echoed through the silent sleeping house.

For a moment afterwards the echoes died, the silence returned and then was split by a chorus of screams from the bedroom of the younger girls across the passage.

"What is it?" bellowed Fred Black, from the big bedroom.

"There's somebody in the house."

"Get him, Fred, don't just lie there."

"Where's my shotgun?"

"Help, papa! Help!"

With a single bound, Mary leapt up from the bedroom floor, snatched her nightgown off the chair and swept it over her head.

"Mary!" Mark sat up, he wanted to explain, to try and tell her about the chaplain. He leaned towards her and even in the faint moonlight he could see the fury that contorted her features.

"Mary—" He did not have time to avoid the blow, it came full-armed and flat-handed, smashing into the side of his head with a force that rattled his teeth and starred his vision. She was a big strong girl. When his head cleared, she was gone, but his ear still sang with the sound of a thousand wild bees.

A dusty Daimler lorry pulled up beside Mark as he trudged along the side of the deeply rutted road with thick grass growing along the central hump.

There was a middle-aged man and his wife in the front seat, and he called to Mark.

"Where are you going, son?"

"Ladyburg, sir."

"Jump in the back, then."

Mark rode the last twenty miles sitting high on bagged maize, with a coop of cackling hens beside him and the wind ruffling his stiff newly cropped hair.

They rattled over the bridge across the Baboon Stroom, and Mark marvelled at how it had all changed. Ladyburg was no longer a village, but a town. It had spread out as far as the stream itself, and there was a huge new goods yard below the escarpment in which half a dozen locomotives busily shunted trucks heavily laden with freshly sawn timber from the mills, or with bagged sugar from the new factory.

The factory itself was a monument to the town's progress, a towering structure of steel girders and huge boilers. Smoke and steam boiled from half a dozen stacks to form a grey mist that smeared away on the gentle breeze.

Mark wrinkled his nose at the faint stink of it on the wind, and then looked with awe down Main Street. There were at least a dozen new buildings, their ornate façades decorated with scrolls of ironwork, and beautifully intricate gables, stained glass in the main doors and the owner's name and date of construction in raised plaster lettering across the front; but these were all overshadowed by a giant structure four stories tall, crusted with ornamentation like a wedding cake of a wealthy bride. Proudly it bore the legend "Ladyburg Farmers Bank." The driver of the truck dropped Mark on the sidewalk in front of it, and left him with a cheery wave.

There were at least a dozen motor vehicles parked among the scotch-carts and horse-drawn carriages, and the people on the streets were well dressed and cheerful-looking, the citizens of a prosperous and thriving community.

Mark knew one or two of them from the old days, and as he trudged down Main Street with his pack slung over one shoulder, he paused to greet them. There was always a momentary confusion until they recognized him, and then, "But, Marky, we heard—we thought you'd been killed in France. It was in the *Gazette*."

The Land Deeds Registrar's Office was in the sprawled labyrinth of Government offices behind the Magistrate's Court and Police Station. There had been plenty of time to think on the long journey up from Andersland, and Mark knew exactly what he was going to do, and in what order.

There was a cramped space in the front of the office with an uninviting wooden bench, and a plain deal counter. There was an elderly clerk with nearsighted eyes behind steel-rimmed spectacles, and a peaked green eyeshade on his forehead. He looked like an ancient crow in his black alpaca jacket with paper guards over his cuffs, and a bony beak of a nose, as he crouched over his desk making a Herculean task of stamping a pile of documents.

He worked on for a few minutes. Mark patiently read the Government notices that plastered the walls, until the clerk looked up at last with the exasperated air of a man interrupted in a labour that might alter the destiny of mankind.

"I'd like to look at a land deed, please sir."

\* \* \*

*A certain piece of extinguished quit-rent land situate in the division of Ladyburg being Erf. No. 42 of Division A of One. The farm known as ANDERS-LAND . . .*
*Deed of Transfer passed in favour of Ladyburg Estates*

*Ltd registered at Ladyburg on 1st day of June, 1919.
Know all men whom it may concern that DENNIS
PETERSEN appeared before me, Registrar of Deeds,
he, the said appearer, being duly authorized by a
power of attorney executed at Ladyburg on the 12th
day of May, 1919, by JOHN ARCHIBALD AN-
DERS which power was witnessed in accordance with
law . . . and that the said appearer declared that his
principal had truly and legally sold . . .*

Mark turned to the next document.

*Agreement of Sale of Immovable property.
That JOHN ARCHIBALD ANDERS, hereinafter
known as the Seller, and LADYBURG ESTATES
LTD hereinafter known as the Purchaser—the Farm
known as ANDERSLAND—together with all im-
provements and buildings, standing crops, implements
and livestock—for the consideration of Three Thousand Pounds Sterling—*

    *In witness whereof the parties set their hand.
JOHN ARCHIBALD ANDERS (his mark) X
For and on behalf of LADYBURG ESTATES
LTD—
DIRK COURTNEY (DIRECTOR)
As witnesses of the above:—*
    *PIETER ANDRIES GREYLING
    CORNELIUS JOHANNES GREYLING*

Mark frowned at the two names. Piet Greyling and his
son had accompanied the old man up to Chaka's Gate almost immediately after witnessing the Deed of Sale, and
they had found him dead a few days later and buried him
out there in the wilderness.

*General Power of Attorney
in favour of DENNIS PETERSEN.
I, the undersigned, JOHN ARCHIBALD ANDERS*

*do hereby empower the above-mentioned DENNIS ...*
*signed JOHN ARCHIBALD ANDERS X (his mark)*
*as witness PIETER ANDRIES GREYLING.*
                    *CORNELIUS JOHNNES GREYLING*

Mark pored over the bundle of stiff legal parchment with its fancy printing and red wax seals with dangling ribbons of watered silk. Carefully he copied out the names of the parties involved in the transaction into his notebook and when he had finished, the clerk who had been jealously watching his precious papers reclaimed them and reluctantly handed over an official receipt for the five-shilling search fee.

The office of the registrar of companies was directly across the narrow lane, and here Mark was received in a different mood. The keeper of this gloomy cavern was a young lady dressed in severe dove-grey jacket and long sweeping skirt which was at odds with her lively eyes and pert air.

The pretty little face, with freckled snub nose, lit with a quick appreciative smile as Mark came in through the door and within minutes she was helping him in a comradely and conspiratorial manner as he perused the memoranda and articles of association of Ladyburg Estates Ltd.

"Do you live here?" asked the girl. "I haven't seen you before."

"No, I don't," Mark answered warily without looking up at her. He was finding it difficult to concentrate on the documents, and he remembered vividly his last encounter with a young girl.

"You're lucky." The girl sighed dramatically. "It's so dull here, nothing to do after work in the evenings." She waited hopefully, but the silence drew out.

The Directors of Ladyburg Estates were Messrs. Dirk Courtney and Ronald Beresford Pye, but they held only a single share each, just sufficient to qualify them to act as officers of the company.

The other nine hundred and ninety-nine thousand, nine

hundred and ninety-eight ordinary fully paid-up five-shilling shares were held by the Ladyburg Farmers Bank.

"Thank you very much," said Mark, returning the file to the girl while avoiding her frank gaze. "Could I see the file for Ladyburg Farmers Bank please?"

She brought it promptly.

The one million one-pound shares of the Ladyburg Farmers Bank were owned by three men, all of them Directors of the Company.

Dirk Courtney:        600,000 fully paid-up shares
Ronald Beresford Pye:  200,000 fully paid-up shares.
Dennis Petersen:     200,00 fully paid-up shares.

Mark frowned, the web was tangled and intricately woven, the same names again and again. He wrote the names into his notebook.

"My name is Marion, what's yours?"

"Mark—Mark Anders."

"Mark, that's a strong romantic name. Have you read *Julius Caesar*? Mark Antony was such a strong romantic character."

"Yes," agreed Mark. "He was. How much do I owe you for the search fee?"

"Oh, I'll just forget about that."

"No, look don't do that—I want to pay."

"All right then—if you want to."

At the door he paused.

"Thanks," he said shyly. "You were very kind."

"Oh it's a pleasure. If there's anything else—well, you know my name and where to find me." Then suddenly and unaccountably, she blushed scarlet. To hide it, she turned away with the files. When she looked again, he was gone, and she sighed, holding the files to her plump little bosom.

Mark found the accounts of the old man's estate filed with the Master of the Court almost contemptuously under the heading "Intestate Estates less than £100."

On the credit side were listed two rifles and a shotgun,

four trek oxen and scotch-cart—sold at public auction to realize eighty-four pounds sixteen shillings. On the debit side were legal and commission fees accruing to one Dennis Petersen—and costs of winding up the estate. The total was one hundred and twenty-seven pounds; the account had been in deficit—a distribution had been made and the estate closed. John Archibald Anders had gone, and left hardly a ripple behind him, not even the three thousand pounds he had been paid for Andersland.

Mark hefted his pack again and went out into the brilliant sunlight of afternoon. A water cart was moving slowly down Main Street drawn by two oxen, its sprinklers pouring fine jets of water into the roadway to lay the thick dust.

Mark paused and inhaled the smell of water on dry earth, and looked across the street at the towering building of the Ladyburg Farmers Bank.

For a brief moment, he touched the idea of crossing and entering, demanding of the men in there what had made the old man change his firm resolve to die and be buried on Andersland, how the money had been paid to him—and what he had done with it.

But the idea passed swiftly. The men who worked in that building were creatures of a different breed from the penniless grandson of an illiterate hard-scrabble farmer. There were orders in society, unseen barriers which a man could not cross, even if he had a university diploma, a military medal for gallantry and an honourable discharge from the army.

That building was the shrine of wealth and power and influence, where dwelt men like giants, like gods. The likes of Mark Anders did not barge in there demanding answers to unimportant questions about an old man of no account.

"Intestate estate less than £100," Mark whispered aloud, and set off across town, towards the clanking, huffing sounds of the railway goods yard.

"Yes," agreed the station master, "Piet Greyling was a mainline loco driver, and his son fired for him—but they threw in their time months ago, back in 1919, both of them." He rubbed his chin thoughtfully. "No, I don't know where they were headed, just too damned happy to see them go, I guess. Oh, yes, now I come to think on it, the son did say something about they were going up to Rhodesia. Going to buy a farm, or something," and the man chuckled. "Buy a farm! With what, I wonder—wishes and dreams—not on the salary of a loco driver or fireman."

* * *

The board room of the Ladyburg Farmers Bank occupied half of the top floor of the building; one set of floor-to-ceiling windows faced eastwards to catch the cool sea breeze on hot summer days, the other windows faced the tall escarpment. This made a fine backdrop to the town, and gave an interesting aspect to the huge room with its high ornately plastered ceiling where dancing white cherubs bearing bunches of grapes were suspended upside-down, frozen in their endless jollification.

The walls were panelled in dark mahogany that set off the green velvet curtaining with golden corded edges.

The carpet was green also, and thick enough to muffle the hoofs of a cavalry charge. The board room table was of marble with golden ormolu work, vine leaves and nude female figures clambering up the legs, playing harps or dancing demurely.

At one end of the table, a man stood respectfully, a man with the short neck and heavy shoulders of a wrestler. The seat of his khaki breeches was shiny from the saddle, and his boots were dusty from hard riding. He twisted the rim of a slouch hat nervously between his fingers.

Opposite where he stood at the far end of the marble table, another man slouched elegantly in the leather-padded chair. Even seated, it was clear that he was a big man, the shoulders under the expensive British broadcloth were wide and powerful.

However, his head was nicely balanced on these shoulders, a glorious head of lustrous but skilfully barbered hair, dark curls that extended low down on to his cheeks into magnificent sideboards. The strong smoothly shaven chin had the jut and set of a man accustomed to command, a wide determined mouth and perfect white teeth with which he now nibbled thoughtfully at his lower lip. A small frown formed a bird's foot at the bridge of his nose, between the dark intelligent eyes, and one carefully manicured fist supported his chin as he listened quietly.

"Anyway, I thought you might like to know, Mr. Courtney," the speaker ended lamely, and shuffled his dusty boots on the thick carpet. For a long moment there was silence. The man glanced uneasily at the other two gentlemen who flanked Dirk Courtney, but then flicked back to the central figure.

Dirk Courtney dropped his hand into his lap, and the frown cleared. "I suspect you did the right thing, Hobday." He smiled slightly, a smile that enhanced his powerful good looks. "You can rest in the antechamber. The clerk there will find refreshment for you, but I will want to talk to you again later. Wait."

"Yes, sir, Mr. Courtney, sir." The man crossed to the door with alacrity, and as it closed behind him the two men flanking Dirk Courtney burst out together.

"I told you at the time something like this would happen—"

"But you told us he had been killed—"

"I never liked the idea—"

"Oh, I thought it was going too far this time—"

They spoke across each other, quick breathless outbursts while Dirk Courtney sat with an enigmatic half-smile hovering on his lips, examining with attention the diamond on the little finger of his right hand, turning the big white stone to catch the light from the windows so that it flicked spots of brilliant light across the ceiling high above where he sat.

After a few minutes, the two of them faltered into silence, and Dirk Courtney looked up politely.

"Have you both finished? I found that most helpful, constructive, imaginative." He looked from one to the other expectantly, and then when they were silent he went on, "Unfortunately, you are not in possession of all the facts. Here is some more news for you. He arrived in town this morning, and he went straight to the Land Deeds, from there to the Registrar of Companies, the Master's Office—" There was a fresh outburst of lamentation from his listeners, while Dirk Courtney selected a cigar from the humidor and prepared it carefully, cutting the end with a gold-plated pocket-knife and moistening it between his lips, then he held it poised between thumb and forefinger while he waited for silence again.

"Thank you, gentlemen—but as I was saying, the gentleman in question then went down to the goods yard—and began making inquiries about Greyling and son."

This time they were silent, exchanging appalled and disbelieving glances, and the silence drew out while Dirk Courtney struck a Swan Vesta and waited for the sulphur to burn off before he lit the cigar.

"It was all your idea," said Ronald Pye. He was at least thirty years senior to Dirk Courtney. Once prosperously bulging flesh had sagged beneath his expensive waistcoat, his jowls drooped also, like the wattles of a rooster, and his cheeks were mottled with faded freckles and old man's blemishes, little darker liver spots. His hair also had faded and thinned, stained only by residual traces of the fiery ginger it had once been. But his prominent ears stood out from his head, giving him an alert listening look, like a desert fox, and his eyes had a fox's cunning glitter as they watched Dirk Courtney's face.

"Yes," Dirk Courtney agreed. "Most ideas around here are mine indeed. That's why the net reserves of the Farmers Bank have increased from one and a half to fifteen million pounds in the ten years since I started contributing my ideas—"

Ronny Pye went on staring at him, regretting bitterly for the ten thousandth time in those ten years that he had ever been tempted to sell control of the bank to this young adventurer, this elegant buccaneer.

God knows, there had been occasion for doubt, for caution, and he had hesitated long enough before accepting the fantastic offer that Dirk Courtney had made. He had known too much of the lad's history, how he had left his home here in Ladyburg in unsavoury circumstances, estranged from his father and family.

Then, years later, he had sauntered into Ronald Pye's office, unannounced and unheralded, and made his offer.

He had seen at a glance that the boy had grown into a hard man, but the offer had been too good to dismiss, and then immediately after, he had begun to hear the dark rumours that followed the man as vultures follow the lion. He should have been warned; the fact that Dirk Courtney could offer six hundred thousand pounds in cash for sixty per cent of the Bank's shares and support the offer with a bank guarantee from Lloyds Bank of London was, in itself, enough to give substance to the dark rumours. How often does an honest man make that kind of money in a few short years, he asked himself.

In the end the money had tempted Ronny Pye, that and the chance to score over an old enemy, General Sean Courtney. He had delighted in the prospect of settling up the estranged son, setting him up in almost baronial circumstances in the very centre of Courtney country. The delight in doing so had swung the balance, spite and six hundred thousand pounds cash money.

It had been a bad bargain. "I was against this from the beginning," he said now.

"My dear Pye, you are against every new idea—on principle. Yet only a week ago you were swooning like a virgin bride over the balance sheet of Ladyburg Estates, and Zululand sugar."

Dirk stood up from his chair. His full height was imposing; he smoothed his hair lightly with both hands while his cigar was gripped between strong white teeth, then he arranged the folds of his cravat, touching the pearl pin before swinging away and striding to the far wall of the board room.

He drew down the rolled map of Zululand and north Natal that covered half the wall, and stood back from it. The boundary of every farm was marked in large-scale topography. The farms belonging to Ladyburg Estates had been carefully shaded in green chalk. They made an impressive sweep of colour from sea to mountains, a great phalanx of land and natural wealth.

"There it is now, gentlemen—the scheme that you opposed so violently." He smiled again. "It was too rich for your watery blood." The smile faded, and he scowled. When he scowled, the line of the wide mouth became bitter and the set of the lustrous eyes altered, with a mean pinched expression. "The key to the whole thing was here on the Umfolosi—the water, we had to have it or none of it made sense. One stupid, stubborn, uneducated old bastard—" he cut it off abruptly, and in a moment his smile was back, the voice tight with excitement. "It is all ours now, the full south bank of the river, and it's not going to end there!" His spread hands clammed down on the map, hooked like claws. "Here," he said, "and here, and here—" his hands marched northwards greedily.

He swung away from the map, laughing, and cocked his big handsome head at them. "Look at you," he laughed. "It's running down your legs, you're so terrified—and all because I'm making you rich."

Dennis Petersen spoke now. He was the same age as Ronny Pye, married to his sister, and, but for that connection, he would never have been seated at the ormolu marble table, for he was the least significant of the three men. His features were indefinite and slightly blurred, his body in expensive clothing was pudgy and shapeless, while the colour of his eyes was difficult to fathom.

"What are we going to do?" he asked, and though his hands were clasped in his lap, it seemed that he was actually wringing them plantively.

"We?" Dirk asked kindly, and crossed to his chair. "We,

my dear Dennis?" he patted the man's shoulder like a father, despite the age difference. "*We* aren't going to do a thing. You just go back to your own office now—and I will tell you about it once it's over."

"Listen, Dirk." Dennis lifted his chin firmly. "No more of that—that rough stuff, do you hear?" Then he saw Dirk's eyes and dropped his chin. "Please," he mumbled.

Dirk chuckled. "Off you go and do your sums, both of you, add up the money. Don't worry about a thing." He helped them from their seats, a hand on each shoulder, and shepherded them towards the door. "We have a board meeting tomorrow at nine o'clock, Dennis, I will be discussing the new extraction plant at Stanger. I will want the figures, make sure I have them."

Alone for a moment, Dirk Courtney's face changed and the eyes narrowed. He pressed out the stub of the cigar in the onyx ashtray as he crossed to the door that led to the antechamber.

"Hobday," he called softly. "Come in here a moment, please."

\* \* \*

There are occasions in a hunter's experience when a spoor begins hot and true and then fades. Mark remembered a hunt like that which he and the old man had made up near Chaka's Gate.

"Dead spoor, gone away," he muttered aloud now, and stood uncertainly in the main street of Ladyburg. There seemed no way that he might find the old man's grave. No way that he could bring the body back and rebury it beside Alice on Andersland.

Less important was the money that the old man had been paid for Andersland. Three thousand pounds. It was a vast fortune in Mark's eyes and it would be good to know what had happened to it. With that amount, he could afford land of his own somewhere.

Then Mark faced the issue he had avoided up until now

and admitted that there was just one more faint chance, but he felt his stomach tighten at what he had to do. With a physical effort he steeled himself and set off steadily down the street towards the towering building of the Ladyburg Farmers Bank. He had not reached it before the church clock on the spire at the end of the street sounded the hour, five clear chimes that echoed across the valley, and a dozen bank employees came out in a group through the front door, smiling and chatting gaily in the relief of the day's work ended—while a uniformed guard began closing and locking the solid mahogany doors.

Mark felt a sneaking sense of relief, and he turned away. "I'll come back tomorrow," he told himself firmly.

The boarding house behind the church offered dinner and a bed for seven shillings and sixpence, and Mark thought about it for only a moment. The sovereigns that he had from the old man's hoard might have to carry him long and far.

He went on out to the bridge over the Baboon Stroom and climbed down on to the bank, moving upstream to find a place to camp.

There was a fine site, with trees and firewood a quarter of a mile above the bridge, but when Mark went down the bank to the water, he could smell the stink of it before he touched the surface with the canteen; he paused, squatting on his haunches.

There was a thick soapy scum thrown up along the edge, and it had coated the stems of the reeds. For the first time Mark realized that the reeds were dead and brown, and that the water bubbled with sullen beads of gas. He scooped a handful and sniffed at it, then flicked it away with disgust and stood up, wiping his hand on the seat of his pants.

There was a big yellow fish, at least four pounds in weight, its swollen belly upwards and rotting opaque eyes bulging from its head as it floated in the sluggish current, turning gently in the eddy at the edge of the reeds. Mark watched it with a feeling of disquiet, of foreboding, as though that poisoned and rotting carcass had some special significance in his life. He shuddered softly and turned away, climbed the bank again and shouldered his pack.

He made his way upstream, pausing now and then to peer down into the river-bed, until he was opposite the steel structure of the new sugar mill; here the waters of the stream boiled and steamed with wisps of pale gas that hung like mist in the stiff brown reeds. Around the next bend he came upon the effluent pipe, a six-inch black iron pipe that stuck out over the far side of the bank from which the hot, steaming discharge poured in a continuous stream.

A change in the breeze carried the acrid chemical stench of it to where Mark stood, and he coughed and turned away.

A hundred yards further upstream, the clear water chuckled through clean stands of green reeds that bowed and swung gracefully on the breeze, and Mark saw the deep waving shape of an eel in the pool beyond, and watched the small black and pink crabs scurrying across the sugar-white sand below the surface.

He found another camp site on the first slope of the escarpment, beside a waterfall and its slowly swirling pool. In the trees above him, the ferns hung like soft green veils, and when he stripped his clothing and went into the pool, the water was a cool and refreshing delight.

He shaved with the old cut-throat, sitting naked on a mossy rock beside the pool. He dried himself on his shirt and then rinsed it out and hung it beside the small bright fire to dry, and while he waited for the canteen to boil he wandered, bare to the waist, on to the open slope and looked down into the valley.

The sun was already touching the rim of the escarpment, and its low rays were ruddy and warm rose. They burnished the iron roofs of the town, and tinted the column of smoke that rose from the chimney stack of the sugar mill to a beautiful golden bronze. The smoke rose tall into the evening sky, for the breeze had dropped in that peculiar stillness and hush of the African evening.

Movement caught his eye, and he blinked to clear his vision.

There was a hunting party in the open land beyond the town. Even at this distance, Mark could tell they were hunters. Four horsemen moving slowly in a group, one with a rifle or shotgun held against his hip, its barrel pointing to the sky as he leaned forward intently in the saddle. The other three were armed also; he could see the guns in the scabbards at their knees, and they also had that intent air of suppressed excitement, the air of the hunter. Ahead of the group was a single figure, a Zulu in ragged cast-off western clothing but he led the horsemen in the characteristic attitude of the tracker, trotting in that deceptively fast gait of the Zulu, head down, eyes on the ground, carrying a stripped reed in one hand, the tracker's wand to part the grass, or touch the spoor.

Idly Mark wondered what they were hunting, so close to town, and on the bank of that dying and poisoned river, for they were coming along the same trail that Mark had followed to the escarpment.

The light was going swiftly now, the shining beacons of the iron roofs winked out swiftly as the sun went below the crest, but in the last of the light, Mark saw the leader of the group of horsemen rein in his mount and straighten in the saddle. He was a stocky figure, sitting square on his mount. The man looked up towards the escarpment where Mark stood, then the light was gone and the group became a dark blob against the darkening land.

Vaguely disturbed, and troubled by the day just past, by the cold memories of the old man, by the sadness of that dying river, and at last by that distant figure, Mark crouched over his fire, munching his stew of tinned bully and then sipping his coffee.

When at last he pulled on his coat and rolled into his blanket close beside the fire, he could not sleep. The sense of disquiet seemed to grow rather than abate, and he found himself wondering again what four horsemen could find to hunt on the edge of a busy town. Then he thought again about the way that they had followed his own path along the river, and the disquiet deepened, sleep receded.

Suddenly he remembered how the old man would never sleep beside his cooking fire.

"I learned that when we was chasing Boer. A light in the night brings things other than moths—lions, hyenas and men." He could almost hear the old man's voice saying it, and he rose immediately, with the blanket still around his shoulders, and moved away up the slope fifty yards until he found a hollow filled with dead leaves.

Sleep came at last and the soft skirt of it was falling lightly across his eyes when a Scops owl called in the forest near him; instantly he was fully awake. It was a familiar night sound, but this one had jarred some deep chord in him. The imitation had been clever, but it did not deceive an ear so closely tuned to the sounds of the wild.

Tense and listening, Mark lifted his head slowly and peered down the slope. His fire was a puddle of pink embers and above him the shapes of the trees were dark and fluffy against a crisp sky of white stars.

The owl called again down near the pool, and, at the same moment, Mark heard something move stealthily near him in the darkness, something big and heavy, the brush brush of footfalls in the dead leaves. Then there was silence again.

Mark strained his eyes and ears into the darkness, but it was impenetrable under the trees.

Far below in the valley, a locomotive whistled three times, the sound carrying clearly in the stillness, and then there was the huff and puff of the train pulling out from the goods yard and settling into a steady rhythmic beat of boiler and tracks.

Mark tried to put that sound beyond his hearing, trying to filter it out so that he could discern the closer softer sounds in the night around him.

Something moved down the slope; he heard the silky soft whisper of it and then he saw movement, outlined against the glowing ashes of his fire, a man's booted legs stepped out of the darkness and halted beside the fire, standing completely still.

Nearer Mark, there was another movement, a stir of impatient feet in dead leaves—and then, unmistakably, the metallic snick of gun-metal as a safety-catch was slipped to the "fire" position. The sound struck like electricity along Mark's nerve ends, and his breath caught in his throat. It was very close, six feet away, and now he thought he could make out the loom of the man against the stars. He was standing almost on top of Mark's bed in the hollow, staring down at the fire beside the camp.

The man at the fire spoke now, softly, but his voice carried clearly. "The bastard has gone—he's not here." He stooped to the pile of dry firewood that Mark had cut and stacked. He threw a piece on to the embers, and sparks flew upwards in a fiery spiral and the branch flamed, throwing out a circle of yellow light.

Then he exclaimed sharply, "His pack is still here," and he hefted the shotgun expectantly, glaring into the night. "Remember, there's a hundred pounds on it."

The words and the way the man was handling the shotgun made his intention clear beyond doubt. Mark felt the warm flood of adrenalin rush through his body, and he was poised and quivering with suppressed energy, ready to burst into explosive movement in an instant.

The man near him moved again, and Mark heard the muted tap of metal on metal, the sound of the man's breathing also, hoarse with tension—and then suddenly and with devastating shock, bright white light split the darkness. A lantern beam swivelled and then fastened on Mark's blanket-wrapped crouching form.

In the instant before he moved, Mark saw the shape of the man beyond the dazzle of the light. He carried the lantern in his right hand holding it high, at the level of his head, and the rifle was in his left hand, hanging at the trail.

He was completely unprepared to find Mark lying almost at his feet, and his shout was wild.

"He's here. My God." He tried to bring up the rifle, but his right hand held the lantern.

"Shoot! Shoot, damn it!" another voice shouted, a voice somehow familiar, and beside Mark the man dropped the lantern and began to swing up the rifle. Mark launched himself straight at him.

He used the man's own momentum, taking the upswing of the rifle; seizing the muzzle of the barrel in one hand and the stock in the other, he smashed the weapon into the man's face with the full weight and force of his body behind it. He heard gristle and bone crunch, while the solid impact of the steel breech striking into the man's face was transmitted through the rifle into his arms, jarring him to the shoulders.

The man went over backwards, with a cry that bubbled with the quick burst of blood into his nose and mouth. Mark bounded over him and ran at the slope.

Behind him there was a chorus of shouts and cries, and then the blam, blam of a shotgun and the double glow of the muzzle flashes. Mark heard the heavy charges of shot slash into the leaves beside him, and something burned his upper arm like the sting of a wild bee.

"The light. Get the light!"

"There he is, don't let him get away."

A rifle fired three times in quick succession; it sounded like a .303 Lee-Enfield. The bullet hit a rock and howled away into the sky, another thumped into a tree trunk close beside him as he ran.

Mark fell heavily in the dark and felt his ankle go, the pain of it exploded up his leg into his groin and lower belly. He rolled on to his knees, and the beam of the lantern swept over, and then fastened hungrily on him.

"We've got him."

A fusillade of shots, and a triumphant chorus of shouts. The shot and bullets shattered the air around him, one so close that the whip of it deafened one ear and he threw himself forward at the slope.

The pain in his foot made Mark cry out. It was white-hot shooting agony that burst from his ankle and broke like brilliant phosphorescent surf against the roof of his skull, but he drove himself on, soaked with sweat, swerving as he ran, sobbing and hobbling on the damaged leg.

They were spread out in the bush behind him, and it seemed that the slope was tiring them quickly, men accustomed to riding horseback, for the cries were becoming strained and breathless, edged with worry and the first fear that their quarry might escape them.

Mark was trying to think between the bursts of agony with which each step racked him. He thought to drop into thick cover and lie until they passed him, but they were too close for that, and they had a tracker with them, a tracker who had brought them unerringly to his camp, even in darkness. To lie down now would be surrender—and suicide, but he could not go on much longer. Already the pain was threatening to swamp him, there was a sound in his head like great wings and his vision was starting to break up and star.

He fell to his knees and vomited, gagging and choking on the acid gall of it, and within seconds the voice of the pursuit was closer and more urgent. He dragged himself up, and the lantern beam caught him squarely, a rifle bullet disrupted the air about his head so that he staggered as he blundered onwards, using the screen of bush to avoid the beam of light. Quite suddenly he felt the ground tilt upwards sharply under his feet.

He lost his footing again, but in the same movement rolled to his feet and stumbled over a lip on to level ground where there was the sudden sugary crunch of gravel under his feet. Three stumbling paces and he came down heavily, his feet knocked out from under him and as he went down, steel smeared the skin from his outflung forearm.

He lay panting and blinded for long seconds and heard the hunters bay like hounds down the slope. The sound goaded him and he groped with outstretched hands for purchase to push himself on to his feet once more.

He found the cold smooth steel that had tripped him; it

trembled like a living thing under his hands. It came to him then that he had climbed the embankment of the railway line and fallen across the rails of the permanent way.

He pushed himself to his knees, and now he heard the deep panting rush in the night; suddenly the whole slope of the escarpment was lit by reflected light that swung dramatically and brightened like daylight as the locomotive he had heard leaving the goods yard in the valley came roaring out of the deep cutting that skirted the steepest part of the escarpment, before crossing the deep gorge of the river.

The long white beam of the lamp struck him like a solid thing and he flung up his arm to shield his eyes and rolled off the rails, crouching down on the gravel on the opposite side to that of his pursuers.

In the light of the locomotive lamp, Mark saw a stocky agile figure come up the embankment at a run. He ducked across the tracks, directly under the roaring throbbing loco. The dazzle of light prevented Mark seeing his face, yet there was something familiar in the way the man moved and held his shoulders.

The engine came thundering down on Mark, and as it drew level a spurt of steam from the driving pistons scalded him with its hot breath. Then it was past and there was just the dark blurred rush of the boxcars above him.

Mark dragged himself upright, balancing on his good foot and struck the streams of sweat from his eyes, peering upwards to judge his moment.

When it came, he almost missed it; his hands were slippery with sweat and the railing was almost jerked from his grip even though the train had lost much of its speed and power on the slope.

The strain in his shoulder shot an arrow of pain along his arm, and he was torn off his feet, swinging against the side of the boxcar while he grappled wildly for a grip with his other hand.

He found purchase and clung on to the side of the boxcar, his feet still free but scrabbling for the footplates—and at that moment hands like steel claws seized his injured ankle, the full weight of a heavy body bore him down, racking him out against the side of the car.

Mark screamed with the unbearable white-hot pain of the grip on his ankle, and it took all his strength and courage to maintain his double grip on the rail.

His body was penduluming, as the man who held him was himself swung off the ground and then came back to skid and run in the loose gravel of the embankment, as though he were driving a dog-sledge.

Mark twisted his head back and judged the white blob of the man's face and aimed the kick with his free foot, but it was an impossible target. At that instant the sound of the locomotive altered, as it hit the steel of the bridge where it crossed the deep gorge of the river.

The uprights of the bridge sprang out of the rushing corridor of blackness; Mark heard the deadly hiss of the riveted steel girders flit past his head, and at the same moment the grip on his leg was released. He clung with his remaining strength and resolve to the railing of that goods truck, while the train racketed over the bridge and ploughed on steadily up the slope, until it burst at last over the crest on to the level ground of the plateau. It picked up speed sharply, and Mark dragged himself inch by agonized inch up the railing, until at last he tumbled over the side of the open boxcar on to the load of sugar sacks and lay face downwards, sobbing for each breath, while he rode the high storm surf of pain from his leg.

The cold roused him at last. His sweat-sodden coat was turned icy by the rush of night air and he crawled painfully forward towards the shelter of the high steel side of the car. He checked quietly and found with relief that his purse and notebook were still in his pocket.

Suddenly he was aware that he was not alone and fresh panic gripped him.

"Who's that?" he croaked, recoiling quickly into a defensive attitude.

A voice answered quickly in deep Zulu. "I mean no harm, Nkosi," and Mark felt a quick rush of relief. A man crouched against the side of the car, out of the wind, and it was clear that he was as alarmed by Mark's presence as Mark had been by his.

"I mean no harm, lord. I am a poor man without the money to pay to ride the steamer. My father is sick and dying in Tekweni, Durban town."

"Peace," grunted Mark in the same language. "I am a poor man also." He dragged himself into shelter beside the Zulu, and the movement twisted his ankle and he gasped at the fresh pain.

"Hau!" the black man's eyes caught the starlight as he peered at Mark. "You are hurt."

"My leg," Mark grunted, trying to ease it into a more comfortable position—and the Zulu leaned forward and Mark felt his gentle hands on the ankle.

"You are without shoes?" The man was surprised at Mark's torn and bloodied feet.

"I was chased by bad men."

"Ha," the Zulu nodded, and Mark saw in the starlight that he was a young man. "The leg is bad. I do not think the bone is broken, but it is bad."

He untied the small pack beside him and he took out some article of clothing. Deliberately he began to tear the material into strips.

"No," Mark protested sharply. "Do not destroy your clothes for me." He knew how each article of western clothing, however ragged and threadbare, was treasured.

"It is an old shirt," said the Zulu simply and began to bind up the swollen ankle skilfully. When he had finished, it felt easier.

"*Ngi ya bone*—I praise you," Mark told him, and then he shivered violently as the delayed but icy fist of shock clamped down on him; he felt nausea rise in his throat and he shivered again.

The Zulu took the blanket from around his own shoulders and placed it carefully over Mark.

"No. I cannot take your blanket." The blanket smelled

of smoke from a dung fire, and of the Zulu himself—the earthy African tang. "I cannot take it."

"You need it," said the Zulu firmly. "You are sick."

"Very well," Mark muttered, as another shivering fit caught him. "But it is a large blanket, big enough for two—"

"It is not fitting."

"Come," said Mark roughly, and the Zulu hesitated a moment longer before drawing closer and taking up a fold of the woollen blanket.

Shoulder to shoulder, they sat on into the night, and Mark found himself dropping into a haze of exhaustion and pain, for the swollen ankle still beat like a drum. The Zulu beside him was silent, and Mark thought he slept, but as the train slowed after two hours' hard run across the plateau, he whispered quietly,

"This is Sakabula halt. It stops here for to let the other train pass."

Mark remembered the desolate siding with its double loop of line. No buildings and only a signboard to identify it. He would have lapsed once more into half sleep, but something warned him, a strange sense of danger which he had developed so acutely in France.

He shrugged aside the blanket, and dragged himself up on his knees to peer ahead. The track came into the siding on a gentle curve, and the silver rails glittered in the lamp of the locomotive.

Far ahead was the sign-post of the halt, stark white in the beam from the locomotive, but there was something else. Parked on the track beside the halt was a dark vehicle, a heavy lorry, and its headlights still burned. In the puddle of yellow light Mark made out the dark shapes of waiting men. Alarm jarred his bowels and clutched at his chest with a cold cramping fist.

A motor lorry from Ladyburg could not have reached here ahead of them, but a telegraph message could have alerted—

"I must go," Mark blurted, and with stiff fingers he

hooked a sovereign out of his money belt and pressed it quickly into the Zulu's hand.

"There is no call for—" the man began, but Mark cut him off brusquely.

"Stay in peace." He dragged himself to the side of the car furthest from the waiting men, and lowered himself down the steel ladder until he hung just above the tracks.

He waited for the locomotive to slow down, groaning and creaking and sighing steam, and then he braced himself and dropped—trying to take most of his weight on his good leg.

He collapsed forwards as he struck the ground; ducking his head, he rolled on to his shoulders and, drawing up his knees, went down the embankment like a rubber ball.

In the dry pale grass beside the line, he did not rise but dragged himself on elbows and belly to a low dark thorn bush, fifty yards from the rails. Slowly he worked himself under its low spiny branches and lay face down, gritting his teeth against the dull beat of his ankle.

The train had halted with its van level with Mark's hiding place; the guard climbed down, flashing his lantern, while from the head of the train a group of men, each one carrying a lantern, hurried back toward him, searching the open trucks as they came.

Mark could see they were all armed, and their voices carried loudly as they called explanations to the driver and fireman who leaned from the cab of the locomotive.

"What's the trouble?"

"You've got a fugitive from justice aboard."

"Who are you?"

'We're special constables."

"Who's the fellow?"

"He robbed a bank—"

"He killed four men in Ladyburg—"

"He jumped your train on the escarpment—"

"Don't take any chances, you fellows, the bastard is a killer—"

They came swiftly down the train, talking loudly and

calling to each other to bolster their courage, and at the last moment Mark remembered the Zulu. He should have warned the man, but he had been too concerned with his own danger. He wanted to shout now, warn him to run, but he could not bring himself to do it. The Zulu would be all right, they would not shoot when they saw he was a black, they might slap him around a little and throw him off—

The Zulu darted out from between two of the boxcars from where he had climbed down on to the coupling. He was a dark flitting shape, and somebody yelled a warning. Immediately there was a shot.

Mark saw the dust from the bullet fly in the lamplight, and the Zulu swerved and ran directly out into the open grassland. Half a dozen shots ripped the night, the muzzle flashes were angry red blooms in the night, but the Zulu ran on.

One of the men on the track dropped to his knee, and Mark saw his face white and eager in the light of the torches. He aimed deliberately, and his rifle kicked up sharply.

The Zulu collapsed in the grass without a cry, and they raced forward in an excited pack to gather around his body.

"Oh, Jesus, it's only a black." There was confused angry discussion and argument for five minutes, and then four of them took an arm and leg each and carried the Zulu between them to the parked lorry.

The black man's head lolled back, almost sweeping the earth, his mouth gaped open and the blood that dripped from it was black as tar in the lamplight and his head swung loosely to the uneven stride of the men who carried him. They lifted him into the back of the lorry.

The north-bound train came thundering through the siding, its whistle shrilling on a high piercing shriek, and then it was gone on its way to Ladyburg.

The men climbed into the lorry and the engine fired, and

it moved away with its headlights sweeping sky and earth as it pitched over the bumpy track.

The stationary train whistled mournfully and it began to roll forward, rumbling slowly over the tracks. Mark crawled out from his hiding-place beneath the bush, and hopped and stumbled after it, catching it just before its speed built up.

He crawled over the sugar bags into the lee of the steel side, and found the Zulu had left his blanket. As he wrapped it around his icy body, he felt the guilt flood over him, guilt for the man's death, the man who had been a friend—then the guilt turned to anger.

Bitter corrosive anger that sustained him through the night as the train rushed southwards.

\* \* \*

Fordsburg is a squalid suburb of Johannesburg, three hundred miles from the golden grassy hills of Zululand and the beautiful forested valley of Ladyburg. It is an area of mean cottages, tiny workers' houses of galvanized iron on timber frames, each with a bleak little garden. In some of the gardens there were brave and defiant shows of bright blooms, barbeton daisies, cannas and flaming red poinsettia, but in most of them the bare untended earth, patched with blackjack and khakibush, told of the tenants' indifference.

Over the narrow streets and crowded cottages, the mine dumps held majestic sway, towering table-topped mountains of poisonous yellow earth from which the gold had been extracted. The cyanide process of extraction ensured that the earth of the dumps was barren and sterile. No plants grew upon them, and on windy days the yellow dust and grit whipped over the grovelling cottages beneath them.

The dumps dominated the landscape, monument to the antlike endeavours of man, symbols of his eternal greed for gold. The mine headgears were spidery steel structures against the pale cloudless blue of the highveld winter sky. The huge steel wheels on their heights spun endlessly, back and forth, lowering the cages filled with men deep into the earth, and rising again with the ore bins loaded with the gold-rich rock.

Mark made his way slowly down one of the narrow, dusty streets. He still limped slightly, and a cheap cardboard suitcase carried the few possessions he had bought to replace those he had lost on the escarpment.

The clothes he wore were an improvement on the shapeless demobilization suit that the army had given him. His flannels were neatly creased and the blue blazer fitted his good shoulders and narrow flanks, the open-necked white shirt was snowy clean and set off the smooth brown skin of his neck and face.

He reached the cottage numbered fifty-five on the gate, and it was a mirror image of those on each side and opposite. He opened the gate and went up the short flagged path, aware that somebody was watching him from behind the lace curtain in the front room.

However, when he knocked on the front door it was only opened after a delay of many minutes, and Mark blinked at the woman who stood there.

Her dark short hair was freshly combed, and the clothes she wore had clearly been hastily put on in place of dowdier everyday dress. She was still fastening the belt at her slim waist. It was a dress of pale blue with a design of yellow daisies, and it made her appear young and gay, although Mark saw at once that she was at least ten years older than he was.

"Yes?" she asked, tempering the abrupt demand with a smile.

"Does Fergus MacDonald live here?" He saw now that she was good-looking, not pretty, but fine-looking with good bones in her cheeks and dark intelligent eyes.

"Yes, this is Mr. MacDonald's house." There was a foreign inflection in her voice that was intriguing. "I am Mrs. MacDonald."

"Oh," he said, taken by surprise. He had known Fergus was married. He had spoken about it often, but Mark had never really thought about his wife before—not as a real flesh and blood woman, and certainly not one like this. "I am an old friend of Fergus' from the army."

"Oh, I see—" she hesitated.

"My name's Mark, Mark Anders." Instantly her attitude changed, the half smile boomed and lit her whole face. She gave a small gasp of pleasure.

"Mark, of course, Mark." She took his arm impetuously and drew him over the threshold. "He has spoken of you so often—I feel I know you so well. Like a member of the family, like a brother," she still had his arm, standing close to him, laughing up at him. "Come in, Mark, come in. I am Helena."

\* \* \*

Fergus MacDonald sat at the head of the deal table in the dingy kitchen. The table was covered with sheets of newsprint instead of a cloth and Fergus hunched over his plate, and scowled angrily as he listened to Mark's account of his flight from Ladyburg.

"The bastards, they are the enemy, Mark. The new enemy."

His mouth was filled with potato and heavily spiced boerewors, thick farmer's sausage, and he spoke through it.

"We are in another war, lad—and this time they are worse than the bloody Hun."

"More beer, Mark." Helena leaned across to fill his tumbler from the black quart bottle.

"Thank you." Mark watched the foaming head rise in his glass, and he pondered Fergus' statement.

"I don't understand, Fergus. I don't know who these men are, I don't know why they tried to kill me."

"They are the bosses, lad. That's who we are fighting now. The rich, the mine-owners, the bankers, all those who oppress the working man."

Mark took a long swallow of his beer, and Helena smiled at him from across the table.

"Fergus is right, Mark. We have to destroy them." And she began to talk. It was strange confusing talk from a woman, and there was a fanatical light in her dark eyes. The words had a compelling power in her clear articulate voice with its lilting accent, and Mark watched the way she used her hands to emphasize each point. They were neat strong hands with gracefully tapered fingers and short nails. The nails were clean and trimmed but the first two fingers of her right hand were stained pale yellow. Mark wondered at that, until suddenly Helena reached across and took a cigarette from the packet at Fergus' elbow.

Still talking, she lit the cigarette from a match in her cupped hands, and drew deeply before exhaling forcibly through pursed lips. Mark had never seen a woman smoke before, and he stared at her. She shook her head vehemently.

"The history of the people's revolt is written in blood. Look at France, see how the revolution sweeps forward in Russia."

The short dark shining curls danced around her smooth pale cheeks, and she pursed her lips again to drag at the cigarette, and in some strange fashion Mark found the mannish act shocking—and exciting.

He felt his groin clenching, the tight swollen hardening of his flesh, beyond his reason—far beyond his control. His breathing caught with shock and embarrassment, and he leaned back and slipped one hand into his trouser pocket, certain that both of them must be aware of his shameful reaction, but instead Helena reached across the table and seized his other wrist in a surprisingly powerful grip.

"We know our enemy, we know what must be done and how we must do it, Mark."

Her fingers seemed to burn like heated iron into his flesh, he felt dizzy with the force of it. His voice was hoarse as he forced himself to reply.

"They are strong, Helena, powerful—"

"No, no, Mark, the workers are strong, the enemy are weak, and smug. They suspect nothing, they wallow like hogs in the false security of their golden sovereigns, but in reality they are few and unprepared. They do not know their own weakness—and as yet the workers do not realize their great strength. We will teach them."

"You're right, lass." Fergus wiped the gravy from the plate with a crust of bread and stuffed it into his mouth. "Listen to her, Mark, we are building a new world, a brave and beautiful new world."

He belched loudly and pushed his plate away, leaving both elbows on the table. "But first we have to tear down and destroy this rotten, unjust and corrupt society. There will be hard fighting, and we will need good hard fighting men." He laughed harshly and slapped Mark's shoulder. "They'll call for MacDonlad and Anders again, lad, you hear me."

"There is nothing for us to lose, Mark." Helena's cheeks were flushed. "Nothing but our chains—and there is a whole world to win. Karl Marx said that, and it's one of the great truths of history."

"Helena, are you," he hesitated to use the word, "are you and Fergus—well I mean, you aren't Bolsheviks are you?"

"That's what the bosses, and their minions, the police, call us." She laughed contemptuously. "They try to make us criminals, already they fear us. With reason, Mark, we will give them reason."

"No, lad, don't call us Bolsheviks. We are members of the communist party, dedicated to universal communism. I'm the local party secretary and shop steward of the mineworkers' union for the boilermakers' shop."

"Have you read Karl Marx?" Helena demanded.

"No." Mark shook his head, dazed and shocked, but still sexually excited by her to the edge of pain. Fergus a Bolshevik? A bomb-throwing monster? But he knew he was not. He was an old and trusted comrade.

"I will lend you my copy."

"Come on, lass," Fergus chuckled, and shook his head. "We are going too fast for the lad. He's got a right barmy look right now." He leaned over and placed an affectionate arm around Mark's shoulders, drawing him close. "Have you a place to stay, lad? A job? A place to go?"

"No." Mark flushed. "I haven't, Fergus."

"Oh, yes you have," Helena cut in quickly. "I have fixed the bed in the other room—you'll stay there, Mark."

"Oh, but I couldn't—"

"It's done," she said simply.

"You'll stay, lad." Fergus squeezed him hard. "And we'll see about a job for you tomorrow—you're book-learned. You can read and write and figure, it will be easy to fix you. I know they need a clerk up at the pay office, and the paymaster is a comrade, a member of the party."

"I'll pay you for lodging."

"Of course you will," Fergus chuckled again, and filled his glass to the brim with beer. "It's good to see you again, son," and he raised his own glass. "Send down the line for MacDonald and Anders—and warn the bastards we are coming!" He took a long swallow, the pointed Adam's apple bobbing in his throat, then wiped the froth from his upper lip with the back of his hand.

\* \* \*

The regimental chaplain had called it the "sin of Onan," while the rankers had many more ribald terms for it, "toss the caber" or "visit Mrs. Hand and her five daughters." The chaplain had warned of the dire consequences that it would bring—failing sight, and falling hair, a palsied shaking hand and at last idiocy and the insane asylum. Mark lay in the narrow iron bed and stared with unseeing eyes at the faded pink rose-pattern wallpaper of the tiny room. It had the musty smell of being long closed, and there was a wash-basin in an iron frame with an enamel basin against the far wall. A single unshaded bulb hung on a length of flex from the ceiling, and the white plaster around it was fly-speckled; even at the moment three drowsy flies sat on the flex in a stupor. Mark swivelled his attention to them, trying to put aside the waves of temptation that flowed up through his body.

Light steps in the passage stopped opposite his bedroom door, and now there was a tap on the woodwork.

"Mark?"

He sat up quickly, letting the single thin blanket fall to his waist.

"May I come in?"

"Yes," he husked, and the door swung open. Helena crossed to his bed. She wore a gown of light pink shiny material that buttoned down the front; the skirt opened at each step and there was a glimpse of smooth white flesh above her knees.

She carried a slim book in one hand. "I said I would lend it to you," she explained. "Read it, Mark." She held out the volume.

*The Communist Manifesto* was the title, and Mark took it from her, opening it at random. He bowed his head over the open pages to cover the confusion into which her near presence plunged him.

"Thank you, Helena." He used her name for the first time, wanting her to leave and yet hoping she would stay. She leaned over him a little, looking at the open book, and the bodice of her gown fell apart an inch. Mark looked up, and saw the incredibly silky sheen where the beginning of one white breast pressed against the lace that edged the neck of the gown. Swiftly he dropped his eyes again, and they were both silent until Mark could stand it no longer, and he looked up at her.

"Helena," he began, and then stopped. There was a smile, a secret womanly smile on her lips, lips that were slightly parted and moist in the harsh electric light. The dark eyes were half hooded but glowed again with that fierce fanatical light, and her bosom beneath the pink satin rose and fell with quick soundless breathing.

He flushed a sultry red under the dark tan of his cheeks

and he rolled abruptly on to his side, drawing up his knees.

Helena straightened up slowly, still smiling. "Goodnight, Mark." She touched his shoulder, fire sprang afresh from her finger-tips and then she turned and went slowly towards the door. The slippery material of the gown slid softly across the tight double rounds of her buttocks.

"I'll leave the light on." She looked back at him, and now the smile was knowing. "You'll want to read."

* * *

The Pay Office of Crown Deep Mines Ltd was a long austere room where five other clerks worked at high desks set in a line down one wall. They were mostly men in advanced middle age, two of them sufferers from phthisis, that dreaded disease of the miners in which the rock dust from the drills settled in the lungs, building up slowly until the lungs turned to stone and gradually crippled the man. Employment in the mine offices was a form of pension. The other three were grey and drab men, stooped from poring over their ledgers. The atmosphere in the office was quiet and joyless, as in some monastic cloister.

Mark was given charge of the files and personnel R to Z, and the work was dull and repetitive, soon becoming automatic as he calculated overtime and leave pay, made deductions for rent and union fees and struck his totals. It was drudgery, not nearly enough to engage a bright and active young brain, and the narrow confines of the office were a cage for a spirit that was at home in the wide open sweep of sky and veld and had known the cataclysmic universe of the battlefields of France.

On the weekends, he escaped from his cage and rode on an old bicycle for miles into the open veld, following dusty paths along the base of the rocky kopjes on which grew the regal candelabra of giant aloes, their blooms burning in bright scarlet against the clear pale blue of the highveld sky. He sought seclusion, wilderness, secret places far from other men, but it seemed that always there were the barriers of barbed wire to limit his range; the grasslands had gone to the plough, the pale dust devils swirled and danced over red earth from which the harvest had been stripped, leaving the dried sparse stubble of maize stalks.

The great herds of game that once had covered the open grassland to the full range of the eye were long gone, and now small scrub cattle, multi-coloured and scrawny, grazed in mindless bovine herds tended by almost naked black picaninnies who paused to watch Mark pedalling by, and greeted him with solemnity which turned to wide-eyed pleasure when he returned the greeting in their own language.

Once in a while Mark would start a small grey duiker from its lay and send it bounding and bouncing away through the dry grass with small sharp horns and ears erect, or else catch a glimpse of a springbuck drifting elusive as smoke across the plain, lonely survivors of the long rifles. Then the delight of their wild presence stayed long with him, warming him on the dark cold ride home.

He needed these times of quiet and solitude to complete the healing process, not only of the Maxim bullet wounds in his back but of the deeper wounds, soul damage caused by too early an exposure to war in all its horror.

He needed this quietness also to evaluate the swift rush of events that filled his evenings and nights in direct contrast to the grey drudgery of his working days.

Mark was carried along by the fanatical energy of Fergus MacDonald and Helena. Fergus was the comrade who had shared with him experience that most men never knew, the stark and terrible involvement of combat. He was also much older than Mark, a paternal figure, filling a deep need in his life. It was easy to suspend the critical faculties and believe; not to think, but to follow blindly wherever Fergus' bitter restless energy led them.

There was excitement and a sense of commitment in those meetings with men like him, men with an ideal and a sense of destiny. The secret meetings in locked rooms with armed guards at the doors, the atmosphere quivering with the promise of forbidden things. The cigarette-smoke spiralling upwards until it filled the room with a thick blue haze, like incense burning at some mystic rite; the faces shining with sweat and quiet frenzy of the fanatic, as they listened to the speakers.

Harry Fisher, the Chairman of the Party, was a tall fierce man with a heavy gut, the brawny shoulders and hairy muscular arms of a boilermaker, an unkempt shock of coarse wiry black hair laced with strands of silver and dark burning eyes.

"We are the Party, the praetorian guard of the proletariat, and we are not bound by law or the ethical considerations of the bourgeois age. The Party in itself is the new law, the natural law of existence."

Afterwards he shook hands with Mark, while Fergus stood by with paternal pride. Fisher's grip was as fierce as his stare.

"You're a soldier," he nodded. "We will need you again, comrade. There is bloody work ahead."

The disquieting presence of the man stayed to haunt Mark long afterwards, even when they rode home in the crowded tramcar, the three of them squeezed into a double seat so that Helena's thigh was pressed hard against his. When she spoke to him, she leaned sideways, her lips almost touching his cheek, and her breath smelling of licorice and cigarettes, a smell that mingled with the cheap flowery perfume she wore, and the underlying musky warmth of her woman's body.

There were other meetings on the Friday evenings, great raucous shouting gatherings where hundreds of white miners crowded into the huge Fordsburg Trades Union Hall, most of them boozy with cheap brandy, loud and inarticulate and spoiling for trouble. They roared like the crowd at a bull fight as the speakers harangued them; occasionally one of the audience climbed on to his chair to sway there, shouting meaningless confused slogans until his laughing comrades dragged him down.

One of the most popular speakers at these public meetings was Fergus MacDonald; he had a dozen tricks to excite his audience, he probed their secret fears and twisted the probe until they howled half in pain and half in adulation.

"You know what they are planning, the bosses, you know what they are going to do? First they will fragment the trades—"

A thunderous ugly roar, that shook the windows in their frames, and Fergus paused on the stage, sweeping his sparse sandy hair back off his forehead and grinning down at them with his thin bitter mouth until the sound subsided.

"—the trade that took you five years to learn, they will split it up and now there will be three unskilled men to do your job, with only a year's training to learn that fragment, and they will pay them a tenth of the wage you draw."

A storming roar of "No!" and Fergus flung it back at them.

"Yes!" he shouted. "Yes! Yes! And yes again. That is what the bosses are going to do. But that's not all, they are going to use blacks in your jobs, black men are going to take those jobs away from you—black men who will work for a wage that you cannot live on."

They screamed now, frantic with anger, a terrible anger which had no object on which to focus.

"What about your kids, are you going to feed them on mealies, are your wives going to wear limbo? That's what will happen, when the blacks take your jobs!"

"No!" they roared. "No!"

"Workers of the world," Fergus shouted at them, "workers of the world unite—and keep our country white!"

The bellow of applause, the rhythmic stamp of feet on the wooden floor lasted for ten minutes, while Fergus strutted back and forth across the stage, clasping his hands above his head like a prize-fighter. When at last the cheering faltered, he flung back his head and bellowed the opening line of "The Red Flag."

The entire hall came crashing to its feet, and stood at attention to sing the revolutionary song:

*Then raise the scarlet standard high,*
*Within its shade we'll live or die.*
*Tho' cowards flinch and traitors sneer,*
*We'll keep the red flag flying here.*

Mark walked home with the MacDonalds in the frosty night, their breathing smoking like ostrich plumes in the lights of the street lamps. Helena walked between the men, a small dainty figure in her black overcoat with rabbit-fur collar and a knitted cap pulled down over her head.

She had slipped a hand into the crook of the elbows of each of them, a seemingly natural impartial gesture, but there was a disturbing pressure of fingers on the hard muscle of Mark's upper arm, and her hip touched his as she skipped occasionally to catch the longer stride of the men.

"Listen, Fergus, what you were saying there in the hall doesn't make sense, you know," Mark broke the silence, as they turned into the home street. "You can't have it both ways, workers unite and keep it white."

Fergus chuckled appreciatively. "You're a bright lad, comrade Mark."

"But, I'm serious, Fergus—it's not the way Harry Fisher—"

"Of course not, lad. Tonight I was shovelling up swill for the hogs. We need them fighting mad, we have things to tear down, bloody work to do." He stopped and turned to face Mark over the woman's head. "We need cannon fodder, lad, and plenty of it."

"So it won't be like that?" Mark asked.

"No, lad. It will be a beautiful brave new world. All men equal, all men happy, no bosses—a workers' state."

Mark tried to control his pricking nagging doubts.

"You keep talking of fighting, Fergus. Do you mean that, literally? I mean, will it be a shooting war?"

"A shooting war, comrade, a bloody shooting war. Just like the revolution in Russia, where comrade Lenin has shown us the way. We have to burn away the dross, we have to soak this earth with the blood of the rulers and the

bosses, we have to flood it with the blood of their minions—the petit bourgeois officer's class of the police and
military."

"What will—" Mark almost said "we" but it would not
come to his lips. He could not make that commitment.
"What will you fight with?"

Fergus chuckled again, and winked slyly. "Mum's the
word, lad, but it's time you knew a little more." He nodded. "Yes, tomorrow night," he decided.

\* \* \*

On Saturday there was a bazaar being held in the Trades
Hall, a Women's Union fund-raising drive for building the
new church. Where the crazed mob had screamed murder
and bloody revolution the previous night, now there were
long trestle tables set out and the women hovered over
their displays of baked and fancily iced cakes, trays of tarts,
preserved fruit in jars and jams.

Mark bought a packet of tarts for a penny and he and
Fergus munched them as they wandered idly down the
hall, stopping at the piles of second-hand clothing while
Fergus tried a maroon cardigan and, after careful deliberation, purchased it for half a crown. They reached the top of
the hall, and stood beneath the raised stage.

Fergus surveyed the room casually and then took Mark's
arm and led him up the steps. They crossed the stage quietly, and went in through the door in the wings, into a
maze of small union offices and storerooms, all deserted
now on a Saturday afternoon.

Fergus used a key from his watch-chain to unlock a low
iron door, and they stooped through it. Fergus relocked
behind him, and they went down a narrow flight of steps
that descended steeply. There was a smell of damp and
earth, and Mark realized that they were descending to the
cellars.

Fergus tapped on the door at the bottom of the stairs,

and after a moment a single eye regarded them balefully through a peep hole.

"All right, comrade. Fergus MacDonald—a committee member."

There was the rattle of chains and the door opened. A disgruntled, roughly dressed man stood aside for them. He was unshaven and sullen, and against the wall of the tiny room was a table and chair, still spread with the remains of a meal and the crumpled daily newspaper.

The man grunted, and Fergus led Mark across the room and through another door into the cellars.

The floor was earthen and the arched columns were in raw unplastered brick. There was the stench of dust and rats, stale dank air in confined space. A single bulb lit the centre starkly, but left the alcoves behind the arches in shadow.

"Here, lad, this is what we are going to use."

There were wooden cases stacked neatly to the height of a man's head in the alcoves, and the stacks were draped with heavy tarpaulin, obviously stolen from the railway yards for they were stenciled SAR & H.

Fergus lifted the edge of one tarpaulin, and grinned that thin humourless smile.

"Still in the grease, lad." The wooden cases were branded with the distinctive arrow-head and W.D. of the British War Department, and below that the inscription: "6 pieces. Lee-Enfield Mark IV (CNVD)."

Mark was stunned. "Good God, Fergus, there are hundreds of them."

"That's it, lad—and this is only one arsenal. There are others all along the Rand."

He lifted another tarpaulin, walking on down the length of the cellar. The ammunition cases, with the quick-release catches on the detachable lids that were painted: "1000 rounds .303."

"We have enough to do the job." Fergus squeezed Mark's arm, and led him on.

There were racks of rifles now, ready for instant use, blued steel glistening with gun oil in the electric light. Fergus picked out a single rifle and handed it to Mark.

"This one has got your name on it."

Mark took the weapon, and the feel of it in his hands was terribly familiar.

"It's the only one we've got, but the moment I saw it, I thought of you. When the time comes, you'll be using it."

The P.14 sniper's rifle had that special balance that felt just right in his hands but made Mark sick in the stomach. He handed it back to Fergus without a word, but the older man winked at him before racking it again carefully.

Like a showman, Fergus had kept the best for last. With a flourish he whipped the canvas off the heavy weapon, with its thick corrugated water-jacketed barrel, that squatted on its steel tripod. The Maxim machine gun, in its various forms, had the dubious distinction of having killed more human beings than any other single weapon that man's destructive genius had been able to devise.

This was one of that deadly family, the Vickers-Maxim .303 Mark IV.B, and there were boxes stacked beside it, each containing a belt of 250 rounds. The gun could throw those at 2440 feet per second and at a cyclic rate of 750 rounds a minute.

"How about that, comrade? You asked what we are going to fight with—how will that do for a beginning?"

In the silence Mark could hear faintly, but distinctly, the sound of children's laughter from the hall above them.

\*  \*  \*

Mark sat alone upon the highest crest of the low kopjes that stretched into the west, black ironstone ridges breaking out of the flat dry earth like the crested back of a crocodile surfacing from still lake water.

The memory of the hidden arsenal had stayed with him through the night, keeping him from sleep, so that now his eyes felt gritty and his skin stretched tight and dry across the bones of his cheeks.

Lack of sleep had left him with remote feeling, a lightness of thought, detached from reality, so now he sat in the bright sunlight blinking like a day-flying owl, and looking like a stranger into his own mind.

He felt a rising sense of dismay as he realized how idly he had drifted along the path that had brought him here to the very brink of the abyss. It had taken the feel of the P.14 in his hands, and the laughter of children to bring him up at the end of a rope.

All his training, all his deepest beliefs were centred on the sanctity of law, on the order and responsibilities of society. He had fought for that, had spent all of his adult life fighting for that belief. Now suddenly he had drifted, out of apathy, to the camp of the enemy; already he was numbered with the legions of the lawless, already they were arming him to begin the work of destruction. There was no question now that it was merely empty rhetoric shouted at gatherings of drunken labourers—he had seen the guns. It would be cruel and without mercy. He knew Harry Fisher, had recognized the forces that drove him. He knew Fergus MacDonald, the man had killed before and often; he would not flick an eyelid when he killed again.

Mark groaned aloud, aghast at what he had let happen to himself. He who knew what war really was, he had worn the king's uniform, and won his medal for courage.

He felt the oily warmth of shame in his throat, a gagging sensation, and, to arm himself against future weakness of this same kind, he tried to find the reasons why he had been drawn in.

He realized now that he had been lost and alone, without family or home, and Fergus MacDonald had been the only shelter in the cold. Fergus, the older comrade of shared dangers, whom he had trusted without question. Fergus the father figure—and he had followed again, grateful for the guidance, not questioning the destination.

There had, of course, been Helena as well and the hold

she had over him, the tightest grip any human could have over another. He had been, and still was, totally obsessed with her. She had awakened his long suppressed and tightly controlled sexuality. Now it was but a breath away from bursting the wall he had built to dam it; when it burst, it might be a force he could not control, and that thought terrified him almost as much as the other.

He tried now to separate the woman from her womanhood, tried to see the person beyond this devastating web she wove around his senses, and he succeeded inasmuch that he realized that she was not a person he could admire, not the mother he would choose for his children. Also, she was the wife of an old comrade who trusted him completely.

Now he felt he was ready to make the decision to leave, and to carry that resolve through firmly.

He would leave Fordsburg immediately, leave Fergus MacDonald and his dark, cataclysmic schemes. He felt his spirits lighten instantly at the prospect. He would not miss him, nor that drab monastic pay office with its daily penance of boredom and drudgery. He felt the bright young spirit of anticipation flame again.

He would leave Fordsburg on the next train—and Helena. Immediately the flame flickered and his spirit plunged. There was a physical pain in his groin at the prospect, and he felt the cracks open in the dam wall of his passions.

It was dark when he left his bicycle in the garden shed, and he heard voices raised jovially in the house and bursts of laughter. Lights blazed beyond the curtained kitchen windows and when he stepped into the room there were four men at the table. Helena crossed quickly and hugged him impulsively, laughing, with high spots of colour in her cheeks, before taking his hand and leading him to the table.

"Welcome, comrade." Harry Fisher looked up at Mark with those disturbing eyes and the shock of dark wiry hair hanging on to his forehead. "You are in time to join the celebration."

"Grab the lad a glass, Helena," laughed Fergus, and she

dropped his hand and hurried to the cupboard to fetch a glass and fill it with black stout from the bottle.

Harry Fisher raised his own glass to Fergus. "Comrades, I give you the new member of the Central Committee— Fergus MacDonald."

"Isn't it wonderful, Mark?" Helena squeezed Mark's hand.

"He's a good man," growled Harry Fisher. "The appointment isn't too soon. We need men with comrade MacDonald's guts." The others nodded agreement over their stout glasses, the two of them were both members of the local committee of the party; Mark knew them well from the meetings.

"Come, lad." Fergus made room for him at the table and he squeezed in beside him, drawing all their attention.

"And you, young Mark," Harry Fisher laid a powerful hairy hand on his shoulder, "we are going to issue your party card—"

"How about that, lad!" Fergus winked and nudged Mark in the ribs. "Usually it takes two years or more, we don't let the rabble into the party, but you've got friends on the Central Committee now."

Mark was about to speak, to refuse the honour he was being accorded. Nobody had asked him, they had taken it that as he was Fergus' protégé, he was for them. Mark was about to deny it, to tell them the decision he had made that day—when that sense of danger warned him. He had seen the guns; if he was not a friend then he was an enemy with a fatal secret. A secret that they could not risk. He had no doubts at all about these men, now. If he was an enemy, then they would see that he never passed that secret on to another man. But the moment for refusal had passed.

"Comrade MacDonald, I have a mission for you. It is urgent—and vital. Can you leave your work for two weeks?"

"I've got a sick mother," Fergus chuckled. "When do you want me to go, and what do you want me to do?"

"I want you to leave, say Wednesday, that will give me

time to give you your orders and for you to make your arrangements." Harry Fisher took a swallow of stout and the froth stayed on his upper lip. "I'm sending you to visit all the local committees—Capetown, Bloemfontein, Port Elizabeth—so that each of them can be co-ordinated."

Mark felt a guilty lift of relief at the words, there would be no confrontation with Fergus now. He could merely slip away while he was gone on his mission. Then he glanced up and was startled by the gaze that Helena had fastened upon him. She stared at him with the fixed hungry expression of a leopard watching its prey from cover in the last instant before its spring.

Now when their eyes met, she smiled again that secret knowing smile, and the tip of her pink tongue dabbed at her slightly parted lips.

Mark's heart pounded to the point of physical pain and he dropped his eyes hurriedly to his glass. He was to be alone with Helena, and the prospect filled him with dread and a surging passionate heat.

\* \* \*

Mark carried Fergus' cheap and badly battered suitcase down to the station, and as they took the short cut across open veld, the thick frost crunched like sugar under their feet, and sparkled in myriad diamond points of light in the first rays of the sun.

At the station they waited with four other members of the party for the southbound mail, and when at last it came, puffing hoarsely, shooting steam high into the frosty air, it was thirty-five minutes late.

"Thirty-five minutes late is almost early for the railways," Fergus laughed, and shook hands with each of them in turn, slapping their shoulders before scrambling up the steel ladder into the coach. Mark passed his suitcase up through the open window.

"Look after Helena, lad, and yourself."

Mark stood and watched the train run out southwards,

shrinking dramatically in size until the sound of it was a mere whisper fading to nothingness. Then he turned and started up the hill towards the mine just as the hooters began their mournful wailing howl that echoed off the yellow mesas of the dumps, summoning the disorderly columns of men to their appointed labours. Mark walked with them, one in a thousand, distinguished from the others neither in appearance nor achievement. Once again he felt a sense of seething discontent, a vague but growing knowledge that this was not all that was life, not all that he was capable of doing with his youth and energy; and he looked curiously at the men who hurried with him towards the iron gates at the mine hooter's imperious summons.

All of them wore that closed withdrawn look, behind which Mark was convinced lurked the same misgivings as now assaulted him. Surely they also felt the futility of the dull daily repetition—the young ones at least must feel it. The older and greyer must regret it; deep down they must mourn for the long sunny days, now past, spent toiling in endless drudgery for another man's coin. They must mourn the fact that when they went, they would leave no footprints, no ripple on the surface, no monument, except perhaps a few sons to repeat the meaningless cycle, all of them interchangeable, all of them dispensable.

He paused at the gates, standing aside while the stream of humanity flowed past him, and slowly the sense of excitement built up in him, the certainty that there was something, some special and worthwhile task for him to perform. Some special place that waited for him, and he knew he must go on and find it.

He hurried forward, suddenly grateful to Fergus MacDonald for placing this pressure on him, for forcing him to face himself, for breaking the easy drifting course he had taken since his flight from Ladyburg.

"You are late, Anders." The supervisor looked up from his ledgers severely, and each of his juniors repeated the gesture, a long row of them with the same narrow disapproving expressions.

"What have you got to say?"

"I merely called in to clean out my desk," said Mark smiling, the excitement still on him. "And to throw in my time."

The disapproving expressions changed slowly to shock.

\* \* \*

It was dusk when Mark opened the back gate of the cottage and went up the short walk to the kitchen. He had walked all day at random, driven on restlessly by a new torrent of energy and exciting thoughts; he had not realized how hungry he was until he saw the lights in the window and smelled the faint aroma of cooking.

The kitchen was deserted, but Helena called through from the front.

"Mark, is that you?" Before he could answer, she appeared in the kitchen door, and leaned one hip against the jamb. "I thought you weren't coming home tonight."

She wore the blue dress, and Mark knew now that it was her best, reserved for special occasions, and she wore cosmetics—something that Mark had never seen her do before. There were spots of rouge on her cheeks and her lips were painted, giving new lustre to her usually sallow skin. The short dark hair was newly washed, shiny in the lamplight, and brushed back, caught over one ear with a tortoise-shell clasp.

Mark stared at her. Her legs were smooth and sleek in silken stockings, the feet neatly clad in small pumps.

"Why are you staring, Mark?"

"You are—" Mark's voice turned husky, and caught. He cleared his throat. "You are very pretty tonight."

"Thank you, sir." She laughed, a low throaty chuckle, and she did a slow pirouette, flaring the blue filmy skirt above the silken legs. "I'm glad you like it." Then she stopped beside him and took his arm. Her touch was a delicious shock, like diving into a mountain pool.

"Sit down, Mark." She led him to the chair at the head

of the table. "Let me get you a nice beer." She went to the ice box, and while she pulled the cap on the bottle and poured, she ran on gaily. "I found a goose at the butcher's—do you like roast goose?"

Saliva poured from under Mark's tongue. "I love it."

"With roast potato and pumpkin pie."

"For that I would sell my soul."

Helena laughed delightedly; it wasn't one of Mark's usual shy and reserved replies. There was a sense of excitement surrounding him like an aura this evening, echoing her own excitement.

She brought the two glasses, and propped one hip on the table.

"What shall we drink to?"

"To freedom," he said without hesitation, "and a good tomorrow."

"I like that," she said, and clinked his glass, leaning over him so that the bodice of her dress was at the level of his eyes. "But why only tomorrow—why can't the good times start right now this minute?"

Mark laughed. "All right, here's to a good tonight and a good tomorrow."

"Mark!" Helena pursed her lips in mock disapproval, and immediately he blushed and laughed in confusion.

"Oh no, I didn't mean—that sounded dreadful. I didn't—" She did not want to embarrass him and break the mood, so she crossed to the stove.

"It's ready," she announced, "if you want to eat now."

She sat opposite him, anticipating his appetite, buttering the thick slices of bread with yellow farm butter and keeping his glass fully charged.

"Aren't you eating?"

"I'm not hungry."

"It's good—you don't know what you are missing."

"Better than your other girls cooked for you?" she demanded playfully, and Mark dropped his eyes to his plate and busily loaded his fork.

"There weren't any girls."

"Oh, Mark, you don't expect me to believe that! A handsome young fellow like you, and those French girls. I bet you drove them mad."

"We were too busy, and besides—" he stopped.

"Besides what? she insisted, and he looked up at her, silent for a moment, and then he began to talk. It was suddenly so easy to talk to her, and he was buoyed up with his new jubilant mood and relaxed with the food and drink in his belly. He talked to her as he had never talked to another human being, and she answered him with the frankness of another man.

"Oh, Mark, that's nonsense. Not every woman is sick, it's only the street girls."

"Yes, I know. I didn't believe every girl, but well, they are the only ones that a man can—" he broke off. "And the others get babies," he went on lamely.

She laughed and clapped her hands with delight. "Oh, my darling Mark. It's not easy, you know. I have been married for nine years and I've never had a baby."

"Well," Mark hesitated. "Well, you are different. I didn't mean you, when I said those things, I meant other girls."

"I'm not sure if that's meant to be a compliment or an insult," she teased again. She had known he was a virgin, of course. There was that transparent shining innocence that glowed from him, his unpractised and appealing awkwardness in the presence of women, that peculiar shyness that would pass so soon but which now heightened her excitement, rousing her in some perverse way. She knew now why some men paid huge sums of money to despoil innocence; she touched his bared forearm now, delighting in the smooth hardness of young muscle, unable to keep her hands off him.

"Oh, it was a compliment," Mark answered her hurriedly.

"Do you like me, Mark?"

"Oh, yes. I like you more than I've ever liked any other girl."

"You see, Mark," she leaned closer to him, her voice

sinking to a throaty whisper. "I'm not sick, and I'm not going to have a baby—ever." She lifted her hand and touched his cheek. "You are a beautiful man, Mark. I liked you from the first moment I saw you coming up the walk like a stray puppy."

She stood up slowly and crossed to the kitchen door, deliberately she turned the key and flipped up the light switch. The small room was dark, but for the shaft of light from the hallway.

"Come, Mark." She took his hand and drew him to his feet. "We are going to bed now."

At the door to Mark's bedroom she reached up on tiptoe and kissed his cheek lightly, and then without another word she let his hand drop and glided away from him.

Uncertainly Mark watched her go, wanting to call to her to stay, wanting to run after her—and yet relieved that she had gone, that the headlong rush into the unknown had abruptly halted. She reached the door of her own bedroom and went through without looking back.

Torn by conflicting emotions, he turned away and went through into his own room. He undressed slowly, disappointment now stronger than relief, and while he folded his clothing, he listened to her quiet movements in the room beyond the thin wall.

He climbed at last into the narrow iron bed, and lay rigid until he heard the light switch click next door; then he sighed and picked up the book from his bedside table; he had not yet read it through, but now the dull political text might divert his emotions enough to allow him to sleep.

The latch of his door snapped softly. He had not heard her in the passage, and she stepped into the room. She wore the gown of slippery peach-coloured satin and she had recombed her hair and retouched her cheeks and lips.

Carefully, she closed the door and crossed the room with slow swaying hips under the moving satin.

Neither of them spoke as she stopped by the side of his bed.

"Have you read it, Mark?" she asked softly.

"Not all of it." He placed the book aside.

"Well, this isn't the time to finish it," she said, and deliberately opened the gown, slipped it from her shoulders and dropped it over the back of the chair.

She was naked, and Mark gasped. She was so smooth. He had not expected that somehow, and he stared at her as she stood close beside him. Her skin had an olive creaminess, like old porcelain, a sheen that caught the light and glowed. Mark felt his whole body rocked by the exquisite tension of arousal, and he tried feebly to thrust it aside. He tried to think of Fergus, of the trust that had been placed in him.

"Look after Helena, lad, and yourself."

Her breasts were big for the slimness of her body, already they hung heavily, almost overripe, drooping smooth and round with startlingly large nipples, rosy brown and big as ripe grapes. They swung weightily as she moved closer to him, and he saw that there were sparse dark hairs curling from the puckered aureole around the nipples.

There was hair also curling out in little wisps from under her arms, dark glossy hair—and a huge wild bush of it below the smooth creamy slightly bulging belly.

The hair excited him, so dark and crisp against the pale skin, and he stared at it, transfixed. All thoughts of honour and trust faded, he felt the dam wall inside him creak and strain.

She reached out and touched his bare shoulder, and it convulsed his body like a whip-lash.

"Touch me, Mark," she whispered, and he reached out slowly, hesitantly, like a man in a trance, and touched with one finger the smooth ivory warmth of her hip, still staring fixedly at her.

"Yes, Mark. That's right." She took his wrist and slowly drew his hand upwards, so that the tips of his fingers traced featherlike over her flank and the outline of her ribs.

"Here, Mark," she said, "and here." The big dark nipples contracted at the touch of his fingers, changing shape, thrusting out and hardening, swelling and darkening. Mark could not believe it was happening, that woman's flesh could react as swiftly and dramatically as a man's.

He felt the dam break, and the flood came pouring through the breach. Too long contained, too powerful and weighty to resist, it poured through his mind and body, sweeping all restraint before it.

With a choking cry, he seized her around the waist with both arms, and drew her fiercely to him, pressing his face into the smooth soft warmth of her naked belly.

"Oh, Mark!" she cried, and her voice was hoarse and shaking with lust and triumph, as she twisted her fingers into the soft brown hair and stooped over his head.

\* \* \*

The days blurred and telescoped together, and the universe shut down to a tiny cottage in a sordid street. Only their bodies marked the passage of time, sleeping and waking to love until exhaustion overtook them and they slept again to wake hungry, ravenous for both food and loving.

At first he was like a bull, charging with a mindless energy and strength. It frightened her, for she had not expected such strength from that slim and graceful body. She rode with his strength, little by little controlling and directing it, changing its course, and then she began gently to teach.

Long afterwards, Mark would think back on those five incredible days and realize his great good fortune. So many young men must find their own way into the uncharted realms of physical love-making, without guide, accompanied usually by a partner making her own hesitant first journey into the unknown.

"Did you know that there is a tribe in South America, Mark, that have a rule that every married woman must take one young warrior of the tribe and teach him to do what we are doing?" she asked, as she knelt beside him in one of the intervals of quiet between the storms.

"What a shame," he smiled lazily. "I thought we were the first two ever to think of it." He reached out for the pack of Needlepoint cigarettes on the bedside table and lit two of them.

Helena drew upon hers and her expression was fond and proud. He had changed so swiftly and radically in the last few days, and she was responsible for that. This new assurance, this budding strength of purpose. The shyness and reticence were fading. He spoke now in a way that he had never spoken before, calmly and with authority. Swiftly he was becoming a full man—and she had had a hand in it.

Mark believed that each new delight was the ultimate one, but she proved him wrong a dozen times. There were things that, had he heard them spoken of might have appalled and revolted him, but when they happened the way Helena made them happen, they left only wonder and a sense of awe. She taught him a vast new respect for his own body, as it came at last fully alive, and he became aware of new broad reaches and depths of his own mind.

For five days neither of them left the cottage; then on the sixth day there was a letter brought by a uniformed postman on a bicycle and Mark, who accepted it, recognized immediately Fergus MacDonald's cramped and laboured hand. Guilt hit him like a fist in the stomach; the dream shattered like fragile crystal.

Helena sat at the newspaper-covered table in the kitchen with the now soiled peach gown open to the waist and read the letter aloud, mocking the writer with the inflection of her voice as he reported a string of petty achievements, applause at party meetings where a dozen comrades had gathered in a back room, messages of loyalty and dedication to bring back to the Central Committee, commitment to the cause and promises of action when the time to strike was ripe.

Helena mocked him, rolling her eyes and chuckling when he asked after Mark—was he well and happy, was Helena looking after him properly.

She drew deeply on the stub of the cigarette and then

dropped it into the dregs of the coffee cup at her elbow, where it was extinguished with a sharp hiss. This simple action caused in Mark an unnatural reaction of revulsion.

Suddenly he saw her clearly, the sallow skin wrinkled finely in the corners of her eyes as her youth cracked away like old oilpaint; the plum-coloured underlining of the eye sockets, the petulant quirk of her lips and the waspish sting to her voice.

Abruptly, he was aware of the squalid room, with the greasy smell of stale food and unwashed dishes, of the grubby and stained gown and the pendulous droop of the big ivory-coloured breasts beneath the gown.

He stood up and left the room.

"Mark, where are you going?" she called after him.

"I'm going out for a while."

He scrubbed himself in the stained enamel bath, running the water as hot as he could bear it so that his body glowed bright pink as he towelled himself down.

At the railway booking office he stood for nearly half an hour, reading the long lists of closely printed timetables pasted to the wall.

Rhodesia. He had heard they needed men in the new copper mines. There was still a wilderness up there, far horizons and the great wild game, lakes and mountains and room to move.

He moved to the window of the booking-office and the clerk looked out at him expectantly.

"One second-class single to Durban," he said, surprising himself. He was going back to Natal, to Ladyburg. There was unfinished business there, and answers to search for. An unknown enemy to find and confront.

As he paid for the ticket with the old man's sovereigns, he had a vivid mental picture of the old man on the stoep of Andersland—with his great spiky whiskers and the old terai hat pulled low over his pale calm eyes. Mark knew then that this had been only a respite, a hiatus, in which he had found time to heal and gather courage for the task ahead.

He went back to collect his belongings. There was not much to pack, and he was in a consuming hurry now. As he swept his few spare shorts and clean socks into the cardboard suitcase, he was suddenly aware of Helena's presence, and he turned quickly.

She had bathed and dressed and she stood in the doorway watching him, her expression too calm for the loneliness in her voice.

"You are going." It was a statement, not a question.

"Yes," he answered simply, turning to snap the catches on the case.

"I'm coming with you."

"No. I'm going alone."

"But, Mark, what about me?"

"I'm sorry, Helena. I'm truly sorry."

"But don't you see, I love you—" her voice rose in a low wail of despair. "I love you, Mark darling, you can't go." She spread her arms to block the doorway.

"Please, Helena. We both knew it was madness. We both knew there was nothing for us. Don't make it ugly now, please let me go."

"No." She covered her ears with both hands. "No, don't talk like that. I love you. I love you."

Gently he tried to move her from the doorway.

"I have to go. My train—"

Suddenly she flew at him, vicious as a wounded leopard. He was unprepared, and her nails raked long bloody lines across his face, narrowly missing his eyes.

"You bastard, you selfish bastard," she shrieked. "You're like all of them," and she struck again, but he caught her wrists.

"You're all the same, you take—you take—"

He turned her, wildly struggling, and tipped her back on to the unmade bed. Abruptly the fight went out of her and she pressed her face into the pillow. Her sobs followed Mark as he ran down the passage, and out of the open front door.

It was more than three hundred miles to the port of Durban on the coast, and slowly the train huffed up the great barrier of the Drakensberg Mountains, worming its way through the passes until at last it plunged joyously over the escarpment and ran lightly down into the deep grassy bowl of the eastern littoral, dropping less steeply as it neared the sea and emerged at last into the lush semi-tropical hothouse of the sea-board with its snowy white beaches and the warm blue waters of the Mozambique current.

Mark had much time to think on the journey down, and he wasted most of it in vain regrets. Helena's cries and accusations echoed through his mind while the cold grey stone of guilt lay heavily in the pit of his stomach, whenever he thought of Fergus MacDonald.

Then, as they passed through the town of Pietermaritzburg and began the last leg of the journey, Mark put aside guilt and regret, and began to think ahead.

His first intention had been to return directly to Ladyburg, but now he realized that this was folly. There was an enemy there, a murderous enemy, a hidden enemy striking from cover, a rich enemy, a powerful enemy, who could command a bunch of armed men who were ready to kill.

Mark thought then of those bloody attacks that he and Fergus had made in France. Always the first move had been to identify and mark the enemy, locate where he was lying, find his stance and assess him. How good was he, was his technique rigid, or was he quick and changeable? Was he sloppy, so that the hunters could take risks, or were risks suicidal?

"We got to try and guess the way the bastard's thinking, lad—" was Fergus' first concern, before they planned the shoot.

"I've got to find who he is," Mark whispered aloud, "and guess the way the bastard is thinking."

One thing at least was clear, a hundred pounds was too high a price in blood money for such an insignificant person as Mark Anders; the only thing that could possibly make him significant in any way was his relation to the old man and to Andersland. He had been seen at Andersland by both the Hindu babu and the white foreman. Then he had brazened into the town asking questions, perusing documents. Only then had they come after him. The land was the centre of the puzzle, and he had the names of all the men who had any interest in the sale.

Mark lifted his suitcase down from the luggage rack and, holding it on his lap, hunted for and found his notebook. He read the names: DIRK COURTNEY, RONALD PYE, DENNIS PETERSEN, PIET GREYLING and his son CORNELIUS.

His first concern must be to find out all he could about those men, find out where each was lying, find his stance and assess him, decide which of them was the sniper. While he did this, he must keep his own head well down below the parapet. He must keep clear of enemy country, and enemy country was Ladyburg.

His best base would be Durban city itself; it was big enough to absorb him without comment, and, as the capital of Natal, he would have many sources of information there, libraries, government archives, newspaper offices. He began making a list of all possible sources in the back of the notebook, and immediately found himself regretting bitterly that Ladyburg itself was closed to him. Records in the Lands Office and Company Registers for the district were not duplicated in the capital.

Suddenly he had a thought. "Damn it, what was her name!" Mark closed his eyes, and he saw again the bright, friendly and cheerful face of the little girl in the Companies office in Ladyburg.

"Mark, that's a strong romantic name—" He could even hear her voice, but the train was sliding into the platform before her name came to him again.

"Marion!" and he scribbled it into the notebook.

He climbed down on to the platform, carrying his case, and joined the jostling throng of travellers and welcomers. Then he set out to find lodgings in the city.

A penny copy of the *Natal Mercury* led him through its small advertisements to a rooming house in Point Road, down by the docks. The room was small, dark and smelled of those gargantuan cockroaches that infest the city, swarming up from the sewers each evening in shiny black hordes, but the rental was only a guinea a week, and he had the use of the lavatory and shower room across the small enclosed yard.

That night he wrote a letter:

> Dear Marion,
>     I don't suppose you remember me, my name is Mark Anders, the same as Mark Antony! I have thought of you often since I was compelled to leave Ladyburg unexpectedly before I had a chance to see you again—"

Tactfully he avoided any mention of the research work he wanted undertaken. That could wait for the next letter. He had learned much about women recently, and he addressed the letter simply to "Miss Marion, Company Registrar's Office, Ladyburg."

\* \* \*

Mark started the following morning at the City Library, walking up Smith Street to the four-storied edifice of the Municipal Buildings. It looked like a palace flanked by the equally imposing buildings of the Royal Hotel and the cathedral, with the garden square neatly laid out in front of it, bright with spring blooms.

He had another inspiration as he approached the librarian's desk.

"I'm doing research for a book I intend writing—"

Immediately the grey-haired lady who presided over the dim halls and ceiling-high racks of books softened her severe expression. She was a book person, and book people love other book people. Mark had the key to one of the reading rooms given him, and the back copies of all the Natal newspapers, going back to the time of the first British occupation, were put at his disposal.

There was immediately a temptation for Mark, voracious reader that he was, to lose himself in the fascination of history printed as urgent headlines—for history had been one of Mark's favourite subjects both at Ladyburg School and at University College.

He resisted the temptation and went at once to the drawers that contained the copies of the *Ladyburg Lantern and Recorder*. The first copies were already yellowing with age and tore easily, so he handled them with care.

The first mention of the name "Courtney" leapt at him in thick black headlines on one of the earliest copies from 1879.

> *Ladyburg Mounted Rifles massacred at Isandhlwana.*
> *Colonel Waite Courtney and his men cut down to a man*
> *Blood-crazed Impis on the rampage.*

Mark guessed that this must refer to the founder of the family in Ladyburg; after that the name cropped up in nearly every issue, there were many Courtneys and all of them lived in the Ladyburg district, but the first mention of Dirk Courtney came in 1900.

> Ladyburg welcomes one of its Favourite Sons.
> Hero of the Anglo-Boer War Returns.
> Colonel Sean Courtney purchases Lion Kop Ranch.
> Ladyburg welcomes the return of one of her favourite sons after an absence of many years. There are very few of us who are not acquainted with the exploits of Colonel Sean Courtney, D.S.O., D.C.M., and all will

recall the major role he played in the establishment of the prosperous gold-mining industry on the Witwatersrand . . .

A long recital of the man's deeds and reputation followed, and the report ended,

> Colonel Courtney has purchased the ranch Lion Kop from the Ladyburg Farmers Bank. He intends making this his home and will plant the land to timber. Major Courtney is a widower and is accompanied by his ten-year-old son, Dirk.

The ancient report shocked Mark. He had not realized that Dirk Courtney was the son of his old General. The big, bearded, hook-nosed man he had met that snowy night in France, the man whom he had immediately respected and liked—no, more than liked. The man whose vital force and presence, together with his reputation, had roused in him an almost religious awe.

His instant reaction was to wonder if the General himself was in any way involved in the murderous attack he had survived on the escarpment; and the thought disturbed him so that he left the library and went down to the palm-lined esplanade and found a bench overlooking the quiet sheltered waters of the bay, with the great whale-backed mountain of the bluff beyond.

He watched the shipping, as he pondered the tangled web that was centred in Ladyburg, where the hidden spider sat. He knew that his investigations were going to take time. The reading was a slow business and it would be days before he could expect to have a reply to his letter to Marion.

Later, in his dingy room, he counted the remaining sovereigns in his money belt, and knew that living in the city they would not last him long.

He needed a job.

The floor manager had the beer belly and flash clothing that seem always to go with salesmen in the motor industry; Mark answered his questions with extreme politeness and a false cheerfulness, but with despair below the surface.

He had trudged the city for five days, from one faint prospect of work to another.

"Times are hard," almost every prospective employer told him at the beginning of the interview, "and we are looking for a man with experience."

Mark had no time to pursue his quest at the library. Now he sat on the front edge of his chair waiting to thank the man and say goodbye as soon as he was dismissed, but the man went on talking long after he should have closed the interview. He was talking about the salesmen's commission, and how it was so generous that there was plenty for two.

"—if you know what I mean." The man winked and fitted a cigarette into his ivory holder.

"Yes, of course," Mark nodded vehemently, having absolutely no idea what the man meant, but eager to please.

"Of course, I'd be looking after you personally. If we came to some sort of arrangement, right?"

"Right," Mark agreed, and only then did he realize that the manager was soliciting a kick-back off Mark's commission. He was going to get the job.

"Of course, sir." He wanted to leap up and dance. "I'd like to think we were equal partners."

"Good." Fifty per cent of Mark's commission was more than the manager had expected. "Start Monday, nine o'clock sharp," he said quickly, and beamed at Mark.

Mark wrung his hand gratefully, but as he was leaving the little cubicle of the office the manager called after him.

"You do have a decent suit, Anders, don't you?"

"Of course," Mark lied quickly.

"Wear it."

He found a Hindu tailor at the Indian market who ran up a grey three-piece suit overnight, and charged him thirty-two shillings.

"You wear clothes beautiful, sir. Like a royal duke," the tailor told him, as he pointed Mark at the fly-blown mirror in his fitting-room, standing behind him and skilfully holding a fold of surplus material at the small of Mark's back to give the front of the suit a fashionable drape. "You will be an extremely first class advertisement for my humble skills."

* * *

"You can drive a car, of course?" the manager, whose name was Dicky Lancome, asked him casually as they crossed the showroom floor to the glistening Cadillac.

"Of course," Mark agreed.

"Of course," Dicky agreed. "Otherwise you wouldn't have applied for a job as a car salesman, would you?"

"Of course not."

"Hop in then," Dicky invited. "And whip us around the block."

Mark reeled mentally, but his tongue was quick enough to rescue him.

"I'd prefer you to point out the special features first. I've never driven a Cadillac before." Which was for once the literal truth. He had never driven a Cadillac, or any other motor vehicle, before.

"Righty ho," Dicky agreed, and as they sped down the Marine Parade with Dicky whistling and tipping his hat to the pretty girls on the sidewalk, Mark watched his every action with wheels and pedal avidly.

Back at the showrooms in West Street, Dicky flicked casually through a bunch of forms.

"If you make a sale, you fill in one of these—and make sure you get the money." Then he pulled out his watch.

"God, it's late. I've got a desperately important lunch date," it was a little after eleven o'clock, "very important client." Then he dropped his voice, "Blonde, actually. Smasher!" and he winked again. "See you later."

"But what about prices, and that sort of thing?" Mark called desperately after him.

"There is a pamphlet on my desk. Gives you all that stuff. Ta-ta!" and Dicky disappeared through the back door.

Mark was circling the Cadillac uncertainly, utterly engrossed with the pamphlet, muttering aloud as he tried to master the operating instructions and identify the various component parts of the vehicle from the line-drawing and numerated list, when there was a tap on his arm.

"Excuse me, young man, but are you the salesman?" Before him stood an elderly couple, the man dressed in beautifully tailored dark cloth, a carnation in his buttonhole and a cane in one hand.

"We would like a drive in the motor vehicle—before we decide," said the elegant lady beside him, smiling at Mark in a motherly fashion through the light veil that draped down over her eyes from the brimmed hat. The hat was decorated with artificial flowers, and her hair below the brim was washed silver and neatly waved.

Mark felt waves of panic threaten to engulf him. He looked about desperately for an escape, but already the gentleman was handing his wife into the front seat of the Cadillac.

Mark closed the doors on the couple, and ducked behind the machine for one last brief perusal of the operating pamphlet. "Depress clutch pedal with left foot, engage gear lever up and left, depress accelerator pedal firmly with right foot, release clutch pedal," he muttered, stuffed the pamphlet into his pocket and hurried to the driver's seat.

The gentleman sat forward in the centre of the back seat, both hands resting on the head of his cane, grave and attentive as a judge.

His wife beamed kindly at Mark. "How old are you, young man?"

"Twenty, ma'am, almost twenty-one." Mark pressed the

starter and the engine growled, so she had to raise her voice.

"My," she nodded, "the same age as my own son."

Mark gave her a pale and sickly grin, as he silently repeated the instructions in his mind.

"—accelerate firmly." The engine beat rose to a deafening bellow, and Mark clung to the driving wheel until the knuckles of both hands blanched with the pressure of his grip.

"Do you live at home?" asked his passenger.

"No, ma'am," Mark answered and let out the clutch. The back wheels screeched like a wounded stallion, and a blue cloud blew out from behind as the entire machine seemed to rear upwards, and then hurl itself, slewing wildly, towards the street doors, leaving two long black rubber smears across the polished showroom floor.

Mark fought the wheel and the Cadillac swayed and skidded, lined up with the doors at the last possible moment and careered into the street, moving sideways like a crab. A team of horses drawing a passing coach shied out of the path of the roaring machine, and behind Mark the elderly gentleman managed to struggle up into a sitting position again and find his cane.

"Good acceleration!" Mark shouted above the roar of the engine.

"Excellent," agreed his passenger, his eyes popping in the rear view mirror.

His wife adjusted her flowered hat that had come down over her eyes, and shook her head sadly.

"You young boys! As soon as you leave home you starve yourselves. I could tell you are living on your own—you are as thin as—"

Mark took the intersection of Smith and Aliwal at the charge, but halfway through it a heavily laden lorry lumbered across their front and Mark spun the wheel nimbly. The Cadillac changed direction ninety degrees and ducked into Aliwal on two wheels.

"—as a rake," said the lady, holding firmly to the door

handle with one hand, and with the other to her hat. "You should come up to the house one Sunday for a decent meal."

"Thank you, ma'am, that's very kind."

When Mark stopped the Cadillac against the pavement in front of the showrooms at last, his hand was shaking so feverishly that he had to make a second effort to earth the magneto. He could feel the damp of nervous sweat soaking through the jacket of his new suit, and he had not the strength to let himself out of the cab.

"Incredible," said the elderly gentleman in the back seat. "What control, what mastery—I feel quite young again."

"It was very nice, dear," his wife agreed.

"We'll take her," her husband decided impulsively, and Mark could not believe he had heard right. He had made his first sale.

"Wouldn't it be nice if this young man would come to us as a chauffeur. He is such an excellent driver."

"No, ma'am," Mark nearly panicked again. "I couldn't think of leaving my job here—thank you all the same."

* * *

"Jolly good show, old man." Dicky Lancome folded the two five-pound notes that were his half-share of Mark's commission on the sale of the Cadillac. "I can see a great future ahead for you."

"Oh, I don't know," Mark demurred modestly.

"A great future," Dicky predicted sagely. "But just one thing, old man—that suit," he shuddered gently, "let me introduce you to my tailor, now that you can afford it. No offence, of course, but that looks like you are on your way to a fancy-dress ball."

That evening after close of business Mark hurried back to the library for the first time in a week. The librarian welcomed him with a severe expression like a disapproving school ma'am.

"I thought we had seen the last of you—that you had given up."

"Oh no, by no means," Mark assured her, and again she softened and handed him the key to the reading-room.

Mark had mapped out a family tree for the Courtneys in his notebook, for it was confusing. There was a brother to Sean, who was also a colonel at the end of the Boer War, but also a holder of the Victoria Cross for gallantry—a distinguished family indeed. This brother, Colonel Garrick Courtney, had gradually become a noted and then a famous author of military history and of biographies of other successful soldiers—beginning with his *With Roberts to Pretoria* and *Buller, a Fighting Soldier*, and going on to *Battle for the Somme* and *Kitchener. A Life*. The books were all extensively and glowingly reviewed in the *Lantern*. The author had a single son, Michael Courtney. Prior to 1914, there were references to this son's business activities as managing director of the Courtney Saw Mills in the Ladyburg district, and his skills as an athlete and horseman in many local meetings. Then 1917—LADYBURG HERO DECORATED

> Captain Michael Courtney, son of Colonel Garrick Courtney V.C., was awarded the Distinguished Flying Cross for his exploits with the 21st R.F.C. Fighter Squadron in France. Captain Courtney has been credited with five "kills" of German aircraft, and was described by his commanding officer as a "courageous and dedicated officer of high flying skills." Hero, son of a hero.

Then again, within months, a front-page article outlined in a square of heavy black type.

> It is with great regret that we report the death in action of CAPTAIN MICHAEL COURTNEY D.F.C. It is believed that Captain Courtney was shot down in flames

behind enemy lines and that his executioner was none other than the notorious Baron von Richthofen of bloody reputation. *The Ladyburg Lantern* extends its deepest and sincerest condolences to his father and family. "A Rose plucked in full bloom."

The activities of this branch of the family, its triumphs and tradedies were all reported in detail—and it was the same with the Sean Courtney family for the period from the turn of the century to May of 1910.

Sean Courtney's marriage to Mrs. Ruth Friedman in 1903 was described in loving detail, from the bride's dress to the icing on the cake. "One of the flower girls was Miss Storm Friedman, aged four, who wore an exact replica of her mother's dress. She makes a pretty new sister for Master Dirk Courtney." Again the mention of the name that truly interested Mark, and he noted it, for it was the last until May 1910.

Colonel Sean Courtney's achievements in politics and business and the more serious fields of recreation filled page after page of subsequent editions; his election to the legislative council of Natal, and later to Prime Minister Louis Botha's Cabinet; he became leader of the South Africa Party in Natal—and was a delegate to Whitehall in London, taking his entire family with him, to negotiate the terms of Union.

Sean Courtney's business flourished and multiplied, new sawmills, new plantations, elevation to new offices, the chairman of the first Building Society in Southern Africa, director of Union Castle Shipping Lines, head of the Government Commission on Natural Resources. Chairman of the South African Turf Club, a one hundred and fifty foot luxury yacht built for him by Thesens of Knysna, Commodore of the Royal Natal Yacht Club—but no further mention of Dirk Courtney until May 1910.

*The Ladybug Lantern and Recorder's* front page of the edition of 12th May 1910.

*The Ladyburg Lantern* takes great pleasure in announcing that its entire paid up share capital has been acquired by Mr. Dirk Courtney, who recently returned to Ladyburg after an absence of some years.

Mr. Courtney tells us that the intervening years have been spent in travel, gaining both experience and capital. Clearly they were not wasted, for immediately on his arrival home, Mr. Courtney purchased a controlling interest in the Ladyburg Farmers Bank for a reputed one million pounds sterling in cash.

Ladyburg and all its inhabitants are sure to benefit enormously by the vast energy, wealth and drive that Mr. Dirk Courtney brings to the district.

"I intend taking a close day-to-day interest in all aspects of my companies' operations in Ladyburg," he said, when asked of his future plans. "Progress, Growth, Prosperity for All, are my watchwords."

Mr. Dirk Courtney, *The Ladyburg Lantern* salutes you and welcomes you as a notable ornament to our fair community.

After that, hardly an edition of *The Lantern* did not contain fawning eulogies of Mr. Dirk Courtney—while mention of his father and family was reduced to an occasional small article in the inside pages.

To find news of Sean Courtney, Mark had to turn to the other Natal newspapers. He began with the *Natal Mercury*.

Ladyburg Mounted Rifles Sail for France
General Courtney Takes his Men to War once more

That jolted Mark, he could remember the sea mist on the bay and the ranks of khaki-clad figures climbing the gangways, each of them burdened by kitbag and rifle. The singing, and the cries of the women, paper streamers and flower petals twisting and falling in gay and gaudy clouds about them, and the sound of the fog horns reverberating mournfully from the bluff. It was so clear in his mind still. How soon he was to follow them, after exaggerating his age to a recruiting sergeant who did not inquire too closely.

Ladyburg Rifles Badly Mauled
Attack fails at Delville Wood
General Courtney: "I am proud of them."

Mark felt sudden stinging tears burn his eyelids as he went slowly down the long casualty lists, pausing as he recognized a name—remembering, remembering—lost again in those terrible seas of mud and blood and suffering.

A hand touched his shoulder arousing him, and he straightened up from the reading table, bewildered at his sudden return to the present.

"We are closing now, it's after nine o'clock," said the young assistant librarian softly. "I'm afraid you will have to leave now." Then she peered more closely at him. "Are you all right? Have you been crying?"

"No." Quickly Mark groped for his handkerchief. "It's just the strain of reading."

His landlady shouted down the stairs to him as he let himself into the hall.

"I've got a letter for you."

The letter looked as thick as a complete works of William Shakespeare, but when he opened it there were only twenty-two pages, beginning:

> My dear Mark,
>     Of course I remember you so clearly, and I have thought about you often, wondering what ever had become of you—so your welcome letter came as a marvellous surprise—

Mark felt a guilty twinge at the unrestrained joy that her letter voiced.

I realize that we know so little about each other. You did not even know my name!! Well, it is Marion Littlejohn—silly name, isn't it? I wish I could change it (that's not a hint, silly!) and I was born in Ladyburg (I'm not going to tell you when! A lady never reveals her age!) My father was a farmer, but he sold his farm five years ago, and now he works as a foreman at the sugar mill.

The entire family history, Marion's schooling, the names and estates of all her numerous relatives, Marion's hopes, dreams, aspirations—"I'd love to travel, wouldn't you? Paris, London"—were laid out in daunting detail, much of it in parentheses and liberally punctuated with exclamation and question marks.

Isn't it strange that our names are so similar—Mark and Marion? It does sound rather grand, doesn't it?

Mark had stirrings now of alarm—it seemed he had called the whirlwind when he had merely whistled for a breeze—and yet there was an infectious gaiety and warmth that came through to him strongly, and he regretted that the girl's features were so hazy in his mind. He realized that he might easily pass her in the street without recognizing her.

He replied that night, taking special care with his penmanship. He could not yet blatantly come to the true purpose of his letters, but hinted that he was considering writing a book, but that it would require much research in the Ladyburg archives, and that as yet he did not have either the time nor the capital to make the journey, and he concluded by wondering if she did not have a photograph of herself that he might have.

Her reply must have been written and posted the same day as his letter was received.

"My dearest Mark—" He had been promoted from "Dear Mark."

There was a photograph accompanying the twenty-five pages of closely written text. It was stiffly posed, a young girl in party clothes with a fixed nervous smile on her face, staring into the camera as though it were the muzzle of a loaded howitzer. The focus was slightly misty, but it was good enough to remind him what she looked like, and Mark felt a huge swell of relief.

She was a little plump, but she had a sweet heart-shaped face with a wide friendly mouth and well-spaced intelligent eyes, an alert and lively look about her; and he knew already that she was educated and reasonably well read— and desperately eager to please.

On the back of the photograph he had received further promotion:

> To darling Mark,
> With much love,
> Marion.

Under her name were three neat crosses. The letter was bursting with unbounded admiration for his success as a Cadillac salesman, and with awe for his aspirations to be a writer.

She was anxious to be of help in his researches, he had only to let her know what information he needed. She herself had access to all the Governmental and Municipal archives ("and I won't charge you a search fee this time!"), her elder sister worked in the editorial office of the *Ladyburg Lantern*, and there was an excellent library in the Town Hall building where Marion was well known and where she loved to browse—please would he let her help?

One other thing, did he have a photograph of himself, she would love to have a reminder of him.

For half a crown Mark had a photograph taken of himself at a beachfront open-air studio, dressed in his new suit, and with a straw boater canted at a rakish angle over one eye and a dare-devil grin on his face.

My darling Mark,
How handsome you are!! I have shown all my friends and they are all quite envious.

She had some of the information he requested, and more would follow.

\* \* \*

From Adams Booksellers in Smith Street, Mark purchased a bulky leather-bound notebook, three enormous sheets of cardboard, and a large-scale survey map of Natal and Zululand. These he pinned up on the walls of his room, where he could study them while lying in bed.

On one sheet he laid out the family trees of the Courtneys, the Pyes and the Petersens, all three names associated with the purchase of Andersland on the documents he had seen in Ladyburg Deeds Office.

On one other sheet he built up a pyramid of companies and holdings controlled by the Ladyburg Farmers Bank, and on another he pyramided in the same way the companies and properties of General Sean Courtney's holding company, Natal Timber and Estates Ltd.

On the map he carefully shaded in the actual land holdings of the two groups, red for General Courtney and blue for those controlled by his son, Dirk Courtney Esquire.

It gave him new resolution and determination to continue his search when he carefully shaded with blue the long irregular shape of Andersland, with its convoluted boundary that followed the south bank of the river; and when he had done so and wiped the crayon from his fingers, he was left with the bitter lees of anger in his mouth, a reaffirmation of his conviction that the old man would never have let it go—they would have had to kill him first.

The anger was with him again whenever he filled in another section of the map, or when he lay in bed each night, smoking a last cigarette and studying the blue and red patchwork of Courtney holdings. He smiled grimly when he thought what Fergus MacDonald would say about such wealth in the hands of a single father and son, and then he wrote in the leather-bound notebook any new information that he had accumulated during the day.

He would switch out the light then and lie long awake, and often, when at last he slept, he dreamed of Chaka's Gate, of the great cliffs guarding the river and the tumbled wilderness beyond the gates, that concealed a lonely grave. A grave unmarked, overgrown now with the lush restless vegetation of Africa—or, perhaps, long ago dug open by hyena or the other scavengers.

One day, when Mark spent his customary evening's study in the library reading-room, he turned first to the recent issues of *the Ladyburg Lantern*, searching through those editions covering the week following his flight from Ladyburg, and he almost missed the few lines on an inside page.

Yesterday the funeral service was held of Mr. Jacob Henry Rossouw at the Methodist Church in Pine Street. Mr. Rossouw fell to his death in the gorge of the Baboon Stroom below the new railway bridge while hunting with a party of his friends.

Mr. Rossouw was a bachelor employed by the Zululand Sugar Co. Ltd. The funeral service was attended by the Chairman of the Company, Mr. Dirk Courtney, who made a short but moving tribute at the graveside, once again illustrating his deep concern for even the humblest of the employees of his many prosperous enterprises. "Greatness shows itself in small ways."

The date coincided neatly with his escape from the valley. The man might have been one of his hunters, perhaps the one who had caught his damaged ankle as he hung from the goods truck. If he was, then the connection with Dirk Courtney was direct. Slowly Mark was twisting a rope together, but he needed a head for the noose.

Yet, in one direction, Mark felt easier. There seemed to exist a deep rift between father and son, between General Sean Courtney and Dirk. None of their companies overlapped, none of their directorships interlocked, and each pyramid of companies stood alone and separated. This separation seemed to extend beyond finance or business, and Mark had found no evidence of any contact between the two men at the social level, in fact active hostility between them was indicated by the sudden change in *the Ladyburg Lantern*'s attitude to the father, once the son took control of its editorial policy.

Yet he was not entirely convinced. Fergus MacDonald had repeatedly warned him of the perfidious cunning of the bosses, of all wealthy men. "They will go to any lengths to hide their guilt, Mark, no trick is too low or despicable to cover the stains of honest workers' blood on their hands."

Perhaps Mark's first concern must be to establish beyond doubt that he was hunting only one man. Then, of course, the next move must be to go back to Ladyburg, to try and provoke another attack—but this time he would be ready for it and have some idea from which direction it would come. His mind went back to the way in which he and Fergus MacDonald had used Cuthbert, the dummy, to draw fire and force the enemy to reveal himself, and he grinned ruefully at the thought that this time he must do Cuthbert's job himself. He felt for the first time a fear he had not known in France before a shoot, for he must go out against something more formidable and ruthless than he had ever believed possible before, and the time was fast approaching.

He was distracted then by another massive epistle from Ladyburg, one that gave him honest cause for delaying direct action.

My dearest darling,

What great news I have for you!! If the mountain will not come to Mohammed, then he (or she!) must go to the mountain. My sister and her husband are going to Durban for four days' holiday, and they have asked me to join them. We will arrive on the fourteenth—and will be staying at the Marine Hotel on the Marine Parade—won't we be posh!

Mark surprised himself by the strength of his pleasure and anticipation. He had not realized the affection that he had slowly accumulated at such long remove for this willing and friendly creature. He was surprised again when he met her, both of them dressed with obvious pains and attention to detail, both in an agony of shyness and restraint under the surveillance of Marion's sister.

They sat on the hotel veranda and stiffly sipped tea, making small talk with the sister while surreptitiously examining each other over the rim of their cups.

Marion had lost weight, Mark saw immediately, but would never know that the girl had almost starved herself to do so in anticipation of this moment; and she was pretty—much prettier than he remembered or than her photograph suggested. More important was her transparent wholesomeness and warmth. Mark had been a lonely boy for most of his life, but more particularly so in these last weeks, living in his small dingy room with only the cockroaches and his plans for company.

Now he reacted to her like a traveller coming in out of the snow-storm responds to the tavern fire.

The sister took her duties as chaperone seriously at first, but she was only five or six years older than Mark, and perceptive enough to be aware of the younger people's attraction for each other and to recognize the essential decency of the boy. She was also young enough and herself so recently married as to have sympathy for them.

"I would like to take Marion for a drive—we wouldn't

be gone very long." Marion turned eyes as soulful and pleading as those of a dying gazelle on her sister.

"Oh please, Lyn."

The Cadillac was a demonstration model, and Mark had personally supervised while two of the Zulu employees at Natal Motors had burnished its paintwork to a dazzle.

He drove down as far as the mouth of the Umgeni River, with Marion sitting close and proud and pretty beside him.

Mark felt as good as he ever had in his life; dressed in fashionable style, with gold in his pocket, a big shining automobile under him and a pretty adoring girl beside him.

Adoring was the only word to describe Marion's attitude towards him. She could hardly drag her eyes from his face for a moment, and she glowed every time he glanced across at her.

She had never imagined herself beside such a handsome, sophisticated beau. Not even her most romantic daydreams had ever included a shining Cadillac, and a decorated war hero.

When he parked off the road and they picked a path through the densely overgrown dunes down to the river mouth, she clung to his arm like a drowning sailor.

The river was in spate from some upland rainstorm; half a mile wide and muddy brown as coffee, it surged and swirled down to meet the green thrust of the sea in a leaping ridge of white water. Carried down on the brown water were the debris of the flood, and the carcasses of drowned beasts.

A dozen big black sharks were there to scavenge, pushing high up the river, their dark triangular fins knifing and circling.

Mark and Marion sat side by side on a dune overlooking the estuary.

"Oh," sighed Marion, as though her heart would break, "we've only got four days together."

"Four days is a long time," Mark laughed at her, "I don't know what we are going to do with it all."

They spent nearly every hour of it together. Dicky Lancome was most understanding with his star salesman. "Just show your face here for a few minutes every morning, to keep the boss happy, then you can slip off. I'll hold the fort for you."

"What about the demonstration model?" Mark asked boldly.

"I'll tell him you are making a sale to a rich sugar farmer. Take it, old chap, but for God's sake, don't wrap it round a tree."

"I don't know how I'll ever repay you, Dicky, really I don't."

"Don't worry, old boy, we'll think of a way."

"I won't ask again, its just that this girl is really special."

"I understand." Dicky patted his shoulder in a paternal fashion. "Most important thing in life—a likely bit of crumpet. My heart goes out to you, old son. I'll be cheering you on in spirit every inch of the way."

"It's not like that, Dicky," Mark denied, blushing fiercely.

"Of course not, it never is. But enjoy it anyway," and Dicky winked lasciviously.

Mark and Marion—she was right, it did sound rather grand—spent their days wandering hand in hand through the city. She was delighted by its bustle and energy, enchanted by its sophistication, by its culture, its museums and tropical gardens, by its playground beachfront with myriad fairy lights, the open-air concerts in the gardens of the old fort, by the big departmental stores in West Street, Stuttafords and Ansteys, their windows packed with expensive imported merchandise, by the docks with great merchant ships lining the wharf and the steam cranes huffing and creaking above them.

They watched the Indian fishermen running their surf-boats out from the glistening white beach, through the marching lines of green surf to lay their long nets in a wide semi-circle out into deep water. Then Marion hitched up her skirts and Mark rolled his trousers to the knee to help the half-naked fishermen draw in the long lines, until at last a shimmering silver mound of fish lay on the boat, still quivering and twitching and leaping in the sunlight.

They ate strawberry-flavoured ice cream out of crisp yellow cones, and they rode in an open rickshaw down the Marine Parade, drawn by a leaping howling Zulu dressed in an incredible costume of feathers and beads and horns.

One night they joined Dicky Lancome and a languid siren to whom he was paying court, and the four of them ate grilled crayfish and danced to a jazz band at the Oyster Box Hotel at Umhlanga Rocks, and came roaring home in a Cadillac, tiddly and happy and singing, with Dicky driving like Nuvorelli, rocketing the big car over the dusty rutted road, and Mark and Marion cuddling blissfully in the back seat.

In the lobby of the hotel, under the watchful eye of the night clerk who was poised to intercept Mark if he tried for the elevator, they whispered goodnight to each other.

"I have never been so happy in all my life," she told him simply, and stood on tip-toe to kiss him full on the lips.

Dicky Lancome had disappeared with both Cadillac and lady-friend, probably to some dark and secluded parking place along the sea front, and as Mark walked home alone through the deserted midnight streets, he thought about Marion's words and found himself agreeing. He could not remember being so happy either, but then, he grinned ruefully, it hadn't been a life crowded with wild happiness up to then. To a pauper, a shilling is a fortune.

It was their last day together, and the knowledge weighted their pleasure with poignancy. Mark left the Cadillac at the end of a narrow track in the sugar cane fields and they climbed down to the long white curve of snowy sand beach, guarded at each end by rocky headlands.

The sea was so clear that from the tall dunes they could see deep down to the reefs and sculptured sand banks below the surface. Farther out, the water shaded to a deep indigo blue, that met at last a far horizon piled with a mountainous range of cumulus clouds, purple, blue and silver in the brilliant sunlight.

They walked down barefooted through the crunching
sand, carrying the picnic basket that Marion's hotel had
prepared for them and a threadbare grey blanket from
Mark's bed, and it seemed that they were the only two
persons in the world.

They changed into swimming costumes, modestly sepa-
rating to each side of a dense dark green milk-wood bush,
and then they ran laughing into the warm clear water at
the edge of the beach.

The thin black cotton of Marion's costume clung wetly
to her body, so that it seemed that she was naked, although clothed from mid thigh to neck, and when she
pulled the red rubber bathing cap from her head and shook
out the thick tresses of her hair, Mark found himself physically roused by her for the first time.

Somehow the pleasure he had taken in her up until then
had been that of friendship, and companionship. Her patent
adoration had filled some void in his soul, and he had felt
protective, almost brotherly towards her.

She sensed instantly, with some feminine instinct, the
change in him. The laughter died on her lips, and her eyes
went grave and there were shades in them of fear or apprehension—but she turned to face him, lifting her face to
him, seeming to steel herself with a conscious act of courage.

They lay side by side on the grey blanket, in the heavy
shade of the milk bush, and the midday was heavy and
languorous with heat and the murmur of insects.

The wet bathing-suits were cool against their hot skins,
and when Mark gently peeled hers away, her skin was
damp beneath his fingers, and he was surprised to find her
body so different from Helena's. Her skin was clear milky
white, tipped with palest pink, lightly sugared with white
beach sand, and the hair of her body was fine as silk, light
golden brown and soft as smoke. Her body was soft also,
with the gentle yielding spring of woman's flesh, unlike the
lean hard muscle of Helena's, and it had a different feel to
it, a plasticity that intrigued and excited him.

Only when she gasped, and bit her lip and then turned her face and hid it against his neck did Mark realize suddenly, through the mists of his own arousal, that all the skills Helena had taught him were not moving Marion, as they were him. Her body was rigid, and her face pale and tensed.

"Marion, are you all right?"

"It's all right, Mark."

"You don't like this?"

"It's the first time it's ever happened—"

"We can stop—"

"No."

"We don't have to—"

"No, Mark, go on. It's what you want."

"But you don't want it."

"I want what you want, Mark. Go on. It's for you."

"No—"

"Go on, Mark, please go on." And now she looked at him and he saw her expression was pitiful, her eyes swimming with bright tears and her lips quivering.

"Oh, Marion. I'm sorry." He recoiled from her, horrified by the misery he saw reflected in her expression, but immediately she followed him throwing both arms around his neck, lying half on top of him.

"No, Mark—don't be sorry. I want you to be happy."

"It won't make me happy—if you don't want to."

"Oh, Mark, don't say that. Please don't say that—all I want in the world is to make you happy."

She was brave and enduring, holding him tightly over her, both arms locked around his neck, her body rigid but spread compliantly, and for Mark the ordeal was almost as painful; he suffered for her as he felt the tremble of locked nerves and the small sounds of pain and tension that she tried to keep deep in her throat.

Mercifully for both of them, it was swiftly ended, but still she clung to him.

"Was it good for you, Mark my darling?"

"Oh, yes," he assured her vehemently. "It was wonderful."

"I want so much to be good for you in every way, my darling. Always and in every way, I want to be good for you."

"It was the best thing in my life," he told her, and she stared into his eyes for a moment, searching for assurance, and finding it because she wanted it so terribly.

"I'm so glad, darling," she whispered, and drew his head down on to her damp warm bosom, so soft and pink and comforting. Holding him like that, she began to rock him gently, the way a mother rocks her child. "I'm so glad, Mark, and it will be better and better. I'll learn, you see if I don't, and I'll try so hard for you, darling, always."

Driving home slowly in the dusk, she sat proudly next to him on the wide leather seat, and there was a new air about her, an air of confidence and achievement, as though she had grown from child to matron in the space of a few short hours.

Mark felt a rush of deep affection for her. He felt that he wanted to protect her, to keep that goodness and sweetness from souring, to protect her from unhappiness and wanton damage. For a fleeting moment he felt regret that she had not been able to feed that raging madness of his body, and regret also that he had not been able to lead her through the storm to the same peace. Perhaps that would come, perhaps they would find the way together—and if they didn't, well it wasn't that important. The important thing was the sense of duty he felt towards this woman, she had given him everything of which she was capable, and it was his duty now to give back in equal measure—to protect and cherish her.

"Marion, will you marry me?" he asked quietly, and she began to cry softly, nodding her head vehemently through the tears, unable to speak.

Marion's sister, Lynette, was married to a young lawyer from Ladyburg and the four of them sat up late that night discussing the betrothal.

"Pa won't give permission for you to marry before you are twenty-one, you know how Peter and I had to wait."

Peter Botes, a serious young man, nodded wisely and placed his finger-tips together carefully. He had thin sandy hair, and was as pompous as a judge in scarlet.

"It won't do any harm to wait a few years—"

"Years?" wailed Marion.

"You're only nineteen," Peter reminded her. "And Mark will need to build up some capital before he takes on the responsibility of a family."

"I can go on working," Marion came in hotly.

"They all say that." Peter waggled his head sagely. "And then two months later there's a baby on the way."

"Peter!" His wife rebuked him primly, but he went on calmly.

"And now, Mark, what about your prospects? Marion's father will want to know."

Mark hadn't expected to present an account of his affairs, and on the spur of the moment he could not be certain if his total worth was forty-two pounds twelve shillings—or seven and sixpence.

He saw them off on the Ladyburg train the next morning, with a long lingering embrace and a promise to write every day, while Marion swore she would work at filling her bottom drawer, and at altering her father's prejudice against early marriage. Walking back from the railway, Mark remembered, for no apparent reason, a spring morning in France coming back out of the line to go into reserve, and his shoulders went back and his step quickened and became springy and elastic once more. He was out of the line, and he had survived—that was as far as he could think at that moment.

Dicky Lancome's polished elastic-sided boots were propped on the desk in front of him and fastidiously crossed at the ankles. He looked up from his newspaper, a tea cup held in the other hand with little finger extended delicately.

"Hail the conquering hero comes, his weary weapon slung over his shoulder."

"Oh come on, Dicky!"

"—weak at the knees, bloodshot eye and fevered brow—"

"Any calls?" Mark asked seriously.

"Ah, the giant mind now turns to the more mundane aspects of life."

"Play the game, Dicky." Mark riffled quickly through a small pile of messages that awaited him.

"A surfeit of love, a plethora of passion, and overdose of crumpet, a genital hangover."

"What's this? I can't read your scrawl." Mark averted his eyes, concentrating on his reading.

"Mark my words, Mark, that young lady has got the brood lust. If you turn your back on her for ten minutes, she will be up the nearest tree building a nest."

"Cut it out, Dicky."

"That's precisely what you should do, old boy, unless you can face the prospect of her dropping your whelps all over the scenery." Dicky shuddered theatrically. "Never ride in a saloon if you can drive a sports model, old chap, which reminds me," he dropped the newspaper, checked the watch from his waistcoat pocket, "I have this important client." He inspected his glossy boots a moment, flicked them lightly with the handkerchief from his breast pocket, stood up and adjusted the strawbasher on his head and winked at Mark. "Her husband's gone up country for a week. Hold the fort, old boy, it's my turn now."

He disappeared through the office door into the showroom, and then reappeared instantly, an expression of horror on his face. "Oh God, customers! Get after them, Mark my boy, I'm taking the back door," and he was gone, leaving only the faint perfume of brilliantine lingering on the air.

Mark checked his tie in the sliver of broken mirror wedged in the frame of the window, and adjusted his welcoming smile as he hurried to the door—but at the threshold he stopped as though coming up at the end of a chain. He was listening with the stillness and concentration of a wild gazelle, listening with every fibre and every quivering nerve end to a sound of such aching and penetrating beauty that it seemed to freeze his heart. It lasted only a few seconds, but the sound of it shimmered and thrilled in the air for long seconds afterwards, and only then did Mark's heart beat again, surging heavily against his rib cage.

The sound was the laughter of a girl. It was as though the air around Mark had thickened to honey, for it dragged heavily at his legs as he started forward, and it required a physical effort to draw it down into his lungs.

From the doorway he looked into the showroom. In the centre of the wide floor stood the latest demonstration model Cadillac, and beside it stood a couple.

The man had his back to Mark, and left only the impression of massive size, a towering figure dressed in dark cloth. Beside him, the girl was dainty, almost ethereal, she seemed to float, light and lovely as a humming-bird on invisible wings.

The earth tilted beneath Mark's feet as he gazed at her.

Her head was thrown back to look up at the man. Her throat was long and smooth, balancing the small head with its huge dark eyes and the laughing mouth, small white regular teeth beyond pink lips, a fine bold brow, pale and wide above those haunting eyes—and all of it crowned by a heart-stopping tumble of thick lustrous hair, hair so black that its waves and falls seemed to be sculptured from freshly oiled ebony.

She laughed again, a lovely joyous ripple of sound, and she reached up to touch the man's face. Her hand was narrow, with long tapered fingers, strong capable-looking hands—so that Mark realized that his first impression had been wrong.

The girl was small only in comparison to the man, and her poise heightened the illusion. However, Mark saw now that she was tall, but graceful as a papyrus stem in the wind, supple and slim, with tiny waist and long legs beneath the light floating material of her skirt.

With her finger-tips, she traced the jawline of the man; tilting her head on its long swanlike neck, her beauty was almost unbearable, as her huge eyes shone now with love, and the line of the lips was soft with love.

"Oh Daddy, you are an old-fashioned, grumpy old bear." She spun away from him, lightly as a ballerina, and struck an exaggerated pose beside the huge glistening machine, putting on a comic French accent. "*Regarde! Mon cher papa, c'est très chic—*"

The man growled. "I don't trust these fancy new machines. Give me a Rolls."

"Rolls?" cried the girl, pouting dramatically, "they're so staid! So biblical! Darling Daddy, this is the twentieth century, remember?" Then she drooped like a dying rose in a vase. "How could I hold my head up among my friends if you force me to ride in one of those great sombre coffins?"

At that instant she noticed Mark standing in the doorway of the sales office, and her entire mien changed, the carriage of head and body, the expression of mouth and eye flowing instantly from clown to lady.

"Pater," she said softly, the voice cultivated and the eye cool as it flicked over Mark, a steady encompassing sweep from his head to his feet. "I think the sales person is here." She turned away, and Mark felt his heart convulse again at the way her hip swung and pushed beneath the skirt—and he saw for the first time the cheeky, challenging roll of her small rounded backside as she walked slowly around the Cadillac, calm and aloof, not glancing in his direction again.

Mark stared at her, with fascination, all his emotions in

upheaval. He had never seen anything so beautiful, so completely captivating in all his life.

The man had turned and was glaring at him angrily. He seemed, as the girl had teased him, to be biblical. A gaunt and towering figure with shoulders wide as the gallows tree and the big fierce head exaggerated in size by the slightly twisted hooked nose and the dark thick bush of beard, shot through with grey.

"I know you, dammit!" he growled. The face had been burned almost black by twenty thousand suns, but there were deep white creases in the corners of his eyes and the skin in a line below the thick curls of his silvering hair was white also, protected by the band of a hunter's hat—or a uniform cap.

Mark roused himself, tearing his eyes off the girl, for the fresh shock of recognition. At the time he could only believe it was some monstrous coincidence—but in the years that followed he would know differently. The threads of their lives were plaited, and intertwined. But in this instant the shock, coming so close on the other, unsettled him and his voice croaked.

"Yes, General Courtney, I am——"

"Don't tell me, goddammit," the General cut in, his voice like the crack of a Mauser shooting from cover, and Mark felt his spirit quail before the expression on his face; it was the most formidable he had ever confronted.

"I know—the name is right there!" he glowered at Mark. "I never forget a face." The tremendous force and presence of the man threatened to swamp him.

"It's a sign of old age, Pater," said the girl coolly, glancing over her shoulder without smile or expression.

"Don't you say that, girl," the man rumbled like an active volcano. "Don't you dare say that." He took a threatening step towards Mark, the dark brow corrugated and the blue eyes cutting into his soul like a surgeon's knives. "It's the eyes! Those eyes."

Mark retreated a hurried step before the limping, moun-

tainous advance, not quite sure what to expect, but ready
to believe that Sean Courtney might at any moment lunge
at him with the heavy ebony cane he carried, so murderous
seemed his anger.

"General——"

"Yes!" Sean Courtney snapped his fingers with a crack
like a breaking oak branch, and the scowl smoothed away,
the blue eyes crinkling into a smile of such charisma, of
such infectious and conspiratorial glee, that Mark had to
smile back at him.

"Anders," he said. "Anders and MacDonald. Martin?
Michael? No, Mark Anders!" And he clenched his fist and
struck his own thigh. "Old, is it? Girl—who said old?"

"Pater, you are a marvel." She rolled her eyes, but Sean
Courtney was advancing on Mark, seizing his hand in a
grip that made the bones creak until he recovered himself
and squeezed back, matching the big man's grip.

"It was the eyes," laughed Sean. "You've changed so
much from that day, that night——" and the laughter
dried, as he remembered the boy in the stretcher, pale and
moribund, smeared with mud and thick drying blood, and
heard again his own voice, "He's dead!" He drove back the
image.

"How are you now, my boy?"

"I'm fine, sir."

"I didn't think you were going to pull through." Sean
peered closely at him. "I'll grant you seem to have made it
with all colours flying. How many did you collect, and
where?"

"Two, sir, high in the back."

"Honourable scars, my boy, we'll compare notes one
day." And then he scowled again, horrendously. "You got
the gong, didn't you?"

"Yes, sir."

"Good, you never know in this man's army. I wrote the
citation that night, but you never know. What did they give
you?" Sean smiled his relief.

"The M.M., sir. I got it at the hospital in England."

"Excellent. That's good!" he nodded, and he let go of Mark's hand, turning to the girl again.

"Darling, this gentleman was with me in France."

"How nice." She touched the design on the radiator of the car with one finger, as she drifted past it, not glancing back at them. "Do you think we might have a drive now, Pater?"

Mark hurried to the back door to hold it open. "I'll drive," she said, and waited for him to jump to the driver's door.

"The starter button is here——" he explained.

"Thank you, I know. Sit in the back, please."

She drove like a man, very fast but skilfully, picking a tight line into the corners and using the gearbox to brake, double declutching with dancing feet on the pedals, and hitting the shift with a quick sure hand.

Beside her the General sat with the set to his shoulders of a younger man.

"You drive too fast," he growled, the ferocious tone given the complete lie by the fond smile he turned on her.

"And you're an old fusspot, Daddy," she laughed again; the thrill of it sang in Mark's ears as she hurled the big powerful machine into the next bend.

"I didn't beat you enough when you were young."

"Well, it's too late now." She touched his cheek with her free hand.

"Don't bank on that, young lady—don't ever take bets on that."

Shaking his head in mock despair, but with the adoration still glowing in his eyes, the General heaved himself around in the seat and subjected Mark to another dark penetrating scrutiny.

"You don't turn out at the weekly parades."

"No, sir."

"It's an hour on Friday evenings—half an hour square-bashing and then a lecture."

"Yes, sir?"

"Good fun, really. Tremendous spirit, even though we

have combined with the other peace-time regiments now."

"Yes, sir."

"I'm the Colonel-in-Chief," Sean chuckled. "They couldn't get rid of me that easily."

"No, sir."

"We have a monthly shoot—good prizes, and a barbecue afterwards."

"Is that so, sir?"

"We are sending a team to shoot for the Africa Cup this year, all expenses paid. Marvellous opportunity for the lucky lads who get chosen."

"I'm sure, General."

Sean waited for more, but Mark was silent. He could not meet the big man's fierce, unrelenting gaze, and he shifted his eyes—catching as he did so the girl's face reflected in the rearview mirror.

She was watching him intently, with an unfathomable expression—contempt perhaps, dry amusement, maybe, or something else—something much more intriguing or dangerous. For the split part of an instant, their eyes met, and then her head turned away on the tall graceful column of her neck. The dark shining hair was brushed away from the nape, and there at the juncture with pale skin, the hair was fine and silky, a tiny whorl of it like a question mark at the back of her small sculptured ear.

Mark had an almost insane desire to lean forward and press his lips to it. The thought struck like a physical blow in his groin, and he felt the nerves along his spine racked out cruelly. He realized suddenly then, with a shock that made his senses tilt again, that he was in love with her.

"I want to win that cup," said the General softly, watching him. "The regiment has never won it before."

"I've rather had enough of uniform and war, General." Mark forced his eyes back to meet the General's. "But I do wish you good luck."

the place of the wind, and on the crest of the hills above
Durban town, it would indeed receive the cool blessing of
the sea breezes during the sweltering summer months. The
swinging portion of the gate was two racks of heavy cast-
iron spears, but they stood open now, and Mark crossed
the iron grid which would prevent hooved animals entering
or escaping and started up the gentle curve of the driveway, butter yellow flint pebbles carefully raked and freshly
watered, set on each side with deep beds of cannas which
were now in full bloom. They had been arranged in banks
of solid colour, scarlet and yellow and white, dazzling in
the bright sunshine, and beyond them were lush lawns of
deep tropical green, mown carpet-smooth but studded with
clumps of indigenous trees which had obviously been
spared for their size or beauty or unusual shape. They were
festooned with garlands of lianas, the ubiquitous monkey
rope plants of Natal, and even as Mark watched, a small
blue-grey vervet monkey dropped lithely down one of the
living ropes, and, with its back arched like a cat and its
long tail held high in mock alarm, bounded across an open
stretch of lawn until it reached the next clump of trees
where it shot to the highest branches and chattered inso-
lently at the slowly passing car.

Mark knew from his investigation that this was merely
the Courtney town house, the main family home was at
Ladyburg, and he had not expected anything like this
splendour. And yet why not, he grinned wryly, the man
had everything in the world, this was a mere pied-à-terre.
He twisted his head to look back. The gates were out of
sight behind him now, and there was still no sign of the
house ahead. He was surrounded by a fantasy landscape,
half wild and yet lovingly groomed and tended, and now he
saw the reason for the animal grid at the main gates.

Small herds of semi-domesticated game cropped at the
short grass of the lawn or stood and watched the passing
car with mild curiosity. He saw graceful golden brown impala with snowy bellies and spindly back-curved horns; a
dainty blue duiker as big as a fox terrier with pricked-up

ears and bright button eyes; an eland bull with hanging dewlap, thick twisted horns arming the short heavy head, and a barrel body heavy as a pedigreed Afrikander bull.

He crossed a low bridge over the narrow neck of an artificial lake. The blue water lotus blooms stood high above their huge round green leaves that floated flat on the surface. Their perfume was light and sweet and nostalgic on the bright warm air, and the dark torpedo shapes of bass hung suspended in the clear water below the sheltering lotus leaves.

On the edge of the lake, a black and white spur-winged goose spread its wings, as wide as the reach of a man's arms, and pressed forward with snakelike neck and pink wattled head, threatening flight at the intrusion; then, thinking better of such effort, it furled the great wings again and waggled its tail, satisfied with a single harsh honk of protest as the Cadillac passed.

The roof of the house showed through the trees ahead now, and it was tiled in candy pin, towered and turreted and ridged, like a Spanish palace. The last curve of the driveway brought Mark out into full view of the building. Before it lay an open expanse of blazing flowerbeds. The colour was so vibrant and so concentrated that it daunted the eye, and was relieved only by the tall soft ostrich feathers of spray that poured high into the air from the fountains set in the centre of four round ponds, parapeted in stone. The breeze blew soft wisps of spray like smoke across the flowerbeds, wetting the blooms and enhancing the already dazzling colour.

The house was two stories high, with random towers breaking the solid silhouette and columns, twisted like candy sticks, ornamenting the entrance and supporting the window lintels; it was painted white, and it shone in the sunlight like a block of ice.

It should have given the impression of solid size and ostentatious display, but the design was so cunning that it seemed light as a French pastry—a gay and happy house, built in a spirit of fun and probably of love. A rich man's

gift to a lovely woman, for the feminine touch was everywhere evident, and the great masses of flowers, the fountains and peacocks and marble statues seemed right, the
only setting for such a structure.

Slowly, awed and enchanted, Mark let the Cadillac roll
down the last curve of the driveway, and the light faint
cries of female voices caught his attention.

The tennis courts stood at the end of the lawns, and
there were women at play, their white dresses sparkling in
the sun, their limbs flashing as they ran and swerved and
struck at the ball. Their voices and laughter were sweet and
melodious in the warm hush of the tropical mid-morning.

Mark left the car, and started across the lawn towards
the courts. There were other female figures, also white-
clad, who lolled in deck-chairs in the shade of the banyan
trees, watching the play and conversing languidly as they
sipped at long frosted glasses, waiting their turn on the
courts.

None of them noticed Mark until he was on the edge of
the group.

"Oh, I say, girls." One of them turned quickly in her
chair, and appraised Mark with eyes suddenly no longer
bored, but clear blue and acquisitive. "A man! We *are* in
luck."

Instantly the others changed, each reacting differently: one exaggerating her indifferent and indolent loll in
the low chair, another tugging at her skirt with one hand
and pushing at her hair with the other, smiling brightly and
sucking in her tummy.

They were all young and sleek as cats, glossy with youth
and health and that elusive but unmistakable aura of
wealth and breeding.

"And what is your pleasure, sir?" asked the one with
blue eyes. She was the prettiest of the four, with fine pale
golden hair in a halo around the small neat head and good
white teeth as she smiled.

Mark felt discomforted under their stares, especially
when the speaker turned further in her chair, slowly un-

crossed and crossed her legs, managing to give Mark a flash of white silk panties under the short skirt.

"I am looking for Miss Storm Courtney."

"God," said the smiler. "They all want Storm—why don't any of them ever want me?"

"Storm!" The blonde called out to the court.

Storm Courtney was about to serve, but the call distracted her and she glanced across. She saw Mark and her expression did not change, her attention switched back to the game. She threw the ball high and swung overhand at it, the stroke was fluid and controlled. The racket twanged sharply, and the movement threw her white cotton skirt high against the back of her thighs. Her legs were beautifully moulded, slim ankles and gently swelling calves, knees marked only by symmetrical dimples.

She spun lightly and caught the return of the ball, a long lightly tanned arm flashing in a full sweep and the ball leapt from the racket in a white blur; again her skirt kicked up and Mark shifted slightly on his feet, for the earth had tilted again.

She ran back to the baseline, short neat steps on those long narrow feet, head thrown back to follow the high parabola of the lobbing ball against the blue of the sky. Her dark hair seemed to glow with the metallic sheen of a sunbird's wing as she judged her stroke, and then her whole body went into it, power uncoiling along those long beautiful legs, driven up from tensed and rounded buttocks under the light cotton skirt, through the narrow waist, along young hard back muscles and exploding down through the swinging right arm.

The ball hummed like an arrow, flashed low across the net and kicked a white puff of dust from the baseline.

"Too good!" wailed her opponent despairingly, and Storm laughed, gay and triumphant, and came back to the high fence to pick up the spare balls from the gutter.

"Oh Storm, there's a gentleman here to see you." The blonde called again, and Storm flipped up a ball with the tip of her racket and the side of her foot bouncing it once on the turf of the court and then catching it in her free hand.

"Yes, Irene," she answered lightly. "I know. He's only a sales person. Ask him to wait by the car until I'm ready to deal with him."

She had not looked at Mark again, and now she turned away. "Forty—love," she called gaily, and ran back to the baseline. Her voice had a music and lilt that did nothing to sweeten the sudden flare of anger which made Mark's jaw set grimly.

"If you are a sales person," Irene murmured, "then you can sell me something some time. But right now, darling, I suggest you do what Storm says—otherwise we will all know about it."

When Storm came to where he waited, she was flanked by the other girls, like maids in waiting attending a princess, he thought, and he felt his resentment fade as he watched her. You could forgive somebody like that, somebody so royal and lovely and heart-achingly beautiful—you could forgive them anything.

He stood attentive, waiting for her, and he realized then how tall she was. The top of that glossy head reached to his chin, almost.

"Good morning, Miss Courtney. I have brought your new Cadillac, and all of us at Natal Motors wish you much joy and enjoyment." It was a little speech he always used when making a delivery, and he spoke it with all the warmth and charm and sincerity which had made him in so few months the star salesman of Natal Motors.

"Where are the keys?" Storm Courtney asked, and for the first time looked at him directly. Mark realized that her eyes were that dark, almost black, blue, like the General's. There was no question who her father was.

She opened them a little wider, and in the sunlight they were the colour of polished sapphires or the blue of the Mozambique current, out in the deep water at noon.

"They are in the car," he answered, and his voice

sounded strange in his own ears, as though it came from a distance.

"Get them," she said, and he felt himself start to move, to hurry to her bidding. Then something like that sense of danger he had known and developed in France warned him. Her expression was neutral, completely unconcerned, as though she found the effort of talking directly to him was wasted, just one of these tiresome moments in an otherwise important march of events. Yet the warning was clear as the chime of a bell in his head, and only then he saw something else move in her eyes, something dangerous and exciting like the shape of a leopard hunting in the shadows. A challenge, perhaps, a dare—and suddenly he knew clearly that no daughter of Sean Courtney would be reared to such natural arrogance and rudeness. There was a reason, some design in her attitude.

He felt a lightness of mind, that kind of special madness which had driven away fear of consequence so often in moments of peril or desperate enterprise, and he grinned at her. He did not have to force the grin, it was natural and devilish and challenging.

"Certainly, Miss Courtney. Of course I'll get them, just as soon as you say please."

There was an audible communal gasp from the girls around her, and they stilled with awed delight, their eyes darting to Storm's face and then back to Mark's.

"Say please to the nice man, Stormy." Irene used the patronizing voice for instructing young children, and there was a delighted burst of giggles from the others.

For one unholy instant something burned in the girl's dark blue eyes, something fierce that was not anger. Mark recognized the importance of that flash; although he did not truly know the exact emotion it betrayed, yet he knew it might affect him. Then it was gone and in its place was true unfeigned anger.

"How dare you!" Storm's voice was low and quivering, but her lips were suddenly frosty white as the blood drained away. The anger was too swift, too strong for the occasion, out of all proportion to the mild exchange, and Mark felt a reckless excitement that he had been able to reach her so deeply. He kept the grin mocking and taunting.

"Hit him, darling," Irene teased, and for a moment Mark thought she really might.

"You keep your silly mouth shut, Irene Leuchars."

"Oh la la!" Irene gloated. "Temper!"

Mark turned casually away, and opened the driver's door of the Cadillac.

"Where are you going?"

"Back to town." He started the engine, and looked out of the window at her. There was no doubt now that she was the most beautiful creature he had ever seen. Anger had rouged her cheeks, and the fine dark hair at her temples was still damp from her play on the courts. It was plastered against the smooth skin in tiny curls.

"That is my car!"

"They'll send somebody else up with it, Miss Courtney, I'm used to dealing with ladies."

Again the wondering gasp and burst of giggles.

"Oh, he's a darling!" Irene clapped her hands in applause, but Storm ignored her.

"My father will have you fired."

"Yes, he probably will," he agreed. Mark thought about that solemnly for a moment, then he nodded and he let out the clutch. He looked back in the mirror as he took the first bend in the driveway and they were still standing in a group staring after him in their white dresses, like a group of marble statues. "Nymphs Startled by Satyr" was a fitting title, he thought, and laughed with the reckless mood still on him.

\*   \*   \*

"Jesus," Dicky Lancome whispered, clutching his brow with horror. "What made you do it?" He shook his head slowly, wonderingly.

"She was damned rude."

Dicky dropped his hands and stared at him aghast. "*She* was rude to *you*. Oh my God, I don't think I can stand much more. Don't you realize that if she was rude to you, you should be grateful? Don't you know that there are thousands of peasants like us who go through their entire lives without being insulted by Miss Storm Courtney?"

"I was not going to take that," Mark explained reasonably, but Dicky cut in.

"Look, old bean, I've taught you all I know, and you still know nothing. Not only do you take it, but if Miss Courtney expresses a desire to kick your fat stupid arse, the correct reply is 'certainly, ma'am, but first let me don fresh bags lest I soil your pretty foot!' "

Mark laughed, the reckless mood still there but fading, and Dicky's expression became more lugubrious.

"That's right, have yourself a good laugh. Do you know what happened?" and before Mark could answer he went on, "A summons from on high, the ultimate, the Chairman of the Board himself. So the boss and I dash across town— fear, trepidation, cautious optimism—are we to be fired, promoted, congratulated on the month's sales figures? And there is the Board, the full Board mind you, looking like a convention of undertakers who have just been informed of the discovery of Pasteur's vaccine—"

Dicky stopped, the memory was too painful, and he sighed heavily. "You didn't really tell her to say 'please,' did you?"

Mark nodded.

"You didn't really tell her she was not a lady?"

"Not directly," Mark protested. "But I did imply it."

Dicky Lancome tried to wipe his face off with one hand, starting at the hairline and drawing the palm of his hand down slowly to his chin.

"I've got to fire you, you know that, don't you?"

Mark nodded again.

"Look," said Dicky. "I tried, Mark, I really did. I showed

them your sales figures, I told them you were young, impulsive—I made a speech."

"Thank you, Dicky."

"At the end of the speech, they almost fired me also."

"You shouldn't have stuck your neck out for me."

"Anyone else—you could have picked on anyone else, old chap, you could have punched the mayor, sent abusive letters to the king, but why in the name of all holy things did you have to pick on a Courtney?"

"You know something, Dicky?" and it was Dicky's turn silently to shake his head.

"I loved it—I loved every moment of it."

Dicky groaned aloud, as he took out his silver cigarette case and offered it to Mark. They lit their cigarettes, and smoked in silence for a few moments.

"So I am fired, then?" Mark asked at last.

"That's what I have been trying to tell you for the last ten minutes," Dicky agreed.

Mark began to clear out the drawers in his desk, then stopped and asked impulsively, "Did the General—did General Courtney make the demand for my head?"

"I have no idea, old chap—but sure as hell it was made."

Mark wanted to believe that it had not been the General. It was too mean a gesture from such a big man. He could imagine the General bursting into the showroom, brandishing a horsewhip.

The man who could take such revenge for a small flash of spirit, might be capable of other things—like killing an old man for his land.

The thought sickened Mark, and he tried to thrust it aside.

"Well, then, I suppose I'd better be getting along."

"I'm sorry, old bean." Dicky stood up and offered his hand, then looked embarrassed. "You all right for the filthy lucre? I could let you have a tenner to tide you over."

"Thanks, Dicky, but I'll be all right."

"Look," Dicky blurted out impulsively. "Give it a month

or so, time for the dust to settle, and then if you haven't got yourself fixed, come and see me. I'll try and sneak you in again through the back door—even if we have to write you up on the paysheet under an assumed name."

"Goodbye, Dick, and thanks for everything. I really mean that."

"I'm going to miss you, old chap. Keep your head down below the parapet in future, won't you?"

\* \* \*

The pawn shop was in Soldiers Way, almost directly opposite the railway station. The front room was small and overcrowded with a vast array of valuables, semi-valuables and rubbish left there by the needy over the years.

There was a melancholy about the racks of yellowing wedding dresses, in the dusty glass cases of old wedding rings, engraved watches, cigarette cases and silver drinking flasks—all given in love or respect, each with its own sad story.

"Two pounds," said the pawnbroker, after a single glance at the suit.

"It's only three months old," Mark said softly. "And I paid fifteen."

The man shrugged and the steel-framed spectacles slid down his nose.

"Two pounds," he repeated, and pushed the spectacles up with a thumb that looked grey and dusty as his stock.

"All right—and what about this?"

He opened the small blue case, and showed the bronze disc nestled in a nest of silk, pinned by its gay little ribbon of white and red and blue. The Military Medal for gallantry displayed by non-commissioned officers and other ranks.

"We get a lot of those—not much call for them." The man pursed thin lips. "Twelve pounds ten," he said.

"How long do you keep them before you sell them?" Mark asked, suddenly reluctant to part with the scrap of metal and silk.

"We keep 'em a year."

The last ten days of constant search for employment had depleted Mark's resources of cash and courage.

"All right," he agreed.

The pawnbroker wrote the ticket, while Mark wandered into the back reaches of the shop. He found a bundle of old military haversacks and selected one; then there was a rack of rifles, most of them ancient Martinis and Mausers, veterans of the Boer war—but there was one among them that stood out. The woodwork was hardly marked, and the metal shone smooth and oily, no scratches or pitting of rust, and Mark picked the weapon off the rack and the shape and feel of it brought memories crowding back. He thrust them aside. He would need a rifle where he was going, and it was sensible to have one he knew so well. Fate had put a P.14 there for him, and damn the memories, he decided.

He slipped the bolt from the breech and held the barrel to the light from the doorway, peering into the mouth of the breech. The bore of the barrel was unmarked, the rifling described its clean glistening spirals, again without fouling or pitting. Somebody had cared well for the weapon.

"How much?" he asked the pawnbroker, and the man's eyes turned to lifeless pebbles behind his steel-rimmed spectacles.

"That's a very good rifle," he said, "and I paid a lot of money for it. There's a hundred rounds of ammunition goes with it also."

*　*　*

Mark found he had gone soft in the city, his feet ached within the first five miles and the straps of rifle and haversack cut painfully into his shoulders.

The first night he lay down beside the fire and slept as though he had been clubbed. In the morning he groaned at the effort of sitting upright, the stiffness was in his legs and back and shoulders.

The first mile he hobbled like an old man, until his muscles began to ease, and he was going well by the time he reached the rim of the escarpment and started down into the coastal lowlands.

He kept well away from Andersland, crossing the river five miles upstream. His clothing and rifle and pack were balanced on his head as he waded through a shallow place between white sandbanks, and he dried naked in the sun, sprawled out like a lizard on a rock, before he dressed again and headed north.

The third day, he settled into the long swinging hunter's stride, and the pack rode lightly on his back. The going was hard, the undulating folds of the ground forced him to climb and then descend, taxing every muscle, while the thick thorn scrub made him weave constantly to find a way through, wasting time and almost doubling the distance between point and point. Added to this, the grass was dried and seeding. The seeds were sharp as spears and worked easily through his woollen socks into his flesh. He had to stop every half hour or so to dig them out—but still he made thirty miles that day. In the gathering dusk he crossed another of the countless ridges of higher ground. The distant blue loom of Chaka's Gate almost blended with the darkening clouds of evening.

He camped there that night, sweeping a bed on the bare ground below an acacia thorn tree and eating bully beef and maize porridge by the light of the fire of acacia wood that burned with its characteristic bright white flame and smell of incense.

\* \* \*

General Sean Courtney stood at the heavy teak sideboard, with its tiers of engraved glass mirrors and displays of silver plate. In one hand he held the ivory-handled carving fork and in the other the long Sheffield knife.

He used the knife to illustrate the point he was making to the guest-of-honour at his table.

"I read it through in a single day, had to stay up until after midnight. Believe me, Jan, it's his best work yet. The amount of research—quite extraordinary."

"I look forward to reading it," said the Prime Minister, nodding acknowledgement to the author of the work under discussion.

"It's still in manuscript. I am not entirely satisfied yet, there is still some tidying up to do."

Sean turned back to the roast and, with a single practised stroke of the blade for each, cut five thin slices of pink beef rimmed with a rind of rich yellow fat.

With the fork he lifted the meat on to the Rosenthal porcelain plate and immediately a Zulu servant in a flowing white kanza robe and red pillbox fez carried the plate to Sean's place at the head of the long table.

Sean laid the carving-knife aside, wiped his hands on a linen cloth, and then followed the servant to the table and took his seat.

"We were wondering if you might write a short foreword for the book," Sean said, as he raised a cut crystal glass of glowing red wine to the Prime Minister, and Jan Christiaan Smuts inclined his head on narrow shoulders in an almost birdlike gesture. He was a small man, and the hands laid before him on the table were almost fragile; he had the mien of a philosopher, or a scholar, which was not dispelled by the neat pointed beard.

Yet it was hard to believe that he was small. There was a vital force and awesome presence about him that belied the high, rather thin voice in which he replied,

"Few things would give me as much pleasure. You do me honour."

He seemed to bulk huge in his chair, such was the power of character he commanded.

"I am the one who is honoured," Colonel Garrick Courtney replied gravely from across the table, bowing slightly—and Sean watched his brother fondly.

"Poor Garry," he thought, and then felt a guilty stab. Yet it seemed so natural to think of him in those terms. He was frail and old now, bowed and grey and dried out, so that he seemed smaller even than the little man opposite him.

"Have you a title yet?" asked Jan Smuts.

"I have thought to call it *The Young Eagles*. I hope you do not find that too melodramatic for a history of the Royal Flying Corps."

"By no means," Smuts contradicted him. "I think it excellent."

"Poor Garry," Sean thought again. Since Michael had been shot down, the book filled the terrible gap that his son's death had left; but it had not prevented him from growing old. The book was a memorial to Michael, of course, an act of great love—"This book is dedicated to Captain Michael Courtney D.F.C., one of the Young Eagles who will fly no more." Sean felt the resuscitation of his own grief, and he made a visible effort to suppress it.

His wife saw the effort, and caught his eye down the length of the table. How well she knew him after all these years, how perfectly she could read his emotions, she thought, as she smiled her sympathy for him, and saw him respond, the wide shoulders squaring up and heavy bearded jaws firming as he smiled back at her.

Deftly she changed the mood. "General Smuts has promised to walk around the gardens with me this afternoon, Garry, and advise me on planting out the proteas he brought me from Table Mountain. You are also such a knowledgeable botanist. Will you join us?"

"As I warned you, my dear Ruth," said Jan Smuts in that ready, yet compelling voice, "I do not give much hope for their survival."

"Perhaps the Leucadendrons," ventured Garry, "if we find a cool, dryish place?"

"Yes," agreed the General, and immediately they fell into an animated discussion. She had done it so skilfully, that she seemed to have done nothing.

Sean paused in the doorway of his study and ran a long
lingering gaze over the room. As always, he felt a glow of
pleasure at re-entering this sanctuary.

The glass doors opened now on to the massed banks of
flowers, and the smoking plumes of the fountain, yet the
thick walls ensured that the room remained cool even in
the sleepy hush of midday.

He crossed to the desk of stinkwood—dark and massive
and polished, so that it shone even in the cool gloom—and
he lowered himself into the swivel chair, feeling the fine
leather stretch and give under his weight.

The day's mail was neatly arranged on a silver salver at
his right hand, and he sighed when he saw that, despite the
careful screening by the senior clerk down at the city Head
Office, there were still not much less than a hundred envelopes awaiting him.

He delayed the moment by swinging the chair slowly to
look once again about the room. It was hard to believe it
had been designed and decorated by a woman—unless it
was a woman who loved and understood her man so well
that she could anticipate his slightest whim and fancy.

Most of the books were bound in dark green leather, and
stamped on their spine in gold leaf with Sean's crest. The
exceptions were the three ceiling-high shelves of first editions with African themes. A dealer in London, and another in Amsterdam had *carte blanche* instructions from
Sean to search for these treasures. There were autographed
first editions by Stanley, Livingstone, Cornwallis Harris,
Burchell, Munro and almost every other African explorer
or hunter who had ever published.

The dark panelled woodwork between the book shelves
was studded with the paintings of the early African artists;
the Baines glowed like rich gems in their flamboyant colours and naïve, almost childlike, depiction of animal and
countryside. One of these was set in an intricately carved

frame of Rhodesian redwood and engraved, "To my friend David Livingstone, from Thomas Baines."

These links with history and the past always warmed Sean with pleasure, and he fell into a mild reverie.

The deep carpeting deadened her footsteps, but there was the light perfume on the air that warned Sean of her presence, and he swung his chair back to the desk. She stood beside his chair, slim and straight as a girl still.

"I thought you were walking with Garry and Jan."

Ruth smiled then, and seemed as young and beautiful as when he had first met her so many years before. The cool gloom of the room disguised the little lines at the corners of her eyes and the light streaking of silver in the dark hair drawn back from her temples and caught with a ribbon at the back of her neck.

"They are waiting for me, but I slipped away for a moment to make certain that you had all you wanted." She smiled down at him, and then selected a cigar from the silver humidor and began to prepare it.

"I will need an hour or two," he said, glancing at the pile of mail.

"What you really need, Sean, is an assistant." She cut the cigar carefully, and he grunted.

"You can't trust any of these young people—" and she laughed lightly as she placed the cigar between his lips.

"You sound as old as the prophets." She struck a Vesta and waved it to clear the sulphur before she held it to the tip of the cigar. "It's a sign of old age to mistrust the young."

"With you beside me, I'll be young forever," he told her, still awkward with a compliment after all these years and she felt her heart swell with her love, knowing the effort it had required.

She stooped quickly and kissed his cheek, and with a speed and strength that still astonished her, one of his thickly muscled arms whipped around her waist and she was lifted into his lap.

"You know what happens to forward young ladies—

don't you?" He grinned at her, his eyes crinkling wickedly.

"Sean," she protested, in mock horror. "The servants! Our guests!" She struggled out of his embrace with the warmth and wetness of his kiss still on her lips, together with the tickle of his whiskers and the taste of his cigar, and rearranged her skirts and her hair.

"I'm a fool." She shook her head sorrowfully. "I always trust you." And then they smiled at each other, lost for a moment in their love.

"My guests," she remembered suddenly, a hand flying to her mouth. "May I set the tea for four o'clock? We'll have it down at the lake. It's a lovely day."

When she had gone, Sean wasted another minute staring after her through the empty doorway into the gardens. Then he sighed again, contentedly, and drew the silver salver of mail towards him.

He worked quickly, but with care, pencilling his instructions at the foot of each page and initialling them with a regal "S.C."

"No!—but tell them politely. S.C."

"Let me have the previous year's figures of purchase—and delay the next shipment against bank guarantee. S.C."

"Why did this come to me? Send it to Barnes. S.C."

"Agreed. S.C."

"To Atkinson for comment, please. S.C."

The subjects were as diverse as the writers—politicians, financiers, supplicants, old friends, chancers, beggars—they were all there.

He flicked over a sealed envelope and stared at it for a moment, not recognizing the name or the occasion.

"Mark Anders Esq., Natal Motors, West Street, Durban."

It was written in the hand that was so bold and flourishing that nobody could mistake it for any other but his own, and he remembered sending the letter.

Somebody had written across the envelope. "Left—no forwarding address—return to sender."

Sean clamped the cigar in the corner of his mouth and slit the flap with a Georgian silver paper-knife. The card was embossed with the regimental crest.

> The Colonel-in-Chief and the officers of the Natal Mounted Rifles request the pleasure of *MARK ANDERS ESQ.* at a regimental reunion dinner to be held at the Old Fort . . .

Sean had written in the boy's name in the blank space, and at the end of the card, "Do try to come. S.C."

Now it was returned, and Sean scowled. As always, he was impatient and frustrated by even the slightest check in his plans. Angrily he tossed both card and envelope at the wastepaper bin, and they both missed, fluttering to the carpet.

Surprisingly, even to himself, his mood had altered, and though he worked on, he fumed and gruffed now over his correspondence and his instructions became barbed.

"The man is a fool or a rogue or both—under no circumstances will I recommend him to a post of such importance, *despite* the family connections! S.C."

After another hour, he had finished and the room was hazed with cigar smoke. He lay back in the chair and stretched voluptuously like an old lion, then glanced at the wall clock. It was five minutes short of four o'clock, and he stood up.

The offending card caught his eye again, and he stooped quickly and picked it up, reading it again as he crossed the room, tapping the stiff cardboard thoughtfully on the open palm of his hand as he limped out heavily into the sunlight and across the wide lawns.

The gazebo was set on a constructed island in the centre of the lake with a narrow causeway joining it to the lawns.

Sean's household and guests were gathered there already, sitting about the table in the shade under the crazily contrived roof of the gazebo with its intricate cast-iron work painted with carnival colours. Already a host of wild duck had gathered about the tiny island, quacking loudly for pieces of biscuit and cake.

Storm Courtney saw her father coming across the lawns, and she let out one small excited squeak, leapt from the tea table and flew down the causeway to meet him before he reached the lake.

He lifted her easily, as though she were still a baby, and when he kissed her, she inhaled the smell of him. It was one of the lovely smells of her existence, like the smell of rain on hot dry earth, or horses, or the sea. He had a special perfume like old polished leather.

When he lowered her, she took his arm and pressed close to him, matching her light quick step to his limp.

"How was your lunch appointment?" he asked, looking down on her shining lovely head, and she rolled her eyes and then squinted ferociously.

"He is a very presentable young man," Sean told her sternly. "An excellent young man."

"Oh, Daddy, from you that means he is a weak-minded bore."

"Young lady, I would like to remind you that he is a Rhodes scholar, and that his father is the Chief Justice."

"Oh, I know all that—but, Daddy, he just hasn't got zing!"

Even Sean looked nonplussed for an instant. "And what, may I ask, is 'zing'?"

"Zing is indefinable," she told him seriously, "but you've got zing! You're the zingiest man I know."

And with that statement Sean found all his fatherly advice and disapproving words gone like migrating swallows, and he grinned down at her, shaking his head.

"You don't really believe that I swallow all your soft soap, do you?"

"You'll never believe it, Daddy, but Payne Bros. have got in twelve actual Patou Couture models—they're absolutely exclusive—and Patou is all the rage now—"

"Women in savage, barbaric colours, driven mad by

those machiavellian scheming monsters of Paris," growled Sean, and Storm giggled delightedly.

"You are a scream, Daddy," she told him. "Irene's father had told her she may have one of them—and Mr. Leuchars is a mere tradesman!"

Sean blinked to hear the head of one of the largest import houses in the country so described.

"If Charles Leuchars is a tradesman—what, pray, am I?" he asked curiously.

"You are landed gentry, a Minister of the Crown, a General, a hero—and the zingiest man in the world."

"I see," he could not help but laugh, "that I have a position to uphold. Ask Mr. Payne to send the account to me."

She hugged him again, ecstatically, and then for the first time noticed the card he still held in his hand.

"Oh," she exclaimed. "An invitation!"

"Not for you, my girl," he warned her, but she had taken it from his hand, and her face changed as she read the name. Suddenly she was quiet and subdued.

"You are sending that to that—sales person."

He frowned again, his own mood altering also. "I sent it. It was returned. He has left, without a forwarding address."

"General Smuts is waiting to talk to you." With an effort she recaptured the smile and skipped beside him. "Let's hurry."

\* \* \*

"It's serious, old Sean. They are organized, and there is no question but that they are seeking a direct confrontation." Jan Christiaan Smuts crumbled a biscuit between his fingers, and tossed it to the ducks. They squabbled noisily, splashing in the clear water and chattering their broad flat bills as they dipped for the scraps.

"How many white workers will they lay off?" Sean asked.

"Two thousand, to begin with," Smuts told him. "Probably four thousand, all in all. But the idea is to do it gradually, as the blacks are trained to replace them."

"Two thousand," Sean mused, and he could not help but imagine the wives, and the children—the old mothers, the dependants. Two thousand wage-earners out of work represented much suffering and misery.

"You like it as little as I do." The shrewd little man had read his thoughts; not for nothing did his opponents call him "slim Jannie," or "clever Jannie." "Two thousand unemployed is a serious business," he paused significantly. "But we will find other employment. We need men desperately on the railways and on other projects like the Vaal-Harts irrigation scheme."

"They will not earn there the way they do in the mines," Sean pointed out.

"No," Jan Smuts drew out the negative thoughtfully, "but should we protect the income of two thousand miners, at the cost of closing the mines themselves?"

"Surely it is not that critical?" Sean frowned quickly.

"The Chairman of the Chamber of Mines assures me that it is—and he has shown me figures to support this view."

Sean shook his head, half in incredulity and half in anguish. He had been a mine-owner himself once—and he knew the problem of costs, and also the way that figures can be made to speak the language their manipulators taught.

"You know also, old Sean, you especially—how many others depend for life on those gold mines." It was a hard probing statement, with a point like a stiletto. The previous year, for the first time, the sales of timber pit-props from Sean's sawmills to the gold mines of the Transvaal had exceeded two million pounds sterling. The little General knew it as well as he did.

"How many men are employed by Natal Sawmills, old Sean, twenty thousand?"

"Twenty-four thousand," Sean answered shortly, one blond eyebrow lifted quizzically, and the Prime Minister smiled softly before going on.

"There are other considerations, old friend—that you and I have discussed before. On those occasions, it was you who told me that to succeed in the long term, our nation must become a partnership of black man and white, that our wealth must be shared according to a man's ability rather than the colour of his skin—not so?"

"Yes," Sean agreed.

"It was I who said we must make haste slowly in that direction, and now it is you who hesitates and baulks."

"I also told you that many small steps were surer than a few wild leaps, made under duress, made only with an assegai at your ribs. I said, Jannie, that we should learn to bend so that we might never have to break."

Jannie Smuts turned his attention back to the ducks, and they both watched them distractedly.

"Come, Jannie," Sean said at last. "You mentioned other reasons. Those you have given me so far are good but not deadly urgent and I know you are politician enough to save the best until the end."

Jannie laughed delightedly, almost a giggle, and leaned across to pat Sean's arm. "We know each other too well."

"We should," Sean smiled back at him. "We fought each other hard enough." They both sobered at mention of those terrible days of the civil war. "And we had the same tutor, God bless him."

"God bless him," echoed Jan Smuts, and they remembered for a moment that colossus Louis Botha, warrior and statesman, architect of Union, and first Prime Minister of the new nation.

"Come," Sean insisted. "What is your other reason?"

"It is quite simple. We are about to decide who governs. The duly elected representatives of the people, or a small ruthless band of adventurers who call themselves trade union leaders, representatives of organized labour—or quite simply international communism."

"You put it hard."

"It is hard, Sean. It is very hard. I have intelligence facts that I shall lay before the first meeting of the Cabinet when

Parliament reconvenes. However, I wanted to discuss these with you personally before that meeting. I need your support again, old Sean. I need you with me at that meeting."

"Tell me," invited Sean.

"Firstly, we know that they are arming, with modern weapons, and that they are training and organizing the mineworkers into war commandos." Jan Smuts spoke quickly and urgently for nearly twenty minutes, and when he had finished he looked at Sean.

"Well, old friend, are you behind me?"

Bleakly Sean looked out into the future, seeing with pain the land he loved once more torn by the hatred and misery of civil war. Then he sighed.

"Yes," he nodded heavily, "I am with you, and my hand on it."

"You and your regiment?" Jan Smuts took the big bony hand. "As a Minister of the Government and as a soldier?"

"Both," Sean agreed. "All the way."

* * *

Marion Littlejohn read Mark's letter, sitting on the closed seat of the office toilet, with the door locked, but her love transcended her surroundings, discounted even the hiss and gurgle of water in the cistern suspended on its rusty downpipe above her head.

She read the letter through twice, with eyes misty and a tender smile tugging uncertainly at her lips, then she kissed his name on the final page and carefully folded it back into its envelope, opened her bodice and nestled the paper between her plump little breasts. It made a considerable lump there when she returned to the main office and the supervisor looked out from his glass cubicle and made a show of consulting his watch. It was an acknowledged, if unwritten, rule in the Registrar's office that calls of nature should be answered expeditiously, and in no circumstances should the answer occupy more than four minutes of a person's working day.

The rest of the day dragged painfully for Marion, and every few minutes, she touched the lump in her bodice and smiled secretively. When at last the hour of release came, she hurried down Main Street and arrived breathless just as Miss Lucy was closing the doors of her shop.

"Oh, am I in time?"

"Come in, Marion dear—and how is your young man?"

"I had a letter from him today," she announced proudly, and Miss Lucy nodded her silver curls and beamed through the silver steel frames of her spectacles.

"Yes, the postman told me." Ladyburg was not yet such a large town that it could not take an intimate interest in the affairs of all its sons and daughters. "How is he?"

Marion prattled on, flushing and shiny-eyed, as she inspected once again the four sets of Irish linen sheets that Miss Lucy was holding for her.

"They are beautiful, dear, you can really be proud of them. You'll have fine sons between them." Marion blushed again.

"How much do I still owe you, Miss Lucy?"

"Let's see, dear—you've paid off two pounds and sixpence. That leaves thirty shillings balance."

Marion opened her purse and counted its contents carefully, then after a mental struggle reached a decision and laid a shiny golden half sovereign on the counter.

"That leaves only a pound." She hesitated, flushed again, then blurted out, "Do you think I might take one pair with me now? I would like to begin the embroidery work."

"Of course, child," Miss Lucy agreed immediately. "You have paid for three already. I'll open the packet."

* * *

Marion and her sister Lynette sat side by side on the sofa. Each of them had begun at one side of the sheet and their heads were bent together over it, the embroidery needles flicking in the lamplight as busily as their tongues.

"Mark was most interested in the articles I sent him on

Mr. Dirk Courtney and he says that he feels Mr. Courtney will have a prominent place in the book—"

Across the room, Lyn's husband worked head down over a sheath of legal documents spread on the table before him.

He had lately affected a briar pipe, and it gurgled softly with each puff. His hair was brilliantined and brushed down to a polish with a ruler-straight parting of white scalp dividing it down the middle.

"Oh, Peter," Marion exclaimed suddenly, her hands stilling and her face lighting. "I have just had a wonderful idea."

Peter Botes looked up from his papers, a small frown of annoyance crinkling the serious white brow, a man interrupted at his labour by the silly chatter of woman.

"You do so much work for Mr. Courtney down at the bank. You've even been up to the big house, haven't you? He even greets you on the streets—I've seen that."

Peter nodded importantly, puffing at the pipe. "Yes, Mr. Carter has often remarked that Mr. Courtney seems to like me. I think I will be handling the account more and more in the future."

"Oh, darling, won't you speak to Mr. Courtney and tell him that Mark is doing all this work for his book on Ladyburg, and that he is ever so interested in Mr. Courtney and his family—"

"Oh, come now, Marion." Peter waved the pipe airily. "You can't expect a man like Mr. Courtney—"

"You might find he is flattered to be in Mark's book— please dear. I know Mr. Courtney will listen to you. You might find he likes the idea—and it will reflect credit on you."

Peter paused thoughtfully, weighing carefully the value of impressing the womenfolk with his importance and influence against the dread prospect of speaking on familiar terms with Mr. Dirk Courtney. The thought appalled him. Dirk Courtney terrified him and in his presence he affected a fawning, self-effacing manner which was, he realized, part of the reason why Dirk Courtney liked to work with him; of course, he was also a painstaking meticulous lawyer, but the main reason was his respectful attitude; Mr. Courtney liked respect from his underlings.

"Please, Peter, Mark is going to so much trouble over this book. We must try and help him. I was just telling Lynette that Mark has taken a month's leave from his job to go on an expedition up to Chaka's Gate, just to gather facts for the book."

"He's gone to Chaka's Gate?" Peter looked mystified, and removed the pipe from his mouth. "What on earth for? There is nothing up there but wilderness."

"I'm not sure," admitted Marion, and then quickly, "but it's important for the book. We must try and help him."

"What exactly do you want me to ask Mr. Courtney?"

"Won't you ask him to meet Mark, and sort of tell him his life story in his own words. Imagine how that would be in the book."

Peter swallowed once. "Marion, Mr. Courtney is a busy man, he can't—"

"Oh please." Marion jumped up and crossed the room to kneel beside his chair. "Pretty please, for my sake!"

"Well," he mumbled, "I'll mention it to him."

\* \* \*

Peter Botes stood lika a guardsman beside the head seat of the long ormolu table, bending stiffly from the waist only when it was necessary to turn the page.

"—and here please, Mr. Courtney."

The big man in the chair dashed a careless signature across the foot of the document, hardly glancing at it and without interrupting his conversation with the other fashionably dressed men further down the table.

There was a strong perfume hanging about Dirk Courtney, he wore it with the panache of a cavalry officer's cloak, and Peter tried in vain to identify it. It must be terribly expensive, but it was the smell of success, and he made a resolution to acquire a bottle of whatever it was.

"—and here again, please, sir."

He noticed now at close range how Dirk Courtney's hair was shining and cut longer at the temple, free of brilliantine and allowed to curl into the sideburns. Peter would wash the brilliantine from his own hair tonight, he decided, and let it grow out a little longer.

"That is all, Mr. Courtney. I'll have copies delivered tomorrow."

Dirk Courtney nodded without glancing up at him, and, pushing back his chair, he stood up.

"Well, gentlemen," he addressed the others at the table, "we should not keep the ladies waiting," and they all laughed with that lustful, anticipatory laugh, their eyes gleaming like those of caged lions at feeding time.

Peter had heard in detail of those parties that Dirk Courtney held out at Great Longwood, his big house. There was gaming for high stakes, sometimes dog-fighting—two matched animals in a pit, ripping each other to ribbons of dangling skin and flesh—sometimes cock-fighting, always women—women brought in closed cars from Durban or Johannesburg. Big city women and Peter felt his body stir at the thought. Introductions to the parties were limited to men of importance or influence or wealth, and during the weekend that the revels continued, the grounds were guarded by Dirk Courtney's bully boys.

Peter dreamed sometimes of being invited to one of those parties, of sitting across the green baize table from Dirk Courtney and casually drawing towards him the multi-coloured pile of ivory chips without removing the expensive cigar from his lips, or of sporting among the rustling silks and smooth white limbs—he had heard of the dancers, beautiful women who disrobed as they danced the Seven Veils, and ended mother-naked while the men roared and groped.

Peter roused himself almost too late. Dirk Courtney was across the room, ushering his guests ahead of him, laughing and charming, flashing white teeth from the swarthy handsome face, a servant standing ready with his overcoat,

chauffeurs waiting with the limousines in the street below—about to depart into a realm about which Peter could
only speculate in disturbing erotic detail.

He hurried after him, stammering nervously.

"Mr. Courtney, I have a personal request."

"Come, Charles," Dirk Courtney did not look at Peter,
but smilingly laid a friendly arm across one of his guests'
shoulders. "I trust you are in better luck than last time, I
hate to take a friend's money."

"My wife's sister has a financé, sir," Peter stumbled on
desperately. "He's writing a book about Ladyburg, and he
would like to include an account of your personal experience—"

"Alfred, will you ride with Charles in the first car." Dirk
Courtney buttoned his coat, and adjusted his hat, beginning
to turn towards the door, just a slight crease to his brow
showing his annoyance at Peter's importunity.

"He is a local man," Peter was almost in tears of embarrassment, but he went on doggedly, "with a good war record, you might remember his grandfather John Anders—"

A peculiar expression came over Dirk Courtney's face,
and he turned slowly to look directly at Peter for the first
time. The expression struck instant terror into him; Peter
had never before seen such burning malevolence, such merciless cruelty on a man's face before. It was only for an
instant—and then the big man smiled. Such a smile of
charm and good fellowship that Peter felt dizzy with relief.

"A book about me?" He took Peter's arm in a friendly
grip above the elbow. "Tell me more about this young
man. I presume he is young?"

"Oh yes, sir, quite young."

"Gentlemen." Dirk Courtney smiled apologetically at his
guests. "Can I ask you to go ahead of me. I will follow
shortly. Your rooms are prepared, and please do not feel
you have to await my arrival before sampling the entertainment."

Still holding Peter's arm, he led him courteously back
into the huge board room to a seat in one of the leather

chairs by the fireplace. "Now, young Master Botes, how about a glass of brandy?" and Peter watched bemused as he poured it with his own hands, big strong hands, covered with fine black hair across the back and with a diamond the size of a ripe pea on the little finger.

\* \* \*

With each step northwards, it seemed to Mark that the great bastions of Chaka's Gate changed their aspect gradually, from silhouettes smoked blue with distance until the details of the living rock came into focus.

The twin bluffs faced each other in almost mirror image, each towering a thousand sheer feet but deeply divided by the gorge through which the Bubezi River spilled out on to the coastal lowlands of Zululand and then meandered down a hundred and twenty miles into a maze of swamp and lagoon and mangrove forest, before finally escaping through the narrow mouth of the tidal estuary. The mouth sucked and breathed with the tide, and the ebb blew a stain of discoloured water far out into the electric blue of the Mozambique Current, a brown smear that contrasted sharply with the vivid white rind of sandy beaches that stretched for a thousand miles north and south.

If a man followed the course of the Bubezi up through the portals of Chaka's Gate, as Mark and the old man had done so often before, he came out into a wide basin of land below the main escarpment. Here, among the heavy forests, the Bubezi divided into its two tributaries, the White Bubezi that dropped in a series of cataracts and falls down the escarpment of the continental shield—and the Red Bubezi, which swung away northwards following the line of the escarpment up through more heavy forest and open grassy glades until at last it became the border with the Portuguese colony of Mozambique.

In the flood seasons of high summer, this tributary carried down with it the eroding laterite from deposits deep in

Mozambique; turning to deep bloody red, it pulsed like a living artery, and well earned its name, the Red Bubezi.

Bubezi was the Zulu name for the lion, and indeed Mark had hunted and killed his first lion on its banks, half a mile below the confluence of the two tributaries.

It was almost noon, when at last Mark reached the river at the point where it emerged from the gorge between the gates. He reached for his watch to check the time and then arrested the gesture. Here time was not measured by metal hands, but by the majestic swing of the sun and the eternal round of the seasons.

He dropped his pack and propped the rifle against a tree trunk; the gesture seemed symbolic. With the weight off his shoulders, the dark weight on his heart seemed to slip away also.

He looked up at the rock cliffs that filled half the sky above him, and was lost in awe as he had been when he looked up at the arched stone lattice-work of the Henry VII chapel in Westminster Abbey.

The columns of rock, sculptured down the ages by wind and sun and water, had that same ethereal grace, yet a freedom of line that was not dictated by the strict rules of man's vision of beauty. The cliffs were painted with lichen growth, brilliant smears of red and yellow and silvery grey.

In cracks of irregularities of rock grew stunted trees; hundreds of feet above their peers, they were deformed and crippled by the contingencies of nature as though by the careful skills of a host of Japanese Bonzai gardeners, and they twisted out at impossible angles from the face of the cliff, holding out their branches as if in supplication to the sun.

The rock below some narrow ledges was darkened by the stain of the urine and faeces of the hydrax, the fluffy rock rabbits, which swarmed from every crack and hole in the cliff. Sitting in sleepy ranks, on the very edge of the drop, sunning their fat little bodies and blinking down at the tiny figure of the man in the depth of the gorge.

Following the floating wide-pinioned flight of a vulture, Mark watched it swing in steeply, planing and volleying its great brown wings to meet the eddy of the wind across the cliff face, reaching forward with its talons for a purchase as it pulled up and dropped on to its nesting ledge a hundred and fifty feet above the river, folding its wings neatly and then crouching in that grotesque vulturine attitude with the bald scaly head thrust forward, as it waddled sideways along the rim of its huge shaggy nest of sticks and small branches built into the rockface.

From this angle Mark could not see the chicks in the nest, but clearly he recognized the heaving motions of the bird as it began to regurgitate its cropful of rotten carrion for its young. Gradually a sense of peace settled like a mantle over Mark, and he sat down, his back against the rough bole of a fever tree, and slowly, without sense of urgency, he selected and lit a cigarette, drawing the smoke with an unhurried breath and then letting it trickle out through his nostrils, watching the pale blue tendrils rise and swirl on the lazy air.

He thought perhaps that the nearest human being was forty miles distant, the nearest white man almost a hundred—and the thought was strangely comforting.

He wondered at the way in which all man's petty striving seemed insignificant in this place, in this vast primeval world—and suddenly he thought that if all men, even those who had known nothing but the crowded ratlike scrambling of the cities, could be set down in this place, even for a brief space of time, then they might return to their lives cleansed and refreshed, their subsequent strivings might become less vicious, more attuned to the eternal groundswell of nature.

Suddenly he grunted, his reverie shattered by the burning needle sting in the soft of his neck below the ear, and he slapped at it with open palm. The small flying insect was stunned, its carapace too tough to be crushed, even by a blow that heavy. It fell spinning and buzzing into Mark's lap, and he picked it up between thumb and forefinger, examining it curiously, for it was many years since last he had seen one.

The tsetse fly is slightly larger than the house fly, but it has a sleeker more streamlined body, with transparent wings veined in brown.

"The saviour of Africa," the old man had called it once, and Mark repeated the words aloud as he crushed it between his fingers. It burst in a bright liquid red explosion of the blood it had sucked from his neck. He knew the bite would swell and turn angry red, all the subsequent bites would react in the same way, until swiftly his body rebuilt its immunity. Within a week he would not even notice their stings, and the bite would cause less discomfort than that of a mosquito.

"The saviour of Africa," the old man had told him. "This little bastard was all that saved the whole country being overrun and over-grazed with domestic animals. Cattle first, and after cattle the plough, and after the plough the towns and the railway tracks." The old man had chewed slowly, like a ruminating bull in the light of the camp fire, his face shaded by the spread of the terai hat. "One day they will find some way to kill him, or something to cure the sleeping sickness—the nagana—that he carries. Then the Africa we know will have gone, lad." He spat a long honey-brown spurt of juice into the fire. "What will Africa be without its lonely places and its game? A man might as well go back and live in London town."

Looking with new eyes and new understanding at the majestic indigenous forest around him, Mark saw in his imagination what it might have been like without its tiny brown-winged guardians; the forests chopped out for firewood, and cleared for ox-drawn cultivation, the open land grazed short and the hooves of the cattle opening the ground cover to begin the running ulcers of erosion, the rivers browned and sullied by the bleeding earth and by man's filth.

The game hunted out—for its meat and because it was in direct competition to the domestic animals for grazing. For the Zulu, cattle was wealth, had been for a thousand years, and wherever cattle could thrive, they came with their herds.

Yet it was ironic that this wilderness had had another guardian, apart from the winged legions, and that guardian had been a Zulu. Chaka, the great Zulu king, had come here long ago. Nobody knew when, for the Zulu does not measure time as a white man does, nor record his history in the written word.

The old man had told Mark the story, speaking in Zulu which was fitting for such a story, and his old Zulu gun-bearer had listened and nodded approvingly, or grunted a correction of fact; occasionally he spoke at length embroidering a point in the legend.

In those days there had lived here in the basin a small tribe of hunters and gatherers of wild honey, so they called themselves Inyosi, the bees. They were a poor people but proud, and they resisted the mighty king and his insatiable appetite for conquest and power.

Before his swarming impis, they had withdrawn into the natural fortress of the northern bluff. Remembering the story, Mark raised his eyes and looked across the river at the sheer cliffs.

Twelve hundred men and women and children, they had climbed the only narrow and dangerous path to the summit, the women carrying food upon their heads; a long dark moving file against the rock wall, they had gone up into their sanctuary. And from the summit the Chief and his warriors had shouted their defiance at the king.

Chaka had gone out alone and stood below the cliff, a tall and lithe figure, terrible in the strength of his youth and majesty of his presence.

"Come down, oh Chief, receive the king's blessing and be a chief still—under the sunshine of my love."

The Chief had smiled and called in jest to his warriors around him, "I heard a baboon bark!" Their laughter rang against the rock cliffs. The king turned and strode back to where his impis squatted in long patient ranks, ten thousand strong.

In the night Chaka picked fifty men, calling each softly by name. Those of great heart and fearsome reputation. And he had told them simply, "When the moon is down, my children, we will climb the cliff above the river," and he laughed that low deep laugh, the sound of which so many had heard as their last sound on this earth. "For did not that wise chief call us baboons—and the baboon climbs where no man dares."

The old gunbearer had pointed out to Mark in daylight the exact route that Chaka had taken to the top. It needed binoculars to trace the hairline cracks and the finger-wide ledges.

Mark shuddered now, retracing the route with his eyes, and he remembered that Chaka had led the climb without ropes, in the pitch darkness after the moon, and carrying his shield and his broad-bladed stabbing spear strapped on his back.

Sixteen of his warriors had slipped and fallen during the climb, but such was the mettle of the men that Chaka had chosen that not one of them had uttered a sound during that terrible dark plunge, not a whisper of sound to alert the Inyosi sentries until the final soft thud of flesh on rock down below in the gorge.

In the dawn, while his impis diverted the Inyosi by skirmishing on the pathway, Chaka had slipped over the rim of the cliff, regrouped his remaining warriors and—thirty-five against twelve hundred—carried the summit with a single shattering charge, each stab of the great blades crashing through a body from chest to spine, and the withdrawal sucking the life blood out in a gushing burst of scarlet.

"Ngidhla! I have eaten," roared the king and his men as they worked, and most of the Inyosi threw themselves from the cliff top into the river below, rather than face Chaka's wrath. Those who hesitated to jump were assisted in their decision.

Chaka lifted the chief of the Inyosi with both hands high above his head, and held him easily as he struggled.

"If I am a baboon—then you are a sparrow!"

He roared with savage laughter. "Fly, little sparrow, fly!" and he hurled the man far out into the void.

For once they spared not even the women nor the children, for among the sixteen Zulus who had fallen from the cliff during the climb were those whom Chaka loved.

The old gunbearer had scratched in the debris of the scree face below the cliff and showed Mark in the palms of his hand chips of old bones that might have been human.

After his victory on the summit, Chaka had ordered a great hunt in the basin of the two rivers.

Ten thousand warriors to drive the game, and the hunt had lasted four days. They said that the king alone with his own hands had slain two hundred buffalo. The sport had been such that afterwards he had made the decree:

"This is a royal hunting ground, no man will hunt here again, no man but the king. From the cliffs over which Chaka threw the Inyosi, east to the mountain crests, south and north for as far as a man may run in a day, and a night, and another day, this land is for the king's hunt alone. Let all men hear these words, tremble and obey."

He had left a hundred men under one of his older indunas to police the ground, under the title of "Keeper of the King's Hunt," and Chaka returned again and again, perhaps drawn to this well of peace to refresh and rest his tortured soul with its burning crippling craving for power. He had hunted here, even in that period of dark madness while he mourned his mother Nandi, the Sweet One. He had hunted here nearly every year until at last he had died beneath the assassin's blades wielded by his own brothers.

Probably nearly a century later, the legislative council of Natal, sitting in solemn conclave, hundreds of miles distant from the cliffs of Chaka's Gate, had echoed his decree and proclaimed the area reserved against hunting or despoliation, but they had not policed the Royal Hunt as well as had the old Zulu King. The poachers had been busy over the years, with bow and arrow, with snare and pit, with spear and dog pack, and with high-powered rifled weapons.

Perhaps soon, as the old man had predicted, they would find a cure for the nagana or a means of eradicating tsetse fly. A man-made law would be repealed, and the land given over to the lowing, slow-moving herds of cattle and to the silver-bright blade of the plough. Mark felt a physical sickness of the stomach at the prospect, and he rose and set off along the scree slope to let the sickness pass.

\* \* \*

The old man had always been a creature of habit, even to the clothes he wore and his daily rituals of living. He always camped at the same spot when he travelled a familiar road or returned to a place he had visited before.

Mark went directly to the old camp site above the river junction in the elbow of the main river course, where flood waters had cut a steep high bank and the elevated ground above it formed a plateau shaded by a grove of sycamore fig trees, with stems thick as Nelson's column in Trafalgar Square and the cool green shade below them murmurous with the sound of insects and purple doves.

The hearth stones for the camp fire were still there, scattered a little and blackened with soot. Mark built them back into the correct shape.

There was plenty of firewood, dead and fallen trees and branches, driftwood brought down by the floods and cast up on the high watermark on the bank.

Mark drew clear water from the river, put the billy on to boil for tea, and then, from the side pocket of the pack, brought out the sheath of paper, held together by a clasp and already much fingered and a little tattered, that Marion had sent him.

"Transcript of the evidence from the coroners' inquiry into the death of JOHN ANDERS ESQUIRE of the farm AN-DERSLAND in the district of LADYBURG."

Marion Littlejohn had typed it out laboriously during

her lunch hours, and her lack of skill with the machine was evident in the many erasures and over-types.

Mark had read it so many times before that he could almost repeat the entire text from memory, even the irrelevant remarks from the bench.

> MR. GREYLING (SNR.): We was camped there by the Bubezi River, Judge—
>
> MAGISTRATE: I am not a judge, sir. The correct form of address to this Court is Your Worship.

But now he began again at the beginning, searching carefully for some small clue to what he was seeking that he might have overlooked in his previous readings

But always he came back to the same exchange.

> MAGISTRATE: Will the witness please refer to the deceased as "the deceased" and not "the old man."
>
> MR. GREYLING (SNR.): Sorry, your worship. The deceased left camp early on the Monday morning, he says like he's going to look for kudu along the ridge. It would be a little before lunchtime we hears a shot and my boy, Cornelius, he says—"Sounds like the old man got one"—beg your pardon, I mean the deceased.
>
> MAGISTRATE: You were still in camp at that time?
>
> MR. GREYLING (SNR.): Yes, Your Worship, my boy and me, we was cutting and hanging biltong—we didn't go out that day.

Mark could imagine the butchering of the game carcasses, the raw red meat hacked into long strips, soaked in buckets of brine, and then festooned on the branches of the trees—a scene of carnage he had witnessed so often before. When the meat had dried to black sticks, like chewing tobacco, it was packed into jute sacks for later carriage out on the pack donkeys. The wet meat dried to a quarter of its weight, and the resulting biltong was highly prized through

Africa and commanded such a high price as to make the poaching a lucrative trade.

> MAGISTRATE: When did you become concerned by the deceased's absence?
> MR. GREYLING: Well, he didn't come into camp that night. But we weren't worried like. Thought he might have been spooring up a hit one, and slept up a tree.

Further on in the evidence was the statement:

> MR. GREYLING (SNR.): . . . Well, in the end we didn't find him until the fourth day. It was the assvogels—beg pardon, the vultures—that showed us where to look. He had tried to climb the ridge at a bad place, we found where he had slipped and the gun was still under him. It must have been that shot we heard—we buried him right there, you see he wasn't fit to carry—what with the birds and the sun. We put up a nice cross, carved it myself, and I said the Christian words.

Mark refolded the transcript, and slipped it back into the pack. The tea was brewing and he sweetened it with thick condensed milk and brown sugar.

Blowing on the mug to cool it, and sipping at the sweet liquid, he pondered what he had gleaned. A rocky ridge, a bad place, within sound of gunshot of where he now sat, a cairn of stones, probably, and a wooden cross, perhaps long ago consumed by termites.

He had a month, but he wondered if that was time enough. On such slim directions it was a search that could take years, if luck ran against him.

Even if he was successful, he wasn't yet sure what he would do next. The main concern that drove him on was merely to find where the old man lay. After that he would know what to do.

He worked the ridges and the rocky ground on the south
bank first. For ten days he climbed and descended the rug-
ged rim of the basin, hard going against the grain of the
natural geological formations, and at the end of that time
he was lean as a greyhound, arms and face burned to the
colour of a new loaf by the sun and with a dark crisp pelt
of beard covering his jaw. The legs of his pants were tattered by the coarse, razor-edged grass and by the clumps of
aptly named wait-a-bit thorns, that grabbed at him to delay
his progress.

There was a rich treasure of bird life in the basin; even
in the heated hush of midday, the air rang with their
cries—the fluting mournful whistle of a wood dove or the
high piping chant of a white-headed fish eagle circling high
overhead. In the early morning and again in the cool of the
evening, the bush came alive with the jewelled flash of
feathers—the scarlet breast of the impossibly beautiful Na-
rina Trogon, named long ago for a hottentot beauty by one
of the old travellers, the metallic flash of a sunbird as it
hovered over the pearly fragrant flowers of buffalo creeper, the little speckled woodpeckers tapping furiously with
heads capped in cardinal red, and, in the reeds by the river,
the ebony sheen of the long floating tail feathers of the Sakabula bird. All this helped to lighten the long weary hours
of Mark's search, and a hundred times a day he paused,
enchanted, to watch for a few precious moments.

However, of the larger animals he saw very little, although their sign was there. The big shiny pellets of kudu
dung scattered along their secret pathways through the forest, the dried faeces of a leopard furry with baboon hair
from its kill, the huge midden of a white rhinoceros, a
mountain of scattered dung accumulated over the years as
this strange animal returned to the same place daily to def-
ecate.

Pausing beside the rhinoceros midden, Mark grinned as

he remembered one of the old man's stories, the one that explained why the rhinoceros was so fearful of the porcupine and why he always scattered his own dung.

Once, long ago, he had borrowed from the porcupine a quill to sew up the tear in his skin caused by a red-tipped mimosa thorn. When the job was done the rhinoceros had held the quill between his teeth as he admired his handiwork, but by accident he swallowed the quill.

Now, of course, he runs away to avoid having to face the porcupine's recriminations—and he sifts each load that he drops, to try and recover the missing quill.

The old man had a hundred yarns like that one to delight a small boy, and Mark felt close to him again; his determination to find his grave strengthened, as he shifted the rifle to his other shoulder and turned once more to the rocky ridge of the high ground.

On the tenth day, he was resting in the deep shade at the edge of a clearing of golden grass, when he had his first good sighting of larger game.

A small herd of graceful pale brown impala, led by three impressively horned rams, emerged from the far side of the clearing. They fed cautiously; every few seconds they froze into perfect stillness with only the big scooplike ears moving as they listened for danger, and their wet black noses snuffing silently.

Mark was out of meat, he had eaten the last of the bully the previous day, and he had brought the rifle for just this moment—to relieve a diet of mealy porridge—yet he found himself strangely reluctant to use it now, a reluctance he had never known as a boy. For the first time, he looked with eyes that saw not just meat but rare and unusual beauty.

The three rams moved slowly across the clearing, passing a hundred paces from where Mark sat silently, and then drifted away, pale shadows, into the thorn scrub. The does followed them, trotting to keep up, one with a lamb stumbling on long gawky legs at her flank, and at the rear of the troop was a half-grown doe.

One of her back legs was crippled, it was withered and stunted, swinging free of the ground and the animal was having difficulty keeping up with the herd. It had lost condition badly, bone of rib and spine showed clearly through a hide that lacked the gloss and shine of health.

Mark swung the P.14 and the flat crack of the shot bounced from the cliffs across the river, and startled a flock of white-faced ducks into whistling flight off the river.

Mark stooped over the doe as she lay in the grass and touched the long curled lashes that fringed the dark swimming eyes. There was no reflex blink, and the check for life was routine only. He knew the shot had taken her in the centre of the heart, an instantaneous kill.

"Always make the check." The old man's teachings again. "Percy Young would tell you that himself if he could, but he was sitting there on a dead lion he had just shot, having a quiet pipe, when it came to life again. That's why he isn't around to tell you himself."

Mark rolled the carcass and squatted to examine the back limb. The wire noose had cut through the skin, through sinew and flesh, and had come up hard against the bone as the animal struggled to break out of the snare. Below the wire the leg had gangrened and the smell was nauseous, summoning a black moving wad of flies.

Mark made the shallow gutting stroke, deflecting the blade upwards to avoid puncturing the gut. The belly opened like a purse. He freed the anus and vagina with the deft surgeon strokes, and lifted out bladder and bowel and gut in one scoop. He dissected the purple liver out of the mass of viscera, cut away the gall bladder and tossed it aside. Grilled over the coals, the liver would make a feast for his dinner. He cut away the rotten, stinking hind leg, and then he carefully wiped out the stomach cavity with a handful of dry grass. He cut flaps in the skin of the neck. Using the flaps of skin as handles, he hefted the whole carcass and lugged it down to the camp by the river. Cut and salted and dried, he now had meat for the rest of his stay. He hung the strips of meat high in the sycamore fig to save them from the scavengers who would surely visit the camp during his daily absences, and only when he had finished the task, and he was crouching over his fire with the steaming mug in his hand, did he think again of the sanring wire that had crippled the impala doe.

He felt an indirect flash of anger at the person who had set that noose, and then almost immediately he wondered why he should feel particular anger at the trapper, when a dozen times he had come across the old abandoned camps of white hunters. Always there were the bones, and the piles of rotting worm-riddled horns.

The trapper was clearly a black man, and his need was greater than that of the others who came in to butcher and dry and sell.

Thinking about it, Mark felt a despondency slowly overwhelm him. Even in the few short years since he had first visited this wilderness, the game had been reduced to but a small fraction of its original numbers. Soon it would all be gone—as the old man said, "The great emptiness is coming."

Mark sat at his fireside, and he felt deeply saddened at the inevitable. No creature would ever be allowed to compete with man, and he remembered the old man again.

"Some say the lion, others the leopard. But believe me, my boy, when a man looks in the mirror, he sees the most dangerous and merciless killer in all of nature."

\* \* \*

The pit had been built to resemble a sunken water reservoir. It was fifty feet across and ten feet deep, perfectly circular, plastered and floored in smooth cement.

Although there were water pipes installed and its position on the first slope of the escarpment above Ladyburg was perfectly chosen to provide the correct fall to the big gabled house below, yet it had never held water.

The circular walls were white-washed river sand and neatly raked.

Pine trees had been planted to screen the reservoir. A twelve-stranded barbed wire fence enclosed the whole plantation, and there were two guards at the gate this evening, tough, silent men who checked the guests as the cars brought them up from the big house.

There were forty-eight men and women in the excited, laughing stream that flowed through the gate, and followed the path up among the pines to where the pit was already starkly lit by the brilliant glare of the Petromax lanterns suspended on poles above it.

Dirk Courtney led the revellers. He wore black gaberdine riding breeches and polished knee-length boots to protect his legs from slashing fangs, and his white linen shirt was open almost to the navel, exposing the hard bulging muscle of his chest and the coarse black body hair which curled from the vee of the neck. The sleeves of the shirt were cut full to the wrist, and he rolled a long thin cheroot from one corner of his mouth to the other without touching it, for his arms were around the waists of the women who flanked him, young women with bold eyes and laughing painted mouths.

The dogs heard them coming and bayed at them, leaping against the padded bars of their cages, hysterical with excitement as they tried to reach other through the gaps, snarling and snapping and slavering while the handlers attempted to shout them into silence.

The spectators lined the circular parapet of the pit, hanging over the edge. In the merciless light of the Petromax, the faces were laid bare, every emotion, every stark detail of the blood lust and sadistic anticipation was revealed— the hectic colouring of the women's cheeks, the feverish glitter of the men's eyes, the shrillness of their laughter and the widely exaggerated gesturing.

During the early bouts, the small dark-haired girl beside Dirk screamed and wriggled, holding her clenched fists to her open mouth, moaning and gasping with fascinated, delighted horror. Once she turned and buried her face against Dirk's chest, pressing her body, trembling and shuddering, against him. Dirk laughed and held her around the waist. At the kill she screamed with the rest of them and her back arched; then Dirk half lifted her, as she sobbed breathlessly, and supported her to the refreshment table where there was champagne in silver buckets and sandwiches of brown bread and smoked salmon.

Charles came to where Dirk sat with the girl on his lap, feeding her champagne from a crystal glass, surrounded by a dozen of his sycophants, jovial and expansive, enjoying the rising sense of tension for the final bout of the evening when he would match his own dog, Chaka, against Charles' animal.

"I feel bad, Dirk," Charles told him. "They have just told me that your dog is giving almost ten pounds."

"That mongrel of yours will need every pound, Charles, don't feel bad now—keep it for later, when you'll really need it." Dirk was suddenly bored with the girl, and he pushed her casually from his lap, so that she almost lost her balance and fell. Piqued, she settled her skirts, pouted at Dirk and when she realized he had already forgotten her existence, she flounced away.

"Here." Dirk indicated the chair beside him. "Do have a seat, Charles old boy, and let's discuss your problem."

The crowd drew closer around them, listening eagerly to their banter, and braying slavishly at each sally.

"My problem is that I should like a small wager on the bout, but it does seem most unsporting to bet against a light dog, like yours." Charles grinned as he mopped his streaming red face with a silk handkerchief, sweating heavily with champagne and excitement and the closeness of the humid summer evening.

"We all know that you make your living betting on certainties." Charles was a stock-broker from the Witwatersrand. "However, the expression of such noble sentiment does you great credit." Dirk tapped his shoulder with the hilt of his dogwhip, a familiar condescending gesture that made Charles' grin tighten wolfishly.

"You will accommodate me then?" he asked, nodding

and winking at his own henchmen in the press of listening men. "At even money?"

"Of course, as much as you want."

"My dog Kaiser against your Chaka, to the death. Even money, a wager of—" Charles paused and looked to the ladies, smoothing the crisp little moustache with its lacing of iron grey, drawing out the moment. "One thousand pounds in gold." The crowd gasped and exclaimed, and some of the listeners applauded, a smattering of handclaps.

"No! No!" Dirk Courtney held up both hands in protest. "Not a thousand!" and the listeners groaned, his own claque shocked and crestfallen at this loss of prestige.

"Oh dear," Charles murmured, "too strong for your blood? Name the wager then, old boy."

"Let's have some real interest—say ten thousand in gold." Dirk tapped Charles' shoulder again, and the man's grin froze over. The colour faded from the scarlet face, leaving it blotched purple and puffy white. The small acquisitive eyes darted quickly around the circle of laughing applauding faces, as if seeking an escape, and then slowly, reluctantly returned to Dirk's face. He tried to say something, but his voice squeaked and broke like a pubescent boy.

"Ah, and what exactly does that mean?" Dirk inquired with elaborate politeness. Charles would not trust his voice again, but he nodded jerkily and tried to resurrect his cheeky grin, but it was crooked and tense and hung awkwardly on his face.

Dirk carried the dog under his right arm, enjoying the hard rubbery feel of the animal's compact body, carrying its fifty-pound weight easily, as he dropped lightly down the steps to the floor of the pit.

Every muscle in the dog's body was strained to a fine tension, and Dirk could feel the jump and flutter of nerves and sinew, every limb was stiff and trembling, and the deep crackling snarls kept erupting up the thick throat, shaking the whole body.

He set the dog down on the raked sand, with the leash

twisted securely around his left wrist, and as the dog's paws touched ground he lunged forward, coming up short against the leash so hard that Dirk was almost pulled off his feet.

"Hey, you bastard," he shouted, and pulled the animal back.

Across the pit, Charles and his handler were bringing down Kaiser, and it needed both their strength for he was a big dog, black as hell, and touched with tan at the eyes and chest, a legacy of the Doberman Pinscher in his breeding.

Chaka saw him, his lunges and struggles became wilder and fiercer, and the snarls sounded like thick canvas ripping in a hurricane.

The timekeeper called from the parapet, lifting his voice above the excited buzz of the watchers.

"Very well, gentlemen, bate them!"

The two owners set them at each other with cries of "Sick him up, Kaiser!" and "Get him, boy. Kill! Kill!" but held them double-handed on the leash, driving them into a madness of frustration and anger.

On the short leash, the Doberman weaved and ducked, leggy for a fighting dog, with big shoulders dropping back to lower quarters. He had good teeth, however, and a threatening gape, enough to lock the teeth into the killer grip at the throat. He was fast too, swinging and weaving against the leash, barking and thrusting with the long almost snakelike neck.

Chaka did not bark, but the thick barrel of his chest vibrated to the deep rolling snarls and he stood foursquare on his short legs. He was heavy and low in silhouette, Staffordshire bull terrier blood carefully crossed with mastiff, and his coat was coarse and brindled gold on black. The head was short and thick, like that of a viper, and when he snarled, his upper lip lifted back in deep creases revealing the long ivory yellow fangs and the dark pink gums. He watched the other dog with yellow leopard eyes.

"Bate them! Bate them!" yelled the crowd above, and the owners worked the leashes like jockeys pushing for the post, pointing the animals at each other and driving them on.

Dirk slipped a small steel implement from his pocket, and dropped on his knee beside his dog. Instantly the animal swung on him with gaping jaws but the heavy muzzle caged his fangs. His saliva was beginning to froth, and it splattered the spotless linen of Dirk's shirt.

Dirk reached behind the dog and stabbed the short spur of steel into his flesh, a shallow goading wound at the root of his testicles, just enough to break the skin and draw a drop of blood—the animal snarled on a newer higher note, slashing sideways, and Dirk goaded him again, driving him further and further into the black fighting rage. Now at last he barked, a series of almost maniacal surges of sound from his straining throat.

"Ready to slip," shouted Dirk, struggling to manage his animal.

"Ready here!" Charles panted across the pit, his feet sliding in the sand as Kaiser reared chest high.

"Slip them!" yelled the timekeeper, and at the same instant, both men slipped muzzle and leash and studded collars, leaving both animals free, and unprotected.

Charles turned and scrambled hurriedly out of the pit, but Dirk waited extra seconds, not wanting to miss the moment when they came together.

The Doberman showed his speed across the pit, meeting Chaka in his own ground, bounding in on those long legs, leaning forward so the sloping back was flattened in his run.

He went for the head, slashing open the skin below the eye in a clean sabre-stroke of white teeth, but not holding.

Chaka did not go for a hold either, but turned at the instant of impact; using his shoulder and the massive strength of his squat frame, he hit the bigger dog off-balance, breaking his charge, so that he spun away and would have gone over but the white-washed wall caught him, and saved him—for Chaka had turned neatly to catch him as he fell.

Now, however, Kaiser was up and with a quick shift of weight he was in balance again—and he cut for the face mask, missing as the smaller brindled dog ducked, catching only the short cropped ear and splitting it, so that blood flew in black droplets to splatter the sand.

Again Chaka hit with the shoulder, blood streaming from cheek to ear, as he put his weight into the charge. The bigger dog reared out, declining to meet shoulder with shoulder and as he came over he went for a hold—but the crowd screamed as they saw his mistake.

"Drop it! Drop it!" howled Charles, his face purple as an over-ripe plum—for his dog had got into that thick loose skin, padded with fat between the shoulder, and he growled as he worried it.

"Work him, Chaka. Work him!" howled Dirk, balancing easily on the narrow parapet above them. "Now's your chance, boy."

Locked into his grip the Doberman was holding too high, his neck and head up and off-balance. As he worried the hold, it gave and pulled like rubber, not affording purchase or leverage to throw his weight across and bring down the brindled terrier.

The smaller dog seemed not even to feel the grip, although a small artery had ruptured, sending a fine spurt of blood dancing into the lantern light like a pink flamingo's feather.

"Drop it," screamed Charles again in agony, wringing his hands, sweat dripping from his chin.

"Belly him! Belly him!" exhorted Dirk, and his dog twisted under the big dog's chest, forcing him higher so that his front paws were off the ground, and he hit him in the belly, gaping wide and then plunging his yellow eye-teeth full into the bare, shiny dark skin below the ribs.

The Doberman screamed and dropped his shoulder hold, twisting out violently so that Chaka's fangs tore out of his belly hold, ripping out a flap of stomach-lining through which wet purple entrails bulged immediately—but he beat the terrier's try for the throat, jaw clashing into open snarling jaw, and teeth cracked together, before they spun off and circled.

Both heads were masks of blood now, eyelids blinking rapidly, the eyeballs smeared with flying blood from wound and bite, the fur of the faces plastered with black blood, blood filling the mouths and turning the exposed teeth pink, trickling from the corners of the jaw, staining the froth of saliva bright rose red.

Twice more they came together, each charge initiated by the smaller squatter Chaka, but each time the Doberman avoided the solid contact of chest to chest for which Chaka's instincts dictated that he must keep trying. Instead, Chaka received two more slashes deeply through the brindled skin, into the flesh, down to white bone, so that when his next charge carried him to the wall he left a broad thick smear of red across the white-wash before turning to attack again.

The Dobermann was humped up from the belly wound, arching his back to the agony of it, but fast and lithe still, not trying for another hold since that fool's hold at the shoulder, but cutting hard and deep and keeping off his opponent like a skilled boxer.

Chaka was losing too much blood now, and as he circled again he lolled his tongue for the first time, frothy saliva discoloured with blood dripping from it, and Dirk swore aloud at this sign of weakness and imminent collapse.

Big Kaiser attacked again now, cutting in sharply as though for the throat and then turning in a low dark streak for another weakening flank cut. As he hit, Chaka turned in to him steeply, and snapped at his lean belly again, reaching low and with fortune taking a hold on the bulging entrails that showed in the open flap of the wound.

Instantly the terrier went stiff on his forelegs, and hunched his neck, bringing his chin down on to his chest to hold the grip. The Doberman's charge carried him on and his entrails were pulled out of him, a long thick glistening ribbon in the lantern light—and the women screamed, high with anguished delight, while the men roared.

Chaka crossed the bigger dog's rump now, still holding his guts and tangled his back legs in the slippery rubbery pink tubes that hung out of the stomach cavity, so that he stumbled off-balance—and the terrier lunged forward, hitting him solidly with the chest, knocking him into the air so he dropped on to his back, screaming and kicking.

Chaka's follow-up was so instinctive, so natural to his breed, that it was swift as the flash of a striking adder and he had his killing hold—locked deep and hard into the throat, bearing down with the solid bone of his jaws, snuffling and working his head on the short hunched neck until his long eye-teeth met in the Doberman's windpipe.

Dirk Courtney jumped down lightly from' the parapet, his laugh was pitched unnaturally high and his face was darkened to a congested sullen red as he whipped off his dog, and turned the carcass of the Doberman with the toe of his boot.

"A fair kill?" he laughed up at Charles, and the man glowered down at him a moment before shrugging acknowledgement of defeat and turning away.

\* \* \*

Dicky Lancome sat with the voice-piece of the telephone set on the desk in front of him and the ear-piece held loosely to his cheek, trapped there by a hunched shoulder while he trimmed his finger-nails with a gold-plated penknife.

"What can I say, old girl, except that I am desolate, but then Aunty Hortense was rich as that fellow that turned everything to gold, that's right Midas, or was it Croesus, I just cannot give her funeral a miss, you do understand? You don't?" and he sighed dramatically, as he returned the penknife to his waistcoat pocket and began to thumb through the address book for the other girl's number. "No, old girl, how can you say that? Are you certain? Must have been my sister—"

It was almost noon on Saturday morning and Dicky had

the premises of Natal Motors to himself. He was making his domestic arrangements for the weekend on the firm's telephone account before locking up, and finding some wisdom in the admonition against changing mounts in midstream.

At that moment he was distracted by the crack of footsteps on the marbled floor of the showroom, and he swivelled his chair for a glimpse through the door of his cubicle.

There was no mistaking the tall figure that strode through the street doors, the wide shoulders and thrusting bearded jaw, the dark glint of eyes like those of an old eagle.

"Oh, Lord preserve us," Dicky breathed, his guilty conscience delivering a heavy jolt into his belly, "General Courtney," and he let the ear-piece of the telephone drop and dangle on its cord, while he slid forward stealthily from his chair and crawled into shelter below his desk, knees drawn up to his chin.

He could imagine exactly why General Courtney was calling. He had come to discuss the insult to his daughter in person, and Dicky Lancome had heard enough about the General's temper to want to avoid joining this discussion.

Now he listened like a night animal for the stalk of the leopard, cocking his head for the sound of further footsteps and bating his breath to a shallow cautious trickle, in order not to disclose his hiding-place.

The ear-piece of the telephone still dangled on its cord, and now it emitted the high-pitched distorted voice of an irate female. Without leaving the cover of the desk, he reached out to try and muffle the ear-piece, but it dangled tantalizing inches beyond his finger-tips.

"Dicky Lancome, I know you are there," squawked the tinny voice, and Dick wriggled forward another inch.

A hand, in size not unlike that of a bull gorilla, entered Dicky's field of vision, closed on the ear-piece, and placed it in Dicky's outstretched fingers.

"Please allow me," said a deep gravelly voice from somewhere above the desk.

"Thank you, sir," whispered Dicky, trying not to draw too much attention to himself even at this stage. For want of anything better to do, he listened respectfully to the earpiece.

"It is no good pretending not to be listening," said the female voice. "I know all about you and that blonde hussy—"

"I expect you need this," said the deep voice from on high, and the hand passed the mouthpiece of the telephone down into his hiding-place.

"Thank you, sir," Dicky whispered again, uncertain as to which emotion dominated him at that moment, humiliation or trepidation. He cleared his throat and spoke into the telephone.

"Darling, I have to go now," he croaked. "I have an extremely important client in the shop." He hoped that the touch of flattery might sweeten the coming encounter. He broke the connection and crawled out unwillingly on his hands and knees.

"General Courtney!" He dusted himself down and smoothed his hair, assembled his dignity and salesman's smile. "We are honoured."

"I hope I did not interrupt you in anything important?" Only the sapphire twinkle in the heavily browed eyes betrayed the General's amusement.

"By no means," Dicky assured him, "I was—" he looked around wildly for inspiration, "I was merely meditating."

"Ah!" Sean Courtney nodded. "That explains it."

"How can I be of service to you, General?" Dicky went on hurriedly.

"I wanted to find out about a young salesman of yours—Mark Anders." Dicky's heart was struck by black frost again.

"Don't worry, General, I fired him myself," Dicky blurted out. "But I tore a terrible strip off him first. You can be sure of that." He saw the General's dark beetling brows come together and the forehead crease like an eroded desert landscape, and Dick nearly panicked. "He won't get another job in this town,—he's properly queered around here, he is."

"What on earth are you talking about, man?" the General rumbled, like an uneasy volcano.

"One word from you, sir, was enough." Dicky found that the palms of his hands were cold and slippery with sweat.

"From me?" The rumble rose to a roar and Dicky felt like a peasant, looking fearfully up the slopes of Vesuvius. "What did I have to do with it?"

"Your daughter," choked Dicky, "after what he did to your daughter."

"My daughter?" The huge voice subsided to something that was close to a whisper, but was too cold and intense. It was a fiercer sound than the roar that preceded it. "He molested my daughter?"

"Oh God no, General," Dicky moaned weakly. "No employee of ours would raise a finger to Miss Storm."

"What happened? Tell me exactly."

"He was insolent to your daughter, I thought you knew?"

"Insolent? What did he say?"

"He told her she did not conduct herself like a lady. She must have told you?" Dicky gulped, and the General's fearsome expression melted. He looked stunned and bemused.

"Good God. He said that to Storm? What else?"

"He told her to use the word 'please' when giving orders." Dicky couldn't meet the man's eyes and he lowered his head. "I'm sorry, sir."

There was a strangled growling sound from the General, and Dicky stepped back quickly, ready to defend himself. It took him seconds to realize that the General was struggling with his mirth, gales of laughter that shook his chest—and when at last he let it come, he threw back his head and opened his mouth wide.

Weak with relief, Dicky essayed a restrained and cautious chuckle—in sympathy with the General.

"It's not funny, man," roared Sean Courtney, and instantly Dicky scowled.

"You are much to blame—how can you condemn a man on the whim of a child?" It took Dicky a moment to realize that the child in question was the gorgeous, head-strong, darling of Natal society.

"I understood that the order came from you," stammered Dicky.

"From me!" The laughter stopped abruptly, and the General mopped at his eyes. "You thought I would smash a man because he was man enough to stand up to my daughter's tantrums? You thought that of me?"

"Yes," said Dicky miserably, and then quickly, "No," and then hopelessly, "I didn't know, sir."

Sean Courtney took an envelope from his inside pocket, and looked at it thoughtfully for a moment.

"Anders believed, as you did, that I was responsible for his dismissal?" he asked soberly now.

"Yes, sir. He did."

"Can you contact him? Will you see him again?"

Dicky hesitated, and then steeled himself and took a breath. "I promised him his job back at the end of the month—after we had gone through the motions of dismissal, General. Like you, I didn't think the crime deserved the punishment."

And Sean Courtney looked at him with a new light in his eye, and a grin lifting the corner of his mouth and one eyebrow.

"When you see Mark Anders again, tell him our conversation—and give him this envelope." Dicky took the envelope, and as the General turned away, he heard him mutter darkly, "And now for Mademoiselle Storm." Dicky Lancome felt a comradely pang of sympathy for that young lady.

It was almost noon on a Saturday morning and Ronald Pye
sat in the back seat of the limousine, stiffly as an undertaker in his hearse, and his expression was as lugubrious.
He wore a three-piece suit of dark grey cloth and a high
starched collar with stiff wings; gold rimmed spectacles
glittered on his thin beaky nose.

The chauffeur swung off the main Ladyburg road into
the long straight avenue that led up to the glistening white
buildings of Great Longwood on the lower slopes of the
escarpment. The avenue was lined with cycads that were
at least two hundred years old, thick-stemmed palm-like
plants each with a golden fruit the size of hogshead, like a
monstrous pine cone, nestled in the centre of the graceful
fronds. Dirk Courtney's gardeners had scoured the countryside for a hundred miles in each direction to find them, and
had lifted them, matched them for size and replanted them
here.

The driveway had been smoothed and watered to keep
down the dust, and parked in front of the house were
twenty or thirty expensive motor cars.

"Wait for me," said Ronald Pye. "I won't be long," and
as he alighted, he glanced up at the elegant façade. It was
an exact copy of the historic home of Simon van der Stel,
the first Governor of the Cape of Good Hope, which still
stood at Constantia. Dirk Courtney had his architects measure and copy faithfully every room, every arch and gable.
The cost must have been forbidding.

In the hall, Ronny Pye paused and looked about him
impatiently, for there was nobody to welcome him, although he had been specifically invited—perhaps summoned was a better word—for noon.

The house was alive; there were women's voices and the
tinkling bells of their laughter from deep in the interior,
while closer at hand the deeper growl of men punctuated

by bursts of harsh laughter and voices raised to that reckless, raucous pitch induced by heavy drinking.

The house smelled of perfume and cigar smoke and stale alcohol, and Ronny Pye saw empty crystal glasses standing carelessly on the priceless rosewood hall table, leaving rings of damp on the polished surface—and an abandoned pair of pearly rose women's silk cani-knickers were draped suggestively over the door handle that led to the drawing-room.

While he still hesitated, the door across the hall opened and a young woman entered. She had the dazed, detached air of a sleep-walker, gliding silently into the room on neatly slippered feet. Ronny Pye saw that she was a young girl, not much more than a child, although her cosmetics had run and smeared. Dark rings of mascara gave her a haunted consumptive look, and her lipstick was spread so that her mouth looked like a bruised and overblown rose.

Except for the slippers on her small feet, she was stark naked and her breasts were immature and tender, with pale unformed nipples, and snarled dishevelled tresses of pale blonde hair hung to her shoulders.

Still with slow, drugged movements, she took the knickers from the door handle, and stepped into them. As she pulled them to her waist she saw Ronny Pye standing by the main door, and she grinned at him—a lopsided depraved whore's smile on the smeared and inflamed lips.

"Another one? All right, come along then, love." She took a step in his direction, tottered suddenly and turned away to grab at the table for support, the painted doll's face suddenly white and translucent as alabaster, then slowly she doubled over and vomited on the thick silken expanse of woven Qum carpet.

With an exclamation of disgust, Ronald Pye turned away, and crossed to the doors that led into the drawing-room.

Nobody looked up as he entered, although there were twenty people or more in the room. They were gathered intently about a solid round gaming-table of ebony with ivory and mosaic inlay. The tabletop was scattered with poker chips, brightly coloured ivory counters, and four men sat at the table, each holding a fan of cards to his chest, watching the figure at the head of the table. The tension crackled in the room like static electricity.

He was not surprised to see that one of the men at the table was his brother-in-law. He knew that Dennis Petersen regularly attended the soirées at Great Longwood, and he thought briefly of his pliant dutiful sister and wondered if she knew.

"The man has drawn us all in," Ronny thought bitterly, glancing at Dennis and noticing his bleary, inflamed eyes, the nervous drawn white face. "At least I have withstood this, this final filthy degradation. Whatever other evils he has led me into, I have kept this little shred of my self respect."

"Well, gentlemen, I have bad news to impart, I'm afraid," Dirk Courtney smiled urbanely. "The ladies are with me," and he spread his cards face up on the green baize. The four queens in their fanciful costume stared up with wooden expressions, and the other players peered at them for a moment, and then one at a time, with expressions of disgust, discarded their own hands.

Dennis Petersen was the last to concede defeat, and his face was stricken, his hand shook. And then with a sound that was almost a sob, he let his cards flutter from his fingers, pushed back his chair and blundered towards the door.

Halfway there, he stopped suddenly as he recognized the gaunt forbidding figure of his brother-in-law. He stared at him for a moment, the lips still trembling, blinking his bloodshot eyes; then he shook his head as though doubting his senses.

"You here?"

"Oh yes," Dirk called from the table where he was gathering and stacking the ivory chips. "Did I forget to mention that I had invited Ronald? Forgive me," he told the other players, "I will back in a short while." He stood up from the table, brushed away the clinging hands of one of the women, and came to take the elbows of Ronald Pye and his brother-in-law in a friendly grip, and to guide them out of the drawing-room, down the long flagged passage to his study.

Even at midday, the room was cool and dark, thick stone walls and heavy velvet drapes, dark wooden panelling and deep Persian and Oriental carpeting, sombre smoky-looking oil paintings on the panelling, one of which Ronald Pye knew was a Reynolds, and another a Turner, heavy chunky furniture, with coverings of chocolate-coloured leather—it was a room which always depressed Ronald Pye. He always thought of it as the centre of the web in which he and his family had slowly entangled themselves.

Dennis Petersen slumped into one of the leather chairs, and after a moment's hesitation, Ronald Pye took the one facing him and sat there stiffly, disapprovingly.

Dirk Courtney splashed single malt whiskey into the glasses that were set out on a silver tray on the corner of the big mahogany desk, and made a silent offer to Ronald Pye, who shook his head primly.

Instead, he carried a glass of the glowing amber liquor to Dennis who accepted it with trembling hands, gulped a mouthful and then blurted thickly,

"Why did you do it, Dirk? You promised that nobody would know I was here, and you invited—" he glanced across at the grim countenance of his brother-in-law.

Dirk chuckled. "I always keep my promises—just as long as it pays me to do so." He lifted his own glass. "But between the three of us there should be no secrets. Let's drink to that."

When Dirk lowered his glass, Ronald Pye asked, "Why did you invite me here today?"

"We have a number of problems to discuss—the first of which is dear Dennis here. As a poker player, he makes a fine blacksmith."

"How much?" Ronald Pye asked quietly.

"Tell him, Dennis," Dirk invited him, and they waited while he studied the remaining liquor in his glass.

"Well?" said Ronald Pye again.

"Don't be shy, Dennis, me old cocky diamond," Dirk encouraged him. Dennis mumbled a figure without looking up.

Ronald Pye shifted his weight in the leather chair, and his mouth quivered. "It's a gambling debt. We repudiate it."

"Shall I ask one or two of the young ladies who are my guests here to go down and give your sister a first-hand account of some of the other little tricks Dennis has been up to? Did you know that Dennis likes to have them kneel over—"

"Dirk, you wouldn't," bleated Dennis. "You're not going to do that—" and he sank his face into his hands.

"You will have a cheque tomorrow," said Ronald Pye softly.

"Thank you, Ronny, it really is a pleasure to do business with you."

"Is that all?"

"Oh no," Dirk grinned at him. "By no means." He carried the crystal decanter across to Dennis and recharged his glass. "We have another little money matter to discuss." He filled his own glass with whisky and held it to the light. "Bank business," he said, but Ronny Pye cut in swiftly.

"I think you should know that I am about to retire from the Bank. I have received an offer for my remaining shares, I am negotiating for a vineyard down in the Cape. I will be leaving Ladyburg and taking my family with me."

"No," Dirk shook his head, smiling lightly. "You and I are together for ever. We have a bond that is unbreakable. I want you with me always—somebody I can trust, perhaps the only person in the world I can trust. We share so many secrets, old friend. Including murder."

They both froze at the word, and slowly colour drained from Ronald Pye's face.

"John Anders and his boy," Dirk reminded them, and they both broke in together.

"The boy got away—"

"He's still alive."

"Not for much longer," Dirk assured them. "My man is on the way to him now. This time there will be no further trouble from him."

"You can't do it," Dennis Petersen shook his head vehemently.

"Why, in God's name? Let it be." Ronald Pye was begging now, suddenly all the stiffness going out of his bearing. "Let the boy alone, we have enough—"

"No. He has not left us alone," Dirk explained reasonably. "He has been actively gathering information on all of us and all our activities. By a stroke of fortune I have learned where he is and he is alone, in a lonely place."

They were silent now, and while he waited for them to think it out, Dirk flicked the stub of his cheroot on to the fireplace and lit another.

"What more do you want from us, now?" Ronald asked at last.

"Ah, so at last we can discuss the matter in a business-like fashion?" Dirk propped himself on the edge of the desk and picked up an antique duelling pistol that he used as a paper weight. He spun it on his finger as he talked. "I am short of liquid funds for the expansion programme that I began five years ago. There has been a decline in sugar prices, a reduction in the Bank's investment flow—but you know all this, of course."

Ronald Pye nodded cautiously. "We have already agreed to adapt the land purchases to our cash flow, for the next few years at least. We will be patient."

"I am not a patient man, Ronny."

"We are short two hundred thousand a year over the next three years. We have agreed to cut down," Ronald Pye went on, but Dirk was not listening. He twirled the pistol, aimed at the eye of the portrait above the fireplace and snapped the hammer on the empty cap.

"Two hundred thousand a year for three years is six hundred thousands of sterling," Dirk mused aloud, and lowered the pistol. "Which is by chance exactly the amount paid by me to you for your shares, some ten years ago."

"No," said Ronald Pye, with an edge of panic in his voice. "That's mine, that's my personal capital, it has nothing to do with the Bank."

"You've done very nicely with it too," Dirk congratulated him. "Those Crown Deep shares did you proud, an excellent buy. By my latest calculations, your personal net worth is not much less than eight hundred thousand."

"In trust for my family, my daughter and my grandchildren," said Ronny, his voce edged with desperation.

"I need that money now," Dirk spoke reasonably.

"What about your own personal resources?" Ronald Pye demanded desperately.

"Stretched to their limit, my dear Ronald, all of it invested in land and sugar."

"You could borrow on—"

"Oh, but why should I borrow from strangers, when a dear and trusted friend will make the loan to the Ladyburg Farmers Bank. What finer security than that offered by that venerable institution? A loan, dear Ronald, merely a loan."

"No." Ronald Pye came to his feet. "That money is not mine. It belongs to my family." He turned to his brother-in-law. "Come. I will take you home."

Smiling that charming, sparkling smile, Dirk aimed the duelling pistol between Dennis Petersen's eyes.

"Stay where you are, Dennis," he said, and snapped the hammer again.

"It's all right," said Ronald Pye to Dennis. "We can break away now. If you stick with me." Ronald was panting a little, and sweating like a runner. "If he accuses us of murder, he accuses himself also. We can prove that we were not the planners, not the ones who gave the orders. I think he is bluffing. It's a chance we will have to take to be rid of him." He turned to face Dirk now, and there was the steel of defiance in his eyes. "To be rid of this monster. Let him do his worst, and he damns himself as much as he does us."

"How well conceived a notion!" Dirk laughed delightedly. "And I do really believe that you are foolish enough to mean what you say."

"Come, Dennis. Let him do his worst." Without another glance at either of them, Ronald Pye stalked to the door.

"Which of your grandchildren do you cherish most, Ronny, Natalie or Victoria?" Dirk asked, still laughing. "Or, I imagine, it's the little boy—what's his name? Damn! I should know the brat's name—I am his godfather." He chuckled again, then snapped his fingers as he remembered. "Damn me, of course, Ronald, like his granddaddy. Little Ronald."

Ronlad Pye had turned at the door and was staring across the room at him. Dirk grinned back at him, as though at some delicious joke.

"Little Ronald," he grinned, and aimed the pistol at an imaginary figure in the centre of the open carpet, a diminutive figure it seemed, no higher than a man's knee. "Goodbye, little Ronald," he murmured, and clicked the hammer. "Goodbye, little Natalie." He swung the pistol to another invisible figure and snapped the action. "Goodbye, little Victoria." The pistol clicked again—the metallic sound shockingly loud in the silent room.

"You wouldn't—" Dennis' voice was strangled, "you wouldn't—"

"I need the money very badly," Dirk told him.

"But you wouldn't do that—"

"You keep telling me what I wouldn't do. Since when have you been such a fine judge of my behaviour?"

"Not the children?" pleaded Dennis.

"I've done it before," Dirk pointed out.

"Yes, but not children—not little children."

Ronald Pye stood at the door still. He seemed to have aged ten years in the last few seconds, his shoulders had sagged and his face was grey and deeply lined, the flesh seemed to have fallen in around his eyes, sagging into loose folds.

"Before you leave, Ronny, let me tell you a story you have been desperate to hear for twelve years. I know you have spent much time and money trying to find out already. Return to your chair, please. Listen to my story and then you are free to go—if you still want to do so."

Ronald Pye's hand fell away from the door handle, and he shambled back and dropped into the leather chair as though his limbs did not belong to him.

Dirk filled a spare glass with whisky and placed it on the arm of his chair, within easy reach—and Ronny did not protest.

"It's the story of how a nineteen-year-old-boy made himself a million pounds in cash, and used it to buy a bank. When you have heard it, I want you to ask yourself if there is anything that boy would *not* do." Dirk stood up and began to pace up and down the thick carpeting between their chairs like a caged feline animal, lithe and graceful, but sinister also, and cruel; and he began to speak in that soft purring voice that wove a hypnotic web about them, and their heads swung to follow his regular measured pacing.

"Shall we call the boy Dirk, it's a good name—a tough name for a lad who was thrown out by a tyrannical father and set out to get the things he wanted his own way, a boy who learned quickly and was frightened of nothing, a boy who by his nineteenth birthday was first mate of a beaten-up old coal-burning tramp steamer running dubious cargos to the bad spots of the Orient. A boy who could run a ship single-handed and whip work out of a crew of niggers with a rope end, while the skipper wallowed in gin in his cabin."

He paused beside the desk, refilled his glass with whisky and asked his audience,

"Does the story grip you so far?"

"You are drunk," said Ronald Pye.

"I am never drunk," Dirk contradicted him, and resumed his pacing.

"We will call the steamer *L'Oiseau de Nuit*—'The Bird

of Night,' though, in all truth, it's an unlikely name for a stinking old cow of a boat. Her skipper was Le Doux—the sweet one—again a mild misnomer," and Dirk chuckled reminiscently, and sipped at his glass. "This merry crew discharged a midnight cargo in the Yellow River late in the summer of '09 and next day put into the port of Liang Su for a more legitimate return cargo of tea and silks.

"From the roadstead, they could see that the outskirts of the town was in flames, and they could hear the crackle of small arms fire. The basin was empty of shipping, just a few sampans and one or two small junks, and the fear-crazed population of the city was crowding the wharf, screaming for a berth to safety.

"Hundreds of them plunged into the basin and swam out to where 'The Bird of Night' was hovering. The mate let two of them come aboard and then turned the hoses on the others, driving them off, while he learned what was happening." Dirk paused, remembering how the pressure of the solid jets of water had driven the swimmers under the filthy yellow surface of the basin, and how the others had wailed and tried to swim back. He grinned and roused himself. "The Communist warlord, Han Wang, was attacking the port and had promised the rich merchants an amusing death in the bamboo cages. Now the mate knew just how rich the merchants of Liang Su really were. After consulting the captain, the mate brought 'The Bird of Night' alongside the wharf, clearing it of the peasant scum with steam hoses and a few pistol shots, and he led an armed party of lascars into the city to the guild house where the Chinese tea merchants were gathered, paralysed with terror and already resigned to their fate. Another whisky, Ronny?"

Ronald Pye shook his head, his eyes had not left Dirk's face since the tale began, and now Dirk smiled at him.

"The mate set the passage money so high that only the very richest could afford to pay it, two thousand sovereigns a head—but still ninety-six of them came aboard 'The Bird of Night,' each staggering under the load of his possessions.

Even the children carried their own weight, boxes and bales and sacks—and while we are on the subject of children, there were forty-eight of them in the party, all boys of course, for no sane Chinaman would waste two thousand pounds on a girl child. The little boys ranged from babes to striplings, some of them of an age with your little Ronald." Dirk paused to let it register, then, "It was a close run, for as the last of them came aboard, the mate cast off from the wharf and Han Wang's bandits burst out of the city and hacked and bayoneted their way on to the wharf. Their rifle-fire spattered the upper works, and swept 'The Bird of Night's' decks, sending her newly boarded passengers screaming down into the empty holds, but she made a clear run of it out of the river and by dark was pushing out into a quiet tropical sea.

"Le Doux, the captain, could not believe his fortune— almost two hundred thousand sovereigns in gold, in four tea chests in his cabin, and he promised young Dirk a thousand for himself. But Dirk knew the value of his captain's promises. Nevertheless, he suggested a further avenue of profit.

"Old Le Doux had been a hard man before the drink got to him. He had run slaves out of Africa, opium out of India, but he was soft now, and he was horrified by what his young mate suggested. He blasphemed by praying to God and he wept. 'Les pauvres petits,' he slobbered, and poured gin down his throat until after midnight he collapsed into that stupor that Dirk knew would last for forty-eight hours.

"The mate went up on to the bridge and sounded the ship's siren, shouting to his passengers that there was a government gunboat overtaking them, and driving them from the open deck back into the holds. They went like sheep, clutching their possessions. The mate and his lascars battened down the hatches, closing 'em up tight and solid. Can you guess the rest of it?" he asked. "A guinea for the correct solution."

Ronald Pye licked his dry grey lips and shook his head.

"No?" Dirk teased him. "The easiest guinea you ever

missed—why, it was simple. The mate opened the seacocks and flooded the holds." He watched them curiously, anticipating their reactions. Neither of his listeners could speak, and as Dirk went on, there was a small change in his telling of it. He no longer spoke in the third person. Now it was "we" and "I."

"Of course, we couldn't flood to the top, even in that low sea she might have foundered, and rolled on her back. There must have been a small airspace under the hatch, and they held the children up there. I could hear them through the four-inch timbers of the hatch. For almost half an hour they kept up their howling and screaming until the air went bad and the roll and slosh of the water got them, and when at last it was all over and we opened the hatches, we found that they had torn the woodwork of the underside of the covers with their fingers, ripped and splintered it like a cage full of monkeys."

Dirk turned to the empty chair nearest the fireplace and sank into it. He swilled the whisky in his right hand and then swallowed it. He threw the crystal glass into the empty fireplace and it exploded into diamond fragments. They were all silent, staring at the glass splinters.

"Why?" whispered Dennis huskily at last. "In God's name, why did you kill them?"

Dirk did not look at him, he was lost in the past, reliving a high tide in his life. Then he roused himself and went on, "We pumped out the hold, and I had the lascars carry all the sodden sacks and bales and boxes up into the saloon. God, Ronny, you should have been there. It was a sight to drive a man like you mad with greed. I piled it all up on the saloon table. It was a treasure that had taken fifty cunning men a lifetime to accumulate. There was gold in coin and bar, diamonds like the end of your thumb, rubies to choke a camel, emeralds—well, the merchants of Liang Su were some of the richest in China. Together with the passage money, the loot came to just over a million in sterling—"

"And the captain, Le Doux, his share?" Ronald Pye asked, even in his horror his accountant's mind was working.

"The captain?" Dirk shook his head and smiled that light, boyish smile. "Poor Le Doux, he must have fallen overboard that night. Drunk as he was, he would not have been able to swim—and the sharks were bad out there in the China Sea. God knows that with the water full of dead Chinese, there was enough to attract them. No, there was only one share, not counting a token to the lascars. Two hundred pounds for each of them was a fortune beyond their wildest dreams of avarice. That left a million pounds for a night's work. A million before the age of twenty."

"That's the most terrible story I've ever heard." Ronald Pye's voice shook like the hand that raised the glass to his lips.

"Remember it when next you have naughty thoughts of leaving Ladyburg," Dirk counselled him, and leaned across to pat his shoulder. "We are comrades—unto death," he said.

*   *   *

For Mark the allotted days were running out swiftly. Soon he must leave the valley and return to the world of men, and a quiet desperation came over him. He had searched the south bank and the steep ground above it, now he crossed to the north bank and started there all over again.

Here, for the first time, he had warning that he was not the only human being in the valley. The first day he came across a line of snares laid along the game trails that led down to drinking-places on the river. The wire used was the same as that he had found on the gangrened leg of the crippled impala doe, eighteen-guage galvanized mild steel wire, probably cut from some unsuspecting farmer's fence.

Mark found sixteen snares that day and tore each out, bundled the wire and hurled it into one of the deeper pools of the river.

Two days later, he came across a log deadfall, so cunningly devised and so skilfully set that it had crushed a full-grown otter. Mark used a branch to lever the log clear and drew out the carcass. He stroked the soft, lustrous chocolate fur and felt again the stirring of his anger. Quite unreasonably, he was developing a strange proprietary feeling for the animals of this valley, and a growing hatred for anyone who hunted or molested them.

Now his attention was divided almost equally between his search for his grandfather's grave and for further signs of the illegal trapper. Yet it was almost another week before he had direct sign of the mysterious hunter.

He was crossing the river each morning in the dawn to work the north bank. It might have been easier to abandon the camp under the fig trees, but sentiment kept him there. It was the old man's camp, their old camp together, and in any case he enjoyed the daily crossing and the journey through the swampland formed in the crotch of the two rivers. Although it was only the very edge of this watery world that he moved through, yet he recognized it as the very heart of this wilderness, an endless well of precious water and even more precious life, the last secure refuge of so many creatures of the valley.

He found daily evidence of the big game on the muddy paths through the towering stands of reed and papyrus, which closed overhead to form a cool gloomy tunnel of living green stems. There were Cape buffalo, and twice he heard them crashing away through the papyrus without a glimpse of them. There were hippopotamus and crocodile but they spent the days deep in the dark reed-fringed lakelets and mysterious lily-covered pools. At night he often woke and huddled in his blanket to listen to their harsh grunting bellows resounding through the swampland.

One noonday, sitting on a low promotory of rocky wooded ground that thrust into the swamp, he watched a white rhinoceros bring its calf out of the sheltering reeds to feed on the edge of the bush.

She was a huge old female, her pale grey hide scarred

and scratched, folded and wrinkled over the massive prehistoric body that weighed at least four tons, and she fussed over the calf anxiously, guiding it with her long slightly curved nose horn; the calf was hornless and fat as a piglet. Watching the pair, Mark realized suddenly how deeply this place had touched his life, and the possessive love he was developing for it was reaffirmed.

Here he lived as though he was the first man in all the earth, and it touched some deep atavistic need in his spirit. It was on that same day that he came upon recent signs of the other human presence beyond Chaka's Gate.

He was following one of the faint game paths that skirted another ridge, one of those that joined the main run of ground into the slopes of the escarpment, when he came upon the spoor.

It was barefooted, the flat-arched and broad soles of feet that had never been constricted by leather footwear. Mark went down on his knees to examine it carefully. Too big for a woman, he knew at once.

The stride told him the man was tall. The gait was slightly toe-in and the weight was carried on the ball of the foot, the way an athlete walks. There was no scuff or drag of toe on the forward swing, a high lift and a controlled transfer of weight—a strong, quick, alert man, moving fast and silently.

The spoor was so fresh that at the damp patch where the man had paused to urinate, the butterflies still fluttered in a brilliant cloud for the moisture and salt. Mark was very close behind him, and he felt the hunter's thrill as, without hesitation, he picked up and started to run the spoor.

He was closing quickly. The man he was following was unaware. He had paused to cut a green twig from a wild loquat branch, probably to use as a tooth pick, and the shavings were still wet and bleeding.

Then there was the place where the man had paused, turned back on his own spoor a single pace, paused again, almost certainly to listen, then turned abruptly off the path; within ten more paces the spoor ended, as though the man had launched into flight, or been lifted into the sky by a fiery chariot. His disappearance was almost magical, and though Mark worked for another hour, casting and circling, he found no further sign.

He sat down and lit a cigarette, and found he was sweaty and disgruntled. Although he had used all his bushcraft to come up with his quarry, he had been made to look like an infant. The man had become aware of Mark following, probably from a thousand yards off, and he had jinked and covered his spoor, throwing the pursuit with such casual ease that it was a positive insult.

As he sat, Mark felt his ill-humour harden and become positive hard anger.

"I'll get you yet," he promised the mysterious stranger aloud, and it did not even occur to him what he might do, if he ever did come up with his quarry. All that he knew was that he had been challenged, and he had taken up the challenge.

The man had the cunning of—Mark sought for a simile, a properly disparaging simile—and then grinned as he found a suitable one. The man had the cunning of a jackal, but he was Zulu so Mark used the Zulu word *Pungushe*.

"I'll be watching for you, Pungushe. I'll catch you yet, little jackal.

His mood improved with the insult, and as he crushed out his cigarette, he found himself anticipating the contest of bush skills between himself and Pungushe.

Now, whenever Mark moved through the wilderness, part of his attention was alert for the familiar footprints in the soft earthy places or for the glimpse of movement and the figure of a man among trees. Three times more he cut the spoor, but each time it was cold and wind-eroded, not worth following.

The days passed in majestic circle of sky and mountain, of sun and river and swamp, so that time seemed without end until he counted on his fingers and realized that his month was almost run. Then he felt the dread of leaving, a sinking of the spirits such as a child feels when the moment of return to school comes at the end of an idyllic summer holiday.

That night he returned to the camp below the fig tree with the last of the light, and set his rifle against the stem of the tree. He stood a moment, stretching aching muscles and savouring the coming pleasure of hot coffee and a cheerful fire, when suddenly he stooped and then dropped on one knee to examine the earth, soft and fluffy with leaf mould.

Even in the bad light, there was no mistaking the print of broad bare feet. Quickly, Mark looked up and searched the darkening bush about him, feeling an uneasy chill at the knowledge that he might be observed at this very moment. Satisfied at last that he was alone he backtracked the spoor, and found that the mysterious stranger had searched his camp, had found the pack in the tree and examined its contents, then returned them carefully, each item to its exact place and replaced the pack in the tree. Had Mark not seen the spoor in the earth he would never have suspected that his pack had been touched.

It left him disquieted and ill at ease to know that the man he had tracked and followed had been tracking and probably watching him just as carefully—and with considerably greater success rewarding his efforts.

Mark slept badly that night, troubled by weird dreams in which he followed a dark figure that tap-tapped with a staff on the rocky dangerous path ahead of him, drawing slowly away from Mark without looking back, while Mark tried desperately to call to him to wait, but no sound came from his straining throat.

In the morning he slept late, and rose dull and heavy-headed to look up into a sky filled with slowly moving cumbersome ranges of dark bruised cumulus cloud that rolled in on the south-east wind from off the ocean. He knew soon it would rain, and that he should be going. His time had run, but in the end he promised himself a few last days, for the old man's sake and his own.

It rained that morning before noon, a mere taste of what

was to come, but still a quick cold grey drenching downpour that caught Mark without shelter. Even though the
sun poured through a gap in the clouds immediately afterwards, Mark found that the cold of the rain seemed to have
penetrated his bones, and he shivered like a man with palsy
in his sodden clothing.

Only when the shivering persisted long after his clothes
had dried, did Mark realize that it was exactly twenty-two
days since his first night under the fig tree, and his first
exposure to the river mosquitoes.

Another violent shivering fit caught him, and he realized
that his life probably depended now on the bottle of qui-
nine tablets in the pack high in the branches of the fig tree,
and on whether he could reach it before the malaria struck
with all its malignance.

It was four miles back to camp and he took a short route
through thick thorn and over a rocky ridge, to intersect the
path again on the far side.

By the time he cut the path, he was feeling dizzy and
lightheaded, and he had to rest a moment. The cigarette he
lit tasted bitter and stale, and as he ground the stub under
his heel he saw the other spoor in the path. In this place it
had been protected from the short downpour of rain by the
dense spreading branches of a mahoba hoba tree. It over-
laid his own outward spoor, moving in the same direction
as he had, but the thing that shocked him was that the feet
that had followed his had been booted, and shod with hobnails. They were the narrower elongated feet of a white
man. There seemed in that moment of sickness on the
threshold of malaria to be something monstrously sinister
in those booted tracks.

Another quick fit of shivering caught Mark, and then
passed, leaving him momentarily clear-headed and with the
illusion of strength, but when he stood to go on, his legs
were still leaden. He had gone another five hundred yards
back towards the river when a day-flighting owl called on
the ridge behind him, at the point where he had just
crossed.

Mark stopped abruptly, and tilted his head to listen. A tsetse fly bite at the back of his neck began to itch furiously, but he stood completely still as he listened.

The call of the owl was answered by a mate, the fluting hoot-hoot, skilfully imitated, but without the natural resonance. The second call had come from out on Mark's right, and a new chill that was not malaria rippled up his spine as he remembered the hooting owls on the escarpment above Ladyburg on that night so many months ago.

He began to hurry now, dragging his heavy almost disembodied legs along the winding path. He found that he was panting before he had gone another hundred yards, and that waves of physical nausea flowed upwards from the pit of his belly, gagging in his throat as the fever tightened its grip on him.

His vision began to break up, starring and cracking like shattered mosaic work, irregular patches of darkness edged in bright iridescent colours, with occasional flashes of true vision, as though he looked out through gaps in the mosaic.

He struggled on desperately, expecting at any moment now to feel the spongy swamp grass under his feet and to enter the dark protective tunnels of papyrus which he knew so well, and which would screen him and direct him back to the old camp.

An owl hooted again, much closer this time and from a completely unexpected direction. Confused, and now frightened, Mark sank down at the base of a knob-thorn tree to rest and gather his reserves. His heart was pounding against his ribs, and the nausea was so powerful as almost to force him to retch, but he rode it for a moment longer and miraculously his vision opened as though a dark curtain had been drawn aside, and he realized immediately that in his fever blindness he had lost the path. He had no idea where he was now, or the direction in which he was facing.

Desperately he tried to relate the angle of the sun, or slope of the ground, or find some recognizable landmark, but the branches of the knob-thorn spread overhead and all around him the bush closed in, limiting his vision to about fifty paces.

He dragged himself to his feet and turned up the rocky slope, hoping to reach high ground, and behind him an owl hooted—a mournful, funereal sound.

He was blind and shaking again when he fell, and he knew he had torn his shin for he could feel the slow warm trickle of blood down his ankle, but it seemed unrelated to his present circumstances, and when he lifted his hand to his face, it was shaking so violently that he could not wipe the icy sweat from his eyes.

Out on his left, the owl called again, and his teeth chattered in his head so that the sound was magnified painfully in his ears.

Mark rolled over and peered blindly in the direction of the hooting owl, trying to force back the darkness, blinking the sweat that stung like salt in his eyes.

It was like looking down a long dark tunnel to light at the end, or through the wrong end of a telescope.

Something moved on a field of golden brown grass, and he tried to force his eyes to serve him, but his vision wavered and burned.

There was movement, that was all he was sure of—then silent meteors of light, yellow and red and green, exploded across his mind, and cleared, and suddenly his vision was stark and brilliant, he could see with unnatural almost terrifying clarity.

A man was crossing his flank, a big man, with a head round and heavy as a cannon ball. He had a wrestler's shoulders, and a thick bovine neck. Mark could not see his face. It was turned away from him, yet there was something dreadfully familiar about him.

He wore a bandolier over his shoulder, over the khaki shirt with military-style button-down pockets, and his breeches were tucked into scuffed brown riding-boots. He carried a rifle at high port across his chest, and he moved with a hunter's cautious, exaggerated tread. Mark's vision began to spin and disintegrate again.

He blundered to his feet, dragging himself up the stem of
the knob-thorn and one of the sharp curved thorns stabbed
deeply into the ball of his thumb; the pain was irrelevant
and he began to run.

Behind him there was a shout, the view-halloo of the
hunter and Mark's instinct of survival was just strong
enough to direct his feet. He swung away abruptly, changing direction, and he heard the bullet a split second before
the sound of the shot. It cracked in the air beside his head
like a gigantic bull-whip, and after it, the secondary brittle
snapping bark of the shot.

"Mauser," he thought, and was transported instantly to
another time in another land.

Some time-keeping instinct in his head began counting
the split instants of combat, tolling them off even in his
blindness and sickness, so that without looking back he
knew when his hunter had reloaded and taken his next
aim. Mark jinked again in his stumbling, unseeing run and
again the shot cracked the air beside him, and Mark un-
slung the P.14 from his shoulder and ran on.

Suddenly he was into trees, and beside him a slab of
bark exploded from a trunk, torn loose by the next Mauser
bullet in a spray of flying fragments and sap, leaving a
white wet wound in the tree. But Mark had reached the
ridge, and the instant he dropped over it, he turned at right
angles, doubled up from the waist and dogged away, seeking desperately in the gloom for a secure stance from which
to defend himself.

Suddenly he was deafened by a sound as though the
heavens had cracked open, and the sun had fallen upon
him—sound and light so immense and close that he
thought for an instant that a Mauser bullet had shattered
his brain. He dropped instinctively to his knees.

It was only in the silence that followed that he realized
lightning had struck the ironstone ridge close beside him,
and the electric stench of it filled the air around him, the
rumbling echo of thunder still muttered over the blue wall
of the escarpment and the huge bruised masses of cloud

had tumbled down out of the endless blue vault of the sky to press close against the earth.

The wind came immediately, cold and swiftly rushing, thrashing the branches of the trees above him, and when Mark dragged himself to his feet again, it billowed his shirt and ruffled his hair, inducing another fit of violent shivering. It seemed the sweat on his face had been turned instantly to hoarfrost; in the rush of the wind, an owl hooted somewhere close at hand, and it began to rain again.

In the rain ahead of Mark, there was the gaunt, tortured shape of a dead tree. To his fever-distorted eyes it had the shape of an angry warlock, with threatening arms and twisted frame, but it offered a stance, the best he could hope for at this exposed moment.

For a few blessed moments, the darkness behind his eyes lightened and his vision opened to a limited grey circle.

He realized that he had doubled back and come up against the river. The dead tree against which he stood was on the very brink of the sheer high bank. The river had undercut its roots, killing it, and in time would suck it into the flood and carry it away downstream.

At Mark's back, the river was already high and swift and brown with rain water, cutting off any retreat. He was cornered against the bank while the hunters closed in on him. He knew there were more than one, the owl calls had been signals, just as they had on the escarpment of Ladyburg.

Mark realized that perhaps his only hope was to separate them, and lead them unsuspecting on to his stance, but it must be quick, before the fever tightened its hold on his senses.

He cupped one hand to his mouth and imitated the sad, mournful call of the Scops owl. Then he leaned back against the tree and held the rifle low across one hip. Off on the right his call was answered. Mark did not move. He stood frozen against the tree trunk, only his eyes swivelled to the sound and his forehead creased in his effort to see clearly. Long minutes drew out, and then the owl hoot came, even closer at hand.

The rain came now on the wind, driving in at a steep angle, ice-white lances of slanting rain, tearing at the bush and open grassland beneath it, hammering into Mark's face with sharp needles that stung his eyelids, and yet cleared his vision again so that he could see into the swirling white veils of water. Carefully Mark cupped his mouth and hooted the owl call, bringing his man closer.

"Where are you?" a voice called softly. "Rene, where are you?"

Mark swivelled his eyes to the sound. A human figure loomed out of the sodden trees, half obscured by the sheets of falling rain.

"I heard your shots—did you get him?" He was coming towards Mark, a tall lean man with a very dark brown sun-scorched face, deeply lined and wrinkled around the eyes, with a short scraggy growth of grizzled hair covering his jowls.

He carried a Lee-Metford rifle at the trail in one hand, and a rubber ex-army gas-cape draped over his shoulders, wet and shiny with rain, a man past the prime of his life, with the dull, unintelligent eyes and the coarse almost brutal features of a Russian peasant. The face of one who would kill a man with as little compunction as he would slit a hog's throat.

He had seen Mark against the dead tree trunk, but the swirling rain and the bad light showed him just the dark uncertain shape, and the call of the owl had lulled him.

"Rene?" he called again, and then stopped, for the first time uncertain, and he squinted into the teeming rain with those flat expressionless eyes. Then he swore angrily, and tried to bring up the Lee-Metford, swinging it across his belly and wiping the safety-catch across with one calloused thumb. "It's him!" He recognized Mark, and the dismay was clear to see on his face.

"No," Mark warned him urgently, but the rifle barrel was coming up swiftly, and Mark had heard the metallic snick of the safety-catch and knew that in an instant the man would shoot him down.

He fired with the P.14 still held low across his hip, the man was that close, and the shot crashed out with shocking loudness.

The man was lifted off his feet, thrown backwards with the Lee-Metford spinning from his hands, hitting the rocky ground with his shoulder blades, his heels kicking and drumming wildly on the earth and his eyelids fluttering like the wings of trapped butterflies.

The blood that streamed from his chest soaked into the sodden material of his shirt and diluted immediately to a paler rose pink by the hammering raindrops.

With a final spasm, which arched his back, the man subsided and lay completely still. He seemed to have shrunk in size, looking old and frail, and his lower jaw hung open, revealing the pink rubber gums of a set of tobacco-stained false teeth. The rain beat into the open staring eyes, and Mark felt a familiar sense of dismay. The cold familiar guilt of having inflicted death on another human being. He had an irrational desire to go to the man, to give him succour, though he was far past any human help, to try to explain to him, to justify himself. The impulse was fever-born and carried on wings of rising delirium; he was at the point now where there was no clear dividing line between fantasy and reality.

"You shouldn't have," he blurted, "you shouldn't have tried, I warned you, I warned—" He stepped out from the shelter of the dead tree trunk, forgetting the other man, the man that his senses should have warned him was the more dangerous of the two hunters.

He stood over the man he had killed, swaying on his feet, holding the rifle at high port across his chest.

Hobday had missed with his first three shots, but the range had been two hundred or more and it was up-hill shooting, with intervening bush and tree and shrub, snap shooting at a running, jinking target, worse than jump-shooting for kudu in thick cat bush—a slim swift human shape. He had fired the second and third shots in despair, hoping for a lucky hit before his quarry reached the crest of the ridge and disappeared.

Now he could follow only cautiously, for he had seen the rifle strapped on the boy's back, and he might be lying up on the ridge—waiting his chance for a clear shot. He used all the cover there was, and at last the sheets of falling rain, to reach the rocky crest, at any moment expecting retaliatory fire, for he had shown his own hand clearly. He knew the boy was a trained soldier. He was dangerous and Hobday moved with care.

His relief when he reached the crest was immense, and he lay there on his belly in the wet grass with the reloaded Mauser in front peering down the reverse slope for a sign of his quarry.

He heard the owl hoot out on his left, and frowned irritably. "Stupid old bastard!" he grunted. "Pissing himself with fright still." His partner needed constant reassurance, his old nerves too frayed for this work, and he used no judgement in timing his contact calls. The damned fool! He must have heard the shots and known the critical stage of the hunt was on, yet here he was calling again, like a child whistling in the dark for courage.

He brushed the man from his thoughts and concentrated on searching the rain-swept slope, until he froze with disbelief. The owl call had been answered, from his left, just below the crest.

Hobday came up on his feet. Crouching low, he worked swiftly along the crest.

He saw solid movement in the grey, wind-whipped scrub and dropped into a marksman's squat, drawing swift aim on the indistinct target, blinking the rain out of his eyes, waiting for a clean shot and then grunting with disappointment as he recognized his own partner, bowed under the glistening wet gas-cape, moving heavily as a pregnant woman in the gloom beneath the rain cloud and dense overhead branches.

The man paused to cup his hand over his mouth and call the mournful owl hoot again, and the bearded hunter grinned. "Decoy duck," he whispered aloud, "the stupid old dog!" and he felt no compunction that he was going to let his ally draw fire for him. He watched him carefully, keeping well down on the skyline, the silhouette of his head and shoulders broken by the low bush under which he crouched.

The old man in the gas-cape called again, and then waited listening with his head cocked. The reply called him on, and he hurried forward into the wind and the rain, drawn on to his fate. Hobday grinned as he watched. One share was better than two, he thought, and wiped the clinging raindrops off the rear sight of the Mauser with his thumb.

Suddenly the old man checked and began to swing up the rifle he carried, but the shot crashed out and went down abruptly in the grass. Hobday swore softly, bitterly, he had missed the moment, had not been able to place the spot from which the shot had been fired. Now he waited with a finger on the trigger, screwing up his eyes against the rain, less certain of himself, feeling a new awe and respect for his quarry, and the first tingle of fear. It had been a good kill, that one, leading the old man right in close, calling him up as though he were a hungry leopard coming to the bleat of a duiker horn.

Then suddenly the bearded hunter's doubts were dispelled, and for an instant he could hardly believe his fortune. Just when he had been steeling himself for a dangerous and long-drawn-out duel, his quarry stepped out into the open from the cover of a twisted dead tree trunk on the bank of the river, a childlike, ridiculously artless act—an almost suicidal act, so ingenuous that for a moment he feared some trap.

The young man stood for a moment over the corpse of the man he had killed. Even at this range, it seemed as though he swayed on his feet, his face very pale in the weak grey light but the khaki of his shirt standing out clearly against the back lighting from the surface of the river.

It needed no fancy shooting, the range was less than a hundred and fifty yards and for an instant Hobday held his aim in the centre of the boy's chest, then he squeezed off the shot with exaggerated care, knowing that it was a heart shot. As the rifle pounded back into his shoulder and the brittle crack of the Mauser stung his eardrums, he watched the boy hurled backwards by the shock of the strike and heard the bullet impact with a jarring solid thud.

Mark never even heard the Mauser shot for the bullet came ahead of the sound. There was only the massive shock in the upper part of his body, and then he was hurled backwards with a violence that drove the air from his lungs.

The earth opened behind him, and as he fell, there was the sensation of being engulfed in a swirling vortex of blackness—and he knew for just a fleeting moment of time that he was dead.

Then the icy plunge into the swirling brown current of the river caught him and shocked him back from the edge of blackness. The water engulfed his head and he had the strength to kick away from the muddy bottom. As his head broke the surface, he dragged precious air into his crushed burning lungs and realized that he held the P.14 in both hands still.

The wooden stock of the rifle was directly in front of his eyes, and he saw where the Mauser bullet had smashed into the wood and then flattened against the solid steel of the breech block.

The bullet was squashed to a misshapen lump, like a pellet of wet clay hurled against a brick wall. The rifle had stopped it dead, but the tremendous energy of impact had driven the P.14 into his chest, expelling the air from both lungs and hurling him backwards over the bank.

With enormous relief, Mark let the rifle drop into the muddy bottom below him, and was swept away by the current into a swirling nightmare of malaria and rain and raging brown water. Slowly the darkness overwhelmed him, and his last conscious thought was the irony of being saved from death by rifle shot to be immediately drowned like an unwanted kitten.

The water came up over his mouth again, he felt it burn in his lungs and then he was gone into nothingness.

\* \* \*

There can be few terrors like those of a mind tortured by malaria fever, a mind trapped in an endless nightmare from which there is no escape, never experiencing the relief of waking in the sweat of terror and knowing it was only delirium.

The nightmares of malaria are beyond the creation of the healthy brain, they are unremitting and they are compounded by a consuming thirst. The thirst as the body burns its strength and fluid in the heat of the conflict, a cycle of attack no less terrible for its regular familiar stages: icy chills that begin the cycle, followed by burning Saharan fevers that rocket the body heat to temperatures so high that they can damage the brain, and that are followed by the great sweat, when body fluid streams from every pore of the victim's body, desiccating him and leaving him without the strength to lift head or hand while he awaits the next round of the cycle to begin, the next bout of icy shivering chill.

There were semi-lucid moments for Mark between the periods of heat and cold and nameless terror. Once, when the thirst burned so that every cell of his body shrieked for moisture and his mouth was dry and swollen, it seemed that strong cool hands lifted his head and bitter liquid, bitter but cold and wonderful, flooded his mouth and ran like honey down his throat. At other times in the cold, he pulled his own grey woollen blanket close around his shoulders and the smell of it was familiar and well-beloved—the smell of woodsmoke and cigarette and his own body smell. Often he heard the rain and crash-rumble of thunder, but always he was dry, and then all sound faded and he was swept away on the next cycle of the fever.

He knew it was seventy-two hours after the first chilling onslaught that he came once again fully conscious. The malaria is that predictable in its cycle that he knew when it was to within a few hours.

It was late afternoon and Mark lay wrapped in his blanket on a mattress of fresh-cut grass and aromatic leaves. It was still raining, a steady grey relentless downpouring from the low pregnant cloudbanks that seemed to press against the tree-tops—but Mark was dry.

Above him was a low roof of rock, a roof that had been blackened over the millennium by the wood fires of others who had sought shelter in this shallow cave; the opening of the shelter faced north-west, away from the prevailing rain-bearing winds, and just catching the last glimmerings of light from where the sun was sinking behind the thick cloud-cover.

Mark lifted himself with enormous effort on one elbow and looked about him, bemused. Propped against the rock wall near his head was his pack. He stared at it for a long time, puzzled and completely bewildered. His last coherent memory had been of engulfing icy waters. Closer at hand was a round-bellied beer pot of dark fire-baked clay, and he reached for it immediately, his hands shaking not only from weakness but from the driving need of his thirst.

The liquid was bitter and medicinal, tasting of herbs and sulphur, but he drank it with panting grateful gulps until his belly bulged and ached.

He lowered the pot then and discovered beside it a bowl of stiff cold maize porridge, salted and flavoured with some wild herb that tasted like sage. He ate half of it and then fell asleep, but this time into a deep healing sleep.

When he awoke again, the rain had stopped and the sun was near its zenith, burning down through the gaps and soaring valleys of the towering cloud ranges.

It required an effort, but Mark rose and staggered to the opening of the rock shelter. He looked down into the flooded bed of the Bubezi River, a roaring red-brown torrent in which huge trees swirled and tumbled on their way to the sea, their bared roots lifted like the crooked arthritic fingers of dying beggars.

Mark peered to the north and realized that the whole basin of swamp and bush had been flooded, the papyrus beds were submerged completely under a dull silver sheet of water that dazzled like a vast mirror, even the big trees on the lower ground were covered to their upper branches, and the higher ridges of ground and the low kopjes were islands in the watery waste.

Mark was still too weak to stay on his feet, and he staggered back to his bed of cut grass. Before he slept again he pondered the attack, and the disquieting problem of how the assassins had known he was here at Chaka's Gate; somehow it was all bound up with Andersland and the death of the old man in the wilderness here. He was still pondering it all when sleep overtook him.

When he awoke, it was morning again, and during the night somebody had replenished the beer pot with the bitter liquid and the food bowl with stiff porridge and a few fragments of some roast flesh, that tested like chicken but was probably iguana lizard.

The waters had fallen dramatically, the papyrus beds were visible with their long stems flattened and the fluffy heads wadded down by the flood, and the trees were exposed, the lower ground drying out; the Bubezi River in the deep gorge below Mark's shelter had regained some semblance of sanity.

Mark was suddenly aware of his own nudity, and of the stink of fever and body wastes that clung to him. He went down to the water's edge, a long slow journey during which he had to pause often to regain his strength and for the dizziness to stop singing in his ears.

He bathed away the smell and the filth and examined the dark purple bruise where the Mauser bullet had smashed the P.14 into his chest. Then he dried in the fierce glare of the noon sun. It warmed the last chills of the fever from his body—and he climbed back up to the shelter with a spring and lightness in his step.

In the morning he found that the beer pot and food bowl had disappeared, and he sensed somehow that the gesture was deliberate and carried the message that, as far as his mysterious benefactor was concerned, he was able to fend for himself again, and that he had begun to outlive his welcome.

Mark gathered his possessions, finding that all his clothing had been dried out and stuffed into the canvas pack. His bandolier of ammunition was there also and the bone-handled hunting knife was in its sheath, but his food supply was down to one can of baked beans.

He opened it and ate half, saved the rest for his dinner, left the pack in the back of the shelter, and set out for the far side of the basin.

It took him almost two hours to find the killing ground, and he recognized it at last only by the dead tree with its twisted arthritic limbs. The ground here was lower than he had imagined, and had been swept by the flood waters; the grass was flattened against the earth, as though brilliantined and combed down, some of the weaker trees had been uprooted and swept away and, in the lower branches of the larger stronger trees, the flood debris clung to mark the high-water level.

Mark searched for some evidence of the fight, but there was none, no body nor abandoned rifle, it was as though it had never been . . . Mark began to doubt his own memory until he slipped his hand into the front of his shirt and fingered the tender bruising.

He searched down the track of the waters, following the direction of the swept grass for half a mile. When he saw vultures sitting in the trees and squabbling noisily in the scrub, he hurried forward, but it was only a rhino calf, too young to have swum against the flood, drowned and already beginning to putrefy.

Mark walked back to the dead tree and sat down to smoke the last cigarette in his tin, relishing every draw, stubbing it out half-finished and carefully returning the butt to the flat tin with its picture of the black cat—and the trademark "Craven A."

He was about to stand when something sparkled in the sunlight at his feet, and he dug it out of the still damp earth with his finger.

It was a brass cartridge case, and when he sniffed at it, there was still the faint trace of burned cordite. Stamped into the base was the lettering "Mauser Fabriken. 9mm" and he turned it thoughtfully between his fingers.

The correct thing was to report the whole affair to the nearest police station, but twice already he had learned the folly of calling attention to himself while some remorseless enemy hunted him from cover.

Mark stood up and went down the gentle slope to the edge of the swamp pools. A moment longer he examined the brass cartridge case, then he hurled it far out into the black water.

At the rock shelter he hefted his pack on to his shoulders, bouncing from the knees to settle the straps. Then, as he crossed to the entrance, he saw the footprints in the fine cold ash dust of the fire. Broad, bare-footed, he recognized them instantly.

On an impulse he slipped the sheathed hunting knife off his belt, and laid it carefully exposed in an offertory position at the base of the shelter wall; then, with a stub of charcoal from the dead fire, he traced two ancient symbols on the rock above it—the symbols that old David had told him stood for "The-bowed-slave-who-bears-gifts." He hoped Pungushe, the poacher, would come again to the rock shelter and that he could interpret the symbols and accept the gift.

On the slope of the south butt of Chaka's Gate, Mark paused again and looked back into the great sweep of wilderness, and he spoke aloud, softly, because he knew that if the old man were listening, he would hear, no matter how low the voice. All he had learned and experienced here had hardened his resolve to come to the truth and to unravel the mystery and answer the questions that still hid the facts of the old man's death.

"I'll come again—some day." Then he turned away towards the south, lengthening his stride and swinging into the gait just short of a trot that the Zulus call *Minza umhlabathi*—or "eat the earth greedily."

\* \* \*

The suit felt unfamiliar and confining on his body, and the starched collar was like a slave's ring about Mark's throat, the pavement hard and unyielding to his tread and the clank of the trams and the honk and growl and clash of the train and automobile were almost deafening after the great silences of the bush, and yet there was excitement and stimulation in the hurrying tide of human beings that swirled around him, strident and colourful and alive.

The tropical hot-house of Durban town encouraged all growth of life, and the diversity of human beings that thronged her streets never failed to intrigue Mark; the Hindu women in their shimmering saris of gaudy silk with jewels in their pierced nostrils and golden sandals on their feet; the Zulus, moon-faced and tall, their wives with the conical ochre headdresses of mud and plaited hair that they wore for a lifetime, bare-breasted under their cloaks, big stately breasts fruitful and full as those of the earth mother, to which their infants clung like fat little leeches, and the short leather aprons high on their strong glossy dark thighs swinging as they walked; the men in loin-cloths muscled and dignified—or wearing the cast-off rags of Western clothing with the same jaunty panache and self-conscious assurance that the mayor wore his robes of office; the white women, remote and cool and unhurried, followed by a servant as they shopped or encapsuled in their speeding vehicles; their men in dark suits and the starched collars better suited to the climes of their native north, many of them yellowed with fever and fat with rich foods as they hurried about their affairs, their faces set in that small perpetual frown, each creating for himself an isolation of the spirit in the press of human bodies.

It was strange to be back in the city. Half of Mark's soul hated it while the other half welcomed it, and he hurried to find the human company for which he had sometimes hungered these long weeks just past.

"Good God, my dear old sport." Dicky Lancome, with a red carnation in his button-hole, hurried to meet him across the showroom floor. "I am delighted to have you back. I was expecting you weeks ago. Business has been deadly slow, the girls have been ugly, tiresome and uncooperative, the weather absolutely frightful—you have missed nothing, old son, absolutely nothing." He held Mark off at arm's length and surveyed him with a fond and brotherly eye. "My God, you look as though you've been on the Riviera, brown as a pork sausage but not as fat. God, I do declare you've lost weight again—" and he patted his own waistcoat which was straining its buttons around the growing bulge of his belly. "I must go on a diet—which reminds me, lunch-time! You will be my guest, old boy, I insist—I absolutely insist."

Dicky began his diet with a plate piled high with steaming rice, coloured to light gold and flavoured with saffron; over this was poured rich, chunky mutton curry, redolent with Hindu herbs and garnished with mango chutney, ground coconuts, grated Bombay Duck and half a dozen other sauces, and as the turbaned Indian waiter offered him the silver tray of salads, he loaded his side plate enthusiastically without interrupting his questioning.

"God, I envy you, old boy. Often promised myself that. One man against the wilderness, pioneer stuff, hunting and fishing for the pot." He waved the waiter away and lifted a quart stein of lager beer to salute Mark. "Cheers, old boy, tell me all about it."

Dicky was silent at last, although he did the curry full justice, while Mark told him about it—about the beauty and the solitude, about the bushveld dawn and the starry silent nights, and he sighed occasionally and shook his head wistfully.

"Wish I could do it, old boy."

"You could," Mark pointed out, and Dicky looked startled. "It's out there now. It won't go away."

"But what about my job, old boy? Can't just drop everything and walk away."

"Do you enjoy your job that much?" Mark asked softly. "Does peddling motorcars feed your soul?"

"Hey?" Dicky began to look uncomfortable. "It's not a case of enjoying it. I mean nobody really enjoys having to work, do they? I mean it's just something one does, you know. One is lucky to find something one can do reasonably well where one can earn an honest coin, and one does it."

"I wonder," Mark mused. "Tell me, Dicky, what is most important, the coin or the good feeling down there in your guts?"

Dicky stared at him, his lower jaw sagging slightly, exposing a mouthful of half-masticated rice.

"Out there, I felt clean and tall," Mark went on, fiddling with his beer stein. "There were no bosses, no clients, no hustling for a commission. I don't know, Dicky—out there I felt important."

"Important?" Dicky swallowed the unchewed curry noisily. "Important? Hey now, old boy, they're selling rakes like you and me on the street corners at ninepence a bunch." He washed down the rice with a swallow of beer, and then patted the froth from his upper lip with the crisp white handkerchief from his breast pocket. "Take an old dog's advice, when you say your prayers at night give thanks that you are a good motorcar salesman, and that you have found that out. Just do it, old son, and don't think about it, or it will break your heart." He spoke with an air of finality that declared the subject closed, and stooped to open his briefcase on the floor beside his chair. "Here, I've something for you."

There were a dozen thick letters in Marion Littlejohn's

neat feminine hand, all in blue envelopes, a colour which she had explained in previous letters indicated undying love; there was also an account for a disputed twelve and sixpence which his tailor insisted Mark had underpaid; and there was another envelope of marbled paper, pale beige and watered expensively, with Mark's name blazoned across it in a peremptory, arrogant hand—and no address.

Mark singled it out and turned it over to examine the crest, thickly crusted in heavy embossing that stood out on the flap.

Dicky watched him open it and then leaned forward to read it unashamedly, but Mark saved him the effort and flipped it across to him.

"Regimental dinner," he explained.

"You'll just make it," Dicky pointed out. "Friday the 16th." Then his voice changed, imitating a regimental sergeant-major. "Two oh hundred hours sharpish. Dress formal and R.S. bloody V.P. Take your dressing from the right, you lucky blighter, your guinea has been paid by your Colonel-in-Chief—Lord Muck-a-Muck General Courtney his exalted self. Off you go, my boy, drink his champagne and steal a handful of cigars. Up the workers, say I."

"I think I'll give it a miss," murmured Mark, and placed Marion's letters in his inside pocket, to prevent Dicky reading those also.

"You've gone bush-crazy, the sun touched you, old boy," Dicky declared solemnly. "Think of those three hundred potential owners of Cadillacs sitting around one table, pissed to the wide, and smoking free cigars. Captive audience. Whip around the table and peddle them a Cadillac each while they are still stunned by the speeches."

"Were you in France?" Mark asked.

"Not France." Dicky's expression changed. "Palestine, Gallipoli and suchlike sunny climes." The memory darkened his eyes.

"Then you'll know why I don't feel like going up to the old fort to celebrate the experience," Mark told him, and

Dicky Lancome studied him across the loaded table. He
had made himself a judge of character, of men and their
workings. He had to be a good judge to be a good salesman, so he was surprised that he had not recognized the
change in Mark sooner. Looking at him now, Dicky knew
that he had acquired something, some new reserve of
strength and resolution the likes of which few men gathered
about them in a lifetime. Suddenly he felt a humility in
Mark's presence, and although it was tinged with envy, the
envy was without rancour. Here was a man who was going
somewhere, to a place where he would never be able to
follow, a path that needed a man with a lion's liver to
tread. He wanted to reach across the table and shake
Mark's hand and wish him well on the journey, but instead
he spoke quietly, dropping the usual light and cavalier
façade.

"I wish you'd think about it, Mark. General Courtney
came to see me himself—" and he went on to tell him of
the visit, of Sean Courtney's anger when he had heard that
Mark had been discharged at his daughter's behest. "He
asked for you to be there especially, Mark, and he really
meant it."

\* \* \*

Mark showed his invitation at the gates, and was passed
through the massive stone outer fortifications.

There were fairy lights strung in the trees along the pathway that led through the gardens of the old fort, giving the
evening a frivolous carnival feeling at odds with the usual
atmosphere this bastion had known from the earliest British
occupation, through siege and war with Dutch and Zulu;
many of the Empire's warriors who had paused here on
their occasions.

There were other guests ahead of and behind him on the
pathway, but Mark avoided them, feeling self-conscious in
the dinner-jacket he had hired from the pawnbroker when
he retrieved his decorations. The garment had the venera-

ble greenish tinge of age, and was ventilated in places by
the ravages of moths. It was too tight across the shoulders
and too full in the belly, and it exposed too much cuff and
sock, but when he had pointed this out to the pawnbroker,
the man had asked him to finger the pure silk lining and
had reduced the hire fee to five shillings.

Miserably he joined the file of other dinner-jacketed figures on the steps of the drillhall, and when his turn came,
he stepped up to the reception line.

"So!" said General Sean Courtney. "You came." The
craggy features were suddenly boyish, as he took Mark's
hand in a grip that felt like tortoise-shell, cool and hard
and calloused. He stood at the head of the reception line
like a tower, broad and powerful, resplendent in immacu-
lately cut black and crisp starched white with a gaudy
block of silk ribbons and enamel crosses and orders across
his chest. With a twitch of an imperial eyebrow, he summoned one of his staff.

"This is Mr. Mark Anders," he said. "You remember the
old firm of Anders and MacDonald,1st brigade?"

"Indeed, sir." The officer looked at Mark with quick interest, his eye dropping from his face to the silk ribbons on
his lapel and back to his face.

"Look after him," said General Courtney, and then to
Mark, "Get yourself a drink, son, and I'll talk to you later." He released Mark's hand and turned to the next in
line, but such was the magnetism and charm of the big
man that after the brief contact and the few gruff words,
Mark was no longer the gawky stranger, callow and awkward in cast-off clothes, but an honoured guest, worthy of
special attention.

The subaltern took his charge seriously and led Mark
into the dense crowd of black-clad males, all of them still
subdued and self-conscious in their unaccustomed finery,
standing in stiff knots, although the waiters moved among
them bearing silver trays laden with the regiment's hospitality.

"Whisky, is it?" asked the subaltern, and picked a glass

from one of the trays. "All liquid refreshment tonight is with the General's compliments," and took another glass for himself. "Cheers! Now let's see—1st brigade—" and he looked around. "You must remember Hooper, or Dennison?"

He remembered them and others, dozens of them, some were vaguely familiar features, just shades at the edge of his memory, but others he knew well, had liked, or disliked, and even hated. With some he had shared food, or passed a cigarette butt back and forth, with others he had shared moments of terror or exquisite boredom; the good ones, the workers, the cowards and the shirkers and the bullies were all there—and the whisky came endlessly on silver trays.

They remembered him also, men he had never seen in his life came up to him. "You remember me, I was section leader at D'Arcy Wood when you and MacDonald—" And others, "Are you *the* Anders, I thought you'd be older somehow—your glass is empty," and the whisky kept coming on the silver trays—and Mark felt tall and clever, for men listened when he talked, and witty, for men laughed when he jested.

They sat at a table that stretched the full length of the hall and was covered with a damask cloth of dazzling white; the regimental silver blinked like heliographs in the candlelight, and now it was champagne cascading into crystal glass in showers of golden bubbles. All around, the comradely uproar of laughter and of raised voices—and each time Mark lowered his glass, there was a turbaned figure at his side and a dark hand poising the green bottle over his glass.

He sagged back in his chair with his thumbs hooked in his armpits and a black cigar sticking a foot out of his mouth, "Hear! Hearing!" and "Quite righting!" the after-dinner speakers, as owlish and wise as the best of them, exchanging knowledgeable nods of agreement with his neighbors, while the ruby port smouldered in his glass.

When the General rose from his centre seat at the cross-piece of the table, there was an audible stir in the company which had become heavy and almost somnolent with port and long meandering speeches. They grinned at each other now in anticipation, and though Mark had never heard Sean Courtney speak, he sensed the interest and recharged enthusiasm and he sat up in his chair.

The General did not disappoint them; he started with a story that left them stunned for a moment, gasping for breath, before they could bellow with laughter. Then he went at them in a relaxed easy manner that seemed casual and natural, but using words like a master swordsman using a rapier, a jest, an oath, a solid piece of good sense, something they wanted to hear, followed immediately by something that disturbed them, singling out individuals for praise or gentle censure.

"Third this year in the national polo championships, gentlemen, an honour which the regiment carried easily last year—but a certain gentleman seated at this board has chosen to ride for the sugar planters now, a decision which it is his God-given right to make, and which I am certain not one of us here would condemn," and Sean Courtney paused, grinning evilly and smoothing his whiskers, while the entire company booed raucously and hammered the table with their dessert spoons. The victim flushed to vivid scarlet and squirmed in the cacophony.

"However, good news and great expectations for the Africa Cup this year. By dint of adroit sleuthing, it has been discovered that dwelling in our very midst—" and the next moment the entire hall was slapping palm to palm, a great thunder of sound, and heads were craning down to Mark's end of the table, while the General nodded and beamed at him, and when Mark slumped down quickly in his seat and tried to make his lanky frame fold like a carpenter's ruler, Sean Courtney called, "Stand up, son, let them get a look at you."

Mark rose uncertainly and bobbed his head left and right, and not until later did it occur to him that he had been skilfully maneuvred into accepting their applause,

that in doing so, he was committed. It was the first time he
witnessed from a front-row seat the General handling the
destiny of a man and achieving his object without apparent
effort.

He was pondering this, a little muzzily, as he steered for
the safe base of the next lamp post. It would, of course,
have been wiser and safer to accept the offer made to him
by one of the rickshaw drivers at the gates of the fort, when
he had reeled out into the street two hours after midnight.
However, his recent unemployment and extravagant ex-
penditure on fancy clothing had left him no choice as to his
means of transport. He faced now a walk of some three
miles in the dark, and his progress was erratic enough to
make it a long journey.

. He reached the lamp post and braced himself just as a
black Rolls-Royce stopped beside him and the back door
swung open.

"Get in!" said the General, and as Mark tumbled un-
gracefully into the soft leather seat, an iron grip steadied
him.

"You are not a drinking man." It was a statement, not a
question, and Mark had to agree.

"No, sir."

"You've got a choice," said the General. "Learn, or
leave it alone completely."

Sean had waited for almost half an hour, the Rolls
parked under the banyan trees, for Mark to appear through
the gates, and he had been on the point of abandoning the
evening and giving his driver the order to return to Emoyeni when Mark had tottered out into the street, brushed
away the importunate rickshaw drivers and set off like a
crab along the pavement, travelling further sideways than
forward.

The Rolls had crept silently along behind him with the
headlights dark, and Sean Courtney had watched with a
benevolent smile the young man's erratic progress. He felt
a gentle indulgence for the lad and for himself, for the odd
little quirks and whims with which he still surprised himself

occasionally. At sixty-two years of age, a man should know himself, know every strength and be able to exploit it, know every weakness, and have built a secure buttress against it.

Yet here he was, for no good reason that he could fathom, becoming more and more emotionally involved with a young stranger. Spending time and thought for he was not sure what end.

Perhaps the boy reminded him of himself at the same age, and now he thought about it, he did detect beneath the warm glow of champagne in his belly the nostalgia for that troubled time of doubt and shining ambition when a boy stood on the threshold of manhood.

Perhaps it was that he admired—no, cherished was a better word—cherished special quality in any animal. A fine horse, a good dog, a young man, that excellence that horsemen might call "blood," or a dog-handler "class." He had detected it in Mark Anders, and as even a blood horse might be damaged by bad handling or a class dog spoiled, so a young man who had the same quality needed advice and direction and opportunity to develop his full capability. There was too much mediocrity and too much dross in this world, Sean thought, so that when he found class, he was drawn strongly to it.

Or perhaps again—and suddenly he felt that terrible black wave of mourning sweep over him—or perhaps it is simply that I do not have a son.

There had been three sons: one had died before he had lived, still-born in the great wilderness beyond the Limpopo River. Another had been borne by a woman who was not his wife and the son had called another man father. Here Sean felt the melancholy deepen, laden with guilt; but this son was dead also, burned to a charred black mass in the flimsy machine of wood and canvas in which he had flown the sky. The words of Garry's dedication to his new book were clear in Sean's mind, "This book is dedicated to Captain Michael Courtney, D.F.C., one of the Young Eagles who will fly no more." Michael had been Sean's natural son, made in the belly of his brother's wife.

The third son lived still, but he was a son in name only and Sean would have changed that name had it been within his power. Those ugly incidents that preceded Dirk Courtney's departure from Ladyburg so many years before, among them casual arson and careless murder, were nothing compared to the evil deeds he had perpetrated since his return. Those close to him knew better than to speak the name "Dirk Courtney" in his hearing. Now he felt the melancholy change to the old anger, and to forestall it, he leaned forward in his seat and tapped the chauffeur's shoulder.

"Pull up beside him," he said, pointing to Mark Anders.

"What you need is fresh air," Sean Courtney told Mark. "It will sober you up or make you puke, either of which is desirable."

And by the time the Rolls parked at the foot of West Street pier, Mark had, by dint of enormous mental effort, regained control of his eyes. At first, every time he peered at the General beside him, he had the nauseous certainty that there was a third eye growing in the centre of his forehead, and that he had multiple ears on each side of his head, like ripples on the surface of a pond.

Mark's voice had at first been as uncontrolled, and he had listened with mild disbelief to the odd blurred sounds with which his lips had replied to the General's questions and comments. But when he frowned with the effort, and spoke with exaggerated slowness and articulation, it sounded vaguely intelligible.

However, it was only when they walked side by side down through the loose sand to the edge of the sea where the outgoing tide had left the sand hard and wet and smooth, that he began to listen to what the General was saying and it wasn't tea-party talk.

He was talking of power, and powerful men, he was talking of endeavour and reward, and though his voice was rumbling and relaxed, yet it was like the purr of an old lion who has just killed, and would kill again.

Somehow Mark sensed that what he was hearing was of great value, and he hated himself for the alcohol in his veins that slowed his mind and haltered his tongue. He fought it off actively.

They walked down along the glistening strip of wet smooth sand, that was polished yellow by the sinking glow of the late moon, the sea smelt of salt and iodine, a crisp antiseptic smell, and the little breeze chilled him so that he shivered even in his dinner jacket. But soon his brain was keeping pace with that of the burly figure that limped beside him, and slowly a sense of excitement built up within him as he heard things said that he had only sensed deep in some secret place of his soul, ideas that he recognized but that he had believed were his alone.

His tongue lost its drag and blur and he felt suddenly bright as a blade, and light as the swallow that drinks in flight as it skims the water.

He remembered how he had at one time suspected that this man might have been responsible in some way for the loss of Andersland and the old man's death. But now those suspicions smacked almost of blasphemy, and he thrust them aside to throw all his mind into the discussion in which he found himself so deeply involved.

He never did suspect until long afterwards how important that single night's talk would be in his life, and if he had known perhaps his tongue would have seized up solid in his mouth and his brain refused to keep pace, for he was undergoing a rigorous examination. Ideas thrown at Mark seemingly at random were for him to pick up and carry forward or to reject and leave lying. Every question raked his conscience and bared his principles, and gradually, skilfully, he was forced to commit himself on every subject from religion to politics, from patriotism to morals. Once or twice the General chuckled, "You're a radical, did you know that? But I suppose I was at your age—we all want to change the world. Now tell me what do you think about—" and the next question was not related to the one that preceded it. "There are ten million black men in this

country, and a million whites. How do you think they are
going to be able to live together for the next thousand
years?" Mark gulped at the enormity of the question, and
then began to talk.

The moon paled away in the coming of the dawn, and
Mark walked on into an enchanted world of flaming ideas
and amazing visions. Though he could not know it, his excitement was shared. Louis Botha, the old warrior and
statesman, had said to Sean once, "Even the best of us get
old and tired, Sean, and when that happens, a man should
have somebody to whom he can pass the torch, and let him
carry it on."

With a suddenness that took them both by surprise, the
night was passed, and the sky flamed with gold and pink.
They stood side by side, and watched the rim of the sun
rise from the dark green sea and climb swiftly into the sky.

"I have needed an assistant for many years now. My
wife hounds me," Sean chuckled at the hyperbole, "and I
have promised her I will find one, but I need somebody
quick and bright and trustworthy. They are hard to find."
Sean's cigar was long dead and horribly chewed. He took it
from his mouth and examined it with mild disapproval before tossing it into the creeping wavelets at his feet. "It
would be a hell of a job, no regular hours, no set duties,
and, God knows, I'd hate to work for me, because I am a
cantankerous, unsympathetic old bastard. But on the other
hand one thing I'd guarantee—whoever took the job
wouldn't die of boredom, and he'd get to learn a thing or
two."

He turned now, thrusting his head forward and staring
into Mark's face. The wind had ruffled his beard, and he
had long ago stripped off his black tie and thrust it into a
pocket. The golden rays of the rising sun caught his eyes
and they were a peculiarly beautiful shade of blue.

"Do you want the job?" he demanded.

"Yes, sir," Mark answered instantly, dazzled by the
prospect of an endless association with this incredible man.

"You haven't asked about the money?" growled Sean.

"Oh, the money isn't important."

"Lesson one." Sean cocked a beetling black eyebrow over the amused blue twinkle of his eye. "The money is always important."

\* \* \*

The next time Mark entered the gates of Emoyeni was to enter a new life, an existence beyond any he had ever imagined; and yet, in all the overpowering new experience, even in the whirl of having to adjust to new ideas, to the daunting procession of visitors and endless new tasks, there was one moment that Mark dreaded constantly. This was his next meeting with Miss Storm Courtney.

However, he would never know if it had not been carefully arranged by General Courtney, but Storm was not at Emoyeni on Mark's first day, nor during the days that followed, although the memory of her presence seemed everywhere in the portraits and photographs in every room, especially the full-length oil in the library where Mark spent much of his time. She was dressed in a full-length ivory-coloured dress, seated at the grand piano in the main drawing-room, and the artist had managed to capture a little of her beauty and spirit. Mark found the tantalizing scrutiny which the portrait directed at him disconcerting.

Quickly a relationship was established between Mark and the General, and during the first few days, the last of Sean's misgivings were set at rest. It was seldom that the close proximity of another human being over an extended period of time did not begin to irritate Sean, and yet with this youngster he found himself seeking his company. His first ideas had been that Mark should be taught to deal with day-to-day correspondence and all the other time-consuming trivia, leaving Sean a little more leisure and time to devote to the important areas of business and politics.

Now he would drift through into the library at odd times to discuss an idea with Mark, enjoying seeing it through younger and fresher eyes. Or he might dismiss his chauffeur and have Mark drive the Rolls out to one of the sawmills, or to a board meeting in the city, sitting up front beside him on the journey and reminiscing about those days in France, or going further back to the time before Mark was born, enjoying Mark's engrossing interest in talks of gold-prospecting, and ivory-hunting in the great wilderness beyond the Limpopo River in the north.

"There will be an interesting debate in the Assembly today, Mark. I am going to give that bastard Hendricks hell on the Railway budget. Drive me down, and you can listen from the visitors' gallery.

"Those letters can wait until tomorrow. There's been a breakdown at the Umvoti Sawmill, we'll take the shotguns and on the way back try and pick up a couple of guinea-fowl.

"Drillhall at eight o'clock tonight Mark. If you aren't doing anything important—" which was a command, no matter how delicate the phrasing, and Mark found himself sucked gently back into the ranks of the peace-time regiment. He found it different from France, for he now had powerful patronage. "You are no use to me as third rank marker. You're getting to know the way I work, son, and I want you at hand even when we are playing at soldiers. Besides," and here Sean grinned that evil, knowing grin, "you need a little time for range practice."

At the next turn-out, still not accustomed to the speed with which things happened in the world ruled by Sean Courtney, Mark found himself in the full fig of Second Lieutenant, including Sam Browne cross-strap and shining single pips on his shoulders. He had expected antagonism, or at least condescension from his brother officers, but found that when he was placed in command of range drill, he was received with universal enthusiasm.

In the household Mark's standing was not at first clear. He was awed by the mistress of Emoyeni, by her mature beauty and cool efficiency. She was remote but courteous for the first two weeks or so, referring to him as "Mr. Anders," and any request was preceded by a meticulous "please" and followed by an equally punctilious "thank you."

When the General and Mark were at Emoyeni for the midday meal, Mark was served by one of the servants from a silver tray in the library, and in the evenings, after he had taken his leave from the General, he climbed on the elderly Ariel Square Four motorcycle he had acquired, and clattered off down the hill into the sweltering basin of the city to his verminous lodgings in Point Road.

Ruth Courtney was watching Mark with an even shrewder eye than her husband had used. Had he in any way fallen short of her standards, she would have had no compunction in immediately bringing all her influence to bear on Sean for his dismissal.

One morning while Mark was at work in the library, Ruth came in from the garden with an armful of cut flowers.

"Don't let me disturb you." She began to arrange the flowers in the silver bowl on the central table. For the first few minutes she worked in silence, and then in a natural and friendly manner, she began to chat to Mark, quietly drawing from him the details of his domestic arrangements—where he slept and ate, and who did his laundry, and secretly she was appalled.

"You must bring your laundry up here, to be done with the household washing."

"That's very kind of you, Mrs. Courtney. I don't want to be a nuisance."

"Oh nonsense, there are two dhobi wallahs with nothing else to do but wash and iron."

Even Ruth Courtney, one of the first ladies of Natal, still a renowned beauty as a matron well past forty years of age, was not immune to Mark's unstudied appeal. To his natural charm was added the beneficial effect his coming had upon her own man.

Sean seemed younger, more lighthearted in these last weeks, and watching it, she realized that it was not only the

burden of routine work that had been lifted from him. The
boy was giving him back a little of that spirit of youth, that
freshness of thought, that energy and enthusiasm for the
things of life that had gone slightly stale and seemed no
longer quite worth the effort.

It was their custom to spend the hour before bed in
Ruth's boudoir, Sean lounging in a quilted dressing-gown,
watching her brush out her hair and cream her face, smoking his last cigar, discussing the day's events while he enjoyed her still slim lithe body under the thin silk of her
night-dress, feeling the slow awakening of his own body in
anticipation of the moment when she would turn from
watching him in the mirror and rise, holding out one hand
to him, and lead him through into the bedroom, to the
huge four-poster bed under the draped and tasselled velvet
canopy.

Three or four times in the weeks since Mark's arrival in
the household, Sean had made a remark so radical, so unlike his usual old-fashioned conservative self, that Ruth had
dropped the silver hairbrush into her lap and turned to
stare at him.

Each time he had laughed self-consciously and held up a
hand to prevent her teasing. "All right, I know what you're
going to say, but I was discussing it with young Mark." He
would chuckle again. "That boy talks a lot of good sense."

Then one evening, after Mark had been with them just
over a month, they had sat in companionable silence for a
while when Sean said suddenly, "Young Mark, doesn't he
remind you of Michael?"

"I hadn't noticed—no, I don't think so."

"Oh, I don't mean in looks. It's just something about the
way he thinks."

Ruth felt the old crushing regret welling up within her
like a cold dark tide. She had never given Sean a son. It
was the only true regret, the only shadow on all their sunlit
years together. Her shoulders sagged now, as though under
the burden of her regret, and she looked at herself in the
mirror, seeing the guilt of her inadequacy in her own eyes.

Sean had not noticed, had gone on blithely, "Well, I can hardly wait until February. It's going to break Hamilton's heart to hand over that big silver mug. Mark's changed the whole spirit of the team. They know they can win now, with him shooting number one."

She had listened quietly, hating herself for not being able to give him what he had wanted so badly, and she glanced down at the little carved statue of the God Thor on her dressing-table. It had stood there all these years since Sean had given it to her, a talisman of fertility. Storm had been conceived in the height of a raging electrical thunderstorm, and had been named for it. He had joked that it needed thunder and had given her the little godlet.

"A fat lot of help you were," she thought bitterly, and looked up at her own body under the silk in the mirror.

"So good to look at, and so damned useless!" She did not usually curse, it was a measure of her distress. Lovely as it was, her body would not bear another child. All it was good for now was to give him pleasure. She stood up abruptly, her nightly ritual incomplete, and she crossed to where he sat and removed the cigar from his lips, crushing it out deliberately in the big glass ashtray.

Surprised, he looked up at her, about to ask a question, but the words never reached his lips. Her eyelids were half hooded, they drooped languorously, and her lips pouted slightly to reveal the white small teeth, and there were spots of hectic colour on her high beautifully moulded cheek-bones.

Sean knew this expression and the mood it heralded. He felt his heart lurch and then begin to pound like an animal in the cage of his ribs. Usually their loving was a thing of depth and mutual compassion, a thing grown strong and good over the years, a complete blending of two persons, symbolic of their lives together—but once in a rare while, Ruth would droop her eyelids and pout that way with the colour in her cheeks, and what followed was so wild and wanton and uncontrolled that it reminded him of some devastating natural phenomenon.

She pushed one slim pale hand into his gown, and long nails raked lightly across his stomach so that his skin was instantly tingling and alive, and she leaned forward and with the other hand twined her fingers into his beard and twisted his face up to her and kissed him full on the lips, thrusting a sharp pink tongue deep into his mouth.

Sean let out a growl, and seized her, trying to draw her down into his lap and at the same time pulling open the bodice of her nightdress so that her small pointed breasts fell free, but she was quick and strong, twisting out of his grip, the ivory and pink sheen of her skin glowing through the transparent silk of her gown and her bared breasts joggling delightfully as she flew on long shapely legs into the bedroom, her laughter mocking and goading and inviting.

The following morning, Ruth cut an armful of crimson and white carnations and carried them into the library where young Mark Anders was at work. He stood up immediately and as she replied to his greeting, she studied his face. She had not truly realized how handsome he was, and she saw now that it was a face that would age well. There was a good bone structure and a proud strong nose. He was one of those lucky ones who would improve with the addition of a few wrinkles and lines around the eyes, and a little silver in the hair. That was a long way off, however, now it was the eyes that demanded attention.

"Yes," she thought, looking into his eyes. "Sean is right. He has the same strength and goodness that Michael had."

She watched him surreptitiously as she worked at her flower arrangement, deliberately picking the words as she began to chat to him, and when she had completed the flower bowl, she stood back to admire her work and spoke without looking at him.

"Why don't you join us for lunch on the terrace, Mark?" and the use of his name was deliberate, both of them very conscious of it as it was spoken. "Unless you'd prefer to continue eating here."

Sean glanced up from his newspaper as Mark came out on to the terrace, but his expression did not change as Ruth waved Mark to the seat opposite him and he immediately plunged back into the paper and angrily read out the editorial to them, mocking the writer by his tone and emphasis before crumpling the news sheet and dropping it beside his chair.

"That man's a raving bloody idiot—they should lock him up."

"Well, sir," Mark began delicately.

Ruth sighed a silent breath of relief for she had not consulted Sean on the new luncheon arrangements, but the two of them were instantly in deep discussion, and when the main course was served, Sean growled, "Take care of the chicken, Mark, and I'll handle the duck," so that the two of them were carving and arguing at the same time, like members of the same family, and she covered her smile with her table napkin as Sean ungraciously conceded a debating point to his junior.

"I'm not saying you are right, of course, but if you are, then how do you account for the fact that—"

And he was attacking again from a different direction, and Ruth turned to listen as Mark adroitly defended himself again; as she listened, she began to appreciate a little more why Sean had chosen him.

It was over the coffee that Mark learned at last what had become of Storm Courtney.

Sean suddenly turned to Ruth. "Was there a letter from Storm this morning?" When she shook her head he went on, "That damned uppity little missy must learn a few manners—there hasn't been a letter in nearly two weeks. Just where are they supposed to be now?"

"Rome," said Ruth.

"Rome!" grunted Sean. "With a bunch of Latin lovers pinching her backside."

"Sean!" Ruth reprimanded him primly.

"Beg your pardon." He looked a little abashed, and then grinned wickedly. "But she's probably putting it in the correct position for pinching right at this moment, if I know her."

That night when Mark sat down to write to Marion Littlejohn, he realized how the mere mention of Storm Courtney's name had altered his whole attitude to the girl he was supposed to marry. Under the enormous work-load which Sean Courtney had dropped casually on his shoulders, Mark's letter to Marion was no longer a daily ritual, and at times there were weeks between them.

On the other hand, her letters to him never faltered in regularity and warmth, but he found that it was not really the pressure of work that made him keep deferring their next meeting. He sat now chewing the end of his pen until the wood splintered, seeking words and inspiration, finding it difficult to write down flowery expressions of undying love on every page; each empty page was as daunting as a Saharan crossing, yet it had to be filled.

"We will be travelling to Johannesburg next weekend to compete in the annual shooting match for the Africa Cup," he wrote, and then pondered how to get a little more mileage out of that intelligence. It should be good for at least a page.

Marion Littlejohn belonged to a life that he had left behind him when he passed through the gates of Emoyeni. He faced this fact at last, but was none the less dismayed by the sense of guilt the knowledge brought him, and he tried to deny it and continue with the letter but images kept intruding themselves—and the main of these was a picture of Storm Courtney, gay and sleek, glitteringly beautiful and as unobtainable as the stars.

* * *

The Africa Cup stood almost as high as a man's chest on a base of polished ebony. The Emoyeni houseboys had polished it for three days before they had achieved the lustre that General Courtney found acceptable, and now the cup formed the centre-piece of the buffet table, elevated on a pyramid of yellow roses.

The buffet was set in the antechamber to the main ballroom, and both rooms overflowed with the hundreds of guests that Sean Courtney had invited to celebrate his triumph. He had even invited Colonel Hamilton of the Cape Town Highlanders to bring his senior officers by Union Castle liner, travelling first class, as the General's guests to attend the ball.

Hamilton had refused by means of a polite thank-you note, four lines long, without counting the address and the closing salutation. The cup had been in the Cape Town Castle since it had been presented by Queen Victoria in the first year of the Boer War, and Hamilton's mortification added not a little to Sean Courtney's expansive mood.

For Mark it had been the busiest period he had known since coming to Emoyeni. Ruth Courtney had come to place more and more trust in Mark, and under her supervision he had done much of the work of preparing the invitations and handling the logistics of food and liquor.

Now she had him dancing with all of the ugly girls who would otherwise have sat disconsolately along the wall, and at the end of each dance, the General summoned him with an imperious wave of his cigar above the heads of his guests to the buffet table where he had taken up a permanent stance close to the cup.

"Councillor, I want you to meet my new assistant— Mark, this is Councillor Evans. That's right, Pussy, this is the young fellow who clinched it for us."

And while Mark stood, colouring with embarrassment, the General repeated for the fifth or sixth time that evening a shot by shot account of the final day's competition when the two leading regiments had tied in the team events, and the judges has asked for an individual re-shoot to break the deadlock.

"A cross-wind gusting up to twenty or thirty mles an hour, and the first shoot at two hundred yards—"

Mark marvelled at the intense pleasure this trinket gave the General. A man whose fortune was almost beyond calculation, whose land could be measured by the hundred square miles, who owned priceless paintings and antique books, jewellery and precious stones, houses and horses and yachts—but none of them at this moment as prized as this glittering trifle.

"Well, I was marking myself," the General had taken enough of his own good whisky to begin acting out his story, and he made the gesture of crouching down in the bunker and looking up at the targets, "and I don't mind telling you that it was the worst hour of my life."

Mark smiled in agreement. The Highlander marksman had matched him shot for shot. Each of them signalled as a bullseye by the flags of the markers.

"They both shot possibles at two hundred yards, and then again at five hundred yards, it was only at the thousand-yard targets that young Mark's uncanny ability to judge the cross-wind—" By this time, Sean's audience was cow-eyed with boredom, and there were still ten rounds of deliberate and another ten of rapid fire to hear about. Mark sensed panic signals across the ballroom and he looked up.

Ruth Courtney was beside the main doors of the ballroom and with her was the Zulu butler. A man with warrior blood in his veins and the usual bearing of a chief, now he was grey with some emotion close to fear and his expression was pitiable as he spoke rapidly to his mistress.

Ruth touched his arm in a gesture of comfort and dismissal, and then turned to wait for Mark.

As he hurried to her across the empty dance floor he could not help but notice again how much mother resembled daughter. Ruth Courtney still had the figure of an athletic young woman, kept slim and firm and graceful by hard riding and long walking, and only when he was close to her were the small lines and tiny blemishes in her smooth ivory skin apparent. Her hair was dressed high on her head, scorning the fashionable shorter cut, and her gown had a simple elegance that showed off the lines of her body and the small shapely breasts. One of her guests reached her before Mark did, and she was relaxed and smiling while Mark hovered close at hand until she excused herself and Mark hurried to her.

"Mark." Her worry showed only in her eyes as she looked up at him towering above her, but her smile was light and steady. "There is going to be trouble. We have an unwelcome visitor."

"What do you want me to do?"

"He is in the entrance hall now. Please, take him through to the General's study, and stay with him until I can warn my husband and send him to you. Will you do that?"

"Of course."

She smiled her thanks, and then as Mark turned away she stopped him with a touch.

"Mark, try to stay with them. I don't want them to be alone together. I'm not sure what might happen." Then her reserve cracked. "In God's name why did he have to come here—and tonight when—" She stopped herself then, and the smile firmed on her lips, steady and composed, but they both knew that she had been going to say, "Tonight when Sean has been drinking."

Mark now knew the General well enough to share her concern. When Sean Courtney was drinking, he was capable of anything—from genial and expansive bonhomie to dark, violent and undirected rage.

"I'll do what I can," he agreed, and then, "Tell me, who is it?"

Ruth bit her lower lip, the strain and worry clear on her face for a moment before she checked herself, and her expression was neutral when she replied.

"It's his son—Dirk—Dirk Courtney."

Mark's own shock showed so clearly that she frowned at him.

"What's wrong, Mark? Do you know him?"

Mark recovered quickly. "No. I have heard of him, but I don't know him."

"There is bad blood, Mark. Very bad. Be careful." She left him and drifted quietly away across the floor, nodding to a dowager, stopping to exchange a word and a smile, and then drifting on to where Sean Courtney still held court in the buffet room.

Mark paused in the long gallery, and looked at himself in one of the tall gilt-framed mirrors. His face looked pale and strained, and when he smoothed his hair, his fingers were trembling slightly.

Suddenly he realized that he was afraid; dread was like a heavy weight in his bowels, and his breathing was cramped and painful.

He was afraid of the man he was going to meet. The man that he had stalked so long and painstakingly, and who he had come to know so well in his imagination.

In his mind he had built up an awesome figure, a diabolic figure wielding great and malignant power, and now he was consumed by dread at the prospect of meeting him face to face.

He went on down the gallery, his footsteps deadened by the thick pile of the carpet, his eyes not seeing the art treasures that adorned the panelled walls, for a sense of imminent danger blinded him to all else.

At the head of the marble staircase, he paused and leaned out with one hand on the balustrade to look down into the entrance hall.

A man stood alone in the centre of the black and white checkered marble floor. He wore a black overcoat, with a short cape hanging from the shoulders, a garment which enhanced his size.

His hands were clasped behind his back, and he balanced on the balls of his feet with head and jaw thrust forward aggressively, an attitude so like that of his father that Mark blinked in disbelief. His bare head was a magnificent profusion of dark curls which were shot by the overhead candelabra with sparkling chestnut highlights.

Mark started down the wide staircase and the man lifted his head and looked at him.

Mark was struck instantly by the man's fine looks, and then immediately afterwards by his resemblance to the

General. He had the same powerful jaw, and the shape of his head, the set of his eyes and the lines of his mouth were identical, yet the son was infinitely more handsome than the father.

It was the noble head of a Michelangelo statue, the beauty of his David and the magnificent strength of his Moses, yet for all his beauty he was human, not the implacable monster of Mark's imagining, and the unreasonable fear released its grip on Mark's chest, and he could smile a small welcoming smile as he came down the steps.

Dirk watched him without blinking or moving, and it was only when Mark reached the checkered marble floor that he realized how tall the man was. He towered three inches over Mark, and yet his body was so well proportioned that its height did not seem excessive.

"Mr. Courtney?" Mark asked, and the man inclined his head slightly without bothering to reply. The diamond that clasped the white silk cravat at his throat flashed sullenly.

"Who are you, boy?" Dirk Courtney asked, and his voice had the depth and timbre to match his frame.

"I am the General's personal assistant." Mark did not let the disparaging form of address ruffle his polite smile, though he knew that Dirk Courtney was his senior by less than ten years. Dirk Courtney ran an unhurried glance from his head to his shoes, taking in the cut of Mark's evening dress and every other detail in one casual sweep before dismissing him as unimportant.

"Where is my father?" He turned to adjust his cravat in the nearest mirror. "Does he know I've been waiting here for almost twenty minutes?"

"The General is entertaining, but he will see you presently. In the meantime, will you care to wait in the General's study? If you will follow me."

Dirk Courtney stood in the middle of the study floor and looked about him. "The old boy is keeping grand style these days." He smiled with a flash of startlingly white teeth and then crossed to one of the studded leather armchairs by the stone fireplace. "Get me a brandy and soda, boy."

Mark swung open the dummy-fronted bookcase, selected a Courvoisier Cognac from the orderly ranks of bottles, poured some into a goblet, squirting soda on top of it, and carried it to Dirk Courtney.

He sipped the drink and nodded, sprawling in the big leather chair with the insolent grace of a resting leopard, and then once again he surveyed the room. His gaze, checking at each of the paintings, at each of the items of value which decorated the room, was calculating and thoughtful, and he asked his next question carelessly, not really interested in the answer.

"What did you say your name was?"

Mark stepped sideways, so that his view of the man's face was uninterrupted, and he watched carefully as he replied.

"My name is Anders—Mark Anders."

For a second the name had no effect, then it struck Dirk and a remarkable transformation passed over his features. Watching it happen, Mark's fear was regenerated in full strength.

When he had been a lad, the old man had snared a marauding leopard in a heavy steel spring-tooth trap, and when they had walked up to the site the following morning, the leopard had charged them, coming up short against the heavy retaining chain within three feet of Mark and with its eyes almost on a level with his own. He had never forgotten the terrible blazing malevolence in those eyes.

Now he was seeing the same expression, an emotion so murderous and unpeakably evil that he drew back involuntarily.

It lasted only an instant, but it seemed that the entire face changed, from extravagant beauty to grotesque ugliness and back to beauty in the time it takes to draw breath. Dirk's voice, when he spoke, was measured and controlled, the eyes veiled and the expression of polite indifference.

"Anders? I've heard the name before—" He thought for a

moment, as though trying to place it, and then dismissed it as unimportant, his attention returning to the Thomas Baines painting above the fireplace—but in that instant Mark had learned with complete certainty that the vague, unformed suspicions he had harboured so long were based on hard cold fact. He knew now beyond any doubt that something evil had happened, that the sale of Andersland and the old man's death and burial in an unmarked grave were the result of deliberate planning, and that the men who had hunted him on the Ladyburg escarpment and again in the wilderness beyond Chaka's Gate were all part of a design engineered by this man.

He knew that at last he had identified his adversary, yet to hunt him down and bring him to retribution was to be a task that might be beyond his capability, for the adversary seemed invincible in his strength and power.

He turned away to tidy the pile of documents on the General's desk, not trusting himself to look again at his enemy, lest he betray himself completely.

Already he had exposed himself dangerously, but it had been necessary, an opportunity too heaven-sent to allow to pass. In exchange for exposing himself he had forced his enemy to do the same, he had forced him into the open, and he counted himself the winner in the exchange.

There was another factor now that had made his exposure less than suicidal. Whereas before he had been friendless and alone, now he was protected by his mere association with Sean Courtney.

If they had succeeded that night on the Ladyburg escarpment or again at Chaka's Gate, it would be the unimportant passing of a rootless vagrant; now his death or disappearance would rouse the immediate attention of General Courtney, and he doubted if even Dirk Courtney could afford that risk.

Mark looked up quickly from the papers, and Dirk Courtney was watching him again, but now his expression was neutral and his eyes were hooded and guarded. He began to speak, but checked himself as they heard the heavy dragging tread in the passage and they both turned expectantly to the door as it was flung open.

Sean Courtney seemed to fill the entire doorway, the top of the great shaggy head almost touching the lintel and the shoulders wide as the cross-trees of a gallows as he leaned both hands on the head of his cane and glared into the room.

His eyes went immediately to the tall elegant figure that rose from the leather armchair, the craggy sun-browned features darkening with blood as he recognized him.

The two men confronted each other silently, and Mark found himself a fascinated spectator, as he followed intuitively the play of emotions, the reawakening of the memory of ancient wrongs—and of the elemental love and affection of son for father and father for son that had long ago been strangled and buried, but were now exhumed like some loathsome rotting corpse, more horrible for once having lived and been strong.

"Hello, Father," Dirk Courtney spoke first, and at the sound of his voice, the rigidity went out of Sean's shoulders, and the anger out of his eyes to be replaced by a sense of sadness, of regret for something that had once had value but was lost beyond hope, so his question sounded like a sigh.

"Why do you come here?"

"Can we speak alone—without strangers?" Mark left the desk and crossed to the door, but Sean stopped him with a hand on the shoulder.

"There are no strangers here. Stay, Mark." It was the kindest thing that anybody had ever said to Mark Anders, and the strength of the affection he felt for Sean Courtney at that moment was greater than he had ever felt for another human being.

Dirk Courtney shrugged, and smiled for the first time, a light faintly mocking smile.

"You were always too trusting, Father." Sean nodded as he crossed heavily to the chair behind his desk.

"Yes, and who should remember that better than you."

Dirk's smile faded. "I came here hoping that we might forget, that we might look for forgiveness from each other."

"Forgiveness?" Sean asked, looking up quickly. "You will grant me forgiveness—for what?"

"You bred me, Father. I am what you made me—"

Sean shook his head, denying it, and would have spoken, but Dirk stopped him.

"You believe I have wronged you—but I *know* that you have wronged me."

Sean scowled. "You talk in circles. Come to the point. What do you want that brings you uninvited to this house?"

"I am your son. It is unnatural that we should be parted." Dirk was eloquent and convincing, holding out his hands in a gesture of supplication, moving closer to the massive figure at the desk. "I believe I have the right to your consideration—" he broke off and glanced at Mark. "God damn it, can't I speak to you without this gawking audience?"

Sean hesitated a moment, was on the point of asking Mark to leave, and then remembered the promise he had made to Ruth only minutes before. "Don't let him be alone with you for a moment, Sean. Promise me you will keep Mark with you. I don't trust him, not at all. He is evil, Sean, and he brings trouble and unhappiness—I can smell it on him. Don't be alone with him."

"No." He shook his head. "If you have something to say, get it over with. If not, go, and leave us in peace here."

"All right, no more sentiment," Dirk nodded, and the role of the supplicant dropped from him. He turned and began to stride up and down the study floor, hands thrust deep into the pockets of his overcoat. "I'll talk business, and get it over with. You hate me now, but when we have worked together—when I have shared with you the boldest and most imaginative venture this land has ever known—then we will talk again of sentiment."

Sean was silent.

"As a business man now and as a son later. Do you agree?"

"I hear you," said Sean, and Dirk began to talk.

Even Mark could not but stand in admiration of Dirk Courtney's eloquence, and the winning and persuasive manner in which he used his fine deep voice and his magnificent good looks; but these were theatrical tricks, well rehearsed and stagey.

What was spontaneous was the burning, almost fanatical glow of commitment to his own ideas which radiated from him as he talked and gestured. It was easy to believe him, for he so clearly believed himself.

Using his hands and his voice, he conjured up before his father a vast empire, endless expanses of rich land, thousands upon thousands of square miles, a treasure the likes of which few men had ever conceived, planted to cotton and sugar and maize, watered by a gigantic dam that would hold back an inland sea of sweet, fresh water—it was a dream quite breathtaking in its scope and sweep.

"I have half of the land already," Dirk paused and cupped his hands with fingers stiff and grasping as the talons of an eagle, "here in my hands. It's mine. No longer a dream."

"And the rest of it?" Sean asked reluctantly, swept along on the torrent against his will.

"It's there—untouched, ripe, ready." Dirk paused dramatically. "It is as though nature had designed it all for just this purpose. The foundations of the dam are there, built by God as though as a blessing."

"So?" Sean grunted sceptically. "Now you are an instrument of God's will, are you? And where is this empire he has promised you?"

"I own all the land south of the Umkomo River, that is the half I have already." He stopped in front of the mahogany desk and leaned forward with his hands on the polished wood, thrusting a face that glowed with the aura of a religious fanatic towards Sean Courtney.

"We will build a dam between the cliffs of Chaka's Gate

and dam the whole of the Bubezi Valley, a lake one hundred and sixty miles long and a hundred wide—and we'll open the land between there and the Umkomo River and add it to the land I already own in the south. Two million acres of arable and irrigated land! Think of that!"

Mark stared at Dirk Courtney, utterly appalled by what he had just heard, and then his gaze switched to Sean Courtney, appealingly, wanting to hear him reject the whole monstrous idea.

"That's tsetse velt," said Sean Courtney at last.

"Father, in Germany three men, Dressel, Kothe and Rochl, have just perfected and tested a drug called Germanin. It's a complete cure for tsetse-borne sleeping-sickness. It's so secret still that only a handful of men know about it," Dirk told him eagerly, and then went on, "Then we will wipe out the tsetse fly in the whole valley."

"How?" Sean asked, and his genuine interest was evident.

"From the air. Flying machines spraying pythagra extract, or other insect-killers."

It was a staggering concept, and Sean was silent a moment before he asked reluctantly, "Has it been done before?"

"No," Dirk smiled at him. "But we will do it."

"You've thought it out," Sean lay back in his chair and groped absently in the humidor for a cigar, "except for one little detail. The Bubezi Valley is a proclaimed area—has been since the time of Chaka, and most of the other ground between the Bubezi and Nkomo rivers is either tribal trust land, Crown land or forestry reserve."

Dirk Courtney lifted a finger at Mark. "Get me another brandy, boy." Mark glanced at the General. Sean nodded slightly, and there was silence again while Mark poured the brandy and brought the glass to Dirk.

"You trust him?" Dirk asked his father again, indicating Mark with his head as he accepted the glass.

"Get on with it, man," snapped Sean irritably, not both-

ering to answer the question. Dirk saluted his father with
the cut-glass tumbler and smiled knowingly.

"You make the laws, Father, you and your friends in the
Cabinet and in the Provincial Assembly, and you can
change them. That's your end of the bargain."

Sean had drawn a swelling chestful of cigar smoke as
Dirk spoke, and now he let it trickle out so that his head
was wreathed in drifting blue smoke as he replied.

"Let's get this clear. You put up the money and I force
through Parliament legislation repealing the proclamation
of these lands we need between Nkomo and the Bubezi
rivers?"

"And the Bubezi Valley," Dirk cut in.

"And the Bubezi Valley. Then I arrange that some front
company gets control of that land, even if it's only on a
thousand year ground rental?"

Dirk nodded. "Yes, that's it."

"What about the cost of the dam and the new railroad to
the dam—have you got that type of capital?" Mark could
hardly believe what he was hearing, that Sean Courtney
was haggling over the assets of the nation, treasures that
had been entrusted to him as a high representative of the
people. He wanted to shout out, to lash out at them as they
schemed. The deep affection he had felt moments before
turned slowly to a deep sense of outrage and betrayal.

"Nobody has that type of capital," Dirk told him. "I've
had my people work out a rough estimate, and there will
be little change left out of four million pounds. No individual has that sort of money."

"So?" Sean asked, the wreaths of cigar smoke drifted
away from his head and it seemed to Mark that he had
aged suddenly. His face was grey and haggard, the deep-set
eyes turned by a trick of the light into the dark empty eye-
sockets of a skull.

"The Government will build them for us," and Dirk
chuckled richly, as he resumed his pacing. "Or rather,
they'll build dam and railway for the nation. To open up
valuable natural resources." Dirk chuckled again. "And

imagine the prestige of the man that shepherds these measures through Parliament, the man who brings progress and civilization into the wilderness." He picked up the brandy glass and tossed off half the contents. "It would all be named after him—the Sean Courtney Dam perhaps?"

"It sounds impressive."

"A fitting monument, Father." Dirk lifted the glass to his father.

"But what of the tribal lands, Dirk?" Sean used his son's name for the first time, Mark noticed, and glanced sharply at him.

"We'll move the blacks out," Dirk told him casually. "Find a place for them in the hills."

"And the game reserves?"

"Good God, are we going to let a few wild animals stand in the way of a hundred million pounds?" He shook the handsome head of curls in mock dismay. "Before we flood the valley, you can take a hunting safari there. You always did enjoy the hunt, didn't you? I remember you telling me about the big elephant hunts in the old days."

"Yes," Sean nodded heavily. "I killed a lot of elephant."

"So, Father, we are agreed then?" Dirk stopped once more before Sean, and there was for the first time an anxious air, a small frown of worry puckering his bold high forehead. "Do we work together?"

Sean was silent for seconds longer, staring at the blotter on his desk-top, then he raised his head slowly and he looked sick and very old.

"What you have told me—the sheer size of it all—has taken me completely by surprise." He spoke carefully, measuring each word.

"It's big and it's going to take guts," Dirk agreed. "But you have never been frightened before, Father. You told me once, 'If you want something, go out and get it—for one thing is sure as all hell, nobody is going to bring it to you.' "

"I am older now, Dirk, and a man grows tired, loses the strength of his youth."

"You're as strong as a bull."

"I want time to think about it."

"How long?" Dirk demanded.

"Until," Sean faltered, and thought a moment, "until after the next parliamentary sessions. I will need to speak to people, examine the feasibility of the whole idea."

"It's too long," Dirk scowled, and suddenly the face was no longer beautiful, the eyes changed, coming together into a mean ferrety look.

"It's the time I need."

"All right," Dirk agreed, and thrust the scowl aside, smiling down at the massive seated figure. He began the gesture of putting out his right hand, but Sean did not look up and instead he thrust the hand back into his overcoat pocket.

"I am neglecting my guests," said Sean softly. "You must excuse me now. Mark will see you out."

"You will let me know?" Dirk demanded.

"Yes," said Sean heavily, still not looking up. "I will let you know."

Mark led Dirk Courtney down to the front doors, and he felt feverish with anger and hatred for him. They walked in silence, side by side, and Mark fought the wild, dark and violent impulses that kept sweeping over him. He hated him for having tarnished the man he had respected and worshipped, for having smeared him with his own filth. He hated him for the old man and for Andersland, and for the dreadful but unknown deeds he had ordered, and he hated him for what he was about to do to that beloved land beyond Chaka's Gate.

At the front doors, Dirk Courtney took his hat from the table and adjusted it over his eyes as he studied Mark carefully.

"I am a good friend to have," he said softly. "My father trusts you, and I am sure he confides in you. You would find me grateful and generous, and I am sure that, since you overheard our conversation, you will know what small items of information might interest me."

Mark stared at him. His lips felt numb and cold, and his whole body trembled with the effort it took to control himself. He did not trust his own voice to speak.

Dirk Courtney turned away abruptly, not bothering with his reply and he strode lightly down the front steps into the night.

Mark stared after him long after he disappeared. There was the crackling snarl of a powerful engine, the crunch of gravel under spinning wheels, and the twin beams of headlights swept the garden, and were gone.

Mark's feet kept pace with the furious rush of his anger, and he was almost running when he reached the General's study. Without knocking, he pushed open the door.

Words threatened to explode out of him—bitter condemnation, accusation and rejection—and he looked to the General's desk, but it was empty.

He was going to warn the General that he would use any means to expose the foul bargain that had been proposed that evening, he was going to voice his disillusion—his horror that Sean Courtney had even listened to it, let alone given it serious thought and the half-promise of his support.

The General stood at the window, his back to the room and the wide square shoulders slumped. He seemed to have shrunk in size.

"General," Mark's voice was harsh, strident with his anger and determination, "I am leaving now—and I won't be coming back. But before I go, I want to tell you that I will fight you and your son—"

Sean Courtney turned into the room, his shoulders still drooped and his head held at a listening angle, like that of a blind man, and Mark's voice trailed away, his fury evaporating.

"Mark?" Sean Courtney asked, as though he had forgotten his existence, and Mark stared at him, not believing what he was seeing—for Sean Courtney was weeping.

Bright tears had swamped and blinded his eyes and streamed down the lined and sun-seared cheeks, clinging in fat bright droplets to the coarse curls of his beard. It was

one of the most distressing sights Mark had ever witnessed,
so harrowing that he wanted to turn away from it—but
could not.

"Get me a drink, son." Sean Courtney crossed heavily
towards his desk and one of his tears fell to the starched
snowy front of his dress shirt, leaving a wet mark on the
material.

Mark turned away, and made a show of selecting a glass
and pouring whisky from the heavy decanter. He drew the
simple act out and when he turned back Sean Courtney
was at his desk.

He held a crumpled white handkerchief in his hand that
had damp patches on it, but although his cheeks were dry
now, the rims of his eyelids were pink and inflamed and
the marvellous sparkling blue clarity of his eyes was dulled
with swimming liquid.

"Thank you, Mark," he said as he set the glass on the
desk in front of him. Sean did not touch the glass but
stared at it, and when he spoke his voice was low and
husky.

"I brought him into the world with my own hands, there
was no doctor, I caught him in my own hands still wet and
warm and slippery—and I was proud. I carried him on my
shoulder, and taught him to talk and ride and shoot. There
are no words to explain what a man feels for his first-born
son," Sean sighed, a broken gusty sound. "I mourned for
him once before, I mourned him as though he was dead,
and that was many years ago." He drank a little of the
whisky and then went on softly, so softly that Mark could
hardly hear the words. "Now he comes back and forces me
to mourn him again, all over again."

"I am sorry, General. I thought—I believed that you
were going to—bargain with him."

"That thought dishonours me." Sean did not raise his
voice nor his eyes. "Leave me now, please Mark. We'll talk
about this again at some other time."

At the door Mark looked back, but the General was not
aware of his presence. His eyes were still misty, and

seemed to stare at a far horizon. Mark closed the door very softly.

* * *

Despite Sean Courtney's promise to discuss Dirk Courtney's proposition again, long weeks went by without even the mention of his name. However, though the life at Emoyeni seemed to continue in its busy round, yet there were times when Mark entered the panelled and book-lined study to find the General brooding darkly at his desk, beak-nosed and morbid as some roosting bird of prey, and he withdrew quietly, respecting his melancholy, knowing he was still in mouring. Mark realized it would take time before he was ready to talk.

During this period there were small changes in Mark's own circumstances. One night, long after midnight, Sean Courtney had entered his dressing-room, to find the lights were still on in the bedroom and Ruth propped on her pillows and reading.

"You shouldn't have waited up for me," he told her severely. "I could have slept on the couch—"

"I prefer you here." She closed the book.

"What are you reading?" She showed him the title.

"D. H. Lawrence's new novel, *Women in Love*."

Sean grinned as he unbuttoned his shirt. "Did he teach you anything?"

"Not yet, but I'm still hoping." She smiled at him, and he thought how young and lovely she looked in her lace nightdress. "And you? Did you finish your speech?"

"Yes." He sat to remove his boots. "It's a masterpiece— I'm going to tear the bastards to pieces."

"I heard Mark's motorcycle leaving a few minutes ago. You kept him here until midnight."

"He was helping me look up some figures and searching Hansard for me."

"It's awfully late."

"He's young," grunted Sean. "And damned well paid for

it." He picked up his boots and stumped through into the dressing-room, the limp more noticeable now that he was in his stockinged feet. "And I haven't heard him complain yet."

He came back in his night-shirt and slipped into bed beside her.

"If you are going to keep the poor boy to these hours, it's not fair to send him back to town every night."

"What do you suggest?" he asked, as he wound his gold hunter and then placed it on the bedside table.

"I could turn the gate-keeper's cottage into a flat for him. It wouldn't need much, even though it's been deserted for years."

"Good idea," Sean agreed casually. "Keep him on the premises so I can really get some work out of him."

"You're a hard man, General Courtney." He rolled over and kissed her lingeringly, then whispered in her ear.

"I am glad you noticed."

She giggled like a bride and whispered back, "I didn't mean that."

"Let's see if we can teach you something that Mr. Lawrence could not," he suggested.

The cottage, once it was repainted and furnished with discards from the big house, was by Mark's standards palatial, and marvellously free of vermin and cockroaches. It was less than half a mile from the main house, and his hours became as irregular as those of his master, his position each day more trusted and naturally integrated into the household. His duties came to cover the entire spectrum from speech-writing and researching, answering all correspondence that was not important enough for the General's own hand, operating the household accounts, to merely sitting quietly sometimes when Sean Courtney needed somebody to talk to, and acting as a sounding board for arguments and ideas.

Yet there was still time for his old love of reading. There were thousands of volumes that made up the library at Emoyeni and Mark took an armful of them down to the cottage each evening and read until the early hours, devouring with omnivorous appetite history, biography, satire, political treatise, Zane Grey, Kipling and Rider Haggard.

Then suddenly there was a new spirit of excitement and upheaval in Emoyeni as the next session of Parliament approached. This meant that the household must uproot itself, and move almost a thousand miles to Cape Town.

Lightly Ruth Courtney referred to this annual political migration as the "Great Trek," but the description was justified, for it meant moving the family, fifteen of the senior servants, three automobiles, a dozen horses, all the clothing, silver, glassware, papers, books and other incidentals that would be necessary to sustain in the correct style a busy social and political season of many months, while General Courtney and his peers conducted the affairs of the nation. It meant also closing Emoyeni and opening the house in Newlands, below the squat bulk of Table Mountain.

In the middle of all this frantic activity, Storm Courtney arrived home from the grand tour of the British Isles and the Continent on which she and Irene Leuchars had been chaperoned by Irene's mother. In her last letter to Ruth Courtney, Mrs. Leuchars had admitted herself to be both physically and mentally exhausted. "You will never know, my dear, the terrible weight of responsibility I have been under. We have been followed across half the world by droves of eager young men—Americans, Italians, Frenchmen, Counts, Barons, sons of industrialists, and even the son of the dictator of a South American Republic. The strain was such that at one period I could bear it no longer and locked both girls in their room. It was only later that I discovered they had escaped by means of a fire escape and danced until the following morning at some disreputable *boîte de nuit* in Montparnasse." With the tact of a loving wife, Ruth refrained from showing the letter to Sean Courtney and so he prepared to welcome his daughter with all the enthusiasm of a doting father, unclouded by awareness of her recent escapades.

Mark was for once left out of the family preparations and he watched from the library window when Sean handed his wife into the Rolls. He was dressed like a suitor in crisply starched fly-away collar, a gay silk cravat, dark blue suit with white carnation in the button-hole and a beaver tilted jauntily over one eye; his beard was trimmed and shampooed and there was a merry anticipatory sparkle in his eyes, and he twirled his cane lightly as he went round to his own seat.

The Rolls purred away, almost two hours ahead of the time when the mailship was scheduled to berth at No. 1 wharf. It was followed at a respectful distance by the second Rolls which would be needed for the conveyance of Storm Courtney's baggage.

Mark lunched alone in the study and then worked on, but his concentration was broken by the imminent arrival of the returning cavalcade, and when it came, he hurried to the windows.

He caught only a glimpse of Storm as she left the car and danced up the front steps hand in hand with her mother. They were followed immediately by the General, his cane snapping a staccato beat off the marble as he hurried to match their swiftness; on his face he wore an expression that tried to remain severe and stern but kept breaking into a wide beaming grin.

Mark heard the laughter and the excited murmur of the servants assembled to greet her in the entrance hall, and Storm's voice giving a new sweet lilt to the cadence of the Zulu language as she went to each of them in turn.

Mark returned to his open books, but did not look down at them. Instead he was savouring that one glimpse he had of Storm.

She had grown somehow lovelier, he had not believed it possible, but it had happened. It was as though the divine essence of young womanhood had been distilled in her, all the gaiety and grace, all the warmth and smoothness, the texture of skin and silken hair, the perfect moulding of limb and the delicate sculpturing of feature, the musical lilt of her voice, clear as the ring of crystal, the dancing grace of her movements, the very carriage of the small perfect head on bare brown shoulders.

Mark sat bemused, acutely aware of the way in which the whole huge house had changed its mood since she entered it, had become charged with her spirit, as though it had been waiting for this moment.

Mark had excused himself from dinner that evening, not wanting to intrude on the family's first evening together. He intended going down to the drill-hall for the weekly muster, and afterwards he would dine with some of the other young bachelor officers. At four o'clock, he left the house through a side entrance and went down to the cottage to bathe and change into his uniform.

He was thundering out of the gates of Emoyeni on the Ariel Square Four when he remembered that the General had asked for the Railway report to be left on his desk. In the distraction of Storm's arrival, he had forgotten it, and now he swung the heavy machine into a tight turn and tore back up the driveway.

In the paved kitchen yard he pulled the motorcycle up on its stand, and went in through the back door.

He was standing at the library table with the report in his hands, glancing through it quickly to check his own notations, when suddenly the latch on the door clicked. He laid aside the report and turned just as the door swung open.

This close, Storm Courtney was lovelier still. She was three quick light paces into the room before she realized she was not alone, and she paused, startled, poised with the grace of a gazelle on the point of flight.

One hand flew to her mouth, and her fingers were delicately tapered with long nails that gleamed like pink mother of pearl. She touched her lips with the tip of one finger; the lip trembled slightly, wet and smooth and glistening, and her eyes were huge and a dark fearful blue. She looked like a little girl, frightened and alone.

Mark wanted to reassure her, to protect her from her own distress, to say something to comfort her, but he found he could not move or speak.

He need not have worried, her distress lasted only a fleeting beat of time, just long enough for her to realize that the source of her alarm was a tall young man, dashing in the dress uniform he wore, a uniform that set off the slim graceful body, a uniform emblazoned with badges of courage and of responsibility.

Subtly, with barely a shadow of movement, her whole poise changed. The finger on her lip now touched one cheek with an arch gesture, and the trembling lip stilled and parted slightly into a thoughtful pout. The huge eyes, no longer fearful, almost disappeared behind drooping lids, and then examined Mark critically, lifting her chin to look up into his face.

Her stance changed also, one hip thrusting forward an inch, the twin mounds of her breasts lifting and pressing boldly against the gossamer silk of her bodice. The tender taunting line of her lips was enough to make Mark's breath catch in his throat.

"Hello," she said. Her voice, although low and throaty, bounced the word off Mark's heart, drawing it out into two syllables that seemed to hang in the air seconds later.

"Good evening, Miss Courtney," he answered her, surprised that his voice came out level and assured. It was the voice that triggered her memory, and the blue eyes flew wide as she stared at him. Slowly her surprise turned to angry outrage. The eyes snapped sparks and two bright scarlet blotches of crimson burned suddenly on the smooth, almost waxy perfection of her cheeks.

"You?" she asked incredulously. "Here?"

"I'm afraid so," he agreed, and her consternation was so comical that he grinned at her, his own misgivings evaporating. Suddenly he felt relaxed and at his ease.

"What are you doing in this house?" She drew herself up to her full height, and her manner became frostily dignified. The full effect was spoiled by the fact that she had to look up at him, and that her cheeks still burned with agitation.

"I am your father's personal assistant now," and he smiled again. "However, I am sure you will soon become reconciled to my presence."

"We will see about that," she snapped. "I shall speak to my father."

"Oh, I was led to understand that you and the General had already discussed my employment—or rather my unemployment."

"I—" said Storm, and then closed her mouth firmly, the colour spreading from her cheeks down her throat as she remembered with sudden acute discomfort the whole episode. The humiliation was still so intense that she felt herself wilting like a rose on a summer's day, and a small choke of self-pity constricted the back of her throat. It was enough that it had happened, that instead of her father's unquestioning support—something she had been accustomed to since her first childhood memories—he had told her angrily that she had acted like a spoiled child, that she had shamed him by misusing his power and influence, and that the shame had been made more intense by the way she had used it without his knowledge, by sneaking behind his back, as he put it.

She had been frightened, as she always was by his anger, but not seriously disturbed. It was almost ten years since he had last lifted a hand to her.

"A true lady shows consideration to all around her, no matter what their colour or creed or station."

She had heard it often before, and now her fear was turning to irritation.

"Oh, la-di-da, Pater! I'm not a child any more!" she flounced. "He was insolent, and anyone who is insolent to me will damned well pay for it."

"You have made two statements there," the General

noted with deceptive calm, "and both of them need correction. If you are insolent, then you will get back insolence—and you *are* a child still." He rose from his chair behind the desk, and he was huge, like a forest oak, like a mountain. "One other little thing, ladies do not swear, and you are going to be a lady when you grow up. Even if I have to beat it into you."

As he took her wrist, she suddenly realized with a sense of incredulous dismay what was about to happen. It had not happened since she was fourteen years of age, and she had believed it would never happen again.

She tried to pull away, but his strength was enormous, and as he lifted her easily under one arm and carried her to the leather couch, she let out her first squeal of fear and outrage. It changed swiftly to real anguished howls as he positioned her carefully across his lap and swept her skirts up over her head. Her pantaloons were of blue *crêpe de Chine* with little pink roses decorating the target area, and his palm, horny and hard, snapped over the tight double bulge of her buttocks with a sharp rubbery crack. He kept it up until the howling and kicking subsided into heart-racking sobs, and then he lowered her skirts and told her quietly, "If I knew where to find him, I'd send you to apologize to that young man."

Storm remembered that threat, and felt a moment of panic. She knew her father was still quite capable of making her apologize even now, and she nearly turned and rushed out of the library. It required a supreme effort once more to draw herself up and lift her chin defiantly.

"You are right," she said coldly. "The hiring and firing of my father's servants is not a subject with which I should concern myself. Now, if you would kindly stand aside—"

"Of course, forgive me." Still smiling, Mark bowed extravagantly and made way for her to pass.

She tossed her head and swished her skirts as she passed him and, in her agitation, went to the wrong shelves. It was some little time before she realized that she was studying intently a row of bound copies of ten-year old parliamentary white papers, but she would not admit her mistake and humiliate herself further.

Furiously she pondered her next sally, picking and discarding half a dozen disparaging remarks before settling on, "I would be obliged if in future you would address me only when it is absolutely necessary, and right at this moment I should like to be alone." She spoke without interrupting her perusal of the white papers.

There was no reply, and she turned haughtily. "Did you hear what I said?" Then she paused.

She was alone, he had gone silently and she had not even heard the click of the latch.

He had not waited to be dismissed, and Storm felt quite dizzy with anger. Now a whole parade of brilliant and biting insults came readily to her lips, and frustration spiced her anger.

She had to do something to vent it, and she looked around for something to break—and then remembered, just in time, that it was Sean Courtney's library, and everything in it was treasured. So instead, she racked her brain for its foulest oath.

"Bloody Hell!" She stamped her foot, and it was entirely inadequate. Suddenly she remembered her father's favourite.

"The bastard," she added, rolling it thunderously around her tongue as Sean did, and immediately she felt better. She said it again and her anger subsided, leaving an extraordinary new sensation.

There was a disturbing heat in that mysterious area between navel and knees. Flustered and alarmed, she hurried out into the garden. The short glowing tropical dusk gave the familiar lawns and trees an unreal stagelike appearance, and she found herself almost running over the spongy turf, as though to escape from her own sensations.

She stopped beside the lake, and her breathing was quick and shallow, not entirely from her exertions. She leaned on the railing of the bridge and in the rosy light of sunset her reflection was perfectly mirrored in the still pearly waters.

Now the disturbing new sensation had passed, she found herself regretting that she had fled from it. Something like that was what she had hoped for when—

She found herself thinking again of that awkward and embarrassing episode in Monte Carlo; goaded on by Irene Leuchars, teased and tempted, she had been made to feel inadequate because she lacked the experience of men that Irene boasted of. Chiefly to spite Irene, and to defend herself against her jibes, she had slipped away from the Casino with the young Italian Count and made no protest when he parked the Bugatti among the pine trees on the high-level road above Cap Ferrat.

She had hoped for something wild and beautiful, something to bring the moon crashing out of the sky and to make choirs of angels sing.

It had been quick, painful and messy—and neither she nor the Count had spoken to each other on the winding road down to Nice, except to mutter goodbye on the pavement outside the Negresco Hotel. She had not seen him again.

Why she thought of this now she could not understand, and she thrust the memory aside without effort. It was replaced almost instantly with a picture of a tall young man in a handsome uniform, of a cool mocking smile and calm penetrating gaze. Immediately she was aware of the warmth and glow in her lower belly again, and this time she did not attempt to fly from it, but continued leaning on the bridge, smiling at her darkening image in the water.

"You look like a smug old pussy cat," she whispered, and chuckled softly.

* * *

Sean Courtney rode like a Boer, with long stirrups, sitting well back in the saddle with legs thrust out straight in front of him and the reins held loosely in his left hand, the black quirt of hippo-hide dangling from its thong on his wrist so that the point touched the ground. His favourite mount was a big raw-boned stallion of almost eighteen hands with a white blaze and an ugly unpredictable nature that only the General could fathom; but even he had to use an occasional light cut with the quirt to remind the beast of his social obligations.

Mark had an English seat, or, as the General put it, rode like a monkey on a broomstick, and he added darkly, "After only a hundred miles or so perched up like that, your backside will be so hot you could cook your dinner on it. We rode a thousand miles in two weeks when we were chasing General Leroux."

They rode almost daily together, when even the huge rooms of Emoyeni became confining, and the General started to fret at the caging of his big body; then he would shout for the horses.

There were thousands of acres of open ground still backing the big urban estates, and then beyond that there were hundreds of miles of red dirt roads criss-crossing the sugarcane field.

As they rode, the day's work was continued, with only the occasional interruption for a half mile of hard galloping to charge the blood, and then the General would rein in again and they would amble on over the gently undulating hills, knee to knee. Mark carried a small leather-bound notebook in his inside pocket to make notes of what he must write up on their return, but most of it he carried in his head.

The week before the departure to Cape Town had been filled with the implementation of details and of broad policies, the winding up of the domestic business of the provincial legislative council before beginning on the national business of Parliament, and, deep in this discussion, their daily ride had carried them farther than they had ridden together before.

When at last the General reined in, they had reached the crest of a hill, and the view before them spread down to the sea, and away to the far silhouette of the great whale-backed mountain above Durban harbour. Directly below them, a fresh scar had been torn in the earth, like a bold knife stroke through the green carpet of vegetation, into the red fleshy earth.

The steel tracks of the permanent way had reached this far, and as they sat the fidgeting horses, the loco came huffing up to the railhead pushing the track carrier ahead of it under its heavy load of steel.

Neither of them spoke, as the tracks were dumped with a faint clattering roar, and the tiny antlike figures of the track-laying gang swarmed over them, man-handling them on to the orderly parallel rows of timber sleepers. The tap of the swinging hammers began then, a quick rhythmic beat as the fishplates were spiked into place.

"A mile a day," said Sean softly, and Mark saw from his expression that he was thinking once again of another railroad far to the north, and all that it betokened. "Cecil Rhodes dreamed of a railway from Cairo to Cape Town—and I believed once that it was a grand dream." He shook his beard heavily. "God knows, perhaps we were both wrong."

He turned the stallion's head away and they walked back down the hill in silence except for the jingle of harness and the clip of hooves. They were both thinking of Dirk Courtney, but it was another ten minutes before Sean spoke.

"Do you know the Bubezi Valley, beyond Chaka's Gate?"

"Yes," said Mark.

"Tell me," Sean ordered, and then went on, "It is fifty years since I was last there. During the war with the old Zulu king Cetewayo, we chased the remains of his impis up there, and hunted them along the river."

"I was there only a few months ago. Just before I came to you."

Sean turned in the saddle, and his black brows came together sharply.

"What were you doing there?" he demanded harshly.

For an instant Mark was about to blurt out all his suspicions—of Dirk Courtney, of the fate that had overtaken the old man, of his pilgrimage to find the grave and to fathom the mystery beyond Chaka's Gate. Something warned him that to do so would be to alienate Sean Courtney completely. He knew enough about him now to realize that although he might accuse and even reject his own son, he would not listen to nor tolerate those accusations from someone outside the family, particularly if those accusations were without substance or proof. Mark put the temptation aside and instead he explained quietly,

"My grandfather and I went there often when I was a child. I needed to go back—for the silence and the beauty, for the peace."

"Yes." The General understood immediately. "What's the game like there now?"

"Thin," Mark answered. "It's been shot out, trapped and hunted. It's thin and very wild."

"Buffalo?"

"Yes, there are some in the swamps. I think they graze out into the bush in the night but I never saw them."

"In 1901 old Selous wrote that the Cape buffalo was extinct. That was after the rinderpest plague. My God, Mark, when I was your age there were herds of ten and twenty thousand together, the plains along the Limpopo were black with them," and he began to reminisce again. It might have been boring, an old man's musty memories, but he told it so vividly that Mark was carried along, fascinated by the tales of a land where a man would ride with his wagons for six months without meeting another white man.

It was with a sick little slide of regret, of something irretrievably lost that he heard the General say,

"It's all gone now. The railway line is right through to the copperbelt in Northern Rhodesia. Rhodes Column has taken the land between the Zambesi and the Limpopo. Where I camped and hunted, there are towns and mines, and they are ploughing up the old elephant grounds." He shook his head again. "We thought it would never end, and now it's almost gone." He was silent and sad again for a while. "My grandchildren may never see an elephant or hear the roar of a lion."

"My grandfather said that when Africa lost its game, he would go back and live in old London town."

"That's how I feel," Sean agreed. "It's strange but perhaps Dirk has done something of great value to Africa and for mankind." The name seemed to choke in his throat, as though it was an effort to enunciate it—and Mark was silent, respecting that effort. "He has made me think of all this as never before. One of the things that we are going to do during this session of Parliament, Mark, is to make sure that the sanctuary in the Bubezi Valley is ratified, and we are going to get funds to administer it properly, to make sure that nobody, ever, turns it into a sugar cane or cotton field, or floods it beneath the waters of a dam." As he spoke, Mark listened with a soaring sense of destiny and commitment. It was as though he had waited all his life to hear these words.

The General went on, working out what was needed in money and men, deciding where he would lobby for support, which others in the Cabinet could be relied on, the form which the legislation must take, and Mark made a note of each point as it came up, his pencil hurrying to keep pace with the General's random and eclectic thoughts.

Suddenly, in full intellectual flight, the General broke off and laughed aloud. "It's true, you know, Mark. There is nobody so virtuous as a reformed whore. We were the great robber barons—Rhodes and Robertson, Bailey and Barnato, Duff Charleywood and Sean Courtney. We seized the land and then ripped the gold out of the earth, we hunted where we pleased, and burned the finest timber for our camp fires, every man with a rifle in his hand and shoes on his feet was a king—prepared to fight anybody, Boer, Briton or Zulu, for the right of plunder." He shook his head and groped in his pockets before he found his cigars. He laughed no longer, but frowned as he lit the cigar. The big stallion seemed to sense his mood, and he crabbed and bucked awkwardly. Sean rode him easily and quirted him lightly across the flank. "Behave yourself!" he growled, and then when he quieted Sean went on, "The day that I met my first wife, only thirty-two years ago, I hunted with her father and her brother. We rode down a herd of elephant and between the three of us we shot and killed forty-three of them. We cut out the tusks and left the carcasses lying. That's over one hundred and sixty tons of flesh." Again he shook his head. "Only now am I coming to realize the enormity of what we did. There were other things— during the Zulu wars, during the war with Kruger, during Bombata's rebellion in 1906. Things I don't even like to remember. And now perhaps it's too late to make amends. Perhaps also it's just the way of growing old that a man regrets the passing of the old ways. He initiates change when he is young and then mourns that change when he grows old."

Mark was silent, not daring to say a word that might break the mood. He knew that what he was hearing was so important that he could then only guess at the depths of it.

"We must try, Mark, we must try."

"Yes, sir. We will," Mark agreed, and something in his tone made the General glance across at him, mildly surprised.

"This really means something to you." He nodded, confirming his statement. "Yes, I can see that. Strange, a young fellow like you! When I was your age all I ever thought about was a quick sovereign and a likely piece of—" He caught himself before he finished, and coughed to clear his throat.

"Well, sir, you must remember that I had my full share of destruction at an earlier age than you did. The greatest destruction the world has ever known." The General's face darkened as he remembered what they had shared together in France. "When you've seen how easy it is to tear down, it makes the preservation seem worth while." Mark chuckled ruefully. "Perhaps I was born too late."

"No," said the General softly. "I think you were born just in time," and he might have gone on, but high and clear on the heat-hushed air came the musical cry of a girl's voice, and instantly the General's head went up and his expression lightened.

Storm Courtney came at the gallop. She rode with the same light lithe grace which marked all she did. She rode astride, and she wore knee-high boots with baggy gaucho pants tucked into the tops, a hand-embroidered waistcoat in vivid colours over a shirt of white satin with wide sleeves, and a black wide-brimmed vaquero hat hung on her back from a thong around her throat.

She reined in beside her father, laughing and flushed, tossing the hair out of her face, and leaning out of the saddle to kiss him, not even glancing at Mark, and he touched his reins and dropped back tactfully.

"We've been looking for you all over, Pater," she cried. "We went as far as the river—what made you come this way?"

Coming up more sedately behind Storm on a bay mare was the blonde girl whom Mark remembered from that fateful day at the tennis courts. She was more conventionally dressed than Storm in dove-grey riding breeches and tailored jacket, and the wind ruffled the pale silken gold of her cropped hair.

While she made her greetings to the General, her eyes kept swivelling in Mark's direction and he searched for her name and remembered she had been called Irene—and realized she must be the girl who had been Storm's companion on the grand continental tour. A pretty, bright little thing with a gay brittle style and calculating eyes.

"Good afternoon, Miss Leuchars."

"Oh la!" She smiled archly at him now. "Have we met?" Somehow her mare was kneed away from the leading pair, and dropped back beside Mark's mount.

"Briefly, yes, we have," Mark admitted, and suddenly the china-blue eyes flew wide and the girl covered her mouth with a gloved hand.

"You are the one—" then she squealed softly with delight, and mimicked him, "just as soon as you say please!"

Storm Courtney had not looked round, and she was paying exaggerated attention to her father, but Mark watched her small perfect ears turn pink, and she tossed her head again, but this time with an aggressive, angry motion.

"I think we might forget that," Mark murmured.

"Forget it?" chirruped Irene. "I'll never forget it. It was absolutely classic." She leaned over and placed a bold hand on Mark's forearm. At that moment Storm could contain herself no longer; she swivelled in the saddle and was about to speak to Irene, when she saw the hand on Mark's arm.

For a moment Storm's expression was ferocious, and the dark blue eyes snapped with an electric sparkle. Irene held her gaze undaunted, making her own paler blue eyes wide and artless, and deliberately, challengingly, she let her hand linger, squeezing lightly on Mark's sleeve.

The understanding between the two girls was instantaneous. They had played the game before, but this time intuitively Irene realized that she had never been in a stronger position to inflict punishment. She had never seen such a swift and utterly malevolent reaction from Storm— and they knew each other intimately. This time she had Missy Storm in a vise, and she was going to squeeze and squeeze.

She edged her mare in until her knee touched Mark's, and she turned away from Storm, deliberately looking up at the rider beside her.

"I hadn't realized you were so tall," she murmured. "How tall are you?"

"Six foot two." Mark only dimly realized that something mysterious, which promised him many awkward moments, was afoot.

"Oh, I do think height gives a man presence."

Storm was now laughing gaily with her father, and trying to listen to the conversation behind her at the same time. Anger clawed her cruelly and she clutched the riding-crop until her fingers ached. She was not quite sure what had affected her this way, but she would have delighted in lashing the crop across Irene's silly simpering face.

It was certainly not that she felt anything for Mark Anders. He was, after all, merely a hired servant at Emoyeni. He could make an idiot of himself over Irene Leuchars and she would not even glance aside at any other time or place. It was just that there were some things that were not done, the dignity of her position, of her father, and family—yes, that was it, she realized. It was an insult that Irene Leuchars, as a guest in the Courtney home, should make herself free, should flaunt herself, should make it so blatant that she would like to lead Mark Anders along the well-travelled pathway to her steamy—she could not continue the thought, for the vivid mental image of that pale, deceptively fragile-looking body of Irene's spread out, languid and naked, and Mark about to—another wave of anger made her sway in the saddle, and she dropped the riding-crop she carried and turned quickly.

"Oh Mark, I've dropped my crop. Won't you be a dear and fetch it for me?"

Mark was taken aback, not only by the endearment, but also by the stunning smile and warmth of Storm's voice. He almost fell from the saddle in his haste, and when he came alongside Storm to hand the crop back to her, she detained him with a smile of thanks, and a question.

"Mark, won't you help me label my cases? It's only a few days and we'll all be leaving for Cape Town."

"I'm so looking forward to it," Irene agreed as she pushed her mare up on Mark's other side, and Storm smiled sweetly at her.

"It should be fun," she agreed. "I love Cape Town."

"Grand fun," Irene laughed gaily, and Storm regretted bitterly the invitation that would make her a guest for four months in the Courtneys' Cape Town home. Before Storm could find a cutting rejoinder, Irene leaned across to Mark.

"Come on, then," she said, and turned her mare aside.

"Where are you going?" Storm demanded.

"Mark is taking me down to the river to show me the monument where Dick King crossed on his way to fetch the English troops from Grahamstown."

"Oh, Irene darling," Storm dabbed at her eye with the tail of her scarf, "I seem to have something in my eye. Won't you see to it? No, don't wait for us, Mark. Go on ahead with the General. I know he needs you still."

And she turned her small perfect head to Irene for her ministrations.

With patent relief, Mark spurred ahead to catch up with the General, and Irene told Storm in honeyed tones,

"There's nothing in your eye, darling, except a touch of green."

"You bitch," hissed Storm.

"Darling, I don't know what you mean."

\* \* \*

The *Dunottar Castle* trembled under the thrust of her engines and ran southwards over a starlit sea that seemed to be sculpted from wet black obsidian, each crest marched with such weighty dignity as to seem solid and unmoving. It was only when the ship put her sharp prow into them that they burst into creaming white, and hissed back along the speeding hull.

The General paused and looked at the southern sky, to where the great cross burned among its myriad cohorts, and Orion the hunter brandished his sword.

"That's the way the sky should be," he nodded his approval. "I could never get used to the northern skies. It was as though the universe had disintegrated, and the grand designs of nature had been plunged into anarchy."

They went to the rail and paused there to watch the moon rise out of the dark sea, and as it pushed its golden dome clear of the horizon, the General pulled out the gold hunter watch from his waistcoat pocket and grunted. "Twenty-one minutes past midnight, the moon is punctual this morning." Mark smiled at the little joke. Yet he knew that it was part of the General's daily ritual to consult his almanac for sunrise and moonrise, and the moon phases. The man's energy was formidable.

They had worked until just a few minutes previously and had been at it since mid-morning. Mark felt muzzy and woolly-headed with mental effort and the pungent incense of the General's cigars which had filled the suite. .

"I think we overdid it a little today, my boy," Sean Courtney admitted, as though he had read the thought. "But I did want to be up to date before we dock in Table Bay. Thank you, Mark. Now why don't you go down and join the dancing?"

From the boat deck, Mark looked down on to the swirling orderly confusion of dancing couples in the break of the promenade deck. The ship's band was belting out a Strauss waltz and the dancers spun wildly, the women's skirts flaring open like the petals of exotic blooms and their laughing cries a sweet and musical counterpoint to the stirring strains of the waltz.

Mark picked Storm Courtney out of the press, her particular grace making it easy to distinguish her, she lay back in the circle of her partner's arms and spun dizzily, the light catching the dark sparkle of her hair and glowing on the waxy golden perfection of her bare shoulders.

Mark lit a cigarette, and leaned on the rail, watching her. It was strange that he had seldom felt lonely in the great silences and space of the wilderness, and here, surrounded by music and gaiety and the laughter of young people, he knew deep loneliness.

The General's suggestion that he go down and join the dancing had been unwittingly cruel. He would have been out of place there among the rich young clique who had known each other since childhood, a close-knit élite that jealously closed ranks against any intruder, especially one that did not possess the necessary qualifications of wealth and social standing.

He imagined going down and asking Storm Courtney for a waltz, her humiliation at being accosted by her father's secretary, the nudging and the snide exchanges, the patronizing questions. "Do you actually type letters, old boy?"

And he felt himself flushing angrily at the mere thought of it.

Yet he lingered by the rail for another half hour, delighting in each glimpse of Storm, and hating each of her partners with a stony implacable hatred; and when at last he went down to his cabin, he could not sleep. He wrote a letter to Marion Littlejohn, and found himself as warmly disposed towards her as he had been in months. Her gentleness and sincerity, and the genuineness of her affection for him were suddenly very precious assets. On the pages he recalled the visit she had made to Durban just before his departure. The General had been understanding and they had had many hours together during the two days. She had been awed by his new position, and impressed by his surroundings. However, their one further attempt at physical intimacy, even though it had been made in the security and privacy of Mark's cottage, had been, if anything, less successful than the first. Thre had been no opportunity, nor had Mark had the heart to break off their engagement, and in the end Mark had put her on the train to Ladyburg with relief, but now loneliness and distance had enhanced her memory. He wrote with real affection and sincerity, but when he had sealed the envelope, he found that he still had no desire for sleep.

He had found a copy of *Jock of the Bushveld* in the ship's library and was rereading the adventures of man and dog, and the nostalgic and vivid descriptions of African bush and animals with such pleasure, that his loneliness was forgotten. There was a light tap on the door of his cabin.

"Oh Mark, do let me hide in here for a moment." Irene Leuchars pushed quickly past him before he could protest, and she ordered, "Quickly, lock the door." Her tone made him obey immediately, but when he turned back to her he had immediate misgivings.

She had been drinking. The flush of her cheeks was not all rouge, the glitter in her eyes was feverish, and when she laughed it was unnaturally high.

"What's the trouble?" he asked.

"Oh God, darling, I have had the most dreadful time. That Charlie Eastman is absolutely hounding me. I swear I'm terrified to go back to my cabin."

"I'll talk to him," Mark offered, but she stopped him quickly.

"Oh, don't make a scene. He's not worth it." She flicked the tail of the ostrich feather boa over her shoulder. "I'll just sit here for a while, if you don't mind."

Her dress was made of layers of filmy material that floated in a cloud about her as she moved, and her shoulders were bare, the bodice cut so low that her breasts bulged out, very round and smooth and white and deeply divided.

"Do you mind?" she demanded, very aware of the direction of his eyes, and he lifted them quickly to her face. She made a moue of impatience as she waited for his reply. Her lipstick was startling crimson and glossy, so her lips had a full ripe look.

He knew he must get her out of his cabin. He knew that he was in danger. He knew how vulnerable he was, how powerful her family, and he guessed how shallow and callous she could be. But he was lonely, achingly grindingly lonely.

"You can stay, of course," he told her, and she drooped her eyelids and ran a sharp pink tongue across the painted lips.

"Have you got a drink, darling?"

"No, I'm sorry."

"Don't be, don't ever be sorry." She swayed against him and he could smell the liquor on her breath, but it was not offensive and, with her perfume, blended into a spicy fragrance.

"Look," she told him, holding up the silver evening bag she carried. "The 'It' girl with every home comfort," and she took a small silver jewelled flask from the bag. "Every comfort known to man," she repeated, and parted her lips in a lewd but intensely provocative pout.

"Come and I'll give you a little sample." Her voice dropped to a husky whisper, and then she laughed and swirled away in a waltzing turn, humming a bar of the Blue Danube and the gossamer of her skirts floated about her thighs. Clad in silk, her limbs gleamed in the soft light and when she dropped carelessly on to Mark's bunk, her skirts ballooned and then settled so high that he could see that the black elastic suspenderbelt that held her stocking tops was decorated with embroidered butterflies. The butterflies were spangled with brilliant colour and in exotic contrast to the pale soft skin of her inner thighs.

"Come, Markie, come and have a little itsy bitsy drinkie." She patted the bunk beside her and then wriggled her bottom across to make room for him. The skirts rucked up higher and exposed the wedge of her panties between her thighs. The material was so sheer that he could see the pale red-gold curls trapped and flattened by the silk.

Mark felt something crack inside him. For another moment he tried to reckon consequence, to force himself back on to the course that was both moral and safe, but he knew that in reality the decision had been made when he had allowed her to stay.

"Come, Mark." She held the flask like bait, and the light reflected off it in silver splinters that she played into his eyes. The crack opened, and like a bursting dam, all restraint was swept aside. She recognized the moment and her eyes flared with triumph and she welcomed him to the bed with a little animal squeal, and with slim pale arms that wrapped about his neck with startling strength.

She was small and strong, quick and demanding, and as skilled as Helena MacDonald—but she was different, so very different.

Her youth gave her flesh a sweetness and freshness, her skin an unblemished lustre, a luscious plasticity that was made more startling by her pale pigmentation.

When she slipped the strap off one shoulder and popped one of her glossy breasts out of the top of her bodice, offering it to Mark with a sound in her throat which was like the purr of a cat, he gasped aloud. It was white as porcelain and had the same sheen, too large for the slim fragile body but hard and firm and springy to his touch. The nipple was tiny, set like a small jewel in the perfect coin of its aureole, so pale and delicate pink when he remembered Helena, dark and puckered and sprinkled with sparse black hair.

"Wait, Mark. Wait," she chuckled breathlessly, and stood quickly to drop the boa and dress to the cabin floor in one quick movement, and then to slip the sheer underwear to her ankles and kick it carelessly aside. She lifted her hands above her head and twirled slowly in front of him.

"Yes?" she asked.

"Yes," he agreed. "Oh very much yes."

Her body was hairless and smooth except for that pale red mist that hazed the fat mound at the base of her belly, and her breasts rode high and arrogant.

She came back to him, kneeling over him.

"There," she whispered. "There's a good boy," she crooned, but her hands were busy, unbuckling, unbuttoning, questing, finding—and then it was her turn to gasp.

"Oh, Mark, you clever boy—all by yourself too!"

"No," he laughed. "I had a little help."

"And you are going to get a lot more," she promised, and dropped her soft, fluffy golden head over him. He thought that her mouth was as red and voracious as one of those low-tide rock-pool anemones that he had fed with such delight as a child, watching it softy enfold each tidbit, sucking it in deeply.

"Oh God," he croaked, for her mouth was hot—hotter and deeper than any sea animal could ever be.

\* \* \*

Irene Leuchars carried her shoes in one hand and the feather boa hung over her other arm and trailed on the floor behind her. Her hair stood out in a soft pale halo around her head, and her eyes were underlined by dark blue smudges of sleeplessness, while the outline of her mouth was smudged and blurred, her lips puffed and inflamed.

"God," she whispered, "I'm still tiddly," and she giggled, and lurched unsteadily to the roll of the ship. Then she pulled up the strap which had slipped from her shoulder.

Behind her in the long passageway, there was a clatter of china and she glanced back, startled. One of the white-jacketed stewards was pushing a trolley of cups and pots towards her. The morning ritual of tea and biscuits was beginning and she had not realized the hour.

Irene hurried away, turning the corner from the steward's sly and knowing grin, and she reached the door of Storm Courtney's cabin without another encounter.

She hammered on the door with the heel of one shoe, but it was a full five minutes before the door swung open and Storm looked out at her, a gown wrapped around her shoulders and her big dark eyes owlish from sleep.

"Irene, are you crazy?" she asked. "It's still night!" Then she saw Irene's attire and smelled the rich perfume of her breath. "Where on earth have you been?"

Irene pushed the door open and almost tripped over the threshold.

"You're drunk!" accused Storm resignedly, closing the door behind her.

"No." Irene shook her head. "It isn't liquor—it's ecstasy."

"Where have you been?" Storm asked again. "I thought you were in bed hours ago."

"I have flown to the moon," intoned Irene dramatically. "I have run barefooted through the stars, I have soared on eagles' wings above the mountain peaks."

Storm laughed, coming fully awake now, as beautiful even in *déshabillé* as Irene would never be, so graceful and lovely that Irene hated her again. She savoured the moment, drawing out the pleasure of anticipation.

"Where have you been? Storm asked again. "I thought you started to catch the spirit of the moment. Tell all!"

"Through the gates of paradise, to the land of never-never on the continent of always—" Irene's smile became sharp, spiteful and venomous, "in short, darling, Mark Anders has been bouncing me like a rubber ball!"

And the expression on Storm Courtney's face gave her the most intense satisfaction she had known in her life.

* * *

"On the third day of January, the Chamber of Mines deliberately tore up the Agreement that it had come to with your Union to maintain the status quo. It tore that agreement to a thousand pieces and flung them in the faces of the workers." Fergus MacDonald spoke with a controlled icy fury that carried to every corner of the great hall, and it stilled even the rowdies in the back seats who had brought their bottles in brown paper packets. Now they listened with intensity. Big Harry Fisher, sitting beside him on the dais, turned his head slowly to assess the man, peering at him under beetling eyebrows and with the bulldog folds of his face hanging mournfully. He marvelled again at how Fergus MacDonald changed when he stood to speak.

Usually he cut a nondescript figure with the small bulge of a paunch beginning to distort the spare frame, the cheap and ill-fitting suit shiny at the elbows and seat with wear, the collar of the frayed shirt darned, and grease spots on the drab necktie. His hair was thinning, starting up in wispy spikes around the neck, pushing back from the brow and with a pink bare patch in the crown. His face had that grey tone from the embedded filth of the machine shops, but when he stood under the red flag and the emblem of the Amalgamated Mineworkers Union on the raised dais facing the packed hall, he grew in stature, a physical phenomenon that was quite extraordinary. He seemed younger and there was a fierce and smouldering passion which stripped away his shoddy dress and armoured him with presence.

"Brothers!" He raised his voice now. "When the mines reopened after the Christmas recess, two thousand of our members were discharged, thrown out into the street, discarded like worn-out pairs of old boots——"

The hall hummed, the warning sound of a beehive on a hot summer's day, but the stillness of thousands of bodies pressed closely together was more menacing than any movement.

"Brothers!" Fergus moved his hands in a slow hypnotic movement. "Brothers! Beginning at the end of this month, and for every month after that, another six hundred men will be," he paused again and then spat the official word at them, "retrenched."

They seemed to reel with the word, the whole concourse stunned as though by a physical blow, and the silence drew out—until a voice at the back yelled wildly,

"No, brothers. No!"

They roared then, a sound like the surf on a stormy day when it breaks upon a rocky shore.

Fergus let them roar, and he hooked his thumbs into his rumpled waistcoat and watched them, gloating in the feeling of exultation, the euphoria of power. He judged the strength of their reaction, and the moment it began to falter he raised both hands, and almost immediately the silence fell upon the hall again.

"Brothers! Do you know that the wages of a black man are two shillings and two pence a day? Only a black man can live on that wage!" He let it sink in a moment, but not too long before he went on, asking a reasonable question, "Who will take the place of two thousand of our brothers who are now out of work? Who will replace the six hundred that will join them at the end of this month, and the next—and the next? Who will take *your* job," he was picking out individuals, pointing at them with an accuser's finger, "and *yours*, and *yours*? Who will take the food from your children's mouths?" He waited theatrically for an answer, cocking his head, smiling at them while his eyes smouldered.

"Brothers! I tell you who it will be. Two and tuppenny black kaffirs—that's who it will be!"

They came upon their feet, a bench here and there crashing over backwards and their voices were a blood-roar of anger, clenched fists thrust out in fury.

"No, brothers. No!" Their booted feet stamped in unison and they chanted, their fists punching into empty air.

Fergus MacDonald sat down abruptly and Harry Fisher congratulated him silently, squeezing his shoulder in a bear's paw before lumbering to his feet.

"Your executive has recommended that all members of our Union come out on general strike. I put it to you now, brothers, all those in favour—" he bellowed, and his voice was drowned in a thousand others.

"Out, brothers! We're out! Out! Out!"

Fergus leaned forward in his seat and looked down the length of the trestle table.

Helena's dark head was bowed over the minute book, but she sensed his gaze and looked up. Her expression glowed with a fanatic's ecstasy, and there was open adoration in her eyes that he saw only at moments like this. Harry Fisher had told him once, "For all women, power is the ultimate aphrodisiac. No matter how puny in body, no matter what he looks like—power makes a man irresistible."

In the thunder of thousands of voices, the pounding feet and the heady roar of power, Fergus was on his feet again.

"The mine-owners, the bosses have challenged us, they have scorned your executive, they have stated publicly that we are too faint-hearted to rally the workers and come out on general strike! Well, brothers, we are going to show them." The lion's voice of the crowd rose again and he silenced it only after another minute. "First, we are going to drive on the scabs, there are going to be no strike-breakers." When the sound subsided he went on, "Slim Jannie Smuts has talked of force to beat a strike, he has an army, but we are going to have one also. I think the bosses have forgotten that we fought their bloody war for them in

France and East Africa, at Tabora and Delville Wood." The names sobered them and they were listening again. "Last time we fought for them, but this time we are fighting for ourselves. Each one of you will report to his area commander—you will be formed into fighting commandos, each man will know his job, and each man will know what is at stake. We will beat them, brothers, the bloody bosses and their greedy grasping minions. We will fight them and beat them!"

\* \* \*

"They are organized into military-style commandos," said the Prime Minister softly, breaking the crisp brown roll of bread with fingers that were surprisingly small, neat and capable as a woman's. "Of course, we know that George Mason wanted to form labour commandos in 1914. It was the main reason I had him deported." The other guests at the luncheon table were silent. The deportation of Mason was not an episode that reflected credit on Jannie Smuts. "But this is a different animal we are dealing with now. Nearly all the younger members of the unions are trained veterans. Five hundred of them paraded outside the Trade Union Hall in Fordsburg last Saturday." He turned and smiled that impish, irresistible smile at his hostess. "My dear Ruth, you must forgive my bad manners. This talk detracts from the delicious meal you have provided."

The table was set under the oak trees on lawns so vivid green that Ruth always thought of them as "English green." The house itself had the solid imposing bulk of Georgian England, so different from the frivolous fairy castle at Emoyeni; the illusion of old England was spoiled only by the soaring cliffs of grey rock that rose as a backdrop to the scene. The sheer slopes of Table Mountain were softened by the pine trees that clung precariously for footholds on each ledge and in each tiny pocket of soil.

Ruth smiled at him. "In this house, General, you may do as you wish."

"Thank you, my dear." The smile flickered off his face and the merry twinkle of the pale blue eyes changed to the glint of swords, as he turned back to his listeners. "They are seeking confrontation, gentlemen, it's a blatant test of our power and resolution."

Ruth caught Mark's eye at the foot of the table and he rose to refill the glasses with cold pale wine tinged with a touch of green, dry and crisp and refreshing, but as he moved down the board, pausing beside each guest—three Cabinet ministers, a visiting British Earl, the Secretary of the Chamber of Mines—he was listening avidly.

"We can only hope you put it too highly, Prime Minister," Sean Courtney intervened gruffly. "They have only broomsticks with which to drill, and bicycles on which to ride into battle . . ."

And while they laughed, Mark paused behind Sean's chair with the bottle forgotten in his hand. He was remembering the cellars below the Trade Union Hall in Fordsburg, the racks of modern rifles, the gleaming P.14 reserved for him and the sinister squatting Vickers machine gun. When he returned to the present, the conversation had moved on.

Sean Courtney was assuring the company that militant action by the unions was unlikely, and that in the worst circumstances, the army was geared to immediate call-up.

Mark had a small office adjoining the General's study. It had previously been a linen room, but was just large enough to accommodate a desk and several shelves of files. The General had ordered a large window knocked through one wall to give it air and light, and now, with his ankles crossed and propped on the desk-top, Mark was staring thoughtfully out of the window. The view across lawns and through oaks encompassed a sweep of Rhodes Avenue, named after that asthmatic old adventurer who had seized an empire in land and diamonds, and ended up Prime Minister of the first Cape Parliament, before suffocating from his weak lungs and heavy conscience. The Cape home of the Courtneys was named Somerset Lodge after Lord

Charles, the nineteenth-century governor, and the great houses on the opposite side of Rhodes Avenue perpetuated the colonial tradition, Newlands House and Hiddingh House, gracious edifices in spacious grounds.

Looking out at them through the new window, Mark was comparing them with the miners' cottages in Fordsburg Dip. He had not thought of Fergus and Helena in many months, but the conversation at lunch had brought them back forcibly, and he felt himself torn by sharply contradictory loyalties.

He had lived in both worlds now, and seen how each opposed the other. He was trying to think without emotion, but always a single image intruded, the cruel shape of weapons in orderly racks, deep in a dark cellar, and the slick smell of gun oil in his throat.

He lit another cigarette, delaying the decision. Through the solid teak door, the sound of voices from the General's study was muted, the higher clearer tones of the Prime Minister, birdlike almost, set against the rumbling of Sean's replies.

The Prime Minister had stayed on after the other luncheon guests had left, as he often did, but Mark wished that he would leave now, thus deferring the decision with which he was wrestling.

He had been trusted by a comrade, somebody who had shared mortal danger with him, and then had unstintingly shared the hospitality of his home, had trusted him like a brother, had not hesitated to give him access to the direst knowledge, had not hesitated to leave him alone with his wife. Mark had betrayed half of that trust—and he stirred restlessly in his seat as he remembered those wicked stolen days and nights with Helena. Now must he betray the rest of the trust that Fergus MacDonald had placed in him?

Once more the image of racked weapons passed before his eyes; they faded only slowly to be replaced with a vivid shocking picture of a face.

It was the face of a marble angel, smooth and white and strangely beautiful, with blue eyes in pale blue sockets, a

burst of pale golden curls escaping from under the rim of
the steel helmet on to the smooth pale forehead—

Mark dropped his feet from the desk with a crash, fighting away the memory of the young German sniper, forcing
it from his mind, and coming to his feet abruptly.

He found that his hands were shaking and he crushed
out the cigarette and turned to the door. His knock was
over-loud and demanding, and the voice from beyond was
gruff with irritation.

"Come in." He stepped through. "What do you want,
Mark, you know I don't—" Sean Courtney cut himself
short and the tone of his voice changed to concern as he
saw Mark's face. "What is it, my boy?"

"I have to tell you something, sir," he blurted.

They listened with complete attention as he described his
involvement with the executive of the Communist Party,
and then broke off to steel himself for the final betrayal.

"These men were my friends, sir, they treated me as a
comrade. You must understand why I am telling you this,
please."

"Go on, Mark," Sean Courtney nodded, and the Prime
Minister had drawn back in his chair—still and quiet and
unobtrusive, sensing the struggle of conscience in which the
young man was involved.

"I came to believe that much of what they were striving
for was good and just—opportunity and a share of life for
every man, but I could not accept the methods they had
chosen to bring these about."

"What do you mean, Mark?"

"They are planning war, a class war, sir."

"You have proof of that?" Sean's voice did not rise, and
he asked the question carefully.

"Yes, I have." Mark drew a deep breath before he went
on. "I have seen the rifles and machine guns they have
ready for the day."

The Prime Minister shifted in his chair and then was still
again, but now he was leaning forward to listen.

"Go on," Sean nodded, and Mark told them in detail,

stating the unadorned facts, reporting exactly what he had seen and where, accurately estimating the numbers and types of every weapon, and finally ending,

"MacDonald led me to believe that this was only one arsenal, and that there were others, many others, on the Witwatersrand."

Nobody spoke for many seconds, and then the Prime Minister stood up and went to the telephone on Sean's desk. He wound the crank handle, and the whirr-whirr was loud and obtrusive in the silent room.

"This is the Prime Minister, General Smuts, speaking. I want a maximum priority connection with Commissioner Truter, the Chief of the South African Police in Johannesburg," he said, and then listened, his expression bleak and his eyes sparkling angrily. "Get me the Exchange Supervisor," he snapped and then turned to Sean, still holding the earpiece. "The line is down. Floods in the Karroo," he explained, "indefinite delay." Then he turned his attention back to the telephone and spoke quietly for many minutes with the Supervisor, before cradling the earpiece. "They will make the connection as soon as possible."

He returned to his seat by the window and spoke across the room. "You have done the right thing, young man."

"I hope so," Mark answered quietly, and the doubts were obvious, shadows in his eyes and the strains of misery in his voice.

"I'm proud of you, Mark," Sean Courtney agreed. "Once again you have done your duty."

"Will you excuse me now, please, gentlemen?" Mark asked, and without waiting for a reply, crossed to the door of his own office.

The two men stared at the closed teak door long after it had closed, and it was the Prime Minister who spoke first.

"A remarkable young man," he mused aloud. "Compassion and a sense of duty."

"He has qualities that could carry him to great heights, qualities for which one day we may be grateful," Sean nodded. "I sensed them at our first meeting, so strongly that I sought him out."

"We will need him—and others like him in the years ahead, old Sean," Jannie Smuts stated and then switched his attention. "Truter will have a search warrant issued immediately, and with God's help we will crush the head of the snake before it has a chance to strike. We know about this man MacDonald, and of course we have been watching Fisher for years."

\* \* \*

Mark had walked for hours, escaping from the tiny box of his office. He had been driven by his conscience and his fears, striding out under the oaks, following narrow lanes, crossing the little stone bridge over the Liesbeeck stream, torturing himself with thoughts of Judas.

"They hang traitors in Pretoria," he thought suddenly, and he imaged Fergus MacDonald standing on the trap in the barnlike room while the hangman pinioned his arms and ankles. He shuddered miserably and stopped walking, with his hands thrust deeply into his pockets and shoulders hunched, and he looked up to find himself standing outside the Post Office.

Afterwards he realized that it had probably been his destination all along, but now it seemed an omen. He did not hesitate a moment, but hurried into the office and found a pile of telegram forms on the desk. The nib of the pen was faulty and it spluttered the pale watery ink, and stained his fingers.

"MACDONALD 55 LOVERS WALK FORDSBURG.
THEY KNOW WHAT YOU HAVE GOT IN THE CELLAR GET RID OF IT."

He did not sign it.
The Post Office clerk assured him that if he paid the

seven pence for urgent rating, the message would have priority as soon as the northern lines were reinstated.

Mark wandered back into the street, feeling sick and depleted by the crisis of conscience, not certain that he had done the right thing in either circumstance, and he wondered just how futile was his hope that he might have forced Fergus MacDonald to throw that deadly cargo down some disused mine shaft before death and revolution was turned loose upon the land.

* * *

It was almost dark as Fergus MacDonald wheeled his bicycle into the shed and paused in the small back yard to slip the clips off the cuffs of his trousers, before going on to the kitchen door.

The smell of cooking cabbage filled the small room with a steamy moist cloud that made him pause and blink.

Helena was sitting at the kitchen table and she hardly glanced up as he entered. A cigarette dangled from her lips with an inch of grey ash clinging hopelessly to the end of it.

She still wore the grubby dressing-gown she had worn at breakfast, and it was clear that she had neither bathed nor changed since then. Her hair had grown longer and now dangled in oily black snakes to her cheeks. She had grown heavier in the last months, the line of her jaw blurring with a padding of fat and the hair on her upper lip darker and denser, breasts bulging and drooping heavily in the open front of the gown.

"Hello then, love." Fergus shrugged out of his jacket and dropped it across the back of a kitchen chair. She turned the page of the pamphlet she was reading, squinting at the curl of blue smoke that drifted across her eyes.

Fergus opened a black bottle of porter and the gas hissed fiercely. "Anything happened today?"

"Something for you," she nodded at the kitchen dresser, and the cigarette ash dropped down the front of her gown, settling in fine grey flakes.

Carrying the bottle, Fergus crossed to the dresser and fingered the buff envelope.

"One of your popsies," Helena chuckled at the unlikeliness of her sally, and Fergus frowned and tore open the envelope.

He stared at the message for long uncomprehending seconds before he swore bitterly. "Jesus Christ!" He slammed the bottle down on the kitchen table with a crash.

Even this late in the evening, there were small groups on each street corner. They had that disconsolate and bored air of men with too little to fill their days, even the commando drilling and the nightly meetings were beginning to pall. As Fergus MacDonald pedalled furiously through the darkening streets, his first alarm and fright turned to fierce exultation.

The time was right, they were as ready as they would ever be; if time drifted on without decisive action from either side, the long boring days of strike inactivity would erode their determination. What had seemed like disaster merely minutes before, he now saw was a heaven-sent opportunity. *Let them come, we will be ready for them,* he thought, and braked alongside a group of four loungers on the pavement outside the public bar of the Grand Fordsburg Hotel.

"Get a message to all area commanders, they are to assemble at the Trade Hall immediately. It's an emergency. Brothers, hurry."

They scattered quickly, and he pedalled on up the rising ground of the dip, calling out his warning as he went.

In the Trade Union offices, there were still a dozen or so members; most of them were eating sandwiches and drinking Thermos tea, while a few worked on the issue of strike relief coupons to Union families, but the relaxed atmosphere changed as Fergus burst in.

"All right, comrades, it's beginning. The ZARPS* are on their way."

---

*Zuid Afrikaanse Republiek Polisie, used as a derogatory term.

It was classic police tactics. They came in the first light of
dawn. The advance guard rode down into the dip of land
between Fordsburg and the railway crossing, where the Johannesburg road ran down between sleazy cottages and
overgrown plots of open ground, thick with weeds and
mounds of rotting refuse.

There was a heavy ground-mist in the dip, and the nine
troopers on police chargers waded through it, as though
fording the sluggish waters of a river crossing.

They had muted harness and muffled accoutrements, so
that it was in ghostly silence that they breasted the softly
swirling mists. The light was not yet strong enough to pick
out their badges and burnished buttons, it was only the
dark silhouette of their helmets that identified them.

Fifty yards behind the leading troopers followed the two
police carriages. High four-wheelers with barred windows to
hold prisoners, and beside each one of them marched ten
constables. They carried their rifles at the slope, and were
stepping out sharply to keep up with the carriages. As they
entered the dip, the mist engulfed them, chest-high, so that
their disembodied trunks bobbed in the white soft surface.
They looked like strange dark sea-animals, and the mist
muted the tramp of their boots.

Fergus MacDonald's scouts had picked them up before
they reached the railway crossing and for three miles had
been pacing them, slipping back unseen ahead of the advance, runners reporting every few minutes to the cottage
where Fergus had established his advance headquarters.

"All right," Fergus snapped, as another of the dark figures ducked through the hedge of the sanitary lane behind
the cottage and mumbled his report through the open window. "They are all coming in on the main road. Pull the
other pickets out and get them here right away."

The man grunted an acknowledgement and was gone.

Fergus had his pickets on every possible approach to the
town centre. The police might have split into a number of
columns, but it seemed his precautions were unnecessary. Secure in the certainty of complete surprise and in overwhelm-
ing force, they were not bothering with diversion or flanking maneuvres.

Twenty-nine troopers, Fergus calculated, together with
the four drivers, was indeed a formidable force. More than
sufficient, if it had not been for the warning from some
unknown ally.

Fergus hurried through into the front parlour of the cottage. The family had been moved out before midnight, all
the cottages along the road had been cleared. The grumpy
squalling children in pyjamas carried on the shoulders of
their fathers, the women with white frightened faces in the
lamplight, bundling a few precious possessions with them
as they hurried away.

Now the cottages seemed deserted, no lights showed, and
the only sound was the mournful howling of a mongrel dog
down in the dip. Yet in each cottage, at the windows that
faced on to the road, silent men waited.

Fergus spoke to one of them in a whisper and he pointed
down into the misty hollow, then spat and worked a round
into the breech of the Lee-Enfield rifle which was propped
on the windowsill.

The rifle bolt made a small metallic clash that lit a sparkle of memory and made the hair rise on Fergus' neck. It
was all so familiar, the silence, the mist and the night
fraught with the menace of coming violence.

"Only on my order," Fergus warned him softly. "Easy
now, lads. Let them come right in the front door before we
slam it on their heads."

He could see the leading horsemen now, half a mile
away but coming on fast in the strengthening light. It
wasn't shooting light yet, but the sky beyond the dark hills
of the mine dumps was turning to that pale gull's-egg blue
that promised shooting light within minutes.

Fergus looked back at the road. The mist was an added

bonus. He had not counted on that, but often when you did not call for fortune, she came a-knocking. The mist would persist until the first rays of the morning sun warmed and dispersed it—another half hour at least.

"You all know your orders." Fergus raised his voice and they glanced at him, distracted for only a moment from their weapons and the oncoming enemy.

They were all good men, veterans, blooded, as the sanguine generals of France would have it. It flashed through Fergus' mind once again how ironical it was that men who had been trained to fight by the bosses were now about to tear down the structure which the bosses had trained them to defend.

"We will tear down and rebuild," he thought, with exultation tingling in his blood. "We will destroy them with their own weapons, strangle them with their own dirty loot—" he stopped himself, and pulled the dark grey cloth down over his eyes and turned up the collar of his coat.

"Good luck to all of us, brothers," he called softly, and slipped out through the front door.

"That old bugger has got guts," acknowledged one of the soldiers at the window.

"You're right, he ain't afraid of nothing," agreed another, as they watched him dodge under the cover of the hedge and run forward until he reached the ditch beside the road, and jump down into it.

There were a dozen men lying there below the lip, and as he dropped beside them, one of them handed him a pick-handle.

"You strung that wire good and tight?" Fergus asked, and the man grunted.

"Tighter than a monkey's arsehole," the man grinned wolfishly at him, his teeth glinting in the first soft light of morning. "And I checked the pegs meself—they'll hold against a charging elephant."

"Right, brothers," Fergus told them. "With me when I give the word."

And he lifted himself until he could see over the low

blanket of mist. The troopers' helmets bobbed in the mist
as they came on up the slope, and now he could make out
the sparkle of brass cap badges and see the dark sticklike
barrels of their carbines rising above each right shoulder.

Fergus had paced out the ranges himself and marked
them with pieces of rag tied to the telephone posts on the
verge.

As they came up to the one-fifty-yard mark Fergus stood
up from the ditch, and stepped into the middle of the road.
He held his pick-handle above his head and shouted,

"Halt! Stay where you are!"

His men rose out of the mist behind him and moved
swiftly into position like a well-drilled team; dark, ominous
figures standing shoulder to shoulder, blocking the road
from verge to verge, holding their pick-handles ready
across their hips, faces hidden by caps and collars.

The officer in the centre of the squadron of horsemen
raised a hand to halt them and they bunched up and sat
stolidly while the officer rose in his stirrups.

"Who are you?"

"Strikers' Council," Fergus shouted back, "and we'll
have no scabs, black-legs or strike-breakers on this property!"

"I am under orders from the Commissioner of Police,
empowered by a warrant of the Supreme Court." The officer was a heavily built man, with a proud erect seat on his
horse, and a dark waxed moustache with points that stuck
out on each side of his face.

"You're strike-breakers!" Fergus yelled. "And you'll not
set a foot on this property."

"Stand aside!" warned the officer. The light was good
enough now for Fergus to see that he wore the insignia of a
Captain, and that his face was ruddy from sun and beer,
his eyebrows thick and dark and beetling under the brim of
his helmet. "You are obstructing the police. We will charge
if we have to."

"Charge and be damned, puppets of imperialism, running dogs of capitalism—"

"Troop, extend order," called the Captain, and the ranks opened for the second file to come up into a solid line. They sat on the restless horses, knee to knee.

"Strike-breakers!" yelled Fergus. "Your hands will be stained with the blood of innocent workers this day!"

"Batons!" called the Captain sternly, and the troopers drew the long oaken clubs from the scabbards at their knees and held them in the right hand, like cavalry sabres.

"History will remember this atrocity," screamed Fergus, "the blood of the lamb—"

"Walk, march! Forward!" The line of dark horsemen waded forward through the mist as it swirled about their booted legs.

"Gallop, charge!" sang out the Captain, and the riders swung forward in their saddles, the batons extended along the horses' necks, and they plunged forward; now the hooves drummed low thunder as they came down upon the line of standing figures.

The Captain was leading by a length in the centre of the line, and he went on to the wires first.

Fergus' men had driven the steel jumper bars deep into the verge, pounding them in with nine-pound hammers, until only two feet of their six-foot length protruded, and they had strung the barbed wire across the road, treble strands pulled up rigid with the fencing strainers.

It cut the forelegs out from the under the leading charger, the bone broke with a brittle snap, startlingly loud in the dawn, and the horse dropped, going over on to its shoulder still at full gallop.

An instant later the following wave of horsemen went on to the wire, and were cut down as though by a scythe, only three of them managing to wheel away in time. The cries of the men, and the screaming of the horses, mingled with the exultant yells of Fergus' band as they ran forward, swinging their pick-handles.

One of the horses was up, riderless, its stirrups flapping, but it was pinned on its haunches, the broken forelegs flap-

ping and spinning as it pawed in anguish at the air, its
squeals high and pitiful above the cries of fallen men.

Fergus pulled the revolver out of the waist-band of his
trousers, dodged around the crazed screaming animals and
pulled the police Captain to his knees.

He had hit the ground with his shoulder and the side of
his face. The shoulder was smashed, sagging down at a grotesque angle and the arm hanging twisted and lifeless. The
flesh had been shaved from his face, ripped off by stone
and gravel, so that the bone of his jaw was exposed in the
mangled flesh.

"Get up, you bastard," snarled Fergus, thrusting the pistol into the officer's face, grinding the muzzle into the lac-
erated wound. "Get up you bloody black-leg. We'll learn
you a lesson."

The three troopers who had escaped the wire had their
mounts under control, and had circled to pick up their
downed comrades, calling to them by name.

"Grab a stirrup, Heintjie!"

"Come on, Paul. Get up!"

Horses and men, milling and shouting and screaming in
the mist, a savage confused conflict, above which Fergus
raised his voice.

"Stop them, don't let the bastard get away," and his men
swung the pick-handles, dodging forward under the police
batons to thrust and hack at the horsemen, but they were
not quick enough.

With men hanging from each stirrup leather, the horsemen reared and wheeled away, leaving only the badly hurt
officer and another inert body lying among the wires and
the terribly mutilated animals, while the police escort was
doubling forward up the road in two columns.

Fergus saw them and fumed impatiently, trying to force
his captive to his feet, but the man was hardly capable of
sitting unaided.

The twenty constables stopped at fifty yards and one
rank knelt, while the others fell in behind them, rifles at the
ready. The command carried clearly.

"One round. Warning fire!"

The volley of musketry crashed out. Aimed purposely high, it hissed and cracked over the heads of the strikers, and they scattered into the ditch.

For one moment, Fergus hesitated and then he pointed the pistol into the air and fired three shots in rapid succession. It was the agreed signal, and instantly a storm of rifle fire crashed from the silent cottages along the road, the muzzle flashes of the hidden rifles dull angry red in the dawn. The fire swept the road.

Fergus hesitated a second only and then he lowered the pistol. It was a Webley .455, a British officer's sidearm. The police Captain saw his intention in his eyes, the merciless glare of the stooping eagle, and he mumbled a plea through his mangled lips, trying to lift hands to protect his face.

The pistol shot was lost in the storm of rifle fire from the cottages, and the answering police fire as they fell back in confusion into the dip.

The heavy lead bullet smashed into the Captain's open pleading mouth, knocking the two front teeth out of his upper jaw, and then it plunged on into his throat and exited through the back of his skull in a scarlet burst of blood and bone chips, clubbing him down into the dirt of the roadway—while Fergus turned and darted away under the cover of the hedge.

\* \* \*

Only at Fordsburg were the police raids repelled, for at the other centres there had been no warning, and the strikers had not taken even the most elementary precautions of placing sentries.

At the Trades Hall in Johannesburg, almost the entire leadership of the strike was assembled, meeting with the other unions who had not yet come out, but were considering sympathetic action. There were representatives of the Boilermakers' Society, the Building and Allied Trades, the

Typographical Union and half a dozen others—together
with the most dynamic and forceful of the strikers. Harry
Fisher was there, Andrews and Ben Caddy, and all the others.

The police were into the building while they were deep
in dialectic, debating the strategy of the class struggle, and
the first warning they had was the thunderous charge of
booted feet on the wooden staircase.

Harry Fisher was at the head of the conference table,
slumped down in his chair with his tangled wiry hair hanging on to his forehead and his thumbs hooked in his braces,
his sleeves rolled up around the thick hairy arms.

He was the only one to move. He leaned across the table
and grabbed the rubber stamp of the High Council of Action and thrust it into his pocket.

As the rifle butts smashed in the lock of the Council
Chamber, he leapt to his feet and thrust his shoulder into
the shuttered casement. It burst open and, with surprising
nimbleness for such a big man, he slipped through it.

The façade of the Trades Hall was heavily encrusted
with fancy cast-iron grille work, and it gave him hand-
holds. Like a bull gorilla, he swarmed up on to the third-
floor ledge and worked his way to the corner.

Below him he heard the crash of overturning furniture,
the loud challenges of the arresting officers and the outraged cries of the labour leaders.

With his back pressed to the wall and his hands spread
out to balance himself, Harry Fisher peered around the
corner into the main street. It swarmed with uniformed police, and more squads were marching up briskly. An officer
was directing men to the side alleys to surround the building, and Harry Fisher drew back quickly and looked
around him for escape.

It was senseless to re-enter another window, for the
whole building was noisy with the tramp of feet and
shouted orders.

Fifteen feet below him was the roof of a bottle store and

general dealer's shop, but the alleyway between was ten feet wide and the roof of galvanized corrugated iron.

If he jumped, the noise he would make on landing would bring police running from all directions—yet he could not stay where he was. Within minutes the building would be surrounded.

He inched sideways to the nearest downpipe and began to climb. He reached the overhang of the roof and had to lean out to get a grip on the rim of the guttering, then he kicked his feet clear and hung from his arms. The drop of fifty feet below him sucked at his heels, and the guttering creaked and sagged perceptively under his weight—but he drew himself up on his arms, wheezing and straining until he could hook one elbow over the gutter and wriggle the rest of his body up and over the edge.

Still panting from the effort, he crawled slowly round the steeply gabled roof and peered down into the main street, just as the police began hustling the strike leaders out ot the front doors.

Fifty helmeted constables with sloped rifles had formed a hollow square in the road, and the strikers were pushed into it, some of them bare-headed and in their shirt-sleeves.

Already a crowd was forming on the sidewalks, and every minute it swelled, as the news was shouted from door to door and the curious hurried from every alleyway.

Harry Fisher counted the prisoners as they were brought out and the total was twenty before the mood of the crowd began changing.

"That's it, comrades," Harry Fisher grunted, and wished he could have been down there to lead them. They surged angrily up to the police lines, calling to the prisoners and hissing and booing the officer who ordered them, through a speaking trumpet, to disperse.

Mounted police wheeled into line, pushing the crowd back and as the last prisoner was led out, the escort stepped out, maintaining its rigid box-formation which enclosed the dejected huddle of strikers.

Somebody began to sing the "Red Flag," but the voices

that joined in were thin and tuneless, and the escort moved off towards the fort, carrying away not only most of the strike leadership but all of its moderate faction, those who had so far counselled against violence, against criminal activity and bloody revolution.

Harry Fisher watched them go with a rising sense of triumph. In one stroke he had been given a band of martyrs for the cause and had all serious opposition to his extreme views swept away. He had also in his hip pocket the seal of the Action Committee. He smiled a thin, humourless grin and settled down on the canted roof-top to wait for nightfall.

*    *    *

Mark Anders carried the General's heavy crocodile-skin briefcase down the steps to the Rolls and placed it on the seat beside the chauffeur while he gave him his instructions.

"To Groote Schuur first, and then to the City Cub for lunch." He stood back as the General came out of the house and paused on the top step to kiss his wife as though he were about to leave on a crusade to far places. He smothered her in a vast bear-hug and when he released her, he whispered something in her ear that made her bridle and slap his shoulder.

"Off with you, sir," she told him primly, and Sean Courtney came down the steps looking mightily pleased with himself, and grinned at Mark.

"The Prime Minister is making a statement to the House today, Mark. I'll want to see you directly afterwards."

"Very well, sir," Mark returned the grin.

"I'll look for you in the visitors' gallery as soon as he's finished, and give you the nod. Then we'll meet in the lobby and I'll see you up to my office."

Mark helped him into the back seat of the Rolls while he was speaking. He was always clumsy and awkward when moving sideways on to the bad leg, nevertheless he resented the helping hand fiercely, hating any weakness in himself even more than he disliked it in others, and he shrugged Mark's hand away the moment he was comfortably seated.

Mark ignored the gesture and went on levelly,

"Your notes for the Cabinet meeting are in the first folder," he indicated the crocodile bag on the front seat beside the chauffeur, "and you are lunching at the Club with Sir Herbert. The House sits at 2.15 and you have three questions from Opposition members, even Hertzog himself has one for you." Sean growled like an old lion bated by the pack.

"That bastard!"

"I have your replies clipped to your Order Paper. I checked with Erasmus and then I added a few little touches of my own, so please have a look at them before you stand up—you may not approve."

"I hope you stuck it to them hard!"

"Of course," Mark smiled again. "With both barrels."

"Good boy," Sean nodded. "Tell him to drive on."

Mark watched the Rolls go down the driveway, check at the gates and then swing out into Rhodes Avenue, before he turned back into the house.

Instead of going down the passageway to his own office, Mark paused in the hall and glanced guiltily about him. Ruth Courtney had gone back into the domestic depths of the kitchen area and there were no servants in sight.

Mark took the stairs three at a time, swung through the gallery and down to the solid teak door at the end.

He did not knock but turned the handle and went in, closing the door behind him quietly.

The stench of turpentine was a solid shock that made his eyes water for a few seconds until they adjusted.

Mark knew that he was quite safe. Storm Courtney never emerged before mid-morning from that sacrosanct area beyond the double doors that were painted with gold cherubim and flying doves. Since arriving in Cape Town, Storm Courtney had kept such hours that even her father had grumbled and huffed.

Mark found himself lying awake at night, just as he was sure the General did, listening for the crunch of wheels on the gravel drive, straining his ears for the faint sounds of gay voices and mentally judging the length and passion of each farewell, troubled by feelings to which he could not place a name.

His relations with Storm had retrogressed drastically. In Natal there had been the beginnings of a relaxed acceptance and undertones of warmth. It had begun with a smile and a friendly word from Storm, then he had escorted her on the daily ride, driven with her to South Beach to swim in the warm surf and sat in the sun arguing religion with her instead. Storm was going through a fashionable period of spiritualism and Mark had felt it his duty to dissuade her.

From religion, the next step had been when Storm had announced, "I need a partner to practise a new dance with."

Mark had wound the gramophone, changed the needles and danced to Storm's instruction.

"You really are quite good, you know," she had told him magnanimously, smiling up at him, light and graceful in his arms as they spun around the empty ballroom of Emoyeni.

"You would make a crippled blacksmith look good."

"Oh la!" she laughed. "You are the gallant, Mr. Anders!"

This had all changed abruptly. Since they had arrived in Cape Town she had neither smiled nor spoken directly to him, and Irene Leuchars, who was to have been a house guest of Storm's for four months, stayed only one night, and then caught the next mailship home.

Her name had not been mentioned again, and Storm's hostility to Mark had been so intense that she could hardly bear to be in the same room with him.

Now Mark felt like a thief in her studio, but he had not

been able to resist the temptation to steal a glimpse of the progress she had made on her latest canvas.

Full-length windows had been put into the north wall for the light, and they looked out on the mountain. Storm's easel stood in the centre of the bare uncarpeted floor—and the only other items of furniture were the artist's stool, a carpenter's table cluttered with paint pots and a chair on the raised model's dais.

Framed canvases in all sizes and shapes were stacked against the walls, most of them still blank. At one stage, during the period of friendliness, she had even asked Mark to help with the timber framework. He felt a pang when he remembered; she was a ruthless supervisor, checking every joint and tack with a perfectionist's meticulous care.

The canvas was almost completed, and he wondered when she had found time to do so much work in the last few days, and realized that he had misjudged her. She had been working in the mornings when he had believed she was lying abed, but now he became absorbed by the picture.

He stood before it with his hands thrust into his pockets and felt a glow of pleasure spread slowly through his body.

It was a picture of trees, a forest glade with sunlight playing on earth and rock and two figures—a woman in a white dress, stooping to gather wild flowers, while a man sat aside, sprawled against a tree trunk and watching her.

Mark was aware that it was a great advance on anything she had painted before, for although it was a simple picture, it evoked in him an emotion so strong that he felt it choke in his throat. He was awed by the peculiar talent which could have produced this work.

He marvelled at how she had taken reality and refined it, captured its essence and made of it an important occasion.

Mark thought how it was possible for an untrained eye to pick out special talent in any field, just as a person who had never watched *épée* used before would recognize a great swordsman after the first exchange; now Mark, who knew nothing of painting, was moved by the discovery of real beauty.

The latch clicked behind him, and he spun to face it. She was well into the studio before she saw him. She stopped abruptly and her expression changed. Her whole body stiffened and her breathing sounded stifled.

"What are you doing here?"

He had no answer for her, but the mood of the picture was still on him. "I think that you will be a great artist one day."

She faltered, taken completely off balance by the compliment and its obvious sincerity, and her eyes slipped away to the picture. All the antagonism, all the haughtiness drained from her.

Suddenly she was just a very young girl in a baggy smock, smeared and daubed with oil paint, and with a wash of pleased and modest colour spreading over her cheeks.

He had never seen her like this, so artless—so open and vulnerable. It was as though for a moment she had unveiled the secret compartments of her soul to allow him to see where she kept her real treasures.

"Thank you, Mark," she said softly, and she was no longer the glittering butterfly, the spoiled flighty little rich girl, but a creature of substance and warmth.

The rush of his own feelings must have been as obvious—he had almost succumbed to the desire he felt to take her in his arms and hold her hard—for she stepped back a pace, looking flustered and uncertain of herself, as though she had read his intention.

"And yet you won't slide out of it that easily." The curtains were drawn hastily across the secret places, and the old familiar ring was in her voice. "This is my private place, even my father wouldn't dare come in here—without my permission first obtained."

The change was extraordinary. It was like a superb actress slipping into a familiar role, she even stamped her foot, a gesture that he found suddenly insupportable.

"It won't happen again," he assured her brusquely, and he stepped to the doorway, passing her closely. He was so angry he felt himself trembling.

"Mark!" She stopped him imperiously, but it was with an effort he forced himself to turn back; his whole body felt rigid, and his lips were numb and stiff with anger.

"My father asks permission to come in here," she told him, and then she smiled, a slightly tremulous but utterly enchanting thing. "Couldn't you just do the same?"

She had him off balance, his anger not fully aroused before she assuaged it with that smile, he felt the rigidity melting out of his body, but she had turned to the bench and was clattering her pots busily and she spoke without looking up.

"Close the door as you leave," she instructed, a princess tossing an order to a serf. His anger, not yet fully assuaged, flared again brightly and he strode to the door with his heels clashing on the bare boards and he was about to slam it with all of his strength, and hope that it smashed off its hinges, when she stopped him again.

"Mark!"

He stopped, but could not bring himself to answer.

"I will be coming down to Parliament with you this afternoon. We will leave directly after lunch—I want to hear General Smuts' speech, my father says it will be important."

He thought that if he tried to answer her, his lips might tear, they felt as stiff and brittle as parchment.

"Oh dear," she murmured. "I had completely forgotten—when addressing Mark Anders Esquire, one must always say please!"

She crossed her hands demurely in front of her, hung her head in a caricature of contrition and made those dark blue eyes huge and soulful.

"Please may I ride to Parliament with you today? I would be ever so grateful, I really would. And now you can slam the door."

"You should be on the stage—you're wasted as a

painter," he told her, but he closed the door with studied deliberation and she waited to hear the latch click before she dropped into the model's chair, and began to shake with laughter, hugging herself delightedly.

Gradually the laughter dried up, but she was still smiling as she selected a blank canvas from the stock and placed it on the easel.

Working with charcoal, she blocked in the shape of his head, and it was right at the first attempt.

"The eyes," she whispered, "his eyes are the key." And she smiled again as they appeared miraculously out of the blank canvas, surprised that she had them fixed perfectly in her mind. She began to hum softly as she worked, completely absorbed.

\* \* \*

The Assembly Chamber of Parliament House was a high square hall, tiered with the galleries for Press and visitors. It was panelled in dark carved indigenous wood, and the canopy above the Speaker's chair was ornately worked in the same wood.

Softly muted green carpeting set off the richer green leather of the members' benches, and every seat was filled, the galleries crowded, but the silence that gripped that concourse was of extraordinary intensity, a cathedral hush into which the high piping voice of the Prime Minister carried clearly. He made a slight but graceful figure as he stood in his seat below the Speaker's dais.

"The entire Witwatersrand complex is passing slowly into the hands of the red commandos—" He used his hands expressively, and Mark leaned forward to obtain a better view. The movement brought his outer leg against Storm Courtney's, and he was aware of the warmth of her thigh against his during the rest of the speech. "Three members of the police have been killed in a brutal attack at Fordsburg, and two others have been critically injured in clashes with strikers' commandos. These groups are armed with modern pattern military firearms, and they are marching freely through the streets in quasi-military formations, committing acts of outrage on innocent members of the public, on public officers going about their duties, on all who cross their paths. They have interfered with public services, transport, power and communication, and have attacked and occupied police stations."

Sean Courtney, who had been slumped in his front bench seat with one hand covering his eyes, lifted his head and said "Shame!" in a sonorous voice; it was his third-whisky voice, and Mark could not help but grin as he guessed that the club lunch had fortified him for the session.

"Shame indeed," Smuts agreed. "Now the strikers have gathered about them all the feckless and dissolute elements in the community, their mood has become ugly and threatening. Legitimate strike action has given way to a reign of terror and criminal violence. Yet the most disturbing aspect of this terrible business is that the management of this labour dispute—or should I say, the stage-managing of the strike—has passed into the hands of the most reckless and lawless men, and these men seek nothing less than the overthrow of civilized government, and a rule of Bolshevik anarchy."

"Never!" boomed Sean, and the cry was taken up across the assembly.

"This house, and the whole nation is faced by the prospect of bloodshed and violence on a scale which none of us expected or believed possible."

The silence was unbroken now as Smuts went on carefully.

"If any blame attaches to this Government, it is that we have been too patient and shown too much forbearance for the miners' grievances; we have allowed them too much latitude, too much expression of their demands. This was because we have always been aware of the temper of the nation, and the rights of individuals and groups to free expression."

"Quite right too," Sean agreed, and, "Hear! Hear!" answered, "Hoor! Hoor!" across the floor.

"Now, however, we have been forced to reckon the cost of further forbearance—and we have found it unacceptable." He paused and bowed his head for a moment, and when he lifted it again, his expression was bleak and cold. "Therefore a state of martial law now exists throughout the Union of South Africa."

The silence persisted for many seconds, and then a roar of comment and question and interjection filled the house. Even the galleries buzzed with confusion and speculation, and the Press reporters jostled and fought each other at the exit doors in the race to reach a telephone.

Martial law was the weapon of last resort, and had only been used once before, during the 1916 rebellion, when De Wet had raised his commandos again and ridden against Botha and Smuts. Now there were cries of protest and anger from the Opposition benches, Hertzog shaking his fist and his pince-nez glinting, while the Government members were also on their feet voicing their support. The Speaker's vain cries of "Order! Order!" were almost drowned in the uproar.

Sean Courtney was signalling to Mark in the gallery, and he acknowledged and helped Storm to her feet, shielding her through the excited press of bodies as they left the gallery and went down the passage to the staircase.

The General was waiting for them at the visitors' entrance. He was scowling and dark-faced with concern, a measure of his agitation was the perfunctory kiss he dropped on Storm's uplifted face before turning to Mark.

"A pretty business, my boy." He seized his elbow. "Come on, let's go where we can talk," and he led them to the members' entrance, and up the stairs under the portraits of stern-faced Chief Justices to his own office.

Immediately the door was closed, he waved Storm away to one of the chairs, and told Mark, "The regiment was called out at ten o'clock this morning. I managed to get Scott on the telephone at his home—and he's got it in hand. He's a good man. They will be fully mobilized by now, and there is a special train being made up. They will entrain and leave for the Witwatersrand at eleven o'clock tonight, in full battle order."

"What about us?" Mark demanded. Suddenly he was a soldier again and he dropped neatly into the role. His place was with the regiment.

"We'll join there. We leave tonight. We are going up in convoy with the Prime Minister, and we'll travel all night—you will drive one of the cars." Sean was at his desk now, beginning to pack his briefcase. "How long will it take us?"

"It's a thousand miles, sir," Mark pointed out.

"I know that, damn it," snapped Sean. "How long?" Sean had never liked nor understood the internal combustion engine, and his dislike showed in his ignorance of their speed and capability whereas he could finely judge a journey by wagon or horseback.

"We won't be there before tomorrow evening—it's a hell of a road."

"Bloody motorcars," Sean growled. "The regiment will be there before us by rail."

"They've only three hundred miles to go." Mark felt obliged to come to the defence of the car, and Sean grunted.

"I want you to get on home now. Have my wife pack my campaign bag and get your duffle together. We'll leave immediately I get home." He turned to Storm. "Go along with Mark, now, Missy. I'm going to be busy here for a while."

\* \* \*

Mark strapped up his bag, and reflected how his worldly possessions had multiplied since he had joined the Courtney household. There had been a time when he could carry everything he owned in his pockets—the thought was broken by a knock on the door.

"Come in," he called, expecting a servant. Only Ruth Courtney ever came down this end of the house on her weekly inspection, a determined crusade against dust and cockroaches.

"Please take it down to the car," he said in Zulu, adjusting his uniform cap in the mirror above the wash-basin.

"All on my own?" Storm asked sweetly in the same language, and he turned startled.

"You shouldn't be here."

"Why not—am I in danger of violation and ravishment?" She had closed the door and leaned against it, her hands behind her back, but her eyes bold and teasing.

"It would be safer, I should imagine, to attempt to ravish a swarm of hornets."

"That was merely boorish, coarse and insulting," she said. "You really are improving immensely." And she looked at the strapped case on the bed.

"I was going to offer to help you pack—most men are hopeless at that. But I see you've managed. Is there anything else I can do for you?"

"I am sure I could think of something," he said with a solemn expression, but something in the tone of his voice made her smile and caution him.

"Not too much improvement in one day, please." She crossed to the bed and bounced on it experimentally. "God! Who filled it with bricks? No wonder Irene Leuchars went home! The poor darling must have sprained her back!" Her expression was innocent, but her gaze raked him and Mark felt himself blushing furiously. Suddenly, much that had puzzled him was clear, and as he turned back to the mirror, he wondered how she had found out about Irene. For something to do, he tipped the brim of his cap.

"Beautiful," she agreed. "Are you going up there to brutalize those poor strikers—or to bounce on their wives also?" And before he could give expression to the shock he felt she went on, "Funnily enough, I didn't really come down here to fight with you. I once had another old tomcat and I was really very fond of him, but he got run over by a car. Have you got a cigarette, Mark?"

"You don't smoke." He had found it difficult to keep up with the conversation.

"I know—but I have decided to learn. It's so suave, don't you think?" Suave was the fashionable word at that moment.

She held the cigarette with an exaggerated vampish pose after he had lit it.

"How do I look?"

"Bloody awful," he said, and she batted her eyes and took a tentative draw, held it for a moment and then started to cough.

"Here, give it to me." He took it away from her, and it tasted of her mouth. He felt the ache in his body, the terrible wanting, mingled now with a strange tenderness he had never felt before. She seemed, for once, so tender and young.

"Will it be dangerous?" she asked, suddenly serious.

"I don't think so—we'll be just like policemen."

"They are killing policemen." She stood up and walked to the window. "The view is dreadful, unless you like dustbins. I'd complain, if I were you." She turned back to face him.

"I've never seen a man off to war before. What should I say?"

"I don't know. Nobody ever saw me off before."

"What did your mother say?"

"I never knew my mother."

"Oh Mark. I'm sorry. I didn't mean to—" Her voice trailed off, and he was shocked to see that her eyes were brimming with tears.

"It doesn't matter," he assured her quickly, and she turned back to the window.

"Actually, you can just see the top of Devil's Peak, if you twist your head." Her voice was thick and nasal, and it was many seconds before she turned back.

"Well, we're both new to this, so we'll just have to help each other."

"I suppose you should say, 'Come back soon.' "

"Yes, I suppose I should—and then what do I do?"

"You kiss me." It was out before he had thought about it, and he was stunned by his own audacity.

She stood very still, rooted by the words, and when she began to move, it was with the slow deliberation of a sleep-walker, and her eyes were huge and unblinking. She came across the room.

She stopped in front of him, and, as she lifted her arms, she came up on her toes.

The air about her was filled with her fragrance, and her arms were slim and strong about his neck, but it was the softness and the warmth of her lips that amazed him.

Her body swayed against him, and seemed to melt with his own, and the long artistic fingers slowly caressed the nape of his neck.

He passed an arm around her waist, and was again amazed at how narrow and slim it was; but the muscles of her back were firm and pliant as she arched it, pushing forward with her hips.

He heard her gasp as she felt him, and a slow voluptuous shudder shook her. For long moments she lingered, her hips pressed to his and her breasts flattened against his tunic.

He stooped over her, his hands beginning to move up the hard resilient little back, his mouth forcing hers open so the soft lips parted like the fleshy red petals of an exotic blooming orchid.

She shuddered again, but then the sound in her throat turned into a panicky moan of protest and she twisted out of his arms, though he tried desperately to hold her. But she was strong and supple and determined.

At the door, she stopped to stare at him. She was trembling, her eyes were wide and dark, as though she had truly only seen him for the first time. "Oh la! Who was talking about swarms of hornets!" she mocked, but her voice was gusty and unsteady.

She twisted the door open, and tried to smile, but it was a poor lopsided thing, and she did not yet have control of her breathing. "I'm not so sure of that 'Come back soon' any more." She held the door open to give herself courage, and her next smile was more convincing, "Don't get run over, you old tomcat," and she slipped out into the passageway. Her receding footsteps were light and dancing in the silence of the big house, and Mark's own legs were suddenly so weak that he sat down heavily on his bed.

\* \* \*

Mark drove fast, concentrating all his attention on the twisting treacherous road through the mountains, driving the big heavily laden Rolls down the path of its own glaring brass-bound headlights, up Baines Kloof where the mountain fell away on his left hand sheer into the valley, past Worcester with its orderly vineyards standing in dark lines in the moonlight, before the final ascent up the Hex River Mountains to the rim of the flat compacted shield of the African interior.

They came out over the top, and the vast land stretched away ahead of them, the dry treeless karroo, where the flat-topped kopjes made strangely symmetrical shapes against the cold starry sky.

Now at last, Mark could relax in the studded leather driver's seat, driving instinctively, the road pouring endlessly towards him, pale and straight out of the darkness, and he could tune his ears to the voices of the two men in the rear seat.

"What they don't understand, old Sean, is that if we do not employ every black man who offers himself for work—no, more than that, if we don't actively recruit all the native labour we can get hold of—it will result not only in fewer jobs for white men, but, in the long run, it will mean, finally, no jobs at all for the white men of Africa."

A jackal, small and furry as a puppy, lolloped into the path of the headlights with its ears erect, and Mark steered carefully to miss it, his own ears cocked for Sean's reply.

"They think only of today." His voice was deep and grave. "We must plan for ten years from now—for thirty, fifty years ahead, for a nation firm and undivided. We cannot afford once again to have Afrikander against Briton, or worse, we dare not have white against black. It is not enough that we are forced to live together, we must learn to work together."

"Slowly, slowly—old Sean," the Prime Minister chuckled. "Don't let dreams run away with reality."

"I don't deal in dreams, Jannie. You should know that. If we don't want to be torn to pieces by our own people, we must give all of them, black, white and brown, a place and a share."

They ran on hard into the endless land, and the light of a lonely farm house on a dark ridge emphasized how vast and empty it was.

"Those who clamour so loudly for less work and more pay may find that what benefit they get now will have to be paid for a thousand per cent interest some day in the future. A payment in misery and hunger and suffering," Sean Courtner was speaking again. "If we are to steer off the reef of national disaster, then men will have to learn to work again, and to take seriously once more the demands of a disciplined and orderly society."

"Have you ever wondered, Sean, at how many people these days depend for their livelihood on nothing else but finding areas of dispute between the employers and the employed, between labour and management?"

Sean nodded, taking it up where Smuts left off. "As though the two were not shackled to each other with bonds that nothing can break. They travel the same road, to the same goal, bound together irretrievably by destiny. When one stumbles, he brings the other down on bloody knees, when one falls the other comes down with him."

Slowly, as the stars made their circuit of grandeur across

the heavens, the talk in the back seat of the Rolls dwindled into silence.

Mark glanced in the mirror and saw that Sean Courtney was asleep, a travelling rug about his shoulders and his black beard on his chest.

His snores were low and regular and deep, and Mark felt a rush of feeling for the big man. It was a fine mixture of respect and awe, of pride and affection. "I suppose that is what you would feel, if you had a father," he thought, and then, embarrassed by the strength and presumption of his feeling, he once again concentrated all his attention on the road.

The night wind had shifted the sky with fine dust, and the dawn was a thing of unbelievable splendour. From horizon to horizon, and right across the vaulted domes of the heavens, vibrant colour throbbed and glowed and flamed, until at last the sun thrust clear of the horizon.

"We won't stop in Bloemfontein or any of the big towns, Mark. We don't want anybody to see the Prime Minister." Sean leaned across the back of the seat.

"We'll need petrol, General."

"Pick one of the roadside pumps," Sean instructed. "Try and find one with no telephone lines."

It was a tiny iron-roofed general dealer's store set back from the road under two scraggy eucalyptus blue gum trees. There was no other building in sight, and the open empty veld stretched dry and sun-seared to the circle of the horizon. The plaster walls of the store were cracked and in need of whitewash, plastered with advertisement boards for Bovril and Joka tea. The windows were shuttered and the door locked, but there were no telephone lines running from the solitary building to join those that followed the road, and a single red-painted petrol pump stood at rigid attention in the dusty yard below the step.

Mark blew a long continuous blast on the Rolls' horn, and while he was doing so, the Prime Minister's black Cadillac that was following turned off the main road and parked behind them. The driver and the three members of the ministerial staff climbed out and stretched their stiff muscles.

When the proprietor of the store emerged at last, unshaven, red-eyed, but cheerfully doing up his breeches, he spoke no English. Mark asked in Afrikaans,

"Can you fill up both cars?"

While the storekeeper swung the handle of the pump back and forth, and the fuel rose alternatively into the two one-gallon glass bowls on the top of the pump, his wife came out from the store with a tray of steaming coffee mugs and a platter of crisp golden freshly baked rusks. They ate and drank gratefully, and were ready to go on again within twenty minutes.

The storekeeper stood in the yard, scratching the stubble of his beard and watched the twin columns of red dust billowing into the northern sky. His wife came out on to the stoep and he turned to squint up at her.

"Do you know who that was?" he asked, and she shook her head.

"That was Clever Jannie—and his English gunmen. Didn't you see the uniform the young one wore?" He spat into the red dirt, and his phlegm balled and rolled. "Khaki! Damned khaki!" He ripped the word out bitterly, and went around the side of the building to the little lean-to stable.

He was clinching the girth on the old sway-backed grey mare, when she followed him into the stall.

"It's none of our business, Hendrick. Let it stand."

"None of our business?" he demanded indignantly. "Didn't I fight khaki in the English war, didn't I fight it again in 1916 when we rode with old De Wet—isn't my brother a rock-breaker on the Simmer and Jack mine, and isn't that where Clever Jannie is going with his hangmen?"

He swung up on the mare and put his heels to her. She jumped away, and he pointed her at the ridge. It was eight miles to the railway siding, and there was a telegraph in the ganger's cottage; the ganger was a cousin of his. The Railway Workers' Union was out in sympathy with the miners now. The Action Committee would have the news in Johannesburg by lunch time that Clever Jannie was on his way.

* * *

While Mark Anders drank coffee at the wayside store, Fergus MacDonald lay under the hedge at the bottom of a garden ablaze with crimson cannas in orderly beds, and peered through a pair of binoculars down the slope at the Newlands Police Station. They had sand-bagged the windows and doors.

The lady of the house had sat on her veranda the previous evening, drinking coffee and counting forty-seven police constables arriving by motor lorry to reinforce the station. Her son was a shift boss on the Simmer and Jack. Whoever commanded the police at Newlands was no soldier, Fergus decided, and grinned that wolfish wicked grin.

He had seen the dead ground instantly, any soldier would have picked it up at a glance.

"Pass the word for the Mills bombs," he muttered to the striker beside him, and the man crawled away.

Fergus swung the glasses up along the road where it started to climb the kopjes, and grunted with satisfaction. The telephone wires had been cut, along with the power lines. He could see the loose ends dangling from the poles.

The police station was isolated.

The striker crawled back to Fergus' side, dragging a heavy rucksack. He had a tooth missing from his upper jaw, and he grinned gap-toothed at Fergus.

"Give them hell, comrade."

Fergus' face was blackened with soot and his eyelashes were singed away. They had burned the Fordsburg Police Station a little before midnight.

"I want covering fire—on my whistle."

"You'll get it—never fear."

Fergus opened the rucksack and glanced at the steel globes, with their deeply segmented squares for fragmentation, then he slung the strap over his shoulder and adjusted the burden to hang comfortably on his flank.

"Look after it well." He handed his Lee-Enfield rifle to the gap-toothed striker. "We'll need it again today." He crawled away down the shallow drainage ditch that led to a concrete culvert which crossed under the road.

The culvert was lined with circular tubes of rusty corrugated iron, and Fergus wriggled through it carefully, emerging on the far side of the road.

Lying on his side, he raised himself slightly to peer over the edge of the drainage ditch. The police station was a hundred and fifty yards away. The blue light over the front door, with the white lettered "POLICE," was dead, and the flag hung limply on its pole in the still windless morning.

It was fifty yards to the slope of dead ground under the eastern windows of the brick building, and Fergus could see the rifle barrels of the defenders poked through the gaps in the sand-bags.

He pulled the silver whistle from his back pocket by its lanyard, and came up on his knees like a sprinter on the blocks.

He drew a deep breath and blew a long shrill ringing blast on the whistle. Immediately a storm of rifle fire crashed out from the hedges and ditches that surrounded the station.

The blue lamp shattered into flying fragments, and red brick dust popped off the walls like dyed cotton pods.

Fergus came out of the ditch at a run. A bullet kicked dust and stone chips stung his ankles, and another jerked like an impatient hand at the tail of his coat, then he was into the dead ground and out of their field of fire.

He still ran doubled over, however, until he reached the police station. Then he flattened himself against the wall between two of the sand-bagged windows while he struggled with his breathing.

A rifle barrel protruded from the left-hand window as it blazed away up the slope of the kopje. Fergus opened the rucksack and took out a grenade with his left hand. He pulled the pin with his teeth, while he groped for the Webley .455 revolver stuck into the belt of his trousers.

He locked one arm over the barrel of the police rifle, dragging it harmlessly aside, then he stepped into the window, and, still holding the rifle, looked through the narrow hole in the sand-bags.

A young, beardless face stared back at him, the eyes wide with amazement, the mouth hanging open slightly and the police helmet pulled down low over his eyes.

Fergus shot him in the bridge of the nose, between the startled staring eyes, and the head was smashed backwards out of view.

Fergus hurled the grenade through the gap and ducked down. The explosion in the confined space was vicious and ear-numbing, Fergus bobbed up and tossed in another grenade.

Glass and smoke blew from the windows, and from within there were the screams and cries of the trapped police constables, the groans and gasping wails of the wounded.

Fergus threw in a third grenade, and screamed, "Chew on that you bloody strike-breakers." The bomb exploded, shattering out a panel from the front door, and smoke billowed from all windows.

Inside a single voice started screaming. "Stop it! Oh God, stop it! We surrender!"

"Come out with your hands in the air, you bastards!"

A police sergeant staggered out of the shattered doorway. He held one hand above his head, the other hung at his side in a torn and blood-soaked sleeve.

* * *

The last call that went out from Newlands Police Station before the strikers cut the lines was a call for help. The relieving column coming over the ridge from Johannesburg in a convoy of three trucks got as far as the Hotel in Main Street where it was halted by rifle fire, and the moment it stopped, strikers ran out into the roadway behind it and set all the trucks ablaze with petrol bombs.

The police abandoned their vehickles and raced for cover in a cottage beside the road. It was a strong defensive position and they looked set to hold out against even the most determined attacks, but they left three dead constables lying in the road beside the burning trucks, and another two of their number lying near them, so badly wounded they could only cry out for succour.

A white flag waved from across the road, and the police commander stepped out on to the veranda of the cottage.

"What do you want?" he called across.

Fergus MacDonald walked out into the road, still waving the flag, a slight unwarlike figure in shabby suit and cloth cap.

"You can't leave these men out here," he shouted back, pointing at the bodies.

The commander came out with twenty unarmed police into the road to carry away the dead and wounded, and while they worked, strikers under Fergus' orders slipped in through the back of the cottages.

Suddenly Fergus whipped the Webley out from under his coat and pressed it to the commander's head.

"Tell your men to put their hands up—or I'll blow your bloody brains all over the road."

In the cottage, Fergus' men knocked the weapons out of the hands of the police, and in the roadway armed strikers were among them.

"You were under a flag of truce," protested the commander bitterly.

"We aren't playing games, you bloody black-leg," snarled Fergus. "We're fighting for a new world." The commander opened his mouth to protest again and Fergus swung the revolver sideways, slashing the barrel into his face, snapping out the front teeth from his upper jaw, and crushing the lip into a red wet smear. The man dropped to his knees, and Fergus strode among his men.

"We'll siege the Brixton ridge now—and after that Johannesburg. By tonight, we'll have the red flag flying on every public building in town. Onward, comrades, nothing will stop us now."

*   *   *

The Transvaal Scottish detrained at Dunswart Station that same morning to march in and seize the mining town of Benoni, which was under full control of the Action Committee's commandos, but the strikers were waiting for them.

The advancing troops were caught in flank and rear by the cross-fire from hundreds of prepared positions, and fought hard all day to extricate themselves, but it was late afternoon when, still under sniping fire, they were able to retrain at Dunswart.

They carried with them three dead officers and nine other dead rankers. Another thirty were suffering from gunshot wounds, from which many would later die.

*   *   *

From one end to the other of the Witwatersrand, the strikers were on the rampage. The Action Committee controlled that great complex of mining towns and mining properties that follows the sweep of the gold-bearing reef across the bleak African veld, sixty miles from Krugersdorp to Ventersdorp, with the city of Johannesburg at its centre.

It is the richest gold-bearing formation yet discovered by man, a glittering treasure house, the foundation stone of the prosperity of a nation—and now the strikers carried the red flag across it at will, and at every point the force of law and order reeled back.

Every police commander was loath to initiate fire, and every constable loath to act upon the order when it did come. They were firing upon friends, countrymen, brothers.

In the cellars of the Fordsburg Trade Union Hall they were holding a kangaroo court; a traitor was on trial for his life.

Harry Fisher's huge bulk was clad now in a military style bushjacket, with buttoned patch-pockets, over which he wore a bandolier of ammunition. On his right arm was a plain band of red cloth, but his unkempt black hair was uncovered, and his eyes were fierce.

His desk was a packing case, and Helena MacDonald stood behind his stool. She had cropped her hair as short as a man's and she wore breeches tucked into her boots, and the red armband on her tunic. Her face was pale and gaunt, her eyes in deep plum-coloured sockets were invisible in the bad light, but her body was tensed with the nervous energy of a leashed greyhound with the smell of the hare in its nostrils.

The accused was a storekeeper of the town, with pale watery eyes behind the steel-rimmed spectacles which he blinked rapidly as he watched his accuser.

"He asked to be connected with police headquarters in Marshall Square."

"Just a minute," Helena interrupted. "You are on the local telephone exchange, is that right?"

"Yes, that's right. I am Exchange Supervisor." The woman looked like a schoolteacher, iron-haired, neatly dressed, unsmiling.

"Go on."

"I thought I'd better listen in, you know, see what he was up to."

The storekeeper was wringing white bony hands, and chewing nervously on his lower lip. He looked at least sixty years old with the pale silver fluff of hair standing up comically from his bald pink pate.

"Well, when he started giving them the details of what was happening here, I broke the connection."

"What exactly did he say?" Fisher demanded.

"He said that there was a machine gun here."

"He said that?" Fisher's expression was thunderous. He transferred his glare to the storekeeper, and the man quailed.

"My boy is in the police—he's my only boy," he whispered, and then blinked back the tears from the pale eyes.

"That's as good as a confession," said Helena coldly, and Fisher glanced over his shoulder at her and nodded.

"Take him out and shoot him," he said.

The light delivery van bumped along the overgrown track and stopped beside the old abandoned No. 1 shaft on the Crown Mine's property. It had not been used for twelve years, and concrete machinery slabs and the collar of the shaft were thick with rank grass that grew out of the cracks in the concrete and covered the rusted machinery.

Two men dragged the storekeeper to the dilapidated barbed-wire fence that protected the dark black hole of the shaft. No. 1 shaft was fifteen hundred feet deep, but had flooded back to the five-hundred-foot level. The warning notices on the barbed-wire fence were embellished with the skull cross-bones device.

Helena MacDonald stayed at the wheel of the delivery van. She lit a cigarette and stared ahead, waiting without visible emotion for the executioner's shot.

The minutes passed, while the cigarette burned down between her fingers, and she snapped impatiently when one of the armed strikers came to the side window of the van,

"What's keeping you?"

"Begging your pardon, missus, neither of us can do it."

"What do you mean?" Helena demanded.

"Well," the man dropped his eyes. "Old Cohen's been selling me my groceries for ten years now. He always gives the kids a candy bar when they go in—"

With an impatient exclamation, Helena opened the van door and stepped out.

"Give me your revolver," she said, and as she strode to where the second striker guarded the old storekeeper she checked the load and spun the chamber of the pistol.

Cohen started to smile, a mild ingratiating smile as he peered at her face myopically; then he saw her expression and the pistol in her hand.

He dropped to his knees, and he began to urinate in terrified spurts down the front of his baggy grey flannel trousers.

When Helena parked the van in the street behind the market buildings, she was aware immediately of a new charge of excitement in the air. The men at the sand-bagged windows called out to her,

"Your old man's back, missus. He's down in the cellar with the boss!"

Fergus looked up from the large-scale map of the East Rand over which he and Harry Fisher were poring. She hardly recognized him.

He was sooty and grimed as a chimney sweep, and his eyelashes had been burned away, giving him a bland star-tled look. His eyes were bloodshot and there were little wet beads of dirty mucus in the corners.

"Hello, luv," he grinned wearily at her.

"What are you doing here, comrade?" she demanded. "You are supposed to be at Brixton ridge."

Harry Fisher intervened, "Fergus has taken the ridge. He's done fine work, really fine work. But now we have been granted a stroke of really good fortune."

"What is it?" Helena demanded.

"Slim Jannie Smuts is on his way from Cape Town."

"That's bad news," Helena contradicted coolly.

"He's coming by road—and he's got no escort with him," Harry Fisher explained.

"Like a lover—right into our arms," grinned Fergus, and spread his own arms wide. There were dark splotches of dried blood on his sleeves.

* * *

The Prime Minister's aide-de-camp had spelled Mark at the wheel of the Rolls on the long stretch northwards from

Bloemfontein. Mark had been able to sleep, hunched up on the front seat, oblivious of the lurching and shaking over the bad stretches of road, so that he woke refreshed when Sean Courtney stopped the little convoy on a deserted hilltop fifteen miles south of the built-up complex of mines and towns of the Witwatersrand.

It was late afternoon and the lowering sun turned the banks of low false cloud in the north to a sombre purple hue. It was not cloud but the discharge from the hundreds of chimneys of the power stations and refineries, of the coal-burning locomotives and the open fires of tens of thousands of African labourers in their locations, and of burning buildings and vehicles.

Mark wrinkled his nose as he smelled the acrid taint of the city fouling the clean dry air of the highveld.

The entire party took the opportunity to stretch cramped muscles and to relieve other physical needs. Mark noted wryly that nice social distinctions were observed when those members of the party who had general officer's rank and Cabinet Minister's status used the screened side of the parked cars, while the lesser members stood out in the open road.

While they went about their business, there was an argument in progress. Sean was advocating caution and a round-about approach through the suburbs and outlying areas of Johannesburg.

"We should cut across to Standerton and come in on the Natal road—the rebels are holding all the southern suburbs."

"They'll not be expecting us, old Sean. We'll go through fast and be at Marshall Square before they know what's happened," Jannie Smuts decided. "I can't afford the extra two hours it will take us to circle around."

And Sean growled at him, "You always were too damned hot-headed, Jannie. Good God, you were the one who rode into the Cape with a hundred and fifty men in your commando to capture Cape Town from the whole British army."

"Gave them the fright of their lives," the Prime Minister chuckled as he came around the back of the Rolls, buttoning his trousers, and Sean, following him, went on with relish,

"That's right, but when you tried the same tricks on Lettow von Vorbeck in German East Africa, you were the one who got the fright. He roasted your arse for you."

Mark winced at Sean's choice of words, and the Prime Minister's party looked to heaven and earth, anywhere except at their master's suddenly unsmiling countenance.

"We are going into Johannesburg on the Booysens Road," said Jannie Smuts coldly.

"You'll be no damned good to us dead," grumbled Sean.

"That's enough, old Sean. We'll do it my way."

"All right," Sean agreed lugubriously. "But you'll ride in the second car. The Cadillac will lead with your pennant flying." He turned to the Prime Minister's driver, "Flat out, you understand, stop for nothing."

"Yes, sir."

"Have you gentlemen got your music with you?" he demanded, and all of them showed him the sidearms they carried.

"Mark," Sean turned to him. "Get the Mannlicher off the roof." Mark unstrapped the leather case from the luggage rack and assembled the 9.3 mm sporting rifle, the only effective weapon they had been able to find at short notice in Somerset House before leaving. He loaded the magazine and handed the weapon to Sean, then slipped two yellow packets of Eley Kynoch ammunition into his own pockets.

"Good boy," Sean grunted, and peered at him closely. "How are you feeling? Did you get some sleep?"

"I'm fine, sir."

"Take the wheel."

Darkness fell swiftly, smearing the silhouettes of the blue gum trees along the low crests of the rolling open ground, crowding in the circle of their vision.

There were the flickering pinpoints of open cooking fires

from a few of the native shacks among the hills, but these were the only signs of life. The road was deserted, and even when they began to speed past the first brick-built buildings, there were no lights, and the stillness was unnatural and disquieting.

"The main power station has shut down. The coal-miners were limiting supply to fifty tons a day for essential services, but now they've stopped even that," the Prime Minister mused aloud, and neither of them answered him. Mark followed the twinkling red rear-lights of the Cadillac, and the darkness pressed closer. He switched on the main beams of his headlights, and suddenly they were into the narrow streets of Booysens, the southernmost suburb of Johannesburg.

The miners' cottages crowded the road like living and menacing presences. On the left, against the last faint glimmer of the day, Mark could make out the skeletal shape of the steel headgear at Crown Mines' main haulage, and ahead, the low table-like hillocks of the mine dumps gave him a nostalgic twinge.

He thought suddenly of Fergus MacDonald, and Helena, and glanced once again to his left, lifting his eyes from the road a moment.

Just beyond the Crown Deep headgear, not more than a mile away, was the cottage on Lover's Walk where she had taught him he was a man.

The memory was too wrapped around with pain and guilt, and he thrust it aside and turned his full attention back to the road just as the first rifle shots sparkled from the darkened cottage windows on the right side of the road ahead.

Instantly, he was judging the angle and field of the enemy fire, noticing how they had chosen the curve of the road where the vehicles must slow. "Good," he thought dispassionately, applauding the choice, and he hit the gear lever of the Rolls, double declutching into a lower gear to build up revolutions for the turn.

"Get down!" he shouted at his illustrious passengers.

Ahead the Cadillac swerved wildly at the volley and then recovered, and went roaring into the turn.

"Six or seven rifles," Mark estimated, and then saw the high hedge and the open pavement below the cottage windows. He would give them a changing closing target, he decided, and used the power and rush of the Rolls to broadside up on to the pavement, under the cover of the hedge.

Foliage brushed with a light rushing whisper against the side of the roaring vehicle and behind him a service revolver banged lustily as Sean Courtney fired through the open window.

Mark hit the brakes and fanned the back of the Rolls through the turn, bounded off the pavement and let her sway out across the road, to further confuse the riflemen in the cottages. Then he tramped down hard on the accelerator, gunned her through the turn and went howling down into the dark deserted commercial area of Booysens, leaving the stupefied riflemen staring into the deserted bend, and listening to the receding note of the Rolls-Royce engine.

Only two miles and they would be through the danger area, over the ridge and into Johannesburg proper.

Ahead of him, the Cadillac was running through the area of shops and warehouses and small factories, its headlights blazing harshly on the buildings that lined the road, carving a tunnel of light down their avenue to safety.

In the back seat of the Rolls, the two Generals had not taken Mark's advice to seek cover, and were both sitting bolt upright, discussing the situation objectively in cool measured tones.

"That was quick thinking," Smuts said. "They weren't expecting that turn."

"He's a good lad," Sean agreed.

"But you are wasting your time with that pistol."

"Gives me something to do," Sean explained, as he reloaded the chambers of his revolver.

"You should have ridden with my commando, old Sean,

I would have taught you to save ammunition." Smuts sought revenge for Sean's earlier remarks.

The headlights of the Cadillac tipped slightly upwards as it charged through the dip and reached the first rising ground. They all saw the road-block at the same moment.

It was flung up crudely across the road, oil drums, baulks of timber, iron bedsteads, sand-bags and household furniture obviously dragged from the cottages.

Sean swore loudly and with ferocity.

"I can turn now," Mark shouted. "But they'll get us when we slow down—and we'll have to go back through the ambush."

"Watch the Cadillac," Sean shouted back.

The heavy black machine had not hesitated, and it roared up the slope at the barricade, picking the spot which seemed weakest.

"He's going to open a breach! Follow him, Mark."

The Cadillac smashed into the road-block, and tables and chairs flew high into the night. Even above the roar of wind and engine, Mark could hear the tearing crashing impact, and then the Cadillac was through and going on up the ridge, but its speed was bleeding away and a white cloud of steam plumed from the torn radiator.

However, they had forged a breach in the barricade and Mark steered for it, bumping over a mangled mass of timber and then accelerating away up the slope, gaining rapidly on the leading vehicle.

The Cadillac was losing speed, clearly suffering a mortal injury.

"Shall I stop for them?" Mark demanded.

"No," said Sean. "We have to get the Prime Minister—"

"Yes," said Smuts. "We can't leave them."

"Make up your bloody minds," yelled Mark, and there was a stunned disbelieving silence in the back, and Mark began to brake for the pick up.

The machine gun opened from the scrubby bush at the base of the nearest mine dump. The tracer flailed the night, brilliant white fire sweeping down the road in a blinding storm, the high ripping tearing sound was unmistakable and Mark and Sean exclaimed together in appalled disbelief.

"Vickers!"

The Prime Minister's green and golden pennant on the bonnet of the Cadillac drew the deadly sheet of fire, and in the horrified micro-seconds that Mark watched, he saw the car begin to break up. The windshield and side windows blew away in a sparkling cloud of glass fragments, the figures of the three occupants were plucked to pieces like chickens caught in the blades of a threshing-machine.

The Cadillac slewed off the road and crashed headlong into the blank wall of a timber warehouse on the edge of the road, and still the relentless stream of Vickers fire tore into the carcass, punching neat black holes into the metalwork, holes that were rimmed with bare metal that sparkled in the headlights of the Rolls like newly minted silver dollars.

It would only be seconds before the gunner swivelled his Vickers on to the Rolls, Mark realized, and he searched the road ahead for a bolthole.

Between the timber warehouse and the next building was a narrow alleyway, barely wide enough to admit the Rolls. Mark swung out to make a hay-cart turn for the alley, and the gunner guessed his intention, but was stiff and low on his traverse as he swung the Vickers on to the Rolls.

The sheet of bullets ripped the surface of the road, a boiling teeming play of dust and tarmac that ran down under the side of the car.

Before the gunner could correct his aim, the petrol tank of the ruined Cadillac exploded in a woofing clap of sound and a vivid rolling cloud of scarlet flame and dense black smoke.

Under its cover Mark steered for the alleyway, and slammed the Rolls into it although she was suddenly heavy on the steering, and thumping brutally in her front end.

Fifty feet down, the alley was blocked with a heavy haul-

age trailer, piled high with newly sawn timber baulks—
and Mark skidded to a halt, and jumped out.

He saw that for the moment they were covered by the
corner of the warehouse from the Vickers, but the timber
trailer cut off their escape down the alley and it would be
only minutes before the strikers realized their predicament
and moved the Vickers to enfilade the alleyway and shoot
them to pieces. One glance showed him that machine-gun
fire had shredded the off-side leading wheel. Mark jerked
open the rear door and snatched the Mannlicher from
Sean, and paused only a moment to snap at the two Generals,

"Get the wheel changed. I'll try and hold them off."
Then he was sprinting back down the alleyway.

"I shall have to insist that in future, when he gives me an
order, he calls me sir," Sean said with thin humour, and
turned to Smuts. "Have you ever changed a wheel, Jannie?"

"Don't be stupid, old Sean. I'm a horse soldier, and your
superior officer," Smuts smiled back at him, with his
golden beard looking like a refined Viking in the reflected
headlights.

"Bloody hell!" grunted Sean. "You can work the jack."

Mark reached the corner of the warehouse and crouched
against it, checking the load of the Mannlicher before
glancing around.

The Cadillac burned like a huge pyre, and the stink of
burning rubber and oil and human flesh was choking. The
body of the driver still sat at the wheel, but the smoky red
flames rushed and drummed about him so that his head
was blackening and charring, and his body twisted and
writhed in a slow macabre ballet of death.

There was a wind that Mark had not noticed before, a
fitful inconstant wind that gusted and puffed down the
ridge, rolling thick clouds of the stinking black smoke
across the road and then changing strength and direction so
that for a few seconds the smoke pall once again poured
straight upwards into the night sky.

Over all blazed the flickering orange wash of the flames, uncertain light which magnified shadow and offered false perspective.

Mark realized that he had to get across the road into the scrub and eroded ground below the mine dump before he could get a chance at the Vickers gunner. He had to cross fifty open yards before he reached the ground where he could turn the clumsiness and relative immobility of the Vickers to his own account. He waited for the wind.

He saw it coming, rustling the grass tops in the firelight and rolling a dirty ball of newspaper down the road, then it picked up the smoke and wafted it in a stinking black pall across the open roadway.

Mark launched himself from the corner of the warehouse and had run twenty paces before he realized that the wind had tricked him. It was merely a gust, passing in seconds and leaving the night still and silent when it had gone, silent except for the snapping, crackling flames of the burning Cadillac.

He was halfway across as the smoke opened again, and the cold weight of dread in his belly seemed to spread down into his legs and slow them as he ran like a man in shackles; but the battle clock in his head was running clearly, tolling off the seconds, judging finely the instant that the Vickers gunner up on the dump spotted his shadowy running figure, judging the time it took for him to swing and resight the heavy weapon.

"Now!" he thought, and rolled forward from the waist without checking his speed, going on to his shoulder and somersaulting, ducking under the solid blast of machine-gun fire that came at the exact second he had expected it.

The momentum of his fall carried him up on to his feet again, and he knew he had seconds before the unsighted gunner picked him up again. He plunged onwards and lances of pain shot through the old bullet wounds in his back, wounds which he had not felt in over a year; the pain was in anticipation, as well as from the wrench of his fall.

The bank of red earth on the far side of the road seemed

to loom far off while instinct warned him that the Vickers was on to him again. He launched himself feet first, like a baseball player sliding for the plate, and at the same instant the stream of the Vickers' bullets tore a leaping sheet of dust off the lip of the bank, and the ricochets screamed like frustrated banshees and wailed away into the night.

Mark lay under the bank for many seconds with his face cradled in the crook of his arm, sobbing for breath while the pain in his old wounds receded and his heart picked up its normal rhythm. When he lifted his head again, his expression was bleak and his anger was cold and bright and functional.

Fergus MacDonald swore softly with both hands on the firing handles of the Vickers, his forefingers still holding the automatic safety-catch open and his thumbs poised over the firing button. He kept the weapon swinging in short rhythmic traverses back and forth as he peered down the slope, but he was swearing, monotonous profanity in a low tight whisper.

The man beside him was kneeling, ready to feed the belt to the gun, and now he whispered hoarsely, "I think you got him."

"The hell I did," hissed Fergus, and jerked the gun across as something in shadow caught his eye down on the road. He fired a short holding burst, and then muttered,

"Right, let's pull out."

"Damn it, comrade, we've got them—" protested the loader.

"You bloody fool, didn't you see him?" Fergus asked. "Didn't you see the way he crossed the road, don't you realize we've got a real ripe one on our hands? Whoever he is, he's a killer."

"Are we going to let one bastard chase us—"

"You're so right," snapped Fergus. "When it's that bucko down there, I'm not going to risk this gun. It's worth a hundred trained men," he patted the square steel breech block. "We came here to kill Clever Jannie, and he's down there, cooking in his fancy motorcar. Now, let's get the hell out of here—" and he started the complicated process of unloading the Vickers, cranking it once to clear the chamber of its live round and then cranking again to clear the round in the feed block. "Tell the boys to cover us when we pull back," he grunted, as he extracted the ammunition belt from the breech pawls, and then started uncoupling the Vickers from its tripod.

"Come on, work quickly," he snapped at his loader. "That bastard is on his way, I can feel him breathing down my neck already."

There were eight strikers on the slope of the dump, Fergus and two for the Vickers, with five riflemen spread out around the gun to support and cover.

"Right, let's go." Fergus carried the thick-jacketed barrel over one shoulder and a heavy case of ammunition in his left hand; his number two wrestled with the ungainly fifty-pound weight of metal tripod and the number three carried the five-gallon can of cooling water and the second case of ammunition.

"We are pulling out," Fergus called to his riflemen, "look lively, that's a dangerous bastard coming after us!"

They ran in a group, bowed under their burdens, feet slipping in the loose white cyanided sand of the dump.

The shot was from the left, Fergus had not expected that, and it was impossibly high on the dump. The bastard must have grown wings and flown to get there, Fergus thought.

The report was a heavy booming clap, some sort of sporting rifle, and behind him the number three made a strange grunting sound as though his lungs had been forcibly emptied by a heavy blow. Fergus glanced back and saw him down, a dark untidy shape on the white sand.

"Good Christ," gasped Fergus. It had to be flukey shooting at that range, and in this impossible light, just the early stars and the ruddy glow of the burning Cadillac.

The rifle boom boomed again, and he heard one of his riflemen scream and then thrash about wildly in the undergrowth. Fergus knew he had judged his adversary fairly, he was a killer. They were all running now, shouting and firing wildly as they scattered back under the lee of the dump, and Fergus ran with them, only one thought in his mind—he must get his precious Vickers safely away.

The sweat had soaked through his jacket between the shoulders, and had run down from under his cap so that he was blinded, and unable to speak when at last he tumbled into the cover of a deep donga and sat against the earth of the bank, with the machine gun cradled in his arms like an infant.

One after another his riflemen reached the donga and fell thankfully into cover.

"How many were there?" gasped one of them.

"I don't know," panted another, "must have been a dozen ZARPS, at least. They got Alfie."

"And they got Henry also, I saw five of them."

Fergus had recovered his breath enough to speak now. "There was one, only one—but a good 'un."

"Did we get Slim Jannie?"

"Yes," said Fergus grimly. "We got him all right. He was in the first car—I saw his flag and I saw him cooking. We can go home now."

\* \* \*

It was a little before eleven o'clock when the solitary Rolls-Royce was halted at the gates of police headquarters on Marshall Square by the suspicious sentries, but when the occupants were recognized, half a dozen high-ranking police and military officers hurried down the steps to welcome them.

The Prime Minister went directly to the large visitors' drawing-room on the first floor which had been transformed into the headquarters of the military administration, empowered and entrusted by the declaration of martial law with the Government of the nation. The relief on the faces of the assembled officers was undisguised. The situation was a mess, but Smuts was here at last and now they could expect order and direction and sanity to emerge from the chaos.

He listened to their reports quietly, tugging at his little goatee beard, his expression becoming more grim as the full extent of the situation was explained.

He was silent a little longer, brooding over the map, and then he looked up at General van Deventer, an old comrade in arms during two wars, a man who had ridden with him on that historic commando into the Cape in 1901 and who had fought beside him against the wily old German, Lettow von Vorbeck, in German East Africa.

"Jacobus," he said, "you command the East Rand." Van Deventer whispered an acknowledgement, his vocal chords damaged by a British bullet in '01.

"Sean, you have the west. I want the Brixton ridge under our control by noon tomorrow." Then, as an afterthought, "Have your lads arrived from Natal yet?"

"I hope so," said Sean Courtney.

"So do I," Smuts smiled thinly. "You will have a merry time taking the ridge single-handed." The smile flickered off his face. "I want your battle plans presented by breakfast time, gentlemen. I don't have to remind you that, as always, the watchword is speed. We have to cauterize this ulcer and bind it up swiftly."

\* \* \*

In early autumn, the highveld sun has a peculiar brilliance, pouring down through an atmosphere thinned by altitude out of a sky of purest gayest blue.

It was weather for picnicking and for lovers in quiet gardens, but on 14th March 1922 it was not calm, but a stillness of a menacing and ominous intensity which hung over the city of Johannesburg and its satellite towns.

In just two days van Deventer had swept through the East Rand, stunning the strikers with his Boer Commando tactics, rolling up all resistance in Benoni and Dunswart, recapturing Brakpan and the mine, while the Brits column under his command drove through the Modder and Geduld mines and linked with van Deventer at Springs. In two days, they had crushed the revolt on the East Rand, and thousands of strikers came in under the white flag to be marched away to captivity and eventual trial.

But Fordsbug was the heart and the Brixton ridge which commanded it was the key to the revolt.

Now at last, Sean Courtney had the ridge, but it had been two days of hard and bitter fighting. With artillery and air support, they had swept the rocky kopjes, the school buildings, brickfields, the cemetery, the public buildings and the cottages, each of which the strikers had turned into a strongpoint; and in the night they had carried in the dead of both sides, and buried them in the Milner Park cemetery, each with his own comrades, soldier with soldier and striker with striker.

Now Sean was ready for the thrust to the heart, and below them the iron roofs of Fordsburg blinked in the fine clear sunlight.

"Here he comes now," said Mark Anders, and they all lifted their binoculars and searched for the tiny fleck of black in the immense tall sky.

The DH.9 sailed in sedately, banking slowly in from the south and levelling for the run over the cowering cottages of Fordsburg.

Through the lens of his glasses, Mark could make out the head and shoulders of the navigator in the forward cockpit as he hoisted each stack of pamphlets on to the edge of the cockpit, cut the strings and then pushed them over the side. They flurried out in a white storm behind the slow-moving machine, caught in the slipstream, spreading and spinning and drifting like flocks of white doves.

A push of the breeze spread some of the papers towards the ridge, and Mark caught one out of the air and glanced at the crude printing on cheap thick paper.

### MARTIAL LAW
### NOTICE

Women and children and all persons well disposed towards the Government are advised to leave before 11 A.M. today that part of Fordsburg and vicinity where the authority of the Government is defied and where military operations are about to take place. No immunity from punishment or arrest is guaranteed to any person coming in under this notice who has broken the law.

SEAN COURTNEY
CONTROL OFFICER

It was clumsy syntax. Mark wondered who had composed it as he crumpled the notice and dropped it into the grass at his feet.

"What if the pickets won't let them come out, sir?" he asked quietly.

"I don't pay you to be my conscience, young man," Sean growled warningly, and they stood on in silence for a minute. Then Sean sighed and took the cigars from his breast pocket and offered one to Mark as a conciliatory gesture.

"What can I do, Mark? Must I send my lads into those streets without artillery support?" He bit the tip off his cigar and spat it into the grass. "Whose lives are more important—the strikers and their families or men who trust me and honour me with their loyalty?"

"It's much easier to fight people you hate," Mark said softly, and Sean glanced at him sharply.

"Where did you read that?" he demanded, and Mark shook his head.

"At least there are no blacks caught up in this," he said. Mark had personally been in charge of sending disguised black policemen through the lines to warn all tribesmen to evacuate the area.

"Poor blighters," Sean agreed. "I wonder what they make of this white men's madness." Mark strode to the edge of the shallow cliff, ignoring the danger of sniping fire from the buildings below, and glassed the town carefully. Suddenly he exclaimed with relief,

"They're coming out!"

Far below where they stood, the first tiny figures straggled out of the entrance of the Vrededorp subway. The women carried infants and dragged reluctant children at arm's length. Some were burdened with their personal treasures, others brought their pets, canaries in wire cages, dogs on leashes. The first small groups and individuals became a trickle and then a sorry, toiling stream, pushing laden bicycles and hand carts, or simply carrying all the possessions they could fit.

"Send a platoon down to guide them, and give them a hand," Sean ordered quietly, and brooded heavily with his beard on his chest. "I'm glad to see the women out of it," he growled. "But I'm sad for what it means."

"The men are going to fight," Mark said.

"Yes," Sean nodded. "They're going to fight. I had hoped we had had enough slaughter—but they are going to make a bitter ending to a tragic tale." He crushed the stub of his cigar under his heel. "All right, Mark. Go down and tell Molyneux that it's on. Eleven hundred hours we'll open the barrage. Good luck, son."

Mark saluted, and Sean Courtney left him and limped back from the crest to join General Smuts and his staff who had come out to watch the final sweep of the battle.

\* \* \*

The first shrapnel bursts clanged across the sky, and burst in bright gleaming cotton pods of smoke above the roofs of Fordsburg, cracking the sky and the waiting silence, with startling violence.

They were fired by the horse artillery batteries on the ridge, and immediately the other batteries on Sauer Street joined in.

For twenty minutes, the din was appalling and the brilliant air was sullied by the rising mist of smoke and dust. Mark stood in the hastily dug trench and peered over the parapet. There was something so dreadfully familiar in this moment. He had lived it fifty times before, but now he felt his nerves screwing down too tightly and the heavy indigestible lump of fear in his guts nauseated him.

He wanted to duck down below the parapet, cover his head to protect his ears from the metallic hammer-blows of sound, and stay there.

It required an immense effort of will to stand where he was and to keep his expression calm and disinterested—but the men of "A" Company lined the trench on each side of him and, to distract himself, he began to plan his route through the outskirts of the town.

There would be road-blocks at every corner, and every cottage would be held. The artillery barrage would not have affected the strikers under cover, for it was limited to shrapnel bursts. Sean Courtney was concerned with the safety of over a hundred police and military personnel who had been captured by the strikers and were being held somewhere in the town.

·"No high explosive," was the order, and Mark knew his company would be cut to ribbons on the open streets.

He was going to take them through the kitchen yards and down the sanitary lanes to their final objective, the Trades Hall on Commercial and Central Streets.

He checked his watch again, and there were four minutes to go.

"All right, Sergeant," he said quietly.

The order passed quickly down the trench and the men came to their feet, crouching below the parapet.

"Like old times, sir," the Sergeant said affably, and Mark glanced at him. He seemed actually to be enjoying this moment—and Mark found himself hating the man for it.

"Let's go," he said abruptly, as the minute hand of his watch touched the black hair-line division, and the Sergeant blew his whistle shrilly.

Mark put one hand on the parapet and leapt nimbly over the top.

He started to run forward, and from the cottages ahead of him came the harsh crackling of musketry. Suddenly, he realized he was no longer afraid.

\* \* \*

He was little more than a youth, with smooth pink cheeks and the lightest golden fluff of a moustache on his upper lip.

They shoved him down the last few steps into the cellars, and he lost his footing and fell.

"Another yellow belly," called the escort, a strapping bearded fellow with a rifle slung on his shoulder and the red band around his upper arm. "Caught him trying to sneak out of the subway."

The boy scrambled to his feet. He had skinned his knees in his fall and he was close to tears as Harry Fisher towered over him. He carried a long black sjambok in his right hand, a vicious tapered whip of cured hippo-hide.

"A traitor," bellowed Fisher. In the last days of continuous planning and fighting, the strain had started to show. His eyes had taken on a wild fanatical glare, his movements were jerky and exaggerated, and his voice ragged and overloud.

"No, comrade, I swear I'm no traitor," the youth bleated pitifully.

"A coward, then," shouted Fisher, and caught the front of the boy's shirt in one big hairy fist and ripped it open to the waist.

"I didn't have a rifle," protested the boy.

"There'll be rifles for all later—when the first comrades die."

The lash of the sjambok split the smooth white skin of the boy's back like a razor stroke, and the blood rose in a vivid bright line as he fell to his knees.

Harry Fisher stood over him and swung the sjambok un-

til there were no more screams or groans, and the only
sound in the cellar was the hiss and splat of the lash—then
he stood back panting and sweating.

"Take him out so the comrades can see what happens to
traitors and cowards."

A striker took each of the boy's arms and as they
dragged him up the steps, the flesh of his back hung in
ribbons and tatters and the blood ran down over his belt
and soaked into the gaberdine of his breeches.

*　*　*

Mark dropped cat-footed over the back wall into the tiny
paved yard. Cases of empty beer bottles were piled high
along the side walls, and the smell of stale liquor was fruity
and heady in the noon heat.

He had reached the bottle store in Mint Road less than an
hour after the starting time of the drive, and the route he
had led his men, through the backyards and over the roof-
tops, had been more successful than he had dared hope.

They had avoided the road-blocks and twice had out-
flanked groups of strikers dug into strong positions, surprising them completely, and scattering them with a single volley.

Mark ran across the yard and kicked in the back door of
the bottle store, and in the same movement flattened himself against the wall, clear of the gaping doorway and any
striker fire from the interior of the building.

The Sergeant and a dozen men followed him over the
wall, and spread out to cover the doorway and barred windows. He nodded at Mark, and Mark dived through the
doorway sideways with the rifle on his hip, and his eyes
screwed up against the gloom after the bright sunlight outside.

The store was deserted, the shutters bolted down over
the front windows and the shelves of bottles untouched by
looters, in testimony of the strikers' discipline. The tiers of

bottles stood neatly in their gaily coloured labels, glinting in the dusky light.

The last time Mark had been in here was to buy a dozen bottles of porter for Helena MacDonald, but he pushed the thought aside and went to the shuttered windows just as the Sergeant and his squad burst in through the back door.

The shutters had been pierced by random shrapnel and rifle fire, and Mark used one aperture as a peephole.

Fifty yards across the road was the Trades Hall, and the complex of trenches and defences that the strikers had thrown up around the square.

Even the public lavatories had been turned into a block-house, but all the defenders' attention was directed into the streets across the square.

They lined the parapets and were firing frantically at the kilted running figures of the Transvaal Scottish Highlanders racing towards the Square from the station side.

The strikers were dressed in a strange assortment of garb, from greasy working overalls and quasi-military safari jackets, caps and slouch hats and beavers, to Sunday suits, waistcoats and ties. But all of them wore bandoliers of ammunition draped from their shoulders, and their backs were exposed to Mark's attack.

A volley through the bottle-store windows would have done terrible execution among them, and already the Sergeant was directing his men to each of the windows in a fierce and gleeful croak of anticipation.

"I could order up a machine gun," Mark thought, and something in him shied away from the mental image of a Vickers firing into that exposed and unsuspecting group. "If only I hated them."

As he watched, first one and then others of the strikers at the barricades crouched down hopelessly from the withering fire the Highlanders were now pouring on to them.

"Fix bayonets," Mark called to the men, and the steel scraped from the metal scabbards in the sombre gloom of the store. A stray bullet splintered the shutter above Mark's

head and burst a bottle of Scotch whisky on the shelves
behind him. The smell of the spirit was sharp and unpleasant, and Mark called again,

"On my order, break open the windows and doors, and
we'll show them steel."

The shutters crashed back, the main doors flew open,
and Mark led his company in a howling racing line across
the road. Before they reached the first line of sand-bags,
the strikers began throwing down their rifles and jumping
up with their hands lifted above their heads.

Across the square, the Highlanders poured into the street
cheering and shouting and raced for the barricades; Mark
felt a surge of relief that he had taken the risk of going with
the bayonet, rather than ordering his men to shoot down
the exposed strikers.

As his men ran into the square, knocking the weapons
out of their hands and pushing the strikers into sullen
groups, Mark was racing up the front steps of the Trades
Hall.

He paused on the top step, shouted, "Stand back inside"
and fired three rifle bullets into the brass lock.

Harry Fisher leaned against the wall and peered out of
the sand-bagged window into the milling yelling chaos of
the square.

The madness of unbearable despair shook the huge
frame, and he breathed like a wounded bull when it stands
to take the matador's final thrust. He watched his men
throw down their arms, saw them herded like cattle, with
their hands held high, stumbling on weary careless feet,
their faces grey with fatigue and sullen in defeat.

He groaned, a low hollow sound of emotional agony
stretched to its furthest limits, and the thick shoulders
sagged. He seemed to be shrinking in size. The great unkempt head lowered, the blazing vision dimmed in his eyes
as he watched the young lieutenant in barathea battle-dress
race up the stairs below him, and heard the rifle shots shatter
the lock.

He shambled across to his desk and slumped down into

the chair facing the closed door, and his hand was shaking as he drew the service revolver from his belt and cocked the hammer. He laid the weapon carefully on the desk in front of him.

He cocked his head and listened to the shouted orders and the trampling confusion in the square below for a minute, then he heard the rush of booted feet up the wooden staircase beyond the door.

He lifted the revolver from the desk, and leaned both elbows on the desk-top to steady himself.

Mark burst in through the main doors of the hall and stopped in surprise and confusion. The floor was covered with prostrate bodies; it seemed there must be hundreds of them.

As he stared, a Captain of Highlanders and half a dozen men burst in behind him. They stopped also.

"Good God," panted the Captain, and then suddenly Mark realized that the bodies were all uniformed, police khaki, hunting green kilts, barathea.

"They have slaughtered their prisoners," Mark thought with nightmare horror, staring at the mass of bodies, then suddenly a head lifted cautiously and another.

"Oh thank God," breathed the Captain beside Mark, as the prisoners began scrambling to their feet, their faces shining with relief, a single voice immediately becoming a hubbub of nervous gaiety.

They surged for the door, some to embrace their liberators and other merely to run out into the sunlight.

Mark avoided a big police Sergeant with rumpled uniform and three days' growth of beard, ducked under his arms and ran for the staircase.

He took the stairs three at a time, and paused on the landing. The doors to five offices on this floor were standing open, the sixth was closed. He moved swiftly down the corridor, checking each of the rooms.

Cupboards and desks had been ransacked, and the floors were ankle-deep in paper, chairs overturned, drawers pulled from desks and dumped into the litter of paper.

The sixth door at the end of the passage was the only one closed. It was the office of the local Union chairman, Mark knew, Fergus MacDonald's office. The man for whom he was searching, driven by some lingering loyalty, by the dictates of shared comradeship and friendship to find him now—and to give him what help and protection he could.

Mark slipped the safety-catch on the rifle as he approached the door. He reached for the handle, and once again that sense of danger warned him. For a moment he stood with his fingers almost touching the brass lock, then he stepped quietly out of the line of the doorway; reaching sideways he rattled the handle softly and then turned it.

The door was unlocked, and the latch snicked and he pushed the door open. Nothing happened, and Mark grunted with relief and stepped through the doorway.

Harry Fisher sat at the desk facing him, a huge menacing figure, crouching over the desk with the big tousled head lowered on massive shapeless shoulders and the revolver held in both hands, pointing directly at Mark's chest.

Mark knew that to move was death. He could see the rounded leaden noses of the bullets in the loaded chambers of the cylinder and the hammer fully cocked, and he stood frozen.

"It is not defeat," Harry Fisher spoke with a strangled hoarse voice that Mark did not recognize. "We are the dragon's teeth. Wherever you bury one of us, a thousand warriors will spring up."

"It's over, Harry," Mark spoke carefully, trying to distract him, for he knew he could not lift the rifle and fire in the time Harry Fisher could pull the trigger.

"No." Fisher shook the coarse tangled locks of his head. "It is only just beginning."

Mark did not realize what he was doing, until Harry Fisher had reversed the pistol and thrust the muzzle into his own mouth. The explosion was muffled, and Harry

Fisher's head was stretched out of shape, as though it were a rubber ball struck by a bat.

The back of his skull erupted, and a loose mass of bright scarlet and custard yellow splattered the wall behind him.

The impact of the bullet hurled his body backwards and his chair toppled and crashed over.

The stench of burned powder hung in the room on filmy wisps of gunsmoke and Harry Fisher's booted heels kicked and tapped a jerky, uneven little dance on the bare wooden floor.

\* \* \*

"Where is Fergus MacDonald?" Mark asked the question a hundred times of the files of captured strikers. They stared back at him, angry, bitter, some of them still truculent and defiant, but not one of them even deigned to answer.

Mark took three of his men, under the pretext of a mopping-up patrol, down to Lover's Walk as far as the cottage.

The front door was unlocked, and the beds in the front room were unmade. Mark felt a strange repugnance of mind, balanced by a plucking of lust at his loins, when he saw Helena's *crêpe de Chine* dressing-gown thrown across the chair, and a crumpled pair of cotton panties dropped carelessly on the floor beside it.

He turned away quickly, and went through the rest of the house. The dirty dishes in the kitchen had already grown a green fuzz of mould, and the air was stale and disused. Nobody had been in these rooms for days.

A scrap of paper lay on the floor beside the coal-black stove. Mark picked it up and saw the familiar hammer and sickle device on the pamphlet. He screwed it up and hurled it against the wall. His men were waiting for him on the stoep.

The strikers had dynamited the railway lines at Braamfontein station, and at the Church Street level-crossing, so the regiment could not entrain at Fordsburg. Most of the roads were blocked with rubble and the detritus of the final struggle, but most dangerous was the possibility of stubborn strikers still hiding out in the buildings that lined the road through the dip to Johannesburg.

Sean Courtney decided to move his men out up the slope to the open ground of the Crown Deep property.

They marched out of Fordsburg in the darkness, before good shooting light. It had been a long uncomfortable night, and nobody had slept much. Weariness made their packs leaden to carry and shackled their legs. There was less than a mile to go, however.

The motor transport was drawn up in the open ground near the headgear of Crown Mine's main haulage, a towering structure, shaped like the Eiffel Tower, steel girders riveted and herring-boned for strength, rising a hundred feet to the huge wheels of the winching equipment. When the shift was in, these wheels spun back and forth, back and forth, lowering the cages filled with men and equipment, hundreds of feet into the living earth, and raising the millions of tons of gold-bearing rock out of the depths.

Now the great wheels stood motionless, they had been dead for three months now, and the buildings clustered about the tower were gloomy and deserted.

The transport was an assortment of trucks and commercial vans, commandeered under martial law—gravel lorries from the quarries, mining vehicles, even a bakery van, but it was clear that there was not enough to take out six hundred men.

As Mark came up, marching on the flank of "A" Company there were half a dozen officers in discussion at the head of the convoy. Mark recognized the familiar bearded figure of General Courtney standing head and shoulders above the others, and his voice was raised in an angry growl.

"I want all these men moved before noon. They've done fine work, they deserve hot food and a place—"

At that moment he saw Mark, and frowned heavily, waving him over and beginning to speak before he had arrived.

"Where the hell have you been?"

"With the company—"

"I sent you to take a message, and expected you back. You know damned well I didn't mean you to get into the fighting. You are on my staff, sir!"

Mark was tired and irritable, still emotionally disturbed by all that he had seen and done that day, and he was in no mood for one of the General's tantrums.

His rebellious expression was unmistakable. "Sir," he began, and Sean shouted at him,

"And don't take that tone to me, young man!"

An uncaring, completely irresponsible dark rage descended on Mark. He didn't give a damn for the consequences and he leaped forward, pale with fury, and opened his mouth.

The regiment was bunched up now, halted in the open roadway, neat symmetrical blocks of khaki, six hundred men in ranks three deep.

The shouted orders of the N.C.O.s halted each section, one after the other, and stood them at the easy position.

From the top of the steel headgear, they made an unforgettable sight in the rich yellow light of eary morning.

"Ready, luv," whispered Fergus MacDonald, and Helena nodded silently. Reality had long faded and been replaced by this floating dreamlike state. Her shoulders were raw where the carrying straps of the heavy ammunition boxes had bitten into the flesh, but there was no pain, just a blunting numbness of body. Her hands seemed bloated, and clumsy, the nails broken off raggedly and rinded with black half-moons of dirt, and the harsh canvas of the ammunition belts between her fingers felt smooth as silk, the brass cartridge cases cool, so that she felt like pressing them to her dried cracked lips.

Why was Fergus staring at her that way, she wondered with a prickle of irritation that did not last, once again the dreamy floating sensation.

"You can go down now," Fergus said quietly. "You don't have to stay." He looked like a very old man, his face shrivelled and falling in upon itself. The stubble of beard on his lined and haggard cheeks was silvery as diamond chips, but the skin was stained by smoke and dirt and sweat.

Only the eyes below the peak of the cloth cap still burned with the dark fanatic flames.

Helena shook her head. She wanted him to stop talking, the sound intruded, and she turned her head away.

The men below stood shoulder to shoulder in their orderly ranks. The low sun threw long narrow shadows from their feet across the red dust of the roadway.

A second longer Fergus stared at her. She was a pale, wasted stranger, the bones pushing through the smooth drawn flesh of her face, the scarf wound like a gypsy around her head, covering the black cropped hair.

"All right then," he murmured, and tapped the breech of the Vickers, once, twice, training it slightly left.

There was a group of officers near the head of the column. One of them was a big powerful man with a dark beard. The sunlight sparkled on his shoulder-tabs, Fergus lowered his head and looked through the rear sight of the Vickers.

There was a younger slimmer officer with the other, and Fergus blinked twice rapidly, as something stirred deep in his memory.

He hooked his fingers into the automatic safety-bar and lifted it, priming the gun, and he brought his thumbs on to the firing button.

He blinked again. The face of the young officer moved something in him, he felt a softening and blurring of his determination and he rejected it violently and thrust down on the button with both thumbs.

The weapon juddered on its tripod, and the long belt was

sucked greedily into the breech, Helena's small pale hands guiding it carefully, and the empty brass cases spewed out from under the gun, tinkling and ringing and bouncing off the steel girders of the headgear.

The sound was a deafening tearing roar that seemed to fill Helena's head and beat against her eyes, like the frantic wings of a trapped bird.

Even the most skilled marksman must guard against the tendency to ride up on a downhill shot. The angle from the top of the headgear was acute and the soft yellowish early light further confused Fergus' aim. His first burst carried high—shoulder-high instead of belly-high, which is the killing line for machine-gun fire.

The first bullets struck before Mark heard the gun. One of them hit Sean Courtney high up in the big bulky body. It flung him forward, chest to chest with Mark, and both of them went sprawling in the roadway.

Fergus tapped the breech block, dropping his aim a fraction to the belly line, and traversed in a long unhurried sweep along the ranks of standing soldiers, cutting them with the scythe of the Vickers in the eternal seconds that they still stood in stunned paralysis.

The stream of tracer hosed them, and washed them into crazy heaps, piled them on each other, dead and wounded together, their screams high and thin in the rushing hurricans of Vickers fire.

Sean rolled off Mark, and his face was contorted, angry and outraged, as he tried to struggle on to his knees, but his one arm was dangling. His blood splattered them both and he flopped helplessly.

Mark wriggled out from under him, and looked up at the headgear. He saw the tracer flickering like fire-flies and darting into the crowded roadway on the triumphant fluttering roar of the gun. Even in his own confusion and despair, he saw that the gunner had picked a good stance. He would be hard to come at.

Then he looked down the road and a cold fist clenched on his guts as he saw the bloody execution. The ranks had broken, men running and stumbling for what little cover the vehicles and ditches offered, but the road was still filled.

They lay in windrows and piles, they crawled and cried and twisted in the dust which their blood was turning to chocolat-red mud—and the gun swivelled and came back, flickering tracer into the carnage, chopping up the road surface into a spray of dust and leaping gravel, running viciously over the piles of wounded, coming back to where they lay.

Mark twisted up into a crouch, and slipped an arm under the General's chest. The weight of the man was enormous, but Mark found strength that he had not known before, goaded on by the fluttering rushing roar of the Vickers. Sean Courtney leaved himself up like a bull caught in quicksand, and Mark got him to his feet.

Bearing half his weight, Mark steadied him and kept him from falling. He weaved drunkenly, hunched over, bleeding badly, breathing noisily through his mouth, and Mark forced him into an ungainly crouching run.

The gun swept their heels, kicking and smashing into the back of a young lieutenant who was creeping towards the ditch, dragging both useless legs behind him. He dropped face down and lay still.

They reached the drainage ditch and tumbled into it. It was less than eighteen inches deep, not enough to cover the General fully, even when he lay flat on his belly, and the Vickers was still hunting.

After that first long slicing traverse, it was firing short accurate bursts at selected targets, more deadly than random fire, keeping the gun from overheating and preventing a stoppage, conserving ammunition. Mark, weighing it all, realized that there was an old soldier up there in the tower.

"Where are you hit?" he demanded, but Sean struck his hands away irritably, twisting his head to peer up into the tall steel headgear.

"Can you get him, Mark?" he grunted, and pressed his

fingers into his shoulder, where the blood welled up thick and dark as molasses.

"Not from here," Mark answered quickly. It had taken him seconds to assess the shoot. "He's holed up tight."

"Merciful Jesus! My poor boys."

"He's built himself a nest." Mark studied the steelwork. The platform below the winch wheels was covered with heavy timber, fitted loosely into the framework of steel.

The gunner had pulled these up and built himself four walls of wood, perhaps two feet thick. Mark could see the light glimmering through the open gaps in the floorboards, and make out the shape and size of the fortified nest.

"He can hold us here all day!" Sean looked down at the piles of khaki bodies in the roadway, and he knew many of the wounded would bleed to death in that time. Nobody dared go out to them.

The gun came back, ripping a flail across the earth near their heads and they ducked their faces to the ground, pressing their bodies into the shallow ditch.

The ground sloped down very gradually towards the steel tower, only when you lay at ground level like this was the gradient apparent.

"Somebody will have to get under him, or behind him," Mark spoke quickly, thinking it out.

"It's open ground all the way," Sean grunted.

On the opposite side of the road fifty yards away, a narrow-gauge railway ran down the short open grassy slope to the foot of the tower. It was used to truck the waste material from the shaft-head to the rock dump, half a mile away.

Almost opposite where they lay, half a dozen of the steel cocoa pans had been abandoned at the beginning of the strike. They were small four-wheeled tip-trucks, coupled to each other in a line, each of them heaped high with big chunks of blue rock.

Mark realized he was still wearing his pack and he shrugged out of the straps as he planned his stalk, judging angles and range as he groped for the field-dressing and handed it to Sean.

"Use this."

Sean tore open the package and wadded the cotton dressing into the front of his tunic. He fingers were sticky with his own blood.

Mark's P.14 rifle lay in the road where he had dropped it, but there were five clips of ammunition in the pouches on his webbing belt.

"Try and give me some covering fire when I start to go up," he said, and watched the tower for the next burst of tracer.

"You'll never get there," said Sean. "We'll bring up a thirteen-pounder and shoot the bastard out of there."

"That will take until noon, it will be too late for them." He glanced at the wounded in the road, and at that moment a stream of brilliant white tracer flew from the tower, aimed at the far end of the column, and Mark was up and running hard, stooping to gather the rifle at full run, crossing the road in a dozen flying strides, stumbling in the rough ground beyond, catching his balance and sprinting on.

That stumble had cost him a tenth of a second, the margin of life and death perhaps, while the gunner high up in the tower spotted him, swivelled the gun and lined up. The steel cocoa pans were just ahead, fifteen paces, but he wasn't going to make it—the warning flared in his brain, and he dropped into the short grass and rolled sideways, just as the storm of Vickers fire filled the air about him with the lash of a hundred bull-whips.

Mark kept rolling, like a log, and the gun gouged a furrow out of the dry stony earth inches from his shoulder.

He came up against the wheels of the cocoa pan with a force that bruised his hip and made him cry out involuntarily. Vickers bullets hammered and clanged against the steel body of the truck and howled off in ricochet, but Mark was under cover now.

"Mark, are you all right?" the General's bull-bellow carried across the road.

"Give me covering fire."

"You heard him, lads," shouted the General, and one or two rifles began firing spasmodically from the ditches, and from behind the stranded motor lorries.

Mark dragged himself on to his knees, and quickly checked the rifle, brushing the sights with his thumb to make certain they were cleaned of dirt and undamaged in the fall.

Then he worked his way to the coupling of the cocoa pan and threw the release toggle. The brake wheel was stiff and required both his hands to unwind it. The brake chocks squeaked softly as they disengaged, but the slope of the ground was so gentle that the truck did not move until Mark put his shoulder to it.

He strained with all his weight before the steel wheels made a single reluctant revolution, then gravity took her and the cocoa pan began to roll.

"Give the bastard hell!" Sean Courtney yelled, as he realized suddenly what Mark was going to do, and Mark grinned without mirth at that characteristic exhortation, and he trotted along, doubled up behind the heavily-laden steel truck.

A terrible tearing, hammering storm of Vickers broke over the slowly rolling truck, and instinctively Mark ducked lower and steadied himself against the metal side.

He realized that as he came closer to the tower, so the gunner's angle would change until he was shooting almost directly down on top of Mark—then the side of the truck would give him no cover, but he was committed. Nothing would stop the slowly accelerating rush of the cocoa pan down the slope, it had the weight of ten tons of rock behind it and its speed was gathering. Soon he would not be able to keep up with it, already he was running—and the Vickers roared again, the bullets screeching and wailing furiously off the steel body.

Twisting as he ran, he slung the rifle on one shoulder and reached up to hook both hands over the side of the truck. He was pulled instantly off his feet, and they dangled without foothold, in danger of being caught up in the spinning steel wheels. He drew his knees up under his chin, hanging all his weight on his arms and taking the intolerable strain in his belly muscles as the truck flew down into the stretching octopus shadow of the headgear.

Still hanging on his arms, Mark flung his head back and looked up. The tower was foreshortened by perpective, and it crouched over him like some menacing monster, stark against the mellow morning sky, crude black steel and timber baulks pyramiding into the heavens. At its zenith, Mark could see the pale mirrorlike face of the gunner, and the thick water-jacketed barrel of the Vickers trained down at its maximum depression.

The gun flamed, and bullets rang the steel near his head like a great bell. They churned into the blue rock, disintegrating into chips of buzzing metal and shattering the rock into vicious splinters and pellets that cut at his hands so that he screwed his eyes shut and clung helplessly.

Such was the speed of the truck now that he was under fire for only seconds, and the gunner's aim could not follow it, as it raced down on to the concrete loading bank, and slammed into the buffers. The force of the impact was brutal and Mark was hurled from his perch, the rifle-strap snapped and the weapon sailed away, and Mark turned in the air and hit the sloping concrete ramp on his side with a crash that jarred his teeth in his head. The rough concrete ripped away the thick barathea cloth from his hip and leg and shoulder, and seared the flesh beneath with gravel burn.

He came up at last against a stack of yellow-painted oil-drums, and his first concern was to roll onto his back and stare upwards.

He was under the headgear now, protected from the gunner by the legs and intricate steel girders of the tower itself, and he pulled himself to his feet, dreading the give and crippling drag of broken bone. But though his body felt crushed and bruised, he could still move, and he hobbled to where his rifle lay.

The strap was broken, and the butt was cracked and splintered, and as he lifted it, it snapped into two pieces. He could not fire from the shoulder.

The foresight had been knocked off, and the broken metal had a sugary grey crystalline look. He could not aim the weapon. He would have to get close, very close.

There was a deep bright scar in the steel of the breech. He muttered a prayer, "Please God!" as he tried to work the bolt open. It was jammed solid and he struggled with it fruitlessly for precious seconds.

"All right," he thought grimly. "No butt to hold to the shoulder, no foresight with which to aim, and only the one cartridge in the breech—it's going to be interesting." He looked around him quickly.

Beneath the steel tower, the two square openings to the main shaft were set into the concrete collar, protected by screens of steel mesh. The one cage stood at the surface station, doors open, ready for the next shift. The other was at the bottom station, a thousand feet below ground level.

They had stood that way for months now. On the far side was the small service elevator which would take maintenance teams the hundred feet to the summit of the tower in half a minute. However, there was no power on the shaft head, and the elevator was useless.

The only other way up was the emergency ladder. This was an open steel stairway that spiralled up around the central shaft, protected only by a low handrail of inch piping.

High above Mark's head the Vickers fired again, and Mark heard a scream of agony out there on the roadway. It hastened him, and he limped to the stairway.

The steel-mesh gate was open, the padlock shattered, and Mark knew by what route the sniper had reached his roost.

He stepped on to the stairway and began to climb, following the coils up the casing round and round, and up and up.

Always at his right hand, the open black mouth of the shaft gaped, an obscene dark orifice in the earth's surface, dropping straight and sheer into the very bowels, a thousand dark terrifying feet.

Mark tried to ignore it, dragging his bruised and aching body up by the handrail, carrying the broken weapon in his other hand, and strained his neck backwards for the first glimpse of the gunner above.

The Vickers fired again, and Mark glanced sideways. He was high enough now to see into the road.

One of the trucks was burning, a tall dragon's breath of smoke and sullen flame pouring into the sky—and the drab khaki bodies were still strewn in the open, death's discarded toys.

Even as he watched, the Vickers fire thrashed over them, mangling already dead flesh, and Mark's anger became cold and bright as a dagger's blade.

"Keep firing, luv," Fergus croaked in that husky stranger's voice. "Short bursts. Count to twenty slowly, and then a touch on the button. I want him to think that I am still up here." He pulled the Webley from his belt, and crawled on his belly towards the head of the steep staircase.

"Don't leave me, Fergus."

"It'll be all right," he tried to grin, but his face was grey and crumpled. "Just you keep firing. I'm going down to meet him halfway. He'll not expect that."

"I don't want to die alone," she breathed. "Stay with me."

"I'll be back, luv. Don't fuss yourself," and he slid on his belly into the opening of the staircase.

She felt like a child again, in one of those terrible dark nightmares, trapped and enmeshed in her own fate, and she wanted to cry out. The sound reached her lips but died there as a low blubbering moan.

A rifle bullet chunked into the barricade of timber beside her. They were shooting from down below. She could not pick them out, for they were hidden in the ditches and the irregularities of the ground, screened by long purple shadows, and her eyes were blurred with tears and with exhaustion, yet she found the last few grains of her strength and crawled to the gun.

She squatted behind it and her hands were almost too small to reach the firing button. She pressed the barrel downwards, and forced her blearing vision to focus, marvelling at the little toy figures in the field of the sight. The gun juddered in her hands like a living creature.

"A short burst," she whispered to herself, repeating Fergus' instructions, and lifted her thumbs from the firing button. "One—two—three," she began to count to the next burst.

Mark paused at the next burst of firing and stood for a moment staring up. He was over halfway to the top, and now he could make out the floor of the service platform below the winch wheels, the platform on which the Vickers was sited.

There were narrow cracks in the woodwork through which bright lines of open sky showed clearly, and as he watched he saw one of the lines of light interrupted by a dark movement beyond. It was that flicker of movement that caught his attention, and he realized that he was looking at the body of the person who served the gun. He must be squatting directly over one of the narrow joints in the floor of the platform, and his movements blocked out part of that bright line of light.

A bullet through the gap would cripple and pin him, but he glanced at the broken weapon in his hand and knew that he would have to get closer, much closer.

He began to run upwards and though he tried to keep his weight lightly on the balls of his feet, the hobnails in his boots rang on the steel stairs.

Fergus MacDonald heard them and checked his own run, shrinking into the protective lee of one of the steel girders.

"One man only," he muttered. "But coming up fast." He

dropped on one knee and peered down through the gaps between the stairs, hoping for sight of the man whom he was hunting. The steps overlapped each other like fanned playing cards, and the lateral supports of the tower formed an impenetrable steel forest below him.

The only way he could hope for a glimpse was to hang out over the handrail and look down the central shaft-well.

The idea of that thousand-foot black hole repelled him, and he had formed an estimate of his opponent high enough to guess that the reward for putting his head over the side would be a bullet between the eyes.

He edged into a better position where he could cover the next spiral of staircase below him.

"I'll let him come up to me," he decided, and braced his arm against the girder at the level of his chin, and laid the Webley over the crook of his elbow to give the heavy pistol support. He knew that over ten paces it was wildly inaccurate, but the dead rest would give him at least one fair shot.

He cocked his head slightly to listen to the clatter of booted feet on steel, and he judged that the man was very close. One more spiral of the stair would bring him into shot. Carefully, he thumbed back the hammer of the Webley and looked down over the slotted rear-sight.

Above them, the Vickers fired again, and Mark paused to catch his breath and check the situation of the gunner, and to his dismay he realized that he had climbed too high in the tower.

He had changed the angle of sight, and could no longer see through the cracks in the timber platform. He had to retreat carefully down the staircase before once again the bright lines of light opened in the dark underbelly of timber.

A vague blur of movement reassured him that the gunner had not changed his position. He was still squatting over the joint, but the shot was almost impossible.

He was shooting directly upwards, awkward even in the best conditions, but now he had no butt to steady the rifle and no foresight, he was shooting into a single dark mass of timber and had to guess the position of the crack because the gunner's body obscured the light from the far side. The crack itself was only two inches wide, and if he missed by a smallest fraction the bullet would bury itself harmlessly in the thick timber.

He tried not to think that there would be only one shot, the jammed breach made that certain.

He put his hip to the guardrail and leaned out over the open shaft, squinted upwards trying to set the target in his mind as he lifted the broken rifle in an easy natural movement. He knew that he had to make the shot entirely by instinct. He had no chance if he hesitated or tried to hold his aim steadily on the target.

He swept up the shattered weapon and at the moment the long barrel aligned, he pressed the trigger.

In the flash and thunder of the shot a tiny white splinter of wood jumped from the edge of the crack. The bullet had touched wood and Mark felt an instant of utter dismay.

Then the body that had obscured the light was jerked abruptly aside, and the crack was a single uninterrupted line again—and on the platform somebody screamed.

Helena MacDonald had just reached the count of twenty again, and was aiming at a gatherring of men she could see grouping beyond one of the lorries. She squatted low over the gun and was on the point of jamming her thumbs down on the firing button, when the bullet came up through the floor timbers.

It had touched one of the hard mahogany baulks, just enough to split the casing of the bullet and alter its shape, mushrooming it slightly, so that it did not enter her body through a neat round puncture.

It tore a ragged entry into the soft flesh at the juncture of her slightly spread thighs and plunged upwards through her lower abdomen, striking and shattering the thick bony girdle of her pelvis, glancing off the bone with still enough impetus to bruise and weaken the lower branch of the descending aorta, the great artery that runs down from the heart, before going on to embed itself in the muscles high in the left side of her back.

It lifted Helena into the air, and hurled her across the platform on to her face.

"Oh God, oh God, help me! Fergus! Fergus! I don't want to die alone," she screamed, and the sound carried clearly to the two men in the steel tower below her.

Mark recognized the voice instantly. It did not need the name to confirm it.

His mind shied at the enormity of what he had done. The broken rifle almost slipped from his hands, but he saved it and caught at the handrail for support.

Helena cried again, a sound without words—it was exactly that strange wild cry that she had uttered at the zenith of one of their wildest flights of passion together, and for an instant Mark remembered her face shining and triumphant, the dark eyes burning and the open red mouth and the soft pink petal of her tongue aflutter.

Mark started to run, hurling himself upwards.

The screams caught Fergus like a flight of arrows in the heart. A piercing, physical agony, he dropped the pistol to his side and stood irresolute staring upwards, not knowing what had happened, except that Helena was dying. He had heard the death scream too often to have any doubt about that. What he was listening to was mortal agony, and he could not force his body to begin the climb upwards, to the horror he knew waited him there.

While he hesitated, Mark came around the angle of the staircase and Fergus was not ready for him. The pistol was at his side, and he fell back and tried to bring it up, to fire at a point-blank range into the chest of the uniformed figure.

Mark was as off balance as he was. He had not expected to run into another enemy, but he saw the pistol and swung the broken rifle at Fergus' head.

Fergus ducked, and the Webley fired wide, the bullet flew inches past Mark's temple and the report slammed against his eardrum and made him flinch his head. The rifle struck the girder behind Fergus and was jerked from Mark's grip, then they came together chest to chest. Mark seized the wrist of his pistol hand and held with all his strength.

Neither of them had recognized the other. Fergus had aged into a grey caricature of himself and his eyes were shaded by the cloth cap. Mark was in unfamiliar uniform, dusty and bloodied, and he had changed also, youth had become man.

Mark was taller, but they were matched in weight and Fergus was endowed with the terrible fighting rage of the berserker which gave him superhuman strength.

He drove Mark back against the guardrail, and bowed his back out over the open shaft, but Mark still had his pistol wrist, and the weapon was pointed up over his head.

Fergus was sobbing wildly, driving with all the wiry uncanny strength of a body tempered by hard physical work, and fired now by the strength of anger and sorrow and despair.

Mark felt his feet slip, the hobnails of his boots skidding on the steel steps and he went over further, feeling the mesmeric suck of a thousand feet of open space plucking at his back.

Above them, Helena screamed again, and the sound drove like a needle into the base of Fergus' brain, he shuddered, and his body convulsed in one great rigid spasm that Mark could not hope to hold. He went backwards over the guardrail, but still he had his grip on Fergus' gun hand and his other arm he had wound about his shoulders.

They slid into the void, locked together in a horrible parody of a lovers' embrace, but as they started to fall, Mark hooked both legs over the rail, like a trapeze artiste, and jerked to a halt, hanging upside down into the shaft.

Fergus was somersaulted over him by the force of his own thrust; as he turned in the air, the cloth cap flew from his head and he was torn from the arm that Mark had around his shoulder.

He came up with a jerk that almost tore Mark's shoulder from its socket, for some animal instinct had kept Mark's grip locked on the pistol hand, and he dangled from that precarious hold.

The two of them pendulumed out over the black emptiness of the shaft, Mark's legs hooked over the rail, hanging at full stretch, with Fergus' body the next link in the chain.

Fergus' head was thrown back, staring up at Mark, and with the cap gone, his lank sandy hair fell back from his face and Mark felt fresh shock loosen his grip.

"Fergus!" he croaked, but the madman's eyes that stared back at him were devoid of recognition.

"Try and get a grip," Mark pleaded, swinging Fergus towards the staircase. "Grab the rail."

He knew he could not hold many seconds longer, the fall had wrenched and weakened his arm, and the blood was rushing to his head; in this inverted position, he could feel his face swelling and suffusing and the pounding ache in his temples—while the black and hungry mouth of the shaft sickened him; with his other hand he groped and got a second hold on Fergus' wrist.

Fergus twisted in his grip, but instead of going for the rail he reached upwards and took the pistol from his own hand, transferring it to his free hand.

"No," Mark shouted at him. "Fergus, it's me! It's me, Mark!"

But Fergus was far past all reason, as he juggled with the Webley, getting a firing grip on the hilt with his left hand.

"Kill them," he muttered. "Kill all the scabs."

He lifted the barrel to aim upwards at Mark, dangling over the drop, twisting slowly in that double retaining grip.

"No, Fergus!" screamed Mark, and the muzzle of the revolver pointed into his face. At that range, it would tear half his head away, and he saw Fergus' forefinger tighten on the trigger, the knuckle whitening under pressure.

He opened his hands and Fergus' wrist slipped from his fingers.

He spun away, falling swiftly, and the revolver never fired but Fergus began to scream a high thin wail.

Still hanging upside down Mark watched Fergus' body, limbs spread and turning like the spokes of a wheel, as it dropped away, shrinking rapidly in size, and the despairing wailing cry receding with it, dwindling away to a small pale speck, like a dust mote which was swallowed abruptly into the dark mouth of the shaft far below and the wailing cry with it.

In the silence afterwards, Mark hung batlike, blinking the sweat out of his eyes and for many seconds unable to find strength to move. Then from the platform above him came a long shuddering moan and it roused him.

Forcing his bruised body to respond, he managed to get a grip on the guardrail and drag himself up, until he tumbled on to the staircase, and started up it on rubbery legs.

Helena had dragged herself to the pile of timber, leaving a dark wet smear across the platform. The khaki breeches she wore were sodden with blood and it oozed from her still to form a spreading puddle in which she sat.

She lay back against the timber next to the tripoded Vickers in an attitude of utter weariness, and her eyes were closed.

"Helena," Mark called her, and she opened her eyes.

"Mark," she whispered, but she did not seem surprised. It was almost as though she expected him. Her face was completely drained of all colour, the lips seemed rimed with frost, and her skin had an icy sheen to it. "Why did you leave me?" she asked.

Hesitantly, he crossed to her. He knelt beside her, looked down at her lower body and felt the scalding flood of vomit rise into his throat.

"I truly loved you," her voice was so light, breathing soft as the dawn wind in the desert, "and you went away."

He put out his hand to touch her legs, to spread them and examine the wound, but he could not bring himself to do it.

"You won't go away again, Mark?" she asked, and he could hardly catch the words. "I knew you'd come back to me."

"I won't go away again," he promised, not recognizing his own voice, and the smile flickered on her icy lips.

"Hold me, please Mark. I don't want to die alone."

Awkwardly, he put an arm around her shoulders and her head lolled sideways against him.

"Did you ever love me, Mark, even a little bit?"

"Yes, I loved you," he told her, and the lie came easily. Suddenly there was a hissing spurt of brighter redder blood from between her thighs as the damaged artery erupted. She stiffened, her eyes flew wide open, and then her body seemed to melt against him and her head dropped back.

Her eyes were still wide open and dark as a midnight sky. As he stared at it, slowly her face changed. It seemed to melt like white candle wax held too close to the flame, it ran and wavered and reformed—and now it was the face of a marble angel, smooth and white and strangely beautiful, the face of a dead boy in a land far away—and the fabric of Mark's mind pulled and tore.

He began to scream, but no sound came from his throat—the scream was deep down in his soul, and his face was without expression, his eyes dry of tears.

They found him like that an hour later. When the first soldiers climbed cautiously up the iron staircase to the top of the steel tower, he was sitting quietly, holding the woman's dead body in his arms.

\* \* \*

"Well," said Sean Courtney, "they've hanged Taffy Long!" He folded the newspaper with an angry gesture and dropped it on to the paving beside his chair.

In the dark shiny foliage of the loquat tree that spread above them, the little white-eyes pinkled and twittered as they probed the blossoms with sharp busy beaks and their wings fluttered like moths about the candle.

Nobody at the breakfast table spoke. All of them knew how Sean had fought for leniency for those strikers on whom the death sentence had been passed. He had used all his influence and power, but it had not availed against the vindictive and vengeful who wanted full measure of retribution for all the horrors of the revolt. Sean brooded now at the head of the table, hunched in his chair with his beard on his chest, staring out over the Ladyburg valley. His arm was still supported by the linen sling; it had not healed cleanly and the bullet wound was still open and draining. The doctors were anxious about it, but Sean had told them,

"Leopard, and bullet and shrapnel and knife—I've had them all before. Don't twist a gut for me. Old meat heals slowly, but it heals hard."

Ruth Courtney watching him now was not worried about the wounds of the flesh. It was the wounds of the mind that concerned her.

Both the men of her household had come back deeply marked by the lash of guilt and sorrow. She was not sure what had happened during those dark days, for neither man had spoken about it, but the horror of it still stalked even here at Lion Kop, even in the bright soft days, on these lovely dreaming hills where she had brought them to heal and rest.

This was the special place, the centre and fortress of their lives, where Sean had brought her as his bride. They owned other great houses, but this was home, and she had brought Sean here now after the strife and the turmoil. But the guilt and the horror had come with them.

"Madness," muttered Sean. "Utter raving madness. How they cannot see it, I do not know." He shook his head, and was silent a moment. Then he sighed. "We hang them now—and make them live for ever. They'll haunt and hound us all our days."

"You tried, dear," said Ruth softly.

"Trying isn't enough," he growled. "In the long run, all that counts is succeeding."

"Oh Pater, they killed hundreds of people," Storm burst out, shaking her shining head at him, with angry colour in her cheeks. "They even tried to kill you!"

Mark had not spoken since the meal began, but now he

lifted his head and looked at Storm across the table. She checked the other words that sprang to her lips as she saw his expression.

He had changed so much since he had come home. It was as though he had aged a hundred years. Though there was no new line or mark on his face, yet he seemed to have shed all his youth and taken upon himself the full burden of knowledge and earthly experience.

When he looked at her like that, she felt like a child. It was not a feeling she relished. She wanted to pierce this new armour of remoteness that invested him.

"They're just common murderers," she said, addressing the words not to her father.

"We are all murderers," Mark answered quietly, and though his face was still remote, the knife clattered against his plate as he put it down.

"Will you excuse me, please, Mrs. Courtney—" he turned to Ruth, and she frowned quickly.

"Oh Mark, you've not touched your food."

"I'm riding into the village this morning."

"You ate no dinner last night."

"I want the mail to catch the noon train." He folded his napkin, rose quickly and strode away across the lawn—and Ruth watched the tall, graceful figure go with a helpless shrug before turning to Sean.

"He's wound up so tight—like a watch spring about to snap," she said. "What's happening to him, Sean?"

Sean shook his head. "It's something that nobody understands," he explained. "We had so much of it in the trenches. It's as though a man can stand just so much pressure, and then something breaks inside him. We called it shell-shock, for want of a better name, but it's not just the shelling." He paused. "I have never told you about Mark before, about why I picked him, about how and when I first met him—" and he told it to them. Sitting in the cool green shade of the loquat tree, he told them of the mud and the fear and the horror of France. "It's not just for a single time, or a day or a week—but it goes on for what becomes an eternity. But it is worse for a man who has special talents. We, the Generals, have to use them ruthlessly. Mark was one of those—" And he told them how they had used Mark like a hunting dog, and his two women listened intently, all of them bound in the life of the young man who had gradually come to mean so much to each of them. "A man gathers horror and fear like a ship gathers weed. It's below the waterline, you cannot see it, but it is there. Mark carries that burden, and at Fordsburg something happened that brought him close to the breaking-point. He is on the very edge of it now."

"What can we do for him?" asked Ruth softly, watching his face, happy for him that he had a son at last—for she had long known that was what Sean saw in Mark. She loved her husband enough not to resent that it was not her own womb that had given him what he so desperately wanted, glad only that he had it at last, and that she could share it with him.

Sean shook his head. "I don't know." And Storm made an angry hissing sound. They both looked at her.

Sean felt that soft warmth spreading through his chest, a feeling of awe that this lovely child could be part of him. Storm looked so smooth and fragile, yet he knew she had the strength of braided whipcord. He knew also that though she had the innocence of a newly opened bloom, yet she could sting like a serpent; she had the brightness and beauty that dazzled, and yet below that were depths that mystified and awed him; and when her moods changed so swiftly, like this unaccountable spurt of anger, he was enchanted by her, under her fairy spell.

He frowned heavily now to hide his feelings.

"Yes, Missy, what is it now?" he grumped at her.

"He's going away," she said, and Sean blinked at her, swaying back in his chair.

"What are you talking about?" he demanded.

"Mark. He's going away."

"How do you know that?" Something deep inside of Sean cringed at the prospect of losing another son.

"I know, I just know," she said, and came to her feet with a flash of long sleek limbs, like a gazelle rising in alarm from its grassy bed. She stood over him.

"You didn't think he would be your lap dog for ever?" she asked, a biting scorn in her tone that at another time would have brought from him a sharp retort. Now he stared at her speechless.

Then suddenly she was gone, crossing the lawn in the sunlight that gilded her loose dark hair with stark white light and struck through the flimsy stuff of her dress, revealing her long slim body in a stark dark silhouette, surrounding her with a shimmering halo of light, that made her seem like some lovely unearthly vision.

\* \* \*

"Don't you see that it's better you cry a little now—than cry for the rest of your life?" Mark asked gently, trying not to let her see how the tears had eroded his resolve.

"Won't you ever come back?" Marion Littlejohn was not one of those women who cried well. Her little round face seemed to smear and lose its shape like unfired clay, and her eyes swelled and puffed pinkly.

"Marion, I don't even know where I am going. How can I know if I'm coming back?"

"I don't understand, Mark, I truly don't understand." She twisted the damp linen handkerchief in her hands, and she sniffed wetly. "We were so happy. I did everything I knew to make you happy—even that."

"It's not you, Marion," Mark assured her hurriedly. He did not want to be reminded of that which Marion always referred to as "that." It was as though she had loaned him a treasure which had to be returned with interest at usurious rates.

"Didn't I make you happy, Mark? I tried so hard."

"Marion, I keep trying to tell you. You are a fine, pretty girl—you're kind and good and the nicest person I know."

"Then why don't you want to marry me?" Her voice

rose into a wail, and Mark glanced with alarm down the length of the porch. He knew that sisters and brothers-in-law were probably straining their hearing for snatches of the conversation.

"It's that I don't want to marry anybody."

She made a low moaning sound and then blew her nose loudly on the inadequate scrap of sodden linen. Mark took his own hankerchief from his inside pocket, and she accepted it gratefully.

"I don't want to marry anybody, not yet," he repeated.

"Not yet," she seized the words. "But some day?"

"Some day," he agreed. "When I have discovered what it is I want out of my life and how I am going to get it."

"I will wait for you." She tried to smile, a brave watery pink smile. "I'll wait for you, Mark."

"No!" Mark felt alarm fire through every nerve of his body. It had taken all his courage to tell her, and now it seemed that he had achieved nothing. "God knows how long it will be, Marion. There will be dozens of other men—you're a kind sweet loving person—"

"I'll wait for you," she repeated firmly, her features regaining their usual pleasant shape, and her shoulder losing their dejected droop.

"Please, Marion. It's not fair to you." Mark tried desperately to dissuade her, realizing that he had failed dismally. But she gave one last hearty sniff and swallowed what was left of her misery, as though it were a jagged piece of stone. Then she smiled at him, blinking the last tears from her eyes.

"Oh, it doesn't matter. I am a very patient person. You'll see," she told him comfortably.

"You don't understand," Mark shrugged with helpless frustration.

"Oh, I do understand, Mark," she smiled again, but now it was the indulgent smile of a mother for a naughty child. "When you are ready, you come back here to me." She stood up and smoothed down the sensible skirts. "Now come along, they are waiting lunch for us."

Storm had taken great care choosing her position. She had wanted to catch the play of afternoon light and the run of the clouds across the escarpment, and yet to be able to see into the gorge, for the white plume of falling spray to be the focus of the painting.

She wanted also to be able to see down along the Ladyburg road, and yet not be overlooked by a casual observer.

She placed her easel on the lip of a small saucer of folded ground near the eastern boundary peg of Lion Kop, positioning both easel and herself with an artist's eye for aesthetic detail. But when she posed on the lip of the saucer, with the palette cradled in the crook of her left arm and the brush in the other, she lifted her chin and looked up at the powerful sweep of land and forest and sky, at the way the light was working and at the golden-tinged turquoise of the sky—and immediately she was intrigued.

The pose was no longer theatrical, and she began to work, tilting her head to appraise a colour mix, moving about the canvas in a slow ritual, like a temple maid making the sacrifice, so completely absorbed that when she heard the faint putter of Mark's motorcycle, it did not penetrate into the silken cocoon of concentration she had woven about herself.

Although her original intention in coming to this place had been to waylay him, now he was almost past before she was aware of him, and she paused with the brush held high in one hand, caught in the soft golden light of late afternoon, a much more striking picture than she could have composed with studied care.

The dusty strip of road snaked five hundred feet below where she stood, making its first big loop on to the slope of the escarpment, and, as he came into the bend, Mark's eyes were drawn naturally to the small delicate figure on the slope.

There were clouds along the summit of the escarpment, and the late sun burned through the gaps, cutting long shimmering beams across the valley, and one of these fell full on Storm.

She stood completely still, staring down the slope at him, making no gesture of recognition or welcome.

He pulled the big machine into the side of the road, and sat astraddle, pushing the goggles on to his forehead.

Still she did not move, and they stared at each other. Mark made a move at last as though to restart the machine, and Storm felt a shock of deprivation, although it did not show either on her face nor in the stillness of her body.

She exerted all her will, trying consciously to reach him with her mind, and he paused and looked up at her again.

"Come!" she willed him, and with an impatient, almost defiant gesture, he pulled the goggles off his head and stripped the gloves off his hands.

Serenely, she turned back to the painting, a small secret smile playing like light across her softly parted lips and she did not watch him climbing up through the yellow knee-high grass.

She heard his breathing behind her, and she smelled him. He had a special smell that she had learned to know, a floury smell a little like a suckling puppy or freshly polished leather. It made her skin feel hot and sensitized, and put a painful little catch in her breathing.

"That's beautiful," he said, and his voice felt like the touch of fingers along the nape of her neck. She felt the fine soft hair there rise, and the flush of blood spread warmly down her chest and turn her nipples into hard little pebbles. They ached with something which was not pain—something more obsessive. She wanted him to touch her there, and at the thought she felt her legs tremble under her and the muscles cramped deeply in the wedge of her thighs.

"It's truly beautiful," he said again, and he was so close

she could feel his breath stir the fine hair of her neck, and another thrill ran down her spine, this time it was like a claw cutting through her flesh and she clenched her buttocks to ride the shock of it as though she was astride a mettlesome horse.

She stared at the painting, and she saw that he was right. It was beautiful, even though it was half-finished. She could see the rest of it in her mind—and it was beautiful and right, but she wanted the touch of his hands now.

It was as though the painting had heightened her emotional response, opened some last forbidden door and now she wanted his touch with a terribly deep physical ache.

She turned to him, and he was so close and tall that she felt her breathing catch again, and she looked up into his face.

"Touch me," she willed him. "Touch me," she commanded silently, but his hands hung at his side and she could not fathom his eyes.

She could not stand still a moment longer, and she stirred her hips in a slow voluptuous gesture, something was melting and burning deep in her lower body.

"Touch me," she tried to force him silently to her will. "Touch me there where it hurts so fiercely."

But he did not heed her, would not respond to all her silent pleas, and suddenly she was angry.

She wanted to lash out at him, to strike him across that solemn handsome face, she had a mental image of ripping his shirt away and sinking her nails deep into the smoothly muscled chest. She stared now at the vee of his open shirt, at the coils of dark hair, and his skin had an oiled gloss gilded by the sun to warm golden brown.

Her anger flared and focused. He had aroused these surging emotions which she could neither understand nor control, these heady terrifying waves of physical arousal, and she wanted to punish him for it, to make him suffer, to have him mauled by his desires as she was; at the same instant in time, she wanted to take that splendid proud head of his and hold it to her bosom like a mother holds her child, she wanted to cherish, and gentle and love him, and claw and ravage and hurt him, and she was confused and giddy and angry and puzzled—but most of all she was racing high on a wave of physical excitement that turned her birdlike and quick and vital.

"I suppose you've been bouncing about on that fat little trollop of yours," she almost snarled it at him. Immediately the hurt and shock showed in his eyes, and she was pleased and savagely triumphant, but also aching with contrition, wanting to fall at his feet and plead for forgiveness, or to lash out with her nails and raise deep bleeding lines across that smooth brown dearly beloved face.

"Wouldn't it have been wonderful if the providence that gave you your beauty and your talent had thought to make you a nice person at the same time," he said quietly, almost sadly. "Instead of a vicious spoiled little brat."

She gasped with the delicious profane shock of it, the insult gave her cause to discard the last vestige of control. Now she could loose the rein and use lash and spur without restraint.

"Oh you swine!" She flew at him, going for his eyes, knowing he was too quick and strong for her, but forcing violent physical contact on him, forcing him to seize her, and when he held her powerless by both arms, she flung her body against his, driving him back a pace, and she saw the surprise on his face. He had not expected such strength. She turned against him, her body fined and tuned and hardened by physical exercise on the courts and in the saddle, forcing him off balance, and, as he shifted his weight from foot to foot, she hooked one ankle with hers and threw her weight in the opposite direction.

They fell together, tumbling backwards into the grassy saucer of ground, and he released her wrists, using both hands to break their fall and cushion her shock as she landed on her back.

Instantly she was at him with both hands, and her nails stung his neck. He grunted and she saw the first flare of real anger in his eyes. It delighted her, and when he seized her wrist, she twisted and bit him in the hard sinewy muscle of his forearm. Hard enough to break the skin, and leave a double crescent of small neat teeth-marks.

He gasped and his anger mounted as he rolled over her, pinning her lower body with one leg as he fought to hold her flying flailing hands.

She bucked under him, her skirts had pulled up to her waist, one slim smooth thigh thrusting up, natural, untutored, cunning, into his groin, not hard enough to injure him, but enough to make him suddenly conscious of his own arousal.

As he realized what was happening, his grip of her arms slackened and he tried desperately to disengage, but one of her arms slid around his neck and the silken warmth of her cheek was pressed to his.

His hands acted without command, running down the deep groove in the centre of her arched back, following the small hard knuckles of her spine to the rounded divide of her buttocks, felt through the glossy slipperiness of silken underwear.

Her breathing rasped hoarsely as sandpaper, and she shifted her head and her mouth joined his, arching her back and lifting her lower body to let her silk underwear come away freely in his hands.

The waxen fork of her body rose out of the bright disordered petals of her skirts like the stamen of some wondrously exotic orchid; its flowing perfection interrupted only by the deep finely sculptured pit in the centre of the perfect plain of her belly, and below that the shockingly abrupt explosion of dark smoky curls, a fat deep wedge that changed shape as she relaxed in a slow voluptuous movement.

"Oh Mark," she breathed. "Oh Mark, I can't stand it." Her anger had all evaporated, she was soft and breathless, slowly entwining, warm and gentle and loving, but the sound of her voice woke him suddenly to reality. He realized the betrayal of the trust placed in him by Sean Courtney, the abuse of a privileged position, and he pulled away from her, appalled at his own treachery.

"I must be mad," he gasped with horror, and tried to roll away from her. Her response was instantaneous, the instinctive reaction of a deprived lioness, that uncanny ability to go from soft purring repose to dangerous blazing anger in the smallest part of a second.

Her open hand cracked across his face, in an explosion of brilliant catherine wheels of colour that starred his vision, and she screamed at him.

"What kind of a man are you?"

She tried to strike him again, but he was ready for her and they rolled together chest to chest in the grass.

"You're a nothing, and you'll stay like that because you haven't the guts and the strength to be anything else," she hissed at him, and the words hurt a thousand times worse than the blow. His own anger flared to match hers and he came up over her.

"Damn you. How dare you say that!"

She shouted back at him. "At least I dare, you wouldn't dare—" But she broke off then as she felt it happen, then she cried out again but in a different voice.

"Oh God!" Her whole body racked as she locked him to her, enfolding and holding him while she purred and murmured with a voice gone low and husky and victorious.

"Oh Mark, oh darling, darling Mark."

\* \* \*

Sean Courtney sat his horse with the slumping comfortable seat of the African horseman. Long stirrups and legs thrust forward, sitting well back on his mount, sjambok trailing from his left hand and reins held low on the pommel of the saddle.

In the shade of the leadwood tree, his stallion stood with the patience of a trained gun horse, its weight braced on three legs and the fourth cocked at rest, neck stretched against the reins as it reached to crop the fine sweet grass

that covered the upper slopes of the escarpment, its teeth
making a harsh tearing sound with each mouthful.

Sean looked out across the spreading forests and grassland below him, and realized how much it had all changed
since he had run across it barefooted with his hunting dogs
and throwing sticks, a small boisterous child.

Four or five miles away, nestled against the protective
wall of the escarpment, was the homestead of Theunis
Kraal, where he had been born in the old brass bedstead in
the front room, both he and Garrick, his twin brother, in
the course of a single sweltering summer morning, a double
birthing that had killed the mother he had never known.
Garrick lived there still, and at last he had found peace and
pride among his books and his papers. Sean smiled with
affection and sympathy, tinged with ancient guilt—what
might his brother have been if one leg had not been shattered by the careless shotgun that Sean had fired? He
thrust the thought aside, and instead turned in the saddle to
survey his own domain.

The thousands upon thousands of acres that he had
planted to timber, and which had given him the foundation
of his fortune. From where he sat he could see the saw-
mills and timber yards adjoining the railway yards down in
the town, and once again he felt the warm contentment of
a life not thrown to waste, the glow of achievement and
endeavour rewarded. He smiled and lit one of the long
dark cheroots, striking the match off his boot, adjusting
easily to the shifting balance of the horse under him.

A moment longer he indulged this rare moment of self-
gratification, almost as though to avoid thinking of the
most pressing of his problems.

Then he let his eyes drift away across the spreading roof-
tops of Ladyburg to that new ungainly structure of steel
and galvanized sheet iron that rose tall enough to dwarf
any other structure in the valley, even the massive four-
storey block of the new Ladyburg Farmers Bank.

The sugar refinery was like some heathen idol, ugly and
voracious, crouching at the edge of the neat blocks of

planted sugar which stretched away beyond the limit of the eye, carpeting the low rolling hills with waving, moving green that roiled in the wind like the waves of the ocean, planted to feed that eternally hungry structure.

The frown puckered the skin between Sean's eyes at the bridge of his big beaky nose. Where he counted his land in thousands of acres, the man who had once been his son counted his in tens of thousands.

The horse sensed his change of mood and gathered itself, nodding its head extravagantly and skittering a little in the shade, ready to run.

"Easy, boy," Sean growled at him, and gentled him with a hand on his shoulder.

He waited now for that man, having come early to the rendezvous as was always his way. He liked go be there first and let the other man come to him. It was an old trick, to let the other seem the interloper in established territory, while the waiting man had time to consider and arrange his thoughts, and to study the other as he approached.

He had chosen the place and the time with care. He had not been able to sanction the thought of Dirk Courtney riding on to his land again, and entering his home. The aura of evil that hung around the man was contagious, and he did not want that evil to sully the inner sanctum of his life which was the homestead of Lion Kop. He did not even want him on his land, so he had chosen the one small section of boundary where his land actually bordered on that of Dirk Courtney. It was the only half-mile of any land of Sean's along which he had strung barbed wire.

As a cattleman and horseman, he had an aversion to barbed wire, but still he had strung it between his land and that of Dirk Courtney, and when Dirk had written asking him for this meeting, he had chosen this place where there would be a fence between them.

He had chosen the late afternoon with intent also. The low sun would be behind him and shining into the other man's eyes as he came up the slope of the escarpment.

Now Sean drew the watch from his waistcoat and saw it was one minute before four, the appointed time. He looked down into the valley, and scowled. The slope below him was deserted, and he could follow the full length of the road into town beyond that. Since he had seen young Mark puttering past on his motorcycle half an hour before, the road also had been deserted.

He looked beyond the town to the flash of the white walls of the grand mansion that Dirk Courtney had built when first he returned to the valley. Great Longwood, a pretentious name for a pretentious building.

Sean did not like to look at it. To him it seemed that the same aura of evil shimmered about it, even in the daylight an almost palpable thing, and he had heard the stories—they had been repeated to him with glee by the gossip-mongers—about what happened up there under the cover of night.

He believed those stories, for he knew with the deep instinct which had once been love, the man who had once been his son.

He looked again at the watch in his hand, and scowled at it. It was four o'clock. He shook the watch and held it to his ear. It ticked stolidly, and he slipped it back into his pocket and gathered the reins. He wasn't coming, and Sean felt a sneaking coward's relief, because he found any meeting with Dirk Courtney draining and exhausting.

"Good afternoon, Father." The voice startled him, so that he gripped the horse with his knees and jerked the reins. The stallion pranced and circled, tossing his head.

Dirk sat easily on a golden red bay. He had come down out of the nearest edge of the forest, walking his mount carefully and silently over the thick mattress of fallen leaves.

"You're late," growled Sean. "I was just leaving." Dirk must have circled out, climbing the escarpment below the falls on to Lion Kop, avoiding the fence and riding up through the plantations to come to the rendezvous from the opposite direction. Probably he had been sitting among the trees watching Sean for the last half hour.

"What did you want to speak to me about?" He must never again underestimate this man. Sean had done so many times before, each time at terrible cost.

"I think you know," Dirk smiled at him, and Sean was reminded of some beautiful glossy and deadly dangerous animal. He sat his horse with a casual grace, at rest but in complete control—and he was dressed in a hunting-jacket of finely woven thorn-proof tweed, with a yellow silk cravat at the throat; his long powerful legs were encased in polished chocolate leather.

"Remind me," invited Sean, consciously hardening himself against the fatal mesmeric charm that the man could project at will.

"Oh come now, I know you have been busy thrashing the sweating unwashed hordes back into their places. I read with pride of your efforts, Father. Your butcher's bill at Fordsburg was almost as fearsome as when you put down Bombata's rebellion back in 1906. Magnificent stuff—"

"Get on with it." Sean found himself hating again. Dirk Courtney had a high skill at finding weakness or guilt, and exploiting it mercilessly. When he spoke like this of the manner in which Sean had been forced to discharge his duty, it shamed him more painfully than ever.

"Of course it was necessary to get the mines operating again. You do sell most of your timber to the gold mines, I have the exact sales figures somewhere." Dirk laughed lightly. His teeth were perfect and white, and the sunlight played in the shining curls of his big handsome head, back-lighting him and making his looks more theatrically magnificent. "Good on you, dear Papa. You always had a keen eye for the main chance. No future in letting a bunch of wild-eyed reds put us all out of business. Even I am utterly dependent on the gold mines in the long run."

Sean could not bring himself to answer, his anger was choking him. He felt dirtied and ashamed.

"It's one of the many things for which I'm indebted to

you," Dirk went on, watching him carefully, smiling and urbane and deadly. "I am your heir, I have inherited from you the ability to recognize opportunity and to seize it. Do you recall teaching me how to take a snake, how to pin it and hold it with thumb and forefinger at the back of the neck?"

Sean remembered the incident suddenly and vividly. The fearlessness of the child had frightened him even then.

"I see you do remember." The smile faded from Dirk's face, the lightness of his manner was gone with it. "So much, so many little things—do you remember when we were lost after the lions stampeded the horses in the night?"

Sean had forgotten that also. Hunting in Mopani country, the child's first overnight away from the security and safety of the wagons. A little adventure that had turned into nightmare, one horse killed by the lions and the other gone, and a fifty-mile walk back through dry sandveld and thick trackless bush.

"You showed me how to find water. The puddle in the hollow tree—I can still taste the stink of it. The bushmen wells in the sand, sucking it up with a hollow straw."

It all came back, though Sean tried to shut his mind against it. They had gone wrong on the third day, mistaking one small dry stony river bed for another and wandering away into the wilderness to a lingering death.

"I remember you made a sling from your cartridge belt, and carried me on your hip."

When the child's strength had gone, Sean had carried him, mile after mile, day after day in the thick dragging sand. When finally his own great strength had been expended also, he had crouched down over the child, shielding him from the sun with his shadow, and had worked his swollen tongue painfully for each drop of saliva to inject into Dirk's cracked and blackening mouth, keeping him alive just long enough.

"When Mbejane came at last, you wept."

The stampeded horse had reached the wagons with the lion claw-marks slashed deeply across its rump. The old

Zulu gunbearer, himself sick with malaria, had saddled the grey and taken a pack horse on the lead rein. He had back-tracked the loose horse to the lion camp, and then picked up the spoor of man and child, following them for four days along a cold wind-spoiled spoor.

When he reached them, they were huddled together in the sand, under the sun—waiting for death.

"It was the only time in my life I ever saw you cry," Dirk said softly. "But did you ever think how often you made me weep?"

Sean did not want to listen longer. He did not want to be further reminded of that lovely, headstrong, wild and be-loved child whom he had reared as mother and father to-gether, yet Dirk's quiet insidious voice held him captive in a web of memory from which he could not escape.

"Will you ever know how I worshipped you? How my whole life was based on you, how I mimicked every action, how I tried to become you?"

Sean shook his head, trying to deny it, to reject it.

"Yes, I tried to become you. Perhaps I succeeded—"

"No." Sean's voice was strangled and thick.

"Perhaps that's why you rejected me," Dirk told him. "You saw in me the mirror-image of yourself, and you could not bring yourself to accept that. So you turned me away, and left me to weep."

"No. God, no—that's not true. It was not that way at all."

Dirk swung his horse in until his leg touched Sean's.

"Father, we are the same person, we are one—won't you admit that I am you, just as surely as I fell from your loins, just as surely as you trained and moulded me?"

"Dirk," Sean started, but there were no words now, his whole existence had been touched and shaken at its very core.

"Don't you realize that every thing I have ever done was for you? Not only as a child, but as a youth and a man. Did you never think why I came back here to Ladyburg, when I could have gone to any other place in the world—

London, Paris, New York—it was all open to me. Yet I came back here. Why, Father, why did I do that?"

Sean shook his head, unable to answer, staring at this beautiful stranger, with his vital strength and his compelling disturbing presence.

"I came back because you were here."

They were both silent then, holding each other's eyes in a struggle of wills and a turmoil of conflicting emotions. Sean felt his resolve weakening, felt himself sliding slowly under the spell that Dirk was weaving about him. He heeled his horse, forcing it to wheel and break the physical contact of their legs, but Dirk went on remorselessly.

"As a sign of my love, of this love that has been strong enough to stand against all your abuse, against the denials you have made, against every blow you have dealt it—as a sign of that, I come to you now—and I hold out my hand to you. Be my father again, and let me be your son. Let us put our fortunes together and build an empire. There is a land here, a whole land, ripe and ready for us to take."

Dirk reached out across the space between the horses with his right hand, palm upwards, fingers outstretched.

"Take my hand on it, Father," he urged. "Nothing will stop us. Together we will sweep the world from our path, together we will become gods."

"Dirk," Sean found his voice, as he fought himself out of the coils in which he had been trapped. "I have known many men, and not one of them was all good nor completely evil. They were all combinations of those two elements, good and evil—that is, until I came to know you. You are the only man who was totally evil, evil unrelieved by the slightest shading of good. When at last I was forced to face that fact, then I turned my back on you."

"Father."

"Don't call me that. You are not mine, and you never will be again."

"There is a great fortune, one of the great fortunes of the world."

"No," Sean shook his head. "It is not there for either

you or me. It belongs to a people, to many peoples—Zulu, and Englishman and Afrikander—not to me, but especially not to you."

"When I came to see you last, you gave me cause to believe," Dirk began to protest.

"I gave you no cause, I made no promise."

"I told you everything, all my plans."

"Yes," said Sean. "I wanted to hear it, I wanted to know every detail, not so that I could help you—but so that I could stand in your way."

Sean paused for emphasis, and then leaned across so his face was close to Dirk's and he could look into his eyes.

"You will never get the land beyond the Bubezi River. I swear that to you," he said it quietly, but with a force that made every word ring like a cathedral bell.

Dirk recoiled, and the high colour drained away from his face.

"I rejected you because you are evil. I will fight you with all my strength, with my life itself."

Dirk's features changed, the line of the mouth and the set of the jaw altered, the slant and tilt of the eyes became wolfish.

"You deceive youself, Father. You and I are one. If I am evil, then you are the source and fountain and father of the evil. Don't spout noble words to me, don't strike postures. I know you, remember. I know you perfectly—as I know myself." He laughed again, but not the bright easy laughter of before. It was a cruel thin sound and the shape of the mouth did not lose its hard line. "You rejected me for that Jewish whore of yours, and the bastard slut you spawned on her soft white belly."

Sean bellowed, a low dull roar of anger, and the stallion reared under him, coming up high on his hindquarters and cutting at the air, and the bay mare swung away in alarm, milling and trampling as Dirk sawed at its mouth with the curb.

"You say you will fight me with your life," Dirk shouted at his father. "It may just come to that! I warn you."

He brought the horse under control, barging in on the stallion so he could shout again.

"No man stands in my way. I will destroy you—as I have destroyed the others who have tried it. I will destroy you and your Jewish whore."

Sean swung back-handed with the sjambok, a polo cut, using the wrist so the thin black lash of hippo-hide fluted like the wing of a flighting goose. He aimed at the face, at the snarling vicious wolf's head of the man who once had been his son.

Dirk threw up his arm and caught the stroke, it split the woven tweed of his sleeve like a sword cut and bright blood sprang to stain the luxurious cloth, as he kneed the bay away in a wide prancing circle.

He held the wound, pressing the lips of the cut together while he glared at Sean, his face contorted with utter malevolence.

"I'll kill you for that," he said softly, and then he swung the bay away and put her into a dead gallop, straight at the five-stranded, barbed fence.

The bay went up and stretched at the jump, flying free of earth and then landing again on the far side, neatly gathered and fully in hand, reached out again into a run, a superb piece of horsemanship.

Sean walked the stallion, fighting the temptation to lash him into a gallop, following the path over the high ground, a path now almost indiscernible, long overgrown. Only a man who knew it well, who had been along it often before, would know it as a path.

There was nothing left of the huts of Mbejane's kraal, except the outline of building stones, white circles in the grass. They had burned the huts, of course, as is the Zulu custom when a chief is dead.

The wall of the cattle kraal was still intact, the stones carefully and lovingly selected, each piece fitted into the shoulder-high structure.

Sean dismounted and tethered the stallion at the gateway. He saw that his hands were still shaking, as though in high fever, and he felt sick to the gut, the aftermath of that wild storm of emotion.

He found his seat on the stone wall, the same flat rock that seemed moulded to his buttocks, and he lit a cheroot. The fragrant smoke calmed the flutter of his heart, and soothed the tremble in his hands.

He looked down at the floor of the kraal. A Zulu chief is buried in the centre of his cattle kraal, sitting upright facing the rising sun, with his induna's ring still on his head, wrapped in the wet skin of a freshly killed ox, the symbol of his wealth, and with his food pot and his beer pot and his snuff box, his shield and his spears at his side, in readiness for the journey.

"Hello, old friend," said Sean softly. "We reared him, you and I. Yet he killed you. I do not know how, nor can I prove it, but I know he killed you—and now he's vowed to kill me also." And his voice quivered.

\* \* \*

"Well," smiled Sean. "If you have to make an appointment to speak with me, it must be some business of dire consequence."

Through the merry twinkle of his eye, he was examining Mark with a shrewd assessing gaze. Storm had been right, of course. The lad had been gathering himself to make the break. To go off somewhere on his own, like a wounded animal perhaps, or a cub lion leaving the pride at full growth? Which was it, Sean wondered, and how great a wrench would the parting make on the youngster?

"Yes, sir, you could say that," Mark agreed, but he could not meet Sean's eyes for once. The usually bright and candid eyes slid past Sean's and went to the books on the shelves, went on to the windows and the sweeping sunlit view across the tops of the plantations and the valley below. He examined it as though he had never seen it before.

"Come on in then." Sean swivelled his chair away from the desk, and took the steel-rimmed spectacles off his nose and waved with them at the armchair below the window.

"Thank you, sir."

While he crossed to the chair, Sean rose and went to the stinkwood cabinet.

"If it's something that important, we'd best take a dram to steel ourselves—like going over the top." He smiled again.

"It's not yet noon," Mark pointed out. "That's a rule you taught me yourself."

"The man who makes the rules is allowed to change them," said Sean, pouring two huge measures of golden brown spirit, and spurting soda from the siphon. "That's a rule I've just this moment made," and he laughed, a fat contented chuckle, before he went on, "Well, my boy, as it so happens, you have chosen a good day for it." He carried one glass to Mark, and returned to his desk. "I also have dire and important business to discuss."

He took a swallow from his glass, smacked his lips in evident relish, and then wiped his moustaches on the back of his hand.

"As the elder, will it be in order if we discussed my business first?"

"Of course, sir." Mark looked relieved and sipped cautiously at his glass, while Sean beamed at him with ill-concealed self-satisfaction.

Sean had conceived of a scheme so devious and tailored so fittingly to his need, that he was a little in awe of the divine inspiration which had fostered it. He did not want to lose this young man, and yet he knew that the surest way of doing so was trying to hold him too close.

"While we were in Cape Town I had two long discussions with the Prime Minister," he began, "and since then we have exchanged lengthy correspondence. The upshot of all this is that General Smuts has formed a separate portfolio, and placed it under my ministry. It is simply the portfolio of National Parks. There is still legislation to see through Parliament, of course, we will need money and new powers—but I am going ahead right away with a survey and assessment of all proclaimed areas, and we will act on that to develop and protect—" He went on talking for almost fifteen minutes, reading from the Prime Minister's letters and memoranda explaining and expanding, going over the discussions, detailing the planning, while Mark sat forward in his chair, the glass at his side forgotten, listening with a rising sense of destiny at work, hardly daring to breathe as he drank in the great concept that was unfolded for him.

Sean was excited by his own vision, and he sprang up from the desk and paced the yellow wood floor, gesturing, using hands and arms to drive home each point, then stopping suddenly in full flight and turning to stand over Mark.

"General Smuts was impressed with you—that night at Booysens, and before that." He stopped again, and Mark was so engrossed that he did not see the cunning expression on Sean's face. "I had no trouble persuading him that you were the man for the job."

"What job?" Mark demanded eagerly.

"The first area I am concentrating on is Chaka's Gate and the Bubezi valley. Somebody has to go in there and do a survey, so that when we go to Parliament, we know what we are talking about. You know the area well—"

The great silences and peace of the wilderness rushed back to Mark, and he felt himself craving them like a drunkard.

"Of course, once the Bill is through Parliament, I will need a warden to implement the act."

Mark sank slowly back in his chair. Suddenly the search was over. Like a tall ship that has made its offing, he felt himself come about and settle on true course with the wind standing fair for a fine passage.

"Now, what was it you wanted to talk to me about?" Sean asked genially.

"Nothing," said Mark softly. "Nothing at all." And his face was shining like that of a religious convert at the moment of revelation.

Mark Anders had been a stranger to happiness, true happiness, since his childhood. He was like an innocent discovering strong liquor for the first time, and he was almost entirely unequipped to deal with it.

It induced in him a state of euphoria, a giddy elation that transported him to levels of human experience whose existence he had not previously guessed at.

Sean Courtney had engaged a new secretary to take over Mark's duties from him. He was a prematurely bald, unsmiling little man, who affected a shiny black alpaca jacket, an old-fashioned celluloid butterfly collar, a green eye-shade and cuff-protectors. He was silent, intense and totally efficient, and nobody at Lion Kop dreamed of calling him anything but "Mr. Smathers."

Mark was to stay on for a further month to instruct Mr. Smathers in his new duties, and at the same time Mark was to set his own affairs in order and make the preparations for his move to Chaka's Gate.

Mr. Smathers' inhuman efficiency was such that within a week Mark found himself relieved almost completely of his previous duties, and with time to gloat over his new happiness.

Only now that it had been given to him did he realize how those tall stone portals of Chaka's Gate had thrown their shadows across his life, how they had become for him the central towers of his existence, and he longed to be there already, in the silence and the beauty and the peace, building something that would last for ever.

He realized how the recent whirlpool of emotion and action had driven from his mind the duty he had set himself—to find the grave of old Grandfather Anders, and fathom the mystery of his death. It was all now before him, and his life had purpose and direction.

But, this was only the foundation and base of his happiness, from which he could launch himself into the towering heady heights of his love.

True enchantment had sprung from that incredible moment in the grassy saucer on the slopes of the Ladyburg escarpment.

His love, which he had borne secretly, a burden cold and heavy as a stone, had in a single magical instant burst open, flowering like a seed into a growth of such vigour and colour and beauty and excitement, that he could not yet grasp it all.

He and Storm cherished it so dearly that no other must even guess at its existence. They made elaborate plans and pacts, weaved marvellously involved subterfuges about themselves to protect this wondrous treasure of theirs.

They neither spoke to each other, nor even looked at the other in the presence of a third party and the restraint taxed each of them so that the moment they were alone together they fell ravenously each upon the other.

When they were not alone together, they spent most of their time planning and scheming how to be so.

They wrote each other flaming notes which were passed under the table in the presence of Sean and Ruth and should have seared the fingers that touched them. They developed codes and signs, they found secret places, and they took hideous chances. Danger spiced their already piquant banquet of love and delight, and they were both insatiable.

At first, they rode to hidden places in the forest along separate and convoluted pathways and galloped the last mile, arriving breathless and laughing, embracing, still in the saddle while the horses stamped and snorted. The first time they were still locked together when they tumbled from the saddles to the forest bed of dead leaves and ferns, and they left their horses loose. It had been a long walk home, especially as they clung to each other like drunkards, laughing and giggling all the way. Luckily their horses had found a field of lucerne before they reached the homestead, and their riderless return had not alerted the grooms. Their secret remained intact, and after that they wasted a few seconds of their precious time together while Mark hobbled the horses.

Soon it was not enough to have only a stolen hour in the day and they met in Storm's studio. Mark climbed the banyan tree, crawling out along the branch, while Storm held the window open and squealed softly with horror when his foot slipped, or hissed a warning when a servant passed, then clapped her hands and flung her arms around his neck as he came in over the sill.

The studio was furnished with a single wooden chair, the floor was bare and hard, and the danger of sudden intrusion too great for even them to ignore. However, they were undaunted and inventive, and they found almost immediately that Mark was strong enough and she was light enough and that all things are possible.

Once Mark became unsteady at the scorching noonday of their loving and backed her into one of her own unfinished masterpieces. Afterwards, she knelt on the wooden chair holding her skirts to her waist and elevated her perfect little round stern while Mark removed the smudges of burnt umber and prussian blue with a rag moistened with turpentine. Storm was shaking so violently with suppressed laugher that Mark's task was much complicated. She was also blushing so furiously that even her bottom glowed a divine ethereal pink, and for ever afterwards, the smell of turpentine acted on Mark as a powerful aphrodisiac.

On another terrifying occasion, there was the heavy tramp, and the unmistakable limping drag in the passageway beyond the studio door, and they were frozen and ashen-faced, unable to breathe as they listened to its approach.

The peremptory knock on the door almost panicked her and she stared into Mark's face with huge terrified eyes. He took control instantly, realizing just how terrible was the danger. Sean Courtney, faced with the sight of somebody actually tupping his ewe lamb, was fully capable of destroying both them and himself.

The knock came again, impatient, demanding, and Mark whispered quickly as they adjusted their clothing with frantic hands. She responded bravely, though her voice caught and quavered.

"One moment, Daddy."

Mark seized her paint-stained smock and slipped it over her head, grabbed a brush from the pot and put it in her right hand, squeezed her shoulders to brace her, and then pushed her gently towards the door.

There was just enough space between the wall and a canvas for him to crawl in and crouch, trying to still his breathing, while he listened to Storm shoot the door-bolt and greet her father.

"Locking the door now, Missy?" Sean growled at her, throwing a suspicious glance around the bare studio. "Intruding, am I?"

"Never, Pater, not you!"

And they were into the room, Storm following meekly, while Sean gave critical judgment of her work.

"There isn't a tree on Wagon Hill."

"I'm not taking photographs, Daddy. There should be a tree there. It balances the composition. Don't you see?" She had recovered like a champion and Mark loved her to the point of pain.

Mark was emboldened enough to take a cautious glance around the edge of the canvas, and the first thing he saw was a five-guinea pair of cami-knickers in sheer oyster silk, the wide legs cuffed with ivory cambrai lace, lying crumpled and abandoned on the studio floor where Storm had dropped them earlier.

He felt a cold sheen of sweat break out afresh across his brow; on the bare floor, the lovely silk was as conspicuous as a battle ensign. He tried to reach that blatantly sinful little pile, but it was beyond his finger-tips.

Storm was hanging on to her father's arm, probably because her legs were too weak to support her, and she saw what Mark's desperate arm and groping hand protruding from behind the canvas was trying to reach. Her panic flooded back again at high spring tide.

She gabbled meaningless replies to her father's questions and tried to lead him towards the door, but it was like trying to divert a bull elephant from his set purpose. Inexorably Sean bore down upon the discarded knickers and the canvas where Mark cowered.

At his next step, the silk wrapped itself around the toe of his boot. The material was so filmy and light that he did not notice it, and he limped on happily, one foot draped in an exotic piece of feminine underwear, while two young people watched in abject terror the knickers' slow circuit of the room.

At the door, Storm flung her arms around his neck and kissed him, managing to anchor the knickers with the toe of her shoe, and then propelling her father into the passage with indecent despatch and slamming the door behind him.

Weak with terror and laughter, they clung together in the middle of the studio, and Mark was so chastened that, when he regained his voice, he told her sternly,

"We are not going to take any more chances, do you understand?"

"Yes, master," she agreed demurely, but with a wicked sparkle in her eye.

Mark was awakened a few minutes after midnight with a wet pointed tongue probing deeply into his ear and he would have let out a great shout but a strong little hand was pressed firmly across his mouth.

"Are you mad?" he whispered, as he saw her bending over him in the moonlight from the open window, and realized that she had made the journey across the full length of the house, down cavernous passageways and creaking staircases, in pitch darkness and clad only in a gossamer pair of pyjamas.

"Yes," she laughed at him. "I'm mad, completely wonderfully insane, a magnificent noble rage of the mind."

He was only half awake or he would not have asked the next question. "What are you doing here?"

"I have come to ravish you," she said, as she slipped into the bed beside him.

"My feet are cold," she announced regally. "Warm them for me."

"For God's sake, don't make so much noise," he pleaded, which was a ridiculous request in the circumstances, for only minutes later they were both raising such a chorus of cries that should have woken the entire household.

Long afterwards, she murmured in that special purry feline voice of hers that he had come to know so well.

"You really are an amazingly talented man, Mr. Anders. Where ever did you learn to be so utterly depraved?" And then she chuckled sleepily, "If you tell me, I shall probably claw your eyes out of your head."

"You mustn't come here again."

"Why not? It's so much better in bed."

"What will your father do if he finds out?"

"He'll murder you," she said comfortably. "But what on earth has that got to do with it?"

\* \* \*

One of the ancillary benefits which accrued to Storm from this relationship was that she had at last a fine male figure model for her work, something which she had always needed but had never found the courage even to ask her father to give her. She knew exactly what his reaction would be.

Mark was not gushing with enthusiasm for the idea either, and it took all her wheedling and cooing to have him disrobe in cold blood. She had picked one of their secret places in the forest for her figure studio, and Mark perched self-consciously on a fallen log.

"Relax," she pleaded. "Think beautiful thoughts."

"I feel such an ass," he protested, wearing only a pair of striped cotton underpants, at which he had drawn the line, despite her entreaties.

"Anyway, there's nothing under there you could paint on canvas," he pointed out.

"But that's not the point, you're supposed to be an ancient Greek, and who ever saw an Olympic athlete—"

"No," Mark cut her short. "They stay on. That's final." She sighed at the intransigence of men, and applied herself to her paints and canvas. Slowly he did relax, and even began to enjoy the freedom and the feel of the sunlight and the air on his skin.

He enjoyed watching her work also, the little frown of total concentration, the half-closed eyes, the porcelain white teeth nibbling thoughtfully at her lower lip, the almost dancing ritual of movement she performed around the canvas, and while he watched her he fantasized a future in which they walked hand in hand through the garden wilderness beyond Chaka's Gate. A future bright with happiness, and radiant with shared labour and achievement, and he began to tell her about it, letting his thoughts find expression in words, that Storm did not hear. Her ears were closed, her whole existence transferred into eyes and hands, seeing only colour and form, sensitive only to mood.

She saw the awkwardness and rigidity of his body flowing into a pose of natural grace such as she could never have composed; she saw the rapture dawning on his features, and she nodded and murmured agreement softly, not wanting to spoil it or break the mood; her fingers racing to capture the moment, all her mind and art concentrated on that single task; her own rapture rising to complement and buoy his even higher, seemingly bound close and fast by the silken traces of love and common purpose, but in reality as far from each other as earth is from the moon.

"I'll be studying the ground for the exact place to site the homestead," he told her, "and it will take a full year to see it all in every season. Good water in the dry, but safe from flood in the rains. The cool sea breeze in summer and protected from the cold weather in winter."

"Oh yes," she murmured, "that's marvellous." But she was looking at his eyes.

"If only I can capture that fleck of light that makes them shine so," she thought, and dabbed a touch of blue to the white to mix the shade.

"Two rooms to start. One to sleep and one to live. Of course a wide veranda looking out across the valley."

"That's wonderful," she exulted softly, as she touched the eye with the tip of the brush and it came instantly alive, gazing back at her from the canvas with an expression that squeezed her heart.

"I'll quarry the stone from the cliff, but away from the river so there'll be no scar to spoil it, and we'll cut the thatch from the edge of the swamp, and the roof poles from the forest."

The sun had swung to the west and it filtered down through the forest roof with a cool greenish light that touched the smooth hard muscles of his arm and the sculptured marble of his back, and she saw that he was beautiful.

"We can build on slowly, as we need new rooms, I'll design it that way. When the children come, we can change the living room to a nursery and add a new wing."

He could almost smell the aromatic shavings of the witels poles, and the sweet perfume of new cut thatch, and in his mind he saw the bright new roof mellowing and darkening in the weather, feel the cool of the high deep rooms at midday, and hear the crackle of the fiercely burning mimosa thorn in the stone fireplace on the cold and starry nights.

"We'll be happy, Storm, I promise you that." They were the only words she heard—and she lifted her head and looked at him.

"Oh yes. We'll be happy," she echoed, and they smiled at each other in total misunderstanding.

When Sean had told Ruth Courtney that Mark was leaving, her dismay had alarmed him. Sean had not realized that he had taken such a place in her affections also.

"Oh, no, Sean," she had protested.

"It's not as bad as it might have been," he assured her quickly. "We'll not lose him altogether, it's just that he'll be on a longer rein, that's all. He'll still be working for me, but now only in my official capacity." And he explained it all to her. She was silent for a long time when he had finished, considering it from every angle before she gave her opinion.

"He'll be good at that, I think," she nodded at last. "But I had rather got used to having him around us. I'll miss him."

Sean grunted what could have been agreement, not able to make such a sentimental admission outright.

"Well," Ruth went on immediately, her whole attitude becoming businesslike, "I'll have to get on with it," which meant that Mark Anders was to be fitted out for his move to Chaka's Gate by one of the world's leading experts. She had sent her man on campaign or on safari so often, that she knew exactly what was necessary, the absolute bare necessity for survival and comfort in the African bush. She knew that anything more than that would not be used, bundles of luxuries would come home untouched, or be abandoned along the way. Yet everything selected was of the finest quality, for she raided Sean's campaign bag blatantly, justifying each theft with the firm utterance,

"Sean won't be using that again."

The sleeping roll needed darning, and she made the repair a little work of art. Then she applied herself to the one luxury the pack would contain, books. This choice she and Mark discussed at length, for weight and space made it essential that each book must be able to withstand numerous rereadings. They had a wide selection from which to make their choice, hundreds of battered old volumes, stained by rain and mud, spilled tea and, in more than one case, by splotches of dried blood, and faded by sunlight and age, all of them having been carried great distances in Sean's old canvas book-bag.

Macaulay and Gibbon, Kipling and Tennyson, Shakespeare and even a small leather-bound Bible were given place, after being carefully screened by the selection committee, and Mark, whose previous camping equipment had been limited to a blanket, a pot and a spoon, felt as though he had been given a permanent suite at the Dorchester.

Sean provided the other essentials for the expedition. The 9.3 Mannlicher in its leather case and two mules. They were big rangy animals, both hard workers and of equitable temper, both salted by having been deliberately exposed to the bite of the tsetse fly and surviving the onslaught of the disease that resulted. They had cost Sean dearly for this immunity, but then the nagana had an almost ninety per cent mortality rate. Salted animals were essential. It would have been less trouble and had the same end result to shoot them between the eyes, rather than take unsalted animals into the fly belt beyond Chaka's Gate.

Each day, Sean set aside an hour or so to discuss with Mark the objects and the priorities of the expedition. They drew up a list, which was added to daily and, as it grew, so did Sean Courtney's enthusiasm. More than once be broke off to shake his head and grumble. "You lucky blighter, what I wouldn't give to be your age again—and to be going back into the bush."

"You could come and visit me," Mark smiled.

"I might just do that," Sean agreed, and then resettled his spectacles on his nose to bring up the next point for discussion.

The first of Mark's tasks was to compile an estimate of what species of wild animal still existed in the proclaimed area, and how many of each there were. Clearly this was of the utmost importance to any attempt at protection and conservation. All would depend on there being sufficent wild-life surviving to make their efforts worthwhile.

"It may already be too late in the afternoon," Sean pointed out.

"No." Mark would not even listen to the suggestion. "There is game there. Just enough to give us a chance. I'm sure of it."

Next important was for him to contact the people living in the area of Chaka's Gate, the Zulus grazing cattle along the edge of the tsetse fly belt, the native hunters and gatherers living within the belt, each wandering group, each village, each headman, each chief, and hold discussions with them; gauging the attitude of the Zulu people to the stricter administration of the proclaimed area, and warning them that what for many years they and their ancestors had looked upon as commonage and tribal hunting-ground was under new control. Men were no longer free to cut timber and thatch, to gather and hunt at will. Mark's intimate knowledge of the Zulu language would serve him well here.

He was to build temporary accommodation for himself, and conduct a survey to choose the final site for a permanent warden's post. There were fifty other tasks less important, but no less demanding.

It was a programme to excite and intrigue Mark, and make him want to begin, and as the day drew nearer, only one cloud lay dark and heavy on the splendid horizon ahead of him. He would be parting from Storm, but he consoled himself with the sure knowledge that it would not be for long. He was going ahead into Eden to prepare a place for his Eve.

* * *

As Storm watched him sleep flat on his back, spread like a crucifix on the forest floor, without even the cotton underpants between him and nature, the possessive smile of a

mother watching over the child at her breast warmed and
softened Storm's lips.

She was naked also, her clothing scattered around them
like the petals of an overblown rose, thrown there by the
storm winds of passions which were now spent and quies-
cent. She sat over him cross-legged on the corner of the
plaid rug, and she studied his face, wondering at how
young he looked in sleep, feeling a choking of tenderness in
her throat, and the soft melting after-glow of loving deep in
her body where he had been.

She leaned over him, and her breasts swung forward
with a new weightiness, the tips darker and wrinkled like
small pinky brown raisins. She dipped her shoulders and let
the nipples brush lightly across his face, and smiled again as
he screwed up his nose and pursed his lips in his sleep,
snorting as if to blow away a bothersome fly.

He came awake suddenly and as he reached for her, she
squealed softly and plucked her breasts away from him,
slapping at his hands.

"Unhand me, sir, this instant!" she commanded, and he
caught her and pulled her down on to his chest, so that she
could hear his heart beating under her ear.

She snuggled down, making throaty little sounds of comfort. He sighed deeply, and his chest swelled and expanded
under her cheek and she heard the air rush into his lungs.

"Mark?" she said.

"I'm here."

"You're not going. You know that, don't you?"

The air in his lungs stayed there as he held his breath,
and the hand that was stroking lightly up from the small of
her back to the nape of her neck stilled. She could feel the
tension in his fingers.

They stayed like that for many seconds and then he let
the air out of his lungs with an explosive grunt.

"What do you mean?" he asked. "Where am I not
going?"

"This place up there in the bush," she said.

"Chaka's Gate?"

"Yes. You're not going."

"Why not?"

"Because I forbid it."

He sat up abruptly, joggling her roughly off his chest.

They sat facing each other, and he was staring at her with such an expression that she ran her fingers through her hair and then folded her arms across her breasts, covering them protectively.

"Storm, what on earth are you talking about?" he demanded.

"I don't want you to waste any more time," she told him. "You must start making your way now, if you're ever going to amount to anything."

"This is my way—our way," he said, bewildered. "We agreed on it. I will go up there to Chaka's Gate and build our home."

"Home!" She was truly appalled. "Up there in the bush—me in a grass hut? Mark, are you out of your mind?"

"I thought—"

"What you're going to do is start making some money," she told him fiercely, and, picking up her blouse, she pulled it over her head, and as her tousled head emerged she went on, "and forget about little boys' games."

"I'll be making money." His expression was stiff, and becoming hostile.

"What money?" she asked, just as frostily.

"I'll have a salary."

"A salary!" She flung back her head and gave a high peal of scornful laughter. "A salary, forsooth! How much?"

"I don't know," he admitted. "It isn't really all that important."

"You're a child, Mark. Do you know that? A salary, twenty pounds a week? Can you really and truly imagine me living on your salary?" She gave the word a world of contempt. "Do you know who earns salaries? Mr. Smathers earns a salary," she was on her feet now, hopping furiously on one leg as she drew on her knickers, "Daddy's foremen at the saw-mills earn salaries. The servants that wait on the table, the stable-grooms earn salaries."

She was pulling up her riding breeches, and with them all her dignity.

"Real men don't earn salaries, Mark." Her voice was high and shrill. "You know what real men do, don't you?"

He was buttoning his fly of his breeches also, forced to follow her example, and he shook his head silently.

"Real men pay salaries—not take them," she said. "Do you know that when my father was your age he was already a millionaire!"

Mark was never able to fathom what it was that triggered him, perhaps the mention of Sean at that particular moment, but suddenly he lost his temper. He felt it like a hot red fog behind his eyes.

"I'm not your bloody father," he shouted.

"Don't you swear at my father," she shouted back. "He's five times the man you'll ever be."

They were both panting and flushed, clothing rumpled, half-clad, with wild hair and wilder eyes, glaring at each other like animals, speechless with hurt and anger.

Storm made the effort. She swallowed painfully, and held out her hands palms upwards.

"Listen, Mark. I've got it all planned. If you went into timber, selling to the mines, Daddy would give you the agency and we could live in Johannesburg."

But Mark's anger was still on him, and his voice was rough and scaly with it.

"Thank you," he said. "Then I could spend my life grubbing money for you to buy those ridiculous clothes and —"

"Don't you insult me, Mark Anders," she blazed.

"I'm me," Mark told her. "And that's what Im going to be the rest of my life. If you loved me, you'd respect that."

"And if you loved me, you wouldn't want me to live in a grass hut."

"I love you," he shouted her down. "But you'll be my wife and you'll do what I decide."

"Don't challenge me, Mark Anders. I warn you. Don't ever do that!"

"I'll be your husband," he began, but she snatched up her boots and ran to her horse, stooping to loose the hobble and then flinging herself on to its back bare-footed and looked down at him. She was breathless with anger, but she struggled to make her voice icy and cutting.

"Don't take any bets on that!" And she dragged the horse's head around and kicked him into a run.

\* \* \*

"Where is Missy?" Sean demanded as he unfolded his napkin and tucked the corner into his waistcoat, glancing at Storm's empty place at the table.

"She's not feeling very well, dear," Ruth told him, as she began serving the soup, ladling it out of the fat-bellied tureen in a cloud of fragrant steam. "I allowed her to have her dinner sent up to her room."

"What's wrong with her?" Sean looked up with concern creasing his forehead.

"It's nothing serious," said Ruth firmly, closing the door on further discussion. Sean stared at her for a moment, and then understanding dawned.

"Oh!" he said. The functions of the female body had always been shrouded for Sean Courtney in deepest mystery, and awakened in him an abiding awe.

"Oh!" he said again, and leaned forward to blow noisily on a spoonful of soup to cover his embarrassment, and the niggling resentment that his beloved child was a child no longer.

Across the table, Mark applied himself to his spoon with equal determination, but with an empty aching feeling below his ribs.

"Where is Missy tonight?" Sean asked, with what was for him a certain diffidence. "Still not well?"

"She telephoned Irene Leuchars this morning. Apparently the Leuchars are having a huge party tonight and she wanted to go. She left after lunch. She's driving herself back to Durban in the Cadillac."

"Where will she stay?" Sean demanded.

"With the Leuchars, naturally."

"She should have asked me." Sean frowned.

"You were down at the saw-mills all day, dear. The decision had to be made immediately, or she would have missed the party. I knew you wouldn't mind."

Sean minded everything that took his daughter away from him, but he could not say so now. "I thought she hated Irene Leuchars," he complained.

"That was last month," said Ruth.

"I thought she was sick," Sean persisted.

"That was last night."

"When is she coming home?"

"She may stay in town for the race-meeting at Greyville on Saturday."

Mark Anders listened with the empty space in his chest turning to a great bottomless void. Storm had gone back to join that close group of rich, indolent and privileged young people, to their endless games and their eternal round of extravagant partying, and on Saturday Mark was leaving with two mules for the wilderness beyond Chaka's Gate.

\* \* \*

Mark would never fathom how Dirk Courtney knew. To him it seemed further evidence of the man's power, the tentacles of his influence that reached into every corner and crevice.

"I understand you are to make the survey for the Gov-

ernment, to decide whether it's worth developing the proclaimed area beyond Chaka's Gate?" he asked Mark.

Mark could still hardly believe the fact that he stood
unarmed and completely unprotected here at Great Longwood. His skin tingled with warning of deadly danger, his
nerves were drawn like bow-strings, and he walked with
exaggerated care, one hand clenched in the hip-pocket of
his breeches.

Beside him, Dirk Courtney was tall and courteous and
affable. When he turned to make that statement, he smiled,
a warm spread of the wide and handsome mouth—and he
laid a hand on Mark's upper arm. A light but friendly
touch, which shocked Mark as though a mamba had kissed
him with its little flickering black tongue.

"How does he know it?" Mark stared at him, his feet
slowing, so that he pulled gently away from Dirk's touch.

If Dirk noticed the withdrawal, it did not show in his
smile, and he let his hand fall naturally to his side and took
the flat silver cigarette-case from his jacket pocket.

"Try one," he murmured. "They are made especially for
me."

Mark tasted the incense of the sweetish Turkish tobacco,
using the act of lighting the cigarette to cover his uncertainty and surprise. Only Sean Courtney and his close family knew, and of course the Prime Minister's office—the
Prime Minister's office, if that was it, as it seemed it must
be, then Dirk Courtney's tentacles stretched far indeed.

"Your silence I must take as confirmation," Dirk told
him, as they came down the paved alleyway between two
lines of white-washed loose boxes. From over the half-doors,
the horses stretched out their necks to Dirk and he paused
now and then to caress a velvety muzzle with surprisingly
gentle fingers, and to murmur and endearment.

"You are a very silent young man." Dirk smiled that
warm endearing smile again. "I like a man who can keep
his own counsel, and respect the privacy of others." He
turned to confront Mark, forcing him to meet his eyes.

Dirk reminded Mark of some glossy cat, one of the big

predators, not the tabby domestic variety. The leopard, golden and beautiful and cruel. He wondered at his own courage, or foolhardiness, in coming here right into the leopard's lair. A year ago it might have been suicidal to put himself in this man's hands. Even now, without Sean Courtney's protection, he would never have dared. Yet although it was logical to believe that nobody, not even Dirk Courtney, would dare touch him, now that he was Sean Courtney's protégé with all that that implied, yet prickles of apprehension nettled his spine as he looked into those leopard's eyes.

Dirk took his elbow, not giving him opportunity to avoid the touch, and let him through a gateway to the stud pens.

The two pens were enclosed with ten-foot-high pole fences, carefully padded to prevent damage to the expensive animals that would be confined here. The earth within the rectangular enclosures was ankle-deep with fresh sawdust, and though one was empty, there was a group of four grooms busy in the nearest pen.

Two of them had the mare on a double lead rein. She was a young animal, a deep red bay in colour, and she had the beautiful balanced head of the Arab, wide nostrils which promised great heart and stamina, and strong but delicate bones.

Dirk Courtney placed a booted foot on the bottom rail of the pen, and leaned forward to look at her with a gloating pride.

"She cost me a thousand guineas," he said, "and it was a bargain."

The two other grooms had the stallion in check. An old, heavily built animal, with grey dappling his muzzle. He wore a girdle, strapped under his belly, and up between the hindlegs, a cage like an old-fashioned chastity belt of woven light chain that was called the teaser. It would prevent his effectively covering the mare.

The grooms gave him rein to approach the mare, but the instant she felt his gentle nuzzling touch under her tail, she put her head down and lashed out with both back legs, a

murderous hissing cut of hooves that flew within inches of
the stallion's head.

He snorted and backed away. Then, undeterred, he
closed with her once more, reaching out to touch her flank,
running his nose with a gentle lover's touch across the
glossy hide, but the mare made her skin shudder wildly, as
though she were beset by bees, and she let out a screaming
whinny of outrage at the importunate touch on her maid-
enly virtue. One of the grooms was dragged down on his
knees as she flashed at the stallion with terrible yellow
teeth, catching him in the neck and ripping open his old
dappled hide in a shallow bloody cut before they pulled her
off.

"Poor old beggar," murmured Mark, although the injury
was superficial; it was the indignity of the whole business
that aroused Mark's sympathy. The old stallion must en-
dure the kicks and bites, until at last the temperamental filly
was wooed and willing. Then he would be led away, his
work done.

"Never waste sympathy for the losers in this world,"
Dirk advised him. "There are too many of them."

In the sawdust-covered arena, the filly lifted her tail, the
long glossy hairs forming a soft waving plume, and she uri-
nated a sharp spurt that was evidence of her arousal.

The stallion circled her, rolling back his upper lip, exposing his teeth, and his shoulder muscles spasmed violently as
he nodded his head vigorously and reached out to her again.

She stood quietly now, with her tail still raised, and
trembled at the soft loving touch of his muzzle, ready at
last to accept him.

"All right," Dirk shouted. "Take him out." But it required the strength of both grooms to drag his head around
and lead him out of the tall gate that Dirk swung open.

"Strangely enough, I don't believe that you are one of
this life's losers," Dirk told Mark easily, as they waited by
the gate. "That is why you are here at this moment. I only
trouble myself with a certain type of man. Men with either

talent, or strength or vision— or all of those virtues. I believe you may be of that type."

Mark knew then that all this had been carefully arranged, the meeting with Peter Botes, Marion Littlejohn's brother-in-law, outside the post office in Ladyburg, the urgent summons to Dirk Courtney's estate he had delivered, so there was no opportunity to report to Sean Courtney and discuss the invitation, and now this erotic show of mating horses—all of it planned to confuse and unsettle Mark, to keep him unbalanced.

"I think you are more like this," Dirk went on, as the grooms led in the stud stallion, an animal too valued to risk damaging by putting to an unwilling female, a tall horse, black as a rook's wing, high-stepping and proud, kicking the soft sawdust with polished hooves, and then coming up hard and trembling on stiff legs as he smelt the waiting mare, and the great black root grew out of his belly, long as a man's arm and as thick, arrogant, and with a flaring head that pulsed with a life of its own and beat impatiently against the stallion's chest.

"The losers toil, and the winners take the spoil," said Dirk, as the huge beast reared up over the mare. One of the grooms darted forward to guide him, and the mare hunched her back to receive the long gliding penetration.

"The winners and the losers," he repeated, watching the stallion work with glistening bulging quarters, and Dirk's handsome face was flushed with high colour, and his hands gripped the poles of the fence until the knuckles blanched like marble.

When at last the stallion dropped back off the mare on to four legs, Dirk sighed, took Mark's elbow again and led him away.

"You were present when I spoke with my father of my dream."

"I was there," Mark agreed.

"Oh good," Dirk laughed genially. "You have a voice—I was beginning to doubt it. But my information is that you have a good brain also."

Mark glanced at him sharply and Dirk assured him, "Naturally, I have made it my business to find out all about you. You know certain details of my plans. I must be in a position to protect myself."

They skirted the ornamental pond, below the homestead, the surface covered with flat lily pads and the smell of their blooms light and sugary in the afternoon heat, and they went on through the formal rose garden, neither of them speaking again until they had entered the high-ceilinged and over-furnished study; Dirk had closed the wooden shutters against the heat, making the room cool and gloomy, and somehow forbidding.

He waved Mark to a chair across from the fireplace and went to the table on which stood a silver tray of bottles and crystal.

"Drink?" he asked, and Mark shook his head and watched Dirk pour from a black bottle.

"You know my dream," Dirk spoke, still concentrating on his task. "What did you think of it?"

"It's a large concept," Mark said cautiously.

"Large?" Dirk laughed. "It's not the word I would have chosen." He saluted Mark with the glass and sipped at it, watching him over the rim.

"Strange how the fates work," Dirk thought, watching the slim graceful figure. "Twice I tried to be rid of the nuisance he could have caused me. If I had succeeded, I would not be able to use him now."

He hitched one leg over the corner of his desk and set the glass aside carefully to leave both hands free, and he gesticulated as he talked.

"We are talking of opening a whole new frontier, a huge step forward for our nation, work for tens of thousands of people, new towns, new harbours, railways—progress." He spread his hands, a gesture of growth and limitless opportunity. "That one wonderful word that describes it all— progress! And anybody who tries to stop that is worse than a fool, he's a criminal, a traitor to his country, and should be treated as one. He should be brushed mercilessly aside, by any means that comes to hand."

He paused now and glowered at Mark. The threat was barely concealed, and Mark stirred restlessly in his chair.

"On the other hand," Dirk smiled suddenly, like a flooding beam of sunlight bursting through the grey overcast of a storm sky. "Every man who works towards the fulfilment of this huge concept will be fully entitled to a share of the rewards."

"What do you want from me?" Mark asked, and the abrupt question caught Dirk with his hands poised and the next flight of oratory on his lips. He let the hands drop to his sides, and watched Mark's face expectantly, as though there was something still to come. "And what are the rewards you speak of?" Mark went on, and Dirk laughed delightedly, those were the words for which he had been waiting—each man has a coin for which he will work.

"You know what I want from you," he said.

"Yes, I think I do," Mark agreed.

"Tell me what I want," Dirk laughed again.

"You want a report that recommends that the development of the Chaka's Gate proclaimed area as a National Park is not practical."

"You said it, not me." Dirk picked up his glass again and lifted it to Mark. "But, none the less, I'll drink to it."

"And the rewards?" Mark went on.

"The satisfaction of knowing that you are doing your patriotic duty for the peoples of this nation," Dirk told him solemnly.

"I had all the satisfaction I need for a lifetime in France," Mark said softly. "But I found out you can't eat or drink it," and Dirk laughed delightedly.

"That really is choice, I must remember it. Are you certain you won't have a drink?"

Mark smiled for the first time. "Yes, I'll change my mind."

"Whisky?"

"Please."

Dirk stood up and went to the silver tray, and he realized that he felt a sneaking relief. If it had proved that this man had no price, as he had started to believe possible, it would have destroyed one of the headstones on which he had based his whole philosophy of life. But it was all right again now. The man had a price, and he felt a sudden contempt and scorn—it would be money, and a paltry sum at that. There was nothing different about this fellow.

He turned back to Mark.

"Here is something you can drink." He gave him the crystal glass. "Now let's discuss something you can eat."

He went back to the desk, slid open one of the drawers, and took out of it a brown manila envelope, sealed with red wax.

He laid it on the desk-top, and picked up his own glass. "That contains an earnest of my good will," he said.

"How earnest?"

"One thousand pounds," Dirk said. "Enough to buy a mountain of bread."

"One of your companies bought a farm from my grandfather," Mark spoke carefully. "He had promised that farm to me, and he died without leaving any of the money."

Dirk's expression had closed suddenly and his eyes were wary and watchful. For a moment he played with the idea of feigning ignorance, but already he had admitted he had investigated Mark thoroughly.

"Yes," he nodded. "I know about that. The old man wasted it all away."

"The price of that farm was three thousand pounds," Mark went on. "I feel that I am still owed that money."

Dirk dropped his hand into the drawer again, and brought out two identical sealed envelopes. He laid them carefully on top of the first envelope.

"By a strange coincidence," he said. "I just happen to have that exact amount with me."

A paltry sum indeed, he smiled his contempt. What had made him suspect that there was something unusual about this man, he wondered. In the desk drawer were seven other identical manilla envelopes, each containing one hundred ten pound notes. He had been prepared to go that high for the report—no, he corrected himself, I would have been prepared to go further, much further.

"Come," he smiled. "Here it is." And he watched Mark Anders rise from the chair and cross the room, pick up the envelopes and slip them into his pocket.

\* \* \*

Sean Courtney's beard bristled like the quills on the back of an angry porcupine, and his face turned slowly to the colour of a badly fired brick.

"Good God!" he growled, as he stared at the three envelopes on his desk top. The seals had been carefully split and the contents arranged in three purple blue fans of crisp treasury bills. "You took his money?"

"Yes, sir," Mark agreed, standing in front of the desk like a wayward pupil before the head pedagogue.

"Then you have the brass to come to me with it?" Sean made a gesture as though to sweep the piles of bills on to the floor. "Take the filthy stuff away from me."

"Your first lesson, General. The money is always important," Mark said quietly.

"Yes, but what must I do with this?"

"As patron of the Society for the Protection of African Wildlife, your duty would be to send the donor a letter of acceptance and thanks for his generous donation—"

"What on earth are you talking about?" Sean stared at him. "What society is this?"

"I have just formed it, sir, and elected you patron. I am sure we will be able to draw up a suitable memorandum of objects and rules of membership, but what it boils down to is a campaign to make people aware of what we are going to do, to gather public support—" Mark spoke rapidly, pouring it all out, and Sean listened with the brick colour

of his face slowly returning to normal, and a slow but
delighted grin pulling his beard out of shape. "We'll use
this money for advertisements in the press to make people
aware of their heritage," Mark raced on, ideas tumbling
out of him, and immediately spawning new ideas, while
Sean listened, his grin becoming a spasmodic chuckle that
shook his shoulders, and then finally a great peal of laughter,
that went on for many minutes.

"Enough!" at last he bellowed delightedly. "Sit down,
Mark, that's enough for now." And he groped for a handkerchief to mop his eyes and blow the great hooked beak of
a nose like a trumpet, while he recovered his self-control.
"It's indecent," he chortled. "Positively sacrilegious! You
have no respect for money at all. It's unnatural."

"Oh, yes, I have—but money is only a means, not an
end, sir," Mark laughed also, for the General's mirth was
contagious.

"My God, Mark. You are a prize, you really are. Where
ever did I find you?" He gave one last chuckle, and then
grew serious. He drew a clean sheet of paper from the side-
drawer and began to make notes. "As though I haven't
enough work already," he growled. "Now let's draw up a
list of objects for this bloody society of yours."

They worked for nearly three hours, and Ruth Courtney
had to come and call them to the dinner table.

"In a minute, dear," Sean told her, and placed a paper-
weight on the thick pile of notes he had made; he was
about to rise when he frowned at Mark.

"You have chosen a dangerous enemy for yourself,
young man," he warned him.

"Yes, I know," Mark nodded soberly.

"You say that with feeling." He stared at Mark question-
ingly. Mark hesitated a moment and then he began.

"You know my grandfather, John Anders, you spoke of
him once before." Sean nodded, and sank back into the
padded leather chair. "He had land, eight thousand acres,
he called it Andersland—"

Sean nodded again, and Mark went on carefully, telling it all without embellishment, stating the facts, and when he had to guess or make conjecture, stating that it was so. Again Ruth came to call them to dinner, just when Mark was describing the night on the escarpment when the gunmen had come to his camp. She was about to insist they come before the meal spoiled, but then she saw their faces and came silently to stand behind Sean's chair and listen, her face becoming paler and more set.

He told them about Chaka's Gate, how he had searched for his grandfather's grave and the men who had come to hunt him, and when he had finished the story they were all silent, until at last Sean roused himself, sighed—a gusty, sorrowful sound—before he spoke.

"Why didn't you report this?"

"Report what? Who would have believed me?"

"You could have gone to the police."

"I have not a shred of evidence that points to Dirk Courtney, except my own absolute certainty." And he dropped his eyes. "It's such a wild, unlikely story that I was afraid to tell even you, until this moment."

"Yes," Sean nodded. "I can see that. Even now I don't want to believe it is true."

"I'm sorry," said Mark simply.

"I know it's true—but I don't want to believe it." Sean shook his head, and lowered his chin on to his chest. Ruth, standing behind him, placed a comforting hand on his shoulder. "Oh God, how much more must I suffer for him?" he whispered, then lifted his head again.

"You will be in even greater danger now, Mark."

"I don't think so, General. I am under your protection, and he knows it."

"God grant that is enough," Sean muttered, "but what can we do against him? How can we stop this—" Sean paused, seeking the word, and then hissed it savagely, "this monster?"

"There is no evidence," Mark said. "Nothing to use against him. He has been too clever for that by far."

"There is evidence," said Sean with complete certainty. "If all this is true, then there is evidence—somewhere."

* * *

Trojan the mule's broad back felt like a barrel under Mark, and the sun beat through his shirt so that his sweat rose in dark damp patches between his shoulder blades and at his armpits, as he jogged down the bank of the Bubezi with Spartan, the second heavily burdened mule, following him on a lead rein.

In the river bed on one of the sugary white sand-banks, he let the mule wade in knee-deep and begin to drink, sucking up the clear water noisily so that he could feel the animal's belly swelling between his knees.

He pushed his hat on to the back of his head and wiped away the drops from his brow with one thumb as he looked up at the portals of Chaka's Gate. They seemed to fall out of the sky like cascades of stone, sheer and eternal, so vast and solid that they dwarfed the land and the river at their feet.

The double pannier on the back of the lead mule was the less onerous of the burdens that he had brought with him from the teeming reaches of civilization. He had brought also a load of guilt and remorse, the sorrow of a lost love, and the galling of duty left unperformed. But now, beneath the cliffs of Chaka's Gate, he felt his burden lightening, and his shoulders gathering strength.

Something indefinable seemed to reach out to him from across the Bubezi River, a feeling of destiny running its appointed course, or more a sense of home-coming. Yes, he thought, with sudden joy, I am coming home at last.

Abruptly Mark was in a hurry. He pulled up Trojan's reluctant head, with water still pouring from his loose rubbery lips, and kicked him forward into the swirling green eddy of the river, slipping from the saddle to swim beside him when he lost his footing.

As the big soup-plate hooves touched bottom, he threw

his leg back across the saddle and rode up the far bank, his breeches clinging to his thighs and his sodden shirt streaming water.

Suddenly, for the first time in a week, and for no good reason, he laughed, a light unstrained burst of laughter that hung about him like a shimmering halo long afterwards.

\* \* \*

The sound was so low, and the hooves of Trojan the grey mule were plugging into the soft earth along the river with a rhythmic chuffing sound, so that Mark was not sure of what he had heard.

He reined Trojan to a stop and listened. The silence was so complete that it seemed to hiss like static, and when a wood dove gave its melodious and melancholy whistle a mile along the river, it seemed close enough to touch.

Mark shook his head, and flicked the reins. At the first hoof fall, the sound came again—and this time there was no mistaking it. The hair down the nape of Mark's neck prickled, and he straightened quickly out of his comfortable saddle slouch. He had heard that sound only once before, but in circumstances that made certain he would never forget it.

It was close, very close, coming from the patch of thick green riverine bush between him and the river, a tangled thicket of wild loquat and hanging lianas, typical cover for the animal that had called.

It was a weird unearthly sound, a fluid sound, almost like liquor poured from the neck of a stone jug—and only one who had heard it before would recognize the distress and warning call of a fully grown leopard.

Mark swung the mule away, and set him lumbering up the rising ground until he reached the spreading shade of a leadwood, where he tethered him and loosened his girth. Then he slipped the Mannlicher out of its scabbard, and quickly checked the loaded magazine, the fat brass car-

tridges with their copper-jacketed noses were still bright
and slick with wax, and he snapped the bolt closed.

He carried the rifle casually in his left hand, for he had
no intention at all of using it. Instead he was aware of a
pleasurable glow of excitement and anticipation. In the two
months of hard riding and walking since his return to
Chaka's Gate, this was the first chance he had been given
of sighting a leopard.

There were many leopard along the Bubezi, he had seen
their sign almost daily, and heard them sawing and cough-
ing in the night. Always the leopard and the kudu are the
last to give way before man and his civilization. Their superior cunning and natural stealth protect them long after the
other species have succumbed.

Now he had a chance at a sighting. The patch of riverine
bush, though dense, was small, and he longed for a sighting, even if just a flash of yellow in deep shade, something
concrete, a firm entry in his logbook, another species to
add to the growing list of his head count. He circled out
cautiously, his eyes flickering from the thick green wall of
bush to soft ground at his feet, checking for spoor as well
as for actual sight of the yellow cat.

Just above the steep river bank he stopped abruptly, and
stared down before going on to one knee to touch the earth.

They weren't leopard tracks, but others he had grown to
know and recognize. There was no special distinguishing
characteristic, no missing toes, no scarring or deformity,
but Mark's trained eye recognized the shape and size, the
slight splaying toe-in way the man walked, the length of his
stride and a toe-heavy impression, that of a quick alert
tread. The distress call of the animal in the thicket made
sense now. "Pungushe," said Mark quietly. "The jackal at
work again." The tracks were doubled, entering the thicket
and returning. The inward tracks seemed deeper, less extended, as though the man carried a burden, but the outward tracks were lighter, the man walked freely.

Slowly, Mark edged in towards the thicket, following the
man's prints. Pausing for long minutes to examine the un-

dergrowth carefully every few paces, or squatting down to give himself better vision along the ground under the hanging lianas and branches.

Now that he knew what he was going to find, the pleasurable glow of excitement had given way to the chill of anger and the cold knowledge of mortal danger.

Something white caught his eye in the gloomy depths of the thicket. He stared at it moments before he saw the white, bleeding pith of a tree trunk, where it had been ripped by the claws of an anguished beast, long raking marks deep through the dark woody bark. His anger slid in his belly like an uncoiling serpent.

He moved sideways and slowly forward, the rifle held ready now, low across his hips, three paces before he stopped again. On the edge of the thicket there was an area of flattened grass and scrub; the soft black leaf-mould earth had been churned and disturbed, something heavy had been dragged back and forth, and there was a fleck of wet red lit by a single beam of falling sunlight that migh have been the petal of a wild flower—or a drop of blood.

He heard another sound then, the clink of metal on metal, link on link, steel chain moved steadily in the dark depths of the thicket and it sighted him. He knew where the animal was lying now, and he moved out sideways, crabbing step after step, slipping the safety-catch of the rifle, and holding it at high port across his chest.

White again, unnatural white, a round blob of it against dark foliage and he froze staring at it. Long seconds passed before he realized that it was the raw wood of a cut log, a short fork-shaped log as thick as a young girl's waist, so freshly cut that the gum was still bleeding from it in sticky wine-coloured drops. He saw also the twist of stolen fencing wire that held the chain to the log. The log was the anchor, a sliding drag weight which would hold the trapped animal without giving it a solid pull against which to pit itself and tear itself free.

The chain clinked again.

The leopard was within twenty paces of him. He knew

exactly where it was but he could not see it, and as he stared, his mind was racing, remembering everything he had heard about the animal, the old man's stories.

"You won't see him until he comes, and even then he will only be a yellow flash of light, like a sunbeam. He won't warn you with a grunt, not like a lion. He comes absolutely silently, and he won't chew your arm or grab you in the shoulder. He'll go for your head. He knows all about two-legged animals, he feeds mostly on baboon, so he knows where your head is. He'll take the top off your skull quicker than you open your breakfast egg, and for good measure his back legs will be busy on your belly. You've seen a cat lie on his back and hook with his back legs when you scratch his belly. He'll cat you the same way, but he'll strip your guts out of you just like a chicken, and he'll do it so quickly that if there are four of you in the hunting-party he'll kill three of them before the fourth man gets his gun to his shoulder."

Mark stood absolutely still and waited. He could not see the animal, but he could feel it, could feel its eyes, they stung his skin like the feet of poisonous crawling insects, and he remembered the shiny marble white scar tissue that Sean Courtney had shown him once in one of those mellow moments after the fourth whisky, pulling up his shirt and flexing muscle, so the cicatrice bulged with the gloss of satin.

"Leopard," he had said. "Devil cat—the worst bastard in all the bush."

He felt his feet pulling back slowly, and the dead leaves rustled. He could walk away and leave it, come back when the vultures told him the animal was dead or too weak to be a danger. Then he imagined the terror and anguish of the animal—and suddenly it was not the animal, but his animal, his charge, his sacred charge, and he stepped forward.

The chain clinked again and the leopard came. It came with a terrible silent rush, and in the blurring streaming charge, only the eyes blazed, they blazed yellow with

hatred and fear and agony. The chain flailed out behind it, spinning and snapping, and as Mark brought the rifle up the last six inches to his shoulder he saw the trap hanging on its foreleg like a sinister grey metallic crab. The heavy steel trap slowed the charge just that fraction.

Time seemed to pass with a dreamlike slowness, each microsecond falling heavily as drops of thick oil, so that he saw that the leopard's foreleg above the grip of the steel jaws was eaten through. He felt his stomach turn over as he realized that the frenzied animal had gnawed through its own bone and flesh and sinew in its desperate try for freedom. The leg was held by only a thread of bloody ragged skin, and that last thread snapped at the heavy jerk of the steel trap. The leopard was free, mad with pain and fear, as it launched itself at Mark's head.

The muzzle of the Mannlicher almost touched the broad flat forehead; he was so close that he could see the long white whiskers bristling from the puckered snarling lips like grass stalks stiff with the morning frost, and the yellow fangs behind wet black lips, the furry pink tongue arched across the open throat, and the eyes. The terrible hating yellow eyes.

Mark fired and the bullet clubbed the skull open, the yellow eyes blinked tightly at the jarring shock, and the head was wrenched backwards, twisted on the snakelike neck, while the lithe body lost its grace and lightness and turned heavy and shapeless in mid-air.

It fell like a sack at Mark's feet, and tiny droplets of brilliant red blood spattered the scuffed toe cap of Mark's boot, and glittered there like cut rubies.

Mark touched the open staring eye, but the fierce yellow light was fading and there was no blinking reflex of the eyelids with their long beautiful fans of dark lashes. The leopard was dead, and Mark sat down heavily in the leaf-mould beside the carcasss and groped for his cigarette tin. The hand that held the match shook so violently that the flame fluttered like a moth's wing. He shook out the flame, threw the match away, and then stroked his open palm across the soft thick fur, the amber gold dabbed with the distinctive rosettes of black, as though touched by the five bunched fingertips of an angel's right hand.

"Pungushe—you bastard!" he whispered again. The animal had died for that golden dappled hide, for the few silver shillings that it would bring when sold in the village market, at a country railway halt, or on the side of a dusty road. A death in unspeakable agony and terror to make a rug, or a coat for a lady. Mark stroked the glowing fur again, and felt his own fear give way to anger for the man who had saved his life once, and whom he had hunted these two months.

He stood up and went to the steel trap, lying at the end of its chain. The severed leg was still held between the relentless jaws, and Mark squatted to examine it. The trap was the type they call a "Slag Yster," a killing iron, and the spikes of the jaws had been carefully filed to bite but not sever. It weighed at least thirty pounds and it would take a thick branch to lever those jaws open, and reset the mechanism.

The steel was dark and sooty where the poacher had scorched it with a torch of dry grass to kill the man-smell on the metal. Lying at the edge of the thicket was the half decomposed carcass of a baboon, the odiferous bait which had been irresistible to the big yellow cat.

Mark reloaded the Mannlicher, and his anger was so intense that he would have shot down the man who had done this thing, if he had come across him in that moment, despite the fact that he owed him his life.

He walked back up the slope and unsaddled Trojan, hobbled him with the leather straps, and hung his saddlebags in the branches of the leadwood out of the way of a questing hyena or badger.

Then he went back and picked up the poacher's spoor at the edge of the thicket. He knew it would be useless to follow on the mule. The poacher would be alerted at a mile range by that big clumsy animal, but he had a chance on foot.

The spoor was fresh and the poacher's camp would be close, he would not stay far from such a valuable asset as his steel trap. Mark had a very good chance.

He would be cagey, of course, sly and cunning, for he would know that it was now forbidden to hunt in the valley. Mark had visited each village, spoken with each tribal headman and drank his beer while he explained to him the new order.

The poacher knew that he was outside the law. Mark had followed his spoor so often, and the precautions Pungushe took, the elaborate ruses to throw any pursuit, made it clear that he was in guilt, but now Mark had a good chance at him.

The spoor crossed the river half a mile down-stream, and then started to zig-zag back and forth among the scrub and forest and brush as the poacher visited his trap line.

The leopard trap was clearly the centre of his line, but he was noosing for small game, using light galvanized baling wire, probably purchased for a few shillings at a country general dealer's store. He was also using copper telegraph wire, probably obtained by blatantly scaling a telegraph pole in some lonely place.

He was trapping for jackal, baiting with offal, and he was trapping indiscriminately at salt licks and mud wallows, any place that might attract small game.

Following the trap line diligently, Mark sprang every wire noose and ripped it out. He closed rapidly with his quarry, but it was three hours before he found the poacher's camp.

It was under the swollen, bloated reptilian grey branches of a baobab tree. The tree was old and rotten, its huge trunk cleaved by a deep hollow, a cave that the poacher had used to shield his small smokeless cooking fire. The fire was dead now, carefully smothered with sand—but the smell of dead smoke led Mark to it. The ashes were cold.

Tucked away in the deepest recess of the hollow tree were two bundles tied with plaited bark string. One bundle held a greasy grey blanket, a carved wooden head-rest, a

small black three-legged pot and a pouch of impala skin
which contained two or three pounds of yellow maize and
strips of dried meat. The poacher travelled light, and
moved fast.

The other bundle contained fifteen jackal skins, sun-
dried and cracklin stiff, beautiful furs of silver and black
and red, and two leopard skins, a big dark golden tom and
a smaller half-grown female.

Mark relit the fire and threw the blanket, the head-rest
and the bag upon it, deriving a thin vindictive satisfaction
as they smouldered and blackened. He smashed the iron
pot with a rock and then he slung the roll of dried skins on
his shoulder and started back.

It was almost dark when he got back to the leopard
thicket beside the river.

He dropped the heavy bundle of dried skin, which by
this time felt like a hundredweight sack of coal on his
shoulder, and he stared uncomprehendingly at the leopard's
carcass.

It swarmed with big green metallic shiny flies. They were
laying their eggs on the dead flesh, like bunches of white
boiled rice, but what astonished Mark was that the carcass
was naked. It had been expertly stripped of its golden fur,
and now it was a raw pink, laced with yellow fat and the
white tracery of muscle ligaments. The head was bare, the
mask stripped away so that dull startled eyes stared out of
the skull like marbles, and tufts of black hair sprang from
the open ear holes, the fangs were exposed in a fixed yellow
grin.

Quickly Mark ran to the anchor log. The chain and trap
were gone.

It was fully a minute before the next logical step occurred to him. He ran up the slope to the leadwood tree.
Trojan was gone. The hobbling straps had been cut with a
razor-sharp blade and laid out neatly under the leadwood
tree.

Trojan, unexpectedly relieved of his hobble, had reacted
gratefully in a fully predictable manner. He had set off,

arrow-straight through the forest, back home to his rude stable, his nightly ration of grain, and the congenial company of his old buddy Spartan.

It was a fifteen-mile walk back to main camp, and it would be dark in fifteen minutes.

The saddle-bags had been taken down from the tree, and the contents meticulously picked over. What Pungushe had rejected, he had folded and stacked neatly on a flat rock. He clearly did not think much of William Shakespeare, his tragedies had been put aside, and he had left Mark his chamois hunting-jacket, a last minute gift from Ruth Courtney.

He had taken the gentleman's sleeping bag, which had once belonged to General Courtney, with its built-in ground sheet and genuine eider filling, twenty-five guineas' worth from Harrods of London, a good exchange for a threadbare greasy blanket and wooden head-rest.

He had taken the cooking pot, pannikin and cutlery, the salt and flour and bully beef, but had left a single tin of beans.

He had taken the clean shirt and khaki trousers, but had left the spare woollen socks and rubber-soled boots. Perhaps it was chance that the boots pointed down-stream to Mark's camp—or was it mockery? A can of beans and boots to carry Mark home.

Through the red mists of his humiliation and mounting rage, Mark glimpsed suddenly a whimsical sense of humour at work. The man had been watching him. Mark was sure of that now, his selection from the saddle-bags echoed too faithfully what Mark had burned of his.

In his imagination, Mark heard the deep bell of Zulu laughter, and he snatched up the Mannlicher and picked up Pungushe's outgoing spoor.

He followed it for only a hundred yards and then stopped. Pungushe was heavily laden with trap, wet skin, and booty, but he had hit the Zulu's stride *"Minza umhlabathi,"* and he was eating ground to the north at a pace which Mark knew was pointless to try and imitate.

He walked back to the leadwood tree and sank down

beside the trunk. His rage turned to acute discomfort at the thought of the fifteen-mile walk home, carrying the saddle-bags, and the roll of dried skins, for honour dicated he did not abandon his meagre spoils.

Suddenly he began to laugh, a helpless, hopeless shaking of his shoulders, and he laughed until tears ran down his cheeks and his belly ached.

"Pungushe, I'll get even for this," he promised weakly, through his laughter.

\* \* \*

It rained after midnight, a quick hard downpour, just enough to soak Mark and to bow the grass with clinging drops.

Then a small chill wind came nagging like an old wife, and the wet grass soaked his boots until they squelched and chafed with each step, and his cigarettes had disintegrated into a yellow porridge of mangled tobacco and limp rice paper, and the roll of skin and the saddle and the bags cut into his shoulders, and he did not laugh again that night.

In the pre-dawn, the cliffs of Chaka's Gate were purple and milky smooth, flaming suddenly with the sun's ardent kiss in vivid rose and bronze, but Mark plodded on under his burden, tired beyond any appreciation of beauty, beyond feeling or even caring, until he came out of the forest on to the bank of the Bubezi River and stopped in mid-stride.

He sniffed in total disbelief, and was immediately assailed by the demands of his body, the quick flood of saliva from under his tongue and the cramping of his empty belly. It was the most beautiful odour he had ever smelled, bacon frying and eggs in the pan, slowly gelling and firming in the sizzling fat. He knew it was only a figment of his exhaustion, for he had eaten his last bacon six weeks before.

Then his ears played tricks also, he heard the ring of an axe-blade on wood and the faint melody of Zulu voices, and he lifted his head and stared ahead through the forest into his old camp below the wild figs.

There was a cone of pristine white canvas, and officer's bell tent, recently pitched beside his own rudely thatched lean-to shelter. The camp fire had been built up, and Hlubi, the old Zulu cook, was busy with his pans over it, while, beyond the flames, in a collapsible canvas camp chair, sitting comfortably, was the burly figure of General Courtney, watching his breakfast cook with a critical eye.

He looked up and saw Mark, bedraggled and dirty as an urchin at the edge of the camp, and his grin was wide and boyish.

"Hlubi," he said in Zulu. "Another four eggs and a pound of bacon."

Sean Courtney's vast energy and enthusiasm were the beacon flames that made the next week one of the memorable interludes in Mark's life. He would always remember him as he was in those days, belly-laughing at Mark's tale of woe and frustration with Pungushe, and then still chuckling, calling to his servants and repeating the story to them, with his own comments and embellishments, until they rocked and reeled with mirth and old fat Hlubi overturned a pan of eggs, his great paunch bouncing like a ball and his cannon-ball of a head, with its hoar-frosting of pure white wool, rolling uncontrollably from side to side.

Mark, half-starved on a diet of bully and beans, gorged himself on the miraculous food that flowed from Hlubi's spade-sized, pink palmed hands. He was amazed at the style in which Sean Courtney braved the hardships of the African bush, from his full sized hip-bath to the portable kerosene-burning ice-box that delivered endless streams of frothing cold beer against the stunning heat of midday.

"Why travel in steerage, when you can go first class?" Sean asked, and winked at Mark as he spread a large-scale map of northern Zululand on the camp table. "Now, what have you got to tell me?"

Their discussions lasted late into each night, with a Petromax hissing in the tree overhead and the jackals yipping and piping along the river, and in the days they rode the ground. Sean Courtney up on Spartan, so clearly enjoying

every moment of it, with the vitality of a man half his age,
keeping going without a check even in the numbing heat
of noon, inspecting the site that Mark had chosen for the
main camp, arguing as to where the Bubezi bridge should
be built, following the road through the forest where Mark
had blazed the trees, exulting at the sight of a big black
nyala ram with his heavy mane and ghostly stripes, as it
raced away panic-stricken by the approach of man, sitting
in his hip-bath under the fig trees, up to his waist in creaming white suds, with a cigar in his mouth and a long glass
of beer in his hand, bellowing for Hlubi to top up with
boiling water from the big kettle when his bath cooled. Big
and scarred and hairy—and Mark realized then what a
wide space this man had filled in his life.

As the day drew closer when he must leave again, Sean's
mood changed, and in the evenings he brooded over the list
of animals that Mark had compiled.

"Fifty zebra," he read Mark's estimate, and poured the
last few inches of whisky from the pinch-bottle into his
glass. "On the Sabi River in '95 a single herd crossed in
front of my wagons. It took forty minutes at the gallop to
go by, and the leaders were over the horizon when the tail
passed us. There were thirty thousand animals in that one
herd.

"No elephant?" he asked, looking up from the list, and
when Mark shook his head, he went on softly, "We thought
it would last for ever. In '99 when I rode into Pretoria
from the north, I had ten tons of ivory on board. Ten tons,
twenty thousand pounds of ivory.

"No lions there?" and again Mark shook his head.

"I don't think so, General. I've seen no sign of them, nor
heard them in the night, but when I was a boy I shot one
near here. I was with my grandfather."

"Yes," Sean nodded. "When *you* were a boy—but, what
about your son, Mark? Will he ever see a lion in the wild?"

Mark did not answer, and Sean grunted.

"No lions on the Bubezi River, God! What have we done
to this land?" He stared into the fire. "I wonder if it was

mere chance that you and I met, Mark. You have opened my eyes and conscience. It was I, and men like me, that did this—"

He shook that great shaggy head and groped in the side-pocket of his baggy hunting-jacket, and produced a leather-bound pocket-size book, a thick little volume, well-thumbed and shiny with the grease of grubby hands.

Mark did not recognize it for a moment, but when he did, he was startled.

"I did not know you read the Book," he exclaimed, and Sean glanced up at him from under beetling brows.

"I read it," he said gruffly. "The older I get, the more I read it. There is a lot of solace here."

"But, sir," Mark persisted, "you never go to church."

This time Sean frowned as though he resented the prying questions. "I live my religion," he said. "I don't go singing about it on Sunday, and drop it for the rest of the week, like some I know." His tone was final, forbidding further discussion, and he turned his attention to the battered volume.

He had marked his place with a pressed flower, and the Bible fell open at the right page.

"I found it last night," he told Mark, as he propped the steel-rimmed spectacles on his nose. "It seemed like an omen, and I marked it to read to you. Matthew x." He cleared his throat and read slowly:

"Are not two sparrows sold for a farthing?

"And one of them shall not fall on the ground without you, Father."

When he had finished, he tucked the Bible away in his pocket, and they were both silent, thinking about it and watching the shapes in the ashes of the fire.

"Then perhaps he will help us to save the sparrow from its fall, here at Chaka's Gate," said Sean, and he leaned forward to take a burning twig from the fire. He lit a fresh cigar with it and puffed deeply, savouring the taste of wood smoke and tobacco before speaking again.

"It is just unfortunate that it all comes at a time like this.

It will be the end of the next year before we can make an official move to have the proclamation ratified and budget for full development here."

Mark was instantly alert, and his voice sharp as he demanded,

"Next year?"

"I'm afraid so."

"But why so long?"

"The grim reality of politics, son," Sean growled. "We have just recieved a shattering blow, and all else must wait while we play the game of power."

"What has happened?" Mark asked with real concern now. "I haven't read a newspaper in two months."

"I wish I were that lucky." Sean smiled without humour. "There was a by-election in a little place up in the Transvaal. It's a seat that has always been ours, a good safe seat, in the hands of a respected backbencher of great loyalty and little intellect. He had a heart attack in the diningroom of the House, expiring between the soup and the fish. We went to our safe little constituency to elect a new member," here Sean paused, and his expression went bleak, "and we got the trouncing of our lives. A fifteen per cent swing to the Hertzog Party. They fought us on our handling of the strike last year—and it was a disaster."

"I didn't know. I'm sorry."

"If that swing, fifteen per cent, carries for the whole country, then we will be in opposition after the next election. Everything else is of no significance. General Smuts has decided to go to the country next year in March, and we will be fighting for our existence. Until then, we cannot introduce this type of legislation, or ask for funds."

Mark felt cold despair spread out to numb his very fingertips. "What happens here?" he asked. "In the meantime must we stop what I am doing? Do we just leave it? Another year of poaching and hunting, another year without protection or development?"

Sean shook his head. "I've had my people studying the

existing proclamation. We have powers there that we can enforce, but no money to do it."

"You can't do anything without money," said Mark miserably.

"Ah, so at last a little respect for the power of money." Sean shot him a thin smile across the fire, and then went on seriously. "I've decided to finance the development and running of the proclaimed area until I get a budget allocation for it. I'll foot the bill from my own pocket. Perhaps I'll get reimbursed from the budget later, but if I don't," he shrugged, "I reckon I owe that much at least. I've had a pretty good run."

"It won't need much," Mark rushed in eagerly but Sean quieted him irritably.

"You'll get the same salary as before, and we'll make a start on the main camp. I'm going to give you four men to do the work," he went on, speaking quietly. "We'll have to made do without a bridge across the river, and only a wagon track for our first road, but it'll be a start—and let's just hope like hell we win our election."

* * *

On the last day at breakfast, Sean laid a folder in front of Mark.

"I talked Caldwell, the man who did the drawings for *Jock of the Bushveld*, into designing the layout," he smiled, as Mark opened the folder. "I wanted you to get the best for your three thousand pounds."

In the folder was a mock-up of the full-page Press announcement which would launch the "Friends of African Wildlife."

The margin contained magnificent line-drawings of wild animals, and under the heavy typed announcement was set out the objects of the Society, and an eloquent plea for support and membership.

"I had my lawyers draft the articles and draw up the

wording. We'll run it in every newspaper in the country. The Society's address is the Head Office of the Courtney Holdings and I have taken on a full-time clerk to handle all the paper work. I've also got a young journalist to edit the Society's newspaper. He's full of ideas and caught up in the whole thing. With luck, we'll get huge public support behind us."

"It's going to cost more than three thousand pounds." Mark was torn between delight, and concern for the size to which his simple idea had grown.

"Yes," Sean laughed. "It's going to cost more than three thousand pounds, which reminds me. I sent Dirk Courtney a receipt for his money—and a life membership of the Society!" The joke carried them over the awkwardness of the last moments before departure.

Sean's bearers disappeared among the trees, carrying head loads of equipment to where the motor lorry had been left on the nearest road twenty miles beyond the cliffs of Chaka's Gate E, and Sean lingered regretfully.

"I'm sad to go," he admitted. "It's been a good time, but I feel stronger now—ready to face whatever the bastards have got to throw at me." He looked about him, taking farewell of river and mountain and wilderness. "There is magic here." He nodded. "Look after it well, son," and he held out his hand.

It was Mark's last opportunity to ask the question which he had tried to ask a dozen times already, but each time Sean had turned it aside, or simply ignored it. But now he had to have an answer, and he took Sean's big gnarled bony fist in a grip that would not be denied.

"You haven't told me how Storm is, sir. How is she? Is she well? How is her painting?" he blurted.

It seemed even then that Sean would not be drawn. He stiffened angrily, made as if to pull his hand away, and then the anger faded before it reached his eyes. For a moment there showed in the deep-set eyes a dark unfathomable grief, and his grip tightened on Mark's hand like a steel trap.

"Storm was married a month ago. But I have not seen her since you left Lion Kop," he said, and he dropped Mark's hand. Without another word, he turned and walked away. For the first time he went slowly and heavily, swaying against the drag of his bad leg, shuffling like an old man—a very tired old man.

Mark wanted to run after him, but his own heart was breaking and his legs would not carry him.

He stood forlornly and watched Sean Courtney limp away into the trees.

\* \* \*

The Natal Number Two came in along the line, his pony's hooves kicking up little spurts of white marking-lime like a machine gun traversing, and he caught the ball two feet before it dribbled out of play.

He leaned low out of the saddle and took it backhanded under his pony's neck, a full-blooded stroke that finished with the mallet high above his head, and the ball rose in a floating arc, a white blur against the stark blue of summer sky.

From the club house veranda, and the deck-chairs beneath the coloured umbrellas, applause splattered above the drum of hooves, and then rose into a swelling hum as they saw that Derek Hunt had anticipated.

He was coming down in a hard canter with Saladin not yet asked to extend. Saladin was a big pony, with a mean and ugly head that he cocked to watch the flight of the white ball, his over-large nostrils flaring so the shiny red mucous membrane flashed like a flag. The eye that watched the ball rolled in the gaunt skull, giving the horse a wild and half-crazed air. He was of that raggedy roan and grey that no amount of currying would ever brighten into a gloss, and his hooves looked like those of a cart-horse. He had to lift them high in the ungainly action that was quickly carrying him ahead of the hard-running Argentinian pony at his shoulder.

Derek sat him as though he were an armchair, idly penduluming his stick from his wrist, his pith helment hard
down over his ears and strapped up tightly under the chin.
His belly bulged out over the belt of his breeches, his arms
were long and thick as those of a chimpanzee, covered in a
thick fuzz of ginger hair. The skin was heavily freckled and
had a raw red look between the freckles, as though it had
been scalded with boiling water. His face was the same raw
painful looking red, tinged by the purplish gaze of the very
heavy drinker, and he was sweating.

The sweat glistened like early dew on his face and
dripped from his chin. His short-sleeved cotton singlet
looked as though he had been caught in a tropical downpour.
It clung to the thick bearlike shoulders, and was stretched so
tightly over his bulging paunch and so transparent with
wetness, that you could see the deep dark pit of his belly
button from the sidelines.

At each jar, as Saladin's hooves struck the hard-baked
earth, Derek Hunt's great backside in the tight-fighting
white breeches quivered like a jelly in the saddle.

Two Argentinian poines were cutting across field to
cover, their handsome riders olive-skinned and dashing as
cavalry officers, riding with huge verve and excited Spanish
cries, and Derek grinned under his bristling ginger moustache, as the ball started its long plummeting curve back to
earth.

"Christ," drawled one of the members on the club house
steps. "The ugliest horse in Christendom." And he raised
his pink gin to salute Saladin.

"And the ugliest four-goal handicapper in the entire
world on his back," agreed the masher beside him. "Poor
bloody dagoes should turn to stone just looking at them."

Saladin and the Argentinian Number One arrived at the
drop of the ball at exactly the same moment. The Argentinian rose in the saddle to trap the fall, his white teeth
sparkling under the trim black pencil-line of his moustache,
the smooth darkly tanned muscles of his arm bulging as he
prepared to go on to the forehand drive, his sleekly beauti-

ful pony wheeling into line for the shot, nimble and quick
as a ferret.

Then an extraordinary thing happened. Derek Hunt sat
fatgutted and heavy in the saddle and nobody could see the
touch of rein and heel that made Saladin switch his quarters. The Argentinian pony cannoned off him as though she
had hit a granite kopje, and the rider went over her head,
going in an instant from balanced perfection to sprawling
windmilling confusion, falling heavily in a cloud of red dust,
and rolling to his knees to scream hysterical protest to the
umpire and the skies.

Derek leaned slightly and there was the tap of mallet
against bamboo root, a gentle almost self-effacing little tap,
and the ball dropped meekly ahead of Saladin's slugging,
hammering head.

It bounced once, twice, and then came up obediently for
the next light tap that kept it hopping down the field. The
Argentinian Number Four swept in from the right, with all
the smooth-running grace of a charging lioness—and the
roar of the crowd carried across the open field, spurring him
on to make the challenge. He shouted a wild Spanish oath,
his eyes flashing with excitement.

Smoothly, Derek changed the mallet from his right hand
to his left, and tapped the bouncing white ball on to his
off-side, forcing the Argentinian to increase the angle of his
interception.

The instant he was drawn, Derek cropped hard, lofting
the ball in an easy lob high over the Argentinian's head.

He said, "Ha!" but not loudly, and touched Saladin with
his heels. The big ugly roan stretched out his neck and
extended, with Derek moving now to help him push.

They ran past the Argentinian as though he had indeed
turned to stone, they left him floundering in their wake and
picked up the ball beyond him. Tap! Tap! And tap
again, he ran it down through the exact centre of the
stubby goal-posts and then turned and trotted back to the
pony lines.

Chuckling so that his belly bounced, Derek swung one

leg forward over Saladin's neck and slid down to the ground, letting him go free to the grooms.

"I'll take Satan for the next chukka," he shouted in that beery throaty voice.

Storm Courtney saw him coming, and knew what was going to happen. She tried to rise, but she was slow and clumsy, the child in her womb anchored her like a stone.

"One for the poor, what!" shouted Derek, and caught her with one long-ginger-fuzzed, boiled red arm.

The sweat on his face was icy cold and smeared down her own cheek, and he smelled of sour beer and horse. He kissed her with an open mouth, in front of Irene Leuchars and the four other girls, and their husbands, and all the grinning grooms, and the members on the veranda.

She thought desperately that she was going to be ill. The acid vomit rose into her throat, and she thought she was going to throw up in front of them all.

"Derek, my condition!" she whispered desperately, but he held her under his one arm as he took the bottle of beer that one of the white-jacketed club servants brought on a silver tray, and, scorning the glass, he drank straight from the bottle.

She struggled to be free, but he held her easily with immense and careless strength—and he belched, a ripping explosion of gas. "One for the poor," he shouted again, and they all laughed—like courtiers at the king's jest. Good old Derek. Law unto himself, old Derek.

He dropped the empty bottle. "Keep it until I get back, wifey!" he laughed, and took one of her swollen breasts in his huge raw-knuckled, red-boiled hand and squeezed it painfully. She felt cold and trembly and weak with humiliation and hatred.

* * *

She had missed a month many times before, so Storm did not begin to worry until the second blank came up on her pocket diary. She had been about to tell Mark then, but that had been the time they had parted. Still, she had expected it all to resolve itself, but as the weeks passed, the enormity of it all began to reach her in her gold and ivory castle. This sort of thing happened to other girls, common working girls, ordinary girls—it did not happen to Storm Courtney. There were special rules for young ladies like Storm.

When it was certain, beyond all doubt, the first person she thought of was Mark Anders. As the panic caught at her heart with fiery little barbs, she wanted to rush to him and throw her arms about his neck. Then that stubborn and completely uncontrollable pride of the Courtneys smothered the impulse. He must come to her. She had decided, he must come on her terms—and she could not bring herself to change the rules she had laid down. Though still, even in her distress, her chest felt tight and her legs shaky and weak, whenever she thought of Mark.

She had wept, silently in the night, when she had first left Mark—and now she wept again. She longed for him even more now, with his child growing in the secret depths of her body. But that perverse and distorted pride would not release its bulldog hold on her, would not allow her even to let him know of her predicament.

"Don't challenge me, Mark Anders," she had warned him, and he had done it. She hated him, and loved him for that. But now she could not bend.

The next person she thought of was her mother. She and Ruth Courtney had always been close, she had always been able to rely on her mother's loyalty and shrewdly practical hard sense. Then she was stopped dead by the knowledge that if Ruth were told, then her father would know within hours. Ruth Courtney kept nothing from Sean, or he from her.

Storm's soul quailed at the thought of what would happen once her father knew that she carried a bastard. The immense indulgent love he had for her, would make his anger and retribution more terrible.

She knew also Mark would be destroyed by it. Her father was too strong, too persistent and single-minded for her to believe she would be able to keep Mark's name from him. He would squeeze it out of her.

She knew of her father's affection for Mark Anders, it had been apparent for anyone to see, but that affection would not have been sufficient to save either of them.

Sean Courtney's attitude to his daughter was bound by iron laws of conduct, the old-fashioned view of the father that left no latitude for maneuver. Mark Anders had contravened those iron laws and Sean would destroy him, despite the fact he had come to love him, and in doing so, he would destroy a part of himself. He would reject and drive out his own daughter, even though it left him ruined and broken with grief.

So, for her father's sake and for Mark Anders' sake, she could not go for comfort and help to her mother.

She went instead to Irene Leuchars, who listened to Storm's hesitant explanations with rising glee and anticipation.

"But you silly darling, didn't you take precautions?"

Storm shook her head glumly, not quite certain what Irene meant by precautions, but certain only that she hadn't taken them.

"Who was it, darling?" was the next question, and Storm shook her head again, this time fiercely.

"Oh dear," Irene rolled her eyes. "That many candidates for the daddy? You are a dark horse, Storm darling."

"Can't one—well, can't one actually do something?" Storm asked miserably.

"You mean an abortion, darling?" Irene asked brutally, and smiled a sly spiteful smile when Storm nodded.

He was a tall pale man, very grey and stooped, with a reedy voice and hands so white as to be almost transparent. Storm could see the blue veins and the fragile ivory bones through the skin. She tried not to think of those pale transparent hands as they pried and probed, but they were cold and cruelly painful.

Afterwards, he had washed those pale hands at the

kitchen sink of his small grey apartment with such exaggerated care that Storm had felt her pain and embarrassment enhanced by a sense of affront. The cleansing seemed to be a personal insult.

"I imagine you indulge in a great deal of physical activity—horse-riding, tennis?" he asked primly, and when Storm nodded he made a little sucking and glucking sound of disapproval. "The female body was not designed for such endeavour. You are very narrow, and your musculature is highly developed. Furthermore, you are at least ten weeks pregnant." At last he had finished washing, and now he bagan to dry his hands on a threadbare, but clinically white towel.

"Can you help me?" Storm demanded irritably, and he shook his pale grey head slowly from side to side.

"If you had come a little earlier—" and he spread the white transparent hands in a helpless gesture.

They had drawn up a list of names, she and Irene, and each of the men on the list had two things in common. They were in love, or had professed to be in love with Storm, and they were all men of fortune.

There were six names on the list, and Storm had written cards to two of them and received vague replies, polite good wishes, and no definite suggestion for a meeting.

The third man on the list she had contrived to meet at the Umgeni Country Club. She could still wear tennis clothes, and the pregnancy had given her skin a new bloom and lustre, her breasts a fuller ripeness.

She had chatted lightly, flirtatiously, with him, confident and poised, giving him encouragement he had never received from her before. She had not noticed the sly, gloating look in his eyes, until he leaned close to her and asked confidentially,

"Should you be playing tennis—now?"

She had only been able to keep herself from breaking down until she reached the Cadillac parked in the lot behind the courts. She was weeping when she drove out through the gates, and she had to park in the dunes above the ocean.

After the first storm of humilation had passed, she could think clearly.

It had been Irene Leuchars, of course. She must have been blind and stupid not to realize it sooner. Everybody, every single person, would know by now, Irene would have seen to that.

Loneliness and desolation overwhelmed her.

Derek Hunt had not been on the list of six, not because he was not rich, not because he had never shown interest in Storm.

Derek Hunt had shown interest in most pretty girls. He had even married two of them, and both of them had divorced him in separate blazes of notoriety, not before they had, between them, presented him with seven offspring.

Derek Hunt's reputation was every bit as vast and flamboyant as his fortune.

"Look, old girl," he had told Storm reasonably. "You and I have both got a problem. I want you, have always wanted you. Can't sleep at night, strewth!" and his ginger whiskers twitched lasciviously. "And you need me. The word's out about you, old girl. Mark of the beast, condemnation of society, and all that rot, I'm afraid.

"Your loss, my gain. I've never given a stuff for the condemnation of society. I've got seven little bastards already. Another one won't make any difference. What about it, then? One for the poor, what?"

They had driven up to Swaziland, and Derek had been able to get a special licence, lying about her age.

There had been nobody she knew at the ceremony, only five of Derek's cronies—and she had not told her father, nor her mother, nor Mark Anders.

\* \* \*

She heard him coming home, like a Le Mans Grand Prix winner, a long cortege of motor cars roaring up the driveway, then the squeal of brakes, the cannonade of slamming doors, the loud comradely shouts and the snatches of wild song.

Derek's voice, louder and hoarser than the rest. "Caramba, me hearties! Whipped your pants off on the field, going to drink you blind now. This way, the pride of the Argentine—" the stamping and shouting, as they trooped up the front staircase.

Storm lay flat on her back and stared at the plaster cupids on the ceiling. She wanted to run, this senseless panicky urge to get up and run. But there was no place to run to.

She had spoken to her mother three times since the wedding, and each time had been agony for both of them.

"If only you had told us. Daddy might have been able to understand, to forgive—

"Oh darling, if you only knew the plans he used to make for your wedding. He was so proud of you—and then not to be at your wedding. Not even invited—

"Give him time, please, Storm. I am trying for you. Believe me darling. I think it might have been better, if it was anybody in the world but Derek Hunt. You know what Daddy thinks of him."

There was nowhere to run, and she lay quietly, dreading, until at last the heavy unsteady boots came clumping up the staircase, and the door was thrown open.

He had not changed, and he still wore riding-boots. The backside of his breeches was brown with dubbin from the saddle, and the crotch drooped almost to his knees, like a baby's soiled napkin; the sweat had dried in salty white circles on the cotton singlet.

"Wake up, old girl. Time for every good man and true to perform his duty." He let his clothing lie where it fell.

His bulging belly was fish white, and fuzzed with ginger curls. The heavy shoulders were pitted and scarred purple with old cicatrices of myriad carbuncles and small boils, and he was massively virile, thick and hard and callous as the branch of a pine tree.

"One for the poor, what?" he chuckled hoarsely, as he came to the bed.

Suddenly and clearly, she had an image of Mark Anders' slim and graceful body, with the clean shape of young muscle, as he sat in the dappled sunlight of the glade.

She remembered with a terrible pang of loss the lovely head with the fine strong lines of mouth and brow, and the serene poet's eyes.

As the bed dipped beneath the solid weight of her husband, she wanted to scream with despair and the knowledge of coming pain.

\* \* \*

For breakfast Derek Hunt liked a little Black Velvet, mixing the Guinness stout and champagne in a special crystal punch bowl. He always used a Bollinger Vintage 1911 and drank it out of a pewter tankard.

He believed in a substantial breakfast, and this morning it was scrambled eggs, Scotch kippers, devilled kidneys, mushrooms and a large well-done fillet steak—all of it on the same plate.

Although his eyes were watery and pink-rimmed with the previous night's revelry, and his face blazed crimson as the rising sun, he was cheerful and loudly friendly, guffawing at his own jokes, and leaning across the table to prod her with a thick red thumb like a boiled langouste to emphasize a point.

She waited until he had picked up the bowl and tilted the last of the Black Velvet into his tankard, and then she said quietly,

"Derek, I want a divorce."

The grin did not leave his face, and he watched the last drops fall into the tankard.

"Damn stuff evaporates—or the dish has got a hole in it," he wheezed, and then chuckled merrily. "Get it? A hole in it! Good, what?"

"Did you hear what I said? Aren't you going to answer?"

"Needs no answer, old girl. Bargain is a bargain, you've got a name for your bastard—I've still got my share coming."

"You've had that, as many times as you could wish," Storm answered quietly, with a whole world of resignation in her voice. "Won't you let me go now?"

"Good God!" Derek stared at her over the rim of his tankard, his moustache bristling and the pink eyes wide with genuine amazement. "You don't think I was really interested in the crumpet, do you? Can get that anywhere, all of it looks the same in the dark." He snorted with real laughter now. "Good God, old girl—you didn't really think I fancied your lily-white titties that much?"

"Why?" she asked.

"Ten million good reasons, old girl." He gulped a mouthful of scrambled eggs and kidney, "and every single one of them in General Sean Courtney's bank account."

She stared at him. "Daddy's money?"

"Right first time," he grinned. "Up you go to the head of the class."

"But—but—" she made fluttery little gestures of incomprehension with both hands. "I don't understand. You are so rich yourself."

"Was, old girl, used to be—past tense." And he let out another delighted guffaw. "Two loving wives, two unsympathetic divorce judges, seven brats, forty polo ponies, friends with big right hands, rocks that shouldn't have been where the road was going, a mine with no diamonds, a building that fell down, a dam that burst, a reef that pinched out, cattle that got sick and myopic lawyers who don't read the small print, that's the way the money goes, pop goes the weasel!"

"I don't believe it." She was aghast.

"Would never joke about that," he grinned. "Never joke about money, one of my principles. Probably my only principle." And he prodded her. "My only principle—get it?

Skunked, absolutely flatters, I assure you. Daddy is the last resort, old girl—you'll have to speak to him, I'm afraid. Last resort, what? One for the poor, don't you know?"

* * *

There was no answer to the front door and Mark almost turned away and went back into the village, feeling a touch of relief and a lightening of heart that he recognized as cowardice. So instead, he jumped down off the veranda and went around the side of the house.

The stiff collar and tie chafed his throat and the jacket felt unnatural and constricting, so that he shugged his shoulders and ran a finger around inside his collar as he came into the kitchen yard of the cottage. It was five months since last he had worn clothes or trodden on a paved sidewalk—even the sound of women's voices was unfamiliar. He paused and listened to them.

Marion Littlejohn was in the kitchen with her sister, and their merry prattle had a lilt and cadence to which he listened with new ears and fresh pleasure.

The chatter ceased abruptly at his knock, and Marion came to the door.

She wore a gaily striped apron, and her bare arms were floury to the elbows. She had her hair up in a ribbon but tendrils of it had come down in little wisps on to her neck and forehead.

The kitchen was filled with the smell of baking bread, and her cheeks were rosy from the heat of the oven.

"Mark," she said calmly. "How nice," and tried to push the curl of hair off her forehead, leaving a smudge of white flour on the bridge of her nose. It was a strangely appealing gesture, and Mark felt his heart swell.

"Come in." She stood aside, and held the door open for him. Her sister greeted Mark frostily, much more aware of the jilting than Marion herself.

"Doesn't he look well?" Marion asked, and they both

looked Mark over carefully, as he stood in the centre of the kitchen floor.

"He's too thin," her sister judged him waspishly, and began untying her apron-strings.

"Perhaps," Marion agreed comfortably, "he just needs the proper food." And she smiled and nodded as she saw how brown and lean he was, but she recognized also, with eyes as fond as a mother's, the growing weight of maturity in his features. She saw also the sorrow and the loneliness, and she wanted to take him in her arms and hold his head against her bosom.

"There is some lovely butter-milk," she said instead. "Sit down, here where I can see you."

While she poured from the jug, her sister hung the apron behind the door and without looking at Mark said primly,

"We need more eggs. I'll go into the village."

When they were alone, Marion picked up the roller, and stood over the table, leaning and dipping as the pastry spread and rolled out paper thin.

"Tell me what you have been doing," she invited, and he began, hesitantly at first, but with blossoming sureness and enthusiasm, to tell her about Chaka's Gate, about the work and the life he had found there.

"That's nice." She punctuated his glowing account every few minutes, her mind running busily ahead, already making lists and planning supplies, adapting pragmatically to the contingencies of a life lived far from the comforts of civilization, where even the small comforts become luxuries —a glass of fresh milk, a light in the night—all of it has to be planned for and carefully arranged.

Characteristically she felt neither excitement nor dismay at the prospect. She was of pioneer stock. Where a man goes, the woman follows. It was merely work that must be done.

"The site for the homestead is up in the first fold of the hills, but you can see right down the valley, and the cliffs of Chaka's Gate are right above it. It's beautiful, especially in the evenings."

"I'm sure it is."

"I have designed the house so it can be added on to, a room at a time. To begin with there will only be two rooms—"

"Two rooms will be enough to begin with," she agreed, frowning thoughtfully. "But we'll need a separate room for the children."

He broke off and stared at her, not quite certain that he had heard correctly. She paused with the rolling-pin held in both hands and smiled at him.

"Well, that's why you came here today, isn't it?" she asked sweetly.

He dropped his eyes from hers and nodded. "Yes." He sounded bemused. "I suppose it is."

She lost her aplomb only briefly during the ceremony, and that was when she saw General Sean Courtney sitting in the front pew with his wife beside him, Sean in morning suit and with a diamond pin in his cravat, Ruth cool and elegant in a huge wagon-wheel sized hat, the brim thick with white roses.

"He came!" Marion whispered ecstatically, and could not restrain the triumphant glance she threw to her own friends and relatives, like a lady tossing a coin to a beggar. Her social standing had rocketed to dizzying heights.

Afterwards the General had bussed her tenderly on each cheek, before turning to Mark. "You've picked the prettiest girl in the village, my boy." And she had glowed with pleasure, pink and happy and truly as lovely as she had ever been in her life.

With the help of the four Zulu labourers Sean had given him, Mark had opened a rough track in as far as the Bubezi River. He brought his bride to Chaka's Gate on the pillion of the motorcycle, with the side-car piled high with part of her dowry.

Far behind him, the Zulus led Trojan and Spartan under heavy packs, the rest of Marion's baggage.

In the early morning the mist lay dense along the river, still and flat as the surface of a lake, touched to shades of delicate pink and mauve by the fresh new light of coming day.

The great headlands of Chaka's Gate rose sheer out of the mist, dark and mysterious, each wreathed in laurels of golden cloud.

Mark had chosen the hour of return so that she might have the best of it for her first glimpse of her new home. He pulled the cycle and side-car off the narrow, stony track and switched off the motor.

In the silence they sat and watched the sun strike upon the crests of the cliffs, burning like the beacons that the mariner looks for in the watery deserts of the ocean, the lights that beckon him on to his landfall and the quiet anchorage.

"It's very nice, dear," she murmured. "Now show me where the house will be."

She worked with the Zulus, muddy to the elbows as they puddled the clay for the unburned Kimberley bricks, joshing them in their own language and bullying them cheerfully to effort beyond the usual pace of Africa.

She worked behind the mules, handling the traces, dragging up the logs from the valley, her sleeves rolled high on brown smooth arms and a scarf knotted around her head.

She worked over the clay oven, bringing out the fat golden brown loaves on the blade of a long handled spade, and watched with deep contentment as Mark wiped up the last of the stew with the crust.

"Was that good, then, dear?"

In the evenings she sat close to the lantern, with her head bowed over the sewing in her lap, and nodded brightly as he told her of the day's adventures, each little triumph and disappointment.

"What a shame, dear." Or, "How nice for you, dear."

He took her, one bright, cloudless day, up the ancient pathway to the crest of Chaka's Gate. Holding her hand as he led her over the narrow places, where the river flowed six hundred sheer feet below their feet. She tucked her skirts into her bloomers, took a firm hold on the basket she carried and never faltered once on the long climb.

On the summit, he showed her the tumbled stone walls and overgrown caves of the old tribesmen who had defied Chaka, and he told her the story of the old king's climb, pointing out the fearsome path up which he had led his warriors—and finally he described the massacre and pictured for her the rain of human bodies hurled down into the river below.

"How interesting, dear," she murmured, as she spread a cloth from the basket she had carried. "I brought scones and some of that apricot jam you like so much."

Something caught Mark's eye, unusual movement far down in the valley below, and he reached for his binoculars. In the golden grass at the edge of the tall reed beds they looked like a line of fat black bugs on a clean sheet. He knew what they were immediately, and with a surging uplift of excitement he counted them.

"Eighteen!" he shouted aloud. "It's a new herd."

"What is it, dear?" She looked up from the scone she was spreading with jam.

"It's a new herd of buffalo," he exulted. "They must have come in from the north. It's beginning to work already."

In the field of the binoculars he saw one of the great bovine animals emerge into a clearing in the long grass. He could see not only its wide black back, but the heavy head and spreading ears beneath the mournfully drooping horns. The sunlight caught the bosses of the polished black horns so that they glittered like gunmetal.

He felt an enormous proprietary pride. They were his own. The first to come into the sanctuary he was building for them.

"Look." He offered her the binoculars, and she wiped her hands carefully and pointed the glasses over the cliff. "There on the edge of the swamp." He pointed, with the pride and joy shining on his face.

"I can see them," she agreed smiling happily for him. "How nice, dear."

Then she swung the binoculars in a wide sweep across the river to where the roof of the homestead showed above the trees.

"Doesn't it look so nice with its new thatch?" she said proudly. "I just can't wait to move in."

The following day they moved up from the shack of crude thatch and canvas at the old camp under the sycamore fig trees, and a pair of swallows moved in with them. The swiftly darting birds began to build their neat nest with little shiny globs of mud under the eaves of the new yellow thatch against the crisply white-washed wall of Kimberley brick.

"That's the best of all possible luck," Mark laughed.

"They make such a mess," said Marion doubtfully, but that night, for the first time ever, she initiated their lovemaking; rolling comfortably on to her back in the double-bed, drawing up her nightdress to her waist, and spreading her warm womanly thighs.

"It's all right, if you want to, dear." And because she was kind and loved him so, he was as quick and as considerate as he could be.

"Was that good, then, dear?"

"It was wonderful," he told her, and he had a sudden vivid image of a lovely vital woman, with a body that was lithe and swift—and his guilt was brutal like a fist below the heart. He tried to thrust the image away, but it ran ahead of him through his dreams, laughing and dancing and teasing, so that in the morning there were dark blue smears beneath his eyes and he felt fretful and restless.

"I'm going up the valley on patrol." He did not look up from his coffee.

"You only came back last Friday." She was surprised.

"I want to look for those buffalo again," he said.

"Very well, dear. I'll pack your bag—how long will you be gone—I'll put in your sweater and the jacket, it's cool in the evenings—it's a good thing I baked yesterday—" she prattled on cheerfully, and he had a sudden terrible urge to shout at her to be silent. "It will give me a chance to plant out the garden. It will be nice to have fresh vegetables again, and I haven't written a letter for ages. They'll be wondering about us at home." He rose from the table and went out to saddle Trojan.

* * *

The flogging explosion of heavy wings roused Mark from his reverie and he straightened in the saddle just as a dozen of the big birds rose from the edge of the reed-beds.

They were those dirty buff-coloured vultures, powering upwards as they were disturbed by Mark's approach, and undergoing that almost magical transformation from gross ugliness into beautiful planing flight.

Mark tethered Trojan and slipped the Mannlicher from its scabbard as a precaution. He felt a tickle of excitement, hopes high that he had come upon a kill by one of the big predatory cats. Perhaps even a lion, one of the animals for which he still searched the valley in vain.

The buffalo lay at the edge of the damp soft ground, half hidden by the reeds and it was so freshly dead that the vultures had not yet managed to penetrate the thick black hide, nor to spoil the sign which was deeply trodden and torn into the damp earth. They had only gouged out the uppermost eye and, with their beaks, scratched the softer skin around the bull's anus, for that was always their access point to a big thick-skinned carcass.

The buffalo was a big mature bull, the great boss of his horns grown solidly together across the crown of his skull, a huge head of horn, forty-eight inches from tip to tip. He was big in the body also, bigger than a prize Hereford stud bull, and he was bald across the shoulders, the scarred grey hide scabbed with dried mud and bunches of bush ticks.

Mark thrust his hand into the crease of skin between the back legs and felt the residual body warmth.

"He's been dead less than three hours," he decided, and squatted down beside the huge body to determine the cause of death. The bull seemed unmarked until Mark managed to roll him over, exerting all his strength and using the stiffly out-thrust limbs to move the ton and a half of dead weight.

He saw immediately the death wounds, one was behind the shoulder, through the ribs, and Mark's hunter's eye saw instantly that it was a heart-stroke, a wide-lipped wound, driven home deeply; the clotted heart blood that poured from it had jellied on the damp earth.

If there was any doubt at all as to the cause of that injury, it was dispelled instantly when he looked to the second wound. This was a frontal stroke, at the base of the neck, angled in skilfully between bone, to reach the heart again, and the weapon had not been withdrawn, it was still plunged in to the hilt and the shaft was snapped short where the bull had fallen upon it.

Mark grasped the broken shaft, placed one booted foot against the bull's shoulder and grunted with the effort it required to withdraw the blade against the reluctant suck of clinging flesh.

He examined it with interest. It was one on those broad-bladed stabbing spears, the assegai, which had been designed by the old king Chaka himself. Mark remembered Sean Courtney reminiscing about the Zulu wars, Isandhlwana, and Morma Gorge.

"They can put one of those assegais into a man's chest and send the point two feet out between his shoulder blades, and when they clear the blade, the withdrawal seems to suck a man as white as though he had his life blood pumped out of him by a machine." Sean had paused for a moment to stare into the camp fire. "As they clear, they shout 'Ngidhla!' —I have eaten! Once you have heard it, you'll not forget it. Forty years later, the memory still makes the hair come up on the back of my neck."

Now still holding the short heavy assegai, Mark remembered that Chaka himself had hunted the buffalo with a

similar weapon. A casual diversion between campaigns—
and as Mark glanced from the blade to the great black
beast, he felt his anger tempered with reluctant admiration.
His anger was for the wanton destruction of one of his
precious animals, and his admiration was for the special
type of courage that had done the deed.

Thinking of the man, Mark realized that there must have
been special circumstances for that man to abandon such a
valuable, skilfully and lovingly wrought weapon together
with the prize he had risked his life to hunt.

Mark began to back-track the sign in the soft black
earth, and he found where the bull had come up one of the
tunnel-like pathways through the reeds after drinking. He
found where the hunstman had waited in thick cover beside
the path, and his bare footprints were unmistakable.

"Pungushe!" exclaimed Mark.

Pungushe had lain upwind and, as the bull passed, he
had put the steel behind his shoulder, deeply into the heart.

The bull had leapt forward, crashing into a ponderous
gallop as Pungushe cleared his point, and the blood had
sprayed from the wide wound as though the standing reeds
had been hosed by a careless gardener.

The buffalo is one of the few wild animals which will
turn and actively hunt its tormentor. Although the bull
was dead on his feet, spurting blood with every lunging
stride, he had swung wide into the wind to take Pungushe's
scent and when he had it, he had steadied into that terrible
crabbing, nose up, wide-horned, relentless charge that only
death itself will stop.

Pungushe had stood to meet him as he came thundering
down through the reeds, and he had picked the point at the
base of the neck for his second stroke and put the steel in
cleanly to the heart, but the bull had hit him also, before
blundering on a dozen paces and falling to his knees with
that characteristic death bellow.

Mark found where Pungushe had fallen, his body marks
etched clearly in the soft clay.

Mark followed where he had dragged himself out of the

edge of the reed beds and shakily regained his feet.

Slowly Pungushe had turned northwards, but his stride was cramped, he was heeling heavily, not up on his toes, not extended into his normal gait.

He stopped once where he had left his steel-jawed spring trap, and he hid it in an ant bear hole and kicked sand over it, obviously too sick and weak to carry it or to cache the valuable trap more securely. Mark retrieved the trap and, as he tied it on to Trojan's saddle, he wondered briefly to how many of his animals it had dealt hideous death.

A mile farther on, Pungushe paused to gather leaves from one of the little turpentine bushes, a medicinal shrub, and then he had gone on slowly, not using the rocky ridges, not covering or back-tracking as he usually did.

At the sandy crossing of one of the steep narrow dry water courses, Pungushe had dropped on one knee, and had used both hands to push himself upright.

Mark stared at the sign for there was blood now for the first time, black droplets that had formed little pellets of loose sand, and in his anger and jubilation, Mark felt a prick of real concern.

The man was hard hit, and he had once saved Mark's life. Mark could still remember the blessed taste of the bitter medicine in the black baked pot cutting through the terrible thirsts of malaria.

He had been leading Trojan up to this point, to keep down, to show a low silhouette, so as not to telegraph heavy hoofbeats ahead to his quarry.

Now he swung up into the saddle, and kicked the mule into a plunging sway-backed canter.

\* \* \*

Pungushe was down. He had gone down heavily at last, dropping to the sandy earth. He had crawled off the game path, under a low bush out of the sun, and he had pulled the light kaross of monkey-skins over his head, the way a man settles down to sleep—or to die.

He lay so still that Mark thought he was indeed dead. He slipped down off Trojan's back and went up cautiously to the prostrate body. The flies were buzzing and swarming gleefully over the bloody bundle of green turpentine leaves that were bound with strips of bark around the man's flank and across the small of his back.

Mark imagined clearly how he had received that wound, Pungushe standing to meet the charging buffalo, going for the neck with the short heavy-bladed assegai, putting the steel in cleanly and then jumping clear, but the bull pivoting hard on his stubby front legs and hooking with the massive bossed and wickedly curved horns.

Pungushe had taken the hook low in the side, far back behind the hip-bone of the pelvis. The shock would have hurled him clear, giving him time to crawl away while the bull staggered on, fighting the deep steel in his chest, until at last he had gone down on his forelegs with that last defiant death bellow.

Mark shuddered in the harsh sunlight at the wound that bundle of leaves covered, and went down on one knee to brush the flies away.

Now for the first time, he became aware of the man's physique. The kaross covered his head and shoulders only, the great chest was exposed. A loin-cloth of softly tanned leather embroidered with blue beads was drawn up between his legs, leaving free the solid bulge of his buttocks, and the sinewy thews of his thighs and the flat hard plain of the belly.

Each separate muscle was clearly defined, and the ropey veins below the surface of the skin were like bunches of serpents, testimony to the man's tremendous physical development and fitness. The skin itself was lighter than that of the average Zulu. It had the smooth dark buttery colour and lustre of a woman's skin, but tight dark curls covered the chest.

"I baited for a jackal," Mark thought wonderingly, "and

I caught myself a lion, a big old black-maned lion." And now he felt real concern that Pungushe was dead. For such a splendid animal, death was a shabby bargain.

Then he saw the gentle, almost imperceptible rise and fall of the deep muscled chest, and he reached out and touched the shoulder through the kaross.

The man stirred, and then painfully lifted himself on one elbow, letting the kaross fall back, and he looked at Mark.

He was a man in the full noon of his strength and pride and dignity, perhaps forty years of age, with just the first frosts of wisdom touching the short cap of dark wool at his temples.

The agony did not show in his face, the broad forehead was smooth as polished amber, the mouth was in repose, and the eyes were dark and fierce and proud. It was the handsome moon face of the high-bred Zulu.

"Sakubona, Pungushe," said Mark. "I see you, O Jackal."

The man looked at him for a moment, thinking about the name and the style of greeting, the language and the accent in which it was spoken. The calm expression did not change, no smile nor snarl on the thick sculptured lips, only a new light in the dark eyes.

"Sakubona, Jamela. I see you, O Seeker." His voice was deep and low, yet it rang on the still air with the timbre of a bronze gong, and then he went on immediately, "Sakubona, Ngaga."

Mark blinked. It had never occurred to him that the jackal might think of him by a name every bit as derogatory. Ngaga is the pangolin, the scaly ant-eater, a small creature that resembles an armadillo, a nocturnal creature, which if caught out in daylight, scurries around like a bent and wizened old man pausing to peer shortsightedly at any small object in its path, then hurrying on again.

The two names "Jamela" and "Ngaga" used together described with embrassing clarity somebody who ran in small circles, peering at everything and yet blindly seeing nothing.

Suddenly Mark saw himself through the eyes of a hidden

observer, riding a seemingly pointless patrol through the
valley, dismounting to peer at anything that caught his interest, then riding on again—just like an ngaga. It was not
a flattering thought.

He felt with sudden discomfort that despite Pungushe's
wounds, and Mark's position of superiority, so far he had
had the worst of the exchange.

"It seems that ngaga has at last found what he seeks," he
pointed out grimly, and went to the mule for his blanket
roll.

Under the bloody bunch of leaves there was a deep dark
hole where the point of the buffalo horn had driven in. It
might have gone in as far as the kidneys, in which case the
man was as good as dead. Mark thrust the thought aside,
and swabbed out the wound as gently as he could with a
solution of acriflavine.

His spare shirt was snowy white and still crisp from
Marion's meticulous laundering and ironing. He ripped off
the sleeves, folded the body into a wad and placed it over
the gaping hole, binding it up with the torn sleeves.

Pungushe said nothing as he worked, made no protest
nor showed any distress as Mark lifted him into a sitting
position to work more easily. But when Mark ripped the
shirt he murmured regretfully,

"It is a good shirt."

"There was once a young and handsome ngaga who
might have died from the fever," Mark reminded him, "but
a scavenging old jackal carried him to a safe place and
gave him drink and food."

"Ah," Pungushe nodded. "But he was not such a stupid
jackal as to tear a good shirt."

"The ngaga is much concerned that the jackal is in good
health, so that he will be able to labour mightily at the
breaking of rocks and other manly tasks when he is an
honoured guest at the kraal of King Georgey." Mark ended
that subject, and repacked his blanket roll. "Can you make
water, O Jackal? It is necessary to see how deep the buffalo
has speared you."

The urine was tinged pinky brown, but there were no strings of bright blood. It seemed that the kidneys may merely have been badly bruised, and that the thick pad of iron muscle across the Zulu's back had absorbed much of the brutal driving thrust. Mark found himself praying silently that it was so, although he could not imagine why he was so concerned.

Working quickly, he cut two long straight saplings, and plaited a drag litter from strips of wet bark. Then he padded the litter with his own blankets and Pungushe's kaross, before hitching it up to Trojan.

He helped the big Zulu into the litter, surprised to find how tall he was, and how hard was the arm he placed around Mark's shoulder to support himself.

With Pungushe flat in the litter, he led the mule back along the game trail, and the ends of the two saplings left a long snaking drag mark in the soft earth.

It was almost dark when they passed the scene of the buffalo hunt. Looking across the reed banks, Mark could make out the obscene black shapes of the vultures in the trees, waiting their turn at the carcass.

"Why did you kill my buffalo?" he asked, not certain that Pungushe was still conscious. "All men know the new laws. I have travelled to every village, I have spoken with every induna, every chief—all men have heard. All men know the penalty for hunting in this valley."

"If he was your buffalo, why did he not carry the mark of your iron? Surely it is the custom of the *Abelungu*—the white men—to burn their mark upon their cattle?" Pungushe asked from the litter, without a smile nor with any trace of mockery, yet mockery Mark knew it was. He felt his anger stir.

"This place was declared sacred, even by the old king, Chaka."

"No," said Pungushe. "It was declared a royal hunt, and," his voice took a sterner ring, "I am Zulu, of the royal blood. I hunt here by my birthright—it is a man's thing to do."

"No man has the right to hunt here."

"Then what of the white men who have come here with their *isibamu*—their rifles—these past hundred seasons?" asked Pungushe.

"They are evil-doers, even as you are."

"Then why were they not taken to be guests at the kraal of King Georgey, as I am so honoured?"

"They will be in future," Mark assured him.

"Ho!" said Pungushe, and this time his voice was thick with contempt and mockery.

"When I catch them, they will go also," Mark repeated doggedly, but the Zulu made a weary gesture of dismissal with one expressive pink-palmed hand, a hand that said clearly that there were many laws—some for rich, some for poor, some for white and some for black. They were silent again until after dark when Mark had camped for the night, and put Trojan to graze on a head-rope.

As he squatted over the fire, cooking the evening meal for both of them, Pungushe spoke again from his litter in the darkness beyond the firelight.

"For whom do you keep the *silwane*—the wild animals of the valley? Will King Georgey come here to hunt?"

"Nobody will ever hunt here again, no king nor common man."

"Then why do you keep the *silwane*?"

"Because if we do not, then the day will dawn when there will be no more left in this land. No buffalo, no lion, no kudu, nothing. A great emptiness."

Pungushe was silent for the time it took Mark to spoon a slop of maize porridge and bully beef into the lid of the pannikin and take it to the Zulu.

"Eat," he commanded, and sat cross-legged opposite him with his own plate in his lap.

"What you say is true," Pungushe spoke thoughtfully.

"When I was a child—of your age," Mark noted the barb but let it pass, "there were elephant in this valley, great bulls with teeth as long as a throwing-spear, and there were many lions, herds of buffalo like the great king's cattle," he broke off. "They have gone, soon what is left will go also."

"Is that a good thing?" Mark asked.

"It is neither a good thing nor a bad thing." Pungushe shrugged and began to eat. "It is merely the way of the world—and there is little profit in pondering it."

They finished eating in silence and Mark cleared the plates and brought coffee, which Pungushe waved away.

"Drink it," snapped Mark. "You must have it to cleanse the blood from your water."

He gave Pungushe one of his cigarettes, and the Zulu carefully broke off the brown cork tip before putting it between his lips. He wrinkled his broad flat nose at the insipid taste, for he was accustomed to the ropey black native tobacco, but he would not belittle a man's hospitality by making comment.

"When it is all gone, when the great emptiness comes here to this valley, what will become of you, O Jackal?" Mark asked.

"I do not understand your question."

"You are a man of the *silwane*. You are a great hunter. Your life is yoked to the *silwane*, as the herdsman is yoked to his cattle. What will become of you, O mighty hunter, when all your cattle are gone?"

Mark realized that he had reached the Zulu. He saw his nostrils flare, and something burn up brightly within him, but he waited while Pungushe considered the proposition at great length and in every detail.

"I will go to *Igoldi*," said Pungushe at last. "I will go to the gold mines, and become rich."

"They will put you to work deep in the earth, where you cannot see the sun nor feel the wind, and you will break rocks, just as you go now to do at the kraal of King Georgey."

Mark saw the repugnance flit across the Zulu's face.

"I will to to *Tekweni*," Pungushe changed his mind. "I will go to Durban and become a man of much consequence."

"In *Tekweni* you will breathe the smoke of the cane mills into your lungs, and when the fat babu overseer speaks to you, you will reply, *yehbo*, Nkosi—yes, master!"

This time the repugnance on the Zulu's face was deeper still and he smoked his cigarette down to a tiny sliver of paper and ash which he pinched out between thumb and forefinger.

"Jamela," he said sternly. "You speak words that trouble a man."

\* \* \*

Mark knew well that the big Zulu's injury was more serious than his stoic acceptance of it would indicate. It was womanly to show pain.

It would be a long time before he was ready to make the journey by side-car over the rough tracks and rutted dusty roads to the police station and magistrate's court at Ladyburg.

Mark put him into the small lean-to tool-shed that he had built on to the far wall of the mule stables. It was dry and cool, and had a sturdy door with a Yale padlock. He used blankets from Marion's chest and the mattress she had been saving for the children's room, despite her protests. "But he's a native, dear!"

Every evening, he took the prisoner's meal down to him in the pannikin, inspected the wound and dressed it afresh.

Then while he waited for Pungushe to eat, he sat on the top step in the doorway to the shed and they smoked a cigarette while they talked.

"If the valley belongs now to King Georgey, how is it that you build your house here, plant your gardens and graze your mules?"

"I am the king's man," Mark explained.

"You are an induna?" Pungushe paused with a spoon of food halfway to his mouth, and stared at Mark incredulously. "You are one of the king's counsellors?"

"I am the keeper of the royal hunt." Mark used the old Zulu title, and Pungushe shook his head sadly.

"My father's father was once the keeper of the royal hunt—but he was a man of great consequence, with two dozen wives, a man who had fought in a dozen wars and killed so many enemies that his shield was as thick with oxtails as there is grass on the hills in springtime." The oxtail was the decoration which the king grants a warrior to adorn his shield when he has distinguished himself in battle. Pungushe finished his meal and added simply,

"King Chaka knew better than to send a child to do man's work."

"The next evening Mark saw that the wound was healing cleanly and swiftly. The man's tremendous fitness and strength were responsible for that. He was able to sit cross-legged now, and there was a new jauntiness in the way he held his head. It would be sooner than Mark had thought that Pungushe would be fit enough to make the journey to Ladyburg, and Mark felt an odd sinking feeling of regret.

"King Georgey is doubtlessly a great, wise and all-seeing king," Pungushe opened the evening's debate. "Why then does he wait until sundown to begin work that should have been started at dawn? If he wanted to avoid the great emptiness in this valley, his father should have begun the work."

"The king's affairs are many, in far countries. He must rely on indunas to advise him who are not as wise or all-seeing," Mark explained.

"The *Abelungu*—the white men—are like greedy children, grabbing up handfuls of food they cannot eat. Instead they smear it over their faces."

"There are greedy and ingorant black men also," Mark pointed out. "Some who even kill leopards with steel traps for their fur."

"To sell to the greedy white men, to dress their ignorant women," Pungushe agreed, and that makes the score deuce, Mark thought as he gathered up the empty panni-kins.

The next evening Pungushe seemed sad, as at the time of leave-taking.

"You have given me much on which I must think heavily," he said.

"You will have much time to do so," Mark agreed. "In between the breaking of rocks." And Pungushe ignored the reference.

"There is weight in your words, for one who is still young enough to be herding the cattle," he qualified the compliment.

"Out of the mouths of babes and sucklings," Mark translated into Zulu and Pungushe nodded solemnly, and in the morning he was gone.

He had opened the thatch at the back of the roof, and wriggled through the small hole. He had taken his kaross and left Marion's blankets neatly folded on the mattress. He had tried for the steel spring-trap, but Mark had locked it in the kitchen, so he had left it and gone northwards in the night.

Mark was furious for so misjudging his prisoner's recovery, and he muttered darkly as he plunged along after him on Trojan.

"This time I'm going to shoot the bastard on sight," he promised, and realized at that moment that Pungushe had back-tracked on him. He had to dismount and laboriously unravel the confused trail.

Half an hour later, Pungushe led him into the river, and it was well after noon when he at last found where the Zulu had left the water, stepping lightly on a fallen log.

He finally lost the cold spoor in the rocky ground on the far rim of the valley, and it was almost midnight when he rode wearily back to the thatched cottage. Marion had his dinner ready and ten gallons of hot bath water bubbling on the fire.

Six weeks later, Pungushe returned to the valley. Mark sat astounded on the stoep of the cottage, and watched him come.

He walked with the long gliding stride that showed he was fully recovered from his wound. He wore the beaded loin-cloth and the jackal-skin cloak over his shoulders. He carried two of the short-shafted stabbing assegai, with the broad steel blades, and his wives followed at a respectable distance behind him.

There were three of them. They were bare-breasted, with the tall clay headdress of the Zulu matron. The senior was of the same age as her husband, but her dugs were flat and empty as leather pouches and she had lost her front teeth. The youngest wife was a child still in her teens, a pretty plump little thing with jolly melon breasts, and a fat brown infant on her hip.

Every wife carried an enormous bundle on her head, balancing it easily without use of hands, and they were followed by a gaggle of naked and half-naked children. Like their mothers, the little girls each carried a headload, the size of it directly proportional to the age and stature of the bearer. The smallest, perhaps four years of age, carried a beer gourd the size of a grapefruit, echoing faithfully the straight erect carriage and swaying buttocks of her seniors.

Mark counted seven sons and six daughters.

"I see you, Jamela." Pungushe paused below the stoep.

"I see you also, Pungushe," Mark acknowledged cautiously, and the Zulu squatted down comfortably on the lowest step. His wives settled down at the edge of Marion's garden—politely out of earshot. The youngest wife gave one of her fat breasts to the infant and he sucked lustily.

"It will rain tomorrow," said Pungushe. "Unless the wind goes into the north. In which case it will not rain again until the full moon."

"That is so," Mark agreed.

"Rain now would be good for the grazing. It will bring the *silwane* down from the Portuguese territory beyond the Pongola."

Mark's astonishment had now given way to lively curiosity.

"There is talk in the villages, common word among all the people that has only recently come to my ears," Pungushe went on airily. "It is said that Jamela, the new keeper of the royal hunt of King Georgey, is a mighty warrior who has slain great multitudes of the king's enemies in the war beyond the sea." The Jackal paused and then went on, "Albeit, he is still unbearded and green as the first flush of the spring-time grass."

"Is that the word?" Mark inquired politely.

"It is said that King Georgey has granted Jamela a black oxtail to wear on his shield." A black oxtail is the highest honour, and might loosely he considered the equivalent of a M.M.

"I am also a warrior," Pungushe pointed out. "I fought with Bombata at the gorge, and afterwards the soldiers came and took away my cattle. This is how I became a man of *silwane*, and a mighty hunter."

"We are brothers of the spear," Mark conceded. "But now I will make ready my *isi-du-du-du*, my motorcycle, so that we may ride to Ladyburg and speak with the magistrate there of matters of great interest to all of us."

"Jamela!" The Zulu shook his head grievingly, like a father with an obtuse son. "You aspire to be a man of the *silwane*, you aspire to fill the great emptiness—and yet who will there be to teach you, who will open your eyes to see and your ears to hear, if I am in the kraal of King Georgey breaking his rocks?"

"You have come to help me?" Mark asked. "You and your beautiful fat wives, your brave sons and nubile daughters?"

"It is even so."

"This is a noble thought," Mark conceded.

"I am Zulu of royal blood," Pungushe agreed. "Also my

fine steel trap was stolen from me, even as my cattle were stolen, thus making me a poor man once more."

"I see," Mark nodded. "It remains only for me to put out of my mind the business of leopard skins and dead buffalo?"

"It is even so."

"Doubtless I will also find it in my heart, to pay you for this help and advice."

"That also is so."

"What size is the coin in which you will be paid?"

Pungushe shrugged with disinterest. "I am royal Zulu, not a Hindu trader haggling in the market-place. The coin will be just and fair," he paused delicately, "always bearing in mind the multitude of my beautiful wives, my many brave sons and the host of nubile daughters. All of whom have unbelievable appetites."

Mark had to remain silent, not trusting himself to speak until he controlled the violent urge to burst out laughing. He spoke again, solemnly, but with laughter rippling his belly muscles.

"In what style will you address me, Pungushe? When I speak, will you answer, *'Yehbo,* Nkosi—Yes, Master'?"

Pungushe stirred restlessly, and an expression flitted across the broad smooth features like a fastidious eater who has just discovered a large fat worm on his plate. "I will call you Jamela," he said. "And when you speak as you have just spoken, I will answer, 'Jamela, that is a great stupidity.' "

"In what style will I address you?" Mark inquired politely, fighting his mirth.

"You will call me Pungushe. For the jackal is the cleverest and most cunning of all the *silwane,* and it is necessary for you to be reminded of this from time to time."

Then something happened that Mark had not seen before. Pungushe smiled. It was like the break-through of the sun on a grey overcast day. His teeth were big and perfect and white, and the smile stretched so wide that it seemed his face might tear.

Mark could no longer contain it. He laughed out loud, beginning with a strangled chuckle. Hearing it Pungushe laughed also, a great ringing bell of laughter.

The two of them laughed so long and hard, that the wives fell silent and watched in amazement, and Marion came out on to the stoep.

"What is it, dear?"

He could not answer her, and she went away shaking her head at the craziness of men.

At last they both fell silent, exhausted with mirth, and Mark gave Pungushe a cigarette from which he carefully broke the corked tip. They smoked in silence for nearly a minute, then suddenly without warning Mark let out another uncontrolled guffaw, and it started them off again.

The cords of sinew stood out on Pungushe's neck, like columns of carved ebony, and his mouth was a deep pink cavern lined with perfect white teeth. He laughed until the tears ran down his face and dripped from his chin, and when he lost his breath, he let out a great whistling snort like a bull hippo breaking surface, and he wiped the tears away with his thumb and said, "Ee—hee!" and slapped his thigh like a pistol shot, between each fresh paroxysm of laughter.

Mark ended it by reaching out his shaking right hand, and Pungushe took it in a reverse grip, panting and heaving still.

"Pungushe, I am your man," Mark sobbed.

"And I, Jamela, am yours."

*  *  *

There were four men sitting in a semi-circle around the wall of the hotel suite. They were all dressed in such fashion that it seemed a uniform. The dark high-buttoned suits, the glazed celluloid collars and sober neckties. Although their ages were spread over thirty years, although one of them was bald with grey wisps around his ears and another had a fiery red bush of hair, although one wore a prim gold pince-nez pinched on to a thin aquiline nose while another had the open far-seeing gaze of the farmer, yet all of them had those solid hewn calvinistic faces, indomitable, unrelenting and strong as granite.

Dirk Courtney spoke to them in the young language which had only recently received recognition as a separate entity from its parent Dutch, and had been given the name of Afrikaans.

He spoke it with an elegance and precision that softened the reserve in their expressions, and eased the set of jaw and the stiffness in their backs.

"It's a Jingo area," Dirk told them. "There is a Union Jack flying on every roof-top. It's rich constituency, landowners, professional men—your party has no appeal there." He was talking of the parliamentary constituency of Ladyburg. "In the last elections you did not even present a candidate, nobody fool enogh to lose his deposit, and the Smuts Party returned General Courtney unopposed."

The eldest of his listeners nodded over his gold pince-nez, inviting him to continue.

"If you are to fight the Ladyburg seat, you will need a candidate with a different approach, an English speaker, a man of property, somebody with whom the voters can identify—"

It was a beautiful performance. Dirk Courtney, handsome, debonair, articulate in either language, striding back and forth across the carpeted lounge, holding all their attention, stopping dramatically to make a point with a graceful gesture of strong brown hands, then striding on again. He talked for half an hour, and he was watching his audience, noting the reaction of each, judging their weaknesses, their strengths.

At the end of that half hour, he had decided that all four of them were dedicated, completely committed to their political faith. They stirred only at appeals to patriotism, to national interest, at reference to the aspirations of their people.

"So," Dirk Courtney thought comfortably. "It's cheaper

to buy honest men. Rogues cost good bright gold—while honest men can be had with a few fine words and noble sentiments. Give me an honest man every time."

One of the older men leaned forward and asked quietly,

"General Courtney has had the seat since 1910. He is a member of the Smuts Cabinet, a war hero, and a man of huge popular appeal. He is also your father. Do you think the voters will take the young dog when they can have the sire?"

Dirk answered: "I am prepared not only to risk my deposit if I achieve the National Party nomination, but I am confident enough of my eventual success to make a substantial earnest of my serious intentions to the campaign funds of the party." He named a sum of meney that made them exchange quick glances of surprise.

"In exchange for all this?" the elder politican asked.

"Nothing that is not in the best interest of the nation, and of my constituency," Dirk told them soberly, and he pulled down the map that hung on the far wall facing them.

Again he began to speak, but now with the contagious fervour of the zealot. In burning words, he built up a vision of ploughed fields stretching to the horizon, and sweet clean water running deep in endless irrigation furrows. The listeners were all men who had farmed and ploughed the rich but hostile soil of Africa, and all of them had searched blue and cloudless skies with hopeless eyes for the rain clouds that never came. The image of deeply turned furrows and slaking water was irresistible.

"Of course, we will have to repeal the proclamation on the Bubezi Valley," Dirk said it glibly, and not one of them showed shock or concern at the statement. Already they could see the inland sea of sweet limpid water ruffing in the breeze.

"If we win at this election," the eldest politican began.

"No, Menheer," Dirk interrupted gently, "*when* we win."

The man smiled for the first time. "When we win," he agreed.

Dirk Courtney stood high on the platform, with thumbs hooked into his waistcoat. When he smiled and tilted that noble lion head with the shining mane of curls, the women in the audience that packed the church hall rustled like flowers in the breeze.

"The Butcher," said Dirk Courtney, and his voice rang with a depth and resonance that thrilled them all, man and woman, young and old. "The Butcher of Fordsburg, his hands red with blood of our countrymen."

The applause began with the men that Dirk Courtney had in the audience, but it spread quickly.

"I rode with Sean Courtney against Bombata—" one man was on his feet, near the back of the hall. "I went to France with him," he was shouting to be heard above the applause. "And where were you, Mr. Dirk Courtney, when the drums were beating?"

The smile never left Dirk's face, but two little spots of hectic colour rose in his cheeks.

"Ah!" He faced the man across the craning heads of the audience. "One of the gallant General's gunmen. How many women did you shoot down at Fordsburg?"

"That doesn't answer my question," the man shouted back, and Dirk caught the eye of one of the two big men who had risen and were closing in quietly on the questioner.

"Four thousand casualties," said Dirk. "The Government would like to hide that fact from you, but four thousand men, women and children—"

The two big men had closed in on their quarry, and Dirk Courtney drew all eyes with a broad theatrical gesture.

"A Government that has that contempt for the life, property and freedom of its people."

There was a brief scuffle, a yelp of pain and the man was hustled out of the side door into the night.

The newspapers started picking it up almost immediately, the same editorials which had ranted against the "Red Cabal" and the "Bolshevik threat," which had praised Smuts' "direct and timely action," were now remembering "a high-handed and brutal solution."

Across the nation, begun by Dirk Courtney and picked up by all the Hertzogites, the balance of public feeling was swinging back, like a pendulum, or the curved blade of the executioner's axe.

Dirk Courtney spoke in the Town Hall of Durban, to three thousand, in the Church Hall of Ladyburg to three hundred. He spoke at every country church in the constituency, at little crossroad general-dealer shops where a dozen voters assembled for an evening's entertainment, but always the Press was represented.

Dirk Courtney worked slowly northwards, during the day visiting all his land holdings, each of his new cane mills, and each evening he spoke to the little assemblies of voters. Always he was vibrant and compelling, handsome and articulate, and he painted a picture for them of a land crossed with railways and fine roads, of prosperous towns, and busy markets. They listened avidly.

\* \* \*

"There are two," said Pungushe. "One is an old lion. I know him well. He stayed last year in Portuguese territory along the north bank of the Usutu River. He was alone then, but now he has found a mate."

"Where did they cross?" Mark asked.

"They crossed below Ndumu, and came south between the swamp and the river."

The lion was five years old, and very cunning, a lean tom, tall at the shoulder and with a short ruff of reddish mane. There was an ugly bald scar across his forehead, and he favoured his right foreleg where a piece of hammered pot-leg fired from a Tower musket two years previously had lodged against the shoulder joint. He had been hunted by man almost without remission since he was a cub, and he was getting old now, and tired.

He crossed the river in the dark, swimming his lioness ahead of him, going south from the hunters who had assembled to drive the bush along the river the next morning. He could hear the drums still beating, and smell the smoke of their fires. He could hear also the yapping clamour of the dog packs. They had assembled, two or three hundred tribesmen with their hunting dogs and a dozen Portugese half-breeds with breech-loading rifles, for the lions had killed two trek oxen on the outskirts of one of the river villages. In the morning the hunt would begin, and the lion took his mate south.

She was also a big animal, and though she was still very young and not as experienced, yet she was quick and strong, and she learned from him every day. Her hide was still clean and unscarred by claw or thorn. Across the back she was a sleek olive tan shading down to a lovely buttery yellow at the throat and fluffy cream on the belly.

She still had traces of her kttten spots dappling her quarters, but the night they swam the Usutu, she came into season for the first time.

On the south bank, they shook the water from their bodies, with fierce shuddering spasms, and then the lion snuffed at her, drumming softly in his throat and then lifting his snout to the bright white stars, his back arching reflexively at the tantalizing musk of her pale blood-tinged oestrous discharge.

She led him half a mile up one of the thickly wooded tributary valleys, and then she crept into the heart of the thicket of tangled bush, a stronghold guarded by the fierce two-inch, wickedly hooked thorns, tipped in red as though they had already drawn blood.

Here in the dawn, he covered her for the first time. She crouched low against the earth, hissing and crackling with angry snarls, while he came over her, biting her ears and neck, forcing her to submit. Afterwards, she lay close against him, licking at his ears, nuzzling his throat and belly, turning half away from him and nudging him flirtatiously with her hind quarters, until he rose and she crouched down submissively and snarled at him while he mounted her briefly once again.

They mated twenty-three times that day, and in the night they left the thorn thicket and wandered southwards again.

A half hour before the set of the moon, they reached the edge of the ploughed land, and the lion stopped and growled softly at the smell of man and cattle.

Tentatively he reached out one paw and tested the freshly turned earth, then he drew his leg back and made a little troubled mewling sound of indecision. The lioness brushed herself lovingly against him, but he turned aside and led her along the edge of the ploughed land.

"Will they reach the valley, Pungushe?" Mark asked, leaning out of the saddle to speak to the Zulu as he trotted at Trojan's shoulder.

Pungushe spoke easily, despite the fact he had run without rest for nearly three hours. "They must cross almost half a day's march of land where men are working, where the ploughs of the new sugar-growers are busy. Besides, Jamela, they know nothing of your valley, and the mad Ngaga who would welcome them." Mark straightened in the saddle and rode on grimly. He knew that this pair, this mating pair, would be his last chance to have lions in his valley. Yet there was twenty miles of danger to cross such as these animals, coming out of the wilderness of Portuguese Mozambique, would never have experienced before, ploughlands, declared cattle area, where lions were vermin. An area devoid of wild prey, but heavily populated with domestic animals. An area where the cry of "Lion" would send fifty men running eagerly for a rifle, fifty white men competing fiercely for the trophy, hating the big predatory cats with a blind unthinking hatred, welcoming what was probably their only chance at one of them, safe in the knowledge that they were fair game, unprotected by law in the cattle areas.

The lions came to the camp downwind, and they lay flat

in the short grass in the darkness at the edge of the camp.

They listened to the drowsy voices of the men at the fire, and smelled the myriad strange smells, of tobacco smoke, of cooking maize meal and the sour tang of Zulu beer, and they lay very flat and tense against the earth, only their round black-tipped ears cocked and their nostrils flaring and sucking the air.

The oxen were kraaled with a low circular enclosure of the felled thorn trees, arranged with their trunks inward and the bushy thorny tangle outwards. The smell of the cattle was strong and tempting.

There were seventy-two oxen in the kraal, two full spans. They belonged to Ladyburg Sugar Company and they were ploughing the new lands east of Chaka's Gate, after the labour teams had stumped out the standing timber and burned it in long windrows.

The lion waited, patient, but alert and tense and silent, while the silver moon went down below the trees and the men's voices dwindled into silence. He waited while the fires died down into puddles of dull ruddy ash. Then he rose silently.

The lioness did not move, except that the great muscles in her chest and limbs swelled, rigid with tension, and her ears cocked fractionally forward.

The lion circled cautiously upwind of the camp. There was a soft cool wash breeze coming steadily out of the east and he used it skilfully.

The oxen caught the whiff of lion as he moved into the wind, and he heard them coming up, rising in that awkward plunging leap from where they had settled.

Horns clashed together as they swung into a tight group facing upwind, and one of them let out a soft mournful lowing. Immediately it was taken up, and their low bellows woke the men at the fires. Somebody shouted, and threw a log on the fire. A torrent of sparks rose into the dark branches of the mimosa and the log caught, lighting the camp with a yellow leaping dancing light. The ploughmen and the lead boys were gathered fearfully around the fire, still with skin karosses draped around their shoulders, owl-eyed with sleep and alarm.

The lion slipped like a shadow, dark and flat against the earth towards the kraal, and the cattle bunched and bellowed wildly at the sharp rank cat smell

Against the thorny windward side of the kraal, the lion crouched, arched his back and ejected a stream of urine.

The pungent, biting ammoniac stink was too much for the mass of cattle. In a single solid bunch, they swung away downwind and charged the thorny wall of the temporary kraal, crashing through it without check, and they thundered free, quickly spreading, losing the solid formation and scattering away into the night.

The lioness was ready for them, and she streaked in across the flank of the panicking plunging formation, selecting a single victim, a heavy young beast. She drove him onwards, chivvying him like a sheep dog, crossing and recrossing his frantic driving quarters, running him far from the fires and the ploughmen before coming snaking up alongside and hooking expertly at one of his powerfully driving forelegs, and the curved yellow claws biting in just above the hock until they grated against the bone. Then she went back on her own bunched quarters and dragged the leg to cross the other.

The ox dropped as though he had been shot through the brain, and he somersaulted haunch over head, and slid against the earth on his back, all four legs kicking to the starry sky.

In a rubbery flash of supple speed, the cat closed, judging finely the massive hooves that could have crushed her skull and the wide straight horns which could have impaled her rib to rib.

She bit in hard at the base of the skull, driving the long ivory yellow eye teeth into the first and second vertebrae, so they crunched sharply like a walnut in the jaws of the cracker.

When the lion came padding hurriedly out of the night, she had already opened the belly cavity of the ox and her whole head was red and toffee sticky with blood as she went for liver and spleen and kidneys.

She flattened her ears against her bloody skull and snarled murderously at him, but he put his shoulder to her flank and pushed her aside, she snarled again and he cuffed her with a lordly paw and began to feed in the hole she had made.

She glared at him for a second, then her ears came erect and she began to lick his shoulder with long pink voluptuous strokes, purring with a deep soft rattle in her throat, pressing her long sleek body against him. The lion tried to ignore her and fed with snuffling grunts and wet tearing ripping sounds.

But she became bolder, the eternal female taking advantage of her new highly attractive condition, liberties which before would have brought swift and stern disciplinary action.

Desperately the lion tried to restrain her by placing a huge paw on her head, claws carefully retracted, and gulped furiously, trying to eat the entire ox before she could join in, but she wriggled out from under the paw and licked his ear. He growled half-heartedly, flickered the ear. She inched forward and licked his eyes, so he had to close them tightly, furrowing his brow and trying to feed blind, but finally he surrendered to the inevitable and allowed her to force her head into the bloody crater.

Side by side, purring and growling softly, they fed.

\* \* \*

There were eighteen of them, gathered on the wide mosquito-screened veranda of the foreman's cottage under the hissing Petromax lamps. The brandy bottle had been out since sundown, and most of the men were red-faced and bright-eyed as they listened to Dirk Courtney.

"There will be schools and hospitals within a twenty mile ride of everybody," he promised, and the women looked up from their knitting. They knew what it was like to raise a young family out here. "This is the beginning only," he promised the men. "And those of you who were first in will be the first to profit. Once I am in Parliament, you'll have a strong voice speaking up for you. You'll see improvement here you couldn't imagine possible—and quickly."

"You're a rich man, Mr. Courtney," one of them said. He was a small trader, not directly employed by Ladyburg Sugar, but sufficiently reliant on it to phrase his question with respect. "One of the bosses. How come you speak out for the working man?"

"I'm rich because I worked hard, but I know that without you men, I won't be rich much longer. We are linked together like a team."

They nodded and Dirk went on quickly. "One thing I promise you. When I can hire a white man at a decent wage, I won't push in coolie or nigger labour!"

They cheered him then, and filled their glasses to toast him.

"Your present Government, the Smuts men, tried that on the gold mines. Two and tuppence a day for black men, and white men out on the street. When the workers protested, they sent the bloody Butcher of Fordsburg, a man who I am ashamed to call my father—"

There was an urgent hammering on the kitchen door, and the foreman excused himself quietly and hurried out. He was back within a minute and whispered to Dirk Courtney. Dirk grinned and nodded, and turned back to his audience.

"Well, gentlemen, a fine bit of sport in the offing—a lion has killed one of my oxen, down on the new Buli block. The plough boy has just come in to report it. It happened only an hour ago, so we will have an excellent sporting chance at him. May I move closure of this meeting, and we'll meet here again at," he glanced at his watch, "at five o'clock tomorrow morning, every man with a horse and rifle!"

Mark and Pungushe slept, each under a single blanket, on the sunbaked earth, with Trojan cropping the scraggy dry yellow grass nearby. There was a cold little breeze out of the east, and they woke in the total dark of not-yet dawn and sat over the fire drinking coffee and smoking silently until Pungushe could take the spoor again.

From the back of Trojan it was still too dark to see the ground, but Pungushe ran confidently ahead, forcing the mule into a reluctant lumbering trot to keep pace.

At the edge of the ploughed land, he had to cast, but he cut the lion spoor on its new track almost immediately. They went off again, with the sunrise outlining the upper branches of the trees, turning them black and spiky against the ruddy gold.

The soft amber rays were without warmth, and threw long distorted shadows of mule and men on the hard red earth. Mark marvelled once again that the Zulu could run a spoor in this light over such ground, where he could see no mark or sign of the lions' passing.

There was a single gun shot, so faint that Mark thought he might have imagined it, but Pungushe stopped instantly and signalled him to rein in the mule.

They stood and listened intently, and suddenly there was a distant popping fusillade, ten, eleven rifle-shots and then silence again.

Pungushe turned and looked at Mark expressionlessly. The silence was complete, even the morning bird chorus was stilled by the gunfire for a moment. Then as the silence persisted, a troop of little brown francolin started chirruping again on the edge of the ploughed lands.

"Go on!" Mark nodded to Pungushe, trying to keep his face as expressionless, but his voice shook with outrage. They were too late. The last lions south of the Usutu were dead. He felt sick with helpless anger.

They did not notice Mark until he was right up to them. They were too excited, too intent on their work.

There were eight white men, all heavily armed and dressed in rough hunting clothes, with two Zulu grooms holding the horses.

In a trampled opening among the mimosa trees lay the half-eaten carcass of a red and white ox. However, this was not what was engaging their attention. They were grouped in a tight circle beyond the ox, and their voices were raucous, raised in rough jest and cheerful oath.

Mark dismounted and handed the reins to Pungushe. He walked slowly towards the group, dreading what he would find, but he stopped again as one of the men looked up and saw him. He recognized Mark instantly.

"Ah, warden!" Dirk Courtney laughed, tossing that splendid head of glossy curls. "We are doing your job for you." The laughter was sly and spiteful, the malice so apparent that Mark knew he was thinking of the bribe that Mark had accepted and then turned against him.

"Here is one that you can cross off your report," Dirk chuckled again, and gestured for his men to stand aside. The circle opened and Mark stepped into the opening. The men around him were still red-faced and garrulous, and he could smell the stale liquor on them.

"Gentlemen, may I present the newly appointed warden of Chaka's Gate proclaimed area." Dirk stood opposite him, across the circle, with one hand thrust carelessly into the pocket of his chamois-leather jacket, a hand-made double barrelled .450 elephant rifle by Gibbs of London tucked into the crook of his elbow.

The lion lay on its side with all four legs extended. He was an old, scarred tom, so lean and rangy that each rib showed clearly through the short tan hair. There were four bullet-holes in the body, the one behind the shoulder would have raked both lungs, but another heavy bullet had shattered the skull. The mouth hung open slackly and a little blook-stained saliva still oozed out on to the lolling pink tongue.

"Congratulations, gentlemen," Mark nodded, and only Dirk Courtney caught the irony in his voice.

"Yes," he agreed. "The sooner we clear this area and make it safe for settlement—the better for all."

There was a hearty chorus of agreement and one of them produced a brown bottle from his back pocket, and passed it from hand to hand, each in turn pointing its base briefly heavenwards, then exclaiming appreciatively and smacking their lips.

"What about the lioness?" Mark asked quietly, refusing his turn at the bottle.

"Don't worry about her," one of them assured him. "She's down already. I hit her clean in the shoulder. We are just giving her a chance to stiffen up, before we go after her to finish her off." And he drew his sheath knife and began to skin out the carcass of the lion, while his comrades passed loud comment and advice.

Mark walked back to Pungushe who squatted patiently at Trojan's head.

"The lioness is wounded, but has run."

"I have seen the spoor," Pungushe nodded, and pointed it out with his eyes, not moving his head.

"How bad is she hit?"

"I do not know yet. I must see how she settles to run before judging."

"Take the spoor," said Mark. "Let us go quietly, without alerting these mighty hunters."

They drifted away from the clearing, leading the mule casually, Mark following a dozen paces behind the Zulu.

Five hundred yards farther on, Pungushe stopped and spoke quietly.

"She is hit in the right shoulder or leg, but I do not think the bone has gone, for she touches with every second pace. She goes well on three legs, and at first there was a little blood, but it dries quickly."

"Perhaps she bleeds inside?" Mark asked.

"If that is so, we will find her within a short while—dead." Pungushe shrugged.

"All right." Mark swung up into the saddle. "Let us go swiftly, that we may outrun these others, none of them will be able to follow across such hard ground."

He was too late.

"Anders!" Dirk Courtney shouted, riding up at the head of his band. "What the hell do you think you are doing?"

"My job," Mark answered. "I'm following a wounded beast."

"We are coming with you."

Mark glanced at Pungushe, and a silent accord flashed between them, then he turned back to the group.

"You all realize the danger involved? These animals have probably been hunted before, and my tracker thinks the lioness is only lightly hit."

There was a little sobering and hesitation, but all eight of them rode on after Pungushe. He went hard, loping away, *minza umhlabathi*, stretching the horses into an easy canter and after the first hour Dirk Courtney swore bad-temperedly.

"I don't see any blood."

"The blood has dried," Mark told him. "The wound has closed."

The contents of the brown bottle were long ago exhausted. Red faces were sweating heavily in the rising heat, eyes were bloodshot and high good humour turning to headaches and woolly tongues; none of them had remembered to bring a water bottle.

Two of them turned back.

An hour later Dirk Courtney snarled suspiciously, "This bloody nigger is giving us a bum run. Tell him I'll take the horse-whip to him."

"The lioness is going strongly—"

"I don't believe it. I can't see any spoor."

Pungushe stopped abruptly, motioned them to stay and went forward cautiously into a low thicket of waterbessie scrub.

"I've had a guts full of this," muttered one of the hunters miserably.

"Me too."

"I've got work to do."

Three more of them turned back, and those that remained sat their restless horses until Pungushe emerged from the thicket and beckoned them forward.

In the heart of the thicket, impressed deeply into the soft mound of a mole heap he showed them the unmistakable pad of a lioness. It headed relentlessly southward.

"All right," Dirk Courtney acknowledged. "He's still on the spoor. Tell him to keep going."

An hour after noon, the lioness led them on to a low unbroken cap of solid grey granite, and Pungushe sat down wearily. His muscles shone in the sunlight with sweat, as though they had been oiled. He looke up at Mark on the mule and shrugged with an expressive gesture of helplessness.

"Dead spoor," said Mark. "Gone away."

Dirk Courtney pulled up his horse's head with a cruel jerk of the curb, and snapped at Mark.

"Anders. I want to speak to you." He trotted away out of earshot of the group, and Mark followed him.

They stopped and faced each other, and Dirk's mouth was twisted into a pinched and bitter line.

"This is the second time you have been clever at my expense," he started grimly. "You could have had me as an ally—but instead you had my father send me a receipt for my gift. Now you and your savage have pulled another trick. I don't know how you did it, but it's the last time it will happen."

He stared at Mark, and the slant of the eyes altered, once again that mad malevolent light burned in their depths.

"A powerful friend I would have been—but a much more powerful enemy I am now. So far only my father's protection has saved you. That will change. No man stands in my way, I swear that to you."

He wheeled his horse, put spurs to it and galloped away. The other two disconsolate hunters trailed away after him.

Mark rode back to Pungushe, and they drank from the water-bottle and smoked a little before Mark asked, "Where is the lioness?"

"We left her spoor two hours back."

Mark glanced sharply at him, and Pungushe stood up and walked to another mole heap at the edge of the granite. He squatted beside it, and with a roll of his open palm outlined the fleshy pad of a lion paw, then he bunched his knuckles and rolled them for the toe marks.

Miraculously, the spoor of a full-grown lion appeared in the soft earth, and Pungushe looked up at Mark's startled unbelieving expression and let out one of those whistling hippo-snorts of laughter, rocking back on his heels delightedly. "For two hours we followed the Tokoloshe,"* he hooted.

\* \* \*

"I cannot see her," said Mark, carefully glassing the shallow wooded valley below them.

"Oh! Jamela, who cannot see."

"Where is she, Pungushe?"

"Do you see the forked tree, beyond the three round rocks—" A step at a time he directed Mark's gaze, until suddenly he made out just the two dark round blobs of her ears above the short yellow grass, about six hundred yards from where they sat. She was lying close in under the spread of a thorn thicket, and even as he watched, she lowered her head and the ears vanished.

"Now that she is alone, she wishes to return to the place she knows well, beyond the Usutu. That is why she moves always that way, when the pain of the wound allows."

Before they had come up with her, they had found three places where she had lain to rest, and at one such place there had been a smear of blood and a dozen yellow hairs glued into the clot. Pungushe had inspected the hairs, mi-

* A Tokoloshe is a mythical creature from Zulu magical legend.

nutely; by colour and texture he could tell from which part of the lioness' body they had come.

"High in the right shoulder—and if she was bleeding inside she would be down already. But she is in great pain, for she walks short. The wound has stiffened. She cannot go far."

Now Mark swung the glasses towards the west, and longingly stared through them at the blue misty loom of the cliffs of Chaka's Gate, half a dozen miles away.

"So close," he murmured, "so close." But the exhausted cat was dragging herself painfully away from sanctuary, back towards the ploughed lands, towards cattle and men and the dog packs.

Instinctively he turned in that direction now, swinging the binoculars in a long slow traverse across the north and east.

From the low ridge he had a good field of sight, across miles of light forest to the open chocolate expanse of ploughed land.

Something moved in the field of the binoculars and he blinked his eyes and refocused carefully. Three horsemen were coming slowly in their direction, and even at this range Mark could see the dogs running ahead of them.

Quickly he looked back at the leading rider. There was no mistaking that arrogantly erect figure. Dirk Courtney had not given up the hunt. He had merely returned to assemble a hunting-pack, and now the dogs were coming down fast on the smell of the wounded cat.

Mark laid a hand on the hard muscle of Pungushe's shoulder, and with his free hand he pointed. The Zulu stood up and stared for a full minute at the oncoming horsemen, then he began to speak quickly.

"Jamela, I will try to call the lioness, and lead her—"

Mark started to ask a question, but Pungushe stopped him harshly. "Can you pull the dogs away, or stop them?"

Mark thought for a moment, then nodded. "Give me your snuff, Pungushe."

He took the snuff horn that hung on a thong around his neck and handed it to Mark without question.

"Go," said Mark. "Call my lioness for me."

Pungushe slipped away down the ridge and left Mark to hurry to Trojan.

There were three sticks of black dried meat left in Mark's food bag. He found two flat stones and pounded the dry meat into a fine power between them, glancing up every few seconds to see the huntsmen coming on rapidly.

Once the meat was powdered he scooped it into his pannikin and added an ounce of native snuff from the horn, mixing the two powders with his fingers as he ran back down the ridge to intersect the lioness trail at the point they had left it.

When he reached the shoulder of the ridge where the wounded cat had skirted a rocky outcrop, he knelt and made three neat piles of the mixed powder directly in the path of the oncoming dogs.

The dried meat would be irresistible when they reached it, the dogs would sniff at it greedily.

He could hear them already, baying excitedly, coming on swiftly, leading the hunters at a canter. As he ran back up the ridge to where Trojan stood, Mark smiled bleakly. A hound with a good suck of fiery native snuff up his nose wasn't going to smell anything else for at least twelve hours.

\* \* \*

The lioness lay on her side, with her mouth open. She panted for air, and her chest pumped like a blacksmith's bellows, and her eyes were tightly closed.

The bullet had been fired from her right quarter. It was a soft lead slug from a .455 Martini Hendry and it had taken her high in the shoulder, but far forward, cutting in through the heavy muscle and grazing the big joint of the shoulder, lacerating sinew and shattering that extraordinary small floating bone, found only in the shoulder of a lion, the lucky bone so prized as a hunter's talisman.

The bullet had missed the artery as it plunged into the neck and lodged there beneath the skin, a lump the size of the top joint of a man's thumb.

The flies swarmed joyously into the mouth of the wound, and she lifted her head and snapped at them, and then mewing softly at the agony that movement had caused, she began to lick the bullet hole carefully, the long tongue rasping roughly against her hide, curling pink and dextrous as it cleansed the fresh little trickle of watery blood that had sprung from it. Then she sank back wearily and closed her eyes again.

Pungushe was aware of the wind in the same way as the helmsman of a tall ship is, for it was as important to him as it is to a mariner. He knew exactly at each moment of the day its force and direction, anticipated any change before it occurred and he did not have to carry an ash bag nor wet a finger, the knowledge was instinctive.

Now he moved carefully into a downwind position from the wounded animal. It did not occur to him to thank any providence for the constant easterly breeze that put him fairly between the cat and the near boundary of Chaka's Gate.

Silent as the cloud shadow moves across the earth, he moved in on the cat, judging the extreme limit of her acute hearing before kneeling facing where she lay three hundred yards away.

He filled and deflated his lungs rapidly a dozen times, the great muscled chest swelling and subsiding as he built up reserves of oxygen in his blood. Then he caught a full breath and stretched out his neck at a peculiar angle, cupping his hands to his gaping mouth to act as a sounding board.

From the depths of the straining chest issued a low drumming rattle, that rose and sank to a natural rhythm and ended with an abrupt little cough.

The lioness' head came up in a single flash of movement,

her ears erect, her eyes alight with yellow lights, for in her
pain and fear and confusion she had heard the old tom
calling to her, that low, far-carrying assembly call with
which he had directed her hunting so often, and which he
had used to bring her to him when separated in thick bush.

The pain of rising was almost too much for her, the
wound had stiffened and her neck and shoulder and chest
were crushed under a granite boulder of agony, but at that
moment she heard for the first time the distant yelping
chorus of the dog pack. She and the old tom had been
hunted by dogs before, and the sound gave her strength.

She came up and stood for a moment on three legs, fa-
vouring the right fore, panting heavily and then she went
forward, whining softly at the pain, carrying the bad leg
high, lunging for balance at each stride.

Mark watched from the ridge, saw the yellow cat start to
move again, hobbling slowly westwards at last. Far ahead
of her, keeping out of sight, the big Zulu trotted, pausing
whenever she faltered to kneel and repeat the assembly call
of a dominant male lion, and each time the lioness answered him with eager little mewling grunts and hobbled
after him, westward toward the dreaming blue hills that
guarded the Bubezi valley.

Mark had heard the old hunters' stories before; old man
Anders had always claimed that his gunbearer, who had
been killed by an elephant on the Sabi River in '84, could
call lions. However, Mark had never seen it done, and secretly had put the story into the category of the picturesque
but apocryphal.

Now he saw it happening, and still wanted to doubt it.
He watched fascinated from his grandstand upon the ridge,
and only a change in the clamour of the dog pack made
him swing his binoculars back towards the east.

At the rocky shoulder of the ridge, where he had set his
bait of powdered biltong and snuff, the pack milled con-
fusedly. There were eight or nine dogs, a mongrel pack of
terriers and boer hounds and ridgebacks.

The determined hunting chorus had disintegrated into a

cacophony of whines and yelps, while Dirk Courtney over-
rode them, standing in his stirrups to lay about them furiously with the horse-whip.

Mark took Trojan's reins and led him down off the
ridge, using what little cover there was, but confident that
the huntsmen were too involved with their own problems
to look ahead and see him.

When he reached the place beside the thorn thicket
where the lioness had last lain, he cut a branch with his
clasp knife, and used it like a broom to brush away any
sign the cat had left.

He followed slowly westwards towards Chaka's Gate,
pausing every few minutes to listen for the drumming lion
call, watching the ground as he moved, and using the
branch to brush away all lion sign, covering for his lioness,
until in the dusk they climbed a low saddle through the hills
and in slow, drawn-out procession, went down to the Bubezi River.

Pungushe made his last call in darkness, and then ran
out in a wide cirlce, leaving the lioness within a hundred
yards of the river, knowing how she would be burned up
by the heat of the wound and crazed for water.

He found Mark by the glow of his cigarette.

"Get up," said Mark, and gave him an arm. Pungushe
did not argue. He had run almost without a pause since
before dawn, and he swung up behind Mark.

They rode home, two up on Trojan's broad sway back,
and neither of them spoke until they saw the lantern light
in the cottage window.

"Jamela," said Pungushe. "I feel the way I did the day
my first son was born." And there was a tone of wonder in
his voice. "I did not believe a man could feel thus for a
devil that kills cattle and men."

Lying in the darkness, with Marion beside him in the
double bed, Mark told her about it. Trying to convey the
wonder and the sense of achievement. He told her what
Pungushe had said, and stumbled for words to describe his
own feeling, to come haltingly at last into silence.

"That's very nice, dear. When are you going into town again? I want to buy some curtains for the kitchen. I thought a checked gingham would look pretty, what do you think, dear?"

\* \* \*

The lioness gave birth to her cubs in the thick jessie bushes that choked one of the narrow tributary valleys which came down off the escarpment.

There were six cubs, but they were almost three weeks old when Mark first saw them. He and Pungushe lay belly down on the edge of the cliff that overlooked the valley when she led them back from the river in the dawn. The cubs followed her in an untidy straggle spread over a hundred yards. The sinew in her right foreleg had healed crooked and slightly shorter, which gave her a heaviness in her gait, a roll like a sailor's, as she came up the draw. One of the cubs, more persistent than the rest was trying to suckle from her pendulant, heavy, multiple dugs as she walked. He kept making clumsy flying leaps at them as they swung above his head, mostly he fell on his head and got trodden on by his mother's back feet, but once he succeeded and hung like a fat brown tick on one nipple. The lioness whirled about and cuffed him left and right, then began to lick him with a tongue that wrapped around his head entirely and knocked him on his back again.

One of the other cubs was stalking his siblings, crouching in ambush behind a single blade of grass, with flattened ears and viciously slitted eyes. When he leapt out on his brothers and sisters and they totally ignored his warlike maneuvers, he covered his embarrassment by turning back and sniffing the grass blade with such attention that it seemed this had been his original intention.

Three of the others were hunting butterflies. There had been a new hatching of colotis ione. On white and purple wings they fluttered close to the earth and the cubs reared on their hind legs and boxed at them with more gusto than skill, overbalancing at the end of each attack and collapsing in a fluffy tangle of outsized paws.

The sixth cub was hunting the tails of the butterfly-hunters. Every time they slashed their little tufted tails in the feverish excitement of the chase, he pounced upon them with savage growls and they were forced to turn and defend themselves against the sting of his needle-sharp baby teeth.

The progress of the family from river to jessie thicket was a long drawn out series of unseemly brawls, which the lioness finally broke up. She turned back and gave that drumming cough which promised imminent retribution if not obeyed instantly. The cubs abandoned their play, formed an Indian file and trotted after the lioness into the shelter of the jessie.

"I would like to know how many females there are in the litter," Mark whispered, grinning fondly like a new father as he watched them go.

"If you wish, Jamela, I will go down and look under their tails," Pungushe offered solemnly. "And you will treat my widows generously."

Mark chuckled and led the way back down the side of the hill.

They had almost reached the tree where Mark had left Trojan, when something caught his eyes. He turned aside and kicked hopefully at the little heap of stones, before he realized that they had not been erected by human hands, but had been pushed up by the surface roots of a siringa tree.

He gave a grunt of disappointment and turned away. Pungushe watched him speculatively, but made no comment. He had seen Mark perform that strange little ritual a hundred times before, whenever an unusual rock or pile caught his attention.

It had become a custom that every few evenings Mark would wander across from the thatched cottage at main camp, half a mile to where Pungushe's wives had erected the cluster of huts that was the family home.

Each hut was shaped in the perfect cone of a beehive,

long whippy saplings bent in to form the framework and the thatch bound in place by the plaited string of bark stripped from the saplings.

The earth between the huts was smoothed and brushed, and Pungushe's carved wooden stool set before the low doorway of his personal sleeping hut. After Mark's fourth visit another, newly carved stool appeared beside it. Though it was never spoken of, it was immediately apparent that this had been reserved exclusively for Mark's visits.

Once Mark was seated, one of the wives would bring him a bowl to wash his hands. The water had been carried laboriously all the way from the river, and Mark merely damped his finger-tips so that it would not be wasted.

Then the youngest wife knelt in front of him, smiling shyly, and offered with both hands a pot of the delicious sour utshwala, the Zulu millet beer, thick as gruel and mildly alcoholic.

Only when Mark had swallowed the first mouthful would Pungushe look up and greet him.

"I see you, Jamela."

Then they could talk in the relaxed desultory fashion of men totally at ease in each other's company.

"Today, when we came down off the hill after watching the lions, you turned off the path and kicked at some stones. It was for this strange custom I named you, this endless seeking, this looking and never finding."

Pungushe would never ask the direct question, it would have been the grossest bad manners to ask outright what Mark was looking for; only a child or an umlungu, a white man, would be so callow. It had taken him many months to ask the question, and now he framed it in the form of a statement.

Mark took another pull at his beer pot and offered Pungushe his cigarette case. The Zulu declined with an open hand, and instead began to roll his own smoke, coarse tarry black tobacco in a thick roll of brown paper, the size of a Havana cigar. Watching his hands Mark replied:

"My father and my mother died of the white sore throat, diphtheria, when I was a child, and an old man became both father and mother to me." He started to answer the question in as devious a manner as it had been asked, and Pungushe listened, nodding and smoking quietly.

"So this man, my grandfather whom I loved, is buried somewhere in this valley. It is his grave I seek," he ended simply, and realized suddenly that Pungushe was staring at him with a peculiar sombre expression.

"What is it?" Mark asked.

"When did this happen?"

"Six seasons ago."

"Would this old man have camped beneath the wild figs?" Pungushe pointed down the valley. "Where first you camped?"

"Yes," Mark agreed. "He always camped there." He felt the surge of something in his chest, foreknowledge of something momentous about to happen.

"There was a man," said Pungushe, "who wore a hat, a hat under which an impi could have camped—" and he made a circle of his arms, exaggerating only a little the size of a double terai brim, "and who had a beard, shaped thus like the wings of a white egret—" An image of the old man's forked beard, snowy and stained only around the mouth with tobacco jucie, leapt in Mark's mind. "An old man who walked like the secretary bird when it hunts for locusts in the grass." The long thin legs, the stooped arthritic shoulders, the measured stride, the description was perfect.

"Pungushe!" Mark exploded with excitement. "You know him!"

"Nothing moves in this valley, no bird flies, no baboon barks, but the jackal hears and sees."

Mark stared at him, appalled at his own oversight. Of course Pungushe knew everything. Pungushe the silent watcher, why in God's name had he not thought to ask him before?

"He followed this path." Pungushe walked ahead of Mark, and with the natural skill of the born actor he mimicked John Anders, the halting gait, and stooped shoulders of an old man. If Mark half closed his eyes, he could see his grandfather as he had seen him so many times before.

"Here he turned off the path," Pungushe left the game trail and started up one of the narrow dried-out watercourses. Their feet crunched in the sugary sand. Half a mile farther, Pungushe stopped and pointed at one of the shiny water-polished black boulders.

"Here he sat and set his rifle aside. He lit his pipe and smoked."

Pungushe turned and scrambled up the steep bank of the water-course.

"While the old man smoked, the fourth man came up the valley. He came as a hunter, silently, following the easy spoor of the old man." He used the Zulu word of respect for an elder, *ixhegu*.

"Wait, Pungushe," Mark frowned. "You say the fourth man? I am confused. Count the men for me."

They squatted down on the bank and Pungushe took a little snuff, offered the horn to Mark who refused, then sniffed the red powder out of his palm, closing one nostril at a time with his thumb. He screwed his eyes closed and sneezed deliciously before going on.

"There was the old man, your grandfather, *ixhegu*."

"That is one."

"Then there was another old man. Without hair on his head nor on his chin."

"That is two," Mark agreed.

"Then there was a young man with very black hair, a man who laughed all the time and walked with the noise of a buffalo herd."

"Yes. That is three."

"These three came together to the valley. They hunted together and camped together below the wild figs."

Pungushe must be describing the Greylings, the father and son who made the sworn deposition to the Ladyburg magistrate. That was as he had expected, but now he asked, "What of the fourth man, Pungushe?"

"The fourth man followed them secretly and *ixhegu*, your grandfather, did not know of him. He had always the manner of the hunter of men, watching from cover and moving silently. But once when your grandfather, *ixhegu*, had left camp to hunt alone for birds along the river, this secret man came to the camp below the wild figs and all three of them spoke together, quietly but with closed faces and wary eyes of men who discuss affairs of deadly moment. Then the silent man left them again and went to hide in the bush before *ixhegu* returned."

"You saw all this, Pungushe?" Mark asked.

"What I did not see, I read in the spoor."

"Now I understnad about the fourth man. Tell me what happened that day."

"*Ixhegu* was sitting there, smoking his pipe, " Pungushe pointed down into the water-course. "And the silent one came and stood here, even where we now sit, and he looked down at your grandfather without speaking, holding his *isibamu*, his rifle, thus."

"What did *ixhegu* do then?" Mark asked. He felt nauseous with the horror of it.

"He looked up and asked a question in a loud voice, as a man does when he is afraid, but the silent one did not reply."

"Then?"

"I am sorry, Jamela, knowing that *ixhegu* was of your blood, the telling of it gives me pain."

"Go on," said Mark.

"Then the silent one fired once with his rifle, and *ixhegu* fell face down in the sand."

"He was dead?" Mark asked, and Pungushe was silent a moment.

"He was not dead. He was shot here, in the belly. He moved, he cried out."

"The silent one fired again?" Mark felt the acid bit of vomit in the back of his throat.

Pungushe shook his head.

"What did he do?"

"He sat down on the bank, here where we sit, and he smoked silently, watching the old man *izhegu* lying down there in the sand, until he died."

"How long did he take to die?" Mark asked in a choked, angry voice.

Pungushe swept a segment of the sky to indicate two hours of the sun's course. "At the end *ixhegu* was calling out in Zulu as well as his own language."

"What did he say, Pungushe?"

"He asked for water, and he called to God and to a woman who might have been his mother or his wife. Then he died."

Mark thought about it with surges of nausea alternating with flashes of bitter hating anger, and racking grief. He tried to imagine why the killer had let his victim die so slowly, and it was many minutes before he remembered that the story must have already been arranged that the old man was to die in a hunting accident. No man accidentally shoots himself twice. The body was to have only one gunshot wound. But, the stomach was always the most agonizing wound. Mark remembered how the gut-wounded screamed in the trenches as they were being carried back by the stretcher-bearers.

"I grieve with you, Jamela."

Mark roused himself at Pungushe's words.

"What happened after *ixhegu* died?"

"The other two men, the old bald one and the young loud one, came from the camp. All three of them talked here, beside the body. They talked for a long time, with shouting and red angry faces, and they waved their hands thus, and thus." Pungushe imitated men in heated argument. "One pointed here, another pointed there, but in the end the silent one spoke and the other two listened."

"Where did they take him?"

"First they opened his pockets, and took from them some papers and a pouch. They argued again, and the silent one took the papers and put them back in the dead man's pockets—" Mark realized the wisdom of this. An honest man does not rob the corpse of an accident victim. "Then they carried him up the bank, and this way—" Pungushe stood and led Mark four hundred yards into the forest, below the first steep gradient of the escarpment. "Here they found a deep ant-bear hole, and they pushed the old man's body down into it."

"Here?" Mark asked. There was short rank grass and no sign of a cairn nor a mound. "I see nothing."

"They collected rocks from the cliff there and placed them in the hole on top of the body, so that the hyena would not dig it out. Then they covered the rocks with earth, and they smoothed it with a tree branch."

Mark went down on one knee and inspected the ground.

"Yes," he exclaimed. There was a very shallow depression in the earth, as though it had subsided a little over an excavation.

Mark drew his heath-knife and blazed four of the nearest trees, making it easier to return to this place, and he built a small pyramid of rocks on the depressed saucer of earth.

When he had finished, he asked Pungushe, "Why did you not tell anybody of this before? Why did you not go to the police in Ladyburg?"

"Jamela, the madness of white men does not concern me. Also it is a very long journey to Ladyburg, to the policeman who would say, "Ho, kaffir, and what were you doing in the Bubezi valley to see such strange events?" Pungushe shook his head. "No, Jamela, sometimes it better for a man to be blind and deaf."

"Tell me truly, Pungushe. If you saw these men again, would you remember them?"

"All white men have faces like boiled yams, red, lumpy and without shape." Then Pungushe remembered his manners. "Except you, Jamela, who are not so ugly as all that."

"Thank you, Pungushe. So you would not know them again?"

"The old bald one and the young loud one I might know." Pungushe furrowed his brow in thought.

"And the silent one?" Mark asked.

"Ho." Pungushe's brow cleared. "Does one forget what a leopard looks like? Does one forget the killer of men? The silent one I would remember at any time and in any place."

"Good!" Mark nodded. "Go back home now, Pungushe."

He waited until the big Zulu was out of sight among the trees, then Mark went down on his knees and removed his hat.

"Well, Pops," he said, "I'm not very good at this. But I know you'd have liked to have the words said." His voice was so hoarse and low that he had to clear his throat loudly before he went on.

* * *

The house on Lion Kop was shuttered, and the furniture all under white dust sheets, but the head servant met Mark in the kitchen yard.

"Nkosi has gone to *Tekweni*. He left two weeks ago."

He gave Mark a breakfast of grilled bacon and fried eggs. Then Mark went out and mounted his motorcycle again. It was a long hard run down to the coast, and Mark had plenty of time to think as the dusty miles spun away under the wheels of the Ariel Square Four.

He had left Chaka's Gate within hours of finding the old man's grave, going instinctively to one man for advice an guidance.

He had wanted Marion to come with him, at least as far as Ladyburg where she could have stayed with her sister. However Marion had refused to leave her home or her garden, and Mark had felt secure in the knowledge that Pungushe would be sleeping in the toolshed behind the stables to guard the homestead in Mark's absence.

Mark had waded the river and trudged up the slope below to the beginning of the trace where he kept the motorcycle in its thatched shelter.

It had been a slow, bumpy journey in the dark and he had reached Lion Kop in the dawn to fine Sean Courtney had moved his household to Durban.

Mark rode through the gates of Emoyeni in the late afternoon, and it was like coming home again.

Ruth Courtney was in the rose garden, but she dropped the basket of cut flowers and lifted her skirts to her knees as she ran to meet him, the wide-brimmed straw hat flying from her head and hanging by its ribbon around her throat and her delighted spontaneous laughter ringing like a young girl's.

"Oh Mark—we've missed you so." She took him in a motherly embrace, kissing both his cheeks. "How brown and hard you look, and you've filled out beautifully." She held him at arm's length and felt his biceps in mock admiration before embracing him again. "The General will be delighted to see you." She took Mark's arm and led him towards the house. "He hasn't been well, Mark, but seeing you again will be a tonic to him."

Mark stopped involuntarily in the doorway and felt the shock dry the saliva under his tongue.

General Sean Courtney was an old man. He sat at the bay windows of the bedroom suite. He wore a plaid dressing-gown and a mohair rug was tucked around his legs. On the table beside him was a pile of files and reports, Parliamentary White Papers and a sheath of letters, all the documentation of his life that Mark remembered so well, but the General had fallen asleep, and the metal-rimmed spectacles had slid down on to the tip of his nose. He snored softly, his lips fluttering at each breath. His face seemed to have wasted so that the bones of cheek and brow stood out gauntly. His eyes receded into deep plum purple cavities, and his skin had a greyish lifeless tinge to it.

But the truly shocking thing was the colour of his beard and the once thick bush of his hair. On Sean Courtney the late snows were falling. His beard had turned into a silver cascade, and his hair was as white and as thin as the fine sun-bleached grasses of the Kalahari desert.

Ruth crossed to his chair and lifted the spectacles off his nose, then gently, with a loving wife's concern, she touched his shoulder.

"Sean, darling. There is somebody here to see you."

He woke the way an old man wakes, blinking and mumbling, with small inconclusive movements of his hands. Then he saw Mark and his expression firmed, suddenly there was a little of the old sparkle in the dark eyes and the warmth in his smile.

"My boy!" he said, lifting his hands, and Mark stepped forward quite naturally. Then for the first time embraced like father and son, and afterwards Sean beamed at him fondly.

"I was beginning to believe we had lost you forever to the ways of the wild." Then he looked up at Ruth beside his chair. "In celebration I think we can advance the hour a little, my dear. Won't you have Joseph bring up the tray?"

"Sean, you know what the doctor said yesterday." But Sean snorted with disgust.

"For fifty years, man and boy, my stomach has got used to its evening dash of Joh Haig pinch bottle. Lack of it will kill me more swiftly and surely than Doctor Henderson and all his pills and potions and blatant quackeries." He placed one arm about her waist and squeezed her winningly. "There's a bonnie girl!"

When Ruth had gone, smiling and shaking her head disapprovingly, Sean waved Mark to the chair opposite him.

"What does the doctor say is wrong with you, sir?"

"Doctor!" Sean blew through his lips. "The older I get, the less faith I have in the whole sorry bunch." He reached for the cigar box. "They even wanted me to stop these. What on earth is the use of living, if you have to give up all the processes of life—I ask you." He lit the cigar with a flourish and drew on it with relish.

"I'll tell you what's wrong with me, son. Too many years of running hard, of fighting and riding and working. That's all it is. Now I'm having a nice little rest, and in a week or so I'll be chipper and fly as I ever was."

Ruth brought the silver tray and they sat until it was dark, talking and laughing. Mark told them of the life at Chaka's Gate, about each little triumph, describing the cottage and the work done on the roads; he told them of the buffalo and the lioness and the cubs, and Sean told him of the progress made by their Wildlife Society.

"It's disappointing, Mark, nothing like I had hoped for. It's extraordinary just how little people care about things that don't affect their daily lives directly."

"I never expected instant success. How can people care about something they have never seen? Once we have made the wilderness accessible, once people can have the experience, like seeing these cubs, it will begin then."

"Yes," Sean agreed thoughtfully. "That's what the true object of the Society is. To educate them."

They talked on while darkness fell and Ruth closed the shutters and drew the curtains. Mark waited for an opportunity to speak of the true reason for his coming to Emoyeni, but he was uncertain of how it might affect a man who was already sick.

At last he could wait no longer. He drew a deep breath, hoped for grace, and told it quickly and without trimmings, repeating Pungushe's story exactly and describing what he had seen himself.

When he finished, Sean was silent for a long time, staring into his glass. At last he roused himself and began asking questions, shrewd cutting questions that showed his mind was as quick and crisp as it had been before.

"Have you opened the grave?" and Mark shook his head.

"Good," said Sean and went on. "This Zulu, Pungushe, was the only witness. How reliable is he?"

They discussed it for another half hour, before Sean asked the one question he had obviously been avoiding.

"You think Dirk Courtney is responsible for this?"

"Yes," Mark nodded.

"What proof is there?"

"He is the only one who could have profited by my grandfather's murder, and the style is his."

"I asked what proof there is, Mark."

"There is none." he admitted, and Sean was silent again while he weighed it all.

"Mark, I understnad just how you feel—and I think you know how I feel. However, there is nothing we can do now that will have any effect, beyond alerting the murderer, whoever he is." He leaned forward in his chair and stretched out a hand to grip Mark's forearm in a gesture of comfort. "All we have now is the unsupported testimony of a Zulu poacher who speaks no English. A good lawyer would eat him without spitting out the bones, and Dirk Courtney would have the best lawyer, even if we could trace this mysterous 'Silent One' to him and get him into court. We need more than this, Mark."

"I know," Mark nodded. "But I thought we might be able to trace the Greyling father and son. They went to Rhodesia, I believe. The foreman at Ladyburg railway station told me that."

"Yes, I'll get somebody on to that. My lawyers will know a good investigator." He made a note on the pad at his side. "But in the meantime, we can only wait."

They talked on, but it was clear tha the discussion had tired Sean Courtney, and grey and blue shadows etched the lines and wrinkles on his face. He settled down a little deeper in his chair, his beard lowered on to his chest and suddenly he had fallen asleep again. He sagged slowly sideways, the crystal glass fell from his hand to the carpet with a soft thud and splattered a few drops of whisky, and he snored a soft single snort.

Ruth picked up the glass, arranged the rug carefully around his shoulders and signalled Mark to follow her.

In the passage she chatted brightly. "I have told Joseph to make up your bed in the blue room, and there is a good hot bath waiting. There will be only the two of us for dinner, Mark. The General will have a tray in his room."

They had reached the door of the library and Mark could be silent no longer. He caught Ruth's arm.

"Mrs. Courtney," he pleaded. "What is it? What is wrong with him?"

The bright smile faded slowly, and she swayed slightly on her feet. Now for the first time he noticed how the few strands of white had turned to deep iron grey wings at her temples. He saw also the little lines and creases around her eyes, and the deeper furrows of worry across her brow.

"His heart is broken," she said simply, and then she was weeping. No hysterical sobs or wild cries of grief, but a slow deep welling up of tears that was more harrowing, more poignant than any theatrical display.

"They have broken his heart," she repeated, and swayed again, so that Mark caught and steadied her.

She clung to him, her face pressed to his shoulder.

"First the estrangement from Dirk and then Michael's death," she whispered. "He never let it show, but they destroyed some part of him. Now the whole world has turned against him. The people to whom he has devoted his life in peace and war. The newspapers call him the Butcher of Fordsburg, Dirk Courtney has whipped them upon him like a pack of wild dogs."

He led her into the library and made her sit on the low buttoned sofa while he knelt beside her and found a crumpled handkerchief in his jacket pocket.

"On top of it all, there is Storm. The way she ran off and married that man. He was a horrible man, Mark. He even came here asking for money, and there was a terrible scene. That's when Sean had his first attack, that night. Then finally there was further shame, further heartbreak

when Storm was divorced. It was all too much, even for a
man like Sean."

Mark stared at her. "Storm is divorced?" he asked softly.

"Yes," Ruth nodded, and then her expression lightened.
"Oh Mark, I know you and Storm were becoming such
good friends. I am sure she is fond of you. Can't you go to
her? It might be the cure for which we all pray."

\* \* \*

Umhlanga Rocks was one of those little seaside villages
that were scattered along the sandy coast line on each side
of the main port of Durban. Mark crossed the low bridge
over the Umgeni River, and headed north.

The road cut through the thick jungly coastal bush,
dense as an equatorial forest, and hung with ropes of lianas
from which the little blue vervet monkeys swung and chattered.

The road ran parallel with the white beaches, but at the
twelfth milestone Mark reached the turn-off and went directly down to the coast.

The village was clustered around the iron-roofed Oyster
Box Hotel where Mark and Dicky Lancome had danced
and dined with Marion and that other nameless girl so long
ago.

The only other buildings were twenty or thirty cottages
set in large gardesn, over-run by the rampant jungle, and
overlooking the sea with its rowdy frothing surf and rocky
points jutting out from the smooth white beaches.

Ruth had given him accurate directions and Mark
parked the motorcycle on the narrow dusty lane and followed the pathway that wound without apparent direction
through a wild garden of purple bougainvillaea and brilliant poinsettia.

The cottage was small, and the bougainvillaea had
climbed up the pillars of the veranda and spread in brilliant, almost blinding display across the thatched roof.

Mark knew at once that he had the right place, for

Storm's Cadillac was parked in the open under the trees. It looked neglected and in careless disrepair. The thread was worn from the tyres, there was a long deep scratch down one side. A side window was cracked, and the paintwork was dull with dust and splattered with the dung of the fruit bats hanging in the tree above.

Mark stopped and stared at the Cadillac for a full minute. The Storm he had known would have stamped her foot and screamed for her father if anybody had tried to make her ride in that.

Mark climbed the veranda steps, and paused to look about him. It was a peaceful and lovely spot, such as an artist might choose, but in its remoteness and its neglected and untrimmed profusion hardly suitable for one of the elegant young ornaments of society.

Mark knocked on the front door, and heard somebody moving about inside for some minutes before the door was opened.

Storm was more beautiful by far than he had remembered. Her hair was long and bleached at the ends by salt water and sun. Her feet were bare, her arms and legs were tanned and slim and supple as ever, but it was her face that had changed.

Although she wore no cosmetics, the skin had the shine of vibrant youth like the lustre inside a sea shell, and her eyes were clear and bright with health, yet there were new depths to them, the petulant set of her mouth had softened, her arrogance had become dignity.

In that moment as they stared at each other he knew that she had indeed grown from girl to woman in the time since he had last seen her. And he sensed that the process had been agonizing, but that from it all was emerging a new value, a new strength, and the love which had been in him all this time spread out to fill his soul.

"Storm," he said, and her eyes opened wide as she stared at him.

"You!" Her voice was a little cry of pain, and she tried to drag the door closed.

Mark jumped forward and held it.

"Storm, I must speak with you."

She tugged desperately at the door handle.

"Go away, Mark. Please go away." All the new dignity and poise seemed to crumble and she looked at him with the wide frightened eyes of a child waking from a nightmare. At last she knew that she could not force the door against his strength, and she turned away and walked slowly back into the house.

"You shouldn't have come," she said miserably, and the child seemed to sense the changed air. It squalled.

"Oh hush, baby," Storm called softly, but her voice goaded it into a fresh outburst, and she crossed the room on bare feet with the long veil of hair hanging down her back.

The room was starkly furnished, the cement floor bare and cool, no rugs to soften them, but along the walls were stacked her canvases, many of them blank, but others half-finished, or completed, and the familiar evocative smell of turpentine was heavy and pungent.

The child lay belly down on a kaross of monkey skins laid out on the cement floor. Legs and arms were spread in that froglike baby attitude, and except for a towelling napkin around the hips, it was naked and sun-tanned. The head was thrown back angrily, and the face flushed with the force of its yells.

Mark stepped into the room, and stared with sickly fascination at the child. He knew nothing of babies, but he could see that this was a sturdy and aggressively healthy small animal. The limbs were strong, kicking and working with a violent swimming motion, and the back was broad and robust.

"Hush now, darling," cooed Storm, as she knelt beside him, and lifted him under the armpits. The napkin slid down to the child's knees and there was no doubting that he was a boy. His tiny penis stuck out at half mast, like a white finger with its little floppy chef's cap of loose wrinkled skin.

Mark found himself hating this other man's child, with a sudden frightening hatred. Yet he went forward involuntarily to where Storm knelt with the baby in her lap.

Mother's touch had quelled the shouts of anger, and now the boy was smacking his lips and making little anticipatory hunger grunts and pawing demandingly at Storm's bosom.

The child had a fine golden cap of hair, through which Mark could see the perfect round of his skull and the little blue veins under the almost translucent skin. Now that the furious crimson tide of anger had receded from his face, Mark saw how beautiful was the child, as beautiful as the mother—and he hated it, he hated it with a bitter sickening feeling in his stomach, and a corrosive taste in his mouth.

He moved closer, watching Storm wipe a dribble of saliva from the child's chin and hoist up his napkin to his waist.

The child became aware of a stranger. He started and lifted his head to stare at Mark, and there was something hauntingly familar in that face. The eyes that looked at him had looked at him before, he knew them so well.

"You should not have come," said Storm, busy with her baby, not able to lift her eyes to him. "Oh God, Mark, why did you come?"

Mark went down on one knee and stared into the child's face, and it reached out towards him with a pair of plump hands, dimpled and pink and damp with spit.

"What is his name?" Mark asked. Where had he seen those eyes? Involuntarily, he extended his forefinger and the child grabbed it with a fat little chuckle and tried to stuff it into his mouth.

"John," Storm answered, still not looking at him.

"John was my grandfather's name," Mark said huskily.

"Yes," whispered Storm. "You told me."

The words meant nothing for a moment, all he was aware of was that the hatred he felt for this little scrap of humanity slowly faded. In its place there grew something else.

Then suddenly he knew where he had seen those eyes. "Storm?" he asked.

Now she lifted her head, and stared into his face. When she replied she was half proud and half defiant.

"Yes!" she said, and nodded once.

He reached for her clumsily. They knelt facing each other on the monkey-skin kaross, and they embraced fiercely, the child held awkwardly between them, gurgling and hiccuping and drooling merrily as it chewed Mark's finger with greedy toothless gums.

"Oh God, Mark, what have I done to us?" whispered Storm brokenly.

\* \* \*

Baby John woke them in the silvery slippery-grey light of before dawn. Mark was grateful to him, for he did not want to miss a minute of that coming day. He watched Storm light the candle and then work over the cradle.

She made small soothing sounds as she changed the baby, and the candlelight glowed on the sweet clean lines of her naked back. Dark silky hair hung over her shoulders, and he saw that childbirth had not thickened her waist, it still had the flared graceful line, like the neck of a wine bottle above the tight round double bulge of her buttocks.

At last she turned and carried the baby to the bed, smiling at Mark as he lifted the blankets for her.

"Breakfast time," she explained. "Will you excuse us, please?" She sat cross-legged in the bed, and she took one of her nipples between thumb and forefinger and directed it into the open questing mouth.

Mark drew as close as he could and placed one arm around Storm's shoulders. He watched with total fascination. Her breasts were big now, and heavy, jutting out into rounded cones. There was a pale blue dappling of active veins deep below the skin, and the nipples were the colour of almost ripe mulberries, with the same rough shiny texture. The child's tugging induced a sympathetic blue-white drop of milk to well from the tip of her other breast. It glistened there like a pearl in the candlelight.

John fed with tightly closed eyes and piglet grunts and snuffles. The milk ran from the corners of his mouth, and after the first pangs of his hunger were appeased, Storm had to prod him to keep him from falling asleep again.

At each prod, his jaw worked busily for a minute or so, and then the level of activity slowly declined until the next prod.

Storm changed him from one breast to the other and laid her own cheek gratefully against the hard lean muscle of Mark's chest.

"I think I am happy," she murmured. "But I've been unhappy for so long that I am not quite sure."

\* \* \*

John lay in a puddle of sea water two inches deep. He was stark naked and brown all over to prove this was no unusual state. He slapped at the water with both hands, and it splashed into his face so that he gasped and blinked his eyes and licked his lips, uncertain whether to be angry or to cry. Instead he repeated the experiment with exactly the same consequences, and he spluttered sand and sea water.

"Poor little devil," Storm watched him. "He has inherited the Courtney pride and stubbornness. He won't give up until he drowns himself."

She lifted him from the puddle and there was instantly such a howl of protest that she had to return him hurriedly.

"I am sure if you went to the General—with John," Mark persevered.

"You don't really understand us Courtneys." Storm sat back and began to plait her hair over one shoulder. "We don't forget or forgive that easily."

"Storm, won't you try it? Please go to him."

"I know exactly how he is, Mark. Better than you, better than Daddy knows himself. I know him so well as I do myself, because we are one person. I am he, and he is me. If I go to him now, having done what I did—having insulted him, having destroyed all the dreams he wove about me—if I go now, when I am destitute of pride and honour, if I go as a beggar, he will despise me for ever."

"No, Storm, you are wrong."

"On this I am never wrong, Mark darling. He would not want to despise me, just as he does not want to hate me now, but he would not be able to help himself. He is Sean Courtney, and he is trapped in the steel jaws of his own honour."

"He is a sick man—you must give him the chance."

"No, Mark. It would kill him. I know that—and it would destroy me. For both our sakes, I dare not go to him now."

"You don't know know much he cares for you."

"Oh I do, Mark. I also know how much I care for him— and one day, when I am proud again, I will go to him. I promise you that. When I know he can be proud of me, I will take him that as a gift—"

"Oh damn you and your stiff cruel pride, you nearly destroyed us with it also."

"Come, Mark," she stood up. "Take John's other hand."

They walked the child between them along the firm wet sand at the edge of the surf. He hung on their hands, leaning forward to watch his own feet appear and disappear magically below him, and he let out great shouts of triumph at his accomplishment.

The day was bright and clean, and the gulls caught the wind and rode above them on smoky white wings, answering the child's shouts with their own harsh cries.

"Oh, I had so many fine clothes and fancy friends." Storm watched the gulls. "I sold the clothes and lost the friends, and found how little any of it really meant to me. Look at the gulls!" she said, head thrown back. "See the sunlight through the spread feathers. I was so busy that I never had time to see clearly before. I never saw myself, nor those around me. But now I am learning to look."

"I saw that in your painting," Mark said, and lifted John to his chest, delighting in the hot restless little body. "You are painting different subjects."

"I want to be a great artist."

"I think you will be. That Courtney stubbornness again."

"We don't always get what we want," she told him, and the spent surf came sliding up the beach and creamed around their ankles.

\* \* \*

The child slept face down on the monkey-skin kaross, exhausted with sun and sea and play, his belly bulging with food.

Storm worked at the easel under the window with narrowed eyes and cocked head.

"You are my favourite model," she said.

"That's just because I'm so cheap." And she laughed lightly.

"With what I pay you, I could be rich," she pointed out.

"You know what they call ladies who do it for money?" Mark asked lazily and lapsed into silence, giving himself up to the full pleasure of watching her and they were silent for nearly an hour—silent but close and spiritually in tune.

Mark spoke at last. "I know what you mean by seeing more clearly now. That one," he pointed at one of the larger canvases against the wall, "that's probably the best thing you've ever done."

"I hated to sell it—the man who bought it is coming tomorrow."

"You've sold some of your paintings?" he was startled.

"How do you think John and I live?"

"I don't know." He hadn't thought about that. "I supposed your husband—"

Her expression changed, darkening swiftly. "I want nothing from him." And she tossed her head so that the braid of hair flicked like the tail of an angry lioness. "I want nothing from him, and his friends, and my loving friends, all those nice loyal people who stay away from me in droves now that I am the scarlet divorcée. I've learned a lot since last I saw you, and especially I have learned about that kind of person."

"They are rich," Mark pointed out. "You once told me how important that is."

The dark anger went out of her, and she drooped a little, the brush falling to her side.

"Oh Mark, please don't be bitter with me. I don't think I could stand that."

He felt something tear in his chest, and he rose swiftly and went to her, picked her up with a swing of his shoulders and carried her high, through the curtained doorway into the small cool dark bedroom.

It was strange, but their love-making was never the same, always there were new wonders, new accords of desire, the discovery of some little things that excited them both beyond all relation to its apparent significance.

Repetition could not weary nor dull the appetite they had for each other, and even as that appetite was totally satiated, so the endless well of their mutual desire began to fill again.

It would start again immediately with the lazy touch of fingers as they lay curled together like sleepy puppies, the sweat of their loving cooling on their skin, raising little goose bumps around the dark rosy aureoles of her nipples.

A finger drawn lightly down his cheek, rasping on the sandpaper of his beard, and then pushing lightly between his lips, making him turn his head for another gentle kiss, a mere touch of lips and the mingling of their breath so that he could smell that peculiar perfume of passion from her mouth, a smell like newly dug truffles, a mushroomy exciting smell.

She saw the new spark of interest in his eyes and drew softly away to chuckle at him, a throaty sensuous sound, and she drew one sharp finger-nail swiftly down his spine so that little sparks of fire flew along his nerves and his back arched.

"I am going to claw you because you deserve it, you randy old tomcat." She made a growly sound in her throat and curled her nails into a lion's claw, drawing it lightly across his shoulder, and then hard down his belly, so that her nails left red lines against the skin.

She studied the red lines, with her lips parted and the tip of her pink tongue touching her small white teeth. The nipples of her breasts swelled as she watched, growing like new buds, as though they were about to burst. She saw the direction of his eyes, and she put her hand behind his head, drawing him down gently, pulling back her shoulder so that the heavy rounded bosom was offered like a sacrifice.

\* \* \*

Mark took some of the big scaly crayfish from the low-tide pools, and they smelled of kelp and iodine, thumping their tails furiously in his grip, snapping their legs and bubbling at the small mouths with their multiple mandibles.

Mark rose, streaming salt water, from the depths of the pool and handed them up to Storm, who squealed with excitement on the rocky edge of the pool and took them gingerly, using her straw hat as a glove against the spiky carapace and waving legs.

Mark built a fire in a scooped fireplace in the sand, while Storm held John on her lap and fed him through a discreetly unbuttoned blouse, offering advice and ribald comment as he worked.

Mark threw wet seaweed over the coals, put the crayfish on top of that and covered them with another layer of seaweed, topping it off with a final layer of sand, and while they waited for the crayfish to cook and John to finish his noisy guzzling, they drank wine and watched the setting sun turn the sea clouds into a brilliant display.

"God, Nature's an old ham. If I painted like that, they'd say I had no sense of colour, and I could go work for a chocolate company painting boxes."

Afterwards, Storm lay John in the apple basket that

served as a portable cradle and they ate crayfish, pulling the long luscious sticks of white meat from the horny legs and washing it down with the tart white Cape wine.

In the darkness the stars were stark pricks of brilliant white, and the surf boomed in long soft phosphorescent lines.

"It's so wonderfully romantic." Storm watched it, sitting hugging her knees, and then turned her head and smiled wickedly. "And you can take that as a hint, if you want to."

On the rug together she said. "Do you know what some people do?"

"No, what do some people do?" Mark seemed more interested in what he was doing than the actions of the nameless somebodies.

"You don't expect me just to say it out like that."

"Why not?"

"It's rude."

"All right, so whisper it."

So she whispered it, but she was giggling so much that he was not sure he had heard right.

She repeated it, and he had heard right. He was truly stunned, so that he found himself blushing in the dark.

"That's terrible," he answered huskily. "You would never do that!" However, he was over the first shock, and the idea intrigued him.

"Of course not," she whispered, and then after a silence, "Unless of course you want to."

There was another long silence during which Storm made some investigations. "If I'm any judge, and I should be by now, you want to," she stated flatly.

Long afterwards, naked in the dark, they swam together out beyond the first line of breakers. The water was warm as fresh milk and they trod water to kiss with wet salty lips.

On the beach Mark built up the fire and they sat close to it, cuddled together in the yellow light of the flames, and they drank the rest of the wine.

"Mark," she said at last, and there was a sadness in her

voice that he had never heard before. "You have been with us two days now, which is two days too much. Tomorrow I want you to go. Go early before John and I are awake, so we don't have to watch you."

Her words struck like a lash so that he writhed at the sting. He turned to her with a stricken face in the firelight.

"What are you saying? You and John are mine. We belong together the three of us, always."

"You didn't understand a word of what I was saying, did you?" she asked softly. "You didn't understand when I said I must rebuild my pride, refashion my honour?"

"I love you, Storm. I have always loved you."

"You are married to somebody else, Mark."

"That doesn't mean anything," he pleaded.

"Oh yes, it does." She shook her head. "And you know it does."

"I will leave Marion."

"Divorce, Mark?"

"Yes." He was desperate. "I'll ask her for a divorce."

"That way we can both be truly proud. That will be a fine way for me to go to my father. Think how proud we will make him. His daughter, and the sone he never had, for that's the way he thinks of you, both of them divorced. Think of baby John. How high he will hold his head. Think of us—what a noble life we can build on the misery of the girl who was your wife." Looking into her eyes in the firelight, he saw that her pride was iron and her stubbornness was steel.

Mark dressed quietly in the dark, and when he was ready he groped his way to the cradle and kissed his son. The child made a little whimpering sound in his sleep, and he smelt warm and milky, like a new-born kitten.

He thought that Storm was sleeping also as he stooped over her, but then he realized that she was lying rigidly with her face pressed into the pillow to stifle the harsh silent sobs that convulsed her.

She did not lift her face to him and he kissed her hair and neck, then he straightened up and walked out into the dark. The motorcycle started at the first kick and he wheeled it out into the lane.

Storm lay in the dark and listened to the sound of the engine die away into the night, and afterwards there was only the lonely mournful sound of the surf and the clink of the tree frogs outside the window.

\* \* \*

Mark sat on the carved wooden stool in the sunset, in front of Pungushe's hut, and he asked for the first time something that had been in his mind since their first meeting.

"Pungushe, tell me of the time when the Jackal pulled the Ngaga from the flooding river."

And the Zulu shrugged. "What is there to tell? I found you caught in the branches of a flooded tree on the edge of the river—and if I had sense, I would have walked away, for you were clearly a very dead Ngaga and the brown water was washing over your head."

"Did you see how it was that I fell into the river?"

There was a pause, while Pungushe steeled himself to admit ignorance. "It seemed to me that you had been blinded with fever and fallen into the river."

"You did not see the man I killed, nor the man that fired at me with a rifle?"

Pungushe covered his amazement nobly, but shook his head. "A little time before I found you in the river I heard the sound of guns, four, perhaps five shots, from up the valley. This must have been you and the one who hunted you, but I saw no man and the rain washed away all sign, before the next morning. The flood waters would have washed the dead man away and the crocodiles eaten him."

They were silent again while the beer pot passed between them.

"Did you see the man who fired at you?" Pungushe asked.

"Yes," said Mark. "But my eyes were weak with fever, and as you say, it was raining. I did not see him clearly."

Hobday stood within the hall, against the wall, out of the crush of excited bodies. He stood like a rock, solid and immovable, his head lowered on the thick wrestler's neck. His eyes were hooded, as though he were able like a great bird of prey to draw an opaque nictitating membrane across them. Only his jaw made an almost imperceptible chewing motion, grinding the big flat teeth together so that the muscle in the points of his jaw bulged slightly.

He was watching Dirk Courtney across the crowded hall, the way a faithful mastiff watches its master.

Tall and urbane, Dirk Courtney had a warm double handshake for each of those who crowded forward to assure him of support and to wish him luck. His gaze was straight and calm, but it kept flicking back to the long counting tables.

They were trestle tables that had done duty at a thousand church socials, and as many weddings.

Now the scrutineers sat along them, and the last ballot boxes from the outlying areas were carried in through the front doors of the Ladyburg Church Hall.

The sprawling shape of the constituency of Ladyburg meant that some of the boxes had come in sixty miles, and although the voting had closed the previous evening, it was now an hour before noon and no result had yet been announced.

Mark crossed slowly towards where General Sean Courtney sat, pushing his way gently through the throng that lined the roped-off area around the counting tables.

Mark and Marion had come in from Chaka's Gate three days before, especially to assist at the elections. There were never enough helpers, and Marion had been completely at home, cutting sandwiches and dispensing coffee, working with twenty other women under Ruth Courtney's supervision in the kitchens behind the hall.

Mark had scoured the village district with other party

organizers. Like a press gang, they had hunted down missing or recalcitrant voters and brought them into the ballot
stations.

It had been hard work, and then none of them had slept
much the previous night. The dancing and barbecue had
lasted until four in the morning—and after that the anticipation of the announcement of the result had kept most of
them from sleep.

For Mark it all had a special significance. He knew now
with complete certainty, that if Dirk Courtney was returned as the member of Parliament for Ladyburg, then his
dreams for Chaka's Gate were doomed.

As the voters had come in during the day, their hopes
had see-sawed up and down. Often it seemed that the end
of the hall where Dirk Courtney's organizers sat under
huge posters of their candidate was as crowded as Sean
Courtney's end of the hall was deserted.

When this happened, Marion's brother-in-law, Peter
Botes, removed his pipe from his mouth and smirked comfortably at Mark across the length of the hall. He had become an enthusiastic supporter of Dirk Courtney's, and his
circumstances had altered remarkably in the last six
months. He had opened offices of his own on the first floor
of the Ladyburg Farmers Bank. He drove a new Packard
and had moved from the cottage to a fine rambling house
in three acres of garden and orchard, where he had insisted
that Marion and Mark dine with him the previous night.

"The evening star sets, the morning star rises, my dear
Mark. The wise man recognizes that," he had sermonized
as he carved the roast.

"General Courtney's star has not set yet," said Mark
stubbornly.

"Not yet," agreed Peter. "But when it does, you will
need new friends. Powerful friends."

"You can always rely on us," said Marion's sister kindly.
"You don't always have to live out there in the bush."

"You don't understand," Mark interrupted quietly. "My
life's work is out there—in the bush."

"Oh, I wouldn't bank on that." Peter heaped slices of roast beef on to Marks plate. "There are going to be changes in the Ladyburg district when Mr. Dirk Courtney takes over. Big changes!

"Besides, it isn't fair on poor Marion. No woman wants to live out there—"

"Oh, I am quite happy wherever Mark wants to go," Marion murmured.

"Don't worry," Peter assured them. "We'll look after you." And he patted Mark's shoulder in a brotherly fashion.

"Mr. Dirk Courtney thinks the world of Peter," said his wife proudly.

Now as Mark crossed the hall towards General Sean Courtney, he felt the heavy doughy feeling of dread in his guts. He did not want to bear the tidings he had for the General, yet he knew it was better that they came gently from a friend, rather than in gloating triumph from an enemy.

He paused to watch Sean Courtney from a distance, feeling both pity and anger. Sean had rallied strongly since those low days at Emoyeni. His shoulders had regained some of that wide rakish set, and his face had filled out. Some of the gaunt shadows had smoothed away, and he had been in the sun again. The skin was tanned brown against the silver of his beard and his hair.

Yet he was seated now. The strain of the last few days had taxed him sorely. He sat erect on a hard-backed chair, both hands resting on the silver head of his cane. With him were many of his old friends who had gathered to give him support, and he listened seriously to his brother Garrick who sat in the chair beside him, nodding his agreement.

Mark did not want to go to him, he wanted to delay the moment, but then there was a stir across the hall. Mark saw Peter Botes scurrying across to where Dirk Courtney stood, and his face was bright scarlet with excitement. He spoke rapidly, gesticulating widely, and Dirk Courtney leaned forward to listen eagerly.

Mark could not delay a moment longer. He hurried forward and Sean saw him coming.

"Well, my boy, come and sit a while. They tell me the voting is extremely close so far, but we'll have the result before noon." Then he saw Mark's face. "What is it?" he demanded harshly.

Mark stooped over him, his mouth almost touching the General's ear, and his voice croaked in his own ears.

"It's just come in on the telegraph, General. We have lost Johannesburg Central, Doornfontein and Jeppe—" They were all solid safe Smuts seats, they had been South Africa Party since Union in 1910, and now they were gone. It was a disaster, a stunning catastrophe. Sean gripped Mark's forearm as if to take strength from him, and his hand shook in a gentle palsy.

Across the hall they heard the wild gloating cheers start ringing out, and Mark had to hurry.

"That's not all, sir. General Smuts himself has lost his seat." The nation had rejected them, the coalition of the Labour and the National Party under Hertzog were sweeping into power.

"My God," muttered Sean. "It's come. I didn't believe it possible."

Still gripping Mark's arm, he pulled himself to his feet. "Help me out to the car, my boy. I don't think I can bring myself to congratulate the new member for Ladyburg."

But they were too late. The announcement came before they reached the door. It was shouted in a stentorian voice, by the chief scrutineer from the platform at the end of the hall.

"Mr. Dirk Courtney, National Labour Party: 2683 votes. General Sean Courtney, South Africa Party: 2441 votes. I give you the new member for Ladyburg—" And Dirk Courtney leapt lightly on to the platform, clasping both hands above his head like a prize-fighter.

"Well." There was a twisted grin on Sean's face, the skin had that greyish tone again and his shoulders had slumped.

"So, exit the Butcher of Fordsburg—" and Mark took him out to where the Rolls waited in the street.

* * *

The champagne was a Dom Perignon of that superb 1904 vintage, and Sean poured it with his own hands, limping from guest to guest.

"I had hoped to toast victory with it," he smiled. "But it will do as well to drown our sorrows."

There was only a small gathering in the drawing-room of Lion Kop homestead, and the few attempts at joviality were lost in the huge room. The guests left early. Only the family sat down to dinner, with Marion in Storm's old seat and Mark between her and Ruth Courtney.

"Well, my boy, what are your plans now?" Sean abruptly asked in one of the silences, and Mark looked up with genuine astonishment.

"We'll be going back to Chaka's Gate, of course."

"Of course." Sean smiled with the first spontaneous warmth of that dark day. "How foolish of me to think otherwise. But you do realize what this," Sean made a gesture with one hand, unable to say the word defeat, "what this could mean for you?"

"Yes, sir. But you still have enormous influence. There is our Wildlife Society—we can fight. We have to fight to keep Chaka's Gate."

"Yes," Sean nodded, and there was a little sparkle in his eyes again. "We'll fight, but my guess is it will be a hard, dirty fight."

* * *

At first there was no sign of the gathering clouds to darken the tall blue sky above Chaka's Gate. The only change was that Mark was submitting his monthly report, not to Sean Courtney, but to the new Minister of Lands, Peter Grobler, a staunch Hertzog man. His reports were acknowledged formally, but although his salary was still paid regularly by the Department, in a short official letter Mark was informed that the whole question of the proclaimed areas was now under consideration at Cabinet level, and that new legislation would be promulgated at the next session of Parliament. His appointment as game warden was to be considered a temporary post, without pension benefits, and subject to monthly notice.

Mark worked on doggedly, but many nights he sat late in the lantern light writing to General Courtney. The two of them were planning at long distance their campaign to awaken public interest in Chaka's Gate, but when Marion had gone off to bed in the next room, he would take a fresh page and cover it with the small cramped lines to Storm, pouring out to her all his thoughts and dreams and love.

Storm never replied to his letters, he was not even certain that she was still in that thatched cottage above the beach, but he imagined her there, thinking of her at odd hours of the day and the night, seeing her working at her easel, or walking the beach with baby John tottering at her side. One particular night he lay awake and imagined her in the tiny shuttered bedroom with the child at her breast, and the image was too vivid, too painful to allow him sleep.

He rose quietly, left a note for Marion as she slept heavily, and, with Pungushe trotting at Trojan's head, set off up the valley.

Marion woke an hour after he had gone, and her first waking thought was that if there was still no show on this morning then it was certain. She had waited all these weeks for that absolute certainty, before telling Mark. Somehow she had been afraid that if she had spoken of it too soon, it would have been bad luck.

She slipped from the bed and crossed the still dark room to the bathroom. When she returned minutes later she was hugging herself with suppressed joy, and she lit the candle by her bedside, eager to see Mark's face when she woke him to tell him.

Her disappointment when she saw the empty rumpled

bed and the note propped on the pillow was intense, but lasted only a short while before her usual gentle placid nature reasserted itself.

"It will give me more time to enjoy it by myself," she said aloud, and then she spoke again. "Harold—Harold Anders? No, that's too common. I will have to think of a really fine-sounding name."

She hummed happily to herself as she dressed, and then went out into the kitchen yard.

It was a cool still morning with a milky pink sky. A baboon called from the cliffs of Chaka's Gate, the short explosive bark ringing across the valley, a salute to the sunrise that was turning the heights to brazen splendour.

It was good to be alive and to have a child growing on such a day, Marion thought, and she wanted to do something to celebrate it. Mark's note had told her that he would be home by nightfall.

"I'll bake a new batch of bread, and—" She wanted something very special for this day. Then she remembered that it had rained five days previously. There might be wild mushrooms coming up from the rains, those rounded buds with sticky brown tops; the rich meaty flesh was a favourite of Mark's and he had taught her when and where to find them.

She ate her breakfast absentmindedly with Mark's copy of *The Home Doctor* propped against the jam jar, re-reading the section on "The Expectant Mother." Then she began on her housework, taking a comfortable pride in the slippery glaze of the cement floors and the burnish which she had worked on to the wood of the simple furniture, in the neatness and order, the smell of polish, the wild flowers in their vases. She sang as she worked and once laughed out loud for no reason.

It was mid-morning before she tied her sun bonnet under her chin, put a bottle of "Chamberlain's Superior Diarrhoea Remedy" into her basket, and set off up the valley.

She stopped at Pungushe's kraal and the youngest wife brought the baby to her. Marion was relieved to see that he was much improved, and Pungushe's wife assured her that she had given him much liquid to drink. Marion took him in her lap and fed him a spoonful of the diluted remedy, despite his violent protests, and afterwards the five women sat in the sun and talked of children and men and childbirth, of sickness and food and clothing, and all the things that absorb a woman's life.

It was almost an hour later that she left the four Zulu women and went down towards the river.

*　　*　　*

The downpour of rain had disquieted the lioness. Some deep instinct warned her that it was but the harbinger of the great storms to come.

The jessie thickets in the valley were a suitable retreat for her litter no longer. Heavy rain on the escarpment would soon turn the steep narrow valley into a cascading torrent.

Twice already she had tried to lead the cubs away, but they were older now and had developed a stubbornness and tenacity. They clung to the haven of the thick thorny jessie, and her efforts had failed. Within half a mile, one or two of the fainthearts would turn and scurry back to what they considered home. Immediately the lioness turned back to seize the deserter, it precipitated an undignified rush by the others in the same direction, and within five minutes they were all back in the jessie.

The lioness was distracted. This was her first litter, but she was governed by instinct. She knew that it was time to wean her cubs, to take them out of the trap of the narrow valley, to begin their hunting lessons, but she was frustrated by the size of her litter, six-cub litters were a rarity in the wilderness and so far there had been no casualties among the cubs; her family was becoming too ungainly for her to handle.

However, instinct drove her and in the middle of a cool bright morning in which she could smell the rain coming, she tried again. The cubs gambolled along behind her, falling over each other and sparring amicably, as far as the river. This was familiar ground and they went along happily.

When the lioness started out across the open white sandbanks towards the far side, there was immediately the usual crisis in confidence. Three cubs followed her willingly, two stood undecidedly on the high bank and whined and mewled with concern, while the sixth turned and bolted straight back up the valley for the ebony.

The lioness went after him at a gallop and bowled him on his back. Then she took the scruff of his neck and lifted him. The cubs were big now, and although she lifted him to the full stretch of her neck, his backside still bumped on every irregularity of the ground. He curled up his legs, wrapped his tail tightly up under his quarters and closed his eyes, hanging from her mouth as she carried him down into the bed of the Bubezi River.

The river was five hundred yards wide at this point, and almost completely empty at the end of the dry season. There were still deep green pools of water between the snowy-white sand-banks, and the pools were connected by a slow trickle of warm clear water only a few inches deep. While five cubs watched in an agony of indecision from the near bank, the lioness carried the cub through the shallows, soaking his dragging backside so he hissed and wriggled indignantly, then she trotted up the far bank and found a clump of dense wit-els where she placed him.

She turned back to fetch another cub, and he followed her with a panicky rush. She had to stop and box him about the ears, snarling until he squealed and fell on his back. She grabbed him by the neck and dragged him back into the wit-els. She started back across the river to find the cub stumbling along on her heels again. This time she nipped hard enough to really hurt, and bundled him back into the thicket. She nipped again at his hindquarters until he cowered flat on the earth, so subdued and chastened that he could not gather the courage to follow again. He lay under the bush and made distraught little sounds of anguish.

\* \* \*

Marion had never been this far from the cottage alone, but it was such a lovely warm clear morning, peaceful and still, that she wandered on in a mood of enchantment and happiness such as she had seldom known before.

She knew that if she followed the river bank, she could not lose herself, and Mark had taught her that the African bush is a safer place in which to wander abroad than the streets of a city—as long as one followed a few simple rules of the road.

At the branch of the two rivers she stopped for a few minutes to watch a pair of fish eagles on top of their shaggy nest in the main fork of a tall leadwood tree. The white heads of the two birds shone like beacons in contrast to their dark russet plumage, and she thought she could just make out the chirruping sound of the chicks in the cup of the hay-stack nest.

The sound of the young heightened the awareness of the life in her own belly, and she laughed and went on down the branch of the Red Bubezi.

Once a heavy body crashed in the undergrowth nearby, and there was a clatter of hooves on stony earth. She froze with a fleeting chill of fear, and then when the silence returned she regained her courage and laughed a little breathlessly and went on.

There was a perfume on the warm still air, sweet as full-blooming roses, and she followed it, twice going wrong but at last coming on a spreading creeper hanging over a gaunt dead tree. The leaves were dark shiny green and the dense bunches of flowers were pale butter yellow. She had never seen the plant before, nor the swarm of sunbirds that fluttered about it. They were tiny restless darting birds, with bright, metallic, shiny plumage like the little humming-birds of America, and they dipped into the perfumed flowers with long slim curved beaks. Their colours were unbelievable in the sunlight, emerald greens and sapphire blue, black like wet anthracite and red like the blood of kings. They thrust their beaks deep into the open throats of the yellow blooms to sip out the thick clear drops of nectar through their hollow tubular tongues.

Watching them, Marion felt a deep pervading delight, and it was a long time before she moved on again.

She found the first batch of mushrooms a little farther on, and she knelt to snap the stems off at the level of the earth and then hold the umbrella-shaped fleshy plant to her face and inhale the delicious musty odour, before laying it carefully, cap uppermost, in the basket so that grit and dirt would not lodge in the delicately fluted gills. She took two dozen mushrooms from this one patch, but she knew they would cook down to a fraction of their bulk.

She went on, following the lip of the steep bank.

Something hissed close by and her heart skipped again. Her first thought was of a snake, one of those thick bloated reptiles, with the chocolate and yellow markings and flat scaly heads, which blew so loudly that they were called puff-adders.

She began moving backwards carefully staring into the clump of first growth wit-els from which the sound had come. She saw small movement, but it was some seconds before she realized what she was seeing.

The lion cub was flat on its belly in the dappled shadow of the thicket, and its own dappled baby spots blended beautifully against the bed of dried leaves and leaf mould on which it lay.

The cub had learned already the first lesson of concealment, absolute stillness; except for his two round fluffy ears. The ears flicked back and forth, signalling clearly every emotion and intention. He stared at Marion with wide round eyes that had not yet turned the ferocious yellow of full growth, but were still hazed with the bluish glaze of kittenhood. His whiskers bristled stiffly, and his ears signalled wildly conflicting messages.

Flattening against the skull: "One step nearer and I'll tear you to pieces."

Shooting out sideways: "One step nearer and I'll die of fright."

Coming up and cupping forward: "What the hell are you anyway?"

"Oh," exclaimed Marion. "You darling little thing." She set down the basket, and squatted. She extended one hand and made soft cooing noises.

"There's a darling. Are you all alone then, poor baby?" She moved forward slowly, still talking and cooing.

"Nobody's going to hurt you, baby."

The cub was uncertain, its ears rising into an attitude of curiosity and indecision as it stared at her.

"Are you all alone then? You'll make a lovely pet for my own baby, won't you?"

Closer and closer she edged, and the cub warned her with a half-hearted apologetic hiss.

"What a cheeky darling we are," Marion smiled and squatted three feet from the cub.

"How are we going to take you home?" Marion asked. "Will you fit in the basket?"

In the river bed, the lioness carried the second cub through the shallows, and was followed by one of the heroes of the litter, struggling along gamely through the thick white sand. However, when he reached the edge of the shallow stream and tested it with one paw, his new-found courage deserted him at the cold wet touch, and he sat down and wept bitterly.

The lioness, by this time almost wild with distraction and frustration, turned back, and dropped her burden which immediately set off in clumsy gallop for the jessie thicket again, then she seized the weeping hero instead and trotted back through the stream and set off determinedly for the far bank.

Her huge round pads made no sound in the soft earth as she came up the bank, carrying the cub.

Marion heard the crackling spluttering explosion of sound behind her, and she whirled to her feet in one movement.

The lioness crouched on the lip of the bank fifty yards away. It warned her again with that terrible sound.

All that Marion saw were the eyes. They were a blazing yellow, a ferocious terrifying yellow—and she screamed, a wild high ringing, rising sound.

The sound launched the lioness into her charge, and it came with an unbelievably fluid flowing speed that turned into a yellow rushing blur. She snaked in low, and the sand spurted beneath her paws, all claws fully extended, the lips drawn back in a fixed silent snarl, the teeth exposed, long and white and pointed.

Marion turned to run, and had gone five paces when the lioness took her. She pulled her down with a swipe of a forepaw across the small of her back and five curved yellow claws cut deeply—four inches through skin and muscle, opening the abdominal cavity like a sabre cut, crushing the vertebrae and bursting both kidneys instantaneously.

It was a blow that would have killed even a full-grown ox, and it hurled Marion twenty feet forward, but as she fell on her back, the lioness was on her again.

The jaws were wide open, the long white fangs framed the deep wet pink cavern of tongue and throat. In an instant of incredibly heightened perception, Marion saw the smooth ridges of firm pink flesh that covered the arched roof of the lioness' mouth in regular patterns, and she smelt the meaty stink of her breath.

Marion lay twisted under the great yellow cat, she was still screaming and her lower body lay at an odd angle from the shattered spine, but she lifted both arms to protect her face.

The lioness bit into the forearms, just below the elbows and the bone crunched sharply, shattering into slivers and splinters in the mangled flesh, both arms were severed almost through.

Then the lioness seized Marion's shoulder, and worried it until the long eye teeth meshed through broken bone and fat and tissue—and Marion kept screaming, twisting and writhing under the cat.

The lioness took a long time to kill her, confused by her own anger and the unfamiliar taste and shape of the victim. She tore and bit and ripped for almost a minute before she found the throat.

When the lioness stood up at last, her head and neck were a gory mask, her fur sticky and sodden with blood.

Her tail still lashed from side to side in residual anger, but she licked her face with a long dextrous tongue and her lip curled at the sweet unfamiliar flavour. She wiped her face carefully with her paws before trotting back to her cub, and licking him also with long pink protective strokes.

Marion's broken torn body lay where she left it, until Pungushe's wives came, a little before sundown.

*     *     *

Mark and Pungushe crossed the river in darkness with the moonlight turning the sand-banks to ghostly grey, and the round white moon itself reflected perfectly in the still mirror-surface of the pool below the main camp. The turbulence of their fording shattered the image into a thousand points of light, like a crystal glass flung on to a stone floor.

As they rode up the bank, they heard the death wail in the night, that terrible keening, the mourning of Zulu women. The men halted involuntarily, the sound striking dread into both of them.

"Come!" shouted Mark and kicked one foot from the stirrup. Pungushe grabbed the leather and swung off his feet as Mark lashed Trojan into a gallop and they tore up the hill.

The fire that the women had lit threw a grotesque yellow wavering glow, and weird dancing shadows.

The four women sat in a group around the long, kaross-wrapped bundle.

None of them looked up as the men ran forward into the firelight.

"Who is it?" Mark demanded. "What has happened?"

Pungushe seized his eldest wife by the shoulders, and shook her, trying to interrupt the hysteria of mourning, but Mark strode forward impatiently and lifted one end of the kaross.

He stared for a moment, not understanding, not recognizing, then suddenly all colour fled from his face and he turned and ran into the darkness. There he fell to his knees and leaned forward to retch up the bitter bile of horror.

\*   \*   \*

Mark took Marion into Ladyburg, wrapped in a canvas buck-sheet, and strapped into the side-car of the Ariel.

He stayed for the funeral and for the grief and recriminations of her family.

"If only you hadn't taken her out there into the bush—"

"If only you had stayed with her—"

"If only—"

On the third day he went back to Chaka's Gate. Pungushe was waiting for him at the ford of the river.

They sat together in the sunlight under the cliffs, and when Mark gave Pungushe a cigarette, he broke off the cork tip carefully and they smoked in silence until Mark asked,

"Have you read the sign, Pungushe?"

"I have, Jamela."

"Tell me what happened."

"The lioness was moving her little ones, taking them one at a time across the river from the jessie bush." Slowly, accurately, Pungushe reconstructed the tragedy from the marks left in the earth which he had studied in Mark's absence, and when he was finished speaking, they were silent again.

"Where is she now?" Mark asked quietly.

"She has taken the little ones north, but slowly, and three days ago, the day after," Pungushe hesitated, "the day after the thing was done, she killed an impala ram, and the cubs ate a little with her. She begins now to wean them."

Mark stood up and they forded the river, climbing together slowly up through the forest to the cottage.

While Pungushe waited on the front stoep, Mark went into the small deserted home. The wild flowers had died and wilted in their vases, giving the room a sad and dejected feeling. Mark began to gather up all Marion's personal possessions, her clothing, and cheap but treasured jewelery, her combs and brushes, and the few hoarded pots of cosmetics. He packed them carefully into her largest suitcase to take to her sister, and when he was finished he carried the case out and locked it in the tool shed. It was too painful a reminder to keep in the house with him.

Then he went back and changed out of his town clothes. He took the Mannlicher down from the rack and loaded it with brass cartridges from a fresh package. The casings of the cartridges were glistening yellow under their film of wax, the bullets soft-nosed for maximum shock at impact.

When he went out on to the stoep carrying the rifle, Pungushe was still waiting.

"Pungushe," he said. "We have work to do now."

The Zulu stood up slowly, and for a moment they stared at each other. Then Pungushe dropped his eyes and nodded.

"Take the spoor," Mark commanded softly.

\*　　\*　　\*

They found where the lioness had killed the impala, but the scavengers of the bush had cleaned the area effectively. There were a few splinters of bone that had fallen out of the crushing jaws of the hyena, a little hair, pulled out in tufts, a shred of dried skin, and part of the skull with the twisted black horns still intact. But the spoor was cold. Wind and the trampling feet of the scavengers, the jackals, and hyena, the vultures and marabou storks, had wiped sign.

"She will keep going north," said Pungushe, and Mark did not ask how he knew that, for the Zulu could not have answered. He simply knew.

They went slowly on up the valley, Pungushe scouting ahead of the mule, making wide tracks back and forth, casting carefully for the sign, and on the second day he cut the spoor.

"She has turned now." Pungushe squatted over the pug marks, the big saucer-sized pads and the smaller myriad prints of the cubs.

"I think she was going back towards the Usutu." He nodded over the spoor, touching it with the thin reed wand he carried as a tracking stick. "She was taking the little ones back, but now she has changed her mind. She has turned southwards, she must have passed close to where we camped last night. She is staying in the valley. It is her valley now, and she will not leave it."

"No," Mark nodded grimly. "She will not leave the valley again. Follow, Pungushe."

The lioness was moving slowly and the spoor ran hotter every hour. They found where she had hunted without success. Pungushe pointed out where she had stalked, and then the deep driving back claws had raked the earth as she leapt to the back of a full-grown zebra. Twenty paces further, she had fallen heavily, dislodged by the stallion's wild plunging. She had struck shoulder first, Pungushe said, and the zebra had run free but bleeding from the long slash of her claws. The lioness had limped away, and lain under a thorn tree for a long time before rising and going back slowly to where she had left her cubs. Probably she had torn muscle and sinew in that fall.

"When will we come up with her?" Mark asked, his face a stony mask of vengeance.

"Perhaps before sunset." But they lost two hours on a rocky ridge, and Pungushe had to cast widely and work with all his skill to cut the spoor again at the point where it doubled sharply and turned west towards the escarpment.

Pungushe and Mark camped on her spoor with only a tiny fire for comfort and they lay directly on the earth. Mark did not sleep. He lay and watched the waning moon come up over the tree tops, but it was only when Pungushe spoke quietly that he realized that the Zulu also was sleepless.

"The cubs are not weaned," he said. "But they will take a long time to die."

"No," Mark replied. "I will shoot them also."

Pungushe roused himself and took a little snuff, leaning on one elbow and staring into the coals of the fire.

"She has tasted human blood," Mark said at last. Even in his grief and anger, he sensed Pungushe's quiet disapproval and wanted to justify what he was about to do.

"She did not feed," Pungushe stated. Mark felt his gorge rise and the bitter taste of it again as he remembered the terrible mutilation, but Pungushe was right, the lioness had not eaten any of that poor torn flesh.

"Pungushe, she was my wife."

"Yes," Pungushe nodded. "That is so. Also it was her cub."

Mark considered the words, and felt for the first time a confusion of his own objects. The lioness had acted out of one of the oldest instincts of life, the urge to protect her young—but what were his motives?

"I have to kill her, Pungushe," he said flatly, and there was some slimy obscene thing in his belly; it moved there for the first time, and he tried to deny its existence.

Marion was dead. Sweet, loyal, dutiful Marion, who had been all that a man could ask for in a wife. She had died an unspeakable death—and now Mark was alone, or did the word "free" come too readily to his tongue?

Suddenly he had an image of a slim, dark lovely girl and a lusty naked little boy walking in the sunset at the edge of the sea.

Guilt, that slimy thing, uncoiled in his belly and began to ripple and undulate like a serpent, and he could not crush it down.

"She has to die," Mark repeated, and perhaps his own guilt could die in that same purging.

"Very well," Pungushe agreed. "We will find her before noon tomorrow." He lay back and pulled his kaross over his head and his voice was muffled, the words almost lost. "Let us hurry now towards the great emptiness."

\* \* \*

They found the lioness early the next morning. She had moved in close under the hills of the escarpment, and when the first heat of the day made the cubs flag and begin to trail disconsolately along behind her, she had selected an umbrella thorn with a flat-topped mass of foliage spreading from the straight trunk and she had lain in the shade on her side, exposing the soft creamy fur of her belly and the double row of flat black nipples.

Now the cubs were almost satiated, only two of the greediest still suckled valiantly, their bellies bulging and the effort of swallowing almost too much.

The indefatigable hunter of tails was now concentrating all his prowess on his mother's long whip-lash with its fine black tuft of hair which she jerked out from under his nose at the very instant of each attack.

The other three were fighting off sleep, with violent outbursts of undirected energy, succumbing slowly to drooping eyelids and strained bellies, until at last they lay in an untidy heap of fluff and fur.

Mark was one hundred and twenty yards downwind. He lay belly down behind a small ant-heap, and it had taken almost an hour to work in this close. The umbrella thorn was set in an area of short open grassland, and he had been forced to stalk flat, tortoising forward on his elbows with the rifle held across the crook.

"Can we get closer?" Mark asked, his whisper merely a soft breath. The short stiff yellow grass was just high enough to screen the cat when she lay flat on her side.

"Jamela, I could get close enough to touch her." He put the emphasis on the word "I" and left the rest of it unstated.

So they waited in the sun, another twenty minutes until at last the lioness lifted her head.

Perhaps some deep sense of survival had warned her of the presence of the hunters. Her head came up in a flash of yellow movement, the extraordinary swiftness so characteristic of all the big cats, and she stared fixedly downwind, the sector of maximum danger.

For long seconds she watched, and the wide yellow eyes were steady and unblinking. Sensing her concern, two of the cubs sat up sleepily and waited with her.

Mark felt the lioness was looking directly at him, but he obeyed the law of absolute stillness. The first movement of lifting the Mannlicher would send her away in a blur of speed. So Mark waited while the seconds spun out. Then suddenly the lioness dropped her head and stretched out flat once again.

"She is restless," warned Pungushe. "We can get no closer."

"I cannot shoot from here."

"We will wait," said Pungushe.

All the cubs slept now, and the lioness dozed, but always all her senses were working, nostrils tasting carefully each breath of the wind for the taint of danger, the big round ears never still, flicking to the slightest sound of wind or branch, bird or animal.

Mark lay in the direct sunlight, and the sweat rose to stain his shirt. A tsetse fly settled behind his ear and bit into the softness of his neck, but he did not make the movement of brushing it away. It was an hour before his chance came.

The lioness rose suddenly to her full height, and swung her tail from side to side. She was too restless to stay here under the thorn tree any longer. The cubs sat up groggily, and looked to her with puzzled furrowed faces.

The lioness was standing broadside to where Mark lay. She held her head low, and her jaws were a little open as she panted softly in the heat. Mark was close enough to see the dark specks of the tsetse fly sitting on her flanks.

She was still in shadow but now she was backlit by the pale yellow grass beyond her. It was a perfect shot—the point of the elbow the hunters aiming mark; the span of a hand back from there, and the bullet would rake both lungs, the span of a hand lower would take the heart cleanly.

The lungs were certain, but the heart was swift. Mark chose the heart and lifted the rifle to his shoulder. The safety-catch had long before been set at the firing position.

Mark took up the slack in the trigger and felt the final resistance before the mechanism tripped.

The bullet was 230 grains in weight, and the bronze jacket of the slug was tipped with a grey blob of lead so that it would mushroom on impact and open massive damage through the lioness' chest cavity.

The lioness called her cubs with a soft moaning grunt, and they scrambled obediently to their feet, still a little unsteady from sleep.

She walked out into the sunlight, with that loose feline gait, her head swinging from side to side at each pace, the long back slightly swayed and the heavy droop of her full dugs thickening the graceful line of her body.

"No," thought Mark. "I will take the lungs." He lifted his aim a fraction, holding steady and true four inches behind the point of the elbow, swinging the rifle to follow her as she went into a short restless trot.

The cubs tumbled along behind her in disorder.

Mark held his aim until she reached the edge of the bush, and then she was gone with the insubstantial blurred movement of a wisp of brown smoke on the wind.

When she was gone, he lowered the rifle and stared after her.

Pungushe saw the thing break in him at last. The cold stillness of hatred and guilt and horror broke, and Mark began to cry, hacking tearing sobs that scoured and purged.

It is a difficult thing for a man to watch another weep, especially if that man is your friend.

Pungushe stood up quietly and walked back to where they had tethered the mule. He sat alone in the sun and took a little snuff and waited for Mark.

* * *

GOVERNMENT MINISTER SPEAKS ON DUTY TO HUMANITY

The newly appointed Deputy Minister of Lands, Mr. Dirk Courtney, expressed concern today at the mauling of a young woman in the proclaimed area of Northern Zululand.

The woman, Mrs. Marion Anders, was the wife of the Government Ranger in the area. She was mauled to death by a lioness last Friday.

This unfortunate incident underlines the grave danger of allowing wild animals to exist in proximity to settled areas of human habitation.

Residents in these areas will be in constant danger of animal attack, of crop depredation and game-borne diseases of domestic animals as long as this position is allowed to continue.

Mr. Dirk Courtney said that the rinderpest epidemic at the turn of the century had accounted for a loss of domestic cattle estimated to exceed two million head. Rinderpest was a game-borne disease. The minister pointed out, "We cannot risk a repetition of such a calamity."

The proclaimed area of Northern Zululand encompasses both highly valuable arable land, and a major watershed vital to proper conservation of our natural resources. If the full potential of our national assets is to be exploited, these areas must be turned over to properly controlled development. The minister went on, "Your Government has placed priority on this issue, and we will be placing legislation before Parliament at the next sitting."

Mark read the article through carefully. It was placed prominently on the leader page of the *Natal Witness*.

"There are more," General Sean Courtney thumbed open a slim folder with half a dozen other cuttings, "take them with you. You'll see it's all the same general purport. Dirk Courtney is beating the drum with a very big stick, I'm afraid."

"He's in such a position of power now. I never dreamed he would be a Deputy Minister."

"Yes," Sean nodded. "He has rushed to power, but on the other hand we still have a voice. One of our members in a solid seat has stood down for Jannie Smuts, even I have been offered a seat in a safer constituency."

"Will you take it, sir?"

Sean shook his silver beard slowly, "I've had a long time in public life, my boy—and anything you do too long becomes a bore." He nodded as he thought about his words. "Of course, that's not strictly true. I am tired, let the younger ones with more energy pick up the reins now. Jannie Smuts will keep in close touch, he knows he can call on me, but I feel like an old Zulu chief. I just want to sit in the sun, drink beer, grow fat and count my cattle."

"What about Chaka's Gate, sir?" Mark pleaded.

"I have spoken to Jannie Smuts and some of the others, on both sides of the house. We have a lot of support in the new Government as well. I don't want to make it a party issue, I'd like to see it as an issue of each man's own conscience."

They went on talking until Ruth intervened reluctantly. "It's after midnight, dear. You can finish your talk in the morning. When are you leaving, Mark?"

"I should be back at Chaka's Gate tomorrow night." Mark felt a prick of guilt as he lied. He knew damned well he was not going home just yet a while.

"But you'll stay for lunch tomorrow?"

"Yes, I'd like that. Thank you."

As Mark rose he picked up the file of newspaper clippings from Sean's desk. "I'll let you have them back tomorrow, sir."

However, the moment Mark was alone in his room, he dropped into an easy chair and turned avidly to the reverse side of the newspaper cutting he had brought with him. He had not dared to turn over the cutting and read the words that had caught his eye in the General's presence, but now he lingered over them, re-reading and savouring. Part of the article was missing, scissored away when the Deputy Minister's speech had been trimmed, but there was enough.

### EXCEPTIONAL EXHIBITION BY YOUNG ARTIST

Presently showing at the sample rooms of the Marine Hotel on the Marine Parade is an exhibition of thirty paintings by a young lady artist.

For Miss Storm Courtney, it is her first public exhibition and even a much older and more established artist could have been justly gratified with such a reception by the art-lovers of our fair city. After the first five days, twenty-one of her paintings had found enthusiastic purchasers at prices as high as fifty guineas each. Miss Courtney has a classical conception of form, combined with both a sure sense of colour and a mature and confident execution rare in an artist of such tender years.

Worthy of special mention is Number 16, "Greek athlete at rest." This painting, property of the artist and not for sale, is a lyrical composition that would perhaps raise the eyebrows of the more old-fashioned. It is an unashamedly sensual ode to—

Here the scissors had cut through, leaving Mark with a disturbing unfinished feeling. He read it once more, inordinately pleased that Storm had reverted to her maiden name with which to sign her work. Then carefully he folded the cutting into his wallet, and he sat in the chair staring at the wall, until he fell asleep, still fully dressed.

\*     \*     \*

A young Zulu lass, no more than sixteen years of age, opened the door of the cottage. She was dressed in the traditional white cotton dustcoat of the nanny and she carried baby John on her hip.

Both nanny and child regarded Mark with huge solemn eyes, but the nanny's relief was patent when Mark addressed her in fluent Zulu.

At the sound of Mark's voice John let out an excited squawk that could have been recognition, but was probably merely a friendly greeting. He began to leap up and down on the nanny's hip with such force that she had to grab to prevent him taking off like a sky rocket.

He reached out both hands towards Mark, burbling and laughing and shouting, and Mark took him, all warm and wriggling and baby-smelling, from the maid. John immediately seized a handful of Mark's hair and tried to remove it by the roots.

Half an hour later when Mark handed him back to the little moon-faced maid, and went down the steep pathway to the beach, John's indignant howls of protest followed him, only fading with distance.

Mark kicked off his shoes and left them and his shirt above the high-tide mark, then he turned northwards and followed the white sweep of sand, his bare feet leaving wet prints on the smooth firm edge of the seashore.

He had walked a mile, and there was no sign of any other person. The beach sand was rippled by static wind-blown wavelets, and dappled with the webbed prints of seabirds.

On his right hand, the surf rose in long glassy lines, curling green and then dropping over in a crash of white water that shook the sand beneath his feet. On his left hand, the dense, dark green bush rose above the white beach, and again beyond that, the far blue hills and taller bluer sky.

He was alone—until he saw, perhaps a mile ahead, another solitary figure, also following the edge of the sea, a far small and lonely figure, coming towards him, still too distant to tell whether it was man or woman, friend or stranger.

Mark lengthened his stride, and the figure drew nearer, clearer.

Mark began to run, and the figure ahead of him stopped suddenly, and stood with that stillness poised on the edge of flight.

Then suddenly the stillness exploded, and the figure was racing to him.

It was a woman, a woman with dark silky hair streaming in the wind, a woman with outstretched arms and flying bare brown feet, and white teeth and blue, very blue eyes.

\*    \*    \*

They were alone in the bedroom. Baby John's cot had been removed to the small dining-room next door, since he had begun to show an interest in everything that looked like a good romp, hanging on the edge of his cot with shouts of applause and approbation, and then trying his utmost to scale the wooden railings and join the play.

Now they were enjoying those contented minutes between love and sleep, talking softly in the candlelight under a single sheet, lying on their sides facing each other, holding close, with their lips almost touching as they murmured together.

"But darling Mark, it is still a thatched hut, and it is still wild bush."

"It's a big thatched hut," he pointed out.

"I don't know. I just don't know if I have changed that much."

"There is only one way to find out. Come with me."

"But what will people say?"

"The same as they'd say if they could see us now."

She chuckled easily, and snuggled a little closer. "That was a silly question. The old Storm speaking. People have said all there is to say about me, and none of it really mattered a damn."

"There aren't a lot of people out there to sit in judgement. Only Pungushe, and he's a very broad-minded gentleman."

She laughed again sleepily. "Only one person I care about—Daddy mustn't know. I've hurt him enough already."

So Storm came at last to Chaka's Gate. She came in the beaten and neglected Cadillac, with John on the seat beside her, her worldly possessions crammed into the cab or strapped on the roof and Mark riding his motorcycle escort ahead of her over the rude and bumpy track.

Where the track ended above the Bubezi River, she climbed out and looked around her.

"Well," she decided after a long thoughtful survey of the towering cliffs, and the river in its bed of green water and white banks, framed by the tall nodding strands of fluffy-headed reeds and great spreading sycamore figs, "at least it's picturesque."

Mark put John on his shoulder. "Pungushe and I will come back with the mules for the rest of your gear." And he led her down the footpath to the river.

Pungushe was waiting for them under the trees on the far bank, tall and black and imposing in his beaded loin cloth.

"Pungushe, this is my lady and her name is Vungu Vungu—the Storm."

"I see you, Vungu Vungu, I see also that you are misnamed," said Pungushe quietly, "for a storm is an ugly thing which kills and destroys. And you are a lady of beauty."

"Thank you, Pungushe." Storm smiled at him. "But you

are also misnamed, for a jackal is a small mean creature."

"But clever," said Mark solemnly, and John let out a shout of greeting and bounced on Mark's shoulder, reaching out with both hands for Pungushe.

"And this is my son."

Pungushe looked at John. There are two things a Zulu loves dearly, cattle and children. Of the two, he prefers children, preferably boy-children. Of all boy-children, he likes best those that are robust, and bold and agressive.

"Jamela, I should like to hold your son," he said, and Mark gave John to him.

"I see you, Phimbo," Pungushe greeted the child. "I see you little man with a great voice." And then Pungushe smiled that great beaming radiant smile, and John shouted again with joy and thrust his hand in Pungushe's mouth to grab those white shining teeth, but Pungushe swung him up on to his shoulder and laughed with a great hippo-snort and carried him up the hill.

So they came to Chaka's Gate, and there was never any doubt, right from that first day.

Within an hour, there was a polite tap on the screen-door of the kitchen and when Mark opened it there stood in a row on the covered stoep all of Pungushe's daughters, from the eldest who was fourteen to the youngest of four.

"We have come," announced the eldest, "to greet Phimbo."

Mark looked at Storm inquiringly, and she nodded. The eldest daughter swung John up on to her back with a practised action, and strapped him there with a strip of cotton limbo. She had played nurse-maid to all her brothers and sisters, probably knew more about small children than both Storm and Mark combined, and John took to the froglike position on her back as though he had been born Zulu. Then the little girl bobbed a curtsey to Storm and trotted away, with all her sisters in procession, bearing John off to a wonderland peopled entirely with playmates of endless variety and fascination.

On the third day, Storm began sketching, and by the end of the first week she had taken over the household management on a system that Mark referred to as comfortable chaos, alternating with brief periods of pandemonium.

Comfortable chaos was when everybody ate what they wanted, perhaps chocolate biscuits and coffee for dinner one night and a feast of barbecued meat the next. They ate it where they felt like it, perhaps sitting up in bed or lying on a rug on the sand-bank of the river. They ate when they wanted, breakfast at noon or dinner at midnight, if talking and laughing delayed it that long.

Comfortable chaos was when the dusting of furniture or polishing of floors were forgotten in the excitement of living, when clothes that needed mending were tossed into the bottom of the cupboard, when Mark's hair was allowed to grow in points over the back of his collar. Comfortable chaos ended unpredictably and abruptly to be replaced by pandemonium.

Pandemonium began when Storm suddenly got a steely look in her eye and announced, "This place is a pig sty!" followed by the snipping of scissors, buckets of steaming water, clouds of flying dust, banging pots, and flashing needles. Mark was shorn and clad in refurbished clothing, the cottage gleamed and sparkled, and Storm's housekeeping instincts were exhausted for another indefinite period. And the next day she would be up on Spartan's back, John strapped Zulu-fashion behind her, following Mark on patrol up the valley.

The first time John had been taken on patrol, Mark had asked anxiously, "Do you think it's wise to take him, he's still very small?"

And Storm had replied, "I am older and more important than Master John. He fits into my life, not me into his."

So John rode patrol on muleback, slept in his apple basket under the stars at night, and took his daily bath in the cool green pools of the Bubezi River, quickly developed an immunity to the occasional tsetse bite, and flourished.

They climbed the steep pathway to the summit of Chaka's Gate, sat with their feet dangling over that fearful drop, and they looked across the whole valley, the far blue hills and the plains and swamps and the wide winding rivers.

"When I first met you, you were poor," Storm said quietly, leaning against Mark's shoulder with her eyes filled with the peace and wonder of it, "but now you are the richest man in the world, for you are the owner of paradise."

\* \* \*

He took her up the river to the lonely grave below the escarpment. Storm helped him to build a pile of rocks, and to set the cross that Mark had made over it. He told her Pungushe's story of how the old man had been killed, and she cried openly and unashamedly, holding John on her lap, sitting on the gravestone, listening and living every word.

\* \* \*

"I have looked—but never truly seen before," she said, as he showed her the nest of a sunbird, cunningly woven of lichen and spider web, turning it carefully so she could peer into the funnel entrance and see the tiny speckled eggs.

"I never knew what true peace was until I came to this place," she said, as they sat on the bank of the Bubezi in the yellow light of fading day, and watched a kudu bull with long spiral corkscrew horns and chalk-striped shoulders lead his big-eared cows down to the water.

"I did not know what happiness was before," she whispered, when they had woken together a little after midnight for no reason and reached for each other in the darkness.

Then one morning she sat up in the rumpled bed, over which John was rampaging unchecked and sowing crumbles of lightly chewed biscuit, and she looked at Mark seriously.

"You once asked me to marry you," she said. "Would you like to repeat that question, sir?"

And it was later that same day they heard the axeman at work up the valley.

\* \* \*

The blade of a two-handed axe, swung against the bole of a standing hardwood tree, rings like a gunshot, and the sound of it bounced against the cliffs of Chaka's Gate and was flung back to break in dying echoes down the valley, each stroke still lingering on in the air while the next cracked off the grey cliffs. There was more than one axeman at work, so that the din was continuous, like the sounds of battle.

Storm had never before seen such a passion of anger on Mark's face. His skin was drained of blood so that the tan of the sun was fever-yellow and his lips seemed frost-bitten and pinched by the force of it. Yet his eyes blazed, and she had to run to match his angry stride as they went up the scree slope from the river beneath the cliffs, and the sound of the axes broke over them, each separate stroke as brutal and shocking as the ones that preceded it.

Ahead of them, one of the lofty leadwoods quivered as though in agony and moved against the sky. Mark stopped in mid-stride to watch it, with his head thrown back and the same agony twisting his own lips. It was a tree of extraordinary symmetry, the silvery trunk rising with such grace as to seem as slim as a young girl's waist. It had taken two hundred years to reach its towering height. Seventy feet above the ground, it spread into a dark green dome of foliage.

As they watched, the tree shuddered again and the axes fell silent. Slowly, majestically, the leadwood swung into a downward arc, gathering ponderous momentum and the partially severed trunk groaned and popped as the fibres tore; faster and faster still she fell, crashing through the tops of the lesser vegetation below her, the twisting tearing wood shrieking like a living thing until she struck solid earth with a jarring impact they could feel in their guts.

The silence lasted many seconds, and then there was the sound of men's voices, awed voices, as though intimidated by the magnitude of the destruction they had wrought. Then almost immediately after that, the axes started again, fragmenting the great silences of the valley—and Mark began to run. Storm could not keep pace with him.

He came out in an area of devastation, a growing swathe of fallen trees where fifty black men worked like ants, half-naked and burnished with their own sweat, as they stripped the branches and piled them in windrows for burning. The wood chips shone white as bone in the sunlight and the sap that oozed from the axe cuts had the sweetish smell of newly spilled blood.

At the head of the long narrow clearing, a single white man crouched to the eyepiece of a theodolite set on its squat tripod. He was aiming the instrument down the clearing and directing with hand signals the setting of brightly painted markers.

He straightened from the instrument to face Mark—a young man with a mild friendly face, thick spectacles in silver wire frames, lank sandy hair flopping on to his forehead.

"Oh, hello there," he smiled, and then the smile froze as Mark hissed at him.

"Are you in charge here?"

"Well, yes, I suppose I am," the young surveyor stuttered.

"You are under arrest."

"I don't understand."

"It's quite simple," Mark blazed at him. "You are cutting standing timber in a proclaimed area. I am the Government Ranger, and I am placing you under arrest."

"Now look here," the surveyor began placatingly, spreading his open hands in a demonstration of his friendly intentions. "I'm just doing my job."

In his blind wholesale rage, Mark had not noticed the approach of another man, a heavy broad-shouldered man who moved silently out of the uncut brush along the edge of the clearing. However, the thick north-country accent was instantly familiar, and struck sparks along the surface of Mark's skin. He remembered Hobday from that day when first he had returned to Andersland to find his world turned upside down.

"That's all right, chummy. I'll talk to Mister Anders." Hobday touched the young surveyor's shoulder placatingly and smiled at Mark, a smile that exposed the short evenly ground teeth, but was completely lacking in any warmth or humour.

"There is nothing you can tell me," Mark started, and Hobday lifted one hand to stop him.

"I am here in my official capacity as a Provincial Inspector for the Ministry of Lands, Anders. You'd better listen."

The angry words died and Mark stared at him, while Hobday calmly unfolded a letter from his wallet and proffered it to Mark. It was typewritten on Government paper and signed by the Deputy Minister of Lands. The signature was bold and black—Dirk Courtney. Mark read through the letter slowly, with a plunging sense of despair, and when he finished, he handed it back to Hobday. It gave him unlimited powers in the valley, powers backed by all the authority and weight of Government.

"You are going up in the world," he said, "but still working for the same master." And the man nodded complacently, and then his eyes switched away from Mark's face as Storm came up. The expression on his face changed, as he looked at her.

Storm had her hair in thick twin braids, dangling forward on to each breast. The sun had turned her skin to a rich reddish brown, against which her eyes were startlingly blue and clear. Except for the eyes, she looked like a Sioux princess from some romantic novel.

Hobday dropped his eyes slowly over her body, with such intimate lingering insolence that she reached instinctively for Mark's arm and drew closer to him, as though to bring herself under his direct protection.

"What is it, Mark?" She was still breathless from her climb up the slope, and high colour lit her cheeks. "What are they doing here?"

"They're Government men," said Mark heavily. "From the Ministry of Lands."

"But they can't cut our trees," she protested, her voice rising "You've got to stop them, Mark."

"They're cutting survey lines," Mark explained. "They are surveying the valley."

"But those trees—"

"It don't really matter, ma'am," Hobday told her. His voice was lower now with a thick gloating tone, and his eyes were still busy on her body, like insects crawling greedily to the scent of honey, moving over the thin sun-bleached cotton that covered her breasts. "It don't matter a damn," he repeated. "They are all going to be under water anyway, cut or standing—it's all going under." He turned away from her at last, and swept one hand down the rude clearing. "From that side to this," he said, indicating the gap between the towering grey cliffs of Chaka's Gate, "right across it, we're going to build the biggest bloody dam in the whole world."

\*　　\*　　\*

They sat together in darkness, close together as though for comfort, and Mark had not lit the lantern. The reflected glow of stars was thrown in under the thatched veranda of the cottage, giving them just enough light to make out each other's faces.

"We knew it was coming," whispered Storm. "And yet

somehow I did not believe it. Just as though wishing could make it stop."

"I'm going through early tomorrow to see your father," Mark told her. "He has to know."

She nodded. "Yes, we must be ready to confront them."

"What will you do? I can't leave you here with John."

"And you can't take me with you. Not to my father," she agreed. "It's all right, Mark, I'll take John back to the cottage. We'll wait for you."

"I'll come for you there, and next time we return here, you'll be my wife."

She leaned against him. "If there is anything to return to," she whispered. "Oh Mark, Mark—they can't do it! They can't drown all this—this—" The words eluded her and she fell silent, clinging to him.

They did not speak again, until minutes later a low polite cough roused them, and Mark straightened to see the dark familiar bulk of Pungushe standing below the veranda in the starlight.

"Pungushe," he said. "I see you."

"Jamela," the Zulu replied, and there was a tone and tightness in his voice that Mark had never heard before. "I have been to the camp of the strangers. The cutters of wood, the men with painted poles, and bright axes."

He turned his head to look down the valley, and they followed his gaze. The ruddy glow of many camp fires flickered against the lower slopes of the cliffs and on the still night air, the sounds of laughter and men's voices carried faintly.

"Yes?" Mark asked.

"There are two white men there. One of them is young and blind and of no importance—while the other is a square thick man, who stands solid on his feet like a bull buffalo, and yet moves silently, and speaks little and quietly."

"Yes?" Mark asked again.

"I have seen this man before in the valley," Pungushe

paused. "He is the silent one of whom we have spoken. He is the one who shot *ixhegu,* your grandfather—and smoked as he watched him die."

\* \* \*

Hobday moved quietly, solidly, along the edge of the slash-line of the trees. The axes were silent, now, but the end of the noon break would be enforced to the minute. At the stroke of the hour they would be back at work. He was driving them hard, he always worked his gangs hard, took a pride in his ability to extract from each man effort beyond his wage. It was one of the qualities that Dirk Courtney valued in him—that and his loyalty, a fierce unswerving loyalty that baulked at no demand upon it. There was no squeamishness, no hesitating. When Dirk Courtney ordered it, there was no question asked. Hobday's reward was every day more apparent, already he was a man of substance, and when the new land was apportioned, that red sweet well-watered soil, rich as newly butchered beef, then his reward would be complete.

He paused at the spot where the slope increased sharply, angling into its plunge to the river bed below, and he looked out across the land. Involuntarily he licked his lips, like a glutton smelling rich food.

They had worked so long for this, each of them in his own way, led and inspired by Dirk Courtney, and although Hobday's personal share of the spoil would be a minute fraction of a single per cent, yet it was riches such as most other men only dream of.

He licked his lips again, standing very still and silent in the shadows and he looked to the sky. The clouds were piled to the very heavens, mountains of silver, blinding in the sunlight, and as he watched they moved ponderously down on the light wind. He could feel the closeness, and he stirred impatiently. Rain would delay them seriously, and rain was coming, the big torrential summer rains.

Then he was distracted again. Something moved on the

far side of the slash line, and his eye darted to the movement. It was a flash of bright colour like the flick of a sunbird's wing, and his veiled eyes jumped to it instantly, his body without moving became charged with tension.

The girl came out of the brush line, and paused thirty paces away. She had not seen him, and she stood poised, listening, head cocked like a forest animal.

She stood lightly, gracefully, and her limbs were slim and brown, the flesh so firm and young and sweet that he felt the quick bright rush of lust again as he had when, the previous day, he had seen her for the first time.

She wore a loose, wide peasant skirt of gay colour, and a thin cotton bodice pulled low at the front and drawn loosely with a string that left the bulge of bosom pushing free, the fine skin shading from dark ruddy brown to pale cream. She was dressed like a girl going to meet a lover, and there was a deliciously fearful tenseness in the way she took a step forward and stopped again uncertainly. He felt the lust fuelled in his groin, and he was suddenly aware of his own hoarse breathing.

The girl turned her head and looked directly at him, and as she saw him, she started visibly, dropping back a pace with one hand flying to her mouth. She stared at him for fully five seconds, and then slowly a transformation came over her.

The fingers dropped away from her face and she put both hands behind her back, a movement that thrust the pert breasts against the cotton of her bodice so he could see the rosy dark buttons of her nipples through the material. She thrust out one hip at a saucy angle, and lifted her chin boldly. Deliberately she let her eyes slide down his body, let them linger on his groin, and then rise again to his face. It was an invitation as clear as the spoken word, and Hobday heard the blood roaring in his ears.

She tossed her head, flicking the thick braid of hair over her shoulder, and she turned away, walking deliberately back to the tree-line, exaggerating the roll of tight round buttocks under the skirt.

She looked back over her shoulder, and as he started forward to follow, she let out a tingling flirt of laughter and ran lightly on sandalled feet, turning at an angle down the slope and Hobday began to run.

Within fifty yards Storm had lost sight of him in the heavy underbrush, and she stopped to listen, fearful that he might have given up the pursuit. Then there was movement above her, at the crest of the slope, and she realized with the first pang of real alarm that he had moved more swiftly than she had anticipated, and he had not followed her down, but had stayed above her in a position of command.

She went off again, running, and almost immediately she realized that he was ahead of her, moving fast along the crest. From up there, he could trap her by a swift turn directly down the slope.

She felt panic spur her, and started to run in earnest. Immediately the loose scree betrayed her and slipped away under her feet. She fell and rolled, flailing her arms for support and coming up on to her knees the moment her fall was broken.

She let out a little sob of fear. The man had seen her fall and had come down the slope. He was so close that she could see the square white teeth in the brown smooth face. He was grinning, a keen excited grimace, and he was steady and quick, moving down directly into the path along which she must run to safety, cutting her off squarely from where Mark waited.

She jumped to her feet and swirled away, doubling the slope, instinctively turning directly away from her pursuer—and from all help. Suddenly, she was completely alone, fleeing on frantic feet into the lonely spaces of the bush, beyond earshot of succour. Mark had been right, she realized, he had not wanted her to act as the bait. He had known just how dangerous a game she had set out to play, but in her stubborn arrogant way she had insisted, laughing at his protests, belittling his fears, until he had reluctantly agreed. Now she was running, terrified, the terror making her heart pound and squeezing her lungs so that her legs felt weak and rubbery under her.

Once she tried to turn back, but like an old and wily hound coursing a hare, he had anticipated and was there to block her, again she ran and suddenly the river was in front of her. The up-country rains had spated the course of the Bubezi and it rolled past in wide green majesty. She had to turn again along the bank, and was immediately into the area of thick jessie bush. The heavy thorn crowded her closely, leaving only narrow passages, a labyrinth of dark and secret twists and turns in which almost immediately she lost direction. She stopped and stood, trying to listen over the rush of her own breathing, trying to see through the wavering mist of her tears, tears of fear and of helplessness.

Her hair had come down in little wisps over her forehead, her cheeks blazed with high colour, and the tears made her eyes glitter with a feverish sheen.

She heard nothing, and the brown thorn encircled her. She turned slowly, almost like a blind woman, and now she was sobbing softly in her terror; she chose one of the narrow passages for escape and dived into it.

He was waiting for her. She came round the first twist of the pathway and ran almost directly into his chest.

Only at the very last instant she saw the outstretched arms, thick and brown and smooth, with the fingers of both hands hooked to seize her.

She screamed, high and shrill, and spun away, back along the path she had come, but his fingers caught in the thin cotton of her blouse. It tore like paper, and as she ran, the smooth creamy flesh of her back shone through the rent, flashing with a pearly promise that spurred his lust even higher, and when he laughed, it was a hoarse breathless blurt of sound that launched Storm into a fresh paroxysm of terror.

He hunted her through the jessie, and twice when he could have taken her, he deliberately let her slip through his fingers, drawing out the excruciating pleasure of it, cat with mouse, delighting at the way she shrieked at his touch, and at the fresh outburst of frantic terror with which she tried to escape him.

But at last she was finished, and she backed up into a corner of solid impenetrable thorn wall, and crouched there, clutching the shreds of her torn blouse about her, trembling with the wild uncontrollable shudders of a patient in high fever, her face smeared with her tears and her sweat, staring at him with huge dark blue eyes.

He came slowly to her. He stooped and she was unresisting as he placed his big square brown hands on her shoulders.

He was still chuckling, but his own breath was unsteady, and his lips were drawn back from the square white teeth in a grimace of lust and excitement.

He pressed his mouth down over hers, and it was like one of those nightmares in which she could not move nor scream. His teeth crushed painfully against her lips, and she tasted her own blood, a slick metallic salt on her tongue and she felt herself suffocating, his hands were hard and rough as granite on the soft silk of her breasts and she came to life again, tugging unavailingly at his wrists, trying to drag them away.

"Yes," he grunted, in the soft thick choked voice. "Fight. Keep fighting me. Yes. Yes. That's right—struggle—don't stop."

His voice roused her from the hypnotic spell of terror, and she screamed again.

"Yes," he said. "Do that. Scream again." And he turned her across his body, forcing her down until his knee caught her in the small of the back, and her body bent backwards like a drawn bow, her hair sweeping the ground and the curve of her throat was soft and white and vulnerable, he placed his open mouth on her throat.

She was pinned helplessly as with one hand he swept the wide peasant skirt up above her waist.

"Scream!" he whispered gutturally. "Scream again." And with complete and horrified disbelief she felt those thick brown fingers, calloused and deliberately cruel, begin to prise open her body. They seemed to tear her tenderest, most secret flesh, like the talons of an eagle—and she screamed and screamed.

Mark had lost them in the labyrinthine maze of the jessie bush, and there had been silence now for many minutes.

He stood bareheaded and panting, listening with every fibre of his being in the aching silence of the jessie thorn, his eyes were wild, and he hated himself with bitter venom for letting himself be persuaded by Storm.

He had known how dangerous this man was, he was a killer, a coldly competent killer, and he had sent a girl, a young and tender girl, to bait him.

Then Storm screamed, close by in the jessie, and with a violent lift of savage relief, Mark began to run again.

At the last moment Hobday heard him coming, and he dropped Storm's slim abused body and turned with unbelievable speed, dropping into the crouch of a heavyweight prize fighter, solid and low behind lifted arms and hunched shoulders, thick and rubbery with muscle.

Mark swung the weapon he had made the night before, a long sausage of rawhide, the seams double sewn, and then filled with lead buckshot. It weighed two pounds, and it made a sound through the air like the wings of a wild duck and he swung full-armed, the blow given power and weight by his terrible anger and hatred.

Hobday threw up his right arm to catch the blow. The bones of his forearm broke cleanly, with a sharp crackle, but still the force of the blow was not fully expended and the leaded bag flew on, directly into Hobday's face.

Had he not caught the full weight of it on his arm, the blow would have killed him. As it was, his face seemed to collapse and his head snapped backwards to the full stretch of his neck.

Hobday crashed backwards into the wall of jessie and the curved, red-tipped thorns caught in his clothing and flesh and held him there, sprawling like a boneless doll, arms outspread, legs dangling, his face hanging forward on his chest and the thick dark droplets of blood beginning to fall on to his shirt and roll softly downwards across his belly, leaving wet crimson lines down the khaki drill.

\* \* \*

The rain began as they carried Hobday up the track to where the two vehicles were kept under the lee of the cliffs of Chaka's Gate, on the south bank of the Bubezi. It came with the first splattering of fat warm drops, that stung exposed skin with their weight and momentum. It fell heavily and still more heavily, turning the surface of the track to a glaze like melting chocolate, so they slipped under their burden.

Hobday was chained at his ankles with the manacles that Mark used for holding arrested poachers. His good arm was cuffed to the leather belt at his waist, the other arm was crudely splinted and strapped down to the same belt.

Mark had tried to force him to walk, but either he was shamming or he was really too weak. His face was grotesquely distorted, the nose was swollen and pushed to one side, both eyes almost closed and leaden blue with bruises, his lips also were swollen and thickly scabbed with black dried blood where they had been mashed against his teeth, and through the mangled flesh were the dark gaps where five of the big square teeth had been torn out or snapped off level with the gum by the murderous force of Mark's blow.

Pungushe and Mark carried him between them, laboriously up the steep path in the teeming, stinging rain, and behind them trailed Storm with baby John on her hip, her hair melting in long black shiny smears down her face in the rain. She was shivering violently, in sudden uncontrollable spasms, either from the cold or from lingering shock. The child on her hip squalled petulantly, and she covered him with a fold of oilskin and tried to hush him distractedly.

They reached the two vehicles under the crude thatched

shelter Pungushe had built to protect them from the elements. They put Hobday into the side-car of the Ariel, and Mark buttoned the canvas screen over him to protect him from the rain and to hold him secure. He lay like a corpse.

Then Mark crossed to where Storm sat, shivering, and sodden and miserable, behind the wheel of the battered old Cadillac.

"I'm sending Pungushe with you," he said, as he took her in his arms and held her briefly. She did not have the strength or will to argue, and she leaned heavily against Mark's chest for comfort.

"Go to the cottage—and stay there," he instructed. "Don't move out of it until I come for you."

"Yes, Mark," she whispered, and shuddered again.

"Are you strong enough to drive?" he asked with sudden gentleness, and she roused herself and nodded gamely.

"I love you," he said. "More than anything or anybody in this world."

Mark led on the motorcycle over the slippery, muddy track, and it was almost dark when they reached the main road, itself hardly better than a track with deeply churned double ruts in the glutinous mud, and all the time the rain fell.

At the crossroads, Mark pulled the motorcycle off the road, and hurried back to talk to Storm through the open window of the Cadillac.

"It's six hours from here to Umhlanga Rocks in this mud, don't try and push it," he told her, and reached through the window. They embraced awkwardly but fiercely, and then she rolled up the window and the Cadillac pulled away, the rear end sliding and skidding in the mud.

Mark watched it over a rise in the land, and when the rear lights winked out over the ridge, he went back to the motorcycle and kicked the engine to life.

In the sidecar the man stirred, and his voice was mushy and distorted through the mangled lips.

"I'm going to kill you for this," he said.

"Like you killed my grandfather?" Mark asked softly, and wheeled the cycle into the road. He took the fork to Ladyburg, thirty miles away through the darkness and the mud and the rain, and his hatred and anger warmed him all the way like a bonfire in his belly, and he marvelled at his own restraint in resisting the temptation to kill Hobday with the bludgeon when he had the chance.

The man who had tortured and murdered the old man, and who had abused and desecrated Storm was in his power—and still the temptation to avenge himself was fierce. Mark pushed it aside and drove on grimly into the night.

The motorcycle slipped and slid from one verge of the road to the other as he took it up the steep ascent of the Ladyburg escarpment, and below him the lights of the town were blanketed by the falling white fog of rain.

Mark was uncertain as to whether or not the General was in residence at Lion Kop, but as he gunned the machine into the walled kitchen yard he saw lights in the windows, and a clamourous pack of the General's hunting dogs rushed out into the night followed by three Zulu servants with lanterns. Mark shouted at them.

"Is the Nkosi here?"

Their answers were superfluous, for as Mark dismounted, he looked up and saw the bulky familiar beloved shape step into the lighted window of the study, head held low on broad shoulders, as Sean Courtney peered down at him.

Mark ran into the house, stripping off his streaming oilskins, and he burst into the General's study.

"My boy." Sean Courtney hurried to meet him across the huge room. "What is it?" Mark's whole being was charged with a fierce and triumphant purpose.

"I have the man who killed my grandfather," he exulted, and halfway across the study Sean stopped dead and stared at him.

"Is it—" he stopped, and the dread was plain on his face, "is it Dirk Courtney, is it my son?"

The servants carried Hobday's heavy inert body into the study and laid him on the buttoned leather sofa in front of the fire.

"Who put those chains on him?" growled Sean, studying the man, and then without waiting for a reply, "Take them off him. My God, what happened to his face?"

Ruth Courtney came then, awakened by the uproar and excitement, dressed in a long dressing-gown with her night cap still knotted under her chin.

"Good Lord," she stared at Hobday. "His arm is broken, and perhaps his jaw also."

"How did it happen?" Sean demanded.

"I hit him," Mark explained, and Sean was silent for a long moment staring at him, before he spoke again.

"I think you had better tell me the whole story," he said. "From the beginning."

While Ruth Courtney worked quietly over Hobday's broken face, Mark began his explanation to the General.

"His name is Hobday, he works for Dirk Courtney—has done so for years. One of his right-hand men."

"Of course," Sean nodded. "I should have recognized him. It was the swollen face. I've seen him before."

Quietly, quickly, Mark told everything he knew about the man, starting from his first meeting with Hobday at the deserted homestead on Andersland.

"He told you he was working for Dirk Courtney then?" Sean demanded.

"For Ladyburg Sugar," Mark qualified, and Sean nodded his white beard on to his chest.

"Go on."

Mark repeated Pungushe's story of the old man's death, how the three men had come with him to the valley, and how "the silent one" had shot him and waited for him to die, and how they had buried him in an unmarked grave.

However, Sean shook his head, frowning, and Hobday on the couch stirred and tried to sit up. His swollen, distorted jaw worked and the words were blurred.

"It's a bloody nigger lie," he said. "First time I've ever been to Chaka's Gate was three days ago."

Sean Courtney's worry showed clearly on his gaunt features as he turned back to Mark.

"You say you hit this man, that you are responsible for his injuries. How did it happen?"

"When he came to the valley, Pungushe recognized him as the man who killed John Anders. I lured him out of his camp, and Pungushe and I captured him and brought him here."

"After half killing him?" Sean asked, heavily, and did not wait for Mark's reply. "My boy, I think you've put yourself into a very serious position. I cannot see a shred of evidence to support all this, evidence that would convict a man in a court of law—while on the other hand you have assaulted somebody, grievous bodily harm and abduction at the least—"

"Oh, I do have proof," Mark cut in quickly.

"What is it?" Sean asked gruffly.

The man on the couch turned his battered face to Sean, and his voice rose confidently.

"He's a bloody liar. It's all lies—"

"Quiet!" Sean waved him to silence, and looked at Mark again. "Proof?" he asked.

"My proof will be in the fact that Dirk Courtney kills this man, or has him killed, the moment we turn him free."

They all stared at Mark in stunned silence, and Mark went on seriously.

"We all know how Dirk Courtney works. He destroys anything that stands in his way, or that is a danger to him."

Hobday was watching him, and for once the eyes were no longer veiled and cold. His mangled lips quivered and gaped slightly, showing the black gaps where the teeth were missing from his jaw.

"It isn't necessary for this man to confess anything to us. The fact that he has been here, in this house, with the General and myself, in the camp of Dirk Courtney's enemies, the fact that his face bears the marks of heavy persuasion—

that will be enough for Dirk Courtney. Then one phone call is all it would take. Something like this." Mark paused, then went on. " 'Hobday was with us, he is ready to make a sworn statement—about the killing of John Anders.' Then we take Hobday down to the village and leave him there. Dirk Courtney kills him, but this time we are ready. For once we can trace the murder directly to him."

"God damn you," snarled Hobday, struggling into a sitting position. "It's a lie. I haven't confessed anything."

"You can tell that to Dirk Courtney. He might believe you," Mark told him quietly. "On the other hand, if you turned king's evidence and did confess, you'd have the protection of the General and the law, all the force of the law—and we would not turn you loose."

Hobday looked around him wildly, as though some avenue of escape might open miraculously for him, but Mark went on remorselessly.

"You know Dirk Courtney better than any of us, don't you, Hobday? You know how his mind works. Do you think he will take the chance that you didn't confess? Just how useful are you going to be to him in the future? Can you trust his loyalty, now that the shadow of doubt is on you? You know what he is going to do, don't you? If you think about it, you'll realize that your only chance of survival will be to have Dirk Courtney locked up safely, or dancing at the end of a rope."

Hobday glared at him. "You bastard," he hissed through his broken lips, and it was as though a cork had been drawn; a steady stream of obscenity poured from him, vicious filth, the ugly meaningless words repeated over and over again, while his naked eyes glittered with helpless hatred.

Mark stood up and cranked the handset of the telephone on Sean's desk.

"Exchange," he said into the mouthpiece. "Please connect me with the residence of Mister Dirk Courtney."

"No!" choked Hobday. "Don't do that!" and now terror

had replaced hatred, and his face seemed to collapse around the ruined nose and mouth.

Mark made no effort to obey, and clearly everybody in the room heard the click of a connection being made, and then the squawk of a voice distorted by the wires and distance.

"This is the residence of the Honourable Deputy Minister for lands, Mr. Dirk Courtney—"

Hobday lumbered off the couch, and staggered to the desk, he snatched the earpiece from Mark's hand and slammed it back on to its bracket of the telephone.

"No," he panted, with pain and fear. "Please don't do that."

He hung on to the corner of the desk, hunched up with the pain, clutching his broken arm to his chest, his mashed features working convulsively. They waited quietly, Mark and Ruth and Sean, waiting for him to reach his decision.

Hobday turned and staggered heavily back to the sofa. He collapsed upon it with his head hanging forward, almost touching his knees, and his breathing hissed and sobbed in the silence.

"All right," he whispered hoarsely. "What do you want to know?"

General Sean Courtney shook himself as though awaking from a nightmare, but his voice was decisive and brisk.

"Mark, take the Rolls. Go down into town and get me a lawyer. I want this statement drawn up in proper form— I'm still a Justice of the Peace and Commissioner of Oaths. I will witness the document."

*       *       *

Mark parked the Rolls in Peter Botes' gravel driveway of the big new house on the outskirts of town.

The house was dark and silent, but to Mark's heavy knocking on the carved teak front door, a dog began to bark in the house somewhere, and at last a light bloomed in an upstairs window and the sash slid up with a squeal.

"Who is it? What do you want?" Peter's voice was querulous and fuddled with sleep.

"It's Mark," he shouted up at the window. "You've got to come with me, now!"

"My God, Mark, it's after eleven o'clock. Can't it wait until morning?"

"General Courtney wants you, now."

The name had its effect. There was a mumble of voices within the bedroom, Marion's sister protesting sleepily, and then Peter called down again.

"All right, give me a minute to dress, Mark."

As he waited in the driver's seat of the Rolls with the rain slashing down on the roof, and rippling in wavering lines down across the windshield, Mark pondered briefly why he had chosen Peter Botes. It was not only that he knew exactly where to find him so late at night. He realized that he wanted Peter to be here when they tore down his idol, he wanted to rub his nose in it when they proved Dirk Courtney a thief and a murderer. He wanted that satisfaction, and he smiled bleakly without humour in the darkened Rolls.

"I deserve at least that," he whispered to himself, and the front door of the house opened. Peter hurried out, ducking his head against the slanting rain.

"What is it?" he demanded, through the window of the Rolls. "It had better be important—getting me out at this time of night."

"It's important enough," Mark told him, and started the engine. "Get in!"

"I'll follow you in my Packard," Peter told him and ran to the garage.

\*     \*     \*

Peter Botes sat at General Courtney's big desk. Hurriedly dressed, he was without a necktie and his small prosperous paunch bulged the white shirt, pulling it free of his trousers' waistband. His sandy hair was thinning and ruffled, so that pink scalp showed through as he bowed over the fool-scap sheet of paper.

He wrote swiftly, a neat regular script, his features betraying each new shock at the words he was transcribing, his cheeks pale and his mouth set and thin.

Every few minutes he would pause incredulously and stare at Hobday across the room, breathing heavily at some new and terrible admission.

"Have you got that?" the General demanded, and Peter nodded jerkily and began to write again.

The others listened intently. The General slumped in his chair by the fire. His eyes were closed, as though he slept, but the questions he rapped out every few minutes were bright and penetrating as a rapier blade.

Mark stood behind his chair, quiet and intent, his face expressionless, although his anger and his hatred cramped in his guts.

Hobday sat forward on the sofa and his voice was a muffled drone in his thick north-country accent, muted in contrast to the terrible words he spoke.

It was not only the killing of John Anders. There was more, much more. Forgery of State documents, bribery of high officials, direct abuse of public office, and Mark started and leaned forward with shock as Hobday recounted how he had tried on two occasions, following Dirk Courtney's orders, to kill him.

Mark had not realized nor recognized him, but now Hobday's stocky shape tied in his memory with the shadowy faceless hunter in the night on the escarpment—and with the other figure seen through the rain and the fever mists. Hobday did not look up as he told it, and Mark had no questions to ask. It was as though once Hobday had started, he must purge himself of all this filth, as though he were now deriving some perverse satisfaction from the horror his words struck into his audience.

They listened, appalled by the magnitude of it all. Every few minutes, Ruth exclaimed involuntarily, and Sean would open his eyes briefly to stare at her, before closing them again and covering them with one hand.

At last Hobday came to the murder of John Anders, and each detail was exactly as Pungushe had described it. Mark felt sickened and wretched as he listened, but he asked only one question.

"Why did you let him die so slowly—why didn't you finish him?"

"It had to look like an accident." Hobday did not look up. "One bullet only. A man does not shoot himself twice by accident. I had to let him die in his own time."

There was no breadth nor horizon to Mark's anger, and this time Ruth Courtney caught her breath with a sound like a sob. Again Sean Courtney opened his eyes. "Are you all right, my dear?"

She nodded silently, and Sean turned back to Hobday. "Go on," he said.

At the end, Peter Botes read the statement back, his voice quivering and fading at the more horrendous passages, so that Sean had to gruff at him fiercely.

"Speak up, man." He had made two fair copies, and Hobday signed each page with an illiterate scrawl, and then each of them signed below him, and Sean pressed his wax seal of office on to the final page of each copy.

"All right," he said, as he carried the top document to the iron safe built into the wall behind his desk. "I want you to keep and file the other copy," he said to Peter. "Thank you for your help, Mr. Botes." He locked the safe and turned back into the room. "Mark, will you telephone Doctor Acheson now, please? We've got to take care of our witness, I suppose. Though, for my money, I'd just as soon see him suffer."

\* \* \*

When Doctor Acheson arrived at Lion Kop, it was almost two in the morning, and Ruth Courtney took him up to the guest room where Hobday lay.

Neither Sean Courtney nor Mark went up; they stayed in the study, sitting quietly together across the fire which a servant had built. Against the windows, the wind bumped and the rain spattered. Sean was drinking whisky, and Mark had filled his glass twice for him in the last hour. He was slumped down in his favourite chair now, tired and old and bowed with grief, holding the glass with both hands.

"If I had the courage, I would take the rifle to him myself—like a rabid dog. But he is still my son, no matter how often I deny it, he is still of my blood, of my loins."

Mark was silent, and Ruth came into the room.

"Doctor Acheson is setting that man's arm," she said. "He will be another hour, but I think you should come up to bed now, my dear." She crossed to Sean's chair and laid a gentle hand on his shoulder. "We have all had more than enough for one day."

The telephone rang on the desk, a tinny irritant sound that startled them all. They stared at it for a full five seconds, until it rang again demandingly and Ruth crossed to it and lifted the earpiece.

"Mrs. Ruth Courtney," she said softly, almost fearfully.

"Mrs. Courtney, are you the mother of Mrs. Storm Hunt?"

"Yes, this is correct."

"I am afraid we have very bad news. This is the Superintendent of Addington Hospital in Durban. Your daughter has been involved in a motor accident. The rain and the mud, I am afraid. Her son, your grandchild, has been killed outright. Thankfully he suffered no pain, but your daughter is in a critical condition. Can you come to her, as soon as you possibly can? We don't know if she will last the night, I'm afraid."

The telephone dropped from Ruth's hand, and she swayed on her feet, the colour flying from her face, leaving it frosted with icy white.

"Oh God!" she whispered, and she started to fall, her legs collapsed and she crumpled forward. Mark caught her before she hit the floor and lowered her on to the sofa.

Sean crossed to the dangling earpiece and lifted it. "This is General Courtney," he barked angrily. "What is it?"

\*     \*     \*

Mark took the big Rolls down the long slanting right hand turn towards the bridge very fast. The woman he loved, the mother of his dead child, was dying—and Mark's heart was breaking. The road was deep with chocolate mud, and other vehicles had rutted it deeply, churning the mud to a thick ugly porridge. The Rolls flared and kicked in the ruts, but Mark fought the wheel grimly.

The bridge over the Baboon Stroom was five hundred yards ahead of them, still invisible in the endless driving rain. The headlights faded fifty feet ahead, overwhelmed by the flights of white raindrops, thick as javelins.

In the rear seat, Ruth Courtney sat quietly, staring ahead with eyes that did not see. The collar of her fur coat was pulled up around her ears, so she looked small and frail as a child.

General Sean Courtney sat beside Mark, and he was talking quietly, as though to himself.

"I've left it too late. I've been a stubborn old fool. I wanted too much from her—I wanted her to be better than human, and I was too harsh on her when she did not meet the standards I set for her. I should have gone to her long ago, and now perhaps it's too late."

"It's not too late," Mark denied. "She will live, she must live."

"It's too late for my grandson," whispered Sean. "I never saw him—and only now I realize how much I wanted to—"

At the mention of baby John, Mark felt the sickening jolt of despair in his stomach again and he wanted to shout, "He was my son. My first born!" But beside him, Sean was talking again.

"I've been a spiteful and unforgiving old man. God have mercy on me, but I even cut my own daughter out of my will. I disowned her, and now I hate myself for that. If only we can reach her, if only I can talk to her once more. Please, God, grant me that."

Ahead of them the steel guard railings of the bridge loomed out of the torrential darkness, and lightning bounced off the belly of the clouds. For an instant Mark saw the spidery steel tracery of the railway bridge spanning the chasm two hundred yards downstream. Under it, the rocky sides of the gorge dropped almost sheer a hundred and fifty feet to the swollen racing brown flood waters of the Baboon Stroom.

Mark touched the brakes, and then double-declutched the gears, bringing the Rolls under tighter control as he lined up for the entrance to the road bridge.

Suddenly, dazzling light flared from the darkness on the right hand side of the road, and Mark threw up one hand to protect his eyes.

Out of the darkness rushed a great dark shape, with two blazing headlights glaring like malevolent eyes as it came.

With sudden clarity of mind, Mark realized that the Rolls was trapped helplessly on the approach ramp to the bridge, and that on his left hand, only a frail railing of iron pipes screened them from the drop and that the monstrous vehicle racing down from the right would come into a collision which would hurl the Rolls through the railing as though it were a child's toy.

"Hold on!" he screamed, and swung the wheel to meet the roaring towering monster of steel, and the blinding white light cut into his eyes.

\*     \*     \*

Peter Botes pulled off the road into the pine trees and switched off the engine of the Packard. In the silence he could hear the pine branches thrashing restlessly on the wind, and the dislodged rain-drops tapped on the roof.

Peter lit a cigarette and the match danced in his cupped hands. He inhaled deeply, waiting for the calming effect of the tobacco smoke, and he stared ahead up the straight roadway that led to Great Longwood, the homestead of Dirk Courtney.

He sensed that the decision he must make now was the most vital of his entire life. Whichever way he decided, his life was already changed for ever.

When Dirk Courtney fell, he would bring down all those close to him, even the innocent, as he was innocent. The scandal and the guilt would sully him, and he had worked so hard for it. The prestige, the blooming career and all the sweets that he was just now starting to enjoy. All of it would be gone, and he would have to begin again, perhaps in another town, another land, to begin again right at the very bottom. The thought appalled him, he had become used to being a man of substance and importance. He did not know if he could face a new beginning.

On the other hand, if Dirk Courtney did not come down, if he were saved from death and disaster—just how grateful would he be to the man who worked his salvation? He knew the extent of Dirk Courtney's present fortune and power, and it was conceivable that some of that, perhaps a large slice of that might come to him, to Peter Botes, the man who had saved Dirk Courtney, and yet still retained the instrument of his destruction.

It was one of those moments of destiny, Peter realized, that come only occasionally to a chosen few. On one hand dishonour and obscurity—on the other, power and riches, tens of thousands, perhaps even millions.

He started the engine of the Packard and the rear wheels spun in the slimy mud, and then he swerved back on to the driveway, and put the big machine to the hill.

Dirk Courtney sat on the corner of his desk, one foot swinging idly. He wore a dressing-gown of patterned silk, and the lustrous material caught the lamplight as he moved. There was a white silk scarf at his throat, and his eyes were clear and alert in the handsome tanned face, as though he had not just risen from deep sleep.

He spun the duelling pistol on his forefinger as he listened intently.

Peter Botes sat nervously on the edge of the chair, and though there was a fire in the grate that Dirk had poked and fed to a fierce blaze, still he shivered every few moments and rubbed his hands together. The cold was in his soul, he realized, and his voice rose a little as he gabbled on.

Dirk Courtney did not speak, made no comment nor exclamation, asked no question until he was done. He spun the pistol, two turns and the butt snapped into the palm of his hand. Two turns, and snap.

When Peter Botes finished, Dirk cocked the hammer of the pistol and the click of the mechanism was unreasonably loud in the silent room.

"Hobday, my father, his wife, young Anders—and yourself. The only ones that know."

"And the Zulu."

"And the Zulu," Dirk agreed, and dry-fired the pistol. The hammer cracked against the pan.

"How many copies of the statement?"

"One," lied Peter. "In the iron safe of the General's study."

Dirk nodded and re-cocked the pistol. "All right. If there is another copy, you have it," he said. "But we don't lie to each other, do we, Peter?"

It was the first time he had used his given name, there was a familiarity and a threat in it, and Peter could only nod with a dryness in his throat.

Again Dirk dry-fired the pistol, and smiled. It was that warm and charming smile, that frank and friendly smile that Peter knew so well.

"We love each other too much for that, don't we?" He kept smiling. "That's why you came to tell me this, isn't it? Because we love each other?"

Peter said nothing, and Dirk went on, still smiling, "And of course you are going to be a rich man, Peter—if you do as I ask. A very rich man. You will do as I ask, won't you, Peter?"

And Peter nodded again. "Yes, of course," he blurted.

"I want you to make a phone call," said Dirk. "If you speak through a handkerchief, it will sound as though it's long distance, and it will muffle your voice. Nobody will recognize it. Will you do that?"

"Of course," Peter nodded.

"You will phone my father's house, speak either to him or his wife. I want you to pretend that you are the Superintendent of Addington Hospital, and here is what you will tell them—"

\* \* \*

Dirk Courtney sat in the darkened cab of the truck, and listened to the rain as he reviewed his plans and preparations carefully.

He did not like having to move in a hurry, without time for careful planning. It was too easy to overlook some vital detail.

He did not like having to do this type of work himself. It was best to send another. He did not take personal risks, not any more, not unless there was no other way.

Regrets and misgivings were vain and wasted the moments which still remained before action. He turned all his attention back to his planning.

They would use the Rolls, and there would be three of them, the General and his Jewish whore, and that arrogant scheming puppy Anders.

Dirk had picked the spot with care, and the farmyard truck was loaded with fifty sacks of horse-feed. Three tons of dead weight. It would give it irresistible momentum.

Afterwards he must do two things, firstly he must make sure of them. He had a length of lead piping wrapped in hessian packing. It would crack a skull without breaking skin. Then he must take the General's keys. The key of the safe was on the bunch, and it was on his watch chain. The thought of plundering his father's dead body did not cause

him even a tremor. His only concern was that the keys
were retrievable, that there was no fire and that the Rolls
was not submerged in the roaring torrent of the Baboon
Stroom.

If that did happen, he must rely then on the General not
having changed his habits of twenty years before. The spare
key had been kept in the wine cellar then, on the rack
above the champagne bottles. Dirk had discovered it there
when he had used the cellar in a boyhood game, and he
had taken the key twice for his own ends, and returned it
secretly. The General was an old dog, a creature of habit.
It would still be there. Dirk was certain.

All right, then, the safe. Two keys. If neither was avail-
able, then it was an old safe, but he did not want to use
force on it. He must hope for the keys. Anyway, he was
content that he could open it one way or another.

The statement was his, to be carefully burned, and that
left Hobday. Probably in one of the guest rooms, sedated,
helpless. The lead pipe again, and then an overturned par-
affin lamp. It was a big house of old dry wooden beams
and thick thatch. It would burn as a pyre, with Hobday
lying in it like a Viking chieftain.

That left only Peter Botes, Dirk glanced sideways at him.
The situation was containable, it was no worse than fifty
others he had survived. It needed only swift, direct action.
He spoke encouragingly to Peter.

"Don't worry," he said. "After tonight, a new life awaits
you. I'm going to take you with me along the paths of
wealth and power, Peter. You'll never regret this night, I
swear it to you."

He squeezed Peter's upper arm, a comradely gesture in
the darkness. Of course, he had a copy of the statement,
Dirk thought, but afterwards there would be time—plenty
of time to find it and to be rid of the pompous little prig. In
a year or so, when the excitement had died down, another
little accident, and it would all be over.

"Have you got the pistol?" he asked, and Peter gulped

nervously, clutching the bulky military model Smith Wesson with both hands between his knees.

"You are not to use it," Dirk warned again. "Except as the very last resort. We don't want bullet holes to explain. You do understand?"

"Yes, I understand."

"You are insurance, that's all. Final insurance." And out in the darkness, through the slanting arrors of rain a light glowed and faded and grew again higher up the slope.

"Here they come," said Dirk, and started the engine of the truck.

\*   \*   \*

Mark spun the wheel hard right, and thrust the accelerator pedal flat against the floorboards, trying to ride off the collison and beat the great roaring vehicle to the threshold of the bridge.

Behind him Ruth Courtney screamed shrilly, but Mark thought he had made it, he thought for an instant that the sudden acceleration had forged the Rolls ahead, but the truck slewed hard, swinging viciously, and he felt the crack of impact in every bone of his body.

It struck at the level of the rear wheels of the Rolls, and the big heavy car snapped sideways, tearing his hands from the steering-wheel and hurling Mark against the door. He felt bones break in his chest like dry twigs, and then the world turned end over end as the Rolls cartwheeled. A shower of bright white sparks flamed like the tail of a meteor in the darkness as steel brushed murderously against steel. There was another jerk as the Rolls crashed through the guardrail of the bridge and then they were dropping free, plunging silently into black space.

In the rear seat, Ruth Courtney was still screaming, and the Rolls struck, a glancing shuddering blow, bounding off the rock wall of the gorge, and leaping out into space once more.

Mark pressed against the side door, held there by the accelerating dropping force of the plunging Rolls, but at the next impact the door burst open, and Mark was hurled like a stone from a slingshot, out into resounding swirling darkness.

He saw the burning headlights of the Rolls, spinning in a great vortex of blinding white, below him, and the gorge rang with the iron echoes of steel on rock, and the crazy bellowing roar of the Rolls-Royce engine jammed at full power.

He seemed to fall for ever, through darkness, and then suddenly he struck with a force that drove the air from his lungs. The hard, unyielding impact convinced him for a moment that his body was crushed to boneless pulp on the rocky floor of the gorge, but then the cold, tumultuous torrent of racing water overwhelmed him. He had been thrown far enough to fall into the river itself.

Clinging to his last shreds of consciousness, he fought for breath, fought to keep his head above the surface, as the torrent swept him away. Glistening black boulders leapt like predators out of the dark, clawing at his legs, pummelling his injured chest, barging into him with numbing bruising power in the flood, and icy water gushed down his straining throat—burning his lungs, and making him choke and retch for each breath.

He slid down a racing spill of white rapids, feeling skin stripped from his hip and shoulder at the contact of harsh rock and then, at the bottom, he struck again, jammed solid between two monumental rocks. In the darkness, they stood over him like gravestones.

He was held in their jaws, and the water tore furiously at him, as though denied of its prey, trying to pluck him away.

There was light, just enough to make out shapes and distances, and Mark marvelled at that with a brain jellied by pounding and starved of oxygen. Then he looked up, and through streaming eyes saw that the truck was parked on the threshold of the bridge high above the gorge, its headlights struck the ironwork and the light was broken up and diffused by the rain. It cast a vague uncertain glow into the gorge.

Added to this was a closer, more powerful light source. The smashed carapace of the Rolls-Royce lay at the foot of the cliff, half in the water, half upon the rocky ledge. It lay on its back, with all four wheels spiralling idly, but both headlights still burned fiercely, striking the uneven rock walls, providing a dramatic stage lighting.

Mark looked around him, and saw that the current had swept him in under the cliff, and that a ledge of glistening black rock extended out over his head. He reached up with his right hand, and then cried out as his fingers touched the ledge, and bright agony flared in his wrist.

Something was broken there, he realized, as he clung desperately to the slippery boulders, and tried to force the fingers of his right hand to open or close.

The torrent was too strong to resist much longer, and he felt himself starting to slide, dragging over the boulders, on the point of being swept away once more. He knew that less than a hundred yards downstream, the first waterfall plunged, frothing and thundering, down the sheer side of the escarpment.

He released his grip with the left hand, and threw himself upwards with all his strength. His fingers caught on the sharp lip of the ledge above his head, and his body swung like a pendulum, the hungry waters slashing at his knees, testing the strength of his grip, trying to drag him away, trying to break the hooked fingers, tearing the finger-nails loose so that droplets of blood squeezed out from under them.

Slowly, achingly, Mark bent the arm at the elbow, lifting his knees, drawing his feet clear of the water and its murderous drag.

He hung another moment, gathering what was left of his strength and resolve, and then, with one last convulsive heave, he threw his right arm upwards and hooked his elbow over the ledge, and followed it immediately with his left elbow.

Another moment of rest, and then he wriggled painfully out on the ledge and lay face down. He thought he was blind now, or that the lights had been doused, but the darkness was in his head only.

Slowly the darkness cleared, and he lifted his head. The thunder of the river drowned out all other sound, he could not hear the scrabble of loose stone and the slide of booted feet as Dirk Courtney came down the almost vertical pathway below the bridge. It did not surprise Mark that it was him—it seemed only natural that Dirk Courtney should be here, at the scene of disaster. He was dressed in hunting breeches and calf-length boots, a thick navy pea jacket and a woollen cap pulled low over his face.

He slid down the last ten feet of the cliff, keeping his balance, light as a dancer on his feet, and he paused on the ledge beside the shattered Rolls. Carefully he looked about him, flashing a lantern into the shadows and crevices.

Mark flattened himself down on the rock, but he was beyond the range of the lantern beam.

Dirk turned the beam on to the Rolls, and Mark groaned with the shock of it.

General Sean Courtney had been thrown halfway through the windscreen, and then the full weight of the machine had rolled on to his upper torso. His head was almost severed, and the thick white beard was sodden with bright blood, that shone like rubies in the lantern light.

Dirk Courtney stooped over him, and felt for the carotid pulse in the throat. Despite the fearful mutilation, he must have detected some flutter of stubborn life there. Dirk rolled the head sideways, and the eyes were open and startled. Dirk lifted the short thick club he carried in his right hand. It was wrapped in coarse brown hessian, but its weight and heft were obvious, by the way he handled it.

Mark tried to cry out, but his hoarse croak was lost in the roar of waters. Dirk struck his father across the temple, above the right ear, where the wet grey curls were plastered against the skull, and Mark seemed to feel the thud of the blow in his own soul.

Then with one exploring forefinger, Dirk pressed the temple and felt the give of mortal damage, the grating of the rough edges of shattered bone shard deep in his father's head.

Dirk's features were expressionless, cold and remote, but then he did something which seemed to Mark more dreadful, more shocking than the killing blow. With a tender touch of his finger-tips, he closed the eyelids over Sean Courtney's dead staring eyes. Then he went down on one knee and kissed his father's bloodied lips lightly, without a change of expression. It was the act of an unhinged mind. It was only at that moment that Mark realized that Dirk Courtney was insane.

Almost immediately, Dirk's manner changed and his hands lost the gentle touch, becoming once again business-like and precise. He rolled the body, unbuttoned the camel-hair overcoat and searched swiftly through Sean's clothing. Then he drew out a gold watch chain with the keys and gold hunter attached.

He examined the keys briefly and then pushed them into his pocket. He stood and went to the rear door of the Rolls and struggled with the handle. The door burst open at last, and Ruth Courtney's body spilled out sideways and lay at his feet. He took a handful of her thick dark hair and drew her head back. Again he swung the short thick club against her temple, and again he felt the skull like a doctor making his diagnosis, prodding to feel the soft spot of crushed bone.

Satisfied, he lifted Ruth Courtney's limp, childlike body in his arms and carried her to the edge of the water. He dropped her over the side, and she was gone instantly, dashed away on the dark current, down to where the plunging waterfalls would tumble her body into the Lady-burg valley, and the cruel rocks would leave no doubt in a coroner's mind as to how she had died.

Helpless with his injuries and exhaustion, his body battered and strained beyond its natural limits, Mark could not move, could hardly breathe as he watched Dirk Courtney stoop and grasp his father's ankles. He dragged the General's heavy body to the edge of the torrent, straining backwards, against the dead weight.

Mark dropped his face into his hands and found that he was weeping, great racking dry sobs that probed the injuries deep in his chest.

When he looked up again, Sean Courtney's body was gone, and Dirk Courtney was coming towards where he lay, cautiously following the narrow ledge, searching the darkness with the lantern beam, sweeping the dark tumbling waters, examining each foot of the ledge, looking for him—looking for Mark, knowing he had been in the Rolls. The headlights of the truck had struck full into Mark's face in that fatal instant of collision. Dirk Courtney knew he was here—somewhere.

Mark rolled on to his side and tried to unfasten the buttons of his coat, but in his haste he had tried with the right hand, and he whimpered with the pain. With his left hand now, he ripped the buttons away and struggled out of the garment, its wet folds resisting each movement so that when he at last was free of it, Dirk Courtney was only fifty feet away, coming steadily, carefully along the ledge, the lantern in one hand, the short heavy club dangling in the other.

Lying on the edge of the river, Mark flipped the jacket sideways, trying to make it fall on to the rocks in the torrent below, but he had no time to see if he had succeeded. Dirk Courtney was too close.

Mark rolled in towards the foot of the cliff, stifling the cry of pain as his damaged ribs and broken wrist came in rude contact with the rock.

In the lee of the cliff there was a dark shallow chimney, screened from the light of the headlights and lantern. Mark came to his feet. Dirk Courtney was out of sight beyond the angle of the cliff, but the beam of his lantern jumped and swept and swung, bobbing with each pace as he came on.

Mark turned his face to the cliff, gathered himself, and found that some of his dissipated strength was returning, and his anger was still alive, like a small warm flame in his chest. He did not know if it was enough strength, or anger, to carry him through, but he began to climb, slowly, clumsily, like a maimed insect he clung to the cold wet rock and dragged himself upwards.

He was twenty feet up when Dirk Courtney stopped on the ledge directly below him. Mark froze into stillness, the last defence of the helpless animal, but he knew that the instant Dirk lifted the beam, he was discovered. He waited for it, with the numbed resignation of the beast waiting in the abattoir chute.

Dirk made another careful search, swinging the lantern in a full slow traverse of both sides of the river, and he was on the point of lifting the beam to play it on to the cliff where Mark hung, when something caught his attention.

Mark's jacket was caught on one of the boulders, and Dirk went down on one knee to try and reach it with one out-stretched arm.

It was the respite that Mark needed. Dirk's full attention was on the stranded jacket and the rush and roar of water covered the noise of Mark's scrabbling feet and hands on the cliff.

He did not look down again until he had dragged himself fifty feet higher, and then he saw that the jacket had succeeded as a decoy. Dirk Courtney was a hundred feet downstream, standing on the lip of the first steep waterfall, on the very edge of the escarpment. He had the sodden jacket in his hands and he was peering over the fearsome drop. In the lantern light, the water was black and smooth as oil, as it streamed into the abyss, turning slowly to thick white spume as it fell.

Dirk Courtney threw the jacket out into black space and stood back from the drop. He settled down comfortably on his haunches, sheltered by the cliff from rain and wind, and quite calmly he selected and lit a cigar, like a workman taking a break after performing satisfactorily a difficult task.

That casual little act, the flare of a sulphur match, and the contented puff of blue tobacco smoke in the lantern light, probably saved Mark's life. It stoked his anger to the point when it could overcome his agony and bodily exhaustion. It provided him with the will to go on, and he began to climb again.

Sometimes during the climb, reality faded away from Mark. Once a sense of warmth and well-being began to suffuse his whole body, a wonderful feeling, floating as though on the very frontiers of sleep, but he caught himself before he fell, and deliberately punched his right hand against the rock face. He screamed with the pain of it, but with the pain came new resolve.

But resolve faded slowly in the cold and the pain, and fantasy grew again. He believed that he was one of King Chaka's chosen, following the old king up that terrible cliff to the summit of Chaka's Gate, and he found himself talking gibberish in broken Zulu, and in his head he heard the deep resonant voice of the old king calling him on, giving him encouragement, and he knew if he climbed faster he might catch a glimpse of the king's face. He lost his grip in his impatience, and slid away, gathering momentum down the incline, until he crashed into one of the stunted dwarf trees that grew from the cliff face. It broke his fall, but he screamed again at the pain of broken ribs.

He climbed on, and then he heard Storm's voice. It was so clear and close that he stopped, and turned his face up into the rain and darkness. She was there, floating above his head, so beautiful and pale and graceful.

"Come, Mark," she said, and her voice echoed and rang like a silver bell in his head. "Come, my darling."

He knew then that she was alive, that she was not dying in a cold hospital bed, that she was here, come to him in his pain and exhaustion.

"Storm," he cried, and threw himself upwards, falling forward, and lying face down in the short wet grass at the top of the cliff.

He just wanted to lie there, for ever. He was not even sure that he had reached the top, was not sure if this was not yet another fantasy, perhaps he was dead already and this was all there was to it.

Then slowly he was aware of the rain drops on his cheek, and the sound of the little tree frogs clinking in the rain, and the cold breath of the wind, and he realized with regret that he was still alive.

The pain began returning then. It started in his wrist first, and began to spread, and he did not think he had the strength left to ride it.

Then suddenly he had the image, clearly formed in his mind, of Dirk Courtney stooped over his father's body, with the club raised in his hand to strike—and Mark's anger came to save him again.

Mark pushed himself to his knees and looked about him. A hundred yards away, the truck was parked on the threshold of the iron bridge, and in its headlights, he could make out the shape of a man.

With one more huge, draining effort, Mark came to his feet, and stood swaying, gathering himself for his next lumbering step.

Peter Botes stood in the rain, holding the heavy pistol hanging in his right hand. The rain had soaked his fine sandy hair, and it ran down his cheeks and forehead, so he kept wiping it away with his left hand.

The rain had soaked through the shoulders of his overcoat also, and he shivered spasmodically, as much from fear as from cold.

He was caught up in the great swirl of events over which he had no control, an encircling web from which he could see no escape, even though his lawyer's mind twisted and turned.

"Accessory to murder—before and after the fact." He did not want to know what was going on down there at the foot of the cliff, and yet he felt the sick fascination and dread of it.

This was not what he had imagined when he had made the decision to go to Dirk Courtney. He had thought it would be a few words, and he could walk away, pretending it had not happened, crawling back into his wife's warm bed and pulling the blankets over his head.

He had not been prepared for this horror and violence, for a gun in his hand, and this ugly bloody business in the gorge.

"The penalty is death," he thought, and shivered again. He wanted to run, but there was no place to run now.

"Oh God, why did I do it?" he whispered aloud. "I wish, oh God, I wish—" the age-old cry of the weakling, but he did not finish the wish. There was a sound behind him and he began to turn, lifting the pistol and beginning to point it with both arms at full stretch in front of him.

A figure came towards him out of the darkness, and Peter opened his mouth to cry out.

The figure was an apparition of blood and mud, with a distorted pale face, and it came so swiftly that the cry never reached his lips.

Peter Botes was a man of words and ideas, a soft little man of desks and rich foods, and the man who came out of the darkness was a soldier.

Mark knelt over him in the mud, panting and holding his ribs, waiting for the pain of movement to recede, and for his starred vision to clear.

He looked down at the man under him. His face was pressed into the mud, and Mark took a handful of his hair and rolled the head on its narrow shoulders to prevent the man drowning; it was only then that Mark recognized him.

"Peter!" he whispered hoarsely, and felt his senses reel again, uncertain if this was another fantasy.

He touched the unconscious man's lips, and they were warm and soft as a girl's.

"Peter!" he repeated stupidly, and suddenly he knew it all. It did not have to be thought out a step at a time. He understood how Dirk Courtney had known where to set his ambush. He knew that Peter was the traitor, and he knew that the decoy had been Storm and baby John, he knew it was all a lie then. He knew that Storm and her child were safe and sleeping in the tiny bedroom above the beach— and the knowledge buoyed him.

He picked the Smith Wesson revolver out of the mud with his left hand and wiped it carefully on his shirt.

Dirk Courtney paused at the head of the pathway. He was only slightly breathless from the climb, but his boots were thick with mud and raindrops dewed his shoulders, glittering in the burning headlights of the truck.

The headlights dazzled him, and there was an area of unfathomable darkness behind them.

"Peter?" he called, and lifted one arm to shield his eyes. He saw the shadowy figure of the waiting man leaning against the cab of the truck, and he walked forward.

"It's done," he said. "You have nothing to worry about now. I have the key to the safe, it's just the cleaning up left to do."

He stopped abruptly, and peered again at the waiting figure. The man had not moved.

"Peter," his voice cracked. "Come on, man! Pull yourself together. There is still work to do."

And he started forward again, stepping out of the beam of the headlights.

"What time is it?" he asked. "It must be getting late."

"Yes." Mark's voice was thick and slurred. "For you, it's very late." And Dirk stopped again, staring at him. The silence seemed to last for all of eternity, but it was only the instant that it took Dirk to see the revolver and the pale mud-smeared face. He knew that the bullet would come now, and he sought to delay it, just long enough.

"Listen to me," said Dirk urgently. "Wait just one second."

He changed his grip on the lantern in his right hand, and his voice was compelling, the tone quick and persuasive, just enough to hold Mark's finger on the trigger.

"There is something you must know." Dirk made a dis-
arming gesture, swinging the lantern back, and then hurling it forward in a wide arc of his long powerful arm, and,
at the same instant, hurling forward.

The lantern struck Mark on the shoulder, a glancing
blow, just enough to deflect his gun hand as he fired.

But he heard the bullet strike, that muffled thumping
sound of soft lead expanding into living flesh, and he heard
the grunt of air driven forcibly from Dirk Courtney's lungs
by the strike.

Then the man's big hard body crashed into Mark, and as
they reeled sideways, supported by the chassis of the truck,
he felt one arm lock around his chest and hard fingers
close over his gun hand.

In that first moment of direct encounter, Mark knew instantly that Dirk Courtney's strength and weight were far
greater than his own. Even if he had been uninjured, it
would have been no contest, he was so out-matched that he
felt as though he had been caught up in the cogs of a powerful piece of machinery. Dirk Courtney's body seemed not
to be made of flesh and bone, but of brutal iron.

Mark's broken ribs moved in the vast encircling grip,
and he cried out as the sharp edges of splintered bone
lanced into his flesh. He felt his gun hand being forced
back, the muzzle of the pistol training up into his own face,
and Dirk Courtney swung him off his feet, both of them
spinning into a turn like a pair of waltzing dancers, so that
only the wildest effort and a lucky trick of balance allowed
Mark to come down on his feet again. But now he no
longer had the support of the truck chassis and the next
effort would throw him headlong into the mud.

He felt Dirk Courtney gather himself for the next effort, the hard athlete's muscles moving him into perfect
balance. Mark tried desperately to meet it, but it came with
a smooth surge of power as irresistible as a huge comber
rushing towards the beach. Then miraculously, at the moment when he was going, Mark felt the big body hit with a

tremor, heard the sobbing outrush of Dirk Courtney's breath, and almost instantly Mark's stomach was drenched with a copious rush of warm liquid as it poured from his adversary.

The strength melted out of Dirk Courtney's body, Mark could feel his balance go, the grip on his pistol hand relaxed slightly—and Mark realized that his bullet had done damage, and that that last effort had torn something open in Dirk's chest. His life blood was expelled from the wound in thick hissing jets by the powerful pump of his heart, and Mark found he was able, by a supreme effort, to reverse the direction of the pistol barrel, swinging it in a slow arc back, back until pointed into Dirk Courtney's face.

Mark did not believe that he had the strength left to pull the trigger. The weapon seemed to fire of its own accord, and the muzzle flash almost blinded him.

Dirk Courtney's head snapped back as though he had been hit in the mouth with the full swing of a baseball bat. He was hurled backwards, out of the beam of the headlights into the darkness, and Mark heard his body sliding and tumbling down the steep side of the gorge.

The pistol dropped from Mark's hand, and he fell, first on to his knees, and then slowly toppled forward on to his face in the mud.

\* \* \*

*This is the last Will and Testament of SEAN COURTNEY, married out of community of property to RUTH COURTNEY, (formerly FRIEDMAN, born COHEN), and presently residing at Lion Kop Ranch in the district of Ladyburg.*

*...................... I give and bequeath my entire estate and effects, movable or immovable, whether in possession, reversion, expectancy or contingency, whereever situate and of whatever description nothing excepted, to my wife the said RUTH COURTNEY.*

At first light the next morning, Mark led the search party down the steep river banks. His right arm was in a sling, his ribs were strapped tightly under his shirt, and he hobbled painfully with his injuries.

They found Sean Courtney half a mile below the last cataract, where the Baboon Stroom debouched into the valley.

He lay on his back, and there was no blood, the waters had cleansed every drop of it, and even his wounds were clean and washed pale blue. Except for the dent in his temple, his features were almost unmarked, and the white bush of his beard had dried in the early morning sun. It curled proudly on his chest. He looked like a carved stone effigy of a medieval knight laid out with his armour and sword on a sarcophagus in the dim depths of an ancient cathedral.

*In the event of my wife predeceasing me, or dying simultaneously, or within six months of each other—*

The river had been kind and carried her down to the same sand-bank. She was lying face down, half buried in the soft white sand. One slim naked arm was outflung, and on the third finger was the simple band of bright gold. The fingers almost, but not quite, touched her husband's arm.

They buried them together, side by side, in the same deep excavation on the slope of the escarpment, a little way beyond the big house of Lion Kop.

*..................... I direct that the following shall apply in regard to the rest and residue of my estate.*

There followed almost five hundred separate bequests which covered fifty pages, and totalled almost five millions of sterling. Sean Courtney had forgotten nobody. Beginning with the humblest grooms and domestic servants—enough for a piece of ground, a small herd, the equivalent of a life pension.

To those with a lifetime of service and loyalty, the gift was greater, in proportion.

To those who had laboured to build up the various prosperous companies and enterprises, there was a share of those companies, a large share.

He had not forgotten a single friend nor relative—not one of them.

> *I acknowledge that I have one legitimate man-child, though I hesitate to employ the word son—one DIRK COURTNEY, presently residing at Great Longwood in the district of Ladyburg. However, God or the devil has already provided for him so abundantly, that anything I could add would be superfluous. Therefore I leave him nothing—not even my blessing.*

They buried Dirk Courtney in the pine forest, below the dog ring. No priest could be found to recite the office of burial, and the undertaker closed the grave under the curious eyes of a few members of the Press and a throng of sensation-seekers. Though there were many to stare, there was nobody to weep.

> *To my daughter STORM HUNT (born COURT-NEY), who took lightly her filial duties, I, in turn, discharge my paternal duties with the bequest of a single guinea.*

"He did not mean it," Mark whispered to her. "He was talking about you that night—as it happened, he was remembering you."

"I had his love," she said softly. "Even though—at the end—he tried to deny it, I will have it always. That is riches enough. I don't need his money as well."

> *To MARK ANDERS, for whom I have conceived the affection a man usually accords only to his natural son, I leave no money, as I am well aware of the con-*

> *tempt he holds for that commodity. I bequeath to him,*
> *in lieu of cash, all my books, paintings, guns, pistols*
> *and rifles, personal jewelery, and all my domestic ani-*
> *mals, including dogs, horses and cattle.*

The paintings in themselves made up a considerable fortune, and many of the books were unique in rarity and condition.

Mark sold only the cattle and the horses, for they were many and there was no place for them all in the tsetse-infested valley of the Bubezi.

> *The rest and residue of my Estate I bequeath to the*
> *said MARK ANDERS in his capacity as the Trustee*
> *of the Wild Life Protection Society. The bequest to be*
> *used to further the aims of the Society, particularly to*
> *the development and extension of the proclaimed*
> *lands presently known as Chaka's Gate, into a Wild*
> *Life Reservation.*

"No one in Government will want to touch a Bill that was drawn up and piloted by the former Deputy Minister of Lands," General Jannie Smuts prophesied to Mark, as they stood talking quietly together after the funeral. "The man's name will leave a pungent stink on anything he ever touched. Political reputations are too fragile to risk like that—I foresee a stampede by the new Government to dissociate themselves from his memory. We can confidently expect a new Bill being introduced, confirming and upgrading the status of the proclaimed lands of Chaka's Gate, and I can assure you, my boy, that the Bill will have the full support of my party."

As General Smuts had foreseen, the Bill passed through the House at the following Session, becoming law on 31st May 1926, as Act No. 56 of 1926 of the Parliament of the Union of South Africa. Five days later, the telegram from the Minister of Lands arrived at Ladyburg confirming

Mark's appointment as first Warden of Chaka's Gate National Park.

\*     \*     \*

There was no trial at which Hobday could turn king's evidence and claim immunity from the crime of murder; so at Hobday's own trial, the Public Prosecutor asked for the death sentence. In his summing up, the Chief Justice mentioned the evidence given by Sithole Zama, alias Pungushe. "He made an excellent impression on this Court. His answers were clear and precise. At no time did the defence shake his transparent honesty and powers of total recall."

On Christmas Eve in the white-washed room at Pretoria Central Gaol, with his arms and legs pinioned by leather straps, and his head covered by a black cotton bag, Hobday dropped to eternity through the crashing wooden trap.

\*     \*     \*

Peter Botes, cleared of any implication in the crimes of murder and attempted murder by the testimony of Mark Anders, was not placed on trial.

"His crimes were weakness and greed," Mark tried to explain to Storm. "If there were punishment for those, then there would be a gallows waiting for each of us. Besides, there has been enough vengeance and death already."

Peter Botes left Ladyburg immediately after the hearings, and Mark never learned where he went or what became of him.

\*     \*     \*

Now, when you cross the Bubezi River by the low concrete bridge, where Dirk Courtney's dam wall and hydro-electric station might have stood, you will come to the barrier on the far bank.

A Zulu ranger in smart suntans and a slouch hat will

salute you, and give you a smile that sparkles like the Parks Board badge on his hat brim.

When you leave your vehicle and go into the office building of hewn stone and neat thatch to sign the register, look then to the left wall beyond the reception desk. In a glass case there is a permanent display of photographs and memorabilia from the park's early days. The centre-piece of this collection is a large photograph of a sprightly old gentleman, lean and tanned and tough as a strip of rawhide, with a shock of pure white hair and a marvellous pair of spiky moustaches.

His cotton jacket is a little rumpled and fits him as though it was made for his elder brother, the knot of his tie has slipped down an inch and one tab of his shirt collar is slightly awry. Although his smile is impish, his jaw is firm and determined. However, it is the eyes that arrest attention. They are serene and direct, the eyes of a visionary or a prophet.

Under the photograph is the legend: "Colonel Mark Anders, First Warden of Chaka's Gate National Park." And below that again in smaller letters, "Because of this man's energy and far-sightedness, Chaka's Gate National Park has come down to posterity. Colonel Anders served on the Board of the National Parks Trust from its inception in 1926. In 1935, he was elected Chairman. He fought with distinction in two world wars, was severely wounded in one, and commanded his battalion in North Africa and Italy in the second. He is the author of many books on wildlife, including *Sanctuary* and *Vanishing Africa*. He has travelled the world to lecture and to gain support for the work of conservation. He has been honoured by monarchs, and governments and universities."

In the photograph, a tall slim woman stands beside the Colonel. Her hair is streaked with grey and drawn back severely from her face, and although there are crow's-feet at the corners of her eyes and deep lines around her mouth, yet they are the lines of laughter and the planes and angles of her face still show traces of what must once have been great beauty. She leans half protectively, half possessively against the colonel's right arm and below the photograph the legend continues:

"His wife and life-long companion in his work was the internationally celebrated artist, who painted her memorable African landscapes and wildlife studies under her maiden name of Storm Courtney.

"In 1973, Colonel Anders retired from his position of Chairman of the Parks Board, and went with his lady to live in a cottage overlooking the sea at Umhlanga Rocks on the Natal Coast."

When you have read the legend you may go back to your motorcar. The Zulu ranger will salute you again and raise the barrier. Then you too can go, for a short time, into Eden.

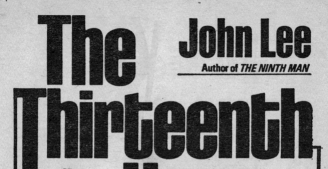

# The Thirteenth Hour

## John Lee
### Author of *THE NINTH MAN*

Pursued by the SS, threatened by the Russian advance, Captain Henry Bascom has only cunning and sheer luck on his side. But when he becomes the sole witness to an incredible Nazi plot to save Hitler, he knows he will need more than cunning and luck to survive!

A Dell Book    $2.50    (18751-6)

---

At your local bookstore or use this handy coupon for ordering: